MW00526813

A CRY OF STONE

A Novel

MICHAEL D. O'BRIEN

A CRY OF STONE

A Novel

IGNATIUS PRESS   SAN FRANCISCO

Frontispiece photograph by John Max
Indian Girl, Mistassini, Quebec
Courtesy of Canadian Museum of Contemporary Photography

Cover art: *Creation*, by Michael D. O'Brien

Cover design by Roxanne Mei Lum

For the unknown martyrs
of North America

I

First she was small. She was very, very small, and that was good because no one could see her. Only Grandma could see her.

No, go farther back than that.

First she was born. She was a seed inside a pod that split open and spilled its contents. Or she was a puppy in a belly, and the long tunnel opened, and she wiggled down it and came into the cold air. Or she was an egg in a circlet of bog cotton, and she tap-tapped until the dome of her prison shattered and she struggled out, wet and ugly, into the blinding light. She lifted her wings. She rode the wind. She was not eaten.

Or she was swept down a river of fire, heard screams, and fell through space pulling her twisting cord after her, until she landed in wrinkled brown hands, and a face with eyes as old as God pressed against her own unknown face and kissed her and cried.

Downwind from the reserve was the cabin where she came into the world and lived with Grandma. There she grew, and there, too, she first saw her own face in the reflection on the kettle or recognized herself in a puddle of rain water and began to know herself a little. Grandma called her *Ogini-wâbigon*, which is the name of the wild roses that grew behind the outhouse. Grandma's name was Oldmary Rabbit, which some white peoples thought was funny because they did not know how beautiful it sounded in the Ojibwe tongue—*Mari-Wâbos.*

Grandma was like a rock that could not be moved. She made a solid place in the great movements of the seasons always wheeling around their home, which was the center of the world. A few other things stayed the same, though imperfectly. There was the water, though its moods were many. And the wind, which had a bad temper. The trees, which simply grew, sighing sometimes, singing sometimes, sleeping sometimes. The sun itself, though it was not dependable. And the moon, which changed its shape. The cabin, though falling apart, was always *there* and always had been.

But Ogini did not remain the same. Her toes sprouted out of the black rubber shoes with the flapping sole, and her pink calico dress grew shorter and shorter until it tickled her knees.

"Little girls grow", Oldmary would say, shaking her head.

"When do they stop growing, Grandma?" Ogini would ask.

"When they are finished", Oldmary would reply, for she was full of knowledge.

"When do they start?"

"They start when they are baby birds."

"Was I a baby bird?"

"Yes, you were once a *bineshi*, a tiny silver bird", Grandma would say, while scrubbing Rose with a soapy rag as she sat in a washtub beside the woodstove.

"Is that how I started?" asked Ogini, dragging her eyes away from Thisdog (the black puppy with white spots) and Thatdog (the white puppy with black spots), who pierced each other's ears with their needle teeth and wrestled over a bone.

"Yes, that is how you started."

"When was that?"

"A long time ago."

"How long ago?"

"Six years ago, in January, when the lake cracked like gun shots, and the land was dreaming under the snow. *Makwa* the bear and *Amik* the beaver slept in their dens."

"And then what happened?"

"Then *Mang* the loon awoke and flew up into the night;

8

high, high he flew and warbled to *Gissis* the moon until she was filled with delight. He begged a piece of silver from her. But being wise she said, 'I would like to give you my silver, but it is a piece of my heart. It is a big thing to give away a piece of my heart. What do you want it for?'

"And Mang said, 'I want it because I come from a dark land that is cold for half of the year, and because we need light.'

" 'How will you care for my light?' asked Gissis. 'I must know, for she is my daughter, this little piece of my heart.'

" 'I will guard her and feed her,' he answered, 'and I will teach her to look up to your face. She will look to you, and your light will shine on her, and she will spread you among the ones who live in the winter and the shadow of winter.'

" 'Did you not know', said Gissis, 'that even my light is a reflection?'

" 'I did not know', said Mang, ashamed.

"So the moon, seeing the loon's humility, fashioned from her heart a tiny bird of silver and blew into its mouth, and it opened its eyes and ruffled its feathers. 'See, I have made you,' said the moon, 'and I send you down into the cold dark land to bring it light.' But though she understood the moon's meaning, the tiny bird did not yet know how to make words.

" 'Go, now,' said the moon, 'to be what you were meant to be.'

"The little bird shivered and lifted its wings, but could not fly.

" 'You must carry her', said Gissis to Mang, 'until she is able to fly.'

"Then the loon put the tiny bird on his back.

" 'Where should I take her?' he asked.

" 'Take her to Mary Wâbos by Threefinger Lake in the Land of Little Trees. There she will grow, and there she will shine her light.'

" 'And what shall we call her?'

9

" 'She will be called *Oginiwâbigon*, which is *Rose-flower*, and she will call me *Ningâ*, which is *my mother.*'

"And so the loon flew down carrying the tiny silver bird who is called Rose. She held tightly to his necklace of diamonds, the *nâbikawâgan*, but faster and faster he flew until his wings cut through the night leaving shimmering curtains of green in the black northern sky, and the diamonds of his neck fell away, and thus was made the *tchibekana*, the river of stars which the white people call the river of milk.

"When the loon came down to the cabin of Mary Wâbos, he tapped on the window pane with his long beak until the old woman awoke. He put the tiny bird on her doorstep and flew away. And when Mary Wâbos opened the door, there was a baby girl."

"Named *Ogini*! Named Rose!" cried Ogini, giggling and squirming and splashing the sudsy water. "Then you took me into your cabin!"

"Then I took you in," said Oldmary.

"And you became my grandma!"

"Yes, I became your grandma."

"You will *always* be my grandma!"

"I will always be your grandma."

"You will always be here!"

Then Oldmary paused. She pulled Ogini onto her lap and wrapped her in a towel and buried the child in her chest, which smelled like smoked fish and tobacco, spruce tea and moose hide.

"You will always be here!" Ogini insisted.

"Sometime, many years from now, I'm going up there", Oldmary pointed. "Into the loon's necklace."

"I'll go too", Ogini said.

"No, you'll come later."

"I don't want to go later. I want to go with you."

"You can't. You have work to do here."

"I would be alone."

"No, you would have light."

"If you went up there," the girl pointed, "if you left me here, I wouldn't have any light."

"You will always have light", the old woman whispered.

When she was seven, Grandma told her about Youngmary-the-mother-of-her-flesh, the one who had brought her into this world. During the early years she didn't know anything about her mother, because Youngmary went away after she was born and left her in the cabin with Grandma and never returned. She could not make a picture of her mother in her mind, even when she sat on the picture-making rock at the lake and squinted her eyes up into the sky that was as blue as Our Lady's dress. When a small cloud appeared out of the south and glided over the lake, it would not change into a mother's face bending over a cradle. Holes opened in it like mouths aching to say the right words, but the branches of vapor that might have become embraces dissolved, and the wind pulled away what was left to other places, leaving Ogini clutching her ankles, chin on knees, staring at the lapping water, beneath which rocks swelled and shrank and flowed, as if everything, everything, were liquid.

Grandma told many stories, on cold mornings and hot nights, sometimes when Ogini picked blueberries, kaplunking, kaplunking into tin cans (she ate more than she saved), or sometimes in the dark when she was frightened of things that cannot be seen. The stories were best on the mountain called the skull, where Grandma sat on a blanket and stared at the rotting trunk of a once-giant tree.

"I saw that pine burn when I was your age, Rose.

"In the autumn of the year when the century turned, after the gathering of *mânowim* the wild rice, and during the time when *wêwe* the wild goose begins to travel south, a thunderstorm tore a path across the bushlands. Some of the white people said it was the edge of a hurricane, but there was not enough wind to confirm this. The destroyer was the Great-Cloud, the thundercloud that is larger and heavier than all the lesser thunderclouds. It rumbled over the villages and camps like waves of coming retribution, or revelation, spitting down lightning to set off many forest fires, then quenching them with much rain as if to show its powers.

"The children shook in fear," said Grandma with her slow voice, her eyes squinting with memory, "among them a little girl known as Mary Wâbos—"

"That was you?" Rose interrupted.

"That was me when I was your age. We children shook with fear in the cabin doors as the green light rolled in. We had never seen such fury, roaring and barking as it tried to snap its chains, though the old people remembered storms that had torn up the big camp tents and thrown them into the lake or sent canoes flying into a heap.

"Toward the end of the day there came a lull in the wind, and the sky broke open to reveal a streak of blue, as blue as the feathers of *ogishkimanissi* the kingfisher. Then it closed over again as a cloud of great darkness moved toward the village. People said later they felt the weight of the air suddenly drop and cold seep into the afternoon like death. The religious ones said it was like the coming of *Dibakonige-gijigad*, the Day of Judgment. First the hail, then the rain again. Then a snake of lightning reached down and struck this old pine. It burned like a torch for a few minutes, lighting up the bush and the clouds, then was doused by the waters that emptied from the heavens.

"When the storm was over, many people came out to see this tree. They stared at the split down the middle, watched the gum go bubbling down the trunk, and heard the branches hissing. As the elders stood around, pointing and commenting, little Mary

Wâbos stepped forward and sniffed the hot sap. It smelled like funeral incense.

" 'It is a church tree', she said aloud.

"A young boy named Kinoje burst out laughing and mocked her, crying 'Io! See the rabbit licking the priest's feet.'

"Some people found this amusing, though most disapproved, for a dying thing deserved respect. A few old men shook their heads, for they had seen themselves in this tallest of trees, this solitary one, and would long lament it."

Grandma sighed and glanced at the stump. "A few more years and it will crumble into the earth. No one will remember it. No one will know it lived here for hundreds of years."

"You will remember it."

"Soon I too will be part of the soil."

"Then I will remember it", Rose said solemnly.

Grandma smiled and stroked the hair back from the girl's forehead.

Their cabin stood in a little clearing in the pines, beside a creek that spilled into Crazyman River. The river was only a short walk down the hill. It flowed into the great waters of Three-finger Lake, which was connected to the distant sea by many routes and vast unthinkable spaces. In all places the waters were full of fish, for water was a home to them as land was a home to people and air was a home to flying things and the black water above the earth was home to the stars and the sun and the moon.

Minnows swelled into big fish that gasped and lashed in the net Rose helped Grandma to pull from the roaring narrows where Crazyman River gushed into Threefinger Lake. With a hatchet she chopped off their heads and split them from the button hole to the pink throat and pulled the guts out. She threw the guts to Thisdog and Thatdog. They tripped all over each other, gulping down the throwaway parts, crunching the fish heads in their wide mouths, whining and waggling their string tails, and yelping with ecstasy. The flesh of *majamegoss* the trout (they were fat and made of aluminum) and the flesh of *kinoje* the jackfish (they were lean and black and their jaws were evil) split equally under the saw-toothed knife and hung like clothes pegs on the drying racks above the willow fire.

And because of this, when the blizzards returned and beat against the log walls and wailed in the chimney, Rose sat with Grandma on the two chairs by the woodstove and held small, salty, golden shards of dry-fish in her mouth and felt them dissolve on her tongue. She tried not to gulp the fried bannock that shone with melting streams of lard and the raspberry jam from a tin that was for Sundays. She chewed it slowly with smiles, and she drank Fort Garry tea with sugar. Grandma let her tear the month-paper from the trading post calendar with the picture of the Parliament buildings and the year numbers, 1944, then 1945, then 1946, because years flowed like water, and because it was her job to measure them.

On a rainy day Rose used her fingers to draw faces in the foggy glass. Later, she scratched pictures of tiny birds flitting in the crystal forests of window frost. She rolled snow and packed and trimmed it into the shapes of bears and wolves and fish. A flaming twig that she pulled from the fire and extinguished in the snow became a charcoal finger that etched waves and wildflowers onto the log walls. Once, before bedtime, she built a house of twigs under a canopy of yellow kerosene light, and with scraps of cloth and thread she made little people to live in it.

When Rose was tired, she saw bad faces in gnarled firewood, and sometimes when she was sick she saw them floating in the air above her bed. She was not sick very often, but when she was, Grandma sat beside her bed, her big black beads clicking through her fingers, her lips whispering, and the faces went away.

Grandma read aloud from a book about a big flood when all the animals went into a boat and were saved with some people, and about a snake that tricked people and made them die, and about a man named Jesus who came from a place far beyond the loon's necklace. He died too, then he came back to life, then went away again, like the geese. But he sent a white bird that spoke words difficult to hear, and the words took the shape of tongues of fire, Grandma said.

That kind of fire did not hurt you, she said.

His name was *Winijishid-Manito*, Holy Ghost God in the white people's tongue, Grandma said.

Sometimes on Sunday, if the weather was good, Grandma would put on her go-to-town parka and her clean rubber boots and pick up her walking stick, and she and Rose would follow the trail through the woods to the reserve, a mile to the east. There, splitting the two dozen cabins, was a dirt road that led farther on around the south rim of the lake to the village where white people lived among the brown people. Usness and themness mixed together. It was a big place with a hundred cabins and, most amazing of all, a red and white airplane rocking on pontoons in front of a fur trader's store on the rocky shore. That was where Grandma exchanged her beaded moccasins for tea, flour, sugar, jam, packets of tiny colored beads, needles, white duffel cloth, and tobacco for her pipe, which she smoked only on Sundays, Christmas, and Easter. Also in that village were a nurse, a policeman, a teacher, a weatherman with balloons and a radio, and a man who built a log chapel with a bell on top. He built it on the stones of an old church that had burned thirty years before.

He was not Jesus, Grandma said. He was a *mekatewikwanaie*, a priest of Jesus. They called him Father Andrei. During the Holy *Anamessikewin*, Rose sat in the back row behind the pump organ, which was the place she liked best, because there she was very, very small and could not be seen, though she could see everything. She could hear the words which Jesus sent by the messenger bird. And as she listened to its words, she felt the opening petals of fire that does not hurt.

Rose did not go to Mass every Sunday because sometimes Grandma's back was sore, and she could not get out of bed. At those times Rose brought her cups of tea and broke stale bannock into small portions and soaked them in the tea and popped them into Grandma's mouth because she had no teeth.

2

Winters were long. Seven, sometimes eight months long. Rose dreamed. She looked at the world. Sometimes she looked within.

She started pretending after the trip to the hospital. But pretending became a window that she looked through too often. Then it grew into a door that she fell through. And then she could not tell whether she was pretending Marleena or Marleena was pretending her.

She called it *falling-into-seeing.*

Marleena did not like winter. Winter came too quickly after the hot summers and the swift autumns. It did not drift in by fits and starts but fell like a harsh scolding on the tail feathers of the departing geese. The first snow fell a foot deep and did not melt, holding the land in a grip that would not loosen.

Marleena's farm was the final outcropping where men turned the soil and drew life from it, saying: here I will stay; I shall not be moved. Beyond its fields the forest stretched in all directions. The trees were tall, and the soil was wet black. North of the farm, there was no living soul other than the poor Indian people in tiny villages scattered around the edges of countless lakes. If Marleena looked there, up to the frozen darkness, only a few people would cross her line of vision in a season: a trapper, perhaps, or a tattered little Indian girl living with her grandmother in a shack at some place called Crazyman River.

The air was cold and bitter in a dawn that resembled night. The girl, awakening in the bite of wind, was breaking snow crust toward the log barn. In one hand she swung the lantern, making pretty patterns on the snow; in the other, a pail of steaming oat mash. Humming to herself, she did not consider the staggering emptiness around her.

The clank of the iron clasp and the creak of the heavy barn door pulled against the wind stirred the animals within. She entered the shelter, its relative warmth formed by the heat of the big smelly bodies, driving out the sting. Singing to the horse and the cow and the barn cats, she pulled down two armloads of hay from a hole in the plank ceiling and threw it into the manger. Beauty nickered and tossed her head. Bossie lowed, breathing soft white plumes between the log stanchions. Marleena pegged Bossie for the milking, and when the mash was placed beneath her dribbling lips, the cow nosed it over greedily.

Seated on the apple box at Bossie's hind end, Marleena butted the flanks, rested her forehead between haunch and swollen rib cage, massaged the old leather bags to let down the milk, and pumped thin white jets into the echoing pail. She could not dislike the poor beast, though she dragged Marleena from her bed every morning, no matter the weather. Even the manure and urine smells rising from the mud of the barn floor were part of the bittersweet ritual. This was the resting time, Marleena's head warm on the hot angular body, closer to sleep than to wakefulness, startled fully awake by a snort of cow impatience with hands dozing and cold on the udder. Whenever Bossie's mild displeasure rose to a level of protest, the cow expressed herself with an unshifting gaze over her right shoulder. Not that Marleena caught her reproachful looks, for her thoughts were usually elsewhere.

The wind howled and rattled the barn rafters. Over and over in her mind, through the last moments of the cow's relief, went the words of the nursery rhyme Granny Crombie liked to recite:

> The north wind doth blow,
> And we shall have snow,

And what will the robin do then, Poor Thing?
He'll sit in a barn,
And keep himself warm,
And hide his head under his wing, Poor Thing!

Marleena unpegged Bossie and led her ambling girth out into the black and white dawn. The cow headed straightway to the stream and pulled long draughts of icy water from the hole Marleena chipped with a hatchet.

The girl crossed the creek on the plank footbridge. Though the water was frozen over, save where the cow was sucking by the bank, she could hear the muffled roar of its passage. The stream was dangerous and had taken more than one young life, according to Pa. Their names the girl did not know. They had been pioneers who had died too long ago to remember. She thought of them at every crossing of the stream—small bare hands reaching out to the sky from the roil of mad waters and muffled screams tumbling down, down and lost. Small coffins, weeping mothers in ankle-length dresses, fathers folding their arms in a lock-grip keeping the pain inside. The scene rose and sank into the stiller pools of her mind, not something a girl had ever witnessed, but real nonetheless. Pa said so. Granny said so, too.

"This land is a friend, if you know it and respect it," was one of Pa's well-worn proverbs, "but she'll kill a fool quicker than a wolf on a sick deer!" Such sayings abounded in him; they were his gee and haw for making one's way in a dangerous land, pulling his children back from carelessness, pushing them forward along the straight and narrow way that must be their life.

Marleena carried the pail of milk up the slope to the house. The old stone building stood against the protective hill, the smoke of the morning fire blowing sideways from the chimney. She shivered and stamped more quickly toward the yellow lamplight of the kitchen window.

By the back door she met her father. Coatless, Pa was coming out into the numbing cold for an armload of birch. He was brave and strong. He never got sick. He couldn't afford to, he said.

"Go ahead, girl", he nodded her through the door into the bright kitchen.

"Morning, Marleena", Ma said, placing bowls of porridge on the table. One sat steaming before her younger brother, Tommy, who sagged in his chair, eyes lidded heavily and both hands dangling like a drunkard's. Marleena glanced at him disapprovingly. She was the oldest and very responsible. She had an eldest daughter's good sense. She pulled her own weight—Ma said so.

Off the kitchen, toward the back of the house, was Granny Crombie's room, where each morning the first rasping coughs erupted from her lungs. In a few moments, she would emerge to begin her day. The old woman ate breakfast late as a rule. The sound of the kettle hissing on the cookstove usually brought her forth by the time the kids were ready to leave for school. After they had pushed back the empty bowls and made the leaving noises, her door opened and she appeared, nodding at them all, looking with a brief scowl toward each. While her daughter-in-law filled a bowl of oatmeal for her, the old woman tilted toward the stove, threw tea leaves into a pot and added boiling water. Granny stared at it until the steaming liquid was nearly black, drew it into a mug, and drank the stuff straight down. Then she slowly made another batch.

"Cold morning", she said, turning to her eldest granddaughter, Marleena. "You going to take the cutter to school?"

"Yes," Marleena answered promptly, "if Pa says I can."

"I need the cutter today", said Pa. "I'll be packing rails out of the bush. You kids can walk it."

"Oh, Pa", groaned the younger ones.

The town lay two miles east by dirt-cart track or cutter trail through snow.

"No bellyaching now. You've made it on colder mornings than this."

The farm was a northern homestead. It seemed a miracle that it was able to grow a few acres of hay and some potatoes, carrots, and beans each short summer. It was sheltered in a basin rimmed by rocky hills, and thus the ravages of winter were broken before they fell on the fertile soil. Each autumn it lit up like fire, the birch, poplar, and maple that fringed the fields igniting into red-gold flames, while the endless stone shield and the black-green army of disapproving conifers surrounded the dance of color like a fire ring. There was, as well, a delicate apple tree, delicate only by comparison, for it was a hardy northern variety which had been planted three decades ago by Grandpa Crombie when he got the land free from the government because he was Scottish Presbyterian and a war hero with three medals. The tree was in memory of him, Granny said. It was coddled, pruned, winter-swaddled in burlap, as if it were a full-standing member of the family. Certainly it was the one well-loved tree in this world of forest. An individual, it had brought a great brightness into their lives. Marleena wanted to give it a Christian name, but that was a silly thought, so she didn't.

In winter, stripped of its leaves, the valley became desolate. In the summer, it resurrected once more to become, briefly, a little Eden. Long ago, the man who became Marleena's grandfather had looked at this spot in the wilderness and seen a future which in time might be understood as more than a dream. It had been a virgin place, untouched. Or so they thought until Pa plowed up a fallen stone cross when he was clearing out the willow thicket, and tiny purple bones appeared, a child of the people who had tried to pioneer here long ago.

"Nothin' remains of them but these", he said to his children, while Ma picked the lichen from letters scratched on the stone.

"Drownd, three yrs old, Apr, 1846", she read in a whisper. That was all, because time had erased everything else there was to be known.

"It's only a small piece of the earth, but it is mine", said Pa. He repeated this from time to time, as reverently as Granny Crombie would quote from the King James. She especially liked the parts where the Chosen People entered the Promised Land and slaughtered the Canaanites. "The Philistines were a bad lot, too", she always added.

The Crombies were like that—religious. The son, Pa or James, was perhaps less so, and all the other members of the family to greater or lesser degrees. Granny had china teeth and slept in a white cap. She was Welsh. She could not tolerate sin, though she liked a dram of whiskey in her tea. There had been moments when Marleena considered the old woman's gaze with a certain reticence, something closer to reverence than to fear. Never, ever, had Granny been a chin-chucker or a tickler. Yet she would sometimes take young Paul or Marleena or Emily or Hilda or Tommy onto her lap, and tell a story, (What did the brave soldier do then, Granny?) and her arms would be around them cool and firm, with never the slightest vibration of possession in her bony fingers, the wiggling blue vein in her brown hands a marvel to behold.

"You got a snake inside you!" Tommy giggled once, and never again, because Granny flushed red and slapped him for the blasphemy. Even so, it was rare that a child would struggle from her arms. The woman would sense any impending inner impulse toward freedom, even before its conception in a young heart, and just as the child was thinking that he might escape, he would find himself being lowered to the floor, with a cashew or a wintergreen lozenge in his hand as a reward.

Sometimes at night, Marleena would stand for a long time in front of her dressing table, in the darkened bedroom where her sisters were sleeping. Brushing and brushing her golden hair, changed to silver in the moonlight streaming through the window, she saw a cabin up in the bush in the empty lands, the kind of shack in which Indians live. The peeled logs sat snugly one on top of the other in alternate layers, the chimney was made of gray river-mud and round black stones, and a rusty tin sleeve roared with dangerous creosote sparks. There was a single small window. She looked through the window, fell in through the window, and tumbled across the floor into a tangle of smelly dogs. And then she and the little Indian girl had a teatime with the miniature china Granny Crombie gave her.

"I am the luckiest girl in the whole wide world", Marleena said to her reflection as she laid the tortoise-shell brush and comb carefully side by side on the dresser. Sighing, she floated to her bed on the sweep and swell of Pa's fiddle playing below the planks of the floor and slipped under the quilts into the generous arms of sleep. And oh, as she fell asleep she wished to see the little Indian girl again. And she said a lovely prayer, thanking God that she was not poor.

All of this was imaginary, of course. Or some of it. It was not Rose's life, but the life of a girl who lived in a place where there were many white people, a town two hundred miles south of Crazyman River. The girl was real enough. Rose had met her once when she was flown out to a hospital for pneumonia, when she was seven. Rose occupied a bed beside Marleena in the children's ward. Marleena was ten years old under a mass of blond ringlets surrounded by flowers and rubber dollies. She had tonsils, she said, and a doctor was going to take them out. She had a cold, so the doctor had to wait three days. And so for three days she told the absolutely silent Rose every detail of her life. Rose was fortunate enough to meet some of the people in Marleena's life. They brought Marleena ginger ale and candy, and animals made of fluffy cloth. Their names were Ma and Pa and Paul and Emily and Hilda and Tommy and Granny

Crombie. Tommy offered Rose a stick of black licorice, but when she opened her mouth to bite it, she coughed a spray onto his hand. His face screwed up in disgust and he said, "Ooo yuck", and went back to his sister's bed.

"Don't bother the little girl, Tommy", said Granny Crombie.

"Poor thing", said Ma to Pa.

After Rose was well again, a floatplane flew her back to Crazyman River, to her real life, and she took Marleena along in her mind. She didn't see anything from the windows, because a nurse who came for the ride said she had to lie down all the way. The roaring, shaking plane was frightening, so she kept her eyes closed and pretended she was with Marleena, or she was Marleena.

She sometimes wondered if it was wrong pretending to be another person. Cuddling in the arms of someone else's family, making up a new past, rearranging the little stick people, hiding them in the twig house behind the stove so Thisdog and Thatdog would not knock over the walls and furniture and chew the tiny mother and father and the many brothers and sisters into pulp.

One winter night, after Rose fell asleep with the creaking of pines and the snuffling of the dogs in her ears, she dreamed a dream. A rolling plain of rock spread toward the north in waves of silent light that could not be seen with the eye. A radiant mountain arose on the horizon. Her heart pounded in unison with its pulsations. Slowly, she spread her arms to embrace it. Fear was a torrent within her, a strange joy-fear containing no terror. As her arms opened, a great tree at the peak of the mountain, the greatest of living trees, was struck by black lightning. It split from top to bottom. It died, and the dying was the end of everything. Then, a tiny sapling, a green fingerling, grew from the crumbling ruins. It grew and grew. It took root in a crack and split the side of the mountain.

From the heart of the broken mountain a stream of blood

gushed toward Rose. The stream grew into a river, sweeping around her and through her, spilling through her mouth and eyes and heart. It did not prompt disgust, for it tasted sweet. Then, from the depths of this river, there emerged a white bird, delicate and strong, formed in the current of blood, yet spotless. It opened wide its wings, turned its turquoise eyes to Rose, and in those eyes she saw stars and galaxies spinning through the universe. The bird's beauty both seared and quenched, hurt and healed. Tears streamed from Rose's eyes and fell into the river as she clasped the bird's neck in her arms. It flexed its wings and climbed into the night sky, bearing her aloft.

Then a roaring wind filled her, louder and louder as she was taken up into a turbulence of lights and bells and rushing air. And there in that place where she had never been before she was filled with sweet fire.

Rose suddenly awoke. Her arms were raised to the ceiling in the darkness, real tears streaming down the sides of her face, and her heart crashing madly. The roar in her ears steadily faded like the sound of a float plane tapering into the horizon, blending into Oldmary's wheezing, asleep in the other bed. Rose lay quietly, listening.

"Ask", the bird sang as it dissolved into a speck of light.

"What should I ask?" Rose whispered.

"For what your heart desires."

But to ask for a mother and a father, Rose knew, was too much.

"I would like a brother", she said. "A brother I could love."

Later, when sun poured onto the blankets through the small unfrosted circle on the windowpane, Rose heard the rumbles of Oldmary's chest. Oldmary hacked, cleared her throat, then made a sign of the cross for her morning prayers. Rose listened a long time to the whispering.

When it was done, Oldmary turned to her and said, "Who is Marleena?"

Then for the first time in her life Rose wanted to tell a lie.

Wanted to say, I don't know, because pretending was a comfort-thing which might be taken away. A secret-thing. Though Grandma had secrets: the ammunition box under the bed, sealed with a rusty padlock, and the leather saddlebag with the letters K. B. on it.

"Who is Marleena?" Grandma asked again.

"A girl", Rose said.

"What girl?" Oldmary asked.

"A girl I think about."

"Is she somebody in the village? I don't know any Marleena living there."

"She is a girl I met when I was sick in hospital."

"You were talking about her when you were asleep."

Rose said nothing.

"Was she nice to you, that girl?"

"Yes," Rose murmured, "she was nice."

"What was she like?"

"She had hair like gold. And dolls."

"Ah", said Oldmary.

"And sometimes . . ."

Rose hesitated. But Oldmary was content to wait.

"Sometimes I pretend I'm her."

She fell silent, embarrassed.

Oldmary pondered this without comment. After clearing her lungs again, she got her legs off the bed and planted her feet onto the floor.

"Come here, Rose."

Rose went over and sat beside her. Oldmary put an arm around her shoulders.

"You don't have to pretend to be somebody else."

"But I like it."

"Yes. But it isn't real."

"It is real", Rose burst out with sudden intensity. "It is! I go there sometimes. To see her. In my mind."

"You mustn't, Rose. It isn't right."

"But it's better there."

At which her grandmother's face twisted and tears filled her old eyes.

"Maybe it feels better for a little while. But after, when you come back to here, here is not so good any more."

"Sometimes," Rose cried, "*there* is more real than *here*."

Then Oldmary did something Rose had never seen before: Her grandmother put her face in her hands and wailed.

But happiness returns. It always does. Usually in the mornings.

The next day was Sunday, and because Oldmary was feeling strong enough for a long walk, they went into the village for Mass. While they were waiting for Fr. Andrei to come, an old man named Mytro Kuchuk, who was half Ukrainian and never came to church, entered noisily. He was dragging a wild creature. They crashed down onto the back pew beside Rose and Oldmary. Kuchuk was out of breath and grumbling as he locked the wild thing in his arms. It thrashed and bit. It was a small boy.

Rose and Grandma watched while the old man and the boy wrestled.

"I think he got a demon", growled Kuchuk.

"Who is he?" Oldmary asked.

"His name is Binemin Edzo. Some people brought him down from Windy Lake last night, had to tie him up to keep him from tipping the canoe. He's out of his mind."

Kuchuk slapped the boy on the back of the head.

"Shut up", he said in Ojibwe. "Stop biting and stop wiggling or I'll beat you good."

The boy looked frightened and froze in Kuchuk's bearlike embrace, though his eyes continued to dart and spin.

Oldmary leaned over and said, "Don't you beat that boy. There are other ways."

"None that work. I tried everything."

27

"What happened to him?"

"I don't know much. He's the grandson of my wife's brother. The ma and pa took off south on a binge and left the kid to starve at their camp on Windy Lake. He was nekked as a skunk, eating raw minnows and berries when some people found him. Had a big chase to catch him. They brought him to me. I'm his only kin, but I ain't even blood kin, 'cause it was by marriage you see, and my wife's dead anyway. What a lunatic he is. Oh, hell, what am I gonna do with him?"

No one had any suggestions. The situation was perplexing. Drunks and madmen were not unusual, but dangerous crazy children were rare. Rose had never seen one before.

The bell rang for the beginning of Mass. The priest came through a side door of the sanctuary and began to pray in Latin. The people rose to their feet. The little madman dropped to the floor and rolled under the pew, where he curled into a fetal position.

Rose watched him. As she gazed at him in wonderment and sadness, the Winijishid-Manito spoke to her. As the words-without-words poured through her she felt them as fire petals unfolding in her heart, like sweet tea or saskatoon-berry jam or the smoke of burning pine gum, or the faint song of south-bound geese flying high over the golden woodlands before the fall of winter, the chant of changing.

This is your little brother, he said.

Rose fell to her knees and peered under the pew. Lying flat on her belly she wiggled under, so close that her face was an inch from his.

"*Nishime*, little brother", she whispered.

His eyes flew open. They were strange eyes for an Indian. They were green-gray, and the shape of his face was like a white man's, though it was as brown as hers.

He snarled—a long, low gargling in the back of his throat. He mouthed a word that was evil.

Rose drew back. Then, reminding herself of the message of the Winijishid-Manito, she put her face close to his again.

"Little brother," she whispered, "Winijishid-Manito has given you to me. I am your sister."

This was countered by more snarls. Kuchuk, hunching uncomfortably through the alien Mass, bent to see what was happening behind his feet and threatened Binemin with a fist, warning him to make no trouble. For all his madness, the boy seemed to understand, though his eyes flared with hatred.

Now all the people knelt for the Consecration. Rose scurried out from under the bench and knelt beside Oldmary. She bowed before the Blessed Sacrament. After that, she went below again and talked to Binemin.

"Did something bad happen to you?" she asked, daring to put a hand on his shoulder. His clothes smelled of woodsmoke. His breath was like rotting fish. His eyes flared again. He rolled over and faced the wall. He shook off her hand. But this time he did not snarl or say the evil word.

Rose left him for a few minutes at Communion time. After receiving the Blessed Sacrament, she knelt beside Oldmary. The fire in her heart was sweeter than anything she had ever known before. And the words-without-words, the song-without-music, continued to flow through her with such force that she gasped for breath.

I ask a sacrifice of you, said the fire-song.

Rose tugged on Grandma's sleeve and asked, "What is a sacrifice?"

"A sacrifice", Oldmary whispered, "is when you take a heavy load on your back, like a hurt or a not-fairness. You give it to God and he puts it on the Cross of Jesus, the Big Sacrifice, and the Mass which is also the Big Sacrifice. Then you have a part in it."

"What kind of part?" Rose whispered.

"Part of mending."

"Like sewing?"

"Yes. Sewing the ripped hide. Sewing the cut flesh. Stopping the blood that is pouring out too fast."

"That is sacrifice?"

"That is sacrifice."

"Does it hurt?"

"Yes."

"Oh."

Rose now wondered if she wanted this thing. This thing had been offered by the song of Manito—Jesus-Manito or Spirit-Manito, she did not know which—it was surely Manito who had asked the question. He had *asked*, not told, which meant that she was free to say no.

She glanced down at the dirty, wild, mad boy lying in the shadow under the bench. She loved him, and, as she loved him, the sweet fire-song swelled in her heart, and she knew that the hurt would be a small thing compared to the love she would have for him, and the life that would come back into him.

She fell-into-seeing inside herself and found the quiet place in her heart where Jesus was.

"Yes, I will", she said in words without words.

After the priest left the altar, Kuchuk pulled Binemin Edzo from under the pew and dragged him outside by the collar of his shirt. There they waited. When Fr. Andrei came to them, his face clouded over with worry as he gazed at the boy thrashing in Kuchuk's fist.

"Let him go", the priest said.

"I can't, Father. He'll run away and bite something or kill somebody. He got a demon inside. Can you cast it out?"

Fr. Andrei closed his eyes. After a moment he opened them. "Little boy, be still", he said in a gentle voice. Binemin ceased to struggle, though his eyes continued to dart this way and that.

"I do not know if it is an evil spirit or a cry from his soul", the priest said, his face stricken with grief. "What has happened to this child?"

Kuchuk told him what he knew. Then the priest raised both of his hands to pray over Binemin Edzo, but the boy twisted suddenly, pulling himself free of Kuchuk's grip, shrieked, and ran into the forest, pursued by several strong men.

The next day Binemin went away in the floatplane to a hospital in the south, and when he returned in the same plane after three months, he no longer snarled and bit or curled into a ball on the floor. He was washed and had nice new clothes. His ma and pa never returned. The police were involved, and somebody else from the government paid for an old couple on the reserve to take him in, to feed him, and to make sure he went to school. It seemed that Rose's little brother was going to be all right. He did whatever people told him to do. He carried firewood into the cabin of his foster parents, who were good to him. He ate a lot. He grew. But he never smiled. And he never talked.

The school was a one-room log structure filled with a dozen long desks and as many benches. Along the wall below the single window was a shelf of textbooks and readers for six grades. Binemin sat at the back because he was big for his age and, of course, because he wished to be unnoticed. Rose sat at the front because she was small, though she would have preferred to be invisible at the back. During classes she never looked around to catch a glimpse of Binemin, though her thoughts often turned to him. She watched him standing by himself in the school yard at recesses and lunch hours, always gazing into the forest as if something would come out of it. Sometimes his eyes would flare and he would growl. He would crouch and grab a stick or a rock. When the school bell rang he would drop his weapon and his face would go blank. He was eight years old, in grade one. But that was all right because a few teenagers were in grade three and four. Everyone had trouble learning to read, so no one thought to tease him for being slow. Besides, they were afraid of him.

Rose was not afraid, because she loved him. She developed a habit of going to the edge of the woods at recess and lunch hour and standing a few feet away from him, saying nothing. Whenever the bile-fire erupted out of his eyes, as green as the gall of a butchered bear—bitter, sour-smelling—the fire inside of her flared stronger and sweeter. She made the rose-fire leap across the great space between them and push back the bile-fire. She told her love to go inside and pour light into him, to warm him up. Deep, deep inside, below the place where words are made, below the locked doors which made him silent, it seemed that he felt what she sent to him. Whenever she stood beside him he would not pick up a stick or a stone, though he never looked at her.

After six months of this, toward the end of winter, she brought to school one day a bundle of charcoal willow sticks wrapped in a scrap of deer hide. At lunch time she hastily ate the hunk of bannock and lard and gulped the tea from the jam jar Grandma had carefully wrapped in rabbit fur and placed into the leather soldier's sack that was Rose's lunch bag, the one with the initials K. B. on it. She went out into the yard and saw Binemin by the edge of the forest eating a chunk of bannock and a rope of dry-meat.

As usual she went and stood beside him. As usual neither of them said a word. After a few minutes, Rose decided to unwrap the bundle of deer hide. The twine that bound it was knotted too tightly. She grunted and pulled clumsily at the knot, but her fingers were numbed by the cold and she could not undo it. Binemin watched her from the corner of his eye.

Rose held the bundle in her hands, frowning down at it.

Slowly, as if coming out of a dream, Binemin reached over and took the bundle. In a moment, he had it undone. He handed it back to her and looked away into the trees.

"Thank you, little brother", she said.

He pretended he had not heard.

She took a charcoal twig from the bundle and walked to the wall of the school building. There she carefully drew a small bird descending. Around it she inscribed a series of flame-like lines, and around them she made a circlet of wild roses. By then she was falling-into-seeing and had become unconscious of the school yard, nor was she aware any longer that she was drawing. She was inside the picture, making a second ring of flowers grow all around the whole.

When she surfaced again, she noticed that Binemin was standing beside her staring at the drawing. He reached into the bundle and took a twig for himself. He paused for a minute staring at it, then slowly put its point to the wall. He drew a crude man-shape, arms and legs extended. Beside it he drew a fire, and it seemed to Rose that as he pressed the stick into this part of his drawing his face began to twist and he pitched forward into his own falling-into-seeing. For the first time, she was frightened of him. The look that came suddenly into his eyes was like the tormented madness she had seen on the day of their first meeting, when the snarls and evil word had come from his mouth.

He put the point of the twig into his fire and glanced swiftly at Rose to see if she had understood. Then with careful deliberation, as if the twig had ignited, he touched the burning point all over the body of the man-shape.

Then he threw the flaming stick into the snow and stared at the ground, a high pitched wail rising in his throat.

"Little brother", Rose whispered. "Did this happen to you?"

At which complete madness possessed him, and he ran away howling into the forest. If she had not been so stunned, Rose would have run after him. But the bell rang then, and, because she was obedient by nature, she returned to the classroom and stared down at her reader, *See Spot run. Run, run, Spot,* until she fell into the abyss of mysterious things that had happened to him, remaining there until the bell at the end of the afternoon.

Three days later, Binemin returned to school and was himself again, or at least his more recent self. He did not speak. He did not look at her. He labored over the torturous alphabet and the numerals as if he were only a slow quiet boy with nothing to say. But Rose now knew what was inside of him. She knew.

At lunch time she brought her bundle of twigs outside and saw that he was waiting for her by the wall. Someone had wiped both of their drawings away.

First, she drew two small figures hand in hand, a boy shape and a girl shape. Boy clothes and girl clothes. Boy hair cut short and girl hair in two braids. Above each she drew a bird. Around the whole she made a circlet of roses. She glanced at him and stood back.

He took a twig in his fingers and stepped toward the wall. He hesitated. His eyes were confused, but not tormented with the madness. He opened his mouth, then closed it again. He dropped the stick into the snow and walked away into the forest. This time he did not howl. Rose walked after him.

She knew that he would not want her to walk beside him. She stayed twenty or thirty feet behind, stepping through the snow humps with care, placing her moccasins in the holes his feet had made. At the edge of the lake, thinking himself alone, he stopped and threw himself into the rippled drifts covering the open expanse of Threefinger Lake. Face down he wailed into the snow, seeming to inhale it, pounding his fists into it as if he wanted to break through it and go down, down into darkness forever. She understood that he wanted to be no more, to remember no more.

Without making a sound, she sat down beside him, and the sweet fire-song grew in her until she was able to turn it toward him, to cover him, to fill him, and with it draw him back up.

34

But the force of his darkness was very great that day, and the rose-fire returned to her without doing what it was for.

Still, she waited by him. Later, the faint ring of the school bell told her it was time to obey. She did not. She knew that her work now was to obey the words-without-words that were the higher commands. If at this point love had no possible action and no possible words, she could at least offer the word of her presence, and this she now realized was no small thing.

When he removed his freezing face from the snow and looked up at her with all wildness burnt out and only hopelessness remaining, he was for an instant startled.

"Little brother", she said. "I will not go away. No, not ever."

He stared at her for a time, then sat up. Eventually he stood. Together they trudged back to the school.

Wild and crazy he was, and everyone knew it. But he was not stupid. In his first year at school he had learned the alphabet, and it was thought that he could count to a hundred. He was nine years old now. No one asked him questions, because they knew that he did not answer questions addressed directly to him. He answered paper questions about letters and numbers. This was a great victory. And now the two old people who looked after him had begun to bring him to Mass, where he sat on the bench by the door, his head tilted back, staring at the sanctuary through half lidded eyes. He did not stand or kneel at the proper moments, and he was the first out the door after the final blessing. But he came. And this too was a great victory, though everyone knew it must not be commented on, for creatures of the forest were easily startled and would run and might not return.

In time, spring arrived. The silver minnows appeared in all flowing water. The school year drew to a close. On Saturday mornings, Binemin would arrive at the edge of the clearing by Oldmary's cabin and wait for Rose to appear. He never approached the cabin, never called or stepped on ground-twigs to make his presence known. When smoke from the morning fire began to rise from the chimney pipe, he would sit and wait for the smells of frying bannock to waft out. He would stare at the door. Oldmary knew he was out there, of course, but she also knew that he needed taming and that he was not ready to be invited in. She prepared extra bannock for him, slathered with jam, and sent it to him in Rose's hands.

When Rose came outside, Binemin would suddenly look away, as if his presence was no more than a coincidence. She was wise about wild creatures and their ways, and so she was always careful to avoid too sudden a meeting. She would stand several paces from him, looking at the river or at the sky. After that she would sit on a rock a few feet away and place the two portions of bannock side by side on a plate of wooden shingle that she had brought for that purpose.

When she sensed that he was ready, she would say simply, "Little brother, eat."

That summer, he began to follow Rose around. It was not exactly that he chased her, because in fact it was she who was taming him and holding him to the world, keeping him from plunging into the underworld, tethering him by a thread. It took the form of rambles. She showed him the pool in Crazy-man River where fat fish swirled their tails in a silent underwater dance. Farther along the river, in a shallow ford, they came upon schools of silver minnows. He squatted by the edge of the water and stared into it for minutes. Rose knelt beside him, wondering what he was doing. Suddenly, his right arm flashed into the water and withdrew a handful of the small fluttering fish. He ate them one by one. Rose watched, aghast. He offered her one. She took it and swallowed it. It wriggled horribly all the way down her throat, but because it was necessary to show him her gratitude, and because this was his first giving of a tangible gift, she forced herself not to gag. She smiled her gratitude and he drank deeply of it. Though he was still incapable of speech.

She took him to the high hill, the skull, where the giant pine had burned when Grandma was a girl, and there they crammed themselves with blueberries. Their mouths were blue. Their eyes were burned with blueness. Rose noticed that Binemin's hair was tinting brown-red under the summer sun and stood straight up in a brush of rusty spikes above his chocolate brow. She made a silly face at him showing her blue teeth.

He stared at her. Then, slowly, his facial muscles contracted into a trembling smile. This too was a great victory. Still he did not speak.

In August there was a big storm and a deluge that fell for two days. When the sun returned on the morning of the third day, Rose went out the cabin door to find a pool of rainwater in the yard. It was about twenty feet across, a foot deep, its bottom carpeted with moss. Many small birds twittered and bathed on the edges. Binemin sat in the leafy shadows on the far side. Holding the shingle of bannock in her left hand she waved at him with her right. He looked away, then looked back. Then nodded.

Rose waded across the pool, placed the bannock on their eating rock, and left him to his breakfast. While he was tearing into the bannock, she walked around the pool to the woodshed and found an old lard bucket and a battered tin water pail. Then she turned toward the path to the river. He got up and followed.

All that morning they walked along the thundering river, and whenever they found a bend where the water had made a beach of tumbled pebbles, Rose would go down on hands and knees and search among them for special stones. Bit by bit, kerplunk, kerplunk, she filled the buckets with small round red and white stones. Binemin watched without contributing. He seemed content simply to be with her. From time to time he would

37

squat and stare into the water, then flash his hand after fish. Once, he swiveled his eyes to Rose, tilted his head back, and dropped a flapping fingerling down his throat.

Rose laughed, and Binemin rewarded her with his halting smile. He offered her a minnow and she ate it in a similar fashion, overcoming revulsion with love, rewarded by another smile, less halting, lingering a little of its own accord.

After that they continued scouting the bank for more pebble beaches. Binemin seemed to get the idea and began to search among the stones for unusual shapes and colors. He found a nearly perfect orb of white quartz, three inches in diameter, and put it into his jacket pocket. Rose wondered if he was keeping it for a weapon, but thought not, because he seemed to be at peace. When they reached the mouth of the river where it surged into the wide lake, they turned onto a sandy beach that was rimmed by a wrack of tiny pieces of driftwood. No larger than a thumbnail in size, each of the millions of fragments was unique, sculpted by the waves. Farther along, the sand ended and round gray stones began. Now and then among them could be found other colors: deep red or black or, rarest of all, pure pink. Rose took some of each. Added to these was an abandoned wasps' nest a foot in diameter. Binemin climbed up a birch tree like a monkey to get it and scrambled back down in the same manner, the nest clenched in his teeth. On the return journey he pried from deep moss a set of green caribou antlers tinted by orange lichen.

They arrived back at the cabin famished and flushed from their excursion. Oldmary came out onto the porch, bent, mumbling to herself, pretending that she did not see Binemin. He looked swiftly away from her but remained sitting on the edge of the porch. She put a pot of fish soup and two bowls and spoons on the step and a basket of broken bannock beside them. A tin can of apricot jam completed the feast. Then she went back inside.

After they had eaten, Rose showed Binemin where she wanted their treasures to be put. By the edge of the pool was an outcropping of stone, no more than a foot in height. Forest flowers grew around it: violets, marsh marigold, and tiny spotted lilies. Rose did not know these names. She called them stars, golds, and trouts. On the moss-capped stone she knelt and emptied her buckets. From the raw materials that she and Binemin had gathered, she now selected certain pieces, first the smallest white stones. These she arranged in a broad circle spaced a few inches apart. Each of the whites was then surrounded by pinks, so that gradually the whole began to emerge as a corona of roses. In the center, she placed the orb of quartz.

"This," she said to Binemin with great solemnity, "is a loon-star. It is a speckle that fell from the *tchibekana*, the necklace, the river of souls. There is only one on earth. It is ours."

He said nothing.

"And this is a garden, little brother", she explained, gazing with concentration as she arranged the tiny wood sculptures into spokes that revolved around the hub.

In the shed there were boxes of garbage. They contained broken crockery, cracked jars, bottle caps, pieces of colored glass, and a tin of moccasin beads that had split and could not hold a thread. Rose selected some of each for her material, placing them into the bucket. Returning to the garden, she arranged them with great care throughout the wheel. At the edge of the rim, farthest from the pool of water, Binemin placed the antlers. For an instant a look of pride crossed his face. Rose saw it and smiled. But he was too engrossed in the act of creation to notice. He placed the wasps' nest into the cradle of the antlers and stood back, hands on his waist, to see what she would do next.

"Our garden", she said.

From the woodshed she brought a rusty tin can and a cola bottle. With the can she gouged a hole in the moss at the base of the loon-star, then parted the moss below it into a miniature creek bed that led to the edge of the rock. Jumping down to the bank of the pool, she squatted and filled the can and the bottle with water. Then she hopped up and poured their contents into the hole. Quickly it filled to the brim, spilled out through the miniature creek bed, ran along it to the edge of the rock, and fell a foot to the pool below. The cascade made a sound like small bells.

Rose knelt down at the edge of the ring. She patted the circle.

"This is the world", she said. Binemin frowned at her in concentration. She put a finger on the loon-star. "And this is us, in the center of the world."

She told him to bring more water. Wordlessly, he obeyed. Taking the can from him she poured its contents slowly over the stone. The water trickled into the hole at its base.

"Underneath is a hidden spring", Rose said in a sing-song. "The spring bubbles up and flows out to the pool." The notes went higher and higher and became a chant. "The pool spills over into the little river. It goes over the waterfall and makes bells. Then it fills the big rain pool. The big rain pool spills into the creek. The creek runs down to the river. The river goes into the lake. The lake spills into the big rivers. The big rivers run to the sea."

She looked up to see if he had understood. His green eyes looked back at her without blinking, which was his way of saying, *Maybe I see, maybe I don't see, but it is enough that you see.*

He gazed at their creation with wonder. He sat down on the moss and took it all in through his eyes, which contained not a hint of madness or hatred. Rose sat beside him, amazed by her powers. The silence stretched until it dissolved into the singing which is presence. They could have remained in this state with perfect contentment, but for Binemin, whose natural state was one of action. He noticed that the waterfall had ceased playing its part in the music and got up, refilled the containers, and poured them over the loon-star. Once again rang the bells of the cascade.

During the following year, Binemin learned to read, to print, to add and subtract. But he never spoke, not even to Rose. It was assumed by all that he was a mute, though clearly he was not deaf. It was acknowledged throughout the village that only Rose Wâbos knew how to bring him out of himself, although this did not mean ordinary interaction. It meant rather a momentary break in his total isolation. Within a year of their meeting, he was attempting fleeting communication, but always through the eyes, by gestures, by presence or nonpresence. He would freeze instantly when others attempted to make him open his mouth.

The only exceptions to this rule were the teacher, to whom he gave the minimal responses necessary for learning, though always without spoken words, and Fr. Andrei, who communicated fluently by his smiling eyes, by a few muttered comments in an alien tongue—some said Polish—and by offering jam and white bread to Rose and Binemin after Mass.

One day, during Rose's eighth year and Binemin's tenth, Fr. Andrei sat down beside Binemin. Together they watched Rose arranging wildflowers in jars on the altar.

"May I pray for you, Binemin Edzo?" the priest asked.

And because Binemin did not refuse or flee, Fr. Andrei placed both hands over the boy's head and began to pray silently. At first Binemin's eyes flew open and the old flaring look returned to them. He flinched, but he did not run away. As the prayers went on, he closed his eyes and began to sigh. Then he grew very still. The priest made the sign of the cross over him and sat back. Neither of them spoke or moved. This was necessary, for silence was the primary language, and the priest knew it.

When sufficient time had elapsed, he said, "I need an altar boy to serve the Mass. Would you help me?"

Binemin looked away and said nothing, which Fr. Andrei suspected meant yes. So began another step. Throughout the following winter the boy listened to the instructions and carefully observed the moves the priest made during the Mass. Then, in his eleventh year, he made his first appearance at the altar. Of course he was not able to say the ritual responses, though he had learned the physical parts of his duties to perfection.

Humor especially was a means of union and growth. Binemin came to depend on his power to make Rose laugh. Although swallowing live minnows was a device that soon lost its appeal for her, he found that whenever he did something precipitous, clownlike, abandoned, and harmless, he could reduce her to giggles. And when she giggled a wave of pleasure surged up and filled for a brief time the empty spaces within him.

Walking along the river, he would pretend to trip on a piece of driftwood and pitch sideways into the water, remain under for a minute, and surface with a small flapping trout in his teeth. In winter, he would pitch headlong over a high bank, she would scream and run to the edge, terrified that he had hurt himself, only to find that he was flat on his back in a deep drift of snow, smiling up at her. She scolded him more than once for frightening her with such tricks, but she did it lightly, for she knew that he could endure only a feather touch.

His favorite means of entertaining her was to become lost during their walks through the forest. Thinking that he was behind her or beside her, she was easily distracted by the many wildflowers that bloomed among the trees. She would look up to find that he was gone. Worried, she would call his name: "Binemin! Little brother! *Nishime!*"

Then he would drop from a high branch in front of her, startling and delighting in a single stroke. At other times he would make bear noises in the thicker bushes, and she would grow terrified. She would walk swiftly away down the forest path, only to hear growling and shaking bushes behind, chasing her, closer and closer until he leaped in front of her with a bear's face. Arms raised, paws clawing the air, he would seem to hang suspended in space above her and fall slowly to the ground, where he would resume his boy shape. It was hard to be amused at this sort of thing, but after a little recovery she would always laugh.

After one such incident she heard the most wonderful sound in the world. That day she was gathering fireweed by the river, alone among the rustling grasses. Suddenly the undergrowth began to shake and a shape came hurtling toward her, a large black shape like a timber wolf, growling and howling and racing closer, closer.

"Nishime!" she cried, shaking with terror. "Nishime! Come quickly, I am afraid!" Then the wolf burst out of the weeds beside her, his wild canine eyes powerful with the bloodlust of the hunt—howl, howl, howl!

"Nishime!" she wailed, fighting back tears. "Stop!" Then the wolf dissolved from his face, he dropped to the ground, and rolled over onto his back with all four paws in the air, whimpering like a pup. This, of course, made her laugh, as he knew it would. And when she did, the wonderful sound came from his mouth. At first it was like the cough of a sick porcupine or the chuckles of Thisdog and Thatdog when they were wrestling with each other. Or a partridge thumping on a hollow log. It was a laugh. It was *his* laugh. Oh, it was so beautiful the fire in her heart grew very strong as they laughed and laughed and laughed together.

Not long after, he let himself go into the cabin with her and, more daringly, let Oldmary put food on the table for him. He sat on one of the chairs and ate, glancing around at the interior of the cabin, staring with special interest at the many pictures charcoaled on the log walls. After the meal, he left. From then on he came inside to eat. And once he even looked at Grandma. She smiled at him, but he looked swiftly away.

They were together every day during the following summer. Not once did he speak to Rose, and not once did he touch her. He was twelve years old now, his body shooting up rapidly. He would be tall one day. He was already many inches higher than Rose. She prayed that he would be pure, because Grandma told her a little about such things. And he was pure, because he still played like a small child, still pretended to be wild things, and still loved to tend the garden with her. He found new and interesting stone shapes, and she could see the pleasure it gave him when he presented them to her. He made a second ring of pebble flowers around the first. Whenever the pool dried up, he carted buckets of creek water to the garden so that together they could listen to the bells.

She often lay awake at night wondering about the horrible things that had happened to him. She sometimes felt it was just her imagining, maybe building a story out of the drawing he had made on the school house wall. Yet at other times she felt sure that what had come into her thoughts was real. Then the doubts would return and she would scold herself, saying that it was nothing more than a picture in her mind, a thought-drawing. But what if it *was* real? Grandma had told her that it was not good to look inside people without their permission. She said it was taking. And the way of love was giving, not taking, she said. This was true, Rose knew. Why, then, had the falling-into-seeing gift been given? Did Manito permit it so that she could love Binemin even more, did Manito want her to know how much her little brother needed her and how much sacrifice would be necessary?

From time to time she felt a hurting in her back. Sometimes it was so bad that she could not sleep, and then she would try to pour the hurting into the darkness in him, to push out the horrible things that had been done to him. But it seemed hard to do. Then she read in a book she found in the church that you had to offer sufferings to Jesus-Manito first, and he would use

44

the sacrifice in the best way of all. When she learned this, she felt peaceful inside and knew that the love was winning. As she grew older, month by month, followed by another year, she began to see the pattern. When she hurt most and poured it into the wounds of Jesus, *he* poured it into Binemin. And soon after, Binemin would make another step, and another, and another.

Someday, maybe, he would speak.

3

Then a wondrous thing occurred. A lady came to the village. She was a teacher.

On a warm afternoon in late August, under clear skies, the native people sensed a hum in the southern sky long before the white people heard it. In small groups, they made their way from the outlying encampments, through the village, to the lake. So that by the time the plane flew low overhead, most of the people had already gathered on the shore by the dock. One by one the whites emerged from their houses and walked down to the edge of water, talking together in excited voices.

The dark blue floatplane, a Norseman, landed far out on the water, then taxied in slowly, and slid toward the dock. Its engine burped and the silver disk of its propeller abruptly ceased to revolve. The trader moored the plane to a pylon. The pilot jumped out, leaped across the pontoons to the passenger side, and opened the door in the craft. A woman popped her head out and then climbed down.

The native people crowded forward, eyeing her curiously.

"Oh, her skin is very bright!" some women mumbled in Ojibwe.

"That is to be expected, she is *waiâbishkiwed*", replied others, marveling.

"Yes, a white woman. A very unusual one. She is so beautiful!"

"But not so young."

"Neither is she old."

The woman, whom everyone knew to be the new teacher, was now shaking hands in a manly way with the policeman and his wife, then the trader and his woman, and the priest.

The native people listened carefully to her words, which were mere pleasantries about weather and travel.

"Hear her, hear her", they commented, "Surely she is a *Jâganâshikwe.*"

"Yes, yes, it is certain. An Englishwoman. Her speech is not like the other *waiâbishkiwedjig.* There is bubbling in it and funny bending."

"Now she meets the *Anishinâbe-ogima,* the Indian agent."

"What is he saying to her?"

"I don't know, I can't hear!"

"*Ay, ay!* Don't push. Let me see her too!"

"He is telling her about the cabin where teachers live. See, he points to it. *Io,* she smiles, and what fine teeth!"

"Hello", the Englishwoman said to certain small children who had dared to press close.

They giggled and looked down at their feet.

She reached out, touched the head of a small girl and ruffled her hair. The child twisted away and ran shrieking with laughter into the crowd.

"She is not shy, this lady."

"No, she is not shy, but even in her kindness she lacks respect. She is, perhaps, *nagânisid*—superior."

"But then, all the whites are like that, the good and the bad."

"This is so."

"*Io!* Such fine cloth she wears. Colored like the early mossberry, and that sweater like *miskobaga,* when the leaves are purple-red."

"And leather moccasins, very shiny."

"A neck like *wâbisi* the swan."

"This one has good breasts", said an old woman. "She will soon be gone. She will marry the *Anishinâbe-ogima!*"

47

The crowd erupted in laughter. Uncomprehending, the teacher smiled at them, which made them laugh louder.

"Or run off with the trader." But this was said sneeringly by Kinoje, the medicine man, and was greeted by less laughter, for many of the people were Christians.

The Englishwoman's eyes swept the crowd of observers, lingering on the children for an extra moment, then she turned away briskly, businesslike, to oversee the unloading of her baggage. The pilot and the Indian agent manhandled three steamer trunks down from the opened side of the plane, followed by cardboard boxes, suitcases upholstered in flowered cloth, and a wire cage.

"Stand back, stand back", people cried. "They are taking her to the teacher's cabin."

The woman was accompanied from the dock by a handful of whites. The crowd of natives parted to let them pass.

"What is in that cage?"

"Small furry animals."

"Yes, yes, they are *wajashk*!"

More laughter.

"How silly is this woman. She brings two muskrats in a wire box when the lake is full of them."

The people crowded close, pointing, staring, laughing.

"The teacher has brought us two *wajashk*!" someone cried loudly.

Great hilarity swept through the people. The woman appeared puzzled and halted, frowning amusedly, allowing them to inspect her cage. Then she smiled broadly and proceeded up the hill to the teacherage.

Classes began on the following Tuesday. Approximately two dozen children straggled into the school throughout the first morning. Though more than a few of them would drop out during the following months, most stayed. Among them was

48

Rose Wâbos. Because the teacher was new, Rose took it upon herself to move from the front row to the back. There she sat on a bench, holding her hands between her knees, making herself very small so that she would not be noticed. She had come only to gaze in wonder at the beautiful *Jâganâshikwe*.

"Children, my name is Miss Gorrel", the teacher explained with an apologetic smile. "Which rhymes with coral. But I shall not expect you to pronounce it correctly at first."

Onto the blackboard she chalked, *Miss Euphrasia Gorrel*.

She looked at each of them.

"Now, I would like to learn your names", she said pleasantly. "Who will be first?"

Though all eyes were on her, no one offered to identify himself.

"Don't be afraid", said the woman. "None of your names, I promise you, could seem more exotic to me than my own."

Of course no one understood what she meant by that.

Strolling to the back of the room, the woman spotted Rose. "What is your name, child?"

The girl looked away and mumbled. Of all the pitifully dressed children in the room, she was the most forlorn. She wore a ragged sweater covered with nubbly lint, unraveling at the grimy sleeves, a patched calico dress from which the brown neck stood up like a pencil. Torn wool socks were covered by oversize rubber slip-on boots.

"Come, tell me your name", said the woman.

"*Oginiwâbigon Wâbos*", Rose whispered.

The woman raised her eyebrows and struggled to repeat it.

After three unsuccessful attempts, she said, "I have brought a dictionary with me, but alas, it is only English-Otchipwe, compiled in 1878 by the missionaries and lacks a pronunciation guide. So, you see, I will need your help, children."

Although she knew a fair amount of simple English, Rose

did not grasp what the woman was saying. She shrank into herself and wished to flee.

"Now, tell me, young lady, what does your name mean in English?"

"*Oginiwâbigon* means rose flower", said an older girl. "*Wâbos* is rabbit."

"Rose Rabbit", the woman's lips trembled. She cleared her throat. "Well, that is a lovely name. We shall soon get to know each other, Rose. And all of you, children. We shall be great friends. I am not an ordinary teacher, as you shall presently discover."

She demonstrated this by walking to the front of the room and removing a silk scarf that covered the cage on her desk.

Inside, two small mounds of fur began to squeak frantically. The children stared openmouthed for a few seconds, then tumbled from their benches and crowded around the cage.

"Allow me to introduce Wallace and Simpson", said Miss Gorrel. "They are guinea pigs."

"They are little *wajashk*", a girl said.

"What is a *wajashk*?" the teacher asked.

"Muskrat."

"Without tails", said another.

"But they are different. This one is the color of the summer fox", said a girl.

"Soft and shining, like the fisher fur."

"Ooh, the other one is like a white weasel with spots."

"If you catch lots of them," said a boy, "you can trade them for money."

"You could make a coat", suggested a girl.

"You could make mittens", ventured another.

Miss Gorrel looked momentarily disturbed. "No, my dears, these are our little friends. We will tame them. They will provide hours of enjoyment. They will teach us much."

"Can you eat them?" asked a small boy.

"No", said the teacher firmly. "Rather, yes. In fact, they are the national dish of Peru."

All eyes turned upon her.

"Did you know, children, that I have been to Peru. I have climbed into the Andes mountains to the lost city of Machu Picchu, where many centuries ago your distant relations built a city in the clouds."

So began their education.

Of the many things they learned that year were certain rudimentary skills in arithmetic, sewing, artwork, and the shape of the planet—the latter was difficult for them to grasp because their eyes told them that it was flat. But they understood that even teachers could not get everything right, that white people often misinterpreted the obvious.

Their reading skills were helped along considerably by the teacher's recitation of several books written and illustrated by a woman named Beatrix Potter, which was a very strange name. The stories were full of characters named Rabbit and Fox and Fisher and even a guinea pig named Podge.

As the last of Indian summer waned, the teacher and the children harvested boxes full of wild grass as hay for the coming winter. The guinea pigs grew fat on it. The female, Wallace, grew fatter than her mate, for reasons that were not immediately obvious.

Miss Gorrel was very good at treating everyone fairly. She had no great favorites, though when the lowered heads of the children scratched tortuously over pencil and paper, she scanned them in search of a soul-mate, or at least a spiritual child in need of rescue. All of them needed her, she knew, yet not a one of them was aware of their need for elevation. But beneath the primitive exteriors, she thought, there would almost certainly be a treasure in the rough. At the many places where she had taught, she had always found this to be so.

The walls of the schoolroom gradually filled with the

children's drawings, which for the most part were incomprehensible gashes, stick humans, or symbolic animals. Rose Rabbit's efforts, however, tended to be the most original. The girl was obsessed with drawing, grinding through boxes of crayons at twice the rate of the other children. She hunched insatiably over her pictures of fish leaping in lashing rivers, bristling porcupines, starry nights, loons and geese, and landscapes that day and night were always dominated by a full whitish moon.

"What is the Ojibwe word for moon?" the teacher asked her one day.

"*Gissis*", Rose murmured, her eyes looking up like two black moons.

"Ah, *gissis*. I see, Rose, that you always put a moon into your compositions. Do you like the moon?"

"I call her *ningâ*."

"*Ningâ?*"

But this was so revealing that Rose instantly retracted, squeezed her mouth shut, looked down, and covered her drawing with both arms.

"It means *my mother*", explained an older girl who was in the first stages of currying favor. "Rose don't gotta mother."

"She gotta grandmother. She got Oldmary", someone else corrected.

Miss Gorrel looked more closely at the small rabbit, said nothing, and went on to approve the art of other children.

There was one boy—a singularly strange looking child of mixed breed—who did not produce art or written compositions. When papers and crayons were handed out, he folded his hands and stared at the desk top. Though he was obviously approaching adolescence, he read at the level of a six- or seven-year-old. Moreover, he never spoke. He was pitiful, yet in his perverse way quite intelligent. The intelligence was all in the eyes, as were the scraps of communication that occasionally flickered on the surface of the dark reservoir within. As the days drew on and the children responded (she knew they would—they always did, wherever she lived), only he remained distant. He hung back from the little throngs that gathered about her desk several times a day, he was indifferent to the usual methods of eliciting childish worship, and he watched her carefully. The large green eyes under the shock of red-brown hair were disturbing, not so much because of their oddity, but because they stared at her continuously.

It was flattering, really. Or perhaps frightening. The Indian agent told her about the boy's background, warned her that he was disturbed, though not prone to violence. A strange case. Very strange. She made a special effort with him, tried to win him, taking her time at it, rewarding him with biscuits and candies whenever his work rose above his usual mediocrity. She paid special attention to the nuances of his nods and frozen stares, the openings and closings of expression. If she stood beside his desk and asked him to speak or read, he merely looked away, making her invisible. But because she was committed on principle to nonviolence, even the emotional kinds of violence, she did not threaten him. Considering his past, any punishment she could offer would be meaningless. He was a challenge. He was the kind of challenge she liked.

He was attached to the little rabbit girl and she to him. It was so very symbiotic, so very obvious that the two outcasts supported each other. At recess and lunch hour, Miss Gorrel watched them from the window of the schoolhouse, noting that they did not join in the games the other children played, but seemed content to walk side by side along the perimeter of the grounds, by the trees. The girl rarely spoke in class and then only when asked a question and always with diffidence. But she chattered happily whenever she walked with the wild boy—"the feral child" as the teacher called him in the privacy of her thoughts. The boy seemed to be listening to her and sometimes responded with hand gestures or jumped about like an animal, though he did not open his mouth.

Week after week, Miss Gorrel thought long and sensitively about the two children, asking herself how she might turn their relationship to her advantage—rather, to their advantage. After class one afternoon, she invited Rose and Binemin to remain behind. She positioned them in two front desks, where they sat patiently looking up at her. She took her desk chair and placed it before them, sat down on it, and arranged her skirt tastefully. Folding her hands, she began.

"My dear children—I call you this for you are, indeed, my children—I want you to know that I think you are my best students."

Disbelief flitted across both sets of eyes. A spark of suspicion ignited in the boy's.

"It is my belief that you, Rose, are very gifted creatively. You are bright and loving and talented."

Though she did not understand everything the teacher had said, Rose smiled shyly with pleasure.

Turning to the boy, the woman continued. "And it is my belief, Binemin, that you are the most intelligent person in our class." She told herself that this was quite true. That he was also damaged, demented, and appallingly underdeveloped were factors that were better left unsaid.

"How far you both shall go in this life! Yes, so very far and high! I am convinced that you can go wherever you wish to go."

She paused.

"You will be successful. And you will be happy, if you choose your path carefully."

Another pause. The children remained silent, waiting.

"Binemin, it is possible that you will go farthest. But there is something you will need on your journey. I see that already you have learned to read and print and do arithmetic. This is excellent. This is the mark of a heroic struggle."

When Miss Gorrel noticed the sudden confusion filling his eyes, she realized that she should not pursue this line too far.

Leaning forward intently, she said to the boy, "But it is not enough. You must learn to speak."

Instantly his eyes shut down and he looked out the window.

"He can't, Miss", Rose explained in a small worried voice.

"Oh, but he can", Miss Gorrel countered with great and kindly authority. "I know that he can. You see, he already speaks, doesn't he."

Perplexed, Rose shook her head.

"He does not speak with words, of course. But he makes sounds, don't you, Binemin? And you talk with your eyes." Miss Gorrel laughed gently. "Yes, I have noticed. I know the greatness inside of you, longing to come out. I am one who recognizes the fugitive veins of gold in the darkened shafts. I have seen it many times, in many places, among several indigenous peoples. And I see it in you."

The two children stared at the teacher, chins down, eyes fixed on her.

"You speak all the time, Binemin. It pours from you. That is language."

"He has no words, Miss", Rose said.

"But he *understands* words, doesn't he, Rose dear. He understands very well."

Furrowing her brow, Rose tried to grasp what the teacher was saying. "You mean the bird songs and the bear and wolf and other animal words?"

"Yes, precisely."

"But that's just playing."

"All language is playing." She patted Rose's knee. "Ah, but I am getting ahead of myself."

"When you were very young," Miss Gorrel said turning to Binemin, "you spoke. You said words from your mouth. But then you stopped. Now you speak only animal and bird language. But we humans are also animals. Wouldn't it be nice if you were to learn to speak our language again?"

At that, Wallace and Simpson began to squeal in high pitched chortles.

Rose giggled. Miraculously, Binemin smiled. Though Miss Gorrel did not believe in miracles, she knew an opportunity when she saw one.

"They are talking to us", she said.

The boy began to chortle to the guinea pigs in perfect imitation. The guinea pigs answered. Rose giggled again, Miss Gorrel threw back her head and laughed, and Binemin made his strange happy noise like the cough of a porcupine or the thrum of a partridge on a log.

"There, you see, wasn't that wonderful? Now why don't we try a human word? You first, Rose."

"What should I say?"

"Anything you wish."

"*Ningâ*", Rose whispered.

"Very good. Now you, Binemin."

His face froze and he stared at the floor. They waited for him. A minute passed, and then another. Miss Gorrel was about to admit defeat when Binemin forced his lips into a tight O and from deep in his throat made a huff–huff, gulp–gulp sound.

"Is that an animal we know?" the woman asked.

He nodded. Her heart leaped. He had replied in the affirmative, though it was not exactly speech.

"Ng-ng-huh-huh", he said. The voice was abrasive from disuse, deep with oncoming adolescence.

Afraid of shattering the delicate moment, Miss Gorrel yearned the sounds out of him. "Yes", she whispered slowly. "There is more, isn't there? You can tell us. You can say it."

"Ng-ng-ing-guhuh-ghuh."

"*Ningâ*", Rose said, wonder filling her eyes.

"Can you say it again, Binemin?" the teacher pressed.

"Ning-ghuh", burst from him. He flushed red beneath the brown skin, his eyes suddenly wild with fear, his lips trembling.

"One more time, now."

"Ningâ!" he howled. It was a cry of agony. He leaped to his feet, knocking the chair to the floor, and ran from the room.

"Oh, dear," Miss Gorrel groaned. "What have I done?" Flustered, she stood and went to the door of the schoolhouse and watched him galloping toward the woods.

"Go to him, Rose. He trusts you."

Rose went out silently and followed him.

He did not reappear in class for a week, and when he did, he was more uncommunicative than ever. But the teacher found some consolation in the fact that he continued to struggle over his school work. Letters and numbers. See Spot run. Run, run, Spot. He still would not make pictures or compose sentences, as the other children did. But sometimes, as the winter fell upon the northlands, and the windows of the classroom frosted thick, she would spy him feeding strands of dried grass to the guinea pigs as they chortled at each other and at him and he to them.

It was her first winter among the natives, a season that offered many opportunities for intelligent pity, for discreet assistance to the underprivileged, and for her primary goal of enlarging small lives. The children were her artwork, and they were responding well. She was happy. Though she did suffer a tragedy of sorts in January when she was sick in bed with the flu for a few days. Upon returning to class, she was met by a small boy who proudly presented her with two circles of willow branch on which the pelts of furred creatures had been stretched by threads of sinew. The fur of one was rusty orange. The other was white with black speckles.

"I see", Miss Gorrel said warmly. "How very clever of you to learn the skills of your ancestors. And what are these creatures? This one, I am certain, is ermine. And the other is fox, is it not?"

"No, Miss, they's *wajashk*!" said the little boy.

"*Wajashk*—oh, yes, muskrat. But such odd colors."

"They's the *wajashk* you bringed on the plane." He pointed to the empty cage at the back of the room.

With a sharp intake of breath she understood, but forced the horror back down her throat.

"We cooked 'em while you was away."

"You cooked them?" she repeated weakly.

"They was good. They was real good."

"Oh", she murmured.

"We saved the hides for you", he added with an adoring smile.

After winter came spring, the return of smells, the return of colors.

On the porch of the trading post three or four raggedy men in red hunting caps and dirty bush jackets were waiting to see what would happen. They sat on benches, rolled cigarettes, and discussed the muskrat harvest and the state of the ice while Oldmary and Rose, hand in hand, stood on the steps waiting for the white lady. A few minutes later Miss Gorrel strode jauntily down the path from the teacherage, smiled broadly from a distance, and waved a girlish flutter of her right palm. Binoculars on straps thumped against her chest. Over her left arm she carried a tartan blanket dominated by greens and yellows, with bobbed fringes. Looped over her waving arm was the long handle of a wicker picnic basket. She wore a sweater of richest maroon (on which was pinned a brooch of tooled Scottish thistle), topped by the white collar of a blouse. Her black-green tartan skirt went halfway down her shins, clipped on the side by a glittering, giant safety pin.

She clomped to the porch in brown oxfords and nodded in a friendly way at the men, who nodded back as if they had no ambition in life, their mouths hanging open in undisguised fascination, smoke trailing from their nostrils.

"Good morning, Mary, good morning, Rose", said the teacher smiling in anticipated pleasure, her chin touching her exquisite collarbone, looking down into their faces, for the natives were, in fact, startlingly short people.

Oldmary nodded and returned the greeting, "Good morning, Miss."

Never had Oldmary looked so bent, so brittled under the persistent wind, like weeds when they have been sun-baked, seed-blown, their purpose fulfilled. Miss Gorrel thought to herself that the dear, dear old woman was as tarnish-brown as a neglected silver tea service.

Rose's eyes flashed, and she blushed, as much as a surge of blood would reveal under bronze cheeks. She squeezed her grandmother's hand tightly and jumped, or was perhaps executing a single skip as an ejaculation of pure joy.

Miss Gorrel extended an arm. Rose took the slender hand tentatively and was absorbed totally by the brief transfer of authority.

"You are a fast walker", Oldmary mumbled to the teacher. "Rose is slow."

"But bright in her heart", Miss Gorrel replied.

"Her back gets tired."

"Then we shall let Rose set the pace, won't we, Rose?"

Rose nodded.

With that, the teacher and the little girl went away, leaving Oldmary staring after them. Miss Gorrel turned once, at the bend in the trail, and waved and directed Rose to do the same, which she did with a tiny smile before they were swallowed by the trees.

Beyond the village, the trail petered out and the massive stone of the shoreline began, swelling to the east, curving around the lake upon which the sun was exploding. The reflection from the rotting ice was too much for direct gaze, but the girl endured it with eyes that became almond slits. The woman dealt with the exaggerated light judiciously, stopping from time to time to raise her free hand above her brow, to shield the eyes, to orient herself by a horizon which was an elegant flourish of mauve ink washed across a pale blue paper sky. Miss Gorrel recognized it as a work of articulation. The land spoke of a piercing loneliness, or perhaps more accurately of a melancholy, but not unsweet, solitude.

So far, the forest struggled unsuccessfully to encroach on the granite of the Precambrian shield, though the humble and deceptively powerless lichen seemed to have no difficulty invading everywhere. As the woman and child walked, the sandpaper rock gritted under their shoes pleasantly, not unlike a stroll on city pavement.

Turning gradually to the northeast, the stone path narrowed until it revealed itself as the spine of the land, rising in jade layers above its own muscles. Now the earlier inclines began to intensify, the rises pitching themselves higher and the dips becoming plunges into furred hollows, which it would be senseless to enter and explore. And so, the printless track of the two humans wound this way and that and climbed. They began to feel their lungs and hear their breath, but they were compensated for their effort by the view from a steadily increasing and possibly exalting height. The wind also increased from the direction of the lake, ice-cooled and fresh. The sun beat on their backs.

The trees became ever more stunted. Here and there were twisted skeletons of trees petrified in the heartrending gestures in which they had burned to death—a flung arm, a cocked elbow, a coil of umbilicus root still clutching the gravel. The trunks were streaked with old black wounds, washed to piebald white and gray, and drowning in the green froth of new growth.

The wind kept the mosquitoes at bay. It was a day for brisk exhalations such as one might take on a high moor with a curdle of sheep shaping and reshaping itself in the lower meadows. But here there were only wild creatures, though none Miss Gorrel could not handle. The animals themselves, perhaps realizing their peril, quickly made themselves invisible. The woman stopped occasionally to peer at the dissolving of a fleeing buck or the liquefying black of a pine marten, using the binoculars with a furrowed brow that in no way indicated displeasure.

They paused to catch their breath at a hummock of rock split with many fierce cracks. A sheaf of brown hair with a thread of premature gray fell down from above Miss Gorrel's left ear; she brushed it back and reproved it with a silver barrette. Still smiling, she shielded her eyes again and scanned the dazzling lake to the north and the heaving undulation to the south.

Looking down at the girl, whose hand was becoming sweaty in her own, she said, "Are you all right, Rose?"

Rose smiled broadly and nodded.

"Are we going too quickly?"

Rose shook her head.

"Brave girl! Then shall we continue?"

A single skip was sufficient reply.

For another hour they climbed until the spine arched upward to a round cranium of rock that ended in a sharp brow. To step beyond it was to pitch headlong down to the lake several hundred feet below. The woman and the girl stood on the edge resisting its pull. The cortex of surrounding trees peeled back from the height, permitting them an all-encompassing view. There, on its uttermost rim, the entire planet and its two representative humans were exposed to the scrutiny of unmediated light.

Miss Gorrel quickly unfurled the tartan blanket in a socket of stone which was shielded a little from the wind. The blanket just escaped being snatched away and tumbled down the mountain to be forever lost, but she caught it decisively, spread it on a patch of moss, and weighted the corners with small stones, adding the basket and binoculars and herself. She patted the spot beside her and Rose obediently sat down.

"Oh, it is too glorious!" the woman cried, lifting her face, eyes closed, to the sun. "Hail thee, festival day!" she cried again, adding her voice to the shrieks of excited gulls.

Rose, observing her, thought that Miss Gorrel was the most beautiful person she had ever seen. The creamy skin of her face was flushed from the exertion of the climb, and her eyes, now blue, now violet, now hazel, drank the horizons hungrily. To the north, above the uncertain line where ice and sky met, a shimmering of air became a silent turbulence that began to engorge into sculpted clouds containing very distant and beautiful storms. All else was palest blue.

"Ah, Rose, is it not perfection?"

Rose nodded.

"Look!" the woman said, rising, pointing, "Now I see why Threefinger Lake is so named! The lake is in the shape of a hand, and at its northernmost shore it extends into three elongated bays. As if a giant rested here once long ago and imprinted it in the stone."

"Or God", Rose said.

"Oh, yes", the woman laughed. "Or God."

Seating herself again she asked, "Are you thirsty?"

"Yes, Miss."

"You may call me Euphrasia", the woman said, as if bestowing a great honor, "because we are friends."

Rose flushed with embarrassment.

"Can you say it?" prompted Miss Gorrel.

Rose forced her lips to mime the difficult syllables.

Ee-you-fray-zee-ah.

"No?" the teacher smiled. "Ah, well, then we shall retain the established formalities."

Miss Gorrel began to unpack the picnic basket, removing from it with unwasted gestures a thermos bottle, several pack-

62

ets of sandwich wrapped neatly in wax paper, two oranges, two apples, and a tin box. The box, like so many of her things, was of plaid design, and printed on its lid was a girl in Scottish dress standing before a castle surrounded by heather. The gold enameled letters read *Dundee Sweet Horehound*. The tin did not contain any candy, however, but instead offered two layers of ivory-colored shortbread, cut into fingers, which melted on their tongues and made them want to eat it all at once, which they did, after the more sensible sandwiches.

As they sipped from two porcelain cups filled with orange squash, Euphrasia Gorrel returned to the sky. Sweeping the dome of blue, though not discounting the towering cumulus which was still distant, letting her eyes sink down again to the miniature forest below, she sighed happily and whispered, "This, then, is *ultima thule*, where one would walk if one wished to be absorbed into absolutes, to be taken, and to be seen no more."

The words moved the speaker to a brim of tears which did not quite spill over the edges of her thick lashes.

Remembering Rose, she said, "You have always lived here. Is it, I wonder, ordinary?"

Rose, struggling to catch the sense of the words, if not the actual meaning, replied, "If you look at it a long time, you go there. In your . . . heart."

"Yes, it is like that", Miss Gorrel said at last. "Very much like that. Sometimes, Rose, sometimes when I am weary of the many artifices of mankind, I desire to walk into that emptiness, or that lavishness which disguises itself as emptiness, and never return."

Rose did not know all of these words, but she struggled to understand something of what the woman meant. Though the words were mystical and wise, they made Rose uneasy. The feeling was similar to what she would have felt while watching a burst of wild flowers fall asleep in a jar and the colors seep away and turn a final black. It was both beautiful and sad.

"You would get lost", Rose said.

The woman laughed suddenly and shook herself.

"Yes, of course. It would be silly, wouldn't it, doing something like that. On a whim. On a sentiment."

"But, if you did, God would be with you."

Miss Gorrel looked into the girl's obsidian eyes and repressed a wave of pity, if not discreet indignation. God again! Must it always be this way? she wondered. Is there only one alternative? Is the only replacement for their pagan religion our own quite primitive faith?

"God?" she murmured.

"He is everywhere", said the girl, with timid enthusiasm, barely restraining a force that Miss Gorrel recognized as naïve joy.

But most moods can be shaken off with an effort of the will. The woman smiled and stroked the girl's arm. She looked into the distance, into the sea of ice.

"When I was your age, Rose, I sat in a cathedral and listened to sermons. A man with white mutton chop whiskers informed me of a God who is everywhere, and who is Law, who is Justice. Later, in a school chapel, I learned from a young divine who had graduated from Oxford that God is everywhere, and he is Love. Which of these two admirable men, do you think, was correct?"

But Rose, straining to grasp the strands of a too complicated question, was unsure.

"Neither or both?" Miss Gorrel prompted gently.

Rose looked down at her empty hands.

"The two men . . . both of them said . . . he is everywhere," Rose offered.

"Yes", the woman replied thoughtfully. "That *was* a convergence of sorts, in certain details."

Rose scampered off into the surrounding bush, laughing at the squirrels who were outraged by the presence of humans, investigating the rubble under upturned tree roots, rearranging pebbles into the shape of flowers and letters: R O S E. She ran off again and returned shyly to present a clutch of actual flowers to the woman.

"That is beautiful, my girl. Very beautiful. Why I believe these white ones are the bloom of the wild strawberry, and this purple spike is, yes, it cannot be but I am sure it *must* be, a woolly lousewort. And this blue one is viper's bugloss." She laughed. "Oh, sometimes I think the people who name flowers should be penalized!"

Then Rose presented the finest gift of all. The three little objects tumbled into Miss Gorrel's open palm.

"What is this?" she asked curiously.

"It's bones", Rose answered. "I found them in the moss."

The bones were tinted palest green with a lacing of rust-orange. They were vertebra of unknown origin.

The woman rolled them in her palm. They clicked.

"Here," said Rose, taking them back, "they fit like this."

Carefully she assembled the pieces until they resembled a portion of spine. She manipulated the parts demonstrating how ingeniously they worked together, how they simulated the moving back of a deer or a wolf.

Rose looked up expectantly, as if the design could not fail to convince Miss Gorrel of the cleverness, if not the existence, of the designer.

"Yes. It is amazing", the woman said without emotion. "Life is always and everywhere amazing."

She observed the dance of bones for quite some time, saying nothing. Eventually she sighed and seemed to change the subject:

"My father used to dig up things", she murmured for no reason whatsoever. "He was an archaeologist. He was absent much of the time."

She sighed again.

"I have lived in many places. I have taught in the hinterland of Australia, in Africa, in South America, on Jersey in the Channel Islands, even the outermost reaches of savage Scotland (she smiled), and now I am here. I have seen many things and known many peoples. I have been shaken by concertos in Salzburg and narrowly escaped being consumed by a crocodile in a ditch on the Nile delta. And once nearly fell headlong into the chiaroscuro of a painting by Caravaggio in Florence. I have won a game of field hockey, galloped a dapple-grey horse, and caught a trout with a fly rod. I have ridden a camel at Giza, knitted a shawl from Aran wool which I carded with my own hands, and purchased the dreamtime paintings of aboriginals drunk on mentholated spirits."

Rose wondered who Miss Gorrel was talking to. Perhaps to a spirit. Regardless, she found the experience so fascinating that she continued to listen with open mouth and adoring eyes.

"I have climbed to the crow's nest of a sailing ship and been lashed through the sky. I have collected painted eggs from the Ukraine. I have sipped sherry while discussing the Palestine problem with a famous politician. Once I split an oyster shell and discovered in its meat a misshapen black pearl, which I kept. My mother and I bred a new peony of an unusual shade of peach. It was afterward named for my mother, *Véronique*, and is famous now in European botanical circles. I have read Stendahl and Fielding, which was daring for a young girl of my generation. I have been courted, wooed, but never won. I have (though you will probably not believe me) met a young prince at Balmoral (we were invited because of the peony). I watched him dance a *schottische*, and a reel, and a highland buck-and-wing, delighting in his perfect timing when he clapped his hands as he wove through the choreography with manful grace. Thus, I fell in love with him, from a distance, in a crowd, as we all did, learning at that instant that I would always be too young or too old for the ones destined to be the ideal form which love does sometimes take. But whether this is by design or accident, I cannot say, do not, in fact, know." She frowned suddenly. "Then he married that American woman."

"Miss?" Rose said tugging at the teacher's sleeve.

Miss Gorrel flushed and blinked. "This is unfair of me", she admonished herself. "It is so unfair to speak of things which you can scarcely imagine, Rose, as if to imply that you are merely a mute receptacle for the self-indulgent musings of a spinster."

Rose did not mind. Her eyes swimming with exotic visions and the unsuspected richness of her teacher's life, she wanted the tale to go on without end. In an act of great daring and intimacy she took Miss Gorrel's hands in her own two small brown paws and squeezed.

"Please, tell me more", she implored.

After consideration, the woman sighed again, as if gearing down for a more difficult terrain of memory. "How much will you remember of this day, child? Perhaps a little. If I speak of these things it is because the reaching itself, Rose, is the true illumination, more significant than the transfer of information."

Miss Gorrel laughed abruptly and scolded herself again: "*Tiens, mais je deviens impossible! La poétesse folle! Le coeur abandonné! Chère pathétique Euphrasia, Mademoiselle Gorreille, dauphine d'ancienne Normandie!* Tell me, how many soliloquies can be absorbed by a little *oiseau sauvage*?"

Rose, undaunted by this paroxysm of self-doubt, pleaded with her eyes and an extra squeeze.

In sadder tones, the woman continued.

"Life is beauty and horror. Of beauty I have seen much and of horror a little. For example, I have seen a golden-haired sailor without a face washed onto the shore of my own native coast. I have stroked a two-headed calf, which during its short life appreciated the illusion of having twice as many mothers as any ordinary calf. I have visited a church in which hundreds of statues had endured the removal of their stone heads, surgically decapitated by religious conviction. I have seen a screaming wallaby split in two with an axe and its young removed from its marsupial pouch and dropped alive into a pot of boiling water. I have seen young black mothers blinded by disease, and worms eating holes into the legs of their children. All flesh is red under the wrappings, did you know. So too, human nature varies little from race to race. The fundamentals of flesh and psyche are the same."

Miss Gorrel realized that she was continuing to be insensitive, insensitive most of all for talking over the child's head with very long words.

"You are one who listens, Rose", she said wistfully. "That is a rare and precious quality."

Raptured by this moving event, Rose knew that she was not understanding much of what the woman was telling her, but did grasp the essential thing, that being invited to participate was itself the gift.

"We shall speak of other things", Miss Gorrel said with finality.

"Did you ever get married?" Rose asked.

Miss Gorrel shifted her body uncomfortably.

"No. Though not from lack of dreaming. Nor lack of being asked."

"Many men asked you?"

"Let us say that a few earnest suitors made preliminary inquiries, and I practically fell."

"You fell down?"

"Actually, I said no."

"Why did you say no?"

"The ones who asked were not the appointed station of my journey."

"Weren't they nice?"

"They were all—well, most of them—nice. But cities breed

68

ciphers, scurriers, tortoise-men, moles, and potentates, the havers and getters before it cloys, you see, who end by choking on their resentment and disillusionment. Wilderness, by contrast, breeds beast-men. There is very little in between."

Rose felt that perhaps this was not a happy thing. "Oh", she said in a small voice. "That is sad."

"Only once," Miss Gorrel went on, "only once did a perfect shape materialize. Only once did fairest love present itself in my path. In that singular being the interior life and the exterior confirmed each other in the ideal form."

"What was it?"

"It was a man."

"What was his name?"

"I never discovered."

Rose puzzled over this.

"It was enough that he existed", Miss Gorrel explained.

"Where did you meet him?" Rose pressed.

Miss Gorrel cleared her throat and gazed into the convolutions of time.

"I was walking on a moor beyond Edinburgh. There were few paths on the heights, but I found one and followed it, going I know not where. The morning was dark and brooding, with a thin rain that was not unpleasant. Yet I was content, warm, bundled well against the weather. I was in my early twenties then, teaching at a private school, my first position, before Australia and Africa. I was young and, I suppose some would say, attractive. I had a hawthorn walking stick which one of the masters had loaned to me for my solitary jaunt. I had a small Swinburne in my pocket and a thermos in the rucksack, for tea on a purple ridge, in the heather, in the mist.

"Then, out of the fog, a white cloud thickened and began to bleat, for it was a flock of sheep with new lambs, from a farm down in the valley, moving to higher ground. And at the head of the flock there was a walking man, a young man easy in his strength, a fern-hillish man, climbing slow in his rough cloth-ing, black rubber boots, and baggy corduroys, a tattered gray sweater of nubbly wool with holes in it and stains at the wrists. For he was that close. When he saw me seated on a rock beside the path, he halted like a startled hart. And looked. He said nothing. His ewes also stopped and looked, though they, poor things, began to gossip one to the other in subdued voices.

"He tipped his cloth cap and said, 'Good morning, Miss.'

" 'It seems far from good, weather-wise,' I rejoined, 'but it is pleasant enough.' At this he smiled and said, 'A person should be cautious about hiking in the wet. There are hollows and cliffs hereabouts, and you might step into one without knowing, till you hit bottom.'

" 'I am not afraid', I said.

" 'May I sit beside you?' he asked, taking a step closer, doffing his cap, pointing to the wide rock on which I was resting.

" 'Sit, then, for the rock is not mine.'

" 'Thank you', he said.

"His voice was deep and calm, neither tense like so many of the ambitious masters, nor lazy and corrupt like the decadent young rich, nor coarse like the locals. I will not describe his physical appearance, for it is enough to say he was a finely wrought balance of strength and harmony. Most of all I was entranced by the eyes, which were Celtic blue, gentle without being weak. In his bearing there was a dignity neither ponder-ous nor timid, nor brash. Merely *itself* in its own reverent power.

" 'I am Euphrasia Gorrel', I said, extending my hand. He shook it once. Firm, warm, but not overpowering. He was the first person in my life who did not laugh at my name, or suppress a laugh, which is the same thing really.

" 'And with whom, pray tell, am I conversing?' I asked.

"He looked thoughtful, then said, 'Names are shapes we give to things unknown.'

"Made breathless by this improbable response, I hastened to collect my wits. 'You are an intellectual, then?'

"'Far from it', he demurred. 'Though I like to read.'

"'What, then, do you read?'

"He removed a battered book from a bag strapped over his shoulder. 'Shakespeare', he said.

"'So you know Shakespeare', I replied, barely suppressing my laughter. 'Which play are you reading?'

"'*A Midsummer Night's Dream*.'

"'Ah, the *Dream*. I know it well.'

"'Do you have a favorite passage in it, Miss?'

"'Yes, the end part. After the play within a play, where Puck apologizes for the fairies. Do you know it?' I asked.

"To my surprise, he looked into the mist above the flock and closed his eyes. Then he recited from memory the lines spoken by Theseus:

> 'More strange than true: I never may believe
> These antique fables, nor these fairy toys.
> Lovers and madmen have such seething brains,
> Such shaping fantasies, that apprehend
> More than cool reason ever comprehends.
> The lunatic, the lover and the poet
> Are of imagination all compact:
> One sees more devils than vast hell can hold,
> That is, the madman: the lover, all as frantic,
> Sees Helen's beauty in a brow of Egypt:
> The poet's eye, in a fine frenzy rolling,
> Doth glance from heaven to earth, from earth to
>   heaven;
> And as imagination bodies forth
> The forms of things unknown, the poet's pen
> Turns them to shapes, and gives to airy nothing
> A local habitation and a name.'

71

"Finished, my nameless companion said no more; he merely opened the book and stared into the pages. But he was not reading, for his eyes were fixed upon some unseen meditation. I did not dare to speak for fear of breaking the spell, and for fear that he might indeed be a lunatic, a compact lover, or a poet in a fine frenzy. He was none of those, of course, but I did not know exactly what he might be.

"At last he looked over at me and said, 'Tis not to airy *nothings* he gives a name.'

"*He?* I wondered. *Whom does he mean?*

"'Oh,' I said too hastily, too noisily, 'that is Shakespeare the artist commenting through his dramatic persona on the nature of art itself. One might disagree with his comment if it were taken in isolation, if one did not know his delightful sense of irony, and if one did not have the body of his plays, which is the fuller context, which testifies over and over again to his belief that drama gives to invisible *realities* a local habitation and a name.'

"Breathless from this academic blurting, I gulped and hiccuped. He laughed, not unkindly.

"'If you see what I mean', I added.

"He laughed louder. Then I laughed too, and it was a moment of inexpressible union. It lasted a few seconds only, but there are seconds which stretch into infinity.

"Then he stood abruptly. 'I have to go', he said. 'I have to take the flock up higher.'

"'But will we meet again?' I asked him. His eyes dropped at the urgency of my voice.

"'Perhaps we'll meet, Miss, another day.'

"He reached out his hand and held mine for a moment.

"'Still, I do not know your name', I said.

"'Names have power. Names and words', he said.

"'Power to change us forever', I answered.

"'If we would permit, and if we would understand', he said.

'For a name can also be an object which is collected in a box with other things.'

" 'Or kept in the heart. As a gift is held in the absence of the giver.'

" 'That too', he replied. 'But your way lies there (he pointed back down the path) and mine there (pointing up into the cloud). Though all paths eventually join at the gate.'

"He turned and moved along the path. His sheep raised their heads and followed. I ached as I watched them leave, the ewes and the bleating lambs. Then he was enfolded in the mist. The flock followed, last of all a single lamb wiggling its dissolving tail, leaving only a faint bleat. And I was left on the moor in the center of a cloud, with no name to keep in the sanctuary of the heart."

Rose, who was surprised to find herself in Miss Gorrel's lap, holding the woman about the waist, feeling drops of water spattering her brow, felt a lump of ache in her throat. She looked up to see the woman weeping.

"Oh, oh, I am a foolish thing!" Miss Gorrel cried as she stroked Rose's curving back with her right hand. "Foolish, foolish me."

Then, startled by an unnatural swerve in the girl's spinal column, the woman awoke from her own pain.

Something is not right, she thought to herself with a pang of concern. *Her bones are misshapen. I must speak to her grandmother about it.*

Easing the girl off her lap, she asked,

"Does your back hurt, Rose?"

"A little bit."

By then the cloud from the north had become a rumbling threat which filled a quarter of the sky. Together the woman and the child brushed away crumbs, folded the blanket, and repacked the hamper. In the process Miss Gorrel reverted to a no-nonsense optimist, sporting a cheery sunburn and perhaps

73

a certain gratitude for the demands imposed by dangerous weather. Pocketing only as an afterthought the difficult vertebrae. Dropping the wilting flowers.

"Rose, dear, quickly now. Let us see if we can outrun this storm."

Which they did, hand in hand, arriving at the porch of the trading post minutes ahead of a curtain of hard rain, frenzied cannon volleys, flashes of steel-blue lightning, flying boards ripped from shacks, a bundle of screaming feathers blown sideways through the screeching wind, and canoes tumbling like toys all along the edge of the lake.

On one cool autumn afternoon, Miss Gorrel took Rose to a point of land below the school, and they sat side by side on the lake shore watching the underwater stones inhale and exhale.

When Rose pointed them out to her, the teacher was delighted by the breathing stones. She rewarded the girl by informing her that she had never before noticed this phenomenon.

"Rose, my child," she said, "you have eyes that see."

From her rucksack the woman removed a roll of paper and the Dundee horehound tin. She placed them on Rose's lap.

"For you", Miss Gorrel smiled. "Open it."

Beneath the tin's heather-girl, Rose found a cedar boxlet full of colored sticks.

She looked up uncomprehending.

"Are they candy?"

"They're oil pastels. With these you can make a picture. Or a memory."

Rose hesitated to touch the colors, as if they were imaginary, for the shock of their brilliance and variety did seem unreal. To touch or eat them was perhaps a kind of violation.

"Don't be shy. They're yours."

Rose picked up a rod that was yellower, more lemony, than the stand of autumn birches on the far shore.

"Go on, try it. Perhaps you would like to draw a wildflower. Or make a picture of the lake."

Rose held the stick in her hand a moment, feeling its lightness, wanting to bite the end of it and chew. She positioned it in her fingers and drew a line of liberated light across the white sheet of paper.

Her heart beat faster.

Another line of yellow. And another. Then a twig of fiery orange lay in her fingers and under their command made a speckling of slashes above the yellow, followed by a flight of birds rendered in teal blue by dot, dot, dot, dot. . . .

"Hold one sideways and it makes a smear, like a band or a roadway in the sky," said the teacher.

Rose chose a pale blue stick, tore the paper wrapper from it, snapped it in half, and pressed its length onto the paper. Then, after hesitating, she pushed. A cloud-front swept across the stippled waxy forest. She churned up the blue with an engorging turbulence of hostile black and ominous purple.

"Oh!" gasped Rose.

After that, the application of white on the remaining empty spaces made a giant bird hovering over the storm, its jeweled eye rendered in turquoise and gentian violet.

Hypnotized by the eye which had come from herself but which was seeing her, Rose plunged through the surface into her fathomless self. Miss Gorrel receded to a vague presence on the edge of her consciousness, all sounds grew thin, and the slow-motion waves, arched into sculpted peaks, practically stood still.

Words were no longer possible, only the short sharp breaths which sustained Rose as a node of pure seeing. It was, at first, a little confusing, because her eyes were captured by the actual forest before her and at the same time tugging down into the landscape of natural memory, the forest of her own unmapped interior. In her attempt to transmit the immediately visible to paper, she tried to scoop up whole lakes and a fistful of trees, gouged the sinewy rocks, scraped the sky. But she did not stop there for more than a few hasty sketches as she passed through the inverse lens to the state which she had previously encountered only with the crude instrument of a smoldering charcoal stick or pieces of garbage arranged beside a puddle. The rods of solidified light moved under the trembling authority of her fingers and revealed things which until then she had not known were there.

Miss Gorrel observed silently. As she pondered the little brown form so totally absorbed by the act of creation, the woman recalled her many exposures to the art of a rather broad range of cultures. At its most profound level, she told herself, it was all the same. It was all, well, *iconographic*—the exteriorizing of the interior icon. She smiled at her cleverness, then recalled suddenly a trek through the islands of Greece, where she had on one occasion been reduced to humble proportions by the severe glance of a Christ Pantocrator on the dome of an apse in Daphni. There she had begun to suspect that a cathedral dome could represent the dome of the actual cosmos, riddled with outpost stars, infinite and impenetrable by physical sight. And there she stopped, glancing back down through the inverted scope to those planes which could be safely observed, those below the station of her own being. Wild Hellenic peas growing by heat-crazed roadsides revealed rows of planets. When the pod split, the seed fell like gunshot into the dust and exploded after the next rain. So too, the pollen of Arctic flowers dusted all suitors, setting the barrens ablaze in their brief season of fertility. Fiery foxes dazzled each other. Trumpeter swans braided their necks. Leviathan sang ballads in the warm seas.

Of the two equally terrifying explanations, she was not sure which was correct: either the unknowable which lay beyond the frontiers of infinity was an impersonal nothingness or it breathed and had a name.

What *was* certain was the existence of an interior universe. The child hunching over paper and colors with such rapture was sufficient evidence of that, as well as Miss Gorrel's own box of memories.

Eventually she stretched out flat on the ground, crossed her ankles, and dozed in the sun, her head resting against a tuft of caribou moss, straw bonnet shading her brow. She awoke some time later to see Rose still huddled, working in controlled frenzy. Around her was a splay of pictures, each sheet held down by a stone. The girl's head was tilted to one side, eyes almost closed, shutting out the distractions of visible stimuli, tapping the unseen sources.

Miss Gorrel observed her until the cessation of brown fingers and the wearing down of color-sticks indicated that she was finished.

"What have you made, Rose?"

"Pictures." Mouth hanging open, eyes dragged back unwillingly to the surrounding world.

"Trees and water and birds in the skies?"

"Some", the girl replied, glancing at the drift of paper.

"And what have you just completed?"

"It is . . . different," the girl said, puzzling over her own creation.

"May I see?"

Shyly, Rose handed the paper to the woman.

"Why, this is amazing!" exclaimed Miss Gorrel, holding a long cream hand to her heart. "Simply amazing."

For a moment she saw only the general structure. Then the dizzying complexity of hairlike strokes flooded in, blurring when she looked too close, sharpening into focus as she held the sheet at arm's length. In the center of the work was a woman clothed in maroon, shot with threads of gold and green. She was sleeping, stretched out across the plane of the image, or rather curved in a half-fetal position, her body embedded in moss, under the halo of a straw bonnet. The face was anguished. Glints of silver spilled from under her eyelids in an overflow of grief. She was no earth-bound creature, for she had wings, though the wings were jutting at broken angles from which dribbles of blood ran down into a pool of violet shadow. Beneath the double sun of her spherical breasts, in the hollow where the heart should be, her two hands gripped fiercely an ugly black stone. It was disturbing, yet permeated by a dreadful beauty. The execution was a mixture of amateurishness and flashes of genius.

A large bird with unfurled wings enveloped the top half of the image, surrounding the sleeping woman, protecting her like two enfolding hands. On the right side of the paper a set of jaws opened wide, bilious green, fanged, wolf-like, eel-like as well, seeking to devour her. Opposing it was the presence on the left side: a young man gazing down at her, his face resolved, his eyes pure and strong, his lips parted, speaking soundless words which flowed from his mouth in the form of golden leaves blown upward into the sky—awake! awake! awake!—which the woman could not hear, being asleep.

After a period of straining to analyze it according to its primitive iconography, Miss Gorrel admitted failure and simply looked.

"It's you", the girl said.

But the confusing mixture of fear and exultation which the image had generated in the woman would not allow her to make an immediate reply. She swallowed a constriction of throat.

"Is this how you see me?" she asked in a too-quiet voice, when she was able.

Rose smiled, "Yes."

Then Miss Gorrel spurted tears, and sucked them back in, and a shudder ran through her. Rose's smile disappeared.

"And thus with the pure eye of childhood I am summarized," the woman sobbed. "A narrow, twisted creature, clutching the flawed black stone of my heart, seeing neither the arms of an enfolding love nor the jaws of a malice which would devour me in the absence of a shepherd's staff. Is this me? Is this, then, how you see me?"

Frightened, Rose made no reply.

"But it must be what you see! Why else would you make such a thing?"

"Because . . ."

"Tell me, why?"

"Because you are beautiful!" the child blurted. "Because I love you."

Horrified by herself, Rose dropped her eyes.

Because I love you hung in the air.

Miss Gorrel dried her eyes and absorbed the words.

Love? What was love? The woman recognized the child's hunger, for the adulation which the girl had offered was a copy of the devotion she had received on many continents, bursting in myriad forms from the raw material of human need. She recalled the trembling mouths of boys and girls as they enunciated the three radioactive words. She saw men saying the same words—the eligible men—the ethereal dons, the hardy cricketeers guzzling stout, the desperate widowers with young children, the aged barristers in whom optimism outweighed realism. Then the ones in between, carrying guns or poetry books, shaking spears or Marxist pamphlets or sieves in which opals did sometimes appear.

And the less eligible: the brooding European philosopher-youths draped in gabardine coats under furred hats, whom she had seen bearing their loads of esoteric books during the year she studied in Vienna and summered in Warsaw. She had feared that they despised her even as they flashed a glance of admiration at her form. There was, as well, a Bengali scholar full of British manners who withdrew politely at the first sign of her uninterest, and an ardent Turk who pinched her hand, enraged at her refusal to be his odalisque, his finest concubine. There had been a painted youth skewering lizards with a spear, longing for pubescent walkabouts in which he could revert without a qualm to nakedness. There had been a young Catholic writer, a Parisian sophisticate who had looked at her with uncomplicated desires or elevated sentiments, then turned away.

All their longings had been encapsulated in the word *love*. She believed that each and every one of them had perceived her only through a golden mist of projection, creating their dream bride or dream mother or dreamtime friend with the raw material of her life. None of them had wished to know her true self. Indeed, how many of them were capable of it? All of them, she felt sure, would have fled at the first strong gust of reality.

But what am I? she asked herself now in the unflinching light of a northern lake. *What is the objective me?*

Rose Wâbos was the very first to see her as she was and, having seen, continued to love. Miss Gorrel realized suddenly that her negative reaction to the picture might have destroyed that love with one blow.

She reached out and touched the girl's greasy hair.

"I love you too, Rose."

The girl looked up cautiously, half-believing.

"This is a wonderful thing you have made. It is an excellent likeness . . . of"—she choked—" . . . of me."

Rose risked a tentative smile.

"Is it good?"

"Oh, yes", the woman breathed, pondering the child with swimming eyes. "It is very good. You are going to be a great artist some day."

"Why did you cry?'

"Because the most beautiful experiences make me cry."

"Are you sad?"

Bravely, Miss Gorrel replied, "No, I am happy."

Rose beamed. Then, overcome with the wonder of it all, she

turned away, drew her legs up under her chin, circled them with her arms, and watched the lake for a time, oblivious of her tragic spine.

Miss Gorrel stared at the spine and the dirty skull with its strings of hair, while her own emotions subsided into the habitual melancholy of her temperament. She recalled a similar stack of hair which she had observed years ago during an excursion through Mexico. In the great plaza of a shrine dedicated to the Virgin of Guadalupe she was surrounded by swarms of beggar children holding up their hands for money. Moved by their eager faces, some more guileless than others, she had fought an impulse to fill the dirty palms with centavos and pesos, resisted a yearning to be for them the great white cornucopia they desired, the goddess who would spill wealth into the lives of the ones who tugged most urgently or pressed closest. The threat of pestilence was real enough. The gummy eyelids. The caked nails. The fleas leaping in ecstasy. Yet it was the agonizing unfairness of life which revolted her most of all, more than the overwhelming stench.

Regardless, she had offered a touch. Reaching out, she stroked the strings of black from the crown of a raggy child, whether girl or boy she could not determine. Tousling the filthy hair, her fingers registered the grit, the grease, and her heart thumped in a surge that was neither pity nor compassion nor a condescending affection. She realized that she, who had been denied none of the advantages of her privileged birth, possessed nothing more than they. Indeed, she wondered if she might even possess less.

The child whom she had tousled dropped his palms and looked up with open mouth, Aztec eyes all black iris, and smiled.

After she had shaken off the beggars like a band of puppies chewing at her hems, she worked up her courage to enter the shrine itself. It was a Spanish baroque building that volcanoes and earthquakes were tipping into the soft soil of the ancient lake bed. She stepped across the threshold tentatively, in the anthropological attitude she had employed while appreciating the tea ceremonies of Kyoto, the dung paintings of Morocco, and the slumbering Buddhas of Ceylon.

She penetrated the dark hush of the interior like a swimmer going down into unknown waters. Curiously sophisticated and primitive, the church was choked with pilgrims moving forward on their knees with arms outstretched toward a distant altar. The atmosphere could have been cut into cubes and sold in the plaza to the devout, it was that thick. It sighed and sang and echoed, breathing its own smoke and beeswax and woolly sweat—the smell of humanity and divinity.

Then she came to the extraordinary image of the woman in blue, who seemed to float out from the plane of the canvas as if she were three dimensional. Euphrasia Gorrel almost gave in to the urge to kneel, to throw herself at the feet of the Mother, and to be gathered into her arms. But she stood firm, fighting that gentle tug of war which is love, and in the end was victorious, for she remained the only one standing, a pillar of enlightenment in all that swarm of pagan Catholicism.

Still, a terrifying thing happened. Feeling dizzy from the close air, she shut her eyes and saw, if *seeing* was the proper word, a hand come out from the image. It reached down and tousled her hair. The Englishwoman leaned into the warm touch, yearning forward. Then, frightened by this turn of events—*if* it was an event and not merely a mild hallucination brought on by traveler's fatigue and lack of oxygen—she stepped backward and commanded her eyes to look elsewhere, to look especially for the exit. Still, for an instant she experienced a touch of purest bliss, before her ample knowledge of human psychology rejected it.

Though she was now fully recovered from that old haunting, Miss Gorrel could not entirely banish it from her memory. She reached out and placed her hand on the top of Rose's head. And gently tousled. Rose looked up with open mouth, Ojibwe eyes all black iris. And like her counterpart, she gazed into the alien woman and smiled.

4

Euphrasia Gorrel did not enjoy mysteries. She had always disliked vagueness, and she valued precision more and more as she got older. She preferred to use the technical terms for archeological ruins, and wildflowers, and the movements of the human mind. She had a well-thumbed copy of *Fowler's English Usage*, which had accompanied her throughout many expeditions, and which she had read with religious devotion in bark huts and palaces. But during her time at Threefinger Lake even these defenses began to fail.

She was lonely.

Which was not unprecedented. But the pressure of an isolation sustained over two years was mounting. During the previous summer, Miss Gorrel had attended a conference on the role of white institutions in the advancement of aboriginal peoples. Educators, churchmen, health professionals, police and other federal agents had gathered in Winnipeg to discuss the problem of the natives.

At the closing banquet she had found herself seated beside a young Anglican minister, originally from Cambridge, presently of an Inuit settlement in the Eastern Arctic. They made polite conversation while she observed his thinning ginger hair, his rumpled tweed suit, and his mukluks with pom-poms. He had a mouth full of teeth like an overcrowded graveyard and his fingernails were untrimmed, but otherwise he was presentable. His diction was the finest, his vocabulary well-stocked, and his personality undoubtedly male in a refined way. She suspected he was a wandering searcher, like herself.

Because it was soon clear that the banqueters on either

side of them were uncomplicated people, or uninterested, they turned again and again to each other and commenced a badminton match of dry wit. Each in turn upped the cleverness of the replies, until the game ended in a tie that left them laughing discreetly, surprised by their good fortune.

"We must meet again", he said at parting, shaking her hand, "and continue this dialogue."

Bowing ironically she batted the shuttlecock. "A rematch?"

"Possibly a match", he swung the racquet swiftly down upon the final word.

"I expect that you do not know your opponent."

"I am willing, Miss, to learn." He added a smile that deliberately covered the teeth.

At the very last moment she said, "Still, I do not know your name." She paused, hiding her trembling behind a semblance of vague interest. "Though names have power," she added, "and can also be objects."

"Mine's Harry", he shot back. "Harry Powys. And you?"

She told him.

"Ornate", he said grinning. "Byzantine. Possibly Baroque."

They exchanged addresses, though nervously because of observers.

On her return to Threefinger Lake, she sat down in the teacherage and gave herself a sensible little lecture: She was in her mid-forties, and, though she looked ten years younger, no man could be fooled for long. Though there were rigorous elements in her personality, she was on the whole emotionally delicate—rather, *refined*. She was a very *cultivated* person, and thus it was improbable that in the dwindling field of suitors there was one who could truly appreciate her qualities. Harold, for example, would surely prove to be no more than a polished version of all the others.

His first letter arrived with the biweekly mail, delivered by the single-engine Norseman shortly after freeze-up. The postmistress, who plied her trade at the end of the canned goods counter, flanked by bales of fur, made no comment when she handed the envelope to the teacher. This woman was known locally as the Trader's Woman, though Miss Gorrel insisted on calling her the Factor's Wife, which was not exactly true. Though curious by nature, the woman did not notice anything unusual about a certain envelope tucked in the middle of Euphrasia Gorrel's incoming stack of mail. The teacher's other envelopes were franked by many nations, illustrated by purple queens or curried elephants, green kangaroos, and a Ceylonese tree dropping orange mangoes. The minister's envelope, by contrast, seemed rather dull, stamped by a monochrome goose. In addition, the italic script of his return address was unreadable to prying eyes. The postmistress, therefore, failed to make note of this development, distracted as she was by the implications of the gaudier braid.

Back in her cabin, Miss Gorrel discovered that the minister's letter was written in the bantering style to which they had grown accustomed during their first meeting. It contained literary allusions of the wittiest sort. Her reply, which contained a pressed wildflower and a quote from Rimbaud, in the suitable context of self-deprecating humor, was mailed two weeks later. Six weeks after that an ironic riposte arrived. She batted the shuttlecock back to him. He met it deftly and returned it. This was followed by several fine strokes that began to resemble a kind of ballet rather than the lurching gestures of crude sport.

Now it must be noted that Miss Gorrel was not liked by the other white women of the community. She was too beautiful, too fragile, and they knew from experience that such women did not last. In addition, their few attempts at sociability had proved uncomfortable due to the teacher's unnerving habit of using difficult words and making painfully obscure references to other worlds while attempting precision and nuance. They suspected her of superiority. Thus, invitations to mug-ups and gossip sessions dwindled to nothing.

By late winter the postmistress had finally noticed something unusual brewing in the mail, had deciphered the name and boreal address, and had begun to simmer fantasies about the elusive Miss Gorrel and her suitor. At one low point she employed steam from her kettle in order to obtain more details. The details were difficult to make out, but revealed enough. Shortly before breakup, having endured an extra long series of unseasonable storms, the postmistress allowed herself a mere slip of the tongue to the nurse. The teacher was in love, she said, and was being pursued by a man. The nurse, who promised to keep the secret, eventually told the wife of the RCMP corporal during an unguarded moment. That woman in turn managed to contain the delectable information for two or three weeks, but broke down under an overdose of coffee, and, in a gleeful conspiratorial voice, she passed it on to the wife of the man in charge of weather.

This man, the government meteorologist, was a decent sort. Made indefinite and philosophical by the weather that was his chief interest in life, he was not easily disturbed by human affairs. But because he was the officer in charge of the station, he was responsible for his two young subordinates. He had noted their interest in the teacher. He knew that they were going strange from lack of recreation, guessed that they were spending too much time lying on their backs in their cells during off-hours, reading sizzling paperbacks, and staring at the lascivious visions taped to their ceilings. These young men, named Robert Duff and Edward Kirkey, known locally as Bob-'n'Eddie, were lusting for the teacher.

Euphrasia Gorrel had early on recognized their motives and despised them. It amused her to think of them as The Suitors, and herself as Queen Penelope, keeping them at arm's length by wile and wit as she awaited the return of her husband Odysseus,

87

who would doubtless slaughter these fools in an appropriate manner. As she passed within feet of them on her way to school she could not very well pretend ignorance of their existence, but would merely nod in a correct, distant manner, offering a chilly "Good morning" as they read thermometers, measured snowfall, or inflated the big flesh-colored helium balloons that bore instruments aloft.

Thinking to nip their passions in the bud, the chief meteorologist reminded them that holidays were only weeks away. He suggested cold showers, and said, by the way, he was pretty sure the teacher was engaged to someone. All those letters, for example.

Bob'n'Eddie snickered and smirked at each other. They knew that courtship was more like tackle football than like ballet.

On the day after the lake was free of ice, the Norseman landed on pontoons, and as it taxied up to the dock the entire village swarmed down to see what it contained. The pilot tossed the mailbags into the arms of the trader, who signaled his Indian assistant to carry them up to the post for sorting. There was twice as much mail as usual, because the plane had been delayed for a month due to a prolonged breakup. When Miss Gorrel retired to her cabin to check hurriedly through her stack of letters in search of the desired one, she found nothing from the Anglican minister. Nor did any other message from him arrive in subsequent weeks. By the end of the school year she was resisting a persistent feeling of anxiety. Perhaps he was ill, she wondered, or had suffered an accident, or been killed. Dismissing the latter as irrational, she began to suspect a more troubling possibility: that he might have met someone else.

She wrote many letters to him and received not a single reply.

"The love notes have stopped", the postmistress informed one of the ladies. "Her 'Arry is backin' out."

This information raced along all the known circuits of the white community and reached the end of the lines within three or four days. No one let on that he knew.

Miss Gorrel did not go south that summer, preferring to save money by spending her vacation in the village and roaming the surrounding hills, reading, canoeing, composing short, hand-bound books that native children could understand. Most of all, she waited for the mail plane.

Frequently she took Rose Wâbos along on her jaunts, though she found it difficult to focus on the girl's presence, saying those pleasant things that encouraged children, acknowledging the strange little drawings the girl continued to make. On a few occasions the feral boy, Binemin Edzo, came with them, cackling at nothing, throwing rocks into ravines, snapping the bones of burnt trees, crushing and sniffing deer pellets in his filthy fingers, sneezing, devouring most of the food, smelling bad, alternately falling behind, then tearing ahead as they mounted "the spine", rummaging noisily in the woods surrounding "the skull".

At one point he brought two handfuls of wild strawberries to share with them. Miss Gorrel declined. Rose accepted a hand-ful in her cupped palms. The teacher observed with distaste the glee with which the two children crammed the fruit into their mouths. The boy scampered away to gather more.

"Tchibi brought us a present", Rose said to Miss Gorrel with a smile of joy.

"Tchibi? Why do you call him Tchibi?"

"Tchibi is from the *tchibekana*, the river of souls, the river of stars, which our people call the loon's necklace. He is like a star to me, because he is like the loon. He does not speak, and he likes to be alone. But his song is sweet."

Miss Gorrel thought she grasped the several loose connec-tions, but probed no more. Rose began to draw a picture of the elusive loon boy—not that he ever stood still long enough for an actual portrait. It was rather the girl's conceptualization of his life. A brutal little life, which Miss Gorrel suspected would be short. Rose used a sheet from the large-size roll of heavy paper the teacher had ordered from an art supply house in Montreal. Working quietly for an hour while the boy galloped about making noises like a wolf or an owl, Rose frowned over the image, slashing with the sticks of color, smudging, rearranging, blending, and even clawing with her fingernails until the unfinishable piece was revealed. She lifted it up and showed it to Miss Gorrel, who was startled by its savagery.

It was a crucifixion, an imaginative representation of the boy's torment, the woman supposed. Obviously Catholic in symbolism, it depicted a writhing brown form nailed to a cabin wall like a beaver hide, covered with wounds that looked like bullet holes. His mouth wide open in a scream that reverberated in razor strokes of sickly green and acid yellow.

Repelled by the image, Miss Gorrel looked away.

"Very expressive, Rose", she murmured. "You have symbolically captured Binemin's pain, if not precisely his experience."

"Would you like it?" the girl asked.

After a considered pause, Miss Gorrel replied tactfully, "No, thank you, dear. It is an interesting piece, but my house is becoming cluttered. Why don't you put it on your wall? If you study it, the strengths and weaknesses of the rendering will emerge, over time. You can learn from it."

One Sunday, learning that Oldmary had been ill with a cough that week, Miss Gorrel hiked to the cabin by Crazyman River and brought Rose back into town with her. Expecting to officiate at tea and art in the teacherage, she was nonplused when the girl insisted that she attend Mass.

Miss Gorrel, remembering the blue woman in Mexico, entered the clapboard church with some reticence, her body dragged along in jerks by Rose's tugging hand, and sat down with her on a bench at the back, behind the pump organ. The priest, whom she had met once or twice in neutral situations, was Polish, she remembered, but he delivered his sermon in fluent Ojibwe. The man limped and was scarred from some dreadful experience in Europe—the war she supposed—but his face radiated serenity and an intelligence that Miss Gorrel did not fail to notice. When the rite was finished, he approached and invited her for a cup of tea in his log rectory. She accepted.

Miss Gorrel and Rose sat at one side of the plank table watching the priest poker about in the firebox of his stove, singing under his breath, making cinders snap and flames leap as if he were a custodian of Purgatory. Then he threw in a chunk of wood, and the kettle soon began to whisper. The room smelled of birch smoke and kerosene fumes. The furnishings were simple, a sleeping bench on which blankets seemed to be the only mattress, a chair, a bookshelf. She tried not to stare at his scars, nor to let on that she was feeling uneasy because of the, well, *hieratic* surroundings—the flaming hearts dripping blood, the tortured corpuses, the various other amulets incongruously intermingled with stacks of books. *A failed scholar*, she thought to herself.

Making pleasant conversation, she found that his English was clear if heavily accented, lapsing only occasionally into slight imperfections of grammar. He told her that he was grateful for her interest in Rose. The girl's "gift", as he called it, was unique, a "profound mystery" which could mature only under a guiding hand.

Catholics, she knew, were forever attributing unexamined things to "mystery".

"It is my understanding," she said in an inoffensive tone, "that mystery is merely a form of ignorance that will be dispelled when sufficient facts and skills are developed."

"Mystery is the gown of Lady Wisdom", the priest replied.

She uttered a strained laugh.

"What, then, is ignorance?" she asked.

"A form of poverty", he said without hesitation. "Of course, there are many kinds of poverty."

He turned away suddenly and looked at a cupboard.

"Bread and jam?"

"I beg your pardon?"

"Would you like some bread and jam? I may have even a can of unopened butter."

She smiled at the syntax. "Oh, yes. Fine. That would be lovely."

The tea arrived, steaming and ruby-colored, sweetened with sugar, beside pieces of torn white bread on a plate. The priest seemed disproportionately pleased to have found the single tin of butter in his rather doleful larder. He cranked it open and brought it to the table, along with a bent knife. Rose led the way, slathering the yellow cream on thickly, followed by blueberry mash from a jar. Swinging her legs, bending forward to protect her spine from the chair's back, eyes bulging, mouth working hard on the paste, she was in a state of pure joy.

Miss Gorrel supposed that the child was feeling fulfillment, psychologically fed by the sensation of a complete, if temporary, family. Here they were, two wildly diverse Europeans gazing at her with such affection that they might have been her mother and father.

This was painful to observe, Miss Gorrel felt, because it would never be enough.

"We give what we can", the priest said for no reason. The woman wondered if he was referring to his hospitality or had read her thoughts.

She cleared her throat and said, "The tea is good."

He smiled.

"The little flowers of summer", he said, offering her the jar of jam. "They may produce a fruit we do not foresee."

"Do not foresee?"

"As with every human life."

"Ah", she nodded.

"Even those which are considered to be of little consequence."

"I see your point," she said carefully. "However, I suspect that existence is nothing more than a shunting of atoms from one empty station to the next."

"How, then, do you explain the presence of beauty?"

"It is an accident."

"A glorious and curiously persistent accident, is it not?" He said it with that gentle smile.

"Perhaps we would find," she countered, "if we were to survive long enough, that it is not so persistent. That everything will end in the cold of space, the fires burnt out to completion and silence."

"And what of the presence of love?"

"Love? I have studied its myriad forms and found that it is all a variation on the one theme."

"Which theme is that?"

"The transfer of energy. One mode of energy consumes another, as fuel, and itself is consumed by another."

He stared at her.

"I do not think you really believe that", he said.

She shrugged. "Ultimately love is cruel. It is a game at best, or a pleasant distraction; at worst a devouring, around which we spin the rituals."

"How has such a person as yourself come to think such things?" he said, sadness filling his eyes.

"Experience."

"Perhaps a lack of it", he replied slowly.

She bristled.

"Love is a chimera. You men do not grasp this, because you are on the dominant end of the illusion. Women, on the other hand, must endure abandonment. It is our lot."

"Abandonment?" he asked with what she considered characteristically male obtuseness.

"Yes, abandonment. The passive must always endure the whims of the active. The lost hopes and broken promises, the harsh reality which appears after the curtain is parted."

"You refer to tragedies", he said.

"Comedies also, which are the subtler form of tragedy."

He pondered that for a while, then answered, "Our perceptions are not always reliable. Tragedies may be the subtler form of comedy."

"Are you Oberon?" she laughed suddenly.

"Please? I do not understand."

"A literary reference", she explained with amusement. "You must forgive me."

"Ah."

"Oberon, King of the Fairies", she said, laughing again. "A character in a play. A comedy. The triumph of love in spite of human folly, you see. Or is it really about the triumph of human folly in spite of love?"

"Ah", he repeated.

The two adults looked down at the uncomprehending Rose, who was still working her way through the loaf of bread.

"Have you considered", he said, "that characters in a play, especially during the tragic acts which are essential to comedy, are often deluded into mistaking the part for the whole?"

"Yes, but we are not fictional characters."

"That is true. But at least you will admit we are not the Author who composed this masterpiece?"

"Masterpiece?" she countered, glancing at Rose. "Look at this deprivation. Show me in this little drama the evidence of benevolence. Tell me, is the Playwright a monster or a lover?"

"Are you not, yourself, present in this play?"

"Have you considered", she proposed after a moment of reflection, "that religion tries to explain everything with pious

94

platitudes and cardboard characters trotted through simplistic morality plays?"

"Oh, no", he relied firmly. "Just the opposite. My faith proposes something more dangerous than that."

"How so?" she replied doubtfully.

"My religion asks us to love in a fallen world, a world that is ignorant and cruel."

"A point that could just as easily reinforce my position, don't you think?" she said with mild disdain. "Why is the world so brutal?"

"Because mankind fears to love."

She waved that away. "I am one", she replied definitively, "who does not fear."

To which he made no reply.

Rose looked up from the last of the loaf.

"My girl," Miss Gorrel tittered nervously, "how you can eat!"

"Are you not a sign of his love for her?" the priest asked.

"Who? Whose love?"

"The Playwright."

She shook her head irritably.

"And what of her grandmother?" he continued. "And what of the food of love which she ate this morning in the Sacrament? Neither she nor the Giver has been destroyed by that consummation. They are alive."

"*That* is theology."

"That is the fire", he replied gently, "of love."

She laughed coldly and sat straighter.

They sipped their tea.

He pointed to a corner of the room, where a rectangle of color lurked in the shadows.

"That was born from her heart", he said.

Miss Gorrel recognized the picture Rose had made of Binemin Edzo.

95

"A crucifixion", the priest added as if to clarify a point.

"The child was crucified literally", she said. "Not theologically."

"Christ is everywhere, in disguise", said the priest.

But this was too much for her. Instinctively, she felt he had crossed a boundary which any cultivated person would recognize as the outer frontier of decorum. He was *sincere*, oh, yes, quite sincere. But his arguments were becoming irritating. They would collapse under the pressure of intelligibility.

"This has been most interesting", she said, standing, brushing crumbs from her skirt. "Some day we must meet again, ages and ages hence, and compare notes. We shall see whether your view of existence or mine is proved correct."

He tilted his head at a contemplative angle before replying.

"Suffering instructs the soul," he said, "if we accept to undergo that education."

She thrust out her hand and shook his. "Thank you, Father, for a rather stimulating, and I might add *unique*, discussion."

He escorted her and Rose to the door.

"Please come again", he said, smiling. "Yes, come any time. You are always welcome."

He stood on the porch of his cabin watching them walk away. Miss Gorrel turned once to see if he had gone back inside. But he had not, and this stillness of observation made her suddenly afraid. And after fear came anger.

In the first week of September, just before classes began, it arrived. Not a letter exactly, but something much better. A gift. A small package wrapped in brown paper and string, sent by Eaton's mail order department, Toronto. Inside was a blue velvet box with a snap-up lid. It contained an engagement ring studded with diamonds and a card with a printed message. The card read:

At the request of Reverend Harold Powys,
Pangnirtung, Northwest Territories

To Euphrasia
Be mine forever,
With undying love,
     Your Harry.

With a gasp, her heart hammering wildly, flooded with many emotions at once, overwhelmed by an exultant joy, Miss Gorrel wept. She removed the ring from its box, kissed it, and put it on her wedding finger.

He was alive! Moreover he felt for her what she had come to feel for him!

She wrote a copious letter in reply and yearned for the coming of the next mail plane, which would speed her answer to him, and as she waited she could feel her heart going like mad, his heart going like mad, and *she said yes, she said yes, yes, I will, Yes.* And if this passionate outburst was borrowed just a little from the very modern novels she had been lately reading, especially James Joyce and D. H. Lawrence, she knew that Harold would be pleased by the literary allusion. Bound together by the ligatures of culture, bound so cleverly that their very cleverness was a protection from submission, they would be happier than any couple who had ever lived. She would pay to have his teeth fixed, and she would talk to him about the pom-poms. The pom-poms, of course, would have to go.

At the end of the month, before the first blows of winter, when the trees were stripped and the lake began to scud into ridges of cruel steel that snapped at the shores and warned of worse to come, the community felt the need for an autumn dance. As was customary whenever a dance was held, the super-structure of social taboos collapsed for a single day and night. Whites, Indians, and Métis would gather at the old metal hangar down by the lake at the edge of town. This rusting Quonset had been erected during the war as an emergency fuel storage depot for air transport bound for bases farther to the north. It was empty now, save for a battered Beaver on skis, its engine missing, its windscreen shattered, parked at the rear of the building's interior. Most people assumed that it was no longer owned by anyone but a distant and nearly abstract government.

On the morning before the dance, dozens of villagers congregated at the hangar door, chatting in various languages, stamping their feet, enjoying the holiday atmosphere that was infecting everyone. Eventually a white man arrived and prybarred the padlock off the door. Then they all went inside, each carrying something: brooms, mops, pails of creek water, powdered carbolic, sacks full of decorations, and kerosene lanterns. Others brought firewood for the barrel heater, and old men who had seen chimney fires kill people banged on the rusty smokestack with sticks, shaking the creosote chips down into the burning chamber. It was colder inside the hall than out, and a fire was soon roaring up the flue. It would take hours to warm the huge volume of air within the building, and it was best to start now. Usually some farsighted person thought to bring along pieces of glass to fix the panes that had been broken since the last dance, and garbage cans to collect the rocks that had been thrown through the windows, and the squirrels' nests that were brushed from the roof joists, and the smashed beer bottles and the rotting sleeping bags left by courting couples.

That evening, as dusk fell, anyone capable of playing a musical instrument was making his way on foot from town and the nearby reserve. The town was noisy, as was the reserve; both communities could hear each other and for once were not inclined to render harsh judgments. Drink was already flowing in both places. Children ran through the shadows of the trees, carrying thin flaming torches, narrowly escaping the conflagration of their hair, dropping sparks that sizzled out on the damp forest floor. Their shouts and laughter warmed the cold night better than the fire and balanced the clamor of the adults.

The policeman and his wife arrived at the hangar in fancy dress, which made the native women grin and ogle with admiration. The trader and his woman strutted in, for he was to be the official master of ceremonies. The head of the reserve band arrived wearing a new red hunting cap and leading his large family. The Métis, the part breeds, and the generally undefinable arrived alone or in groups of two or three. A makeshift stage of plywood hammered onto a dozen packing crates had been erected in front of the Beaver's nose, and onto it the musicians climbed. The policeman had brought his accordion, two men from the reserve had fiddles, the teenage daughter of the Indian agent had a toy xylophone, the head of the meteorological station strummed his guitar, and an assortment of native youths experimented on harmonicas, small drums, dog sled bells, and a single ukulele. Even Miss Gorrel arrived through the main door, dressed in ankle length tartan and a tight plum angora sweater, her slender neck accentuated with a Ceylonese saffron scarf. Striding to the stage, she convinced one of the youths—a student of hers, eighteen years old in grade six—to try an instrument that she held outstretched in her right hand. It was African in origin, a metal can with a long ebony neck strung with three piano wires. When plucked, its high atonal notes brought a hush of fascination and pleasure to the crowd. The youth accepted it and began to experiment.

When the numbers in the hangar seemed close to the two hundred people of the region, and when cigarette smoke began to haze the rafters, and the odors of kerosene and perfume had mingled to the proper mixture, the atmosphere had reached its ignition point. The trader shouted for order.

He made a speech that was forgettable and self-serving, but was part of the ritual and duly appreciated. The policeman walked to center stage and made a short patriotic comment and suggested they all sing "God Save the Queen". Everyone stood to attention, the little boys in the cockpit of the Beaver were told to stop making machine gun noises, babies were hushed. The policeman played the opening cord of the anthem on his accordion, and everyone sang. At first the effort was halting, then it swelled as the singers gained confidence or perhaps were moved by the framed picture of the newly crowned Queen and her consort that someone had hung on the Beaver nose.

When that was finished, people seemed to have thawed sufficiently. Conversation broke out in every direction, bodies became animated, and flasks were uncorked here and there. The fiddlers tuned up. The accordion wheezed. The trader stepped forward and declared he would call a reel.

"Virginia reel!" cried a chorus of elderly Ojibwe women, in English so the whites would understand. Their own name for the dance was *Weaving the Basket*.

"Virginia reel it is!" shouted the policeman, whose name was Bill and who would remain Bill until the following morning, when he would once again become the cop.

And so it went. Dozens shuffled forward into two lines as the music began, mostly native women and their husbands, though children of all the races present hurried forward, and most stunning of all, the very tall and beautiful Miss Gorrel who was always game for unique experiences. As she trotted and spun, ducked and weaved, she glowed with a degree of excitement that the people of Threefinger Lake had never before observed in her, as if she were a woman in love, whose lover would soon stride through the door of the hangar in search of her. As if she were reeling in the ceremonial hall of a castle, eyed by unattached princes, buoyed up by preternatural perfection and the energy infused by her position as an object of envy and desire. Her exultation was contagious, and it was whispered about the hall that she was engaged. Many in the crowd had heard the rumors and informed others that the fiancé was a handsome Englishman who lived somewhere in the high north, and that he was very rich and famous. The younger ones fantasized about such an exalted life, how impossible it would be for them to have such a life, yet they were glad that such a woman existed, and that she was in their midst. If they disliked her momentarily because of the unfairness, they consoled themselves with the knowledge of more dependable and humbler pleasures. The older ones remembered and knew that the keenest joys were to be had in waiting, in anticipation of the one who would come, and that his coming would be an anticlimax, no matter how fine the man she had captured.

When a polka began, Miss Gorrel flung herself out of the dancing crowd and collapsed onto a bench among the native ladies, to catch her breath. They giggled, or smiled sagely, and patted her arms and told her not to wear herself out too quickly—a familiarity which touched her and brought an added flush to her cheeks. She made a joke which they did not understand, though they appreciated her effort.

After that came another polka, which drew just about everyone to the floor. The ratio of male to female was not equal, but that did not matter. Tossed about by the clumsy musical waves, old women danced with old women, children with children, grandfathers with granddaughters, sons with mothers, Whites with Métis and Métis with Ojibwe. Teenage Métis boys with slicked hair tried swing dancing with each other, but quickly abandoned that whenever they found girls who were willing to try the reckless moves. It was crazy and fun and many stopped dancing in order to admire and to clap. But it did not go on for long, because the gymnastics did not suit the spirit of the people.

After the polka, there was another reel.

Fr. Andrei arrived, smiling congenially at everyone. More than once he was invited to dance, but he said that with his bad leg he had best enjoy it from the sidelines. Oldmary Wâbos got into the reel with her granddaughter Rose, the old woman shuffling about with a cane, and the girl doing her best to learn the steps, her back bending in a unnatural curve, which a few elderly women noticed and commented on. Binemin saw it too, for he was seated on the roof of the Beaver's cockpit, straddling it with his legs, staring down at the surging crowd, keeping his eye on Rose, which was not difficult because she was slow.

Rose's back hurt badly that night, but she did not speak to Oldmary about it because her grandmother seemed so happy—bent almost double, her silver hair braided down her back, her wrinkled hands clutching the knobby birch stick with ferocious joy, her eyes squinting with deep pleasure. Other old women came up to her and teased her, asked if she was looking for a husband, said things about the past, about long ago, that made Oldmary laugh. Which surprised Rose, for Oldmary almost never laughed. She went to sit with the oldest of the old women, who were bent like her. Their bodies shook with silent laughter, they showed their toothless grins to each other and talked of vanished times and people who were no more.

Rose wandered over to the big yellow airplane. She thought of Mang the loon who flew up to Gissis the moon, begging a sliver of light, the tiny silver bird who was carried down the necklace of stars to the cabin by Crazyman River in the Land of the Little Trees and became Oginiwâbigon which is the roseflower. And the moon was like a mother, though she was only a reflection of the light, and was not the real mother. Who, then, was the real mother? The mother in whose body she had grown was named Youngmary and had gone away and never come back. Rose wanted to think of her with love, but there was an empty space where her face should be, like a deep lake—so deep that the waters seemed black, though on the shore, when the waves swelled and receded, the rocks breathed, inhaling and exhaling, inhaling and exhaling. *Ningâ,* sighed the stones, *O where are you, Ningâ?*

Underneath, deep below, was the deepest thing of all, but what it was she did not know. It was not a frightening thing. It was merely different and unknown. Was it a stone like the white stone in the garden she and Binemin had made? Was it the greatest and deepest stone from which the springs of all the world poured out and made the sound of bells?

Oginiwâbigon, sang the bells, *you are all little things, small things, weak things. You are the rose flower, and the tiny bird, and the rabbit. These are powerless, and because they are powerless they are strong.*

Rose laughed at herself. All her mind-pictures were swimming, as if they had been swirled together by the reel dance.

How can stones breathe?

How can stones speak?

How can a girl be a bird, a rabbit, and a roseflower?

How can weakness be strong?

How silly her thoughts were!

"Ningâ!" said a voice rising above the music. Rose looked about to see who had spoken. But no one was looking at her, no one speaking to her.

"Ningâ!" It came again. She thought at first that a child in the crowd was calling to its mother, but the cry was deep, like the voice of a young man.

Because there were so many things in life that could not be explained, she turned her thoughts away from the voice and tried to listen to the music.

"Ogini!" cried the voice. It was calling to her, but where did it come from? She looked about in every direction. It seemed to be from above, in the air, in the sky, and if that were so, then perhaps it was an *anjeni,* a bad *anjeni* tormenting her. Or it might be a good *anjeni* sent by Jesus-Manito or the Spirit-Manito. He had spoken before, and so he might speak again, though his voice had not sounded like this voice.

"Ogini", cried the voice from above, "wâbigon."

She looked up at the ceiling of the hangar, but there were no white birds wheeling through the metal ribs.

From the corner of her eye she saw an arm waving halfway to the ceiling and a shape on top of the airplane, sitting on it as men ride horses. The face was turned to her and its mouth was opening and closing, inhaling and exhaling, and the chest was heaving with the labor of making a word come out of the mouth.

"Ogini", the mouth said in the agony of this effort.

"Tchibi!"

"Ningâ. Wâbigon. Ningâwâbigon", he called to her with his mouth, and the mouth issued sweet green fire that hurt him—she could see it was so—hurt him to speak, though the speaking was healing him, and the hurting was pouring out through the crack in the stone that pressed down on his heart. *Oginiwâbigon*, roseflower, *ningâwâbigon*, motherflower, *ogini-ningâwâbigon*, rose-motherflower.

She ran to the airplane and stood looking up at him. He looked down.

"*Mang*, loon-boy!" she cried, skipping once.

He grinned at her and threw his head back and made the song of the loon when it is happy at nightfall calling to its loon wife, when the neck diamonds spill across the black sky to make the *tchibekana*, the river of stars which some call the river of milk, which is the river of souls.

"Come down, Tchibi", she called to him.

He shook his head and made *Come to me* gestures with his wings.

"I can't. I can't climb."

He nodded, made a soft loon call, the sad-song, to tell her that he understood. He bent his wing behind and tapped his back.

"Yes", she said. "It hurts."

He swung his right leg over the top of the plane and slid down the side, dropping four feet to the floor in front of her.

They looked at each other and smiled. He was the first to look away, but the smile did not leave him.

"Can you say it again?" she asked. The music had fallen silent, except for the twanging of the three African wires.

He tilted his head back and began to give the warble of the loon. She stopped him.

"No, the man words, the speaking."

He flushed, fear and hope struggling across his face. He opened his mouth, and again the great struggle began, a birth agony, a shape from inside emerging into the world as a groan. It was harder for him now, because he was not flying high above all peoples, but was standing on the earth, speaking face to face.

At first it was a soundless *O*. Followed slowly by its noise, "O—"

"Say it."

"O-gh-gh-ghin-nee."

"Speak it, Tchibi, to make the hurting in my back go away."

"O-ghin-ee."

"Speak it again."

"Ogini", It was perfect. "Wâ-big-on."

She skipped lightly and waited for more.

"Oginiwâbigon," he said with more steadiness in his throat. "Ningâwâbigon. Ogini-ningâwâbigon."

As he gained confidence, he repeated it over and over, in several variations, as if he were tasting the pleasures of this power for the first time or rediscovering a great treasure that he had lost. Rose saw that as the sweet-fire grew in him, the fear-fire was fading, going—where she did not know, just going. And with it for a time the pain in her back also fled.

Looking up suddenly, she saw that an old man was watching them. He was seated alone on a bench on the far side of the room, his wrinkled face copper brown, his hair white, his eyes peering at her as a weasel would. Rose felt a stab of fear. Something came from his eyes. It rushed toward her like a river of black water. She said a prayer to Manito, and the river was pushed aside; it did not engulf her. It veered toward Binemin, but again she prayed and again the river was pushed away as if it had hit an invisible wall, curved upon itself, and flowed back into the eyes of the old man. When it reached him his eyes flared at her with rage and hatred, and he turned abruptly away, staring into the crowd of dancers.

At the completion of a waltz, Miss Gorrel inclined her head to her partner, the Indian agent, who was short and who had frequently stepped on her toes as he pushed her about the room. He bowed and went away with relief on his face. The teacher, tamping her moist brow with a hanky, took the nearest available bench space, which was beside the old man who had sent the river of black fire. She said something to him. He nodded. She straightened and leaned toward him. She began to speak to him in an animated fashion, gesturing elegantly with her hands. The old man's eyes examined carefully every inflection of her hands as they flitted expressively between them. He began to smile to himself with a slyness that white people often fail to detect.

Oldmary came up to Rose and stood before her, leaning on her cane.

"*Io, bineshi*, small bird, I am tired. Such a dance. It is a joy to have it like the old times."

"Grandmother, who is that man talking with the teacher?"

Oldmary's eyes clouded. "That is Kinoje. The Pike. Why do you ask?"

"He looked at me. He frightened me."

"Ay, ay, ee! That is a wicked man. Stay away from him."

"Why is he wicked?"

"He is one who talks with the *matchi-manito*, the evil spirits, and they speak through him. Why were you frightened? Did he speak to you?"

"He spoke with his eyes. He sent a black river at me."

"Ay, ay, ee! This is not good."

"Do not worry, Grandmother. I prayed to Jesus-Manito, and he pushed the river away. The river turned to Tchibi, but Jesus pushed it away again."

"This is good. Jesus is very strong. He is a mountain, the matchi-manito is a grain of sand. But you must not let the grain into your eye or your heart. Come, let us go home. I am tired."

"Will he send the black river to Miss Gorrel?"

"He might try to, but the *waiâbishkiwed*, the white people, are ignorant. They do not see such things."

"Can they be harmed by what they do not see?"

Oldmary pondered this. "Perhaps. If they have little faith."

"Fr. Andrei has faith."

"Yes, and he sees many things also. Let us go and speak with him."

So the old woman led the two children through the crowded dance floor to the place where Fr. Andrei was drinking a cup of tea beside the food table.

Oldmary came to him and told him in the Ojibwe tongue what had happened. His eyes grew stern but calm as he listened. Then he took her right hand in his and bowed his head. He said a prayer in his own tongue, while Oldmary prayed in hers. Rose also spoke with Jesus-Manito. Binemin stood silently by, watching them. It took a minute or so, and when they had finished, they looked up to see Kinoje walking toward the exit. Before he went outside, however, he stopped and stared at Fr. Andrei. It seemed to Rose that he tried to send a river of black fire at the priest, but Fr. Andrei raised his right hand and made a small sign of the cross in the direction of Kinoje. Kinoje's face hardened, he turned angrily away and stomped out of the hangar.

A moment later, Miss Gorrel came to them, her hand fluttering on her chest.

"Who was that old man?" she asked.

"That is Kinoje", Fr. Andrei replied. "Why do you ask?"

"I've just had a rather odd conversation with him. Of course I know he is an adept of native religion, and as I am interested in such matters, having studied them in a variety of racial groups, I wanted to ask him about the rituals. It is, of course, purely psychic phenomena that these people seem able to tap into. There's not an ounce of supernatural in it, of course, but I do find the symbolism of the subconscious quite fascinating." She stopped to catch her breath.

"And . . . ?" the priest prompted.

"And then he said some very strange things to me."

"What did he say?"

She waved the question away. "It really doesn't matter what he said", she replied emphatically. "It is *how* he said it. The underlying animosity, you see. I do believe Kinoje is a racist."

"Perhaps he is", Fr. Andrei said in a voice designed to calm frayed nerves. "More important, he is a master of illusion. Do not be overly disturbed by anything you hear from him. The spiritual realm is a place of struggle, and deception is part of—"

"Yes, yes, but I am not impressed by that concept. It is all within the dynamics of the mind, as psychology has proved conclusively."

"That is naïve, Miss Gorrel."

She sighed deeply and muttered, "Dear me, two medicine men in one evening." And forced a shrill laugh from her throat.

Rose took the teacher's hand in both of hers. "What did he say to you, Miss? Was it about a river, about black fire?"

"River? Black fire? No, not at all. He was talking nonsense. Complete nonsense. He told me that a great flesh thing, a giant bladder, a lung eater, would greet me when I returned home. It was going to eat me, he said." She laughed shortly. "What, pray tell, is a lung eater?"

"I do not know," said the priest. "Do you, Mary?"

Oldmary shook her head and shrugged.

"You see, sheer nonsense", declared Miss Gorrel. "Something he made up to frighten a silly white woman, I suppose. Well, I am certainly *not* frightened!"

She put on a cheery face, tilted her chin at a good angle, and surveyed the crowd in hope of another fast dance.

"Did he say anything else?" Rose persisted, squeezing the woman's hand too tightly.

"Nothing, dear, nothing. Oh, a little thing about my fiancé, which I suppose he has picked up on the grapevine."

"What did he say about your fiancé?" Oldmary asked in a low voice.

Miss Gorrel smiled archly. "He said that there was no fiancé. Imagine! How patently false, when I have his engagement ring on my very finger. See!" She showed it to them.

Fr. Andrei was about to say something, but Miss Gorrel turned abruptly away. The music had started up again, and she was eyeing with distaste the snickering Suitors, who muttered conspiratorially by the stage and sipped from flasks, which they were also offering to the native youths.

Oldmary and Rose left shortly after, feeling their way along the dark path to their cabin, going by memory. Binemin came with them part of the way, and Rose told Oldmary the wonderful news about his speaking. They stopped in a clearing on the shore of the lake, dimly lit by a sickle moon and the stars.

"Can you speak to my grandmother, Tchibi?" Rose asked.

They listened together for a minute until Binemin cleared his throat and said in a rasping adolescent voice, "Ogini."

"*Io! Io!*" Oldmary exclaimed.

"Ogini," he said shyly. "Ogini-wâbigon."

"Io! Io!"

"Ningâwâbigon."

With each utterance he seemed to shed more of his hesitation.

"Ogini-ningâwâbigon."

Even in the dark, Rose knew that Oldmary was grinning from ear to ear.

Binemin concluded by giving a loon call, wheeled, and returned to the hangar where he was to join his foster parents for their walk to the opposite side of the reserve. Rose took Oldmary's hand, and together they went on to their cabin by Crazyman River.

She fell asleep quickly, thinking of the white bird with the jewel eye, and the promise that had been made to her so long ago, the promise now fulfilled. She had a little brother whom she loved, though he was no longer little. And she had loved him well, offering the hurting to Jesus who joined it to his own hurting and poured it like a cascade into Tchibi's hurting so that he no longer hurt so much. And now he could speak. Soon he would speak many words. Soon he would hurt only a little, and in time there would be no more hurt. Then he too would love, and the rivulets would spill into creeks and creeks into rivers and rivers into lakes that spilled into great rivers, and across the wide world all moving waters, all pure water, would pour into the sea which was Love. Yes.

She slept only on her side now, to keep the spine from digging, but tonight the hurting was almost nothing. How peaceful she felt. How happy. She said thank you to Manito for loving so much, so much, and for asking her to be part of it.

In the night Rose heard a scream, a high, horrible scream that was like deer hide ripping, or a rabbit dying slowly in the claws of a wolverine. She sat up in bed straining to hear. The sound faded away almost at once, and as she listened to Grandma's snoring she knew that the scream had come from inside her ears, not from without. She prayed for whoever or whatever had screamed, and her back began to hurt more than ever.

On Monday, Rose awoke and peered out of the frosted window to find a dusting of powder snow lying on the world. She thrilled with the beauty of it, especially because the lines of the garden stood out in sharp relief.

Grandma fed her extra tea and bundled her up warmly before sending her off on the path to town. Arriving at the school yard, Rose found the other children on the porch, whispering to each other. No smoke came from the chimneys of the schoolhouse or the teacher's cabin on the other side of the yard.

"Where is Miss Gorrel?" she asked the little boy who had butchered Wallace and Simpson.

"She's gone away. She went south in a plane yesterday."

"Where did she go?"

"She's in a hospital."

Rose cried, "Is she sick?"

"She's gone crazy", the little boy said.

Giggling erupted from the direction of the teacherage, where five older girls were standing by the door, pointing to it. Rose went over to them to see if she could learn anything more. The girls turned to her and covered their mouths to suppress their mirth, for they knew that Rose Wâbos was a favorite of the teacher.

"Is it true that she has gone away?" Rose asked.

"Yes, the *kikinoamagekwe*, the Big Miss, has gone crazy," said one.

"Kinoje sent a devil to her, and it beat her and drove her out. How strong are the *matchi-manito* and the medicine men!"

They pointed to a drawing on the door: the outline of a pike. The half eaten body of a naked woman was crammed in its open jaws, clamped by the needle teeth.

"The jackfish is Kinoje's sign", said one of the girls.

"The woman is Big Miss", said another.

"Kinoje is a grain of sand," Rose murmured, "and his *matchi-manito* are smaller grains of sand. Jesus-Manito is bigger than the whole world."

"Then why did she run away?"

"Because she does not know about Jesus", Rose said.

"But she is a white woman!"

"The trader is white. He is bad and stupid", said one of the girls.

"This is so", said another. "Not all white people know Jesus."

"They are a strange people."

"Though they are very powerful."

But this was a well-worn topic, and Rose grew impatient with it.

"How did Kinoje frighten her?" she asked.

"We don't know, we don't know", said a chorus of voices.

"In her cabin is the secret, maybe", said one. "Let's look inside."

None of them wanted to be first. They all stepped back a few paces.

"The devil is in there", said one.

"If he is," said Rose, "we will step on his head, for he is smaller than Jesus. And Jesus is inside us."

"He is not inside us", argued one.

This was true, Rose realized, for some of the girls were not Christian.

While they were all thinking about this, an older girl, a teenager who liked to drink with wild boys, strode over and said, "Ho! So frightened, little stupids, *pingoshens*, little flies!" She walked to the door, turned the handle, and threw it open.

She grinned at them and stepped inside. Everyone held her breath, eyes wide open, mouths thinned with terror. Seconds later the big girl screamed and came flying out.

"*Run!*" she screamed, "*Neshiwed! A neshiwed* is in there!"

Neshiwed! A killer of men!

Everyone stampeded and fled. A large shape came bulging and wobbling and wibbling to the door, huge, a great flesh thing, a giant bladder. Ay! Ay! A lung eater!

Rose cried and ran. Halfway across the yard she bumped into Binemin, who was standing motionless staring at the door. She fell down.

"Run, Tchibi, run!" she screamed.

But he did not hear. He stared at the doorway with hate-green fire in his eyes. He took a big knife from his belt, a hunting knife with a bone handle, its blade inches long. Gripping it fiercely in his right hand, he stalked toward the teacher's cabin. He reached the door, braced his legs wide, and lifted the knife.

"Come back, Tchibi!" Rose cried. "Come back!"

He stabbed the shadow of the open door and took a step farther into the cabin. Then he stabbed and stabbed again and went deeper into the shadows and was seen no more.

There was a hiss and growl and then a longer hissing, and Rose buried her face in her hands and wept and wept for the death of her beloved little brother.

Now there were many cries in the school yard and many feet running toward the cabin. But Rose could not bear to look.

"Ogini", said the voice of Tchibi. "Ogini, stand up."

She looked up between her fingers.

He stood there—alive—with sweet-fire in his eyes. In his right hand was the knife, and in his left was the pelt of the dead *neshiwed*. She stared at it in horror. It was very great and terrible, a long bag of dead skin with all the evil bled out of it. The dead lung eater, the bladder, the great flesh thing was enormous, for its skin trailed all the way back into the cabin.

"Come, Ogini, come and see", Tchibi said, smiling. "It won't hurt you. I killed it."

Then he laughed his partridge laugh, low and drumming.

He took her arm and helped her up from the ground.

She was frightened, but she followed him to the cabin.

Inside, the floor of the main room was filled with the hide of the beast, its horrible body flattened and coiling into the other rooms.

"What is it?" Rose cried. "Never have I seen such a thing."

"You have seen it before. It is the balloon which the weather men send up into the sky. There are many here. I have stabbed them all."

The partridge laughed again, drumming in his throat. Then Rose marveled, for she understood. Then she marveled more because Tchibi had said many words to her, and said them without hesitation, for he was filled with his courage, the sweet-fire that comes of defeating a monster.

"Oh, look!" cried one of the older girls who had entered with the crowd of children. "Kinoje has tricked her, and he has left a letter for her."

"What letter, what letter, let me see, let me see!" cried the children, though some could not yet read.

"It is not from Kinoje", said another.

"Read it to us! Read it to us!"

"These are the words", said the older girl: "'O Darling Euphrasia'!" This caused an uproar of giggling. "'O Darling Euphrasia, prim and proper, Harry your beau has come a cropper. We made the affair and bought you the ring, the wedding is off, it was only a fling. Check out the bill below if you don't believe us. Fooled you! With love undying, Bob and Eddie'."

"Who are Bob and Eddie?" asked one.

"The weather boys", said another.

"The ones who are always chasing Indian girls."

"See this other paper. It says, 'Shipped to Miss Euphrasia Gorrel, Threefinger Lake, Ontario, one cut glass ring, dollar ninety-five, paid in full by Robert Duff. Timothy Eaton Company, Toronto'."

Tears began to fall from Rose's eyes.

"But why? Why did they do it?" she whispered.

The hurting in her spine was terrible for three days after that, and she hardly slept at all. She offered it for Miss Gorrel, begging Jesus to send her back to Threefinger Lake. But he did not. Later in the week the mail plane landed, and Rose went down to the dock to meet it. Only the pilot was on board. In the afternoon, the policeman and the Indian agent helped the pilot to load three big trunks into the plane, along with an empty wire cage.

"Where is Miss?" Rose asked the agent.

"Gone away and never comin' back", he replied with a smile that is a kind of slyness native people cannot understand.

5

Rose tried to make pictures with the remaining paper and color-sticks that Euphrasia had given to her, but her heart was often overwhelmed with longing whenever she did. She no longer thought of the teacher as Miss Gorrel, for memory was changing the woman in her mind, revealing what she had always been—a beloved friend. How confused this made Rose feel, for when Euphrasia had been near in flesh, she had been separate, her teacherness and her whiteness making a little barrier. Now that she was gone, the barrier seemed to have dissolved, the memory of her grew and grew, and with it came an ache that did not cease.

There were times when she felt angry at Euphrasia for running away and leaving her without a word of explanation. Why had the false *neshiwed* so frightened her? Why had she not returned after recovering from her fright? Surely she was no longer crazy, for even crazy people were not always crazy, and many ceased being so altogether. Euphrasia was strong, the strongest woman Rose had ever met, and thus it was impossible that she was still crazy. Why would she not return to the people she loved more than anything else in the world?

For two months after the killing of the *neshiwed*, Rose went down to the dock to meet the weekly mail plane, her disappointment growing as each time it arrived without Euphrasia. By the end of November, she lost all confidence that her friend would return, though she did nurse a hope that a letter would come in the mail, or perhaps even a small Christmas gift, possibly more color-sticks, or a book that Euphrasia had once planned to write for her—the tale of a native girl who lived on the edge of a land of little trees and who ran straight up the loon's necklace into the stars, where she gathered colors as others gather flowers in the forest and returned to her cabin with the star colors and made beautiful pictures with them. Euphrasia had said that Rose must make the pictures for it, but Rose had not made the pictures because first she wanted to have the words on paper, so that the shapes could be placed properly between them, as lakes are placed between the trees.

But now she understood this was not to be. Euphrasia, like Youngmary-the-mother-of-her-flesh, had gone away and would never return. In the dark, after Grandma began to snore, Rose would weep silently. Whenever an angry feeling arose, she overcame it by offering the pain of her spine for Euphrasia and Grandma and Tchibi and the many other people who needed it.

Because she missed Euphrasia so much, she tried hard to make a falling-into-seeing that would take her far across the forest to wherever she was. But it did not happen; the only thing she saw was the afternoon when she had drawn the woman sleeping, clutching the black pearl to her heart. The picture merely flashed and sank back down into the tin box of memories. Thus Rose learned that she could not force a falling-into-seeing, that it was not her power but a gift that was loaned to her only when it was needed. Did this mean that Manito did not want her to know what was happening to Euphrasia? She was not sure if this was so. She continued to pray for a glimpse of her beloved friend, but Manito still would not give her one. It was as if he was telling her something. What was it? Perhaps he was saying that the image of black stone in Euphrasia's heart was all she needed to know.

That winter was the bitterest in living memory. The lake froze early, and the rivers became solid highways soon after.

Snow fell heavily on the woodlands and the waters, and refused to let even a bit of sun poke through a rip in the blanket-cloud that rolled in from the south, slamming into the deadly cold air from the north, precisely over Threefinger Lake. In early December the deep cold began, thirty and forty below zero every day, week after week.

There was a new teacher at the school, an old lady with a bad temper. This, combined with the weather, provided Rose with an excuse to avoid going to school. She stayed indoors mostly, tending the cabin stove which was kept roaring to beat back the chill that tried to get inside everything, even her bones. Oldmary was sick with colds, and her back ached nearly as much as Rose's. But neither of them complained. Grandma prayed her beads morning and night and read her Bible whenever she was able to sit up in a chair by the window. Rose scraped the thick frost from it so that more light would come in.

Tchibi had ceased to visit after the heavy snows, though whenever Rose went to Mass they would stand together outside the front door of the church and chat about little things, stamping their feet to keep them from freezing. He made small sentences now, stringing two or three words together, and sometimes four. Always her heart leaped high when he did this, and she told him with her eyes how happy it made her. Sometimes there was a sadness in him, but this was not greatly troubling, because all people are sad at times. There were frightening moments when his eyes flashed with a hint of the old bile-fire. But the look in his eyes was never as crazy as it had been when she first met him, or before the killing of the *neshiwed*, when he found his courage.

When the worst of the cold snap was over, he came to visit at the cabin, ate Grandma's bannock and jam, and grinned as the slivers of golden dry-fish went down his throat like minnows. He sometimes brought spruce cones that he had crammed into his pockets or bits of broken glass that he had found at the village dump. He made a pile of them in the snow beside the cabin door and told her they would add them to the garden in the spring when they could once again make the bells ring.

In mid-December she finished the socks she had been knitting for him, and though she wanted to give them to him at Christmas, she did not wait. He needed them now, for on his feet he wore only burlap sacking tied with string inside his rubber slip-on boots. They too were torn, as were his dirty pants and jacket which he kept closed across his chest with store-bought safety pins. He did not own a hat, so Grandma knitted one for him, a wool tuque with a long braided cord of red and white yarn that hung down his back. He said nothing when they gave their gifts to him, just sat down on the kitchen chair and stared at the socks and tuque lying in his hands, his eyes filling with tears—the first time Rose had seen such a thing in him.

He was fourteen years old now, and she was twelve. He would not stop growing, like a tea bush shooting up from the bogs, which was, Grandma said, because of the white blood that was in him. The reddish tint in his hair faded away without the summer sun to set it on fire and became brown-black, though not as black as the hair of the other native boys. His skin paled more quickly than theirs, but his eyes were always green—*sweet-green* Rose called it. Like the gold-green of blueberries before they ripen.

But Rose herself seemed to have stopped growing. She was no more than four feet in height, while other girls her age were a head or more taller. It was her spine, of course, which wanted to bend the wrong way. Often, when no one was looking, she craned her neck backward and went up on tiptoes, straining her muscles to make herself straight, but the pain was very bad whenever she did that.

On Christmas Eve, Rose pulled Oldmary on the toboggan

into town, where they attended Midnight Mass. A lady from the reserve named Mrs. Otter played the pump organ. Everyone sang "O Come, O Come, Emmanuel", each in his own language: Ojibwe, English, French, and Polish. Tchibi served very well that night, though he had not yet learned to say the Latin responses that altar boys must say, or perhaps he had refused to learn them. He looked uncomfortable in the red robe and white lace coverlet; he looked like the statue of the little boy-king of Prague that sat on a shelf to the right of the altar, between the statues of St. Jean de Brébeuf, St. Isaac Jogues, and Kateri, the Lily of the Mohawks.

At the end of Mass they all sang the "Huron Carol", which contained words that were close to the Ojibwe tongue, though they said *Gitchi-Manitou* instead of *Kije-Manito*, which is the proper way for the Ojibwe. But it did not matter, because all people were as one at Christmas. Afterward, everyone went next door to squeeze into Fr. Andrei's little cabin. Father had made Polish honey cakes and a flat Bethlehem bread with a picture of the Holy Family stamped on it, which each person broke a piece from and ate. Tchibi brought Rose a cup of tea from the big billy can that bubbled on the stove. He lifted the cuffs of his trousers and showed her the thick socks on his feet. He grinned with his eyes at her, but said little, for there were too many people in the room, and he did not like to be heard by more than one when he spoke.

From his jacket pocket he took a lump wrapped in newspaper tied with red cord.

"For you, Ogini", he said with mouth shapes, though no sound came with it.

She held it in her hands, marveling. It was heavy.

"Do you want me to open it?" she asked.

He shook his head abruptly.

"I will open it later, tomorrow morning," she said to him.

He nodded and went away.

Next morning, the holy morning, the wind howled hard from the north, and Thisdog and Thatdog were curled up outside the door with their tails over their noses and drifts covering their backs. Grandma told Rose to bring them inside because it was a special day and even animals as badly behaved as Thisdog and Thatdog were smart enough to know it. They would be good. And so they were. Huffing and puffing with gratitude, they threw themselves down on the floor in front of the stove and made themselves content chewing on the old fish skins that Grandma gave to them as a treat.

They did not have a Christmas tree as many people in the village did and as a few on the reserve did. It was enough for Rose and Oldmary to pray their morning prayers by the large star Rose had scratched in the window frost. On the table they had placed a candle in a jar, and from the rafter poles pine cones dangled on long braids of red and white yarn. Rose had decorated the cones with the remaining bits of her color-sticks.

Grandma opened her present from Rose: a smoke pipe that the girl had found on the pebbled beach after a party of fishermen had flown in to Threefinger Lake before freeze-up. The pipe was purple-red with a black stem curved like a swan's neck, though the burning bowl was cracked.

"Io! Io!" Oldmary showed her gums. "It is a great gift, a very great gift! O my *Oginiwâbigon*, I kiss you." And so she did. Then she found her tobacco pouch and stuffed some into the bowl and lit it. The room filled with smoke, which Rose sniffed with pleasure, for it was the smell of important days.

Then Oldmary brought out from under the bed her gift for Rose. It was a large sack made of smooth deerskin with a flap that buttoned and hide straps for carrying it over the shoulder. Its front was beaded with pink, white, and red beads—a wild rose.

Oldmary explained: "It is for you to keep the paper and

color-sticks in and the other things that you find in the bush for your garden."

Rose kissed Grandma and skipped, once, for joy.

Then, both of them looked at the lump of newspaper that Tchibi had given to Rose.

When it was opened and lay on the table between them, they frowned and puzzled over it.

It was a stone. It was as large as Oldmary's hand, larger than Rose's, a flat green oval with a small bulge at one end. The surface was smooth and shining, though it seemed to be covered with gray dust.

"Is it for your garden?" Oldmary asked.

"I do not know. It is unlike any other stone in the garden."

"I see a cloud shape in it, or a bird. Yes, it's a bird-shape. Maybe a partridge."

"It *is* a partridge!" Rose exclaimed, her eyes kindling brightly. "It's a *binemin*."

"Now I understand his word in this. He tells you that it is himself."

"See the little eye, Grandma, see how it is green."

"Io, so much work! So many little holes in it! He has drilled them with an awl, like the carvers do. He makes speckles on the partridge feathers, I think."

"But he has made them all over. And so deep," Rose murmured to herself.

"He puts a word of himself in your hand", mused Oldmary.

As Rose warmed the stone between her palms, Oldmary relit her pipe, eyeing the girl thoughtfully. She hesitated before speaking:

"This boy is your friend, Ogini, but—"

"He is my little brother, Grandma."

"But he is a boy who is not really your brother. And he is no longer little. Besides, you are younger."

"I am *ningâ* to him, a little mother as well as sister and friend."

"The *ningâ* way is for a time, and perhaps it is still to be for a time, but it will not always be. Boys become men."

"I will always be his sister."

"Perhaps", said Oldmary puffing her pipe, staring at the stone.

As the end of winter approached, the Indian agent sent a note to Grandma demanding to know why Rose had not been attending school. Oldmary said to Rose that it was no business of his, that people were not to be owned by other people, that owning people was not good for anyone, it was not Jesus' mind. So she did not reply to the letter. Thisdog ate it and spat out the bits when he tasted the ink.

Once Fr. Andrei asked Oldmary if she thought it would be a good idea for Rose to attend school again. Great as her respect for him was, she said, no, she thought that Rose needed quietness this year, needed to learn to sew better and make pictures again.

Fr. Andrei nodded, for he greatly respected the wisdom of Oldmary. He asked if Rose needed more paper for her pictures.

Oldmary said yes, the girl had run out of paper months ago. But that was all right because Rose had not felt much like drawing since the Englishwoman went away. Even so, Oldmary said, she was saving pennies because she hoped to order pads of writing paper from the catalogue book at the trader's post. Maybe the fresh paper would spark Rose's interest again.

Fr. Andrei suggested that she not order paper from the catalogue because he could beg better paper from people he knew in Montreal and Toronto. He would write to them and send the letters on the next plane going south. He was sure that once they learned of Rose's gift they would be willing to donate artists' paper, which was larger and of better quality.

Oldmary agreed.

"I will ask for books also", said Fr. Andrei. "For Rose is very bright, and she sees far. She must learn many things for her mission in life to be fulfilled."

"Mission?" asked Oldmary curiously. "What mission is this?"

"I sense it only", he replied. "I believe she will do much good in this world and bring back certain souls from the regions of the lost."

Oldmary's eyes opened wide in surprise.

"Do you think it or see it with the heart, Father?"

"Both."

"She is very small."

"Yes, she is. Thus, she will be a fitting vessel."

"And what of the fire? Will there be love for her?"

"Yes, God's love and human love. She has this already, does she not?"

"It is untested."

"She has been tested many times", said the priest. "Daily love grows in her. Under her care Binemin Edzo has come out of the regions of the broken ones."

"Io! Io! This is true, but I fear it. I fear that boy."

"Do you fear him? Then do as Rose does—continue to love him and then there will be nothing in him for you to fear."

The old woman nodded once, grimly, and went away.

A few weeks later a cardboard box addressed to Fr. Andrei arrived on the mail plane. It contained a roll of art paper and a box of color-sticks, which he gave to Rose after Mass.

Rose was distressed by the arrival of the new paper and color-sticks. She understood Fr. Andrei's kind act and was grateful for it, yet it only served to increase her grief, for the gifts had not come from Euphrasia, and her old pain, which had slept for a time, was rekindled. During the night after she received the gifts, she had a dream.

She walked along the stone spine that curved up the back of the earth toward the skull. The day was hot. She was happy, because she carried in her new deer-hide sack many color-sticks and a roll of paper. Euphrasia would be waiting for her at the top, because she had promised she would be there. And Rose knew that when they met they would eat a picnic on the blanket and feel the wind blowing upon them as they gazed out across the lake to the north. Rose would draw a very beautiful picture of the land and sky and the woman lying asleep, with no sadness in her. No black stone in her heart. A new white bird in her heart. And a little flame inside the breast of the bird.

But when she arrived at the top of the skull, it was deserted. Euphrasia had not come, and Rose understood finally that she would never come, because she had moved on to another place where there were new children and new experiences that she could collect in her tin box.

Bitter, bitter were the tears that Rose wept. Anger arose in her, then fear, then a sick dull dreadful aching that pulled her heart down into the burned lands where ashes rule, where snakes lurk under rocks, and wolverines prowl.

Io! The pulling sickness dragged her over the edge of a cliff and down she went, falling, falling, bumping, spinning head over heels. She fell for many seconds through space and landed on her back. This was pain as she had never before known it. This was fire in her back that did not go out, and she cried aloud, "O Manito, am I a nothing that you throw me down and break me, am I worthless?"

Ay, ay, worthless—not the smallness of beloveds, but the nothingness of the unbeloveds, those who are despised.

"I am a bent and ugly girl. I am slow of speech and not smart. Those who love me all go away. Soon I will die. I will not fly up to Gissis, to meet my mother. I will be no more, it will be as if I had never existed. *Ay! Ay! Nin tchagidabadan,* we all die away!"

Weeping, her hands covering her face, she heard the crackling of a fire. Looking up, she saw that the forest was in flames all around her. Now terror was added to the pain.

It was true, then, that Manito did not answer her prayers, for she was a throwaway, a garbage that no one wanted. Oldmary had died away, Youngmary and Euphrasia had gone away, and all sweetness had died away within her and none could bring it to life again.

The fire raged, and she huddled in a circle of dry moss that was as yet untouched, Ay, ay, she was like Tchibi on the day they first brought him to the church, the day he was full of madness curled under the bench, and Kuchuk kicked him to make him quiet.

"Oginiwâbigon", said the wind and the many bells.

Then Tchibi stood in the fire; he stood in it and was burning. His feathers were speckled with fire, burning holes in his flesh, though his eyes were filled with sweet-green fire.

"I came for you, Ogini. Do not fear."

Then he lifted her in his arms and pressed her to himself, and the wings that were also part of him spread and raised into the sky, carrying her far above the *winewishkotewin*, which is the evil fire, the impure fire that destroys.

Then she awoke, filled with sadness and joy.

"Grandma, do you ever have dreams?" she asked the next morning.

Oldmary pulled the pipe stem from her mouth and cradled its cracked bowl in her palm. Her feet thumped on the floor, stopping the motion of the chair. Thisdog yelped and yanked his tail from beneath the curved willow striplings that Grandma had nailed to the feet of the chair to turn it into a rocker.

She looked at Rose steadily.

"What do you mean, dreams?"

"When you sleep."

"Oh, them. I have lots of them."

"Do you ever have a dream that comes to you again and again, and when you think about it your heart starts beating fast?"

"Sometimes it is so. Did such a dream come to you?"

"I don't know for sure."

She wanted to tell Grandma, but there was a holding back, a fear that somewhere in the gulf between speaking and hearing the dream might dissolve.

Oldmary began to rock again, sucking hot air into the bowl, brown smoke out through her wide nostrils.

"Most dreams are like a sleeping dog's, like Thisdog and Thatdog chasing rabbits. It can seem real until you wake up. Then you know it is just storytelling in a tired head."

"I dream those all the time", Rose said.

"Yes, everybody does. But the others are different. In my whole life I have had them five, maybe six times . . . always before big turnings, big changes."

"Like what, Grandma?"

"One time I woke up in the middle of a night, this was a long time after I was married, my husband was sleeping beside me, and in my dream I see my mother come to me. Yet, after I am awake I can still see her standing at the foot of our bed. She is looking at me. She says, 'Mary, pray your beads for me, I am going on now.' Only she says it inside of me, without any talking. And then she was gone like fog on the wind."

Oldmary closed her eyes and rocked. Rose understood by the set of her grandmother's thin brown lips that she was feeling it as if it were happening now.

"I had not seen her for years. And it was weeks before the Indian agent come our way with the news. My mother died on the night of that dream, hundreds of miles away in the TB hospital."

Rose continued to sit on a stump of firewood by Oldmary's

feet, feeling the weight of ignorance which lay on human beings, their mortal frailty in the face of the spirit world.

The old woman smiled suddenly.

"Another time, just after your grandfather asked me to marry him. Well, I will tell you, I was not in love with him. In those days we did not think the way people do now; you did not have to have all that. I looked at him, and I saw a good enough man, an honest one. Though he was crazy sometimes, he never hurt me. I knew he would be a good father and husband and look after us. So I said yes. But the closer to the day I got, Rose, the scareder I got."

She looked at her granddaughter and smiled, as if the girl were tangible proof of her sound judgment and would dispel any sting in the memory of her foolish fears. She looked away into the window glass.

"I got so scared I was set to call it off. Then one night, just before the wedding, I dreamed I was standing in a river. It was not cold or warm, just cool and sweet. I jumped into the deepest part of the river. And I swam. I laughed.

"Then a voice said, *you will be married and the spirit will fill you.* So I woke up with my heart going terrible fast and the voice echoing in my ears, and I could even hear the sound of the river."

They were silent again. The stove spat.

"So you married him?" Rose prompted.

"I married him. A white man."

"What was he like?"

"He was a trapper, came up by canoe from Sioux Narrows after a war. He told me once he should have died in it, but he ran away when they were shooting at him."

"Who was shooting at him?"

"Soldiers. Ay, ay! He used to say to me, 'Man was not made for war.' He was not a talker, but he told me that much. He was from a place called Berksher."

"Where is that?"

"It's on an island, far away in the east."

"Oh."

"He would not tell me about his family back there on that island. He said they did not want to see him again because the war had made him crazy, and they were ashamed of him. He said he wanted to forget the past. But he brought some bits of it with him. In his head. And some poems he made when he was a boy."

"Were you happy, you and the whiteman?"

"For a time. Then he died."

"How did he die?"

"Influenza. It nearly killed me too. It took him in our seventh year of marriage."

"Did you have many children?"

"Yes. They were the color of deerskin, not brown like you and me. Two died while still babies. One was born dead."

"Maybe they were from God and went back to him."

Oldmary squinted at her.

"They are *all* from God," she said firmly. "Even the unfinished ones."

Oldmary rocked a little more, turning her black eyes upon Rose. "But not everybody goes back to him", she added.

"If your babies died, who then is my mother?"

"There was a fourth who lived—Youngmary-the-mother-of-your-flesh."

Which made Rose unable to think about it any more.

"About dreams, maybe you should ask Fr. Andrei", Oldmary said, finally.

Rose loved Fr. Andrei. She had tried falling-into-seeing through the windows of his eyes, once, but had been unable to go very far. It was rich and warm inside, and good. Something had told her that she would not understand much of what she saw in there. He did not need her falling-into-seeing for himself, but for his work among the *Anishinâbi*. Manito had permitted it, she guessed, because she was to pray for him, as if he were a fisherman who had thrown a great net into the lake, and her prayers would help to fill it with fish.

Fr. Andrei seemed to know she was seeing inside of him—he was the only person who was ever able to detect it—and his eyes told her that falling-into-seeing was not always the right thing to do.

"God wants us to understand many things", he said to her gently. "But there are ways of seeing that are his ways. It must come in the right order, and only enough to guide your prayer."

Then she understood what he was telling her. To peer into the windows without being asked, or to climb through them while the soul inside was sleeping, was like breaking into a house. The kind of seeing God allowed was only a glimpse, like a flash of light on waves or a lick of lightning in the sky, just enough for you to see a thing that needed prayers. Euphrasia's black pearl. Tchibi's body burning. The locked box under Grandma's bed.

But Rose saw far enough into Fr. Andrei to get a picture. She saw a boy lying on the steps of a big church. There was blood on him. Bad boys had beaten him. Then he was a man in a jail, with bad men beating him. She saw him on a boat coming here; he was sighing and looking at the sea. If she looked into his eyes, she always saw his kindness. She saw that he loved her. She saw that he would never hurt her. He was a man going down into poverty and accepting it as a great gift, for he loved greatly. Rose saw this much, but nothing more.

"There is danger in it, Rose", he went on. "For pictures in the mind can come to you from many places."

Her eyes, widening as far as they could go, asked him to explain.

"The pictures can come from God, or from your own feelings and imaginings. And sometimes they can be false, sent by the matchi-manito, the evil one, to lead you from the safe path."

"How can . . ." she began in a trembling voice, for she had never before dared to ask such a difficult question of him. "How can I tell the good pictures from the bad?"

He thought for a time, and answered, "Pray, and do not cease to pray. Then, if the picture is bad it will go away. If it is good, it will be very simple, to guide your prayer and nothing more. If it is mixed, if it is only feelings and imaginings, even though it offers you pleasure, still you will have no peace in it. But in all of these pray, and then it will become clearer."

"Like the river when it is muddy?"

"Like that."

Music was frozen in all things, waiting to be thawed. Under the late March sun, ribbons of crystal water began to unravel from the drifts. They curled and lengthened and ever sought to run away in all directions. First the very small silver bells, then the larger brass bells, then the booming golden bells. It spilled from the high places into the low, swelling up swamps into sodden snow-covered lakes, turning crevices into treacherous pools. Grandma warned Rose to stay on the known paths or she could sink into slush and icy water much deeper than she would care to guess. Crazyman River now opened, the slashing water doing what the new sun had failed to accomplish, so that until next winter there would be no need for axing and splintering ice, or melting snow for tea.

Layer by layer the snow in the bush melted down, uncovering a saga of inverse animal tracks. Here, a wolf had circled their yard unseen on a late snowy night, compressing the white granules beneath its pads, forming the compact, sunken molds. There, a snowshoe hare had zigzagged across the clearing. Now as the warming days wrestled with the last of winter, the softer snow around the tracks melted away more quickly, leaving the field a crosshatched history of silent travelers.

No longer was there such a thing as pure white snow. The growing light made mauve and robin's-egg blue of the shadows where the pines cast their images across the trail, and in the deeper nooks it would be purple or cobalt, as if someone had made them with giant color-sticks. But where the sun struck full force on the planes of snow there was blinding yellow brilliance. Grandma told Rose that before going out in its glare all day she must smudge soot on the bones below her eyes to cut its power. Snow blindness was like hot sand under the eyelids, so it was worth looking like a raccoon as she walked to the trading post, where white people laughed at the masked faces of the natives and sometimes smiled in pity at Rose's patched calf-length skirt, torn deerskin mitts, and homemade socks stuffed inside the falling-apart rubber boots.

By late April, only a few snow humps in the shadows of the bush remained, where they whispered as they melted. Warm breezes and cool braided together in and out of the trees. The lake groaned, then roared, one night, and in the morning was free of ice.

Sometimes she thought of Euphrasia with love and sometimes with hurt, and sometimes with a gentle sadness that contained love. Or was it a gentle love that contained sadness? And sometimes, though not as often, she remembered Marleena. Then she realized that memories melt like ice under light. They thaw slowly and never entirely disappear, becoming instead a different form of water.

Now Rose was free to walk in a world no longer a prison of straight lines and a few safe paths. She went to school sometimes, and on those mornings when she was not moved to do so, she ambled for hours through the damp woods, eyes looking, looking, soaking up the brown mat on every foot of the forest floor. The green of moss, the rust of rock, the blueness of the wet air. Her lungs felt too small to take in all the pungent herbal smells. Wherever she went, she carried the deer-hide sack, the beaded rose turned outward so that if she were to meet any people they would admire it and think highly of Grandma.

One morning, as she entered the village, Rose felt a great restlessness within. When she came to the school yard, she flashed a look at the children playing there, but proceeded onward and entered the border of trees at the edge of the cabins. She went like the spring wind, into the low bog places where black spruce grows, and up the rocky slopes through the jack pine ridges and birch copses. Climbing onto the stone causeway that ascended into the northeast, she felt a sudden longing to see the skull again. She had not returned to it since the departure of Euphrasia, when life resumed its slow pace of revolving seasons, and the thrill of foreign worlds fell back into the deeper waters of memory.

When she came to the skull, she found that it had not changed. Except for the absence. She sat down in the socket and gazed out over the lake. She opened the tin box in which the new color-sticks lay. She removed a sheet of paper from the roll Fr. Andrei had given her. She flattened it on her knee and divided it evenly into three sheets.

On the first she drew a bird.

On the second the burnt pine tree.

On the third the face of Euphrasia.

But the eruption of love and longing caused by the latter work was too painful.

Rose stuffed the bird and the tree into the deer-hide sack.

Then she stabbed the portrait of Euphrasia, stabbed and stabbed as if the color-sticks were knives—red slashes, orange slashes, purple slashes. In a fury, she tore up Euphrasia and threw her in pieces to the wind.

Frightened by what she had done, she left the brow of the skull hastily, scrambling down the east slope into the bush at the base of the hill. From there she ran panting through the forest in a direction she had never gone before, heading for the place Euphrasia had called *ultima thule*, where one would walk if one wished to be absorbed into absolutes, to be taken, and to be seen no more.

She stopped eventually, because stones and fallen trees tripped her. She fell to her knees and caught her breath. Why was she doing this? Where was she going? Veins of granite ran like hard rivers in many directions, always spreading and reaching toward the ultimate north, but joining in places around the thickets of hoary bush, thrusts of birch spears, or wells of black water. It was dangerous. It was confusing. Turning back to face the south, she saw that the skull was a tiny knob in the distance, beside a line of silver that was the lake. She realized that she was now entering the place of absolutes, where no human eyes had ever penetrated. She feared that she would soon be lost. Her back ached, but the greater pain was caused by what she had done. She cried in sickness and shame, because for an instant she had hated Euphrasia, she had wanted to kill Euphrasia—Euphrasia whom she loved.

Then she saw the pool. It lay hidden in the granite, a few yards across and surrounded by sighing wands of sapling birches. The hollow of transparent water was placid, crystal clear to the bottom, reflecting the blue sky above. In it she saw a high white speck flying overhead.

"*Oshkinjigokâde!*" she whispered, wiping her wet face on her sleeve. "It is made like an eye!"

"*Oshkinjigokijê-Manito*, the Eye of God", sang the high white bird. But when she looked swiftly upward to find it, it was gone.

Green moss fought the brittle caribou moss for domination of the rocks. She sat down on the softer patches, dangling her legs toward the surface of the water. Then on an impulse, she stripped off her clothes. Intending to enter and swim if she could brace herself, she lingered for a moment on the sun-warmed rocks, waiting for courage, looking down her legs crossed like the brown ivory feet of a stained crucifix. She plunged into the waist-deep water. She thrust herself entirely under, screamed silently in its icy depths, then shot upward, shattering the surface, gasps and shouts mixing with the cries of alarmed piper-birds. Jumping up and down, crying with exhilaration that was both pain and joy. Holding her nose between thumb and forefinger, she forced herself under again and crouched on the bottom, looking about at the jade water garden until her lungs were ready to burst. Up! she cried into the air, and her cry split the stone, split the air, rose up to meet the downward plunging cry of a great white bird with turquoise fire-eye, who dissolved in the sparkles of the water beads. Gasping, she pulled herself onto the rocks toward the healing sun and shook herself dry. Standing, shivering by the water's edge, she gazed into the pool which flattened into a mirror, and saw the strange S of a spine that twisted around a naked body. And struggled into her clothing with blue lips and red eyes.

Rose built a fire of twigs and lit it with a wooden match. Her hands still shaking, she fed the flames with dead pine twigs and the petrified sponges of moss. It roared in the hollow of rock and heated her slowly as she sat in its smoke, hugging her knees. Shivering. Watching the white pebbles at the bottom of the pool inhale and exhale.

Hours later she broke through the line of trees into the clearing of the cabin by Crazyman River.

"Where have you been?" Grandma asked, scowling with worry. "You smell like moose hide!"

But Rose could answer only by showing the two drawings.

Grandma looked, then looked away, which was her way.

Tchibi came to the cabin more often now, because the weather was warmer and the beginning of good things had come to the earth again, as it always does. Together he and Rose made the cascade of their garden ring with bells. Rose crooned small wordless tunes to accompany the music of falling water.

The tentative spring grew confident. The early summer light, running through the bush with its torch, ignited new fires of life: first the yellow trout-lily, then the green jack-in-the-pulpit, then the trillium, lady's slipper, Indian pipeweed, purple fireweed, arctic cotton—an abundance of first signs. Then the mountain ash and white maple budded modestly. The poplar and birch exploded in roaring crowds of green flags. The mosquitoes came out in force with the leaves, whining their bloodlust. There was a persistent desire to swat, to scratch, and to hate. Grandma said, as she did every year, that if people would only just allow a few to bite and ignore the rest, the mosquitoes and the humans would hardly notice each other until the end of summer.

Fish filled the nets and were smoked. Thisdog and Thatdog were once again ribby heaving forces that shouldered each other aside, snarled over scraps, or came panting into the cabin with mangled squirrels dripping from their grinning jaws. Grandma wore sweaters with holes instead of the heavy parka. She sewed moccasins and beaded them. And traded them for sugar and tea. They went to Mass every Sunday. School guilt evaporated.

Then the hotter days began. In the evenings, Oldmary and Rose would sit on the porch, sipping tea and talking in the setting sun. Grandma speaking of her lungs and bones, and how lately her eyes had not been what they used to be, her blue pipe smoke wafting into the cool dusk, telling stories, some familiar, some new.

Even so, a restlessness would come upon Rose, most often in the nights when she lay hot and sleepless in the dark room, listening to the sigh of Oldmary's breath or the clicking of rosary beads above the mad humming of the mosquitoes. And sniffing the heavy air that carried in green smells, baked pine

136

bark, dead fish, and the scent of Thisdog's and Thatdog's matted fur and droppings. Anger and fear returned whenever she remembered the stabbing of Euphrasia.

On a Saturday in August, Tchibi knocked on the frame of the open door and said in his soft deep voice, "Ogini, come and walk by the river—the minnows are fat."

This was a very long sentence, and she rejoiced because of it.

"Oh, yes, let's go to the river and farther if you want", she said.

"Will you draw today?" he asked, pointing at the deer-hide bag she was slinging over her shoulder.

"I don't like to make pictures any more."

He puzzled over this, but said nothing. She saw him cast a glance at the stone partridge he had given her, sitting now on the window sill.

"It hurts when I make pictures", she said. "I don't know why."

"It's because of the Big Miss", he replied slowly, staring at the floor so as not to offend her.

"No", she shook her head. Though in her heart she knew he was right.

"Yes", he corrected her. "She gave you the color-sticks."

"This is true."

"You want to forget her."

"No", Rose replied with a hint of anger.

"She went away and left you", he said.

"She went away from all of us."

"But you were like a daughter to her."

How could Tchibi know such things, she wondered. Then she remembered that he too had been abandoned.

"She left you the color-sticks," he said. "You still have *them*."

The mildness in his voice and eyes surprised her, for he was the boy who had barked and snarled at her only a few years before.

"She left me color-sticks a long time ago", Rose said. "The color went from them and they are no more. These are the sticks that Fr. Andrei gave to me."

"Then it is a different thing, Ogini", he said. "You can make pictures without the hurting."

"Let's go for the walk", she said.

They followed the creek down through the lodgepole pines to Crazyman River, picking wild raspberries as they went, going slowly, for in summer all time ceased to exist; indeed, it never had existed. The river flowed green, the water two or three feet lower than usual, uncovering shoals of small stones that had been unreachable until now. They glistened in the spray.

Stepping off the edge of the forest floor, Tchibi slid down the high sandy banks to the beach of pebbles. Rose followed more carefully. The narrow stretch of stones extended without interruption for a half mile to the east, where it bent before its big push into Threefinger Lake. By unspoken agreement Rose and Tchibi walked in that direction. From time to time, they were forced to climb over the trunks and splayed roots of trees that had fallen from the banks above. Taking her by the hand, Tchibi helped her up and over. They walked on, bending often to pick up pebbles of unusual shapes and colors.

Farther along they came to a spit of land that jutted into the river and formed a small sandy cove. It was covered with grass and wild strawberries. Crickets and grasshoppers were making a high singing that flowed along with the burble of the river.

They sat in the grass by the cove and watched the water.

Tchibi lay back and covered his eyes with his forearm. Rose took a piece of paper and the box of color-sticks from the sack. It was the metal container that Euphrasia had given her. Rose had hardly looked at it since the teacher went away. Now she looked closely, examining the Scottish girl on the lid and the plaid design and the gold letters. She opened the lid and stared into the memory box from which many things flew out at her, containing mostly pain. It was very difficult not to cry. And harder still to select some color-sticks and force them across the paper.

She drew the shape of Tchibi sleeping in the grass, his chest rising and falling under the tattered white T-shirt, his ankles scratched and bare above the socks she had made for him. They were his only socks and were disintegrating.

There were many small round holes on the skin of his shins and arms.

"Poor partridge", she whispered. "*Nishime*, my brother."

She tried to force the falling-into-seeing, to see again the things that had been done to him, but she could not. She had already seen, or at least she had imagined what it had been. Was it imagining, or was it true seeing? Was it good, was it bad? She no longer knew for sure. Lately, it was as if the falling-into-seeing was being taken from her. It was fading away. But was the fading like a cloud sliding over the horizon leaving blue sky, or was it like blue sky disappearing over the horizon while a cloud blanket covered everything?

The drawing of Tchibi was not very accurate. A stick boy with holes on his skin. She tore it up and let the wind take the bits of paper. She wondered if Manito had taken away the picture gift as well.

Why was he taking things away?

Why was he giving her more pain in her back and in her heart?

Does love do such things?

She reminded herself that the love-fire always returned, and that in the hidden-way, the blessing-way, he was asking her to be part of his work. If he was allowing her to be smaller and poorer and to bear more suffering, he would use it for a good purpose, take it into the Big Sacrifice, and from there he would pour more healing into others.

She closed her eyes and prayed for Tchibi, offering the having-nothing-way for him.

A few minutes later a grasshopper landed on his nose, startling him awake. Rose laughed. He laughed too, the partridge drumming. They got up and went back to their homes without another word.

Rose thought sometimes of the boys in the village, and though she was careful to keep from her mind the thoughts that Grandma said were impure and would sicken you, she wished she could attract their eyes. She thought it would be a warm thing if they would look at her and say, Ogini is like a wild flower, she is a friend to all, she is our little sister. Most of all she wished that her body would move more gracefully, like normal girls who walked beside their mothers to the store. Or who raced screaming around the dusty baseball diamond behind the school. Io! It was hard not to be like that.

But she reminded herself that she had been given a very great gift in Grandma, who was like a saint, and in a little brother who, if not exactly a saint, was one who cared for her and in whose eyes could be seen, from time to time, the glow of sweet-fire. And she must not forget Euphrasia, who had loved her for a time, a woman who was very great and very beautiful. A woman she had killed. But not quite killed. For paper murder is not the same as the acts of a *neshiwed*. The confession and the sign of the cross Father made over her had absolved her.

"Hatred is wrong, Rose", he had said. "She did not understand how much hurt she would cause. Forgive her."

And so Rose had decided to forgive Euphrasia and let her go. The anger-fear and the turbulent memories subsided into a bittersweetness. She must seek the love that lay everywhere about her in the world, she decided. But love, as Grandma told her so often, was full of difficulties and false words. Finding your way through the forest of difficulties and false words was part of finding love. Hidden within the forest were deep swamps in which you could die, but there were also crystal pools and rivulets of singing bells.

She tried not to look too closely, but never before had boys' legs seemed so powerful. Or a brown arm poking from a tattered sweater. And hair, black like a fan of charcoal strokes as it flashed in the sun. Boys, straining their muscles as they strung their homemade bows, preparing to chase hares hotly through the hotter bush. Men and boys stabbing the lake with paddles as they drove their canoes away from the dock into the north to their fish camps, to their real life. Why did her heart beat so swiftly when these images came to her in half-sleep, the falling-into-dreaming time? The more she thought of them, the more the yearning fires would deepen. Was it death-fire or life-fire? She wasn't sure. Wanting to fall asleep, she would force her mind away to other things.

One night she dreamed about Tchibi, or perhaps it was a half-dream, half-imagining, in the place between sleep and wake. He knelt beside her at the burned tree on the top of the skull, while she drew frenzied storms on large rolls of white paper. He took her hand in his. She stood up, her back straighter than a pine, and was not ashamed. He stood up too, facing her, strong and handsome, clean and combed and dressed in fresh trading post clothes. He smiled at her, and the craziness was gone from his eyes. He was totally healed by God.

"Will you marry me, Rose?" he said in a deep man-voice.

"Oh, yes, Binemin Edzo, Oh, yes," she cried. "I will."

"Let us go down to the church where Fr. Andrei waits for us, Oginiwâbigon Wâbos," he said with love in his eyes. "Let us go unto God, the joy of our youth, and be wed."

And the bells pealed out across the void.

Then she woke up.

She always woke up, though the dreams remained her own. To keep. They were her private fire, a fire which did not eat its fuel. It was burning and sweet with something wild in it straining to break free. A person must tame the sweet-fire, she often reminded herself. Tame it like a wild hare, if she caught one, say, down by the edge of the deep grass behind the outhouse, hiding and thinking it was undiscovered until her hands grabbed it. The hare would be wild with terror, eyes bulging, legs kicking, trying to rake those hind claws down her arms. But she would hold its head in the bend of her elbow so it would believe it was safe in a hole, and she would lay her hand on the brown fur and feel the heart banging in the frail rib cage. And she would whisper to it or sing, and it would gradually stop trembling under the warmth of her hand, and the terror would seep out of it until it no longer believed it would be eaten. Then maybe it would look, but only after the longest time, her arms aching from holding. At last it would sit in the corral of her legs and nibble grass by her toes, a tiny *wâbos* nibbling the petals of the *ogini* flower. And so the hare would become her own, if the dogs did not get it first.

A warm south wind greeted Rose as she climbed toward the skull. Far behind, the village simmered quietly beneath the August sun. Ahead, to the north, the ocean of pine and spruce surged over the land, reaching for the barren lands which lay beyond the curve of the earth. Their tops swayed in humility beneath the waves of the wind, and Rose moved with them. All morning she walked the ribs and backbones that were just barely contained within the skin of the world. She stayed on the higher pathways, which were dry and open. She walked farther than she had ever gone before, farther than the skull, farther even than the pool where she had been cleansed of Euphrasia's murder.

Five or six miles past it, the land reached an escarpment and plunged down into a vast plain filled with swamps drained by countless creeks threading northward to the Hudson Bay basin, to the Arctic sea. She came to a halt on a high, glacier-worn plateau of bare granite. In crannies where a little soil had collected over millennia, blueberries were dusky ripe. She picked and ate them. When she was full she lay down in a pocket of moss and let her face bake in the sun, while there lingered behind her eyes a hallucination of blue pearls burned upon the retina. When she sat up and gazed farther east along the long table of rock, she suspected a similar illusion in what she saw.

A square of white light rested there on a projection of granite, not too distant, perhaps only a few minutes walk away. She blinked twice but the perfect shape, a design alien to these regions, did not disappear. She lurched to her feet and began to walk toward it, feeling a moment of disquiet. She picked her way along the edge of the cliff, training her eyes on the object, but taking care where she placed her feet. She progressed in this manner for half an hour, and began to wonder if the thing was great in size, then considered that its shininess might make it appear larger or closer then it was.

When she reached it, stopping a dozen feet away, its true dimensions were revealed. It was the square end of a long rectangular crate as gray-white as driftwood, the weathered planks glowing softly in the late afternoon sun. A few boards from the top were strewn around and one side had been broken inward. It had been there for years, sunken in the moss. As Rose approached, she saw that stamped on the sides were the words *Fort Garry Tea*, the ink long washed from it but the letters still impressed into the wood.

Then she realized what it was. A coffin. She knew also that if she looked inside she would see a corrupt body or a skeleton. She was not afraid, but her heart thumped harder in the hot wind blowing up the slope from the barrens, and something caught in her throat. She knelt down beside the box and slowly peered inside.

There were, she saw first, two skeletal hands crossed upon a field of rotting cloth. She knew it was a woman's body by the ragged calico dress, as blue as the sky, as flowered as Arctic summer, weathered over her bones, torn through in places. There were scraps of a disintegrated caribou-skin parka. The white of facial bones was not grotesque, merely odd and sad and perfectly still. The wind stirred the corolla of fur circling the ropes of hair which bordered a cap of parchment skin on the top of the skull, gray braids curling down around the shoulders onto a moldering sweater, upon which a green oxidized cross and chain glowed dully in the sun.

Why had the box been left here? The woman must have died in winter, when the ground was too frozen to dig a grave. Perhaps this had occurred during the years when there was no priest at Threefinger Lake. Or it might have been that she belonged to a family travelling across the edge of the barrens and that she had died only a few miles from a village unknown to the wanderers. They had put her on a high place, closer to the eyes of Manito.

Rose knelt a long time, sensing the corpse's dignity, listening to the wind. Birds penetrated the stillness with soft chanting. She was suddenly aware that no wild creatures had disturbed the corpse, scattering bones as they would with any other carrion. Why had they not done so, she wondered. And why had the planks been torn off, who or what had done this, maybe a wolf or bear? But if they had broken open the box of memories, why had they not eaten the colors they had found inside? There was no damage within, save for that done by death itself.

It is holy here, Rose thought.

All sacred things were placed in boxes, for safekeeping, for a sign. Jesus in the tabernacle. The holy souls in their coffins. Color-sticks. And memories.

A small porcelain cup lay at the foot of the box and the caribou moss had grown up around it. In the bottom lay a few scraps of brown fiber, held in place by a stone. Rose sniffed the fiber. It was tobacco.

Who had put it there? It was not a Christian thing to do, yet the woman had been a Christian. Perhaps, many years after she had been left in the wind, her husband or children had returned to offer a gift to her spirit and to sing for her spirit in sacred fragile summer. Was it because they were pagans, or half-pagans? It would seem so. On the other hand, they might have recalled how she liked to smoke, and the offering was nothing more than a sign—a little memory.

Rose knelt down, bent over the moss, and prayed for the woman's soul. Then, quickly, without looking into the box again, she turned and walked back in the direction from which she had come.

One day, Rose happened to be climbing the front steps of the trader's store, where Grandma had sent her to exchange bead-work for tea. Just as she entered, an old man pushed his way out. It was Kinoje. They were alone. He stared at her with a sly scowl. His eyes held her.

"Little girl", he said in a low voice like a dog's growl. "You are a no-thing. Your mother is a no-thing, and your grand-mother is a no-thing."

Rose's throat closed in fear. She tried to slip by him, but his clawlike hand gripped her wrist.

"Tell that old woman, tell her I forget nothing. Tell her I have much to say about the Crazyman." Kinoje cackled. "Your grandfather, the mad owl—the *kokoko*—he used to fire bullets at the sky and scream at the Manito." He laughed again. "The influenza took him before he could put a bullet in his own brain."

Tears spurting from her eyes, Rose pulled away.

"Tell her, little girl, tell Oldmary that Manito is weak and growing weaker. Say to her this: 'Your prayers did not save the Crazyman. Neither will your prayers save the brood that came from him, for I have cursed you.' Tell her that."

Eyes wide with terror, Rose fled from the post and stumbled through the thick clutching trees to the cabin by Crazyman River. As she ran, the words *Crazyman, Crazyman*, cackled over and over in her mind, in Kinoje's voice, and she feared that the name and the voice were now within her. Always she had believed that a hundred years ago, near the beginning of the world, a trapper, a crazy man, had lived upon the river bank somewhere to the northwest, for rivers are long and time is long, and many people, mad or not, come and go on them.

"Grandmother!" she cried when she arrived huffing and puffing in the clearing by the cabin. Oldmary was gutting fish over a tub. She straightened.

"What is wrong?" she asked, her eyes narrowed.

"I have spoken with Kinoje", she sobbed.

"Ay, ay-ee! Why did you speak with that wicked man, when I warned you against him?"

Rose rubbed her wrist. "I did not want to, Grandmother, but he held my arm so that I could not run from him."

Fire flashed in Oldmary's eyes. "What did he say to you?"

"He told me of my grandfather, your husband."

In a low voice Oldmary asked, "What did he say of him?"

Rose told her everything. Oldmary sat down in the dust of the yard among the fish guts. She shielded her eyes with her wrinkled hand.

"Ee, ee, that Kinoje! When he was a small boy he mocked me. Now I am an old woman and still he mocks me."

"Is it true what he said, Grandmother?"

"It is true in part. The river is named for the man who was my husband. In those days the river was called *Swift-water-over-*

bright-pebbles. It was easier for people to say *Crazyman*. So they did. It became a saying in the village. Now it is a name on the white people's map."

"Did he shoot his gun at Manito?" Rose asked with dread.

"This is a thing he did after the baby boy died—Oliver. The madness came upon him, though it swiftly passed. Kinoje saw it. People are like this, Rose—they see part of a thing and make a whole of it."

"Then he was not always mad?"

Oldmary shook her head. "No. Rarely was he mad, and then only for a little time. It came on him whenever the world seemed a darkness to him. He fired his gun in that way—in the blaspheme-way—only once. He was afterward greatly ashamed of it."

"Kinoje said he cursed you."

Once again the fire blazed in Oldmary's eyes. "If Kinoje cursed me, I have not felt it. The waters of baptism cover me. The Holy Communion fills me. He has no power over this."

"Then he lied."

Oldmary nodded. "Yes, he lied. Kinoje is a liar. He is a word-*neshiwed*, for he serves the spirit of the *neshiwed*, the *matchi-manito*—Satan. He has power only where his lie is believed. You need not fear that man's curses."

"Can you tell me about my grandfather?"

"He had a wound in his mind. But he would hurt no one."

"Can you tell me more?"

Oldmary seemed suddenly drained. "Another day," she said with finality.

During that summer another event occurred, and it too would leave its mark. Arriving at the trading post one morning, a week or so after her meeting with Kinoje, Rose saw Mytro Kuchuk sitting in his flat-bottomed duck boat, a stone's throw from shore. He was drinking and fishing, mumbling to himself all the while. In his right hand he held the bottle, and in his left the rod. Its line fell straight down into the water, which was smooth as glass. There was no wind. All else was silent, save for the humming of mosquitoes, so she heard the old man's every word.

Much of it she did not understand, for he spoke in his native tongue, which was Ukrainian.

It sounded at first as if he was cursing or making a nonsense rhyme: "Kvassy-Kuchuki-kavassy-kuchinsky. . . ."

Then he switched to English. "Kuchuk, he goes to da water each day, he fishes and fishes, but de fishies never come his way. . . ." Then he said an evil word about his luck, and a more evil thing against God.

Without being seen, Rose walked toward the shore, listening, saying a prayer for him. As Kuchuk took a swig from his bottle, the pole suddenly bent into a quivering bow and began to whip this way and that. He yelled, dropped the bottle into the bottom of the boat, and grabbed the pole with both hands.

It was a mighty fish, zigging and zagging under water, slowly pulling the boat around in a wide circle. As it rounded near shore, she saw that Kuchuk's face was stunned, flushing red, then yellow, then red again.

Io, his yellow face was frightening, as if happiness and rage were the same thing in him. Rose sat down on the pebbled beach and watched. Bit by bit the fish tired, and the old man began to reel it in a little at a time. When it was near the boat, its body rolling sideways in exhaustion near the gunwale, Kuchuk grabbed a hammer from the bottom of the boat and banged hard on the fish's head.

Then he laughed. His face drained from bright red into yellow again. He reached into the water and stuck a finger into the gills. As he began to pull it up, the boat tipped and nearly overturned. Up and up came the fish; long and black it was, fat too, which was strange, for it was a jackfish.

"Biggest pike ever caught at Threefinger!" he bellowed to the native people who had noticed the commotion and were ambling down to see. They squatted by the shore, observing the old man as he hauled the great fish into the boat at last.

"It *is* big", said one man. "Truly this *kinoje* is one of the biggest ever taken from these waters."

"Twenty, thirty pounds", said another.

"No, forty."

Kuchuk poled his boat toward shore, leaning on the oar. When the prow rumbled on the pebbles, he got out onto solid ground and dragged the fish after him. It was nearly as tall as he. It twitched where it lay, its gills opening and closing. Kuchuk hit it with the hammer one more time, then threaded a rope through the gills and mouth. Than done, he hoisted it over his shoulder and bent under its weight as he headed toward the trees in the direction of his cabin. More people had gathered, and many raised their voices in praise of him.

As Kuchuk went past, Rose stood up and gazed in wonder at the fish. Its eyes stared at her, and its mouth spoke to her.

"*Death*", it hissed.

With a cry of fear, Rose jumped backward and ran all the way home.

In September, when the geese had reversed their direction, there came a gathering of tension in the air, the usual engorging of towering cumulus in the hot afternoons, its nimbus not yet mature, its storm still leashed. The nights were colder and there was frost on the ground in the mornings.

"How is your back, Rose?" Grandma would say. "The nurse was asking me today if it hurts you."

Or, "There is a new teacher in the village. She told me the government wants all children to go to school."

Or, "Fr. Andrei says we should think about taking you to a doctor."

"There are no doctors here", Rose answered quickly. "Besides, we have no money."

"Father says he can beg some."

"For us?"

"Yes. For us. He is good."

This was true, Rose knew. She believed that he was good, but she had come to believe more in the permanence of her twisted spine. She knew that her life would continue as it had, that she would become a woman who stripped fish nets, picked berries, cut lodgepole pine into firewood with a bow saw, fed the stove, baked bannock, and when the artist papers and the store-bought color-sticks were used up, she would collect paper bags on which she would always draw with charcoal.

She accepted the model of womanhood provided by Grandma. You grew into a bent woman. That was, after all, the shape of love.

That winter the owl came. It appeared at the edge of the lake ice one day and was soon surrounded by barking dogs too wary of it to attack. It was larger than forest owls, its feathers pure white. It seemed confused. Perhaps it was lost or sick. As Rose stepped toward it, her arms outstretched as if to enfold and protect it, the bird swivelled its head to stare at her, its yellow eyes blinked, and black speckles appeared on its body.

The whole village came running to see the marvel, circling around it in a wide slow arc, followed always by the revolving head of the owl, its body motionless. It was a species few of the people of Threefinger Lake had ever seen before. The Weatherman said it was a Great Snowy Owl. The Trader said it was from the Arctic tundra, a long way from its home. He approached with a burlap sack and tossed it over the creature. It began to thrash inside the bag. Its talons ripped through the weave, yet it could not escape. The Trader carried the bag gingerly toward his store and threw it down on the steps. On a log stringer he nailed a wire rabbit cage, and into its open door he dumped the owl.

Trembling inside this prison, the owl opened its beak and screamed without a sound. Its eyes were outraged. They pleaded with Rose, who stood at the edge of the porch, aching for it. People brought strips of fish and dry-meat and dropped them through the wires. The owl would not eat. Rose determined to set it free when no one was watching. The next morning, on her way to Mass, she tiptoed onto the porch of the store, intending to open the cage door, only to find that the creature had sunk into the wire grid of the floor, petrified by death, a wing propped up like an abandoned illusion of freedom.

"There is a mission school", Grandma said one night as they sipped tea by the roaring wood stove. A fierce wind howled outside, rattling the panes of glass against the window's crossbars. "It is far, far away to the south, by the great lakes where the sisters have built a house for Indian girls."

"I do not want to go to such a house", Rose said.

"You do not have to," Grandma said. "But. . . ."

Weeks went by. Storm after storm blotted out all horizons.

"At that school they would take you to a doctor", Grandma said.

"I do not need a doctor", Rose replied firmly.

"You need to get your back fixed. I will not always be here."

"You will always be here!" Rose insisted.

"Sometime, many years from now, I am going up there", Oldmary pointed. "Into the loon's necklace."

"I will go too."

"No, you will come later."

"I do not want to go later. I want to go with you."

"You cannot. You have work to do here."

"I would be alone."

"No, you would have light."

"If you went up there," Rose pointed, "if you left me here, I would not have any light."

But this old game was useless.

The following spring Oldmary happened to be walking back from the village alone. Praying her rosary, eyes closed, feeling her way along the familiar trail by touch of feet and by memory, she was distracted by a holy mystery and wandered off into the flanking bush. Hearing a thrashing sound and a faint bleating, she opened her eyes and saw a fawn caught in a trap someone had left cocked near a deer trail. The little body was nearly dead, its leg too ragged for any hope of nursing back to health. She would have liked to pump the speckled glory full of powdered store milk and splint the leg, but it was too far gone from loss of blood, its eyes bulging brown under the delicate lashes, kicking weakly against the iron jaws.

Kneeling, she held its head up and away from her, the long slender neck heart-sickeningly beautiful. She covered its eyes with her left hand. She opened her jackknife and cut quickly through a vein in the sandy neck, spilling the last of its life into the pine needles. And wept the dull groaning tears of the very old.

The pain of it cut into Oldmary deeply. It was the pain you felt as you watched some young captive walk, innocent and mute, to its sacrificing. Like the Lamb of God packing his Cross with a worldful of sins on his shoulders, walking with full knowledge toward his last mountain. But this was different. These little ones could not see, had not lived more than a breath, like her three dead babies. No, they had not chosen. Where was the meaning in that? Where was the reason for all the numberless victims, unable to understand their pain, crying out in a million unknown reaches of the earth?

By the end of that summer, Rose's spine had become obvious to everyone. White people disapproved. Fr. Andrei begged money.

Grandma said Rose *had* to go for her own good, to see if that bone could be straightened out, and to learn to read and write better.

"I can read and write, Grandma", she argued.

"Only a little bit. You need more."

"I do not want more."

"Do you want to carry that back around all your life?" Grandma said cruelly.

Rose cried. Grandma cried. And one day in September they stood on the dock by the trading post, hands dangling, saying nothing, waiting, like the mossless sides of tree trunks. They cried without sounds because people were watching. The watching people felt lumps in their throats. The flag rolled and snapped above the trading post. The sky was heavy lead. No one said much of anything but they all turned more or less toward the plane that skidded in on the water. When it arrived and became silent, and the usual things were accomplished, the pilot pitched a mail sack and Rose's cardboard box of belongings into the plane and climbed back into the cockpit.

Fr. Andrei made the sign of the cross over Rose. Tchibi stood at the edge of the crowd staring at her, his eyes blazing bile-green as if he were about to go wild, though his face had become as stone. Grandma pulled Rose to her, held her head firmly in her hands and mumbled over her in Ojibwe. Rose heard the word for God and then her name. Then Grandma, who was strong, made Rose go up through the door of the plane, which was no longer a Norseman but a new mustard-yellow Beaver.

When the door slammed shut, Rose pressed her face to the glass and burst into tears, but no one heard because the engine was screaming, and the plane rotated its nose toward the lake and began to shudder as its floats gathered speed, slapped the waves, and lifted from the water.

Then Rose saw for the first time the whole shape of the

world as white birds see it in their turquoise eyes. And for the first time she knew what Euphrasia Gorrel had felt on the day she went up into the sky and disappeared forever. Wiping away tears, she glanced from heaven to earth, from earth to heaven, seeking the forms of things unknown, her eyes straining to turn them to familiar shapes. And though her heart was in a frenzy, she knew that within her there was the memory of her place and of her name.

Her name in fact was written on a card pinned to her jacket, and on another card tied by string to her box, which contained the washed clothes, the Scottish tin of sacred memories, and the deer-hide sack with bits of color-sticks that were now no more than nuggets. A long time later, the plane circled over a larger lake and a town which had roads, the smoking stacks of a mill, a mine, and a railroad. A nurse met Rose at the dock and took her in a truck to a train station.

As Rose stood waiting on a gravel siding for the train to arrive, she experienced one of the lowest moments of her life. The nurse stood beside her, and though she was not an unkind person, she did not know how to draw brokenhearted, taciturn children out of themselves. The ferrying of natives in various states of difficulty was a regular part of her duties, and in her experience she had learned not to count overmuch on conversation. The train was due in about half an hour, and the minutes crawled by with excruciating slowness.

Rose was distracted by a big automobile that rumbled to a halt near the siding, about twenty feet away from where she stood. A family tumbled out of it, a man and woman, and several children, followed by an elderly lady who was—Rose's heart skipped a beat—Granny Crombie.

Could it be? Was it really her? Yes, yes it was! They were the same people who had visited Marleena in the hospital many years ago.

Then Rose saw Marleena herself, a tall girl jiggling up and down in shiny black pump shoes, wearing a flowered dress, white stockings with lacy cuffs just below the red knees, red with the cold and with the excitement of meeting someone who was arriving on the train.

Io, what joy flooded Rose's heart! What happiness to see an old friend. How lovely and graceful Marleena still was after all these years. She wore a flawless coat of pale blue cloth, with a black fur collar, red fingergloves on her hands, and a fluffy white angora cap on the top of her ringlets. The ringlets had grown during the years of their separation, falling down in sheafs of gold to the base of her straight spine. Yes, her red cheeks and clear complexion were the same, the sky-blue eyes and long lashes, the perfectly rounded forehead and pencil-thin brows, the tiny dimpled chin; yes, they were all the same.

"But what if it doesn't come?" cried Marleena to her father. "What if they forgot to send it?"

"Don't worry, sweetheart, it'll be on the train. And if it isn't, I'm gonna raise hell with those—"

"James," said the younger Mrs. Crombie, "watch your language, please."

"And it *has* to be a CCM," Marleena cried in a mock wail, to show that she was only joking. Everyone smiled at her. "And it *has* to be fire engine red, just like it shows in the catalogue."

Io, she was as beautiful as a doll in the Eaton's catalogue, the one you could flip through at the trader's post whenever he was in a good mood, Oh, the beautiful, beautiful dolls, hopelessly expensive and inaccessible, though you could admire from a distance.

But why should there be a distance? Rose now asked herself. Did she not know all about Marleena's life? Marleena had told her everything, without ceasing, for three whole days.

Rose looked up at the nurse, who was also enjoying watching the Crombies.

"I know those people", Rose whispered.

"Pardon me, dear?" the nurse said bending to hear.

"I know them, those people."

The nurse smiled, "Oh, I don't think so, dear."

"That is Mr. and Mrs. Crombie and Granny Crombie and Hilda and Emily and Tommy and Paul—and Marleena." *Marleena* was said in a tone of hushed reverence.

This evoked a curious look from the nurse, and from a few of the Crombies as well. Marleena continued to bounce up and down, unable to contain her excitement.

"With an air pump and a bell—you *said* I could have them, Pa!"

"Oh, it'll have them all right", grumbled Pa.

"And a generator for the front and back lights?"

"Well, I don't know about the generator. They cost a pretty penny—"

"But you promised, you promised!"

"James—"

Rose gathered all her courage and walked over to them. She went up to Marleena and smiled. Marleena looked down at the strange little Indian girl who was staring at her. She did not mind the staring, because people always stared at her, but the smell wasn't very nice, not very nice at all. She wrinkled her nose, frowned, and looked away, straining her eyes for a glimpse of the train which was just nosing around a corner far down the tracks.

"It's coming, it's coming!" Marleena cried, bouncing frantically, clapping her hands.

"Toot-toot!" said Tommy.

Granny Crombie looked at Rose with distaste, then at the nurse. The nurse led Rose away.

When the screeching train was before them, blocking off

everything, steaming and whistling, the nurse took Rose by the hand, helped her climb the steps into the passenger car, and led her to a seat. Rose pulled her feet up on the seat, put her head between her knees, wrapped her arms around them, and hid her face. The nurse patted her and smiled and said things that are supposed to make you not afraid.

"You'll be there in five hours", she said. "Try not to worry. Everything will be fine."

Then the train began to roar and shake and the forest became terrifying by flowing past—a moving forest—which was very strange. Then Rose's eyes adjusted, and she saw that she was moving and the forest remained still, as forests usually do.

After the airplane with Rose in its belly had shrunk to the size of a flea and the droning in the southern sky had faded to nothing, Fr. Andrei asked Oldmary if she would like him to walk back with her to the cabin. She said no. But thank you. Would you like a cup of tea, he asked. No, she said again, she would rather be by herself just now.

The old woman went down the trail alone. After she had gone a way into the privacy of the trees, she stopped and sobbed. Turning her face to the heavy clouds she felt the first cold drops of rain, knowing that the sweater was not going to be enough shelter.

"Lord," she said, turning her face to the sky, "I know you have something to say to me."

Hard balls of rain landed in the trail. The zing-zings of pine siskins swept through the branches, and blanket clouds rolled overhead.

"And I know it's about Rose", she prodded the sky.

Often, in her later years, a wind in her heart had driven her out into the wilder places to listen, though these were not the same solitudes where Rose had gone. She never could tell when the wind-word would come to her, though she could sometimes guess why he wished to speak. Whenever she felt the patient calming, the stillness entering her soul, she knew he had a word for her, the knowing-speech that is without words. It took a while usually, but if she sat on a rock looking to a horizon line or into a quiet stream, the worry slipped away like silt falling to the bottom of water, leaving her clear and tender with existence. Then the great one, Manito, would speak deeper than thought-words, and it would be what he wanted her to see, and she would see it, taking something home in her heart that she had not gone out there with.

This gray morning she was in turmoil and felt incapable of sloughing off her worries. The rain began to strike on her back. It stung her scalp. She veered off the trail and hid beneath a spruce. She crouched and sat down on dry needles, brown-spirited like them, in the unquiet light.

"Something in me is unsettled by her going, Lord", she murmured.

She laid her head against the scratch of the trunk, her silver braids hanging down her chest, and tears streaming too, like a more merciful rain.

"*Ay! Nind agoski!* I am afraid!"

The wind's great moan tore the little moans from the woman's mouth, as if God were saying that his grief was larger than hers. Oldmary uttered a half-laugh, though humbly because you should not laugh at God, even when it is his joke.

"*Ni sessessakis!* I burn and weep. I am hurting. She is a rabbit like me. Who will understand her?"

And suddenly within her there flashed a memory of Rose in diapers, during the time after Youngmary went away to the city. After Youngmary had slapped her mother hard in the face and screamed that she was sick of being poor, sick of living with a stupid old woman, sick of the baby she never asked for.

Who is the father? Oldmary had asked. Youngmary would not tell and perhaps did not know. One of the boys from the bush, she said. One of the many. And laughed a hate-laugh as she departed, though Oldmary's prayers followed hard on her heels.

My daughter! O my daughter, where are you?

Words shrieked in the heart that day and cried in the heart every day since.

Leaving the bitter gift of this child no one ever expected, this little *ogini* who sat alone in a pool of dust, unheeding, unaware of her loss, singing baby songs to herself. Playing with mounds of pine mulch or mud or bits of garbage. Making pleasure gardens. Stories already taking shape within her, though she had no words. Or was it all seeing? Large eyes drinking everything, making no judgments on what she took in. Telling it to nobody. Not knowing her grandmother was watching silently, listening to her sing her wordless tunes. Then Oldmary coughed and spat, and baby Rose turned toward the sound and saw Grandma. And smiled her little smile, her eyes looking up tranquil and innocent, like a deep lake at nightfall. Then a fountain of love had rushed up from somewhere inside of Oldmary, yes, from even her old dry breasts, sweeping away all bitterness. At that moment, too, the seed of a story had stirred within her—Gissis and Mang and a silver *bineshi*.

"Little piece of my heart", she had whispered to the baby.

Now Rose too was gone. She had sent her away, and how could Rose ever understand why she had done it!

My granddaughter! O my daughter's daughter, where are you?

Oldmary crawled out into the rain and hobbled along the path. Her hands were cramping with chill. She hid them clenched under her arms. Tempted momentarily to doubt, to question, she stopped and turned her face to the sky.

"You say your eye is on the sparrow! Why have you taken my little bird, my *bineshi* from me? Will your eye be upon her in the far places, in the dark places where none know her, where she knows not a soul?"

But Manito did not answer.

"I am cold, I am cold! Do you not see? Do you not care?"

Ay, ay, the silence of God was a terrible thing!

"Are you there?" she cried. "Lamb of God?"

Then she saw something which instantly wiped the questions from her mind. She looked at it in disbelief until it was absorbed. Two small birds lay unmarked in the mud of the trail. Side by side, apparently dead or stunned. By what? Why were they here?

What did it mean? Was this natural death or an evil sign?

She stooped down and picked them up. Their small brown bodies were still warm, and they eased her aching hands. Then for a moment she was frightened. Did the great Lord have to take the lives of two little feathered things to warm her complaining old paws, to prove to her his care? Was that it?

"*Ay, ay! Nin agatchitawa!*" she wailed, "I am ashamed before him!"

6

Rose was frightened by her first sight of Fort William, which the Anishinâbe people called Thunder Bay. It was a city of immense size, containing countless houses and huge buildings, situated on the northwest banks of Otchipwe-Kitchigami, the Sea of the Ojibwe, which the white people call Superior. In its harbor large ships floated beside cement towers that stood by the shore. Other rail lines met here, some from the west, where it was said that bread-wheat grew from horizon to horizon. The wheat came in the trains, filled the towers, poured out of them again, filled the ships, and these in turn sailed to the east of the inland seas and came by many rivers, after long journeys, to the true sea. Beyond that, Rose's mind could not travel, though she knew the world was very large, and that peoples of many sorts dwelled in various places, even in a distant land called Berksher.

The school where she now lived was a two-story red brick building on a hill at the edge of the city, surrounded by trees. It was built like the letter H, its arms containing different kinds of children—junior girls and senior girls, junior boys and senior boys. The girls were separated from the boys by fences and corridors and doors and long, long hallways. The crossbar between the upright arms of the H was the place where all ate together and prayed together, for there was a church within the school, which the sisters called the *chapel*. Hundreds of people, small and large, dwelled together under one roof. It was an amazing thing, the most amazing Rose had ever seen.

In the center, behind the eating hall, was a kitchen so vast that it took twelve people to cook the food in it, some of whom were women in black dresses who wore veils on their heads. The kitchen was ruled by a powerful lady who wore her silver hair in a bun. She spoke no native tongues, and her English was very strange. The lady spoke rudely to the women in black dresses, but they did not complain. The little girls thought she was *Jâganâshikwedjig*, an Englishwoman, though the older girls tittered and said no, she is an Irishwoman, which is something different.

In this central section were also the offices of the priests and nuns. On the top floors were the schoolrooms, where the children took their classes according to their ages. The boys and girls did not share the same classrooms and met only when they ate, prayed, or gathered together in the auditorium for concerts. At all times they sat or stood or knelt in separate groups according to their *dorms*, as they were called.

Whenever Rose saw the boys across wide aisles, she marveled at the rich variety of native faces, some pure Indian of different tribes, and some a mixture of races, including white blood, for among them were boys not unlike Tchibi.

She missed him greatly. And Grandma. And Fr. Andrei. She felt very lonely, and sometimes would cry herself to sleep after lights-out in the big room, where she slept with thirty other senior girls. She was fourteen years old now, and thus she was an older girl, though she was the youngest among them, and the shortest by far. Several junior girls were taller.

Some of the girls were kind and others were not, which was the same everywhere. This was also true of the sisters, though the nots were few in number, and among the kind there were women of unusual goodness. They were not as beautiful as Euphrasia, but a few of them spoke like her, though they were French.

One of the nuns was named Sister Superior, and Rose thought she must have been named for the lake or the lake for her. She had another name which was stranger still, Sister John they called her—a boy's name. The nuns called her Mère Jean de la Croix. It was confusing.

But Mère Jean, though she was a person of great power in the school, was also very kind. She taught the older girls sewing and catechism and a private and humbling subject called *personal hygiene*, which made Rose blush.

After Rose had lived in this place for several weeks, she stopped crying at night. The pain in her heart began to fade, and the pain in her back also declined a little. She was growing accustomed to the food, though there was no bannock, only white bread, and not as much fish as she was used to. There was meat now and then, which was a great luxury, for in the past she and Grandma had eaten it only whenever someone from the reserve thought to give them a little after hunting.

Most of all Rose was happy to be warm, always warm, and always clothed in the clean uniform. The hard leather shoes hurt her feet, though, and these never grew comfortable. Still, the showers of hot water and perfumed soap were like a miracle that never went away, and the minty toothpowder made her mouth tingle. The chapel was so overheated by the big clanking radiator pipes that she often fell asleep during night prayers.

Her reading skills, which had been poor until then, began to improve. She was not only the smallest of the big girls, but she also considered herself to be the most stupid. The sisters told her this was not so, for she learned quickly. Mère Jean gave her an extra class all by herself twice a week and was very patient. She also read to her from a book about the Canadian martyrs, some of whom were native people, though they were Huron. The Iroquois had slaughtered them, said Sister. In those days the Iroquois were fierce and warlike and wiped out other tribes. The Huron were more gentle, like the Cree and the Chippewa—the Ojibwe. Many of them were Christians. The Iroquois were pagans.

Io, there was so much to learn!

One night after catechism class, Mère Jean took Rose aside to speak to her alone. She had a long, thin face and many downward lines, though her blue eyes were intelligent and gentle, with a hint of joking in them. Rose had seen this combination in only a few people, including Fr. Andrei. A wisp of gray hair fell out by accident over Sister's forehead, from under the wimple and veil, which was a shocking thing, for the nuns were supposed to be bald. It was said by an older girl that it was a sin to see their hair if it grew back in, as it sometimes did on the skulls of the ones who were less holy.

"Rose, I have received a letter from your parish priest", said Mère Jean, bending at the waist to enable a meeting of eyes. "Fr. Andrei tells me wonderful things about you. He says you have faith. This I already know, for you are always the last girl to leave chapel after Mass and evening prayers. But he tells me also that you are a gifted artist."

Rose looked at the floor. She regretted that Fr. Andrei had told the sister this, for her pictures were too much like the falling-into-seeing that was not permitted; pictures were always sliding out of the right order into the taking-stealing kind of seeing. Worse, she had found that whenever she put the seeing onto paper, others realized their secrets had been revealed. She understood now why Euphrasia had cried when she saw the picture of herself sleeping on the skull, clutching the black pearl to her heart, the demon opening wide its pike-jaws to swallow her, and the shepherd on the other side calling to her, and the white bird hovering high above.

Rose understood that her gift could hurt others. And she knew its power to wound her own heart, for she had learned that in the making was suffering. Moreover, there was good making and bad making. There was good suffering and bad suffering, and who could tell the difference? Who could explain it? It was too confusing. It was better to leave it all behind.

"Would you like to join the girls who take the special art class on Saturday morning?" asked Mère Jean.

Rose shook her head.

"Are you sure? Sister Madeleine is in her own right a superb artist. You could learn much from her."

She shook her head again.

"*Tiens*, if you wish. But at any time you may join."

Sister Madeleine was a round sister, very, very round, and her cheeks were as round as the apples that were given out on Sundays after Mass. She was often laughing, often smiling, and she, too, fell asleep during evening prayers, which was extremely embarrassing for her because she was a nun, and it was a fault.

One Saturday morning, when a blizzard was howling outside, and it was too cold to play in the senior girls' yard, and Rose did not know what to do with herself, she climbed the stairs to the school floor and went down a long waxy hallway to the wooden door of the art room and knocked.

Sister Madeleine opened it, threw open her arms and embraced Rose to her ample bosom, crying many incomprehensible things in her native tongue.

"*Ah, mais c'est fantastique! La petite fleur du nord! Quelle surprise! Entrez, entrez! Maintenant nous avons une autre. Bon, bon, bon, entrez!*"

Sister Madeleine loved painting and loved the girls and loved her faith, and on Saturday mornings she loved combining all of these materials into one great work of art that stood in jolly retribution against the storms of life.

"We will have the good *fête* now, Rose Wâbos!" she cried, drawing her inside the room. "Come and see what the girls are making."

At the long worktable five native girls were mucking about in wet clay, making shapes, grinning, giggling, smearing themselves to the elbows. Sister took Rose to an empty chair and, pushing back the sleeves of Rose's tunic, fixed them above the elbows with black elastic bands. After that she raised her own arms to heaven, letting the cuffs of her habit fall back, squeezed them tight to her sides, and grabbed a lump of clay from a bucket. She threw it down on the table before Rose.

"*Tiens!* Make! Anything you want. *Ainsi soit-il! C'est le premier jour de la Création!*"

And giggled uproariously, which set all the girls giggling in unison.

"*C'est bon. Le Seigneur a dit, 'C'est bon'.*"

Rose put her hands on the mound of red clay. It felt wonderful. Like playing in mud, like spring, like the beginnings of things. Her hands took to the clay as they had once taken to bits and pieces of forest refuse and garbage when making her garden. Her hands wanted it badly, though she felt a moment of hesitation. Would this kind of making hurt her?

It did not, for the laughter that filled the room drove away any pain that sought to seep in through the secret entrances of her heart. Pain was also banned by the plate of cream biscuits, and the glasses of warm milk, and the bonbons that Sister popped into their mouths and into her own, regularly.

Rose's hands pressed the cold clay. At first she did not know what to make, for there was no thought in her mind, no picture to inform her hands. So the hands did as they wished and squeezed the lump into curves and hollows. Then she slipped down inside of herself, connected to the clay only by her eyes and fingers, and lost all awareness of the others in the room. The curves and hollows warmed under her touch, became a large red bird, then a face, then a head as it shaped and reshaped itself with a little assistance from Rose. It was alive when joined to her, as if it were flowing from her, or she were flowing from it.

When she surfaced for air, she stood back breathing shallowly, staring at what she had made, or what had made her. Slowly she became aware that the other girls had gathered around and were whispering to each other. Sister Madeleine was standing beside her, arms akimbo, shaking her head. Rose felt frightened, for it seemed that Sister did not like what she had made.

This was not so.

"*Formidable*," Sister whispered. "*Une portrait de l'âme. Excusez-moi,* Rose, pardon, I should speak in the English. I wish to say it is wonderful. It is the portrait of a soul. Is it *Notre Seigneur*?"

"Who is *Notre Seigneur*?" Rose asked.

"Our Savior, the Lord Jesus."

"It is a friend of mine", Rose said shyly.

"Ah, *un petit camarade, un ami. Quelle tristesse*, such a suffering face. Your friend has suffered, Rose?"

"Yes."

"You have shown us, you have shown us very well."

Sister patted Rose's shoulder with many small flutters of her chubby hand.

"*C'est incroyable, la compassion, l'empathie*", Sister muttered to herself. "*La technique est primitive mais la maturité. . . .*"

Shaking herself suddenly, she spun and reached for the plate of chocolate bonbons. Bursting into hot-cheeked cheer she cried, "*Une fête*, my girls, a feast! Now, now, be careful, don't grab, one at a time, one for each!" But there was no grabbing and reaching, because everyone's hands were covered in clay. Sister popped the candy into each open mouth as if she were feeding her baby birds.

Their mouths full of pleasure, oozing chocolatey syrup, the girls ran to the big stainless steel sinks at the end of the room and began to wash up.

Sister returned to Rose's sculpture and stared at it thoughtfully. Rose stared too.

"Wash your hands, *mon enfant*", she smiled at Rose. "Go now, and after we will turn to the colors."

The colors were liquid, almost as bright as color-sticks, and poured from glass bottles into tin cups, eight cups per girl, eight colors.

"You may paint with hands or with brushes, girls", Sister declared with an adventurous twinkle. "I shall lock the door, there shall be no critics to observe. *Tiens*, now *nous faisons la création primordiale!* Such fun we shall have."

And it was a delight to splatter with her hands, to smear and shape and reshape the paint that ran like water. It was more difficult than clay, which was obedient, though its color was dull. These fiery colors were wild and sloshed into each other if she did not keep the shiny paper flat on the table. Within a few minutes most of the girls were struggling unsuccessfully to keep their works from becoming a uniform brown. Rose understood the laws of ponds, creeks, streams and rivers, and lakes and seas, and though there were a few unexpected blendings and slops upon her own sheet, for the most part she made the waters flow where she wanted. It was the largest sheet of paper Rose had ever seen, and it begged to be filled. For the most part she used the pads of her fingertips, but scratching with fingernails was the best for making finer details.

It was a portrait of home, a clearing under a sky full of whirling stars and fireballs, a plunging moon-bird, and forests of purple trees, a miniature garden where two figures knelt. When it was completed Sister Madeleine praised Rose again. She did not forget to praise the other girls as well, and she praised God more formally just before the dinner bell rang.

As the girls filed out in the direction of the refectory, Sister held Rose back and said, "The picture is beautiful, *ma petite*. May I put it on the wall?"

Rose frowned.

"You do not wish?" Sister prompted.

Rose bit her lip, trying to decide.

"The two figures, are they you and your friend?"

Rose nodded.

"Your friend?" Sister asked, pointing at the clay portrait. "The same?"

Rose nodded again.

"Ah, *bon*", Sister mused, smiling into her eyes. Then, after a pause, "Will you come back to our little class?"

"Yes."

And so, without thinking, without hesitating, she decided that she would. And that night, her heart was full of the old joy, and she fell asleep without an ache in her heart or her body.

After the airplane fell from the heavens and landed on the gravel runway in a place with no name, Tchibi was taken to a train and put inside of it. It carried him deep through the rock and pine, snaked around countless small lakes and hills, curved so wide for some that when he pressed his cheek to the window, he could see the *ishkote-odâbân*, the fire-carriage several cars ahead. The powerful beams of its headlamps swept along the track in the twilight, and occasionally points of shining red and green lit up in the bush where they caught the eyes of a deer or fox. Tchibi could see a streak of rose color in the west where the sun had sunk beneath the edge of the cloud layer.

The clatter of wheels on the rough track had became part of him now. He no longer heard it consciously, the noise and endless vibration had merged into his general numbness. He was not allowing himself to be afraid, though at one point he could not stop himself from whimpering, "*Ay, ay! Matchi aiiwishiwan*, it is a wicked thing!"

What he meant by this he could not have explained, even to himself. It was, perhaps, a wicked thing to be taken alone from home, even though it was not a place of happiness. Or the train was wicked because it was too much like a *kinoje*, a pike, a jackfish, and he was in its belly.

His heart beat faster as he stared into the night ahead. Ogini would be there, he knew. She was the reason he had agreed to go to a special school for native children, a place where he would learn things that were not taught at the little cabin school of Threefinger Lake.

"You are fifteen, Binemin", the agent had said. "You have completed grade six—to the best of your ability. But in the new age that is coming, grade six will not be enough for you to make your way in life. There are no jobs in Threefinger. You have no family."

No family, no family, no family, because they had all died away or gone away after doing the things they did to him or because they were in jail someplace. And because the couple who had been paid to care for him no longer wished to do so, for they were now old and sick, and because he had once been crazy and might become so again.

Ogini was at that school. And so he said yes.

He regretted it now, because he was alone.

"Ogini", he reminded himself, "is waiting at the place where the train stops."

A woman seated across the aisle had been looking at him for the last little while. She saw his hair spiking out in all directions, his wild eyes searching through the window into the lowering darkness, hands squeezed together between his thighs. The poor moccasins, sockless, the stained pants ripped at the knee, the checkered bush jacket, equally tattered—these awakened some concern in her. She leaned across to him and offered a sandwich wrapped in wax paper. Tchibi was startled for a moment and wary of strangers. Though he had not eaten since dawn, he shook his head and looked back steadily through his face in the glass. In the distance he saw the red winking lights of a tower and the glow of a city spreading upon the sky. He thought that it must be the reflection of a terrible forest fire, and that it was a dangerous thing to ride toward it. But there was no way to escape from the belly of the *kinoje*.

There was a man, a middle-aged priest, standing beneath the spotlight of the depot.

"I am Fr. Morin, the rector of the school", he said, stretching out his arm to shake Tchibi's hand. "Though you have arrived later than the others, we are glad to have you." He glanced down at a sheet of paper in his hand. "We are glad to have you with us, Binemin Edzo."

As they drove in a car through the lighted streets of the city, Tchibi stared in wonder. A forest of buildings spread in every direction. He could scarcely believe that so many people lived together in one place. The priest turned to him and, with doubt in his eyes, said that he hoped Tchibi would not find it too difficult adapting to his new home. The boy looked back uncomprehendingly, thinking, "What does he mean, does he know about me, has he heard that I once was crazy?"

They soon came to a gate on a hillside at the edge of the city, drove through into a fenced compound, and parked before a large building that stood against a wall of trees. Light poured from countless windows. Tchibi felt a sudden contraction of his heart, a rush of blood to his face. There was too much light, and it was hard cold light, not like the single kerosene lantern in the cabin where he had lived.

The priest led him into the residence through the main entrance and then turned right onto a shining corridor, passing an immense dining room. After that, they went through two sets of doors and entered a separate wing of the building. Tchibi looked in every direction, searching for a glimpse of Ogini, but he saw no children, only a lady in a long black robe floating toward them, smiling at him as she passed. She was a frightening creature, because only her face was human. The rest of her was shaped like a black spruce, and she had no feet, but moved by a power he did not understand.

"What is that?" he asked the priest.

"That", said the priest, "is a nun."

As they passed through another set of double doors, Tchibi noticed at the end of a hallway a large room filled with row after row of beds, uniformly neat, bare of any clutter or decoration. As they moved toward it, they passed a room filled with desks. Tchibi saw within it rows of native boys who looked up from their books to peer curiously and silently at him.

"The boys' study hall", the priest explained.

In the wall between the study hall and the room of beds there was a closed door. The priest stopped before it and knocked. As they waited for an answer, Tchibi listened. It was very quiet throughout the whole wing. When the door opened, a man in his early thirties came out, stared at the priest with a neutral expression, then looked intensely at Tchibi.

"Here is your new charge", the priest said. "His name is Binemin Edzo. I'll leave him with you." He patted the boy on the shoulder. "This is Mr. McKenna, your supervisor."

When the priest departed, the supervisor appraised Tchibi up and down.

"Come in", he ordered and drew him into a private bedroom. When the door was shut they stood for a moment looking at each other.

What a strange name, Tchibi thought to himself, to be called *mikana—agassademo mikana*, the difficult road.

The man was neither young nor old. Though he was taller than Tchibi, his body was soft and his fingers were as round as venison sausage. There was a puffiness about his cheeks, and his lips were almost pretty and very pink. His eyes were palest blue, bracketed by blond brows and lashes. His hair was a shade of white gold with bronze glints, now lit up by the light behind him, like the aureole of the statues of the saints in the church at Threefinger Lake.

The room was small and nearly bare, though there were several pocket books stacked beside the bed, and a framed photograph of a woman's face above a desk. Through a window on one wall Tchibi saw the long room full of many beds. Another window overlooked the tables of boys bent over their homework.

"This is study hour", the man said. "You'll meet them later."

He closed the curtains, a smile flickering on his lips.

"Time for health inspection", he said casually in a low voice. "Take your clothes off."

Instinctively, Tchibi's hands flew to the strings that bound the buttonholes of his shirt and gripped them firmly. The terror leaping in the boy's eyes gave the supervisor a moment's pause. As did the chest, which began to ventilate rapidly. Shoulders arched high, Tchibi took a step back.

"All right", the man murmured nervously. "Later, then."

He threw open the door and led Tchibi into the dormitory. There he showed him the bed that was to be his. Folded on the pillow was a towel, a washcloth, and clothing, the uniform which all the boys wore: dark blue trousers, gray shirt, white underclothes and socks. Beside the bed was a tall metal box on which a pair of shiny black leather shoes stood at attention. The box, said the Mikana, was a locker, a place in which he could store his belongings. Tchibi had nothing of his own except for a pair of tattered wool socks that he had wrapped in a scrap of deer hide, a small round white stone, and the sheathed hunting knife that hung from his cord belt.

"I'll take that," said the Mikana-Supervisor, holding out his hand, index finger pointing to Tchibi's right thigh.

His meaning was difficult to grasp.

"The knife. Give me the knife. Students aren't allowed to have weapons. It'll be returned to you when you leave."

Reluctantly, Tchibi undid the cord, slipped the knife from it, and handed it to the man.

The Mikana looked him up and down and wrinkled his nose.

"Bring your towel and come to the showers."

Tchibi did as he was told and followed him into a huge washroom full of sinks and mirrors. The light was too bright and hurt his eyes. Through an open doorway he saw another tiled room, where dozens of shower heads were blasting jets of hot water.

"Well, Jesse James, let's see what you're made of", the Mikana said with a small crooked smile as he leaned against the ceramic wall.

Tchibi did not understand.

"Come on, you can't delay it forever", he said in a harder voice.

The boy stared at him blankly.

"Take your clothes off", the man barked, his fingers curling into fists.

Tchibi's thoughts flashed through the possibilities. What would happen if he refused to obey? His knife had been taken so he could not defend himself with it. He was alone in an alien land with strange and powerful people. Would the Mikana call the police? Would they come and bind him, strip him, cast him forever into a hospital?

With sickness in his heart, keeping his eyes to the floor, he removed his clothing with trembling hands. When he was completely naked, his bare feet stinging on the cold tiles, he began to shake violently, his teeth to chatter. Only once before had this happened, when *they*—the ones who—the burning ones who had—Yes, and afterward when he was crazy, the village men found him and took him by canoe, bound in ropes, to Threefinger Lake and from there to the hospital where the doctors and the police had looked closely at what *they* had done to him. He was naked and bound then also, and for this reason nakedness was always a horror, it was to be a thing, no, worse than a thing—a nothing—in the eyes of strangers, in an echoing shining room, with all his familiar landmarks gone.

Now he saw in an instant of loneliness too deep for utterance

174

the lamplit kitchen of Fr. Andrei's cabin, the cookstove roaring under a kettle, wild strawberry jam on white bread, the altar of the church at Threefinger Lake, the red vigil lamp, and finally Rose's face in his heart. When he saw her there, he knew that he could endure the nakedness a little, if it did not last long.

The man waited and watched, his eyes flickering all over Tchibi's body as the boy cringed to hide what was unhideable, the marks, the many marks, and the secrets, the many secrets. Suddenly, he stepped back with a look of disgust.

"Filthy", he grumbled. "You stink."

And because stink was better than wounds—all men stink— Tchibi was relieved, for the man did not seem to notice the other things, the things that made him a no-thing. Then the pale blue eyes inspected him more closely, and a gasp came from the rounded lips with the curls at the edges.

"God, what are those?"

Tchibi froze and said nothing, for to speak of it was to open his mouth to the terror that was always trying to get back inside.

"Can't you say anything? Speak up, what are those things all over you? How gross! How utterly repulsive! Did you have smallpox or something? I heard Indians are more likely to get it. But how come the scars are so—? Well, anyway, get inside."

Get inside?

"The shower, stupid."

The man pointed to the shower room and Tchibi entered shivering into the warm steam. The Mikana stood at the door watching. Tchibi turned away, not knowing what to do next. His flesh crept up and down his back. He was sure that if he looked toward the dark shape at the door, the pale eyes would be upon him.

Other boys began to trickle into the shower room saying, "'Scuze me, sir", as they passed under the supervisor's gaze. Some looked at Tchibi out of the corner of their eyes, but no one spoke, not even to each other.

After soaping and scrubbing, the boys lined up in wet formations by the door and were marched one by one through a blast of icy water from the last shower head. In silence they grabbed their towels, dried themselves off, and made their way to the dormitory.

Later, they lay in their beds. The lights had been turned out. The Mikana had gone back to his room, leaving only the dim red glow of the exit lights in the hallway. They saw his bedroom window go dark, then slowly an inch or two of curtain parted.

"He's watching", someone whispered in the next bed.

"What's your name?" another whispered loudly in English from across the aisle. A chorus of murmurs rose and fell in the room, which to the eye, especially one man's eye, might be no more alive than a field of humps.

"What's your name?" the voice came again.

"I am Binemin Edzo."

"Anishinâbe?" the voice asked in the Ojibwe tongue.

"Mostly," he replied.

"Métis?"

"A little."

Which caused an outbreak of muffled laughter.

The beating of his heart slowed then for the first time since he had left the train. Later, when the sighs and snores of the others filled the room, he lay awake looking up at the black ceiling, thinking about Rose. He hoped he would be able to see her tomorrow. "Ogini", he whispered and fell into a troubled sleep.

All the world had changed, the very nature of life itself. This Tchibi knew in every waking moment, filled with a glut of rules and boundaries which the Mikana said were good for you and were called *discipline*. Within the first days Tchibi's fear declined, and he began to adapt. Yet at every turn he discovered how much he did not belong.

There seemed no room for gaping and dreaming here. He could not wander around as he liked. He could not go out into the forest that was so close he could almost touch it. There were high fences and locked gates. Whenever he expressed his wildness, impulsively breaking into a run in the hallway, for example, the Mikana shouted at him and slapped the back of his head. Each day brought new forbidden things that he had not suspected were wrong. It was an offense to climb the chain link fences, to ask for food between meals, to talk in the study hall and the shower room, or to whisper from bed to bed in the dormitory. It was a special offense to look across the wide spaces of the dining room or the chapel to the block of senior girls.

Once, when he grinned at Rose as they passed in the main hallway, sharp knuckles rapped the back of his head. His heart nearly tore from his chest as it sought to follow her, though his body obediently marched straight ahead. Another day, he saw her walking to classes and called to her, earning himself a slap. Not long after, she managed to slip a little note to him in the corridor outside the chapel, after night prayers. This, fortunately, was unseen. There was no time to talk because the girls were being swept away by the nuns.

Nishime, my brother,
   Do not be afraid. I love you.
   Ogini

Lest anyone discover it, he ran to the toilets and locked himself into a cubicle. He read and reread the note a dozen times in the space of a few minutes. Then he ate it.

After that he began to sleep more regularly.

There was much talk of girls among the older boys. They hinted at the presence of something called *saltpeter* in the beans that took your desire away. They poison us, said one boy. This is a prison, said another. This is a torture place, said a third. It seemed to Tchibi that the school combined all of this, for he remembered well another institution where both torture and locked doors had kept him inside his personal horror. Here, too, it was a forbidden act to leave the building, though you could be "expelled" if you escaped.

This was confusing.

"Don't any of you try sneaking off to town", said Mikana with a cold sneer, "If you do, you little rebels, out you go! Back to whatever filthy shacks you crawled here from." Tchibi longed to be so wild they would have to expel him, but remembered that he no longer had a home.

The boys walked to and from their meals, to chapel, and to classes in neat lines. The supervisor was always behind them, and sometimes, like a frenzied dog, he raced up and down the line in a fit of snapping, slapping, and pushing. Order, straightness! It was usually the smallest or the most timid who drew his violence. Yet it was not so much the actual blows but the threat of them which were his power. Humiliation was his weapon of choice, used with fine skill on those creatures most vulnerable, of all living things, to the approval of their peers. They failed to notice, however, that these eruptions were never witnessed by other adults. It was always a private matter, and perhaps they were grateful for this.

Each night the Mikana observed the private entertainment of the showers, his lips glowing with pleasure, his eyes hot-cold. It was his practice to make of nakedness an art form. As the boys exited the blast of icy water, he would sometimes grab one or another by the shoulders and push him against the wall of the washroom. Then another and another, until he had created a gradation of colors ranging from darkest brown to tan.

"Love", he declared in such situations, "knows no boundaries." He threw his head back and from his throat there came a guttural laugh that contained no joy. "Or is it lust?" he smirked, scattering them all to bed with a wave of his hand, half caress, half blow.

But the material of his art was not entirely docile. One night Tchibi was startled by a growl in the air above his bed. Looking up he saw the shadow of an apelike creature hanging there. The building's main water pipe ran the length of the hostel suspended a few inches from the ceilings, and along this someone was now swinging hand over hand.

"Tarzan! Tarzan!" cried the voices in the surrounding beds.

Their laughter was not quite loud enough to rouse the supervisor from his room, but when a metallic clank and a great roar exploded in the dormitory, the Mikana came in a rage. The pipe had broken, sending tons of water crashing across the room in a torrent which knocked one boy from his bed and left another, the culprit, sprawling dazed on his back in a spreading pool of water. The whole place was in an uproar, lights flashing, alarm bell ringing, staff crowding into the room. Fr. Morin arrived, shocked and full of timid questions. Soaked boys stood around the walls holding the cuffs of their pajamas above the rising flood.

Someone finally thought to open the emergency exit door, and the water poured outside. Throughout the night the boys mopped up as the Mikana conducted his investigation. By dawn they were all more or less in order again and deliriously happy.

But the guilty party had been found out. His name was Archie Kakeg, a tall boy with bristling black hair and enormous white teeth in a face that was pure Cree. He was only superficially intimidated by Mikana's temper. The supervisor sensed this and was afraid of him. He did not dare to punish him with the ultimate violence, the strap he constantly threatened them with and sometimes used, for a more anarchic violence simmered behind Archie's eyes. It might explode in the man's face, tearing open the fear that lurked behind his own mask. So he ordered them all to the study hall and made them kneel down by their chairs.

"Kakeg, come here", he said in a deceptively quiet voice. Archie came slowly and knelt where he had been told, by the man's feet, facing the other boys. He obeyed, they knew, because he was very smart, because he was in the ninth grade and wished to go all the way through high school and get a job and become rich. To do so, he often said, you must play the white-man's game.

"When you came here, Kakeg, you stank", sneered the Supervisor. "Your clothes were dirty black till the sisters washed them for you." He spat these words, accompanied by a racial and sexual slur. Archie looked steadily at the floor, his lips a thin line.

"And it's only because you're an ignorant savage that I'm going to let you go." He pointed him out the door. Archie left the room with a measured walk, his shoulders thrown back, but not in a way that expressed open defiance. Then the supervisor, his face straining red, took a wide belt from his back pocket.

"Hands out!" he roared.

Every boy extended his arms, the palms of their hands held upward. The Mikana went from one to the next, giving to each a single ferocious down-lash. Younger boys whimpered, older boys turned to stone, betraying no emotion. Tchibi, among the youngest, saw flames leap where the leather struck his flesh. He opened his mouth to scream, then closed it, pushing the bile-fire deep inside.

"You can thank Archie Kakeg for that!" said the Mikana when he was finished with them.

But Archie was too big and dangerous to hate.

The question of why this should be endured was unasked, unanswered, as they mutely adapted to the man's system of control. If they ever pondered the possibility of complaint, they would feel certain that one white adult's word carried greater weight than a rebel's. Or else it was fear. Afraid, as were most people, to be the first to move against violence, armed with little save the truth—a truth which no one would believe from an Indian.

Tchibi learned that the supervisor's name was not Mikana, but McKenna, though in private the other boys never called him that. They called him *omakaki* the frog. Sometimes the poison frog, sometimes the little frog or the fat frog or the frog that ate boys like flies.

They had names for Tchibi also, but these were not excessively cruel. They called him Pockmark or Green-eyes or Fire-hair. They had worse things to say about others, but no one took great offense at this custom. It was not uncommon for those who were treated badly to invent smaller cruelties to inflict upon each other, as a reminder that they were still above the level of nothingness.

After the first showers no one asked Tchibi about the scars on his body, for he would not answer them. And other boys had scars from smallpox and knives and axes and fires, because to live in the bush is dangerous. To live is to receive wounds.

The mild-mannered Fr. Morin had not reflected on the question of why thirty teenage boys, Indian and Métis, should appear each day at the chapel and refectory in such sober formation. Their docility appealed to his sense of order. It spoke well of his administration. This was a relief to the priest in his first term as rector. Years in the south as a bursar for his Order had given him a need for efficient organization.

There had been times when, called upon by duty, he had assisted with the major work of his colleagues, the education of high school students in the larger cities to the south. This had involved a few hours of teaching a week, and though it was his desire to impart his love of algebra and trigonometry, these hours had been most painful. His delight in the beauty of numbers, of their marvelous and intricate dependability, did not infect his students. Sensing his timidity, they had raised sheer hell in his classroom. With the passing of weeks incessant whispering had grown to uninhibited conversation, and desk-lid slamming had reached earthquake proportions. Anonymous puns and animal noises rang out continually, bringing down gales of laughter. He felt beaten before he had begun. His name was Basil and they would mock his name, drawing out the vowels like a bleating sheep—*Baaaazzzil!* Or answer his questions in the language of cartoon characters they had learned at the cinemas.

Too ashamed to report the growing disorder, abandoning his hope of improving their young minds, he had continued to teach the handful of faithful students who gathered about him in the front rows. He did not make any attempt at discipline, which he felt sure would produce only more humiliation for himself. By midwinter, his superior had called him into the office and with great tact had taken these burdens of duty from his shoulders. The priest's relief had been visible. Those in authority, sensing that his gifts were for finance and administration, had sent him north to their mission school at Fort William. The rector there had just died after a year of illness, leaving the records in a shambles, and they saw in the appointment of Fr. Morin an opportunity to help both him and themselves. Thus, with trepidation, he had undertaken the stewardship of some two hundred children combed out of the bush.

The responsibility was staggering, only here was the blessed miracle that the institution seemed to run by itself. This was largely due to the congregation of nuns who laundered, cooked, and mothered for them all. They also supervised the two girls' dormitories. A religious brother cared for the junior boys. The lone layman on staff was the taciturn Mr. McKenna, who supervised the senior boys. The man was uncommunicative, perhaps, but had managed nevertheless to maintain a valuable peace. And so the priest felt that authority had been safely delegated; he could devote his first year to righting the disorder in the financial records.

Mr. McKenna was pleased by the temperament of the new rector, whose personality he assessed with accuracy. His own experience of rectors, and indeed of any kind of authority, was an inward struggle of smoldering resentment. Always he had hoped and dreaded that they would be something for him beyond the function of executive. Why this had not happened over many years he could not say. Was there something in his manner that unconsciously repelled them? Was it his appearance? Were they jealous? Could they read his most secret thoughts as easily as he read theirs?

Healing never came, nothing but the inevitable power struggles. Thus his disbelief before any friendliness from men in authority had become a relentless theme within him. They never saw it. He was polite and obedient, his excesses mostly hidden from each successive rector. There might be complaints now and then from a barely literate parent or a hotheaded youth, but there was always a bad element in any group. And of course there was that ever-present order which seemed to promulgate its own defense. Each of the rectors had halted before it.

The new rector was the least meddlesome of all. In the beginning, when the supervisor had resisted him on a significant matter, the older man had backed down.

"Mr. McKenna", he had said. "Once a week I would like to spend an evening with your boys. Perhaps a little discussion group. Some catechism. It's my way of getting to know them, and, of course, you."

The response, a rigid silence, had embarrassed Fr. Morin.

"My boys have a very full schedule as it is, Father", said the supervisor, struggling over the last word.

"Yes, well . . . of course . . . perhaps on a Sunday evening, then?" Fr. Morin had smiled nervously at the younger man. McKenna frowned unhappily.

His voice rising dangerously, he said, "If you are calling into question my competence as supervisor—"

"No, no, of course not!" the priest hastened to reassure him. "In fact, considering your thoughts on the matter, and given the large task before us all, I am most happy to leave the supervising to those who know it best." And smiled his most sheeplike smile. McKenna had nodded woodenly and left. In the windowless hallway where he paused for a moment or two, the knowledge came to him that his own authority in this wing of the house had increased. To his delight and terror, his power had become almost total.

As the months passed and the snows arrived, an uneasiness worked within Fr. Morin. He felt vaguely guilty that he had not been more insistent with the supervisor, felt confirmed more than ever in his conception of himself as inept in human relations. But after all, he thought, the man was doing a good job, and those boys were the best behaved group in the residence. There was none of the rowdiness that usually erupted from male adolescents. Such thoughts moved restlessly on the edge of his mind. Not until many months later did he begin to ponder seriously their inscrutable native faces, and only then did his uneasiness grow into suspicion.

By mid-December, Tchibi had not once been outside the school's compound. Since his arrival, all his needs had been met within it. From the high windows he could gaze over the fence tops at an anonymous sky and the line of bush that stretched away into the north, but it was a view through glass, and the land was alien. The boys were regularly driven outdoors for a ration of fresh cold air, to shovel snow or to wobble around the school rink. But life was lived mostly indoors, and for only fleeting moments could he run in the wind and feel the satisfying crunch of snow under the feet. Io! To be again in the freedom of the bush!

The school was too much like the hospital where he had been locked inside with his craziness. Hard light hurt his eyes, hard shoes hurt his feet, hardest of all were the hard rules that hurt his heart because he could almost never see Ogini, and then only for a few stolen seconds. She too was a captive, though he could tell from the look of her eyes that she was happy here. Why was she happy in this place of hardness? How had she remained the Ogini he had known? How had she remained kind and gentle among all these rules and slaps, all this clank of radiators and the rhythmic sluicing of water in the very strange and bright bathrooms? No longer the rush of cascading creeks, no longer the moon pouring through window frost under the cabin eaves, no longer the garden by Crazyman River, but instead the polished hallways and alarm bells and the red planets of night over fire doors saying *Exit*.

Exit, an older boy told him, meant *Go home*. If only it were true, Tchibi thought. Then he would strip off these cold clean clothes and jump into his old rough wool pants smelling of smoke. Then he would leave, disappear into the night and the bush. North he would go, where all of winged creation moved each spring. But it was not spring, he sighed, and he had no money for a train ticket nor courage to ride on the back of Kinoje, freezing in the winter wind.

Christmas was full of singing in the chapel and a dish of ice cream after supper. Each boy was given a box containing new socks and underwear and a chocolate bar. From Rose, Tchibi received a roll of paper bound with a red ribbon, which she gave to him in the hallway as lines of girls passed lines of boys going in opposite directions. When he unrolled it in the privacy of a bathroom cubicle, he saw that it was a painting of the cabin at Crazyman River, himself and Ogini working on their garden under the stars. He rolled it up carefully and hid it in the bottom of his locker.

Mr. McKenna had gone to confession on the twentieth of December and did not attend the nightly showers from that day until the New Year. No one could explain this. When he returned to his post by the shower-room door on January third, life resumed as usual.

A month went by, then another. Tchibi grew accustomed to his new home. He learned that some boys were quiet, some noisy, some were smart, some slow of wit, some full of passionate feelings, some as calm as a pond. Some were even brave. Archie Kakeg's arrogance, walking the fine line between pride and insolence, was his way of defending his dignity. Tchibi's admiration for him, extravagant and unexpressed, was fueled by the older boy's growing habit of pushing at the boundaries. He made faces behind Mikana's back. He ogled girls whenever he could. He broke a window. He left taps running.

It was impossible to become Archie's friend; it was too dangerous. Moreover, friendship of any kind was discouraged, as everyone knew, because Mikana would quickly separate boys who had taken to sitting together regularly at meals, chatting quietly about fishing or hunting or someone they both knew back home. He had a piercing discernment for the buds of affection; sensing danger in it, he made abortions of it with clinical efficiency, for friendships enjoyed by others would have revealed too clearly the barren state of his own life. What self-explanations he made for these acts was impossible to know. Perhaps he did not stop to consider it, but only slaved thoughtlessly to the impulses of his hurt.

It seemed to Tchibi that Mikana had a soul. He came with the boys to the chapel each day, herding them down the main hall like a predator compelling migrating caribou single file into a narrow ravine. And there he knelt and stood at the proper

186

moments and sang songs from the hymnal along with the others on the staff.

Once a month they went to confession. The chaplain was a frail old man who suffered from poor hearing—a most embarrassing situation. The boys were made to sit on the far side of the room in order to distance them from the loud whispering in the confessional. It was a moment of strain for every soul.

Once Tchibi watched as the supervisor slipped into the box, the red light winking on. He marveled as the supervisor reemerged, his hair smoking in the golden glass light, his face as pure and still as a holy card, his hands clasped in front like a child's.

One of the boys—a very simple boy—said of the Mikana, "He looks so holy."

Some of the older boys snorted. But Tchibi could not help staring at the lowered eyes with their curling blonde lashes and the utterly gentle look on the man's face.

Mister McKenna does not want to hit us, he thought. *Perhaps it is we who are to blame.*

The older boys sniggered more loudly and whispered to each other, "See *omakaki* praying. How pure he is! Be careful, flies, soon he will be hungry again."

That night, the supervisor lined them all up in the study hall and gave a near hysterical lecture on sin, yelling at one point, "Hell is burning full of people whose sins of the flesh are putrefaction; their stench goes up to heaven and pollutes the world. Forever they will burn in the fire that never ceases, and the worm that does not die shall eat their flesh—" And so forth.

He went on and on, bellowing at their downturned faces, dismaying the experienced, terrifying the innocent. Some of them recalled similar sermons, though never had they been delivered with rage, and always they had concluded with a reminder of the Mercy of Manito. Not this sermon. It was holiness and terror, it was bile-fire, it was wild-fire without life-fire. When he was finished, the supervisor turned abruptly on his heel and left, leaving them rooted with no command to dismiss.

"*Omakaki* is croaking loud tonight", one of the older boys whispered to another. "Soon he will desire us."

"It will be you tonight."

"No, you."

A half-hour later the supervisor remembered them, came back, and told them to go to bed.

But nothing happened that night or the next.

One late afternoon they were lined up in the dorm waiting for Mikana to take them to supper. He was nowhere to be seen and they were getting restless. Archie, standing in front of Tchibi, turned with a glint in his eyes and said, "Hey, Pockmark, you want a biting contest?"

"What is that?" Tchibi replied.

Archie unbuttoned his shirt and exposed a bare shoulder muscle.

"Bite", he said.

"I do not want to bite."

"You bite me, and I bite you. The first one to quit is a coward."

The other boys crowded around.

"Who is the stronger," Archie challenged haughtily, "your people or my people?"

"Our people are the same," Tchibi said in a shaking voice. "Our speech is close."

"We are not the same. You are a little bit *Otchipwe*. And me—" He thumped his chest. "Me, I am what?"

"You are *Kinishtino*—Cree."

"Right! So let us see which is the greater."

"No."

188

"Come on, are you a coward? Maybe you are a coward because you are *giminidjagan,* a bastard."

"I am not *giminidjagan!*" Tchibi cried.

"Who is your mother?"

"I do not know. She went away."

"Who is your father?"

"I do not know, I do not know!"

"You see!" Archie sneered. "Look at you—you have *Anishi-nâbi* skin but green eyes and porcupine quills in your hair. You have dirty whiteman's blood in you."

At that, Tchibi reverted to the feral boy, snarling, baring his teeth, the hair on the back of his neck bristling. He unbuttoned his shirt and exposed his shoulder. He bit down hard on the cocoa-colored skin of his hero, who sunk his own teeth into Tchibi's muscle, biting harder and harder to the hilarity of the onlookers. The pain in Tchibi's shoulder became unbearable and he shrieked, letting the older boy go. But the other did not open his jaws until he heard the supervisor's door scrape open suddenly, and they all stampeded back into line.

Standing behind Tchibi was an older boy named Gordon Kitagakons. Gordon was one of the silent ones. His communication was limited to the few necessary words, to answering yes or no whenever he was asked a question by members of the staff. His name, which the official records translated into Youngdeer, was more accurately Spotted Fawn, though he was neither fragile, spotted, nor anyone's prey. The *omakaki* part of the supervisor had either missed seeing him altogether or was afraid of him. He was not in the least bit menacing, nor did he practice those tough postures meant to convince the world of something worth treating with respect. He was merely into himself, enduring the school until he could return to his father's trap lines. He was the kind of boy who had wrestled his father's dogs into their traces and sat on his haunches in the snow around a willow fire drinking tea and spruce needles

189

from a tin mug with a .22 strapped to his back. There wa
something in him that no man or boy touched. So he wa
consigned to the background, uninvolved, observing, obeying
any order that was not a direct assault on his pride.

As the line shuffled forward into the hallway leading to th
refectory, Tchibi turned to see Gordon looking at him withou
emotion, saying something with his eyes—not sympathy, bu
what? A light flashed from horizon to horizon and was gon
quicker than understanding.

Shortly after the biting incident, Tchibi was awakened by one o
the "underlings". These were six of the older boys, in their lat
teens. They were Mikana's deputies, overseeing the cleanin
duties, assigning younger boys to sweeping the floors or latrin
scrubbing. Deciding who would help pull the hot water barre
on its squeaking balloon tires across the rink ice, who woul
have first place at the ping-pong table and last in the meal line
There were little records of demerits and awards. It encourage
the admirable order. They were willing. But they were not
unlike most underlings in the service of a tyrant, overly imperious in their duties or vicious. They made attempts at fairness
knowing perhaps that their term of office would have its end n
matter how interminable it might seem. They were from different tribes and spoke different dialects, and their only commo
quality seemed to be that they were all handsome muscular fel-
lows. It was they who had given the name frog to their lord
Despite the disgust they felt for him, there were privileges tha
came with the job that made it a most attractive position in
very bleak house.

They met in Mikana's bedroom once a week after lights-
out. They drank hot chocolate and ate hardtack biscuits with
cheese and laughed at his jokes. Often they would lift weight
in there, barbells and dumbbells, coming afterward into th

dark whispering dormitory, sweating, bare-chested, swinging their pajama tops lazily from their hands.

"Dumbbells!" someone would always say, usually someone at the back of the room. Probably a Métis, for they knew far more English than the pure blooded. It was too late anyway to find out who had dared to mock the supervisor's favorite boys. They did not really care about their critics, for they were a superior class, not that they were ever insolent with the *omakaki* or were permitted to rise to the level of familiarity. But for one evening a week they were older and freer, playing the man's games, claiming with him, for a moment of illusion, to be men. In the mornings they would watch uncomfortably as he slapped some frightened smaller boy.

There were times when the frog was hungry and ate a fly, usually very late at night. These incidents were known only to the initiated, the six who were bound to him by guilt as well as by their desire for comfort.

One night, Tchibi lay in bed unable to sleep, watching the window of the supervisor's room where muffled laughter and the shadow forms of torsos were moving behind the curtains. A shape came unsteadily down the dark aisle to Tchibi's bed, stood topless in sweat, and leaned over him exhaling the smell of wine.

"Hey, wake up!"

Tchibi sat up in bed.

"Come with me, Edzo."

"Why should I come with you?"

"Because you have to."

"I do not have to."

"Come on, pretty boy, Mr. McKenna wants you."

"Why does he want me?"

"You don't ask why", the older boy slurred, his eyes shining in the dull red glow of the night light. "You just come."

"Why?"

"Because he said so. I knew you were crazy, green-eyes, but I didn't know you were stupid too."

"I do not want to come."

"Sure you want to come. You'll like it. Candy. Tobacco. Wine. Fun."

"Why me?"

"Because he thinks you're crazy, and he likes crazy boys. You're the craziest of them all. He wants to see your skin."

Tchibi froze. He lay down and turned his back to the underling.

"Get out of bed. Now! If you don't, you'll make him mad."

"It is night. Go away."

"This is your last chance, Pockmark."

"No", Tchibi said pulling the blanket tight across his shoulders, preparing to die.

Strangely, no storm of fury erupted from the supervisor's room. Nothing happened. Nothing at all. So Tchibi fell asleep. His refusal, an act of rejection which was no small matter, called down neither sudden wrath nor comment nor glance from the supervisor in the morning. But later that day when it became necessary for the man to give an order to Tchibi, he said loudly, in front of all, "Hey you! Yes, you, pretty boy, whiteman!" The last word he executed like a hammer smashing on glass and looked at Tchibi with contempt. The boy did not at first know whom he meant, but as all eyes were now turned to him he jumped and did whatever it was he had been ordered to do. Yet he was not this thing the man had said, he was not a pretty boy, nor a whiteman. He was Binemin, and the white in his blood was only an accident.

The supervisor pulled him out of the lineup the next day, twisting his collar and grinding it into his neck.

"You won't get any special privileges here, whiteman!" he growled and slammed him against the wall.

I am not a whiteman! I am not a whiteman! Tchibi screamed

silently, choking back tears. He would have reverted to the feral boy, if the shock of the accusation had not totally confused him. McKenna let him slide down the wall, and moved on, swaying his buttocks along the hall, his malice slaked.

Looking up, Tchibi saw Gordon Kitagons gazing at him, deep and expressionless.

In the night, Tchibi had a dream. In it he stood by a stone wall while warriors ran toward him with spears, arrows, and burning torches in their hands, intent on taking his life. His rage boiled up, and he knew that he would fight them. The knife clenched in his right hand would take down these *neshiwed*, these killers of men. At least one of them would die as they killed him, and he would maim the others. But during the long minute as they charged upon him, he felt someone standing by his side, and he knew without looking that this man was Jesus-Manito. He turned toward Tchibi, his hand firm on the wounded shoulder. His eyes said, *Do not hate them. I am with you.*

Tchibi saw his eyes and rough woolen garment by a seeing of the heart, though he could not actually turn toward the face. He could not imagine the exact details of the face, but felt that it would have some of Fr. Andrei in it, and some of Rose, and some of Gordon. He let the knife fall from his hand and gazed in stillness of spirit at his murderers as they fell upon him, and he was suddenly risen. *Alleluia! Alleluia!* shouted the chorus of *anjeni*, the holy *anjeni* who sing always in praise of the victory of the Lamb Who Was Slain, and he woke in the dark panting with exultation and terror.

His new name was used with greater frequency, even by some of the boys. Tchibi felt that they hated him, despising his green eyes and the brown hair shot with spikes of red. Perhaps they merely wished to taste, for a change, the sweet poison of power. He walked downhearted, week in, week out. The supervisor was cold and merciless, smiling throughout the little skirmishes in which Tchibi was always the loser.

During lunch hour in the refectory, it was the man's habit to call this or that boy to come to the senior boys' head table to pick up their mail. One day he called out, "Letter for you too, whiteman!"

Tchibi did not move. He continued to eat his meal staring at his plate. The man's voice rose sharply in pitch and he barked, "Whiteman, come here!"

Tchibi forced himself not to hear, his heart crashing suicidally, *that is not my name, that is not my name.* There was no face that was not suddenly bowed over the table, afraid for him, perhaps ashamed for the implications of their submission now being made public. Even the noisy happy blocks of the other children had become quieter. Senior girls watched with interest. Junior girls giggled. Junior boys craned their necks. Some of the sisters turned the black funnels of their veils toward the senior boys. Rose too was watching, her eyes red with helpless longing.

Whiteman! the pressure demanded.

That is not my name, that is not my name, the inner resistance demanded.

"That is not my name!" Tchibi said loudly in English. Then he repeated it in the Ojibwe tongue. There was a moment of total silence.

The man's voice replied like a falling axe, "When I call your name, whiteman, you will come to me!"

Tchibi shook with fear. His words were tiny flies, the power of the *omakaki* was too big for him. Head bowed, he got up and walked slowly to the supervisor's table. The Mikana said an ugly thing to him, words which meant *fatherlessness.* The man threw the letter across the table, his eyes snapping, golden lashes fluttering above the flaming skin.

Tchibi took the letter and returned to his own table. As the clatter of cutlery and children's voices resumed normal volume, he laid the letter beside his empty plate, staring at it. Then hot silent tears splashed onto the handwriting and ran down blue into the whiteness of the dish. He raised his eyes and looked at all the bowed heads, eating quietly, not wanting to see. Only Gordon Kitagons sitting across from him looked into his eyes, saying nothing until they both looked away.

After the meal the senior boys returned to the dormitory and Tchibi bolted for the toilets, locking himself into the cubicle. The letter was from Fr. Andrei.

Dear Binemin,

I pray for you every day. I am sure that many things are different in your new life. Many of them may be difficult for you. Have courage, my friend. Pray every day to Jesus Kijê–Manito. Resist the *matchi-manito*, the devil. Go to the sacraments. Do not be afraid. I send you this little medal of Kateri, the Lily of the Mohawks, who is a great saint. Pray to her. I will see you in the summer.

God protect you,

Fr. Andrei

He reread the letter several times, then ate it. He pocketed the medal. And from then on, he would not answer to the name of whiteman. This brought upon him many slaps. But he did not flinch or retaliate. Having learned much from the demeanor of Gordon Kitagakons, he bore it all, and eventually Mikana gave up. In time the name fell into disuse, and in the days which followed the final slap, the supervisor became polite in a stiff sort of way and said without looking at the boy, "Edzo, you are a crazy person. You do not exist."

But this had no power over him because it contained a contradiction, words that wiped each other out: You are and you are not. It signaled that he had overcome the supervisor.

7

Tchibi wanted to follow Fr. Andrei's instructions, but his pain absorbed much of his attention. Though the supervisor no longer hit or mocked him, he acted as if Tchibi was invisible. As his hatred for the man grew, the bile-fire that had dried up within him began to run again. The feeling came and went, but increased steadily in power. Silent rage gave way to thoughts of vengeance.

It was difficult to understand why Kijê-Manito did not act. Why did he permit a man who served the spirit of the *neshiwed* to have so much power? Why did the priests and the nuns not see the *matchi-manito* behind his mask?

There were times when Tchibi wondered if Jesus was really with him as the dream had promised. He thought that maybe Jesus was a kind of temporary shelter you lived in for a time, then you left it, just as you moved from foster home to foster home. He felt condemned to a prison, his only crime was in being himself, fatherless, motherless, a *giminidjagan*, an orphan bastard who was neither Indian nor white.

The passage of days became an eternity, the impatient counting of them a torment of repetition. And so he tried to abandon himself to forgetfulness and raw sensation. The flesh provided diversions and imagination even more. He pined for those hot summer days when he had ripped through the forest growling and leaping, and hurling himself into pools of minnows cupped in the three fingers of God. Or walked beside the river with Rose, making little gardens. This part of his past was lavish, yet the future always loomed ahead like a shapeless darkness oozing out to meet him.

The only thing he could cling to was the little medallion of the Indian saint, though she was, he thought, dead and powerless. The comforting memory of guttering red lights, bread and jam, the eyes of an old priest, and Rose's words had steadied him in the past. Now they were exchanged for the eyes of his new friend. But Gordon's friendship would not be seized and used like salve on burn holes. He must accept it exactly as it was given.

All others ignored him. Even Archie, who stared through him or walked past him as if he were not there. There were no more tormentings, merely an isolation relieved only by the rare glances from Gordon.

By March, Tchibi had learned to live as an almost-nothing. He attended Mass and prayers obediently, but no longer felt the warmth that had come to him from the tabernacle in the past, though even then it had been infrequent. No longer could he bring himself to do what Fr. Andrei had suggested and go to the sacraments. The supervisor took the sacraments, and they did not make him better.

In his thoughts he began to call the supervisor *omakaki* and nothing but *omakaki*. Drifting off to sleep each night, he imagined the ways he would kill him. It was almost always with his knife, though sometimes in the darkest and most sensual moments it was with slow tormenting fire, an orgy of a thousand burning holes. Whenever the memory of the dream surged stronger than the bile-fire, he dropped the knife and the burning sticks and the bloodied rocks for a time. Yet he always picked them up again.

Alone in the chapel Tchibi prayed. "Jesus-Manito, I do not understand. The *omakaki* is a strange man, and I too am strange. And in this place only Rose and Gordon are good. Why is goodness so difficult to find?"

If he, Tchibi, was not good—most of his experience had shown him this—then what was the purpose of struggling against the current of bile-fire? Why should he try to be good when he was without power to make himself good? Of course, it was a lie that he was a no-thing, but neither was he a good-thing. Could a person become a something by choosing the not-good? The *omakaki* seemed to have chosen this way, had he not? The *omakaki* did many things and said many things that were not good. He commanded obedience, yet he himself was disobedient to the blessing-way and no punishment fell upon him. Perhaps Jesus-Manito was only a picture in the mind, and if this was so, then disobedience did not matter.

Thus Tchibi began to consider another way of living, and these thoughts opened to him secret passageways of delicious disobedience. Once, while mopping the toilet cubicles he found an opening in the wall. A sliver of reflected light glinted through the metal grate that covered it. Looking through the bars, he saw a five-cent coin. His fingers could not reach it. When he tried rattling the grate, he found that it could be removed. He locked the door of the cubicle and pulled off the grate. Pocketing the nickel, he stuck his head inside the hole to see where it led. It was dark inside. He extended his arm as far as it would go, but his fingers touched nothing.

He replaced the cover and went away.

Later that day he approached a boy who kept an army flash-light in his locker. He offered to trade the nickel for a hour's use of the flashlight that night. The boy agreed.

After lights-out, he went to the toilets and opened the cover. He squeezed through the opening and entered a tunnel. Shining the flashlight in all directions, he saw that it was large enough for a man to crawl through on hands and knees. It contained ropes of electric wires and large black metal pipes running from under the toilets and disappearing into the dark-ness. He followed the tunnel for several feet until he came to a junction and turned left into a larger passage which contained many more pipes and wires. Down this avenue he moved with greater speed and within five minutes came to more holes in the wall covered by grates, all of which opened into dark rooms. Some were offices, one was the chapel, another the dining room. Turning into a smaller side tunnel he arrived at a grate through which came the low humming of motors. The room was dark. Flashing his light through the slats he saw that it was the kitchen.

He shook the grate from its frame, gasping when it fell outward onto the kitchen floor with a clatter. Paralyzed with fear, he waited for the sound of hurrying footsteps, but none came. Slowly, his heart pounding hard, he squeezed through and stood upright. The double doors to the dining hall were on the left. He went to them and found them locked, as was the door to the outside porch at the far end of the room, and the door of the corridor that led to the cook's bedroom.

He was alone. The light of the full moon spilled in through the high windows, shining on the bank of electric stoves and a row of steel doors along one wall. He opened the first. A blast of frosty air rushed out and enveloped him. It was a refrigerator so large that a family could have comfortably lived in one. It smelled of meat. Inside, he saw sides of butchered animals hanging from ceiling hooks.

In another refrigerator room, he came upon shelves of eggs, what seemed like thousands upon thousands of eggs. In another he found bins containing countless vegetables. In a fourth, the coldest of all, like winter inside, he came upon a great prize. Within it were metal tubs of the ice cream that was given out at Christmas and other feast days. Here too were shelves of sweet biscuits, buckets of jam, and hundreds of loaves of bread.

He pulled the lid from a tub of ice cream and shone the light inside. It was more than three quarters full of the substance white people called chocolate. The next contained vanilla. The third was strawberry. He dipped his hand into this one and scraped out a wad. It tasted a little like the wild fruit. It was very sweet with the sweetness of summer. He ate more and more. After that he broke open a biscuit box and ate a white wafer. It was hard as rock but the fragments melted quickly in his mouth. He ate more of them until his belly was full.

Then he retraced his steps, covering his tracks as best he could, squeezed into the hole in the wall, pulled the grate into place behind him, and returned to the toilet in his dorm. Later, he lay in bed feeling a great happiness. He knew a thing which no other child knew, and probably few of the staff knew. It was a discovery of such importance that he swelled up with the largeness of it. He thought also that he would like to share this secret with someone. With Gordon perhaps, but he and Gordon had not yet spoken. The language of their eyes had communicated something mysterious, a word-without-words that told him he was not alone, but it had revealed little else about Gordon. Would Gordon betray the secret? Was he too good for such a secret? Would he look down upon stealing?

With a start Tchibi realized that he had stolen. Had he committed a great sin—a mortal sin? Why, then, if the sin was evil, did it feel so good? Why had it made him so happy?

Rose would know. She would explain. She was good, and she understood many things, even the confusing things. He must tell her, he must take her with him to the great prize, and together they would eat the sweetness of summer in the midst of winter, as once they had crammed their mouths with the wild strawberries that grew on the skull at Threefinger Lake in the time when they had been happy.

The next day he wrote a note.

Ogini, I have found a secret treasure and a secret way. Will you meet me in the chapel after night prayers?

He went early to night prayers and finding himself alone in the chapel he dashed across the center aisle and dropped the note on the pew in the spot where she always sat. He worried that someone else would find it, but felt reassured that no one would know that Ogini meant Rose Wâbos. It was unsigned. She would know who had sent it.

When the children and nuns arrived, Tchibi watched Rose take her usual place. How beautiful she was. Her hair was braided and shining. Her face when she looked at the tabernacle shone brighter. At the end of prayers, when the children began to leave, she saw the note, opened it and read it, then put it into the pocket of her uniform. She remained praying on her knees until the chapel was almost deserted. Then she stood, genuflected, and turned to leave. As she went up the aisle toward the exit she cast a swift glance in Tchibi's direction, then went out. He got up and followed. In the main hallway he saw that she had already gone back to the girls' wing, a place where he could never go.

For several days he waited. On the fifth day, she was again the last girl to leave after night prayers. They were alone together. Once again she glanced at him, hesitated, and walked slowly to the back of the chapel where she stood by the door, her face worried. When he came to her, he flashed the sweet-fire at her, and she smiled slightly, though her brow did not unfurrow.

"Nishime, it is not permitted", she whispered.

"I must show you the secret way", he whispered.

"We cannot. It is wrong. In summer we will meet."

"Summer is too far away. It is forever away."

"Not forever."

He reached out and grabbed her hand, a thing which he had never done before.

"Please, Ogini, please", he cried. "It is wonderful. I eat berries in winter. It is like the mountain where we ate strawberries."

"We cannot leave the school or its grounds."

"It is not outside. It is within."

"Within?" she said, puzzled.

"Come, I will show you."

He led her to a grate in the wall. Bending, he jiggled the frame off and grinned at her.

"A tunnel", he said. "We will go inside to the secret place."

Glancing about Rose said, "Not here, not in the holy place. It is forbidden."

"Who has forbidden it? I know of no rule which speaks against it."

"But they would speak against it if they knew."

"Please, Ogini. You will be happy. You will say I have given you a great gift."

"We are not permitted to be together, the boys and the girls."

He sat back on his haunches and bile-fire stirred in his eyes. Then a thought came to him. "We are not like boys and girls. We are brother and sister."

She considered this. "Nishime——"

He laughed. "You call me little brother, though I am older and taller. You are my little sister."

"I don't know. . . ." she said uncertainly.

He pulled a flashlight from his pants pocket, flattened himself on the floor, and wriggled through the hole.

"Tchibi, come back!" she cried to the soles of his shoes, as they disappeared into the darkness.

His partridge laugh was the only reply. Flashes of light flickered inside.

"Come back!" she called again.

"Come inside, Ogini!" he called. "Come and I will show you a garden."

Poking her head inside she saw him crawling away. She wiggled into the tunnel and followed. He waited for her at a junction, and when she caught up, he turned left into a wider tunnel. The flashlight thumped in his hand as he crawled along, bumping his head.

"Ouch! Look out, Rose, watch your head."

At the moment when he said *ouch*, she knew that he was receiving blows for her sake and that she must follow him.

When they arrived at the kitchen grate, Tchibi pried it open.

"See, it is easy," he said. "Now we go through."

When he was standing in the dark kitchen, he beckoned her with his hand. She remained inside the tunnel, staring at the machines and metal doors lit up by moonlight streaming through the windows.

"Oh, it is a beautiful place", Rose gasped. "Where are we?"

"The palace."

"A palace inside the school?"

"The palace of the moon. It is the Gissis-place."

"It is not, Tchibi. You are mistaken."

"Come", he laughed. "They have made a feast for us."

"Who?"

"The loons."

He softly warbled his loon cry, the song of the father loon seeking his bride.

"I cannot", she shook her head. "It is not permitted."

Frowning down at her, he whispered, "Then I will bring you the feast."

He disappeared inside one of the rooms with metal doors and returned minutes later with a large tin bowl. He pushed it through the hole into her hands, then crawled in after her, pulling the grate closed behind him. This was not a moment too soon, for they heard a rattling at the door and the lights in the kitchen came on with terrifying brightness. They retreated a few feet down the tunnel.

Thumping feet entered the room, then stopped. A thick voice muttered, opening and closing cupboard doors. "Here, what'r dese crumbs?"

More thumps and a refrigerator door opening and banging closed.

"Moice!" growled the terrible voice. "More loik rats it is! Or

203

is it the two-legged jabberwockies? It makes no sense t' me, for tis locked. Is it the gremlins, Oi'm wonderin', or the brownies and sprites? Oi'll kill 'em all, fairies or not."

Tchibi peered out.

"Io!" he gasped, the sound drowned by the thumping and grumbling. "Ogini, it is the great *waiâbishkiwed*! The white monster lady, the one they say is *Irishwoman*!"

"The cook?" Rose whispered.

"Yes, her."

"It is Mrs. Boyle. She is very dangerous."

"Shhh."

The cook opened a cupboard above the stove, took a bottle from it, uncorked it, and put it to her mouth. She took a swig, then another, then tilted it up so that the red liquor glugged straight down her throat.

"Io, she drinks", Tchibi said in a low voice.

"Nishime, let us go", Rose pleaded. "Quickly!"

They withdrew still farther down the tunnel, Tchibi dragging the metal bowl after him. But this was a mistake, for it rattled loudly.

"Whatinahell is dat!" came a great bellow from behind. Looking back they saw a large round face pressed to the bars of the grate.

"Rats it is! Ye little bastards, Oi'll get ye. Oi'll get ye yet!"

Tchibi and Rose crawled as fast as they could back to the chapel, bumping all the way through the featureless dark.

Seated on the floor at the back of the unlit room, Tchibi placed the bowl in Rose's lap.

"Eat, Ogini", he whispered.

"Oh, I cannot. You took it without asking."

"They took *me* without asking."

"What do you mean, Tchibi? I do not understand."

"That is because you are good."

She did not reply to this.

"Eat. It is strawberries. It is the taste of summer in winter."

"I cannot."

He flicked the switch of the flashlight and showed her the contents of the bowl. It was full of ice cream and biscuits of many kinds.

He dug his hand into the pink cream and crammed it into his mouth.

"It is so sweet!" he said, his eyes dancing. "But it hurts, it is so cold."

Again and again he offered. Each time she refused.

He was full by the time he had eaten less than half of it.

He scooped a drop of ice cream on the end of his index finger and put it to her lips. She could not help but taste it.

"More?"

She shook her head.

"I am happy now", he said. "Because we have taken from them."

"Why do you say this, Nishime?"

"Because I hate them."

"Why do you hate them?"

"I do not hate all of them. One I hate more than the others, and him the most. The supervisor, the one we call the frog. He is evil. He beats us, he mocks us, and some he takes into his room where secret things are done. What these are I do not know. I know only that he is all full of the *matchi-manito*."

"He cannot be so," Rose replied. "How can a person be all full of the evil spirits?"

He shrugged.

Rose rushed to explain. "Those spirits push him and pull him, and he listens to them. But *he* is not a devil."

"He is *omakaki*!"

"I think you are wrong about this, Tchibi. I have seen inside him."

"What do you mean, you have 'seen inside him'?"

"I cannot speak of it."

"I am your brother; you can speak of it to me."

A long silence ensued.

"You must not hate him, Nishime", Rose said at last. "The hate would poison you. Also, it is not-correct-seeing. You do not understand him."

"I understand his blows and his hatred of me."

"He does not hate you. He hates himself, and himself only."

"How do you know this?"

"It was shown to me so that I might pray for him."

"Who showed it to you?"

"Jesus-Manito—I think. I hope it is he who showed it to me, though I am not sure. It is dangerous. One can see too far, and then the seeing turns to not-seeing, and the praying turns to sickness. Like a muddy river and a clear river. Muddy rivers can become clear, and clear rivers can become muddy."

"What are you talking about?"

Again she fell silent. He shook her arm. "Tell me."

"I will tell you", she said reluctantly. "For it may help you not to hate him. I do not want the poison to come into you, Nishime. Once, soon after you arrived in this place, I was praying for you, and a picture came into my mind about the supervisor. Then I knew in my heart that I must pray for him if I would protect you."

"You would protect *me*?"

"Yes."

Again she fell silent.

"What did you see, what did the picture show you?"

"I saw the empty place in him which he tries to fill with not-goodness, with the bending of things into wrong-shapes and wrong-deeds. I did not see the deeds themselves, only the cloud of wrongness that covered them and hid them from my eyes. And it was given to me to see his life, though whether it is his true life or just a likeness I do not know. His name is Martin."

Martin? Tchibi felt the shock of hearing for the first time the man's name, an unwanted knowledge. Pitiful, frail like a baby's name. Had someone actually given him a name, leaned over the *omakaki* uttering tender words of love?

"Think of a little boy, Tchibi, a boy smaller than you are. He is afraid of the world around him. He lives in a village in the lands where wheat grows in fields as wide as the Sea of the Ojibwe. And he walks to the eating-place where his mother works. Always he walks behind her with his face looking to the ground, because he is afraid, Tchibi. He is ashamed. And see how young he is, like a little bird pushed from its nest and told to fly into the storms with such small wings. He has no father."

I do not have a father, Tchibi said in his mind. *Nor do you, Oginiwâbigon.*

"When he is mocked, he has no one to run home to."

Nor do I have a home.

"He cannot speak of the hurt to his mother, for it is she who is mocked. People laugh at her because she drinks too much alcohol or because her lips are painted bright red. They say cruel things about her. The mother does not hear of it, but the son hears everything."

"How do you know this?" Tchibi demanded.

"I saw it."

Tchibi snorted.

Rose's eyes were now closed, concentrating on what she was seeing within.

"See him, Tchibi, see him walk the outcast-way, with his mother ruined in his eyes, her painted nails stroking his forehead in the nights, in a room where they live above a store. She feeds him on old bread and soup that she saves from the eating place. He reads the bad magazines she brings home, and sometimes he falls asleep looking at the holy cards he found in a church where he goes for shelter when she has been drinking.

Yes, there he looks up at the man on the cross over the high altar."

Tchibi stared into the darkness as the words poured from her lips. It seemed that they were hers but something more than hers, for she spoke as Fr. Andrei spoke when the spirit o Manito was strong in him.

"He grows from childhood into a youth without purpose drifting with her from town to town, until he works shoveling wheat in the grain towers, while his mother sits in her room and drinks and sinks in a river of black pictures in her mind."

"This is him?" Tchibi murmured when she was finished. He shook his head. "I do not believe it. You are thinking these thoughts of him. He is not what you think."

"He once was a child like you."

Silenced for a moment, Tchibi scowled.

"You must have mercy—even for the merciless", Rose went on.

"No. He does not deserve mercy."

"Have pity on him, Tchibi."

"I hate him!" he said sharply. "I do not believe in your pictures. How do you know they are not lies?"

"I do not know for certain."

"Always you have made pictures. Now you make them in your mind."

"The pictures come from somewhere. I have seen many pictures of you."

"What pictures?" he said irritably.

"I have seen—"

"What did you see?"

"I saw what *they* did to you, the man and the woman."

"You cannot know, for only they and I know."

"When you lived with them, the man and the woman, they drank often. The man beat the woman and sometimes the woman beat the man."

"Everyone knows this. Many people do such things."

"The last time was the worst. At the camp where you lived with them, they drank for many days. They fought, and you ran into the forest where you slept beneath a tree. But they came upon you as you slept and caught you and bound you. In the cabin they took your clothing from you and tied your hands and feet to the wall with ropes and hung you on nails."

"Stop!" Tchibi shouted. "It is enough."

Crying out, Rose wrapped her arms around him.

"Nishime, *ni sessessakis!*" she wailed, "They burned you with fire, making fire holes all over you. I hear you screaming! I hear it! I hear it!"

Tchibi struggled to free himself from her grip, but it was amazingly strong.

"What they did to you! Oh, oh, it is *matchi*! It is evil! They kept you on the wall for days, without food, without drink, only whiskey they poured into your throat between the burnings. Then they went away and left you there alone in the cabin, screaming day after day until a fisherman found you. When he untied your hands and feet, you ran away into the forest. You were naked. You ate raw fish and berries. You were as wild as an animal when they found you again. Oh, I thought they had burned your heart forever when they brought you to Fr. Andrei for prayers, and you hid under the bench because you were small and afraid. O Tchibi, your mind, I thought they had broken it, and when you went away to the hospital I died, I died with you. I offered my back to Jesus for you, and he took the sacrifice and he told me it would not be in vain."

A cry of agony leaped from Tchibi's throat.

"And when you returned from the hospital I came back to life again, for though the burning was still inside you, it was less. You were silent. You did not speak. Then I begged the Lord to let me give him more for you, and he said yes. He said I was too

209

small for it, yet he would make me a little stronger that it might be so."

"Ogini", Tchibi sobbed in a low voice. "Say nothing more."

"Only a little more I will say. Tchibi, you have come back from the place of the burned people. Do not let it be a waste, do not let the hatred come inside you again, for then the burning will take you away from me *forever*!"

He put his arms around her and rocked her. He felt the twist of her spine with his fingertips and knew that it was this way because of him, that she had let it be so for him.

They stood and shook themselves and quietly opened the door to the main hallway. Tchibi stuck his head out and listened for sounds, but there were none. He and Rose stepped into the hall, embraced quickly, then turned away from each other and went back without a sound to their dormitories.

Then came a miraculous day. That it invaded the limitless winter was marvel enough for Tchibi, but that it brought freedom with it one Friday evening was beyond all expectation.

The supervisor informed them grimly that as a special privilege the rector had granted permission for twelve senior boys to spend a weekend at the school cottage. This was a shack on a lake three miles north, deep in the forest.

"You are a tribe of idiots", scowled the supervisor. "Not one of you would pass in a normal school. But some of you are less idiotic than others. You have the highest marks for your grades, such as they are, which is meaningless. And because *I* am not the one who decides things here, my wishes have been overridden. It has been ordained and sealed by higher powers. You are to be rewarded for your *accomplishments*."

The sarcastic tone switched to one of ominous threat when he added that some of the chosen would be weeded out. This last punishment was for any unforgiven or suspected rebellion. They were all guilty, the man's face seemed to say, though guilty of what they could not begin to guess. Guilty of failing to be the love he sought. Guilty of leanness and virility. And most of them, though not all, were guilty of innocence.

Tchibi was amazed that he was not among the mute and blamed who had to remain behind. He was further astonished that they would go unsupervised, except for the six underlings, solemn with responsibility as they stood taking last-minute instructions from the Mikana. Despite its weight, these older boys went wild with grinning anarchy as soon as the school was out of sight. They danced and hooted on their snowshoes as they charged along the forest trail, packing the snow for those who followed. The others were strung out behind, pulling toboggans piled with sleeping bags, blankets, food boxes, bow saw, matches, and a kerosene lantern. Laughter, brazen or timid from hibernation, crept out of them and swelled and rose high into the tops of the black pines.

Gordon packed the trail ahead of Tchibi. Despite their language of eyes, they had not yet spoken. A mile from the school, Gordon stepped from the trail and snowshoed several paces into the trees. He turned around and looked at Tchibi. Tchibi stepped off the path and followed him. They waited while the other boys passed.

When they were alone, Gordon looked into the distance and said, "*Kissina!* It is cold!"

"Soon it will be spring", Tchibi murmured.

"How is your shoulder, *Nishime*?"

Only one other had ever called him little brother.

"It no longer hurts", he replied, shrugging. "It is healed."

"That is good."

They said no more for a time. Gordon continued to gaze up into the tree tops. Tchibi wondered why the older boy did not resume the journey. Nor did he understand the silence.

"You say nothing to me", he blurted. "Why do you say nothing?"

"We speak, Binemin green-eyes. For a long time we have spoken."

"We do not speak with the mouth", Tchibi said.

"We are in the house of the white people. They speak much, but see little. They know much, but understand little."

Tchibi nodded.

"When that man, the *nâganisid*, hurts you," Gordon raised his voice with surprising strength, "I am angry."

Tchibi could not believe that anyone would be angry for his sake. His mind went blank.

"Soon it will be *Pak*", Gordon continued in a lower voice. "The grave opens and the dead come forth. Life begins again."

"Are you *anjeni*?" Tchibi stammered.

Gordon burst out laughing.

"An angel? No, I am a man. I am Gordon Kitagakons." He laughed again.

Then, after considering his thoughts, he added solemnly: "I will not return here. Five years I have lived among these people, and this winter has been the worst. This summer I am going with my family farther north, to hunt the *atik* on the edge of the barrens."

"I would go with you."

"No, you cannot, *Nishime*, but I wish that you could."

"Please, let me go with you!"

"You must return to the place from which you came. To your own people."

"I have no people!" Tchibi cried.

Gordon's eyes grew sad. He thought long before answering.

"On *Abitchibawinigijigad*, the day of resurrection, you will have a people. All peoples will be as one."

"We are a nothing-people", Tchibi cried again. "*Nin tchagi-dabadan!* We all die away!"

Again Gordon fixed him with the look of deep sadness. "Not all. Everything that is good will remain."

But Tchibi, certain that he himself was not good, was dismayed by this.

"Do not return here, green-eyes", Gordon said.

With that, he returned to the trail, Tchibi following close behind. A mile farther on they came to a round lake, white and brilliant as an exposed host. They crossed it, and on the far side came to an old cabin in a stand of pines. Tchibi stood stiffly before the building, inspecting its big hacked logs. It was a white-man's place, long a hunter's lodge, now owned by the school.

Inside, it was empty of furniture, dirty with the trash of rummaging vermin. A scuffle of boys broke out around the pot-bellied stove, a desperate and happy struggle for the privilege of setting the fire, of creating the familiar smell of wood smoke. A dozen hands fought, and matches flared in the iron belly. When the kindling ignited, they all stood back smiling and vaguely homesick as the stove belched smoke into the room. There was a riot of banging on the rusty stovepipe to free it of a squirrel's nest, and boys spilled smoke-weeping out into the snow. Then as the room heated and cleared there was a confusion of sawing and chopping, and tall slender trees pitched round the shack. The boys ignored the stove wood that someone had long ago stacked beside the front door, because cutting fresh wood was one of the lost pleasures.

The older ones lit a second blaze in the clearing outside the front door, mixing the green with the dry. Onto it they tossed log after log, watching deliriously as the flames roared high, and they threw on heaps of fir bows just to hear the spit and crackle. The eruption of natural light nursed their bush memories, warmed more than their bones. It calmed and obsessed them, flaring brighter in the dying afternoon, turning the surrounding trees to flickering orange. As the boys gathered about the fire in knee-deep snow, the burning pine gum hissed with such power that they became drunk on its perfume. They would have eaten it if they could.

Someone was moved to pull out a plastic bag and pass it around. "*Monswiias*, moose. Dry-meat", he said. The others did not exactly look at Tchibi, for he was still partly invisible. But they did allow him to take a fingerful of meat. Tchibi wondered at the substance as it came into his hands, for it was not like the salty dry-meat of the people at Threefinger Lake, which was made of *atik* the deer and shredded like tobacco. This was plain strips sweetened with brown sugar. It was wild and good in a new way.

As he chewed it slowly, he heard the word *giminidjagan* in his mind, like a river that broke suddenly through an ice dam and began to surge into black whirlpools. You are a bastard, you have no mother, no father, and soon this elder brother will be taken from you. You are not Cree, you are not Anishinâbi, you are not white, you are nothing, you are a mistake, you should not have been born.

Then he saw Rose's face in his mind, and for a time the black water turned aside and went elsewhere.

The older boys set a tea pail to boil, swinging and singing on the crotch of a stick. Stew bubbled on the cabin stove. Someone swept, unbidden, the dirt and seeds from the corners, and another spread the big patchwork of blankets and sleeping bags. Others packed firewood into their shelter for the oncoming night. Though by day the soft snow sank and the jays flew promisingly through the trees, under the stars winter still proclaimed in frosty breaths: *You see, all things end, and begin, and end again. I, winter, rule everything.*

Tchibi walked quietly into the cabin, which was not a frightening place, for there were no ropes and nails in it, and it was full of laughter and free talking. Stew was passed about in bowls. Soon, boys were climbing inside their sleeping bags. Tchibi found a heap of blankets in the corner farthest from the stove, farthest from the lantern, farthest from the others, and crawled under. He lay on his back, feeling warm, his body

214

smoke-tanned like deer hide, and his face hot with wind, sun, and fire. He stared up into the shadows in the rafters as stories arose like lazy smoke.

"One time, my dad nearly got killed", someone said.

First this story, then that story, until the small stories melted into one great tale which was known to all. There were jokes too, the darting whimsy which analyzed the foolishness of people they had known, turning corners in the mind, finding with a look of surprise their own faces looking back. In time the talk began to circle warily around the subject of the man who governed them.

And finally, bluntly, someone said outright, "*Matchi aiiwishi-wan!* It is a wicked thing! *He* does a wicked thing!"

Total silence ensued, broken only by the crackling stove and the wind.

"It is good he is not here!" someone else muttered.

This was an invitation to death. This was suicide. Several of the boys were considering the possibility that the underlings might report the insolence. But then one of *his* boys, one of *them*, said, "He is like *omakaki* the frog. Big noise, small heart."

The boys laughed, and they were free. A storm of judgment broke upon the specter of their supervisor, as they exposed him in their midst.

"Some of the medicine men go both ways, but this one is worse than them."

"He plays with us. We are things to him."

"He has no respect."

"He is *mo!* Big *mo!*" Which was untranslatable and sparked gales of crueler laughter.

"He is *ogowessi*, the bedbug!"

The laughter which greeted this went on for some time.

"Well, maybe he's not all bad", one said at last.

"And wolves look like dogs", growled another.

Someone blew the light out. Boys began to drift off in a

wreath of deep sighs or snores, while others continued to talk quietly in the moonlight that came through the window, spilling a long realm of silver across the legs and arms in the stillness.

Tchibi smelled the fragrance of bread toasting on the rust of the stove and saw a tall shadow tending the pieces. They crisped toward the edge of burnt, then they were turned, sending baked fragrance into the other smells of wet socks, wood smoke, and sweat. It was an inexpressibly beautiful smell, and he hungered for it.

The boy who had made it came to a pile of blankets beside Tchibi and knelt there in the rivulets of cold air which swirled from under the door. Fumbling in the poor light, he took Tchibi's hand and placed into it a hot piece of toast. It was covered with strawberry jam. Tchibi took a bite, tasting summer in winter. As he rose on one elbow, curious to see who had given him this bread, he suddenly knew who it was. It was Gordon. After a moment or two the older boy slipped without a word into his own blankets, turned away, and slept. For a long time Tchibi lay awake, feeling the bread in his stomach, watching the high tongues of fire as they danced from the cracks in the stove, up into the vast dark fields above.

By the beginning of June, the snow was all gone, and the school yard was a swamp of mud. The mosquitoes arrived in clouds. He wrote the tests the teachers gave and failed most of them. He also allowed himself the luxury of thought. Soon he would return to Threefinger Lake. Maybe to another foster home. Soon he and Rose would make the bells ring in their garden. With this came an eruption of anguished longing. Each day became such a distraction of slowness that it seemed eternal. He did not return to the tunnels, having lost all desire to steal food. His only pleasures in life were the moments when he saw Rose across the wide spaces that separated them.

From time to time he would catch her eye and she would smile. At school, disgusted with books, his attention was mostly fixed on the windows.

One day Mère Jean called to him at the end of class.

"Sit down, please, here at this desk." She pointed to one in the front row. When all the other students had gone, she smiled at him and said, "Is there something you are looking for out that window?"

He shook his head.

"You are a long way from home, Binemin. I shall ask your supervisor to let you have a little more free time. You could perhaps go for more walks."

"It is not permitted", Tchibi murmured, staring at the floor.

"Surely you boys go for walks", said the nun. "I take the senior girls for hikes in the forest every weekend.

"We do not."

"I will speak to Mr. McKenna about it", she said encouragingly.

At the mention of the supervisor's name she noticed the boy's eyes look up darkly, his fingers curling in tension.

"Is there something wrong?" she asked, haunted by a feeling of disquiet that had no obvious cause.

Tchibi's answer burst out like a gunshot. "He hates me!" he cried, shocking himself as well as her.

"Oh, no, Binemin, he does not hate you! Why would he hate you?"

"He hits boys. He always hits boys with his strap. And makes us walk naked before his eyes. One time he ran into the shower—"

He stopped himself. He said no more. His chin quivered. You did not speak of nakedness to women. You especially did not speak of it to nuns.

He saw again the raging man's shirt plastered against his round belly in shower water, flailing about him the strap, laying red welts across the backs of fleeing boys. Screaming about their impurity, their lust, which was untrue, for the *winewishkotewn*, the impure fire, was in the supervisor's mind.

The nun bent toward him, her eyes intense with sudden suspicion, her understanding growing second by second. And then she knew. Sitting in the ticking of the school clock as the too-big, too-wild boy began to control himself, she knew. When he could meet her gaze, she reached for his hand, cupping it in hers.

"I did not know this thing about him", she said. Then her eyes hardened. "No one knew . . . Martin is . . . I cannot. . . ."

Martin, the martin-child burning in the hot yellow light of prairie fires.

"Pray for him, Binemin", said Mère Jean, her eyes full of pity.

He nodded and fled to the chapel, where he begged for a father for the child who had been nailed to a wall and burned, crying, why have you forsaken me, him, everybody, why? The burning, the hunger, the screaming? Why? Why?

But nothing changed in the following days. The supervisor did not become transformed into a companion in the secret fraternity of victimhood, nor into an incarnation of fatherhood, but wielded his powers as usual. A slap or two was sufficient to drive out the trace of Tchibi's religious sentiment, though he kept his desire for vengeance in check, for Rose had taken it all upon her back.

One morning, the Mikana came to Tchibi and handed him the knife he had taken away ten months before.

"You're going home," he said tonelessly.

When the hour came for Tchibi's departure he went outside and stood waiting by the idling car that would take him to the train station. He paused and looked back at the school. A few boys had gathered on the steps of the porch. They watched with various expressions on their faces, some curious, most indifferent. As the car pulled away with Tchibi in the passenger eat, Archie shot a final sneer. The supervisor stood by the railing, his arms crossed, scowling. But the last thing Tchibi saw was a diminishing Gordon, standing square with his arms dropped, his eyes two black points of substance and light.

The driver was Fr. Morin. As they approached the station, Tchibi worked up the courage to ask, "Why are you sending me away?"

"You must leave a week before the others", the priest replied, "because of the transportation problems in returning you to Threefinger Lake."

"When is Ogini coming?"

"Ogini? Who is Ogini?"

"Rose Wâbos."

"Ah, yes, the little girl from your village. Unfortunately, she must stay. Because of her back, which the doctors must try to correct."

Later that day, Tchibi climbed into a pontoon plane and went up into the sky. Then he felt a certain consolation, because he found that Rose's face and Gordon's face came with him in his mind.

When the plane coughed him out onto the dock at Three-finger Lake, he stood wondering who would claim him. In the swirling universe, it was possible that no one would.

Fr. Andrei arrived on the dock, bustling down its creaking boards, arms wide, smiling at him.

"Welcome, Binemin Edzo", he said in Ojibwe. "Welcome home."

Oldmary Wâbos came, welcomed him also, and asked about Rose. Tchibi, who had become momentarily incapable of words, merely stared at the water.

The new Indian agent ran onto the dock with a file under his arms.

"Edzo? Where is the boy Edzo?" he said loudly to everyone

Oldmary and the priest put hands on Tchibi's shoulders.

"He is here", said Fr. Andrei.

The agent consulted his paper and made a check mark with a pencil.

"He's a bit of a problem", the man said over Tchibi's head "He doesn't seem to belong to anyone."

No one knew what to say—well, not in front of the boy.

"Doesn't he have any family around here?"

"The whereabouts of his parents are unknown", said the priest.

"His stepuncle, Kuchuk, is dead," said Oldmary.

The other people who had gathered to listen shook their heads.

"It says here on his file that he was living in a foster home but those people have moved to Sandy Lake."

"He can stay with me", the priest offered.

"Sorry, Father. It's not in the regulations."

Oldmary stepped forward.

"He can stay with me", she said.

"Well, uh, I don't think so, really. You're getting on in years Ma'am."

"Mary Wâbos would be ideal", the priest interjected.

"No way. She's on her last legs. This kid needs a family. I'd better get busy and find a foster home."

"If you do not yet have one for him, perhaps he could spend the day with me, until you have found a family."

The agent's face soured. "All right. I suppose he could. . . ."

Fr. Andrei and Oldmary took Tchibi up the slope to the rectory of the mission, leaving the agent to scout around for a willing family.

"Good wages", he offered to the crowd. "Thirty bucks a month, plus food allowance."

No one was interested, though the money was tempting.

Over tea in the priest's kitchen, Oldmary and Fr. Andrei turned to the boy and asked about his year at school.

"There was a man there", Tchibi said, staring at the floor.

Then he began to speak. It poured from him haltingly at first, then in a rush. The stories were disjointed, but little by little they painted a picture, a picture that the priest understood better than the boy. By the time the agent arrived a few hours later, he had told them everything. Fr. Andrei took the man aside and recounted Tchibi's description of life in the senior boys' dorm. The man grew furious and swore and said he was going to see about that.

"A call to the police wouldn't be out of order. An investigation is long overdue. Those residences are archaic, medieval, staffed by—" He stopped himself. "In the meantime," he said. "I've got someone who's willing to take the boy."

He pointed out the window to a couple who were coming up the path. It was Kinoje and his wife.

Oldmary uttered a cry.

"They are not suitable", the priest said.

"What do you mean not suitable? They have a house. They're decent, law-abiding people. I don't see any problem. They offered."

"But their spiritual activities—" the priest protested.

The man leveled a cold look at him and said, "Just leave your religion out of this, will you. I don't have time to be choosy."

The agent took Tchibi out the door and gave him to Kinoje. With a single backward glance, the boy walked away with them into the surrounding woods. Kinoje, too, looked back, once, shooting a leer at the priest.

When Fr. Andrei and Oldmary were alone, they sat down on kitchen chairs.

"We must pray", the old woman said. They prayed. But the atmosphere of gloom did not lift. Water filled Oldmary's eyes.

"Eeeeee!" she wailed.

The priest wrestled silently with his own anguish. Eventually Oldmary stood up, hobbled to the kitchen window, and peered out.

"*Ay, ay!*" she cried.

"What do you see, Mary?" Fr. Andrei asked.

The old woman replied with a sound too low for understanding. When he asked again, she said more loudly, "*Swing-waage!*"

The priest stiffened and bent toward the window, but the village seemed quiet.

"A wolverine? I do not see it."

"Not the kind you can see," she said, staring not through the glass, but into it.

"You mean the man at the school?"

Oldmary turned to him and murmured, "No. The thing that made him what he is."

"And Kinoje?"

"Him too, and the thing in him. *Ay, ay!* What will become of that boy?"

8

All the other children went home, and most of the staff disappeared as well. Only Mrs. Boyle the cook remained, resting in her private room off the kitchen, grumbling down the hallway in her house-dress and carpet slippers, muttering about the rats, putting in an appearance at Sunday Mass whenever she was not in town on mysterious errands. Svend, the boiler-man, who had been entirely invisible during the winter, now appeared like an unhibernated bear, dismantling and repairing the heating plant, taking out garbage, cutting up logs with his screaming buzz-saw, stacking firewood in the shed behind the school, muttering to himself in Swedish, and casting resentful looks at any nun who dared to interrupt his comings and goings. Sister Madeleine said that he was a Protestant and that all the sisters were praying for his conversion.

"*Quel dommage!*" she would chirp to Rose as they peeled carrots together in the pantry. "He is a good worker, but—tsk!—*si crasseux et crapuleux! Tiens, tiens, tiens!* Tsk-tsk."

Rose remained at the school in Thunder Bay throughout the summer. Between visits to doctors, she practiced her reading and sewing, read more lives of the saints, and lived with the sisters in their cloister on the second floor. There were eight sisters in all, each with her own room on a corridor that echoed with the footsteps of their shiny black shoes and the clinking of the huge rosary beads hanging from their belts. At the end of the corridor was a statue of the Blessed Virgin, who was the Mother of all the mothers. Rose slept in a room that had belonged to an elderly sister who had died the year before. It contained a single bed, a prie-dieu, a crucifix, a dresser, and a rag mat to warm her feet in the mornings. The bed was hard, harder even than the cot in the cabin at Crazyman River, yet it was piled high with woolen blankets and down comforters. How amazing it all was—to live with the sisters almost as one of them! Suddenly she had more mothers than she could have hoped for. Io, to have become as rich and pampered as Marleena Crombie! It was a miracle!

Even so, she missed Oldmary very much, and during the first few days of summer, she cried whenever she thought about her. But Mère Jean de la Croix helped Rose write a beautiful letter to Grandma explaining everything. After that she did not cry so much. And during that first summer with the sisters, she began to think of Mère Jean with another name—*Ningâ*, my mother. Or simply, Mother.

She missed Tchibi also, but she did not cry for him, because her back was now hurting all the time and she knew that the pain was going up to Jesus like a letter that he would deliver straight to Tchibi's heart.

One of the sisters—old Sister Clothilde, who had had a stroke and was slow—made a doll to welcome Rose among them. It had black wool braids and its skin was made of brown cotton. Its dress was pink calico that ended in lace at the ankles. Rose named her *Bineshi*, which meant tiny silver bird. When she heard the name, Sister Clothilde smiled with half of her face because the other side did not work. Like Tchibi, Sister Clothilde did not often speak, but her eyes said much. After Mère Jean and Sister Madeleine, she was Rose's favorite.

Some of the other sisters were quiet people and some were noisy. Some were smart and some not so smart, but they all liked to laugh during recreation in the parlor, where they sewed and did picture puzzles, and told stories and jokes, and listened carefully with many oohs and ahs whenever Rose could be coaxed to tell one of her own stories. About Mang the loon and Gissis the moon, and about the great white bird that hovered over the whole world gazing upon all things with his blue, blue eyes.

They kissed her and cuddled her and told her stories about Jesus and the Holy Family, and about some of their sisters who had been killed by a very bad man named Hitler only a few years ago.

"The time flies swiftly, day unto day, moon unto moon", sighed Sister Madeleine tsk-tsking over a stitch of crochet, "season unto season. *Les petites martyres* have gone from us now these eight-nine years. You were alive when the *monstre, le grand fasciste*, has done his foul deeds, *ma chérie*. A little girl in the bushland, *la terre sauvage*, so innocent, *si douce comme les bonbons*, while the evil ones do their business. *Les martyres* were dying when you were three years old. Thank the Good God that you have lived where you have lived, and *le Sale Bosche* did not turn their evil eyes upon you."

Rose learned more about martyrs from the sisters, and she realized that many people in this world did what she did: offered their suffering for the good of others. It was a great discovery, this, for she had sometimes wondered if it was too strange a thing to do, that she was perhaps doing something forbidden, like falling-into-seeing in such a way that it became stealing. Now she knew that it was right, because there was not a bit of taking in it, only a giving. A very powerful giving, no matter how small a person was.

Rose loved the five times a day when she went with the sisters to the chapel, once for Holy Mass, and four other times for prayer. Each day, moon unto moon, season unto season, the hours of prayer were the most beautiful times of her life, and she was happy—except for the brief moments when she thought about Grandma and Tchibi. But even then she was comforted, for in chapel she felt them very near, knowing that Grandma was herself often sitting in front of the Blessed Sacrament praying for Rose, as she sat praying for Grandma. So they were brought close by the Beating Heart in the tabernacle, who linked together all places, as if there were no distance anywhere in the world that could not be crossed instantly by love.

Whenever she knelt before the Lord Jesus in his Sacrament, she prayed especially for Tchibi, because, well, to tell the truth she was very worried about him. The falling-into-seeing was almost nothing now, just repetitions of what had come to her before. Yet a new way was growing stronger all the time, a knowing about things without many pictures. When she prayed, a person's face would come into her mind-heart or heart-mind, and she would hold him as if they were resting together in a pool of light in spring after a long winter. If she prayed long enough and was very quiet inside, a knowing would arise inside of her and light up the pool, as sunshine turns meltwater to gold sometimes. Then she would send back a beam to the source of the light, the beam saying, *Please send Tchibi someone who will make socks for him, so he will not be cold.* Or, *Thank you for helping Sister Clothilde get over her flu.* Or, *How beautiful is the forest when you make the little leaves burst out of all the branches and then send the wind to sing in them. Greenlight, sweetlight, songlight*, she sang to him. How happy she felt, she wanted to skip, once, for joy, though she was kneeling in chapel and could only send the feeling of a skip to him who was singing inside the tabernacle, telling her how much he loved her.

At other times, the knowing was something darker, like a shadow moving under the deep waters, like a storm brewing, or like a stick stirring a sediment of decaying things, rousing black clouds, and exuding a foul smell.

Every afternoon, except Sundays, Rose and Sister Madeleine went to the art room. Sometimes they threw clay into new shapes. Usually these were animals or the faces of people. Sister put them into a brick oven, and they came out hard. Then they glazed them and baked them again, and they turned shiny and different colors than they were before. Best of all were the gouaches and the little tubes of water paint that Sister said had eggs in them, though the eggs could not be seen. Like color-sticks, they had the brightest colors of all, more colors than Rose had thought possible. There were ten different kinds of green and sixteen kinds of reds, and, oh, it was like being too rich!

Rose spent hours splashing the thick rag paper with waving wildflowers and upwinging birds and lashing trees that un-leashed their many thousand bolts of tinted leaf and seed and berry.

"*C'est joli!*" exclaimed Sister Madeleine, admiring what she herself could never have done, her forte being a careful execu-tion in silverpen on Ingres paper—the Madonnas, the busts of Plato, and the gods and goddesses of the Parthenon that she had learned to copy at L'École des Beaux-Arts in Paris.

Seeing Rose beam with pleasure at her praise, Sister Made-leine would sometimes warn, "*La vie de l'artiste est une fête de l'orgueil, ma chérie*—the satisfaction. One is a little like God, and this is dangerous. The satisfaction easily becomes *la fière arro-gance*—the deadly pride."

Then Sister would grin, "*Tiens*, he keeps me humble by keeping me fat.

There were days when the weather was gray inside Rose's heart, cold with the weight of all falling things. Then she painted purple and gray skies, storms scudding from the north above a weeping forest, and a small figure walking the stone spine of the land toward a high bare hill, in the place of almost-nowhere, where she would walk if she wished to be seen no more.

Whenever she painted a picture like this, Sister Madeleine would chirp like a bird and make her lips into scolding shapes and say, "*Si mélancolique, ma chérie!* Tsk-tsk-tsk!" and pop a bon-bon between Rose's lips and clamp the little girl to her breast, not always remembering to avoid the spine as she thumped Rose's back with hands as small, round, and vulnerable as a porcupine's paws.

On occasion Rose attempted a religious motif, of which she felt unworthy, but tried because she knew it would please Sister Madeleine. There was a Nativity in a forest shack, surrounded by the worshipping deer and hare and fox and lynx. This elicited much praise. There was a flaming heart, surrounded by the thorns of wild raspberry, which made Sister gasp and shed tears of gratitude. There was a crucifixion upon a log wall, which made sister gasp again, her hand fluttering on her chest in profound empathy, though she was puzzled by the work, and asked Rose why she had made *le Bon Seigneur* so young and why there were so many little holes upon his body. But before such questions Rose had already learned to withdraw into inscrutable silence. Sister did not insist upon an answer, for she too had suffered many tortures explaining her own work.

In July, two policemen came to the school to speak with Fr. Morin and Mère Jean about Mr. McKenna, who had gone away for the summer. One evening at recreation Rose overheard the sisters whispering to each other about it.

"He will go to jail", said one.

"Yes, surely, and may it be for life!" said another.

"*Monstre!*"

"*Bête!*" exclaimed Sister Madeleine, who now showed herself capable of breathing fire with a frightful scowl.

All at once the sisters glanced at Rose, who was struggling valiantly over a rat's nest of yarn and a cumbersome crochet hook. They reverted entirely to French.

"*Mon Dieu! La corruption des innocents! Et dans notre maison!*"

"*Les pauvres garçons, les pauvres petits garçons!*"

"*Cet homme, ce méchant McKenna, a grand besoin d'être flagellé.*"

"We must be merciful, my sisters", cautioned Mère Jean in a quiet voice, as she needled the petit point of an altar linen. "If Monsieur McKenna repents of his crimes, will not God himself grant mercy to him? Are you more just than *le Bon Dieu*?"

"*Ma Mère!*" Sister Madeleine protested. "Think of the little ones whose lives he has wounded so dreadfully!"

"I know, it is terrible—"

And so the chorus of voices continued back and forth between the equally incomprehensible poles of mercy and justice, leaving Rose uncertain about what had disturbed them so greatly. She knew, of course, what had been shown to her in her prayer: the hole in Mr. McKenna's heart that he had tried to fill with the bending of shapes into wrong-shapes and wrong-deeds, though the actual pictures were clouded by the stirring of silt in the rotting bottom of the pond.

It was enough to know that an offering was needed. Her pain was given for him that day, and the next and the next, though on Sunday she forgot to offer because there was a picnic and a boat ride on the Sea of the Ojibwe and because usually on Sundays there was little or no pain. On Fridays, it was worse, especially when offered for a very difficult, very clouded thing.

In August, a doctor fitted her into a back brace that was made of thick leather pads and metal clips. It hurt so much when he strapped it onto her body, over the thin linen slip the sisters had made for her modesty, that Rose cried out. She offered the embarrassment and hurting for Mr. McKenna.

"It may take years, Mère Jean", the doctor said. "Even then, we can't promise perfect results. It was left too long, you see. Already the bones are setting, the muscles growing in a false delineation. But we can try to make some correction. She is now old—?" He consulted the chart. "Ah, yes, fourteen."

He spoke as if she were not there, or as if she were a lump of fish drying on a willow rack. She offered this as well.

"A pity to see such retarded development in one so young", he went on. "It's often the way with natives—"

"She understands everything", Mère Jean said to him in a reproving voice.

Ignoring the nun's correction, he went on in a lecturing

tone. "The genetic defect is only part of it. There is, of course, the malnutrition, the neglect."

"She has been much loved", Mère Jean murmured, "by her family."

"Man does not live by love alone", he replied, "but by vitamins and minerals and fresh air. Her lungs are bad. A poorly ventilated cabin, no doubt, full of smoke."

Mère Jean stood abruptly, her hand on Rose's shoulder.

"Thank you for your time, doctor. When shall we see you again?"

"Once a month. As the back grows and adjusts we tighten the straps, put pressure here, ease it there." He pointed here and pointed there, frowning with sadness over the little Indian girl, the almost no-thing.

"Once a month", Mère Jean murmured, glancing down at Rose. "This will be hard on her. Her home is very far away."

He shrugged.

"Do the best you can", he said, smiled, shook Sister's hand, and left the office.

Sister seemed too silent and distracted during the drive back to the school.

"When will I go home to Grandma?" Rose asked.

"I do not know, *ma chérie*. I must write to your grandmother. We shall see."

But life itself answered the question. A letter came to Mère Jean just before the resumption of classes. Fr. Andrei wrote to say that Oldmary had died in her sleep a few days before. The village nurse believed it was her heart or a burst blood vessel in the lungs. He wrote about other details, which Mère Jean told Rose only in small bits and pieces during the months that followed. The police at Threefinger Lake had shot Thisdog and Thatdog, who were running wild in the village. The Indian agent had ordered the cabin burned down because it was infested with rats and squirrels, and the roof was collapsing, and besides it was an illegal cabin on Crown land.

In September, the other children returned, Svend became invisible, Mrs. Boyle became very visible, a religious brother arrived as the new supervisor of the senior boys, Fr. Morin was transferred to another city, and a new priest, a bustling man from France, arrived to take on the responsibility of the entire institution.

It was hard for Rose to concentrate on her studies, because of the brace and because she was now back in the dorm and the sisters did not have as much time to spend with her and because she thought continually about Grandma. She wept herself to sleep every night during the following weeks, for Grandma had done just as she had always said she would do, climbed up on the loon's necklace into the river of stars, leaving Rose alone in the world.

Grandma came to her in dreams so many times during this period that Rose often awoke believing the letter was untrue, though after a minute or two, as she slipped her uniform over the bulky brace, she knew that Fr. Andrei was never untrue and that Grandma had gone up, up, up beyond the stars.

In the first dream Grandma came to her and said, "Pray for me, Rose."

"If you are in heaven, Grandmother, why must I pray for you?"

"*Sasagakwane*, the flame is ascending high, Ogini", Grandma said. "I am being cleansed by fire. In this way am I made ready for the great singing."

"But why must I *pray* for you?"

"The prayers help me fly higher, more quickly, for the flames are love, and love is the purifying fire; it is like the wind."

"Does it hurt you?"

"Ay! Ay, it hurts! Yet it is a good hurt, for it speeds me on my way. You may join your hurt to mine that I may soon reach the singing love. The Holy Mass, *Anamessikewin*, is the most power-ful prayer, and after this, the beads of the Mother. Also, you must ask the little mothers to pray for me, for the sins of my youth were many."

This was a frightening thing to dream, but it contained a strange peace as well, and she did as Grandma asked her.

In other dreams she merely remembered:

"Grandma, where do the roses come from?"

"From seeds."

"I mean before the seeds."

Oldmary raised both arms to the stars, and she splayed her purple fingers with their orange tobacco-stained nails as if spreading a fan of partridge feathers.

"From the stars, and beyond the stars", she said, dropping her arms, and her eyes, as if she had said too much.

On the second day of November a final dream came to Rose. Grandma appeared with her face full of light.

"*Nin gassiiakis*! I am cleansed by fire. It is done. Great my joy. Great, also, will be your joy when you come to me."

"Will it be soon?"

"You will come later."

"I do not want to come later. I want to go with you now."

"You cannot. You have work to do."

"I will be alone."

"You will have light."

"But you have gone from me, and the light has departed with you."

Grandma smiled at her. "The light has not departed from you. It is with you and in you. Never turn from the knowledge of it, Oginiwâbigon, little piece of my heart, my daughter, my daughter's daughter."

"O let me come to you!" Rose wailed.

"If you were to come to me, a sliver of the light would be absent from the earth. You are sent down into the cold dark world to bring it light, though you are but a reflection. Ogini, in many times and many places you will not see the light that you bring, for it is hidden from your eyes so that others may receive it."

Then Grandma departed from that dream never to return, and from it Rose awoke to another day and the first falling of snow, for it was a late autumn, between the time when the geese flee to the south and icebreakers appear in the harbor and the earth goes to sleep.

On the third day of November, the day after the last dream, Mère Jean brought to Rose a cardboard box which had arrived in the mail. It was from Fr. Andrei and it contained Grandma's belongings. His letter to Rose was beautiful and sad, and it gave her new heart, for it showed her that she was not entirely alone, that she was not forgotten.

Mère Jean let Rose open the box in her private office opposite the dining hall and left her by herself to see what it contained. It held many things that she recognized and others that were new to her. Among the familiar were Grandma's rosary and Bible, her last pair of beaded moccasins, with only a small hole in each heel, and a yellow envelope containing documents of birth and baptism and marriage. There was also a roll of drawings that Rose had colored over the years. She looked in vain for the partridge stone that Tchibi had once given her for Christmas, and for the round quartz stone, the loon-star that had been the centerpiece of the garden, but she realized that Fr. Andrei could not have known their value.

The unfamiliar items were few in number. One of these was a ring of pale gold, so thin as to be almost a wire. Another was a silver medal that had a face on it, a man with a crown on his head, and a bar that said *The Somme*. A third thing was a dented cigarette lighter, a piece of gray metal embedded in the dent. In addition, there was a gold coin with another crowned head on it, that said *George V Rex*. Finally, there was an envelope that contained photographs.

These were black and white, and yellowing, some of them stained with water droplets that had dried long ago.

In one picture Rose recognized Grandma's face, though her hair was black. She was standing beside a lake, by a tangle of fish nets draped between two lodgepole pines. There was a wind, because the nets billowed and Grandma's dress was blowing sideways, revealing her shins above rubber boots. She wore a white kerchief on her head and a heavy old sweater. She was not bent. Her shoulders were wide, and her hands dangled down by her sides. She was looking at Rose across thirty-five years or more, with the large eyes of a woman in her twenties, a thin woman, a hard worker, her face beautiful but already lined, her skin dark, darker than Rose ever remembered it. Behind her on a pebbled beach was an upturned canoe, a shotgun propped against it. In the foreground a human shadow stretched toward Grandma, the shape of the one who had taken the photograph.

In another, a man stood beside Grandma with his arm around her shoulder. He was much taller than she. She held a baby in her arms. Her face was gazing at it with a look that Rose knew well—the wave of warmth which had always banished her fears. On the reverse was printed *Mary & me, Threefinger Lake, 1921*.

In another picture there was a log church, and beyond it the shape of the trading post at Threefinger. *Burned in 1923*.

There were several others:

Grandma picking blueberries on the skull beside the stump of a huge pine tree. Her belly was very large. *Mary, July, 1922, Threefinger Lake, Ont.*

A black dog with a white spot on its nose, sitting on its haunches with a grouse lying at its feet. *Sergeant.*

After this were more photographs of dogs and groups of soldiers.

The face of a smiling baby in a cradle, swaddled in native fashion. *Oliver, d. winter, 1922.*

There were two more babies in other pictures—*Hugh* and *Ethel,* with the dates of their burials, 1923 and 1924, the word *influenza* under one. Finally, a small, sweet Indian face, a bundled papoose. *Mary Junior, b. 1925.*

There was a very old photograph of a stone house on a hill surrounded by rows of trees and fields in which there were many sheep. In front of it two people stood, a man with a white beard and a woman in a long black dress. On the back: *Our place, Berkshire, 1913, Mother and Father.*

A young man in a military uniform. *Ned, paid the supreme sacrifice, Passchendaele, 12 October 1917. My beloved brother.*

A young man with an unsmiling face standing by the ramp of a great ship. He was dressed in a tight fitting suit and carried a small suitcase in one hand. His eyes were strained as he gazed at the camera. *Liverpool, Sept., 1919, leaving on the SS Empress of Canada.* Rose looked deep into the eyes of the young man, but no falling-into-seeing was ever possible with photographs, though she knew he would soon stand by a northern lake with his arm around Grandma, staring down at a baby he would bury the following winter.

These, then, were her ancestors—her white ancestors. It struck Rose that they were a part of her, and yet she knew almost nothing about them. Why had Grandma never shown her these pictures? And why did Grandma have an Ojibwe name, if she had married the man from Berksher? She looked into the envelope that contained documents and found the marriage paper. In the signature section Grandma's name was printed Mary Wâbos followed by an X. Beside it was the signature of a man, but the last name was scribbled over with pen strokes, leaving only the first name—Kyle. In other documents, his family name was also scribbled or torn out.

Rose pondered this for many minutes, until it came to her

that Grandma might have wanted to break the thread that connected Rose to a part of her past. Or perhaps the man named Kyle had done it. If so, why had he done it? Had he wanted to forget where he had come from, the land where people killed other people? Was Berksher a place of great evil? His face was haunted by it. Rose, straining with all her might to fall-into-seeing, understood finally that *he* was not evil, only hurt by something evil that had happened to him, for his eyes were a little like Tchibi's before he found his courage.

In another envelope, fat and bound by a red cord, she found a packet of yellow newspaper clippings. Each of them was a poem, each was written by a person who called himself Anonymous.

Rose held the clippings one by one to the light of the window. She read them slowly, hunching over the harder words, mouthing the letters carefully. Their dates, written across the margins in purple script, spanned a period from 1918 to 1919. There were words about "the clash of men's arms" and "incarnadine wounds" and "the sea of mud". One, titled "Cain in Berkshire", spoke of "a barter of medallions for sons, the flow of blood on chalk-stone runs, they wish me dead for I have fled, no more to battle armor wed."

She heard the report of guns, and geese toppled out of the sky like falling stars hissing into the steel waters by the edge of the lake, their long cries trailing down until the splash echoed and reechoed across the many waters. Then she saw in her mind disemboweled rabbits, and sparrows falling from their nests into the jaws of foxes and wolverines. She saw all falling things and wondered why the world was full of this falling. She saw the indignity of death and the terrible and greater indignity of the *neshiwed*-spirit that tempted men to take up the ways of death and drove them to roam ever after through the ultimate places searching for forgetfulness, though the mark of the *neshiwed* was within them.

236

Rose's heart thumped. If this was true of her grandfather, then a little of the *neshiwed* had come down to her through his blood. She quickly scraped Grandma's things into the box and ran with it to the darkened chapel. There she knelt down at the communion rail and yearned upward toward the tabernacle, where the Beating Heart always waited for her.

"O Jesus-Manito, I did not know this thing about myself, I did not know the *neshiwed* was in my blood. Is there a cup of it, or a drop of it, in me?"

Io! It hurt to think of it.

"Ay! Ay!" she cried, remembering the time she had stabbed the picture of Euphrasia.

Then the light of his presence comforted her and told her to be at peace, for the spirit of the *neshiwed* that is passed through the blood is cleansed by the waters of baptism. This was a great relief, though she cried and prayed for the soul of her grandfather who had no name, who might even now be hurting in the purifying fire because the sins of his youth may have been many and the voice of the *neshiwed* strong in his ears, and if he had obeyed it, he might still be far from the great singing. Thus she took another soul onto her back, and the weight of him was great.

That autumn was milder than usual and the heavy snows did not arrive until mid-November. In the weeks preceding, it had rained incessantly during the days, alternating with freezing nights when all the world became a sea of ice. Because of the danger of slipping, and the more imminent danger of sheets of lethal ice sliding from the roof, the children were confined to the building.

On Saturday mornings, Rose resumed her painting and drawing classes with Sister Madeleine but was often to be found with her elbows on the windowsill of the art room, staring out at the drizzle and mist.

"What are you looking at, *ma chérie*?" Sister would ask, stroking her fingertips along the girl's spine, her heart contracting whenever she touched a cruel buckle.

"Strawberries", Rose said.

"*Ah, bon*, why don't you make a picture of them? *Voici*, here are the pinks and reds, so many, many hues. And green for the leaves, white for the strawberry blossom. Come, give it a try."

"No, thank you, Sister."

"You are sad? About the *Grandmaman*?"

"Yes."

"You are thinking of her?"

"Yes. I am thinking of the strawberries she made into jam. And the blueberry and the bog-berry and partridge-berry. For the partridge-berry you need much sugar."

"The partridge-berry is like the strawberry, *non*?"

"No, it is like a drop of blood. It is the *binemin*."

"It is your favorite?"

"It is my favorite to *see*. The strawberry is my favorite to *taste*."

"*Ah, c'est bon*, but it is impossible to have the strawberries in winter. So we make a picture of it to remember us by."

"Sister?" Rose turned to her with a thought sparking in her eyes. "We eat strawberry ice cream in winter, don't we?"

"Yes, but that is for Christmas and Easter only."

"Could we get some today?"

Sister pursed her lips and furrowed her brow. "I think not, Rose, because it would be a special privilege, and we cannot have favorites here, for the other girls would be jealous."

"Could we buy some at a store in Thunder Bay?"

"*Oui*, I suppose we could, but I have no money and you have no money, and I do not think Mère Jean would give us any. Such a thing is not done."

"But I do have money. I have a gold coin that my grandmother gave to me."

238

Sister's eyebrows flew up, and her hands fluttered.

"*Ah, oui?*" she gasped in astonishment. "But you are rich, Rose!"

Together they giggled.

"*Tiens*, if you wish I shall ask Mère Jean of the Cross to make n exception." She paused. "It is from your *Grandmaman, n'est-e pas*? So, we shall say that it is in memory of her."

Rose skipped in delight.

"But what will you do with it? Will you eat it all at once?" ister teased, wagging her finger.

"No, I will give it to Mrs. Boyle."

"You will give it to Mrs. Boyle?" murmured Sister, com-letely puzzled.

Mrs. Boyle, as everyone knew, was the tyrant of the kitchen, hough her power extended beyond it. Her dangerous glances, er imperious gestures with ladle and cleaver, her lips poised on he brink of inventive cruel remarks all contributed to her im-act on those people foolish enough to cross the border of her ingdom without permission. She was a personage of great au-hority and knew it. Relishing power, she used it.

Any staff member unwise enough to complain about the ood or to contradict her, or who failed to show her proper eference, would learn soon enough the cost of rebellion. From hen on his portion of the pudding would be consistently maller, his fried eggs (slammed down in front of him by a surly ervant of Mrs. Boyle) would be rubbery, or running with iquid albumin, or arrive with yolks broken and mingled. His offee would be lukewarm and not infrequently he would find a ly in his soup.

If he were then reckless enough to say, "Tell Mrs. Boyle here's a fly in my soup!" she would catapult through the kitchen doors, and snarl at him, "Shut yer trap, er everyone'll be wantin' one!"

Few were willing to endure a demolishing stare from th eyes of Mrs. Boyle, who could reduce the bravest of men t quivering uncertainty or ineffectual rage. Those who presse their case beyond the point of no return received a scathin tongue-lashing about "complainers" and "whiners" and th "kitchen budget" and the despicable character of "certai greedy types, I ain't sayin' who, who're ferever pesterin' me fe special privileges".

The young religious brother, the new supervisor of th senior boys, refused to be intimidated, but he did not last long He applied for a transfer after discovering a half-melted cub of chocolate-flavored laxative in his cocoa pudding and under standing why he had spent an inordinate amount of time i the bathroom during the previous month.

It was to her advantage that the priests, the nuns, and the la staff ate in separate dining rooms, the priests remotest of a from the central power source, for their refectory was on th other side of the dining hall, a long way down a side corrido paved in battleship linoleum. It was just within earshot, but fa enough from painful scenes to allow Mrs. Boyle certain person ality changes which she could accomplish in a split second. A all non-priests in the house soon learned, a cougar can becom a wounded kitten at the sound of steps in the hall.

The new rector, who was unable to make sense of th complaints made against her, was in the habit of encouragin people to learn to get along together. Mrs. Boyle was alway exquisitely polite to him. She cultivated the nuns as well. Som of them understood her perfectly, though they did not knov what to do about it. To depose a tyrant such as this and not fa into grave sin was a formidable challenge. They prayed for he dismissal, and in weaker moments the less sanctified of the nun daydreamed about the cook's early demise.

Mrs. Boyle understood them perfectly in turn, played witl their emotions only so far, just short of outright confrontation she smiled grimly at the thought of their prayers, absorbing them effortlessly, as she did everything else, into her vast political system of control. She knew that drinking on the job was a cause for dismissal and had trained herself to drink the cooking sherry only at night, in her private room beside the kitchen. If there were sometimes questions from the bursar about the unusual quantity of this condiment on the monthly purchase orders, his timid inquiries were always deflected by smoldering emanations and abrupt counter-questions regarding the chocolate consumption in the cloister. Besides, said Mrs. Boyle, the French Fathers liked the special sauces, which would be inedible without the sherry.

It was whispered in the parlor that the cook had lost a son in a car accident, and another son was in prison in Kingston penitentiary. There were several children, all scattered. And a husband who had deserted very early on. "*Madame Boyle est une abandonnée*", said Sister Clothilde, with a painful effort to control her damaged mouth. Mère Jean was the most patient with the cook, overlooked her many failings, and frequently counseled the other nuns about charity. Mère Jean of the Cross was Mrs. Boyle's protector, for she knew her whole story, though she never spoke of it.

"What sort of religious are we, my sisters, if we cannot love our enemies?" she once said.

"Then you *admit*, Mère Jean, that Madame Boyle *is* our enemy?" countered indignant Sister Madeleine.

"Only in the sense that anyone who disturbs one's peace is an enemy", Mère Jean replied serenely, her arms folded within the cuffs of her habit, "Thus, she is doubly in need of our kindness."

When Mère Jean granted permission, Rose went with Sister Madeleine in the staff car to the grocery store downtown in Thunder Bay. Never in her life had she seen such a variety of foods. Filled with wonder, she walked from aisle to aisle shaking her small head in disbelief.

"Close your mouth, Rose, it is unladylike", said Siste Madeleine.

In a freezer box Sister located a large-size tub of strawberr ice cream, and Rose handed her the gold coin to pay fo it. She felt a little pain in parting with the coin, for it ha belonged to Grandma and was very old, with the picture of king on it.

"*La crème-glacée* is expensive", Sister said with a doubting look as they approached the sales counter. "Are you sure, *ma petite?*"

"Yes", Rose replied in a small voice.

Later, upon returning to the school, Sister led her to the double doors of the kitchen, braced her shoulders, took a deep breath, and pushed through into the other kingdom.

The eyes of the hired kitchen staff looked up with surprise.

"Where is Madame Boyle?" Sister asked.

"It's her nap time", said a char girl, with a jerk of a thumb.

To the private room of the cook Sister now strode with determination, carrying the tub in her ample arms, Rose tim idly following. She knocked.

"Yer souls t' the divil, ye scullions!" came a dull bellow from within.

"Madame Boyle, it is Sister Madeleine of the Infant Jesus. wish to speak with you, Madame."

"Arra, 'tis the great bleatin' noon and th'Infant Jesus is it Well, the Lord kin come in, if he loiks, but the fat arty kin stay outside."

Sister Madeleine's eyes bulged.

"Madame", she said sharply, rapping on the door with un precedented severity. "You will open the door *immediatement* o I shall be forced to speak with Mère Jean of the Cross about your insolence."

"Insolence is it! Insolence be damned, Oi'll give ye inso lence! Go away an' paint yer purty pictures, ye blimp."

"Madame Boyle, I give you one chance and one only. Open

his door or we shall be forced to discuss the subject of the herry."

"*Chérie, ma chérie?* What is the *chérie*?"

"The drink, Madame, the drink that you take in the secret of our private room, and sometimes not so private. I am disgust, Madame, and I am chagrin, and I am, how you say—*fed up*!"

Sister yelled the final two words, making Rose jump and someone drop a utensil. Silence reigned, and all eyes in the kitchen were turned to the door.

A thumping and grumbling came from within. The door was thrown open to reveal a hot-faced, blowzy woman tugging at her sleeves as a prize fighter might, chin down on her chest, brows beetling in a single line, her mouth cocked at a dangerous angle. She was breathing heavily. The smell of alcohol wafted outward.

"Wadderya want, ye smarmy noon?"

"You have a visitor", said Sister in tones of righteous indignation. "An *orpheline*."

"Wot in the hell is an *orpheline*?" snarled Mrs. Boyle.

"This", declared Sister, her eyes slitted as she stepped aside to reveal Rose, "is an *orpheline*. A child without *maman* or *papa*."

Mrs. Boyle said nothing, scowling down at the little Indian girl.

"And woi would the orpheline be visitin' the loiks o' me?" he said sarcastically.

"Because," Sister said, "she asked to see you."

"Asked to see me?" Mrs. Boyle growled in a threatening one. "Is it a young whiner, is it? Is it wantin' somethin' special, is it? Well it won't be tuggin' at these heartstrings, Oi kin promise ye. Get out!"

"*Non*, Madame, we do not get out. She brings you a gift."

Mrs. Boyle snorted, but the snort was interrupted by a dawn of genuine surprise. Her lips began to tremble, possibly with age.

Suddenly her shoulders sagged, and a great sigh whistled from her chest.

"A gift?"

"*Oui*, a gift."

"Why?"

"I do not know, Madame. Will you give her a minute of your time?"

Flushing red, casting a glance over her shoulder at the room within, she mumbled, "Oll right. But only a minute." She wheeled, trudged back inside, and dropped into an armchair. At her feet were a brass Scottie dog and a single red silk shoe.

Sister prodded Rose's back, forcing her inside the room. She put the tub of ice cream into the girl's arms and withdrew, closing the door behind her.

When Rose was alone with the cook, she wished that she had not come. Then she looked into the eyes of the frightening old woman and fell (a little) into seeing. And what she saw made her take a few steps forward.

The eyes were staring at Rose, perplexed, yet also half staring at the floor.

"Wot is it ye got t'say t'me, girl?" the woman said in a little bark that was not really as dangerous as it sounded.

Rose knelt in front of her and put the tub of ice cream on the cook's lap.

"Wot is this?"

"It's for you, Mrs. Boyle," Rose whispered in a trembling voice. "It's strawberry ice cream."

"Did the noons put ye up t'this?" the cook asked suspiciously.

"No, Missus."

"They gave ye the money for it, then?"

"No, it was my own money that my Grandma sent me when she died."

"Doid, is it? Then yer really an orfin?"

Rose nodded.

Suddenly Mrs. Boyle began to cry. At first it was a watering that seeped into her red eyes, then a spilling over, then a roaring sob.

"How did ye know?"

But Rose did not know. She shook her head.

"How did ye know?" Mrs. Boyle said again, staring at the ice cream.

"I do not know anything, Mrs. Boyle", Rose trembled.

"But how could ye know 'tis me Danny boy's day, dead on his black afternoon these eighteen years?"

Rose saw a car exploding and a soul rising into flames of purifying fire, but this flash of seeing was cut short.

"Who told ye? Give me the truth, now. Was it the Mudder John, then?"

"No one told me. I saw a car on fire."

Mrs. Boyle spurted more tears. "You can't o' seen it, for ye re only a choild, girl. He doid before ye was born."

"And a soul going up", Rose whispered.

"Up, not down, ye say?"

"It seemed like up to me."

Then Mrs. Boyle collapsed and gave full vent to her grief. Rose scrambled forward and put her hands on the woman's knees, looking into her face. She began to cry with her, though gently, for the weight of grief was great upon Mrs. Boyle. When she had collected herself, the cook dried her eyes on the eeves of her housecoat, and looked down at the girl.

"It is meltin', and awrful cold on me legs. Put it on the oor."

Rose obeyed.

"Oi'm a ridicerlus creature, to be sure", said Mrs. Boyle in a ttle voice. "You won't be tellin' people about me blubberin'?"

"I won't, Mrs. Boyle."

"An' lookit you, blubberin' too. Wot a fine pair we are. Would you loik a scoop o' that ice cream?"

"No, it's for you."

"For me? All of it, then, for me? You're a strange orfin t'b sure, fer never have I knowed a nipper t'be turnin' down the ic cream."

Rose dried her eyes.

"It was Danny's favorite, the strawberry. Oi was always pack in' the stuff into him on the birthdays, and nothin' else woul make him happy, he was that spoilt after his Dad took off o me, but you wouldn't be knowin' nothin' about that, to be sure wouldya?"

Open-mouthed, Rose shook her head.

"Come here, girl", said Mrs. Boyle, pulling Rose onto he huge lap. "Fer I haven't felt a noice choild on me lap in ages an ages. Six Oi raised an' six are gone, one way or t'other."

Rose sat uncomfortably on the lap, though she thought it fel nice and that Mrs. Boyle was really a very kind person after al The old woman put her arms around her and held her close.

"Poor little defective!" she murmured through her tears "Poor tykey, poor nipperkin with such an awrful hump on ye back!"

She rocked Rose for a long time.

Eventually the woman shook herself and said in a quie voice, "The beans. Those scullies will be burnin' the beans. O hafter go, girl."

Rose slipped to the floor. Mrs. Boyle stood up with groans

"Oi've enjoyed our little visit—wot's yer name, choild?"

"Rose."

"Rose, is it? Well, you'll come back an' visit me again, won you, Rose?"

"I will, Mrs. Boyle."

And so she did.

At Christmas, Mrs. Boyle went away on a visit to a plac called Kingston, so Rose was not able to give her the picture o a shamrock that Sister Madeleine suggested she make for th cook. But under the Christmas tree in the sisters' parlor there was a package for Rose, containing cookies and a pair of knitted pink mittens with red strawberries stitched on them.

In the winter that followed, Mrs. Boyle became more and more good, and the bursar noticed that the Fathers' sauces needed less and less sherry. Mère Jean noticed that Mrs. Boyle snarled only rarely, and the kitchen help were occasionally caught in the act of smiling for no reason whatsoever. It was the beginning of a tearful lavishness which was the first fruit of genuine repentance. Mysteriously, the egg yolks began to stand up like bulging puppy eyes, the coffee became strong and hot, the puddings no longer provoked diarrhea, and the cuts of the pie grew more than fair; indeed, they were generous. In this way, even former enemies were disarmed without a struggle, for Mrs. Boyle had forgiven them with as much absoluteness as she had once hated them.

Her one partiality was for the "orfin" in the senior girls, to whom she slipped little boxes of chocolates from time to time. Rose always passed these around in the dorm or slipped them in turn to Sister Madeleine on Saturday mornings. Between the cook and the art teacher there remained a cool armistice, though Mrs. Boyle made her efforts, as did Sister Madeleine.

"Madame Boyle has made the peace, *Deo gratias*", murmured the latter during recreation one evening, as she put the final piece into a picture puzzle. "It is, as they say, *about time!*"

"She has suffered, *ma Soeur*", said Mère Jean, peering through her bifocals at a difficult stitch of embroidery.

"*Oui*", admitted Sister Madeleine in a casual tone. "But I think Madame Boyle has discovered a great secret of the universe."

"What secret is this?" Mère Jean smiled.

"There are wars you cannot win."

"And other wars that you can win, Madeleine, but in the winning you lose everything. One might even win the whole world, and pacify it, and earn the hatred of everyone. By the same token, there are wars that you lose and in the losing win everything."

Sister Madeleine squinted suspiciously at Mère Jean, wondering if her superior was administering a veiled rebuke.

In the spring, the cook offered her letter of resignation and was gone by the end of the school year, taking with her a small pension, a trunk full of mementos, the brass Scottie, the red silk shoe, and an embroidered Sacred Heart with fire and thorns around it, which the little defective girl stitched for her as a good-bye present.

Mrs. Boyle took up residence in a boarding house that offered a majestic view of brooding Thunder Mountain across the bay. She had adopted several prayer devotions, abandoned all cooking save what was necessary for the preservation of life, nursed a bad tempered, three-legged mongrel dog named Long John, whom she had found abandoned on the street, and knitted socks for the schoolchildren. She contented herself in her two rooms, among potted ferns and *patience* plants, piles of *Reader's Digest*, and many brightly-colored crocheted throws.

She entertained a modest stream of visitors who came hesitantly at first, and then with dedication: former inmates of the school, admiring scullery maids, charitable nuns, and a hostage child or two. When discussing her past, she fell into the habit of dwelling fondly on her happy days with "the orfins", and sometimes she would shed a tear. Mère Jean was her most frequent visitor, and Rose was often brought along.

"Do you find time long on your hands, Madame Boyle?" Mère Jean once asked.

"Oi ain't been bored a minute", Mrs. Boyle replied, pointing at a stack of thick tomes under the reading lamp. "Oi'm improvin' me moind. It's the condensed ones they are, with the large print that's good fer me eyes which are fadin', but all the good parts are left in. Duster Evsky is me favorite. Oi loik his Doll's Toy too, with the Warren Peas. It makes yer heart feel grand, loik goin' to the movies, loik *Gone Wit' t' Wind*."

When Rose was fifteen years of age, she graduated from grade six. Also during that year she was confirmed by the local bishop and took the name of Kateri as her sacred name, for she prayed often to the Mohawk saint and loved her with a mysterious love that she told to no one. It seemed to her that she now had a sister of the heart, that she and Tchibi and Kateri were united in a way that needed no meetings on this earth. She divided her offerings for Tchibi and Mrs. Boyle and felt that now she could know no greater happiness, for her life was clearly not a no-thing, but a something, though its meaning was hidden from all save the Heart that never ceased beating within the tabernacle.

Of Tchibi she thought a great deal, longing for a sight of the sweet-green fire in his eyes, wondering sometimes why he did not reply to her notes. She understood that his not-writing was a part of his not-speaking way. Though he had been released from the prison of total silence, he was never one who looked for words when other kinds of speech were possible. But no other kinds were now possible between them, she reminded herself. Why then did he not write? She knew that he could. He had written the little note to her when he lived at the school and took her through the tunnel to the palace of the moon. That he did not reply to her letters hurt her, though she converted this additional suffering into an offering for him.

She wrote to Fr. Andrei at least twice a year, Christmas and Easter, and he always replied with wise and warm words. He asked her to pray earnestly for Binemin Edzo because her little brother no longer attended Mass. Father told her that he saw Binemin now and then, passing in the village, often with Kinoje, or with some other young people who had become attached to the medicine man. It worried the priest greatly. During this past winter, the boy had moved to another place with Kinoje's clan, no one knew where. It was rumored that they had gone south to the larger communities of the Anishinâbe, where the old religion was reviving, the *matchi-manito* way that the pagans denied was a darkness-way, though it was. Then Father wrote to say that he too was going away to a place in the mountains far to the west. He would never forget her, he said. He would write to her from there, and he would pray daily throughout his life for the rose of the Ojibwe.

All of this was a losing-pain, a letting-go-of-things-pain, for now that Father and Tchibi were gone from the place of her birth there was no living thread tying her to it. In the church graveyard Grandma's bones were buried, but that was the only binding-thing left. Perhaps in the yard of the ruined cabin by Crazyman River the garden that she and Tchibi had made still remained. On the grayest days of winter she liked to recall the water cascading from the white stone over the lip of rock into the rainwater pool, making the sound of small bells. But she did not often turn to this memory, for it contained an equal mixture of pain and joy, as the mixing of blue and yellow made a third thing, a green which was sometimes the color of spring and sometimes the color of bile.

9

When she was sixteen years of age, Rose graduated from grade seven. During the winters, she lived in the dorm with the other girls. Though she was the oldest, she was still the shortest. Sometimes girls teased her, but she did not mind and soon they stopped. The ones who teased hardest often became her closest friends.

Each summer, when the students left for their homes, she moved upstairs to the sisters' cloister and became one of them again. It was as if she were always one of them now, and the ten months that she spent in the dorm merely a private joke that she and the sisters played. In autumns, when she returned to the dorm, she was granted certain freedoms that were not granted to, or desired by, the others. She was permitted to spend long hours in the chapel each night after lights-out. She was, as well, the sacristan, a task which gave her joy. It was a great privilege to fill the gold ciborium with the small white hosts that would become the Body of Christ at *Anamessikewin* and to fill a cruet with the wine that would become his Blood.

Io! Sometimes it was too much, the beauty and the stillness of it in the glow of the chapel, when the electric lights were turned off, and all that remained were the golden glass vigil candles and the red tabernacle lamp and the invisible light that shocked her sweetly like a rising sun when she knelt before it.

Io, she said to herself, *why do the others not desire to be here with him?*

She was (just a little) grateful that they did not desire it as she did, for it meant she was often alone with him, he who was the burning core of perfect love.

Io! Like the great pine that was split like lightning, he burned, he suffered, he died, he fell into the earth as all things fell in the great and continuous falling which was this life. He fell down with her, with all men, down into the darkness. Then on the day of *Pak*, on the day of forth-bursting, the impossible day, he rose. Then he went up, he went up beyond the stars.

He went up but remained among them, his heart a sweet-fire above all sweet fires, heating the cold, dark, barren earth, and any cold, dark, barren hearts who would come to him.

He does not force himself upon us, she thought to herself. No, for Love does not force.

It gave her joy to bend (when no one was watching) and put her face onto the cold tiles of the chapel floor, and whisper words of love to him, feeling the tiles grow warm by her breath.

What was this thing that happened between them, whenever she bent before him?

Once, when Sister Madeleine caught her doing this, the nun fluttered her hand on her breast, saying, "*Ah, mon Dieu, regarde cette petite adoratrice de votre coeur!*"

Sister cried tears and made Rose get up off the floor and kneel in the pew.

"That is for the advanced, *ma chérie*", she whispered, brushing the dust from Rose's cheeks. "Little bird, you must not fly too far too fast, for you might fall."

But this was not an obedience-thing, this was a friend-thing, a loving-thing, a caution like the warnings in winter when the sisters scolded all the girls about walking beneath the roof eaves from which sheaves of ice did sometimes slide, plunging thirty feet to the earth, where they could slice off a little head.

"Be content that you are small", Mère Jean said, smiling at Rose when she heard of the pray-bending. "*Notre Seigneur*, he desires your love, as you desire his. But he knows that you are little. You need not give him *les grandes expressions*."

But it gave Rose great joy to bend before the presence.

"I like to give to him", she replied.

"*L'adoration*", Mère Jean said. "Worship, it is named in English, is the *langue de l'amour*. It is the gesture of love. This must come from within, Rose, lest it remain only a shell, a beautiful shell, but empty."

How wise was Mère Jean de la Croix.

Mère Jean said that all men were created for worship.

For to worship was to love.

And to love was to worship.

And to have this was to have everything.

So, Rose thought to herself, echoing and adapting from Mère Jean, *to worship is to become what you were intended to be from the beginning, before the great falling of all things into the cold and darkness.*

In obedience to Mère Jean, she did not often bend, for it hurt her back terribly and retarded its correction. In obedience she made cloth dolls for the small ones in junior girls. By her own choice, Rose had limited herself to a little dish of vanilla ice cream at Easter, though not at Christmas, when she had a big bowl of strawberry. But once, Sister Madeleine scolded her for not accepting more ice cream at Easter, told her that a good Catholic girl knows how to celebrate the great feasts. "Obedience is the better sacrifice," she had said, "and *ma chérie, voilà*, here is a second bowl with the chocolate sprinkles on top and a maraschino cherry." Then Rose obeyed, with pleasure.

During the three years after taking the brace upon herself, Rose felt it shaping and reshaping her, always with pain, except on Sundays when it faded to almost nothing. Several times the buckles and straps were changed, and the leather pads enlarged. Sister Clothilde made a new uniform for her that spread like a camp tent; it was loose and billowed, though it was navy blue, not canvas white. It had a cloth belt also and a pale blue linen blouse. Sister embroidered small white roses and tiny birds on each collar.

"*Bineshi*", Sister said with her twisted lips.

Bineshi was a word like Binemin, but this was only likeness
sound, for the meanings were apart.

Tiny bird and partridge-berry.

White wing and blood droplet.

Names were poems. All words—except evil words—con
tained the many poems, as the deep ice of lakes containe
masses of water waiting for the swelling sun. The deepest wor
was in the heart, where the sun always throbbed as pulsin
blood, the words thawing and running like the many water
overflowing from rainwater pools, spilling into rivulets, int
creeks, into rivers, into lakes, and from there into greater river
and lakes until all waters came finally to the sea, which sang an
danced and laughed beneath the unsetting sun.

When she was seventeen years of age, Rose began to conside
her future. It had seemed to her that she would always live witl
the sisters, but now she wondered if she might do so as one c
them—as a nun. She did not speak of this, for it might hav
been an arrogant thought, a pride-way, for they were very grea
women and beloved by God in a way that all the other beloved
of the world could not be. Everyone was beloved—all people—
but there were some who flew up into the heavens and som
who swam in the deep waters and others who merely walke
across the stone earth. More and more she mused on images c
her future life: Rose in the black and brown habit of the Orde
Rose with a large rosary hanging from her belt, Rose peekin
out from the cave of the white wimple, a joy-fire hidden dee
inside. Rose being a mother to the orphelines who would com
to them, who always came, for there was a constant source.

"Io! I dare not ask it", she cried once in chapel when th
longing became too great. She almost feared to make such
request because she felt too small and unworthy of the religiou
life.

So she made an act of faith, returned to silence, and waited for him to reveal his will.

The making of pictures was a consolation, because time and the several forms of pain disappeared whenever she painted or threw clay into lumps that warmed in her hands and flowed and shaped themselves into the faces of love.

Yet the faces that looked at Rose had come from her. It was confusing, but Mère Jean once said it was not necessary to understand everything, for it was all contained within the shaping hands of love.

"*Tiens, le Bon Dieu* is a potter", Sister Madeleine said.

"And a painter", said Rose who was dreamily staring out the windows of the art room at a sunset.

"Yes, and a singer", said Sister, who was frowning at the stainless steel sink as she washed the drying clay bits from her hands.

"And the poem maker," said Rose, "as poems are frozen inside all words, like ice waiting for the sun."

Sister glanced swiftly at her and paused.

"*Oui, c'est comme ça.* A little bit like that. He is the *Artiste*, the Maker of all things."

"The world is beautiful", Rose sighed, tears streaming down her cheeks as she watched the globe of fire sink below the bay beside brooding Thunder Mountain.

And Sister cast a worried look at her.

In her nineteenth year, she graduated from grade eight. That was a good year, for the doctor told Mère Jean that Rose had stopped growing and that the brace could be removed permanently.

"She will always be deformed", he said.

Mère Jean shot him a look. "Then it has been a waste?" she said, controlling her anger.

"No, not exactly. Of course we don't really know, do we,

what would have happened without the appliance. Still, it is no longer helpful."

"She may remove it?"

"Yes, she may remove it. We've done what we could."

"Thank you, Doctor", Mère Jean said formally, standing. "Let us go, Rose."

"Good-bye, Sister", said the doctor, failing as always to speak to Rose. But Sister for once did not hear him and left through the clinic door with great dignity, holding Rose's hand in her own.

That night in the parlor there was a little party to celebrate. All the sisters gathered around Rose as she sat among them as a princess, delighting in the small sandwiches cut into heart and diamond shapes. The tea was flavored with *bergamot*, which a sister's relative had sent from France. To sweeten the tea there was honey from a small clay pot. They told jokes and kissed Rose's cheeks many times, and toasted her liberation with a single glass of white wine for each. The wine made Rose's head swim, though it was not much more than a thimbleful. How the sisters giggled that evening, all except Mère Jean, who smiled her usual smile but did not laugh.

The big black leather brace sat on a footstool, ugly enough to make some sisters shiver. In a fit of impatience, or perhaps under the influence of wine, Sister Madeleine leaped to her feet at a climactic moment and kicked the brace heartily so that it toppled end over end before collapsing with a tinkle of buckles on the far side of the room.

"*Sale torticolis!*" she cried. "Be gone!"

"*Soeur Madeleine* has become *une exorciste!*" shouted another sister. And the community roared with laughter. All except Mère Jean, who smiled and checked her watch and reminded them that it was time for night prayers.

How light Rose felt, how free! For more than five years she had scarcely been without the brace, and it now felt as if a ortion of her body had been cleaved from her. Only for a few minutes a week, during her shower, had she known this amazing levity, this weightlessness which seemed to pull her upward, as if she were a balloon. She laughed in chapel, which drew the eyes of the sisters and their smiles, for they understood what relief had come to her.

Still, her spine continued to ache, and, without the support of the brace, she was forced to make her muscles work as they had never worked before. This strain caused other, though smaller, pains. She was still bent, but the bending of her flesh was not so severe as to make it impossible to live a normal life. In the bathroom mirror she saw that the base of her neck had sunken into her shoulder bones, and tilted forward a little. Turning sideways, she saw that the brace had left dents in the flesh that covered her ribs, and the skin had been rubbed to the consistency of tough hide. The twist in the track of her spine had made a hump that was disfiguring, but aside from this she felt sure that she could do all that the sisters did. This was good, for she now determined to speak with Mère Jean about entering the Order.

In July, after the students left, Rose went one evening to Mère Jean's office. When they were settled on chairs facing each other across the desk, Rose swallowed hard and spoke of her desire.

A look of joy lit up Mère Jean's face, then was swept aside by subtler look, a caution-way, a worry-way.

"This is a good desire, my Rose, but is it clearly the plan of *le Bon Dieu* for you?"

"I do not know, Mother."

"You are praying very much to know his will, I am certain."

"Yes, I am, Mother."

"A vocation to the religious life is never a question of what one desires, but rather what God desires. It is frequently obscure."

"Does he speak of this desire in one's heart?" Rose asked.

Mère Jean nodded. "Sometimes. For most girls who wish to enter, it is a matter of faith."

"I have faith, Mère Jean", Rose offered timidly.

"Yes, very great faith", Mère Jean said, leaning forward lacing her fingers together. "In this regard, I mean the faith to *try* one's vocation without certainty."

"Like walking into the place of no-where, putting one foot ahead of the other, not knowing if you step on a stone-way or bog-berry swamp and will rise or sink."

"Yes, like that. Although," she smiled, "if one sinks, like Saint Peter in the waves, *le Seigneur* will catch your hand and lift you up."

"Then I may try?"

"It is my great desire that you try, Rose. But the Order has rules. A novice must have good health."

"I am healthy, Mother."

"You bear burdens in your body, my child. It is possible but . . ."

"Then it *is* possible!" Rose cried.

"It is not a decision I can make. I must write to the Mother house. All of us will pray. Then we shall see."

Mère Jean wrote a letter to France. A reply did not come for many months. On Thursday of Holy Week it arrived, a lovely blue envelope stamped with a rooster. When Rose entered Mère Jean's office she saw it lying on the desk and knew that it was the letter they had awaited. The joy she felt was indescribable.

"It has come?" she breathed with ardor.

"Yes, it has come", said Mère Jean. Her eyes, Rose saw, were filled with the answer. They were misted with the sad-sadness.

"They have said no?"

"It is your health, my Rose. The Order is shrinking. Some say it is dying, and most of the sisters are growing old. The

258

Mother General regrets, but she believes we must have novices who are strong, strong enough to meet the demands of the coming times."

Too shocked to feel anything, Rose sat down and stared out the window at a late snowstorm.

"But I *am* strong", she murmured.

"You are strong of spirit, you are *la petite légionnaire*, it is doubtless. This I told the General, but she has discerned otherwise. It is not to be."

Rose bowed her head, fighting the upwelling tears.

"I am sorry, Rose."

"Thank you, Mother", she said, drying her eyes on the sleeve of her uniform. "It is the will of *le Bon Dieu*. It is his way with me."

"He will have another way for you, a better way for his roseflower."

But for the moment Rose could not be consoled. "There is nothing better than to be a sister!" she sobbed.

Mère Jean knelt beside Rose and put her arms around her shoulders.

"Ah, do not cry, *ma petite*. Do not cry—*ah, bon, bon, bon, la tristesse devenue la joie du printemps*. The winter is upon you now, but the spring is coming."

"Io, ay, ay!"

"It is coming, it is coming. Do not fear."

"I am not afraid, Mère Jean. I am filled with the sad-sad, for he does not want me to come close to him."

"*Ma petite*, you do not yet understand his ways, for his mind is not our mind—"

"But his heart is like our hearts—"

"*Oui*, this is true. Yet he sees farther and higher, and all the horizons of the world are in his eyes, and all the future is in his hand, like a little rose petal in his palm."

"Or a stone."

"*Comme ça*. A round stone, like the earth, and all the live that are upon it, each in its path, each with its *mission*. You cannot yet see his plans for you. They may bring you closer to him than we are to him."

"This I do not understand, Mother."

Mère Jean patted Rose's hands. "In time you will understand and you will thank him for *la petite blessure*, the little wounding. After this will come the great blessing. This I know, for I have never seen him fail in it."

But the great blessing did not seem to come. On Easter Sunday more bad news arrived. On that day Mrs. Boyle died in her room at the boarding house. This was a shock, for Mrs. Boyle was eternal. None of the sisters seemed relieved by the demise of their former cook, as they might have been only a few years before. Neither were they unduly stricken. They were reserved and philosophical.

"It is a mercy", said Sister Madeleine. "She suffered so much. She was lonely."

"But what is to become of *le pauvre chien, le* Long John?" Sister Clothilde asked.

"We will take him in. He will chase the rats", said a practical sister.

"On three legs he will chase the rats!" huffed Sister Madeleine, causing some of the less sensitive sisters to laugh.

"Let us go to the chapel and pray for her soul, *mes soeurs*", said Mère Jean. Which they all did without complaint.

The entire staff of the school attended the funeral at a church in town, followed the hearse in the staff cars to the burial, and from there they went to the reception. The ladies of the parish served coffee and sandwiches and spoke at length about the saintliness of Mrs. Boyle, who had done so much good for the underprivileged and the shut-ins. Representing the family there was only an unshaven young man in rough but clean

lothes who was Mrs. Boyle's son. The sisters surrounded
im and offered many condolences. He stared at them as if they
rightened him, but this was not a new experience for the sis-
ers, and so it did not prevent them from plying him with many
uestions. They told him stories about his mother that made
im smile, shyly at first, then with broad grins that lacked a few
eeth. Finally, they coaxed from him his personal account, as
ffortlessly as if he were their own long-lost child. They learned
hat he was working in Kingston, after a prolonged engagement
n what he called, vaguely, "a government institution".

"Poor Mr. Boyle is an *ex-con*", whispered Sister Madeleine to
ister Clothilde. After bathing him in sympathetic looks, they
luttered around him chirping about the prayers that they would
ay for his "vocation in life".

Svend the boiler man attended the funeral in a suit, hat in
and, and left wordlessly after the sandwiches. He took Long
ohn to live with him in his cottage behind the wood shed.
Long John was happy there, it was plain to see, and Svend was a
nore pleasant man because of it, the sisters noted, and the
quirrels rummaging in the trash cans declined in number.

Two weeks after the funeral the great blessing came. A lawyer
elephoned to Mère Jean and asked for a meeting. At parlor that
ight, Mère Jean informed the sisters and Rose that Mrs. Boyle
ad won a certain amount of money in the Irish Sweepstakes a
ear ago. A good deal of it had been spent, she said, but the
isters had been mentioned in the will. There was a sizable gift,
nough to paint the school and replace the boiler. Moreover,
Mrs. Boyle had stated in the will that "a little something"
hould go to "the orfin".

All eyes now turned upon Rose, and the sisters' faces broke
pen into smiles and exclamations of delight.

Mère Jean came to Rose and embraced her.

"It is a formidable gift", she whispered. "You see how *le Bon
Dieu* never fails."

"What is the gift?" Rose asked. In her weakest moment, succumbing to a most selfish temptation, she had hoped for new mittens, or the brass Scottie, or the red shoe.

"Do you remember how I told you he has another way for you, a better way for his roseflower?"

Rose nodded.

"It has come. This is a doorway that opens; a path leads from it. The gift is financial. It is a means for you to go out into the world."

"But I do not want to go into the world."

"Yes, at this moment you feel that the school is all there is, but it will not always be so."

"Do you *want* me to go?"

"*Mais certainement pas!*" Mère Jean scolded. "You may stay with us as long as you wish."

"But not as a sister."

"I regret . . . *Tiens*, let us not speak of that. The gift is one of money. It will make studies possible for you."

"Then I will study here. You will keep the money."

"No, that is not my meaning. A year or two or three and you will be finished with high school."

"After that I will ask you for a job. I will work in the kitchen, I will be a char. I would be so happy there—"

"Ah, *non-non-non!*" Mère Jean murmured. "Rose, God has given you a treasure, a talent which must not be buried. You are, I believe—and Soeur Madeleine believes also—an artist."

But *la vie de l'artiste*, thought Rose, recalling the warning Sister Madeleine had once given her, was a feast of dangerous satisfaction, easily leading to deadly pride—*la fière arrogance*.

"No, Mother", she trembled. "I cannot. I do not want to become arrogant."

Mère Jean patted her arm. "Let the good Lord deal with *l'arrogance*. He is good at that." She smiled. "He will not fail you."

"*Chérie*", said Sister Madeleine, who drew up beside them. "I ask you a difficult question."

Rose and Mère Jean looked at her curiously.

"Tell me, *petite*, who is the proud girl? Is it the girl who goes out into the world to give it a treasure? Or is it the girl who spurns the gift of *le Bon Dieu* because it might be *dangereux*?"

This was confusing.

"Enough," said Mère Jean clapping her hands together. "Enough for one night. Now it is time for Compline."

Later, in a private meeting, Mère Jean told Rose that the gift was five thousand dollars. A small fortune, she said. This was a legacy that must be used wisely, she cautioned. Rose was now of legal age to take the money and do what she liked with it, but if she wished, Mère Jean would go with her to a bank in the city and open an account in the name of Rose Wâbos.

"Then, when you are ready, when you have prayed and listened carefully, and we have watched and waited for the opening doorways, then and only then should you begin to spend it."

"I want to give it to you", Rose said.

Mother squeezed her hands gently and looked into her eyes with emotion.

"That is a beautiful thought, my daughter. It is because your heart is not attached to any thing. But I cannot accept. Madame Boyle has provided very well for our needs. *Non*, the gift is for your future."

When Rose knelt before the Presence in the chapel, she asked him about this. What future did he desire for her? Why did he not desire that she stay close to him, here with her sisters and Mère Jean?

Had she disappointed him so much? Had she ceased to love as he had showed her? Had the seed of the spirit of *neshiwed* sprouted in her when, upon learning of Mrs. Boyle's death, she had yearned for a pair of mittens, or a brass Scottie, or a red shoe? The smallness of what she had desired did not change the nature of what was in her—the grasping for things that were not hers. Oh, it was shameful! But she had confessed it the same day, and the peace that returned with absolution had made her think that nothing was changed between them, that the Beating Heart loved her as much as ever.

Why, then, these new movements? This falling-way, this losing-way? It was hurrying toward her, eating up time and space, like a storm on the horizon bearing with it the threat of thunder, the thunder rumbling its cruel words louder and louder, *you must go, you will go, you are cast out from this place into the cold dark barren lands*.

She prayed long that night, with cries and beseeching, for if the not-speaking flow of love was impossible for the moment, she could always use the language of spoken words. But even this he would not answer.

Unable to bear the anguish of this inexplicable silence, she spoke to Mère Jean about it in confused phrases.

"It is the little desolation, Rose", Mère Jean explained. "It is normal. He loves you no less, but he has permitted a time when you must grow. If you always have consolations, you will grow a little, but not far. In the desolations he takes you farther."

"I do not understand. It does not sound like love to me."

Mère Jean smiled sadly. "That is true, it does not sound, nor does it feel. But it is. In time you will understand."

But it was very difficult to understand. Rose grieved, as if someone near had died. She felt the emptiness she had known in the wake of other departures. Then she struggled against a new foe—despondency. Day after day she went as usual to the chapel, and day after day the feeling of absence grew. She cried no more tears, for she was moving beyond the out-bursting and the overflowing. Yet in all of this she continued to offer her sufferings for others.

There were times during the year that followed when Rose felt the return of consolations, the sweet-fire, the light-fire, and even on Easter Sunday a burst of the song-fire. This lifted her heart greatly and reassured her that she had not fallen from the hands of his love. Still, it was brief, and she was returned to the world of everyday things on the following Monday. The world was still beautiful, which she took as a sign that he was everywhere within it. Though he was not *it*, he had made it, and it belonged to him, and he guided it and fed it and hovered over it, as he hovered over all things.

After Easter the consolations did not return; they seemed to have dried up like an unwatered garden. Rose asked Kateri to help her, and she did. The helping took the form of a new kind of peace. It was the peace of calm acceptance, accepting that she was a smaller beloved than all the other beloveds, yet still a beloved. And the lover was so great that even to be least in his eyes was a treasure more vast that one could hold. She learned to send the beam of her love to the Beating Heart regardless of his response. She told him that she would never cease to love him, for he was beautiful beyond all imagining; and she had tasted his fire, and it was good. If he chose to keep it from her, this was good also; she thanked him for it, because it gave her a chance to show him that she loved him for himself, and not for his gifts to her.

And so she grew, and the world widened and deepened in her understanding, and her heart became firmer, like chafed skin under the buckles of restraint, for no longer could she fall-into-seeing or rise-into-singing at will. In fact, never. Yet she knew that she had been blessed as few others had been—to live among sisters who loved her, to live with the freedom to paint and draw and make clay shapes. These were her riches!

Rose felt no affection for the money that lay in a vault in Thunder Bay, waiting for her future. She dreaded it, knowing that it was changing everything, knowing also that it could lead her into the world in a way that she had neither foreseen nor wanted. It was dangerous. It was a tainted thing—Jesus had said so himself.

In Rose's twenty-first year, after all the students went home, Mère Jean said that a thought had come to her about Rose's future. Furthermore, she said, when she had spoken to Sister Madeleine about this thought, the art teacher had been surprised, for the same thought had come to her in recent weeks.

"What is the thought?" Rose asked.

"It has come to us, separately, and with a certain peace, that you might wish to attend an art school."

Rose frowned and shook her head.

"My studies—"

"You have completed the twelfth grade, my dear. You have completed high school."

"Why do I need to go higher?"

"Because you have a responsibility."

"The gift?" Rose said sadly.

"Yes, the gift."

"Is it not possible to use my gift here, with you?"

"*Oui*, it is possible. But I doubt you would be happy."

"I would be very happy."

"Possibly, but if the *Bon Dieu* is calling you to learn more than we can teach you, I think you would not be happy to ignore him."

This was unanswerable.

"Do you want me to go?"

Mère Jean's eyes filled with tears. "*Non*, my child. I do not want you to go. But it is my sense that God thinks otherwise."

"But where would I go, Mother?"

"This brings us to the original thought which has come to Soeur Madeleine and myself. Let us go discuss it with her."

266

In the art room, Sister Madeleine was on hands and knees, scraping dry clay from the floor. She was sweating heavily, red-faced, her voluminous apron thrown over her shoulder. A box of bonbons lay open on the floor beside her. She was chewing.

"Soeur Madeleine", Mère Jean called. "We are here for the consultation. Are we interrupting?"

"Please, interrupt", Sister said, struggling to her feet. "Ah, Rose, it is you."

When they were seated on three wooden stools facing each other, Mère Jean asked Sister Madeleine to describe the thought that had come to them both.

"*Une école des beaux-arts*—an art school", she said gravely. "It is my opinion, Rose, and Mère Jean de la Croix agrees, that there is nothing further you can learn from me."

"This is not true", Rose burst out. "You are a great artist!"

Sister Madeleine tittered; Mère Jean smiled.

"I am not the great artist, Rose. I am—how do you say—*not bad*. I am *okay*. I am making the pretty pictures that decorate the walls. This is not a small thing, yet neither is it a great thing." She turned to Mère Jean for confirmation.

"Rose, we are not blind", said Mère Jean. "Your gift is very great, for to look upon your work, especially the color pastels, is to fall into them. One does not wish to leave them. They live in our minds. All the sisters speak of it."

"It is a miracle!" Sister Madeleine exclaimed. "No one decides to have this power. No school can teach it."

"Then why should I go to a school if it is already within me?" Rose asked.

"Because your gift is uneven. It is *primitif*, it is, how do you say, like a fire in the woods, and it must become a fire within a stove—ah, tsk, my poor *vocabulaire*!"

"I think Soeur Madeleine means to say, Rose, that even the greatest gift needs discipline, training, *la technique*. In the cities are great masters who can teach you what we cannot."

"But why do I need to learn more, if my paintings already please?"

The two nuns looked at her, unable to answer. Silence fell on all three.

Eventually, as if groping for the truth of what she felt in her soul, Mère Jean said, "A great mystery lies at the heart of every life. As one approaches the mystery, one must go reverently and carefully. This is most difficult when one is pondering one's own self, one's *mission* in life. We are your sisters and your mother *en l'esprit*. We love you. But at best all we can offer are our intuitions, flashes of insight. Each person is a *géographie de l'âme*, Rose, an entire universe."

"Is there not a duty," Sister Madeleine cut in, "to give to the world what God has given to you? If you can go farther in life, then you must, for then the harvest will be greater."

"What do you mean, harvest?" Rose asked.

"The good that you will do for the souls who look into your pictures—*non*, who fall into your pictures."

"But falling is—"

"And in the pictures they will find the words that point them to *la géographie de l'amour*. The country of love. The hope. The rising."

"But I am too small."

Both nuns nodded simultaneously.

"*C'est correct*", said Sister Madeleine.

"*Précisément*", said Mère Jean. "Rose, surely you understand this. Surely, you know this is true, for it is the same in the life of prayer."

"To be small is to make more space for him?"

Once again they nodded.

"I do not know. . . ." Rose murmured doubtfully.

The sisters left her alone with her thoughts. When the sound of their footsteps and clinking rosary beads had disappeared down the hall, Rose sat for a while looking up at the walls of the art room, on which many of her pictures were pinned. Some of them were from her first year at the school, eight years ago. Others were recent, and more dated from the years between. If there was a unifying theme in them it was that the earth was afire with beauty, a savage beauty, falling and rising and ever changing into other forms. Birds swam, fish flew, trees danced, the sky breathed. All things moved as the poetry in them thawed.

The pictures of people were insideness pictures, the states of their hearts, their souls, their minds. Their shattering beauty. Grandma and Tchibi as they were, Kateri as she imagined her, Jesus as she saw him with the insideness seeing, not the seeing that is confused by the eyes.

Io, it *was* beautiful, she could not argue with that. Was it not enough to make these! Was there more?

In the chapel she knelt for many hours and sat longer, until light grew in the east windows, and it was time for her to set out the holy things for the *Anamessikiwin*. When the sisters began to arrive for their prayers before Mass, it seemed to Rose that life would always be this way; she would always pray beside them in the golden light, in desolation and consolation, in the safe hands of love, never falling through his fingers, never drifting from the sound of his Beating Heart.

Surely it could not be otherwise. Surely he would not ask such a thing of her, to leave, to go out into the places of nowhere, the dark and barren country where the many *neshiweds* roamed and so many souls fell in the great falling that was the world.

What was he asking of her?

At the great offering, at the elevation of his sacred Body and Blood, she knew.

10

And so, in her twenty-second year of life, Rose Wâbos found herself one September evening standing alone in a rented room on the third floor of a tenement in the great and terrifying city of Toronto. Unlike the land around Thunder Bay, the land around this city was flat, its horizon broken only by the tall buildings that rose to the east of the street where she lived. Like Thunder Bay, it was situated on the banks of an inland sea, a different body of water from the Sea of the Ojibwe. Across the water was the country of the United States of America, though the sea was so wide that the pale line of it appeared only on the clearest of days.

Rose's room had green walls, bare linoleum floors in a checkerboard pattern, a wash stand, and a narrow squeaking bed. The bed came with two clean sheets, a gray wool blanket, and a pillow without a slip. It smelled of old feathers and mothballs. A closet contained rattling wire coat hangers and a mousetrap covered with cobwebs. The only other furniture was a chrome table and a wooden chair beside the single window. On the sill was a plug-in hot plate and a kettle with which she could make tea. Down the hall were a bathroom and a refrigerator shared by the four tenants who lived on this floor.

Tacked to the wall over the bed was a calendar that had been left there by the previous resident. It was three years old—1958—a picture of a waterfall called Niagara. The ceiling was ten feet high, which made the room feel larger than it really was, for it was eight feet square. The window opened onto an alleyway, letting in the muffled roar of automobiles, the complaints of spatting cats, and the chirping of sparrows. The view as restricted by the brick wall of a neighboring tenement, though if Rose pushed up the sash window and stretched her neck outside as far as the pain would permit, she was able to see both ends of the alley: on one side a slit of street with constantly moving traffic passing to and fro, and in the opposite direction a slit containing the softer motion of red leaves. Autumn in the south was not yellow, though there was some yellow in the city parks, gold as well, and, less frequently, plum purple. An amazing variety of reds and oranges dominated, like the most expensive box of color-sticks one could imagine.

Her room was on King Street, a few blocks north of the lake, deep in a maze of square, flat-topped, reddish-brown houses of great age. The Art Institute of Ontario was three blocks to the east. Rose had gone there the day before to register, and her first sight of it had not dispelled a feeling of unease. It was a four-story factory building that had been converted into a college several decades earlier, and even then was long past its prime. The ground floor contained offices and an exhibition hall. There was an Indonesian gong-bell in the lobby by the secretary's office. A sign beneath it read *It tolls for thee*. Beside the gong was an eight-foot-high papier-mâché gorilla with a toy airplane in one hand and a doll in the other. Written on a piece of paper taped to its chest was the word *Principal*. A line had been drawn through it, and scribbled beneath was the word *rinciple*.

The second and third floors were classrooms and studios, the fourth was private, containing apartments for a few of the teachers. They were called professors—four women and three men. They were very gifted people. Yet Rose found them a little frightening, for their faces were tense, even when they said friendly things to her and welcomed her and told her how wonderful it was that she had come. They were so unlike the sisters they seemed to be a different species. Rose sensed it before she understood it. The way they held their heads, as if daring anyone to question their authority. The inflexions of their lips were sometimes tight, sometimes crooked and laughing, but always cool. Their eyes were intelligent but distant, guarded, even when they were feigning warmth. Was it pretend warmth, Rose asked herself. Maybe it was real warmth, she answered, and the professors were merely burdened with the weight of their responsibilities, with no time to seek the silence within. Worst of all, she saw in the eyes of some a thing that worried her—a look like Kinoje's slyness and his cruelty. She reprimanded herself for such judgments, told herself that these people were not malicious, that their ways were simply the fruit of ignorance. Or was it, perhaps, the *fête* of satisfaction, *l'arrogance*.

There were one hundred twenty-eight students, a majority of them young women. It seemed to Rose that many of them were copying the professors, trying on the masks of satisfaction and arrogance, though they did not really understand what they were doing. It was play acting, it was pretending that the future was already within themselves. For this and other reasons Rose did not like the atmosphere of the place, despite the excitement that ran through the air like the secret shapes of the wind. Ice she remembered the clean cold wind of home, when the white powder of blowing snow gave it a visible form, created arabesques and spumes and streamers, braiding through the forest pines, leaping along snowbanks into a sky full of rolling moon as large as gold coins.

But that was the view from the cabin at Crazyman River, which had gone up in the smoke of sacrifices that are perpetually offered by time.

Rose found a new penny lying on the sidewalk by the steps of the school the first morning. It was shiny, the crisp picture of the queen and the date reminding her that the world was very large and time very long. When she held it to her eye, she discovered that even a penny can blot out the sun.

The first weeks of study were comprised mainly of drawing classes. This proved to be more difficult than Rose had anticipated, for the objects arranged on the display table did not capture her eye or her heart. The teacher of the course was a middle-aged woman who wore an orange, flowing, see-through shirt over yellow leotards that clung to her like skin. This woman walked always in bare feet when she was within the building, because cultural norms must be shattered if the eye was to be freed, she said. And because she also said that the eye must be trained to see things as they are, Rose obediently sketched vases and apples with charcoal on large buff sheets of newsprint. This art was good. She knew that beginnings often asked one to go back to other beginnings. It was like a return to her childhood, when she had scraped burnt sticks on the logs of the cabin.

Io, I miss your face! she cried silently to Oldmary at times, feeling the weight of an ancient threat fulfilled, for, in the absence of the sisters, Rose knew as never before that Oldmary had indeed gone up beyond the *tchibekana*, leaving her alone.

At lunchtime in the basement cafeteria, the other students eyed her curiously, her bending back, her little lunch box—a plaid tin that was chipped and rusted along the edges. No one came to sit with her or speak to her. It was painful. But she ate her sandwiches and apple and drank the bottle of made-from powder milk without seeking attention. She kept her eyes on the tin's picture, the Scottish girl in the heather who had become her friend. She was perhaps Euphrasia when she was young. Rose had never asked about the girl, because the actual Euphrasia had been enough. Now the longing she had once felt returned with greater force than ever, though the details of Euphrasia's face were blurred and the things she had said were fading.

Rose made herself look back upon other things that had been, in order to find strength for the things that were coming. Tchibi bounding through the burned stumps, making wild-animal sounds. Tchibi exploding out of the underbrush, leaping toward her, landing on his feet. Tchibi tipping a dirty handful of raspberries or strawberries into her upturned palm, grinning with a mouth painted by blueberries. Sitting side by side on the heights of the skull, eating bannock chunks, gazing without words at the convulsing sky.

"*Pagamânimad*, a strong wind is coming", she would say to him, and he would stand erect and arch his back and make a loon cry into the face of the storm.

Together by the river, she drawing with blunted color-sticks, creating the world, drinking the world, aching with love for the long trembling land, Tchibi plunging with his mouth open, catching little fish in his teeth. The memory made Rose laugh. And the other students looked at her, the solitary native woman seated at a corner table, staring into a tin box, laughing.

Late every afternoon, Rose walked the three blocks to her room, feeling the loneliness eat at her from within, but resisting it with the knowledge that tomorrow morning she would be able to attend Mass. Holy Family parish was five blocks in the other direction. Zig and zag. Back and forth, a lot of walking. But the zig was necessary if she hoped to persevere in the zag.

On Saturdays, she walked many blocks to a museum that contained the mummies of dead Egyptian kings and a Babylonian wall with blue lions, the swords of different nations, the clay images hand-shaped by the peoples of many ages, and countless other things that startled and amazed. The world and its past were far greater than she had supposed, despite the numerous books that she had read at the school in Thunder Bay or in the Sisters' private library.

On Sundays, she wrote to Mère Jean and Sister Madeleine, a letter each, telling the details of all that she was learning. These were long letters, for everything was interesting and everything was new. She placed their replies in a stack beneath the little

atue of the Sacred Heart that she kept on the wash stand. It
as comforting. She was bound to them in this way. And they
 her.

One day in the fourth week, the cafeteria was especially
owded at lunchtime, for it was raining heavily outside. A girl
t down beside her and said, "Hope you don't mind. Not
uch room."

Rose smiled at her and shifted her chair to make a place.

The girl had curly red hair, freckled skin, and a small nose
at turned upward at the end. She wore blue canvas pants
d a floppy sweater smeared with paint. She ate a banana and
ank from a bottle of Coke, while staring across the room, not
actly looking at Rose. This was, of course, the way of city
ople, for there were so many of them that it was impossible
r each to know each. Thus, they had learned to act as if all
hers were not real, until the others spoke to them or they
oke to the others, making them real.

"First year?" the girl said as she squashed a ball of wax paper.

"Yes", Rose answered shyly.

"Long way from home?"

"Yes."

"You're native, aren't you?" the girl said turning to her for
e first time.

Rose nodded.

"I like natives", the girl said.

Rose was not unfamiliar with the condescension of some
hite people, the kindness that made you smaller. She stood
 go.

"Tell you what", said the girl. "I've been watching you sit
ere all alone, day after day. Would you like to take in a pik?"

"What is a pik?" Rose asked doubtfully.

"A pik—flik, film, movie."

Rose had seen a motion picture before. On a few occasions
ver the years, the sisters had rented a projector and screen. The

275

whirring wheels of film often broke, but were easily repaire
with tape. It was a great marvel. She saw *The Song of Bernadett*
which made all the sisters cry, and some of the girls also, thoug
not Rose, who had found great joy in what she saw. There w
Miracle on 34th Street, which was not as easy to understand. An
Meet John Doe, which made Sister Madeleine sigh with emo
tion, and Mère Jean frown, for there were scenes in which Joh
Doe kissed a lady. He was a good man—men are like that, eve
the good ones.

"How about I pick you up on the front steps of the Institut
seven o'clock sharp, Friday night? Okay?"

"Oh, yes, I would be happy to go with you", Rose replie
blushing with gratitude.

"Hey, that's great! See you then."

"What is your name?" Rose called after her as the red-haire
girl rushed away. But she did not hear.

On Friday evening the introductions were made.

"Rose—hey, I like that. Kind of old-fashioned but folkish
said the red-haired girl. "I'm Deirdre."

Deirdre liked to move fast along the sidewalks, leaning for
ward, her chin thrust out, nose tilted high, tossing her re
ringlets, which were coppery under the yellow light of th
street lamps. At an intersection, she ignored a red light, graspe
Rose by the hand, and dragged her across a six-lane avenu
dodging cars left and right. It was frightening at first, bu
Deirdre was very good at it. On the other side, she turned an
went south toward the downtown core. Trying to keep u
Rose huffed and puffed. Her back began to scream in protes
Her head swam with the noise of roaring traffic.

"Is it a far place?" she asked breathlessly.

"Not too far, six more blocks."

"May we walk slowly?" Rose pleaded.

"Oh, yeah, sure. Your back slows you down, huh?"

"It does. I'm sorry."

"Not a problem. Hope there won't be a lineup."

But there was. Hundreds of people, one behind the other, ailed down a city block and around a corner. Deirdre and ose went to the end of the line.

Deirdre seemed irritated.

"I'm sorry", Rose said.

Deirdre shrugged. "Hope we get a seat."

She fumbled in her purse and withdrew a package of ciga-ttes. Pall Mall Plains, said the wrapper. It was purple-red. She one and popped another from the package, offering it to ose.

"Want one?"

Rose shook her head, Tchibi's skin flashing before her eyes.

"You're a good girl, huh?"

Without waiting for a reply, Rose's friend tossed her hair, her es darting in all directions. She had darkened her eyelashes d painted her lips bright red. She wore a thin blouse cut very w. Her pants were tight. Every so often she glanced at Rose's ess and the fine white blouse with the embroidered roses and rds on the collars. The old school uniform was the best thing e owned. She wondered if Deirdre envied her for it. At the stitute she wore the large pale-blue studio smock that Sister ladeleine had made for her—a copy of the one Sister had orn at art school in Paris. It was like a tent with a hole for the eck to go through and bound by a cracked leather belt around e waist, adorned with very large pockets for pencils and ushes. But the uniform was elegant. Rose worried that she as becoming a little too proud of it.

"We're in luck", Deirdre said as they edged toward the mar-uee. "It's a double bill. Do you like Elvis?"

"What is elvis?" Rose asked.

Which sent Deirdre into peels of laughter.

"Elvis is a *guy*!" she said too loudly, making other people ok at her. "He's just the most gorgeous guy you ever saw in

your life." She rolled her eyes in ecstasy. "He's the hottes
coolest thing that ever hit this dull old town."

Although the description contained a contradiction that pu:
zled Rose, she understood that the person Deirdre admired w
an actor.

At the ticket window under the marquee, Deirdre steppe
forward and said to the lady inside, "Two. Students."

Then she fumbled in her purse, rummaging and frowning.

"Damn!" she mumbled. "Oh, daaammit! Oh, double damn
She turned to Rose. "Wouldn't you know it. I forgot my walle
You have any spare cash on you?"

Rose opened the deer-hide sack that Grandma had made f
her and took out the roll of money that she always carried in i
She undid the rubber bands and offered Deirdre a five-doll:
bill. Deirdre stared at the roll, chewing gum absentmindedly.

"Oh, great, that's fab, you're a lifesaver. And here I thought
was going to treat you. Thanks a million, Rosy!" She paid f
the tickets and led the way into the theater.

"There's a little change", Deirdre said. "Why don't I get
some popcorn and drinks?"

"Yes, please," said Rose, grateful that Deirdre was such
capable person. It would have been impossible for her to ha
done any of this by herself.

When they were seated in the top row of the balcony, an
the house lights went down, a cartoon began. It was a stor
about some animals that talked like humans, dressed up :
people of the Wild West. They fought an Indian who wa
unlike any Indian Rose had ever known. The people in th
theater laughed loudly whenever the pioneers fooled the In
dian. He was, she saw, very much like a clown, not intelligen
and easily tricked.

This was followed by the movie.

Rose was surprised to see that Elvis was a handicappe
person. His lips did not form words properly; he spoke much :

Sister Clothilde did. Sadly, his bones did not move properly either. They were deformed, especially his hips and legs. Still, Rose thought he was very handsome. He was a nice boy, that was plain to see, though there were parts in the movie when he tried to kiss a girl. Rose knew about such things—all men are like this, even the good ones—and she lowered her eyes as Deirdre strained forward.

The other movie was about several young people who lived by an ocean. They spent a lot of time singing and strumming guitars, telling smart jokes to each other, playing in the sand, and rolling about in blankets. They wore very little clothing. Rose did not see much of this.

When it was over, she and Deirdre got up and went out onto the streets with the crowd leaving the theater. It was a little frightening to be in a river of so many people. Rose did not feel that she had enjoyed herself as much as she had hoped. Yet it had been a great gift to be with someone who acknowledged her presence and talked with her. It was a warming thing to find a friend.

Deirdre walked her back to her room on King Street. When they said good-bye to each other, Rose asked Deirdre where she lived.

"In a dump on Spadina", her friend answered. "With a bunch of other girls from the Institute. You gotta come over sometime. Get out, meet new people."

"I would like to very much, Deirdre. Thank you for asking me."

"Don't mention it, Rosy. See you Monday."

About once a week during that autumn, Deirdre came and sat beside her at lunch, and talked a great deal, though she rarely asked questions about Rose's life. This was understandable because Deirdre was a very busy and talented person, and Rose knew that she herself was rather dull in comparison to the red-haired girl. Deirdre was in second year, and Rose in first, so they did not share classes.

Yet it seemed that Deirdre, for all their differences, liked her and wanted to spend time with her. She invited Rose to go with her to the movies every Friday night, but Rose declined saying that she was not that interested in movies. She asked if Deirdre would like to accompany her to the Art Gallery of Ontario on Saturday mornings. Or perhaps to the Zoo, or the Royal Ontario Museum, which was said to be one of the best in the world.

Deirdre rolled her eyes and said, "Thanks a mill, Rosy, but I've had it up to the eyeballs with the culture stuff."

Rose liked the way Deirdre could turn anything into a joke.

"Don't you want to see the paintings, Deirdre?"

"Seen one, seen 'em all."

"I'm different from you in this", Rose replied. "Many of the paintings are like worlds. You can fall into them, and each time you do it's like a new journey. For with every passing day our eyes change, and so what we see is always changing."

Deirdre chewed her gum harder. "Well, maybe you like that stuff, but it sure isn't my ball o' wax."

Puzzled, Rose said, "But you're an artist, Deirdre."

The red-haired girl laughed. "Just puttin' in time, Rosy. My old man pays for the education, glad to get me off his hands. And when I get a paper from the Institute, I move on. I'm going to a design school after this. I want to be a fashion designer or maybe a model, if I make enough money and can get my nose fixed, the freckles bleached."

Rose felt a sadness for Deirdre, realizing that she was a creative person who did not yet know her path in life. This was because she was not organized, as could be seen in the way she was always forgetting to bring her wallet, or missing classes, or borrowing a sandwich when she neglected to bring a lunch for herself.

In late December, Rose realized that she was learning a great deal in the city. In her classes, she noticed an increasing swiftness in the way her mind-pictures connected to her fingers, directing the pencil or charcoal on the paper without thought. She walked for hours each day, looking at shapes, seeing the forms of man-made things—squares, cubes, spheres, cones, rhomboids. Seeing, as well, the many forms of humanity. Io! This was the most moving part, for man was both beautiful and sad in his continual falling—and rising, though there was less rising, it seemed, than falling. Still, beauty flooded everything, even the parts which were ugly. As Tchibi's heart beat beneath the damaged skin. As Jesus' Heart beat within a metal box.

Io, the city was not as beautiful as the wild lands, but it teemed with life, and life was always beautiful even when wounded and assaulted by the *matchi-manito*, who sought in all places to spread the spirit of the *neshiwed*. Always the greater number of men struggled against this spirit, and only a few gave in to it completely. Of these she saw a handful during her first term; of the good she saw tens of thousands.

Her landlady, for example, a lady like Mrs. Boyle, though very thin. How swiftly she had been thawed. On the first day, last September, the woman had said, "Cash in advance, Miss. I been burned before." Now it was, "Hello, Rose, care for a cup of tea?" Rose enjoyed visits in the landlady's parlor, sitting on a purple velvet fancy chair, her toes just touching the floor, drinking green Chinese tea from a cup and saucer on which two red birds kissed in the air. Lace curtains blowing against the geranium, and listening to the little stories the landlady told between the sparking electric trams that rumbled past the front window. There were always stories, for the landlady's life had been full of experience. She was a widow and childless, and thus she had suffered. She, too, went to Holy Family church for Mass. How surprised she had been to see Rose there the first time. How kind she had become from then on.

"You see," Rose told herself, "in all places good people are present."

Of Rose's five thousand dollars, about half remained. How swiftly it had poured through her fingers. The tuition for the institute, rent, art supplies, trolley fare, food, and the little borrowings that Deirdre asked of her. But that, of course, would be paid back.

In her purse she kept a thousand dollars, because the trip to the bank downtown was too far to walk and cost a quarter each way on the trolley. It was foolish to waste money on the fare and time was also needlessly lost. Rose was not so simple minded as to think there was no thievery in the world, and thus she kept the money in her deer-hide bag, which was always with her. The door to her room was locked when she was not at home or was in the bathroom down the hall or in the cellar washing clothes.

Eighteen hundred dollars remained in the bank. If she were careful she would be able to pay for a second year. If she were very careful and obtained part-time work, say in the grocery store run by the Lebanese people at the corner, she might be able to stretch her inheritance to the end of a third year. And when she graduated she would truly be an artist. Because of this, people might buy her pictures, which would enable her to buy more materials and continue to live as she had begun, developing the great gift, offering it to the world, which was the will of Manito. It would be a suffering to part with her pictures, to send them off into the world with strangers, for they were like children to her, and her suffering was in them. Yet it was his holy will, and thus he would provide for all her needs from his riches, in Christ Jesus-Manito—a promise she had read in Grandma's Bible.

At the end of fall term, in mid-December, classes were suspended for the holiday, and Rose became more alone than she had been since arriving in the city. She did not know the ther tenants on her floor, except to nod at them as they passed. They always nodded back, but did not speak, for they were busy people. At first Rose could not decide what to do with her free time. She tried to fill the days by reading the art books her teachers recommended, the ones that explained about art in this century. But the explanations filled her with confusion and sadness.

It was too cold in the parks and streets for sketching. She tried it once, but her fingers froze quickly, and when she attempted to draw while wearing gloves, the pencils and charcoal became disobedient in her fingers, and the pictures were feless. Then she wondered if she would be permitted to draw in the art gallery or the museum, and was happy to discover that this was a common practice. It was a great pleasure for her to spend hours sitting on a folding stool, heedless of the ticking antique clocks or the passing of hundreds of feet back and forth around her. She did not see the many people, especially the elderly and the very young, who glanced over her shoulder and whispered their admiration.

In the Royal Ontario Museum she came upon an amazing thing. It was a totem that rose from the stone roots under the city, deep in the bottom of the museum, and towered upward floor after floor through a canyon of balconies. It had been made long ago by native people from the west coast. It was very ancient, blackened by smoke and age. It was unlike the other totems, for it was unadorned with the birds and animals that were usually carved on them.

Seeking to understand it, Rose climbed several flights of stairs circling the totem, her right hand on the brass banister, her eyes sweeping ever upward. High above the main floor she came to a figure carved into the wood at the peak of the column. It was a dark face, as dark as the night sky. Two stick arms were thrust out from beneath the face. The totem's hands held a small manshape. The manshape dangled over the abyss.

He looked up into the face of the great totem person. Bot[
regarded each other with solemnity.

"Io!" Rose thought with a sudden thumping of her heart. "I
is a man in the arms of the universe."

The universe was so large, the human so tiny.

"Yes", she whispered after a moment's reflection. "That is i[
word, and thus, that is its name."

Man in the arms of the universe.

This was a great discovery. It thrilled her to know that ther[
were levels of meaning, floors upon floors of words that wer[
layered above each other all the way up to paradise. And tha[
one of these words said the universe was a face behind whic[
the creator dwelled, high, high above the *tchibekana*.

On December twentieth, the landlady went away to anothe[
city to spend Christmas with her sister. All the other tenants le[
for the holidays. The house was full of creakings and groaning[
The emptiness grew and grew. She began to weep for lack [
anyone to speak with. Only at daily Mass was there alleviatio[
of her loneliness, a very brief consolation after Communion[
Aside from this, the Lord had permitted a time of feeling
apartness, even from him. It too was offered, but it was a gre[
burden.

Unable to bear it any longer, counting her money, she de[
cided to spend some of it on a round-trip train ticket to Thun[
der Bay. Mère Jean had often told her that she was to regard th[
school and the convent as her home. She was free to return a[
any time. So she did.

How blessed was the reunion! How shining the sisters' face[
how bright their exclamations of welcome. How calming th[
hushed interior of the chapel at Midnight Mass. And O! th[
consolation after Communion, longer and deeper than it ha[
been in years.

O Jesus, why have you asked me to go from this place? For the world
cold and dark and barren, though your children are in all places
eautiful beneath the wounds they bear.

And, O the tree on Christmas morning! There was a gift for
er beneath it, a new painting smock from Sister Madeleine,
nd a more grown-up dress that had been made by Sister
Clothilde. It was forest green, with little birds and animals
mbroidered in many colors on the shoulder straps.

"*Ce n'est pas un* 'dress', *ma chérie. C'est un* 'jumper'," said
ister Clothilde. "One needs the modest blouse beneath. Or
ie sweater."

"It is beautiful, Sister", Rose cried, kissing the old cheeks
own which two silver tears rolled.

On January first, there was a grand *fête*, a party with sand-
riches cut into amusing shapes, a single glass of wine for each,
nd piano music. Sister Madeleine surprised everyone by danc-
ıg a Breton jig, which made them all clap in time to the music,
nd laugh so hard they held their sides—even Mère Jean could
ot help herself.

Yet once the crest of the year was passed, the downward slide
egan, the acceleration of time. Rose dreaded the approach of
er departure date, hoping the sisters would plead with her to
bandon this foolishness of seeking an education. Not so. They
ere terrible—they were brave and selfless. Fighting their own
ffection for her, they encouraged her to resume her studies, to
ıke heart, to work hard, to be a great artist, and to do much
ood in the world.

It was the will of *le Bon Dieu.*

On the eve of her departure, Rose was asked by Mère Jean to
ome with her to the chapel. They knelt before the presence
nd prayed for a time. Then Mère Jean sat on the pew and Rose
ıt beside her.

"*Ma petite*", she said. "There is something I must tell you. It is
ot happy news. The other sisters do not yet know of it, but

tomorrow you leave us and so I thought it best to speak face to face."

Her hands folded tensely on her knees, she said, "We are being withdrawn from the school, the sisters and I. The government is replacing us with lay teachers. At the end of classes our community is returning to France."

When she could overcome her trembling, Rose cried, "You cannot go! You are my only family!"

"My daughter, you will always be in our hearts."

"Then I will come with you!" Rose declared.

"How I wish this could be. But where would you live? The superior of our Order is not disposed to it, for she has decided you do not have a vocation with us."

"I will live near you. I will live in France."

Mère Jean reflected for a few moments. "This is not impossible. We would see each other in the parlor from time to time. But life in the Motherhouse is very different from life in a small community in the provinces. In addition, France is not your native land. You do not speak our tongue."

"*Je parle un petit peu, ma mère.* For many years I have listened to you speak."

"Yes, you speak a little, but not enough. Your life is already full of difficulty. In a foreign land there would be more. Would not those struggles deflect you from your course?"

"What is my course?"

"The way the Lord has set before you. To go with him into the country which is your own, to become an artist, to make words that give life. To love in the barren lands."

"I no longer know anyone in the land of little trees."

"I mean the spiritual barrenness, in the cities."

At this Rose began to cry.

"I am too small. It frightens me."

Mère Jean patted Rose's arm with affection. "This smallness is also his way for you. In this is your strength."

286

"I do not understand. Why does he take all from me?"

"If he takes all from you, it is because he will in his time give
all back to you, and it shall be greater than what has been taken.
Do you not understand, you who have spoken with him in the
long hours of the night, in the silence?"

"Do you also speak with him, Mother?"

"Yes, in the silence that is the language of love."

"But it is easy for you! You are great! You are holy!"

Mère Jean smiled gently and shook her head. "I am not great,
Rose. I am not holy. I am a little person."

Though a certain grief remained, Rose could not deny that her
return to the city and to classes distracted her somewhat from
the terrible news. The *Bon Dieu* had not taken the gift from
her, and this was no small thing. It meant he had his eye on her.
Moreover, he had provided the means to continue to learn.

Rose was required to take a short series of workshops called
"Perceptual Dissonance", which the professor said would break
the fetters of ordinary seeing. Some of what he taught she
already knew, for example, the drawing of the spaces around the
solider shapes. Rose had done this since childhood, and even
more had she developed this habit under the tutelage of Sister
Madeleine. But, unlike Sister, this teacher seemed to emphasize
the breaking of fetters, as if the absences were far more important than the presences.

Some of these sessions were helpful, others were not. Rose
especially disliked the one in which the students were told to
tear up prints of old art masterpieces and glue them back
together in different shapes—whatever shape they wanted. This
was called *collage*. It was an interesting experiment, but lo! she
did not like the way a human body could become a thing one
broke, a human face could become an animal, a garden of
flowers a heap of rubble.

In a class called "free form", where the professor let them, or

rather commanded them, to draw, paint, sling matter at canva
board, or paper in any manner they wished, on any subject c
nonsubject whatsoever, she was most at home. She chose thic
rag paper and color-sticks, the flamboyant oil pastels containin
memories. This sort of creation demanded everything of he
not because it was technically difficult but because every lev
of her self was engaged. To go inward was more difficult in th
city, in a room full of noisy students, among accomplishe
artist-teachers who had not seen what she had seen.

Nothing exhilarated and exhausted her as much as this worl
The return to the original making that she had known as a chil
by the waters of Threefinger Lake produced images crowde
with the human scenes she had absorbed in her walks throug
the city, mixed with imaginings and longings. White birds an
moons above burning tenements. Rivers of people streamin
into the open jaws of theater marquees. Trees in parks beneat
which lovers strolled hand in hand. She sometimes turned t
familiar subjects—tossing forests, water turbulent with gold an
silver minnows. She did worry that such pictures might b
meaningful to herself alone. On occasion, a professor stoppe
by her drawing board to offer a helpful critique. Often th
teacher seemed impressed and gave compliments in a tone th;
was not used on the others.

When praised, Rose sometimes felt an odd glow of warmt
that prompted dark thoughts. She had developed her art lon
before going to school, she recalled, and she had done it on he
own. No, she corrected, there was the encouragement Euphra
sia had given, and the training supplied by Sister Madeleine. O
the other hand, their help would not have achieved much if th
original gift had not been as great as it was. Surely that coul
not be denied. And was it not also true that many of thes
privileged students did not possess the gift? It was impossibl
not to notice.

With such thoughts her peace departed, and in its place ther

ame a desire to seek more approval, to impress the professors
with images that startled, intrigued, and invited their admira-
on. Admiration? She recoiled, searching within herself for the
uiet place where the core of radiant love resided. When she
ound it, the shame she felt, the sadness too, revealed her vanity.
he trembled at the ease with which praise had drawn her
oward the thing she had been warned about by Sister Made-
eine, the dangerous satisfaction. From then on she practiced
urning away from this temptation. The pain in her back, and
he deeper pain of her losses, also helped.

She rarely saw Deirdre. It seemed that her friend had lost
interest in her. But this was not so. In March, she reappeared
a Rose's life, as the early spring of the south began to turn
he streets into a network of melting slush. Invitations to the
ovies resumed. Rose always thanked her and declined. Even
o, Deirdre would come to the cellar lunch table at least once a
week, and chatter, and crumple wax balls, and make repetitious
ompliments about the beadwork on Rose's deer-hide bag.

In May, when the trees in the parks budded and the nights
were warm, and young people raced up and down the streets in
ars, squealing their tires and playing loud music on their radios,
Rose felt the summer drawing close. Soon the sisters would
eave for France. Their letters did not cease to come, but she
wondered if this would always be so, especially when an ocean
was between them. She continued to write to them on Sun-
ays, describing the details of her classes and the myriad human
cenes that she had witnessed in her rambles throughout the
ity. There were beggars and mad people here, she told them, as
here were in the north. Usually these people were polite and
grateful for anything she could offer.

In a note to Mère Jean she described an incident which had
uzzled her.

In Queen's Park, by the provincial legislature, there were
any large trees, among them several giant oaks. These were

new to Rose, who was most familiar with the smaller, thinne
scratchy pines, and the fluttering birches. The oaks exhale
deep old sighs that were like the most ancient groaning of th
earth.

On a Saturday afternoon, she sat before one such tree t
draw it. As always, she fell in love with her subject. She coul
only draw or paint what she loved. She *became* what she loved
or was it that she already was what she loved?

When she had sketched a flock of sparrows winging into th
branches, she felt it was complete. She straightened her back
little and inhaled deeply of the spring smells. At that point sh
became aware of two men standing beside her, one on eac
side. They were looking down at the drawing.

The man on the left was old and poor. The smell of him wa
like the smell of the yard at Crazyman River, fish flesh and do
fur, and too many months since clothes had been washed in th
tub by the stove. His face was wrinkled, his beard as white
yellow as antler bones. His eyes were watery and brown, lik
aging purple velvet. He looked like a wandering man who ha
been many places and done many things. He glanced at her an
smiled. It was a warm smile, though it contained a history c
losings. He was standing close, this stranger, perhaps a little to
close.

On her right was the other man. He was young and dresse
in a new black suit, carrying a briefcase. His hair was a sheaf c
gold, and his clean, shining face more handsome than any sh
had ever seen, with eyes as dark as lakes at nightfall when n
wind stirs the surface. But his eyes contained no singing, whic
was odd, for all riches had been given to him, everything that
man may desire in this world was his. Like the old man, he als
smiled at her. Like the old man's, his smile seemed warm
though it did not feel the same as the other's. A strange aur
clung to him, it made Rose feel beautiful and exciting, mad
her glow. Whatever it was, it was a new thing, a thrilling thing

1 order to understand him, she would have tried (only a little)
) fall-into-seeing, but he broke her concentration.

"This is extraordinary work", he said in a melodious voice.

"Thank you", she said, feeling the odd warmth rise in her
reast, the tug of desire for admiration.

Strangely, the old man stared at the other as if he had offered
1 insult.

"It is a true work", he rumbled in his chest, coughing.

"What do you mean, *true*?" the young man asked.

"This eye regards all wounded, untamed things and rever-
1ces them," said the old man.

"She will become great", said the other.

Rose blushed and repeated his compliment to herself.

"She will not be what you desire", said the old man.

"And what do you suppose *she* will desire?" said the young
1an archly.

Now Rose's heart began to beat more quickly, for this was a
2ry strange conversation.

"She will desire what is true and beautiful and good", said the
ld man. "She will be great, but by a different measure."

The young man withdrew a step and folded his arms, smiling
) himself as he gazed at the floor of the park, which was
)vered with split black acorns and rotting leaves.

"She will rise", he said, "and rise steadily."

The old man shook his head. "That is not her task."

The young man laughed once, though the sound of it was
ollow.

Utterly perplexed, Rose tried to make sense of the argu-
1ent, for an argument it had swiftly become. She looked at the
ld man, who was not attractive. She looked at the young man
'ho was immensely so. It seemed that death was upon the old
1an and life upon the young one. The young man stared at the
ld man, shot a look of contempt at him, and turned on his
eels. He walked away, chin high, his stride unhurried but

determined. Rose watched until he rounded a corner. When he was no longer in sight she turned to the old man only to find that he too was gone.

Did not the appearances of things reveal their inner condition? Rose asked herself. Was not the golden-haired man visible form of the beauty of life and its ever renewed power? Was not the old man an image of weakness and decay? As Rose pondered these questions, she realized that appearances both revealed and misled. She reminded herself that the surface images of her many beloveds were not beautiful. They were lovely in her eyes because something within them had quickened her heart.

"What *is* beauty?" she asked in great perplexity.

There were so many other interesting things to tell the sisters. There were the antics of squirrels to relate, and the complicated histories of various cats in the alley, each of whom she had named, for the naming of things had not ceased to be habit of hers. Then there were the outdoor markets with the foreigners and many tongues. And the little crimes witnessed along the street. And the beautiful liturgical events in the parish, at which she was always a silent participant, seated in the back pew. And into each letter she put a description of painting that had moved her during the previous week: An iris flower, by an artist named Vincent. A finger plunged into the wound in Christ's side, by a man named Caravaggio. A northern bush scene burning with a savage and dangerous beauty painted by a man who had drowned in a wilderness lake not long after he had painted it.

One morning in June, Rose went to the Institute to pick up the sheet of paper on which the teachers had printed her final marks. The numbers meant little, but the teachers' comments told her that they were expecting her back in September for her second year of studies. She did not attend the student-faculty

arty that afternoon, because she wanted to see a special exhibit
lat was opening at the Art Gallery of Ontario. She was going
way tomorrow, going home to the north, and this was her only
pportunity to see the paintings of a man named Goya.

The travelling exhibition had been drawn from collections in
pain, France, England, and elsewhere. The paintings were full
f rich earth colors, and pain and blood. This in itself did
ot attract her to them. She was drawn to the way the artist saw
e fallingness of things. There were black-ink etchings of the
orrors of war. There was an execution by a firing squad,
eople raving in a madhouse, the grotesque gaiety of the Mardi
ras, a man wrestling with thoughts that took the form of bats
d devils. A bitter pessimism was in many of the works,
pecially when the follies of mankind were the subject matter.
et Rose felt in every canvas the artist's grief over those follies.

After wandering through the exhibition for several hours,
e was strained, emotionally exhausted, and firmly convinced
at she did not wish to paint like this. Goya's work contained
uch truth, much protest against a violated world, yet in its
arkest moods it seemed to say that the *neshiwed*-spirit was too
owerful for man, the darkness was winning. Still, she reminded
erself, the artist showed that darkness was darkness and that all
en must strive to shun it.

Finally she came to a painting that struck her like a physical
low. Indeed, she staggered back from it and lowered her eyes.
was called *Saturn Devouring His Children*. In this work a huge
iant rose up over a black horizon. In his hands he held a small
aked man. The giant's mouth was open, blood and gore run-
ing from it. The mannikin was decapitated. The giant's eyes
ere crazed. It ate and ate and ate. Ay, ay! The whole world was
lunged into an endless night of horror and madness.

Stricken, Rose fled from the gallery.

Io! she reprimanded herself as she hastened along the side-
alk. *Bineshi, little bird, why are you so frightened? Why do you run?*

Back and forth she argued: Was it not better to look only a the good and beautiful things of life, as the holy book said Surely this was so. But was not the little mannikin a sufferer Was there not sympathy in the painting? Did the picture rejoic in the devouring or did it expose it? What, then, did it sa about the world? In its form it was similar to the totem, ye which of the two was the true image? Man in the arms of th universe—the totem universe? Or man in the arms of the paga death-god—the killer universe? In both images, man was in th hands of great and high powers. In both, man learned that h was not God.

The totem spoke. It said, *See, O man, that you are small, th you live and move and have your being in the arms of an immens mystery.*

The Goya also spoke. It said, *See, O man, that you are smal beware, there is a killer in the world, and you must recognize him if yo would escape the devouring.*

As Rose passed the Institute on the way home to her room her inner debate was broken by the music blaring from its ope windows, the shouting and wild laughter, and all the othe sounds that would have come from Goya's painting of th Mardi Gras, had it been able to speak on the level of noise Through an open window, she saw Deirdre's red curls tossing a she danced and screamed. Rose hurried on.

I I

Summer came at last. Because Rose had paid for a full year's rent, the landlady agreed to hold the room for her until September. If Rose had another nine hundred and sixty dollars, she could keep it for another year.

"I been burned before, you understand", said the old woman.

Rose stored a roll of drawings in the closet, gathered what clothing she could carry into a cardboard suitcase, and put some art supplies into the deer-hide sack. Then she splurged on trolley fare, went downtown to the train station, and bought a ticket for Thunder Bay. A day and a half later, when she arrived at her old school, she discovered to her dismay that classes had finished the week before and that the sisters had left on a train bound for the east, where they were to board a ship for France. Letters and many small gifts were waiting for Rose. These tokens cheered her a little, but they were not enough to dispel the deep disappointment.

Now I am alone, she said to herself. *Now I am launched into the world. Io, I wish it were not so.*

The new director of the school told her that she was welcome to sleep for a night in the cloister (the sisters had asked him for this favor, on the chance that Rose would return). He did not seem happy about it, and cautioned her against making a habit of it. The times had changed, he said, this was now a federal institution, and the way the sisters had done things was over. He suggested that Rose leave tomorrow morning, because renovations were about to begin. He did not mean it unkindly, only for clarification.

That night she spent many hours sitting in the chapel, which was now filled with scaffolding and canvas dropsheets. On the entrance door was pinned a piece of paper that said *New Library. Remove altar. Install bookshelves.*

Gazing at the tabernacle with its open brass door, she felt the absence keenly, sensed the lamenting of an abandoned house. The saturated walls still seemed to breathe, but the breathing was memory.

Ay, ay, it was bitter.

She knew that Jesus was within her in the tabernacle of the heart, yet he was silent. Did he sleep within her? It seemed so. More and more during the past year she talked to him without hearing a response. Perhaps he did speak, but she had become deafened by the noise of the city.

The next day she caught a train that would take her north to the end of the rail line. As she rode through the sun-roused land, she observed with fresh interest the ambling rivers and the towns from which paths streaked off toward the horizon. It seemed to Rose that holy priests would always walk these byways, to tea and stories with old pilgrims in cabins, as jets made trails in the sky above and cargo trains rumbled southward with ore and lumber.

There was a fitful sleep with periodic awakenings. A baby cried from the back of the coach, one note only, a church swung by, its tall spire flashing blinding moonlight off aluminum sheets. Long shadows lashed the passing train, telegraph poles bent in deference.

When she awoke, she saw that the land had become crowded with smaller trees bristling upon the humping shoulders of the earth, wounded by lakes and rills and rushing rivers. Isolated dwellings appeared in the dawn. A cabin passed, in its yard an old woman chopping firewood on a stump by her back door. She did not look up. Minutes later the train squealed to a halt at the last station of all.

From there Rose caught the weekly mail plane to Three-finger Lake. It was a slender little Cessna on large pontoons. The takeoff was noisy but smooth. She could not help feeling a burst of happiness when they rose up over the endless bushlands and unnamed waterways, for this was so much like hovering over the world that the joy of it could not be denied, however transient it might be. The flight took less time than those she remembered from the days she had flown in the Beaver and the Norseman many years ago. The Cessna circled the end of the lake, and as it tilted at a dizzying angle, Rose caught a glimpse of the spine and the skull rising along the east shore north of the village. She could almost see a tiny girl clinging to a beautiful woman who had held her in her arms, *my Ningâ, my English mother, my teacher, who went away.*

All things change, Rose thought. *Even I have gone away. Though now I return.*

The plane roared low above the roofs of the village. Another circle and the lake rose up to greet the shuddering pontoons. They bounced as they hit the waves and bounced again, then settled, the engine roared, and the world slowed. The pilot cut the throttle about ten yards from the dock and the propeller ceased revolving. The lapping of water, the sound of wind, and the cry of a seagull entered in.

As usual, a crowd of natives and a scattering of whites were waiting. A whiteman caught the rope the pilot threw to him from the pontoon. When Rose struggled down out of the plane and jumped to the dock, she looked around at the faces observing her. She did not recognize many, others seemed vaguely familiar. Only the old had not aged. A woman with white hair approached—it was Mrs. Otter, the church organist—and asked with curiosity in her eyes, "Are you Anishinâbe? Who are you?"

"I am Rose Wâbos, granddaughter of Oldmary Wâbos."

"Ee-ee, now I know you. How you have grown! Oldmary is

297

gone these many years, and we thought you were dead or living in the south."

"I am here", Rose smiled, touching her arm.

The old woman nodded, and went away. Her manner seemed to say, such is life. People come and go. People are born and die. I cannot keep track of them all.

Rose carried her suitcase and deer-hide sack up the slope to the church where she had been baptized and had received First Communion, where Manito had given Tchibi to her as her little brother, and where Grandma had been buried. As she stood peering in through the cracked glass of the front door, some elderly native people called to her, saying that the church was closed. A priest came once a month to pray the *Anamessi-kewin*, they said.

Rose breathed deeply the scent of pine needles and the smell of the lake. The wind sighed, the siskins zinged in the branches. It was home. Yet it was no longer home. She went around behind the church to the thicket of wooden crosses, many of which had fallen. At the back of the field she found Grandma's grave among the wildflowers, cadmium and purple, aster-blue and red, sprayed like blood across the ragged green grass. A dwarf-sized wooden cross was Oldmary's only memorial, painted white, her name and dates written in a fine black script that had been varnished for preservation. Already it was crackling.

Rose knelt. She felt nothing at first, for her eyes saw only deep grass, pine cones, and twigs. But gravestones seldom lie. Grandma was in the earth, she who had found Rose on the steps of the cabin in the cold winter when Mang the loon brought her down from Gissis the moon, leaving the *tchibekana* trail, the necklace, the river of stars, the river of souls, in the black sky.

Many memory-sounds clamored for Rose's attention: Raven wings beating the crisp air. The chee-chee of a fish hawk. The long-silent bell banging in the church steeple.

"I saw that pine burn when I was your age", she heard Grandma say. "It was older than old. Now I too am older than old. A few more years and it will crumble into the earth. No one will remember it. No one will know it lived here for hundreds of years."

"You will remember it", Rose said solemnly.

"Soon I too will be part of the soil."

"Then I will remember you."

Grandma smiled and stroked the hair from Rose's forehead.

Rose hiked to the place where the cabin had stood beside the creek running into Crazyman River. Her progress was slow, because of her fatigue and the weight of the suitcase. As she made her way along the overgrown footpath, the twilight fell. In the west, behind a pall of overcast, the sun was setting. In the east, a summer storm fretted over the forest, veins of lightning spitting down to the earth. It was only minutes away when she arrived at the clearing. There she found a heap of charred log ends where once the cabin had stood. Rockets of purple fireweed grew from the ashes.

This, then, was the moment of knowledge, when the contents of all letters became solid. Aching, she looked about the clearing in search of anything that remained. The woodshed had collapsed. The garden that she and Tchibi had made was no more, or was overgrown with tall weeds. She walked to it, and brushed aside the grasses with her feet.

Bits of glass glittered here and there. A broken nimbus of pebbles. A spot of pink. A spot of white. Little by little she uncovered its pattern, until finally she came to the center of the radial arms. In the core was a hole. The round white stone which she had called the loon-star was gone. A speckle of the loon's necklace that had come down to earth and rested here was gone. Ay, ay, it was gone! Who had taken it? Who?

Rose sat down in the weeds and cried. She cried long and

hard, and it seemed to her that the storm in her soul, and a rising fear, were worse than she had ever felt.

Thunder rumbled. Strokes of wind and spatterings of rain blew in sideways. Hugging her knees as she had done as a child, Rose slipped into the halfway state between observer and participant at nature's great bathing of its body. Now the first black drops appeared on the heap of ashes. Her eyes widened in the growing darkness, shining at the corners where they picked up bits of yellow light from the lightning flashes over the distant skull. The birches began to whisper, the lodgepole pines to sway and creak. The first waves hit, a hard rain sweeping over the ridge, drawing with it the fragrance of rain-smashed herbs and berries. The cold water plastered her hair in long runnels, her eyes closed to the small slaps, nostrils dilating, sucking in the baptized air. Ah, the river of water, the hurting that heals, the cleansing, consoling tears of the mother.

Rose got up and moved to the ruins of the woodshed, where she found a sheet of rusting tin. She sat on a stump and pulled the tin over her. Then the voiceless things appeared, though keeping to themselves until they looked her over. Mice and squirrels scurried under toppled planks and into clever channels in the rotting logs. When the shower eased a little, Rose peered out into the gloom and saw a fox prancing along the edge of the clearing, a mouse dangling from its delicate jaws, head low and sideways for a cautious look at the haunted ruins.

Soaked, yet too tired to make a fire, she pulled a blanket from the suitcase, rolled herself in it, and lay down under the tin sheet. She slept.

In the morning she awoke stiff and sore, her back screaming, her mind clearer. She struggled along the overgrown path to the river and came to the high embankment where one summer she and Tchibi had tumbled down to the beach of pebbles. She descended carefully, for she was older now and not as limber as she once had been. Arriving at the banks she lay on her belly and thrust her head deep into the water. She drank. It made her teeth chatter. Then along the shore she walked for half an hour until she came to a sand bank which curled about a sandy cove. It was the place where they had eaten wild strawberries, where Tchibi had slept in the sun as she drew him. She remembered his sleep as the language of trust, for it said that he knew she would never harm him.

"Io, loon-boy, where are you?" she whispered. Minnows flashed in the stream.

She walked to the village of Threefinger Lake and purchased a white camp tent, a kerosene lantern, a bow saw, a kettle and frying pan, and various foods: a bucket of lard and another of jam, a sack of flour, a bag of sugar, and a little box of tea. Io, it was good to drink tea that had been boiled in a billy can over a fire. Throw the leaves in and watch them dance. Pour the red water into a tin mug and sip it sweet with white store sugar. It woke her up! It made her feel that she could walk forever into the unknown places and never grow tired.

It hurt to spend so much money, almost two hundred dollars for everything, but there was no choice. She must live. She could not eat memories or swallow live minnows and cram her mouth with berries only.

She hired two teenage boys to haul her equipment to the clearing at Crazyman River. They were energetic and full of fun, and they were happy with the dollars she put into their grubby hands. How torn their clothing—they were like Tchibi had been many years ago, though they were all brown, no white blood in them. They regarded her as a strange person, Rose could see, but they treated her with respect. Was it only because of the dollars, she wondered.

"You want us to kill a rabbit for you, for supper?" one of them asked eagerly.

"No, thank you", said Rose. "I have bannock."

"I will catch fish for you", the other offered.

301

"Yes, I would like a fish and will pay you for it", she said.

"Do you want *atikameg* or *kinoje*?"

"*Atikameg*," she answered. "And *majamegoss*, if you can catch him."

They ran away to find their strings and bait. Hours later they returned with two fat whitefish and a lean trout skewered on sticks. They helped Rose make a fire pit by gathering stones, brought deadwood from the forest, and asked if they could light it. When they had got it burning, and glowing embers were filling up the pit, they set the skewered fish to broil. After that, they erected the tent on the rise of stone near the ruins of the cabin, not far from the garden she and Tchibi had made so long ago. The boys did not want to take her coins for their services, but in the end accepted them.

When they left for the village, Rose ate the trout and saved the whitefish for another day. She made tea and sat down on the grass sipping it with gratitude. The day was sunny, with small white clouds brushing across the underside of the sky. Slipping into memory, she saw Grandma at sunset coming from the cabin door and offering a slice of the saskatoon-berry pie that she had made especially for Corpus Christi. The flies crawling into the pastry slits and out again, though Ogini did not notice, did not care. What is a berry? What is a fly? It all tastes sweet.

Hoping to restore some order to the clearing, she took the bow saw and hacked away the saplings that had sprung up during her years of absence. All one morning she worked in a sweat, cutting down the wrist-thick and finger-thin trees. Throughout the afternoon she bundled little sticks for kindling, stacked small logs in heaps, and covered them with the tin sheet to dry in the wind. After that, she set fire to the dead grass, watching closely as it crawled through the accumulation of old weed, devouring the brittle textures in a wide circle around the hub of the ancient garden. Its wheel was exposed the black ash. Still there was no loon-star in it. This was an absence within the larger absence. Yet how hot and happy her face felt, with soot on her hands and cheeks. And in the dirt was written, *O my daughter, the splendor of the earth was made for you*. And in the heap of dead white fire was written, *O daughter of man, you are but dust and ashes*.

The wildflowers put out buds and blossoms, and the soft night air carried their perfume through the open windows of the tent, along with the mosquito's song, high as the highest note Sister Clothilde used to play on the organ. The tent had mosquito netting, for which Rose was grateful. At night she sometimes lay awake for hours, listening. Listening to the listening within the tabernacle of her heart, though he was silent.

I turn to you, she said to him. *Yet I do not hear you, do not feel you. When will you speak to me again?*

Only the wind replied, singing,

> *I am with you, I am with you,*
> *Do you remember,*
> *O daughter of man,*
> *do you remember,*
> *the child who climbed the heights,*
> *and swam in the pool of cleansing,*
> *and saw the face of death on the border*
> *   of the land of little trees,*
> *and learned of me?*
> *A time to be born and a time to die,*
> *a time to cast away stones and a time*
> *to gather stones together. . . .*

At other times, the wind walloped the tent under an overcast sky, and the lamp-black squirrels galloped upside down on the branches, and it seemed that strangeness and darkness had descended over the world. She recalled the nights of childhood when the pines had creaked and cracked on the *windigo*-terror trail. Then she forced herself to remember how she had felt when seeing the cabin window glowing golden in the distance as she found her way home out of the blackest woods. Or in winter the soft heart-light of the sanctuary when the people sang the Huron Carol, *'Twas in the moon of wintertime when all the birds had fled, that mighty Kije-Manito sent angel choirs instead. Before their light the stars grew dim, and wandering hunters heard the hymn: Jesus your King is born, Jesus is born!*

Jesous Ahatonhia!

He comes, he comes!

She sat by the campfire and drank tea, watching the petals of red light dance on the trunks of the surrounding trees. She glanced up at the loon's necklace, from which long ago a star had fallen into the garden of the world. The evil star, the *matchi manito*, had fallen; so too had many lesser evil stars. But small good stars had been cast down by the lash of his tail as he raged against God, striking, striking, striking at God's beloved as he fell.

Tchibi! Tchibi! Where are you?

There was no Mass that Sunday, or the next. Rose felt keenly the absence of the sacrifice-way, the Great Offering-way, and the Communion. For the first time in more than ten years she was without daily Mass. Perhaps this was the reason she struggled against grief and fear and the small wrestlings of the mind. Surely it was so. But why had he permitted it? Had she misunderstood his will? She had believed he wanted her to return here, but now she was not so sure.

Oh, why does he not speak clearly?

One morning in the third week, she walked northeast into the upper tablelands of bush, climbing the spine toward the place of the skull. The journey was longer than she remembered it

...d made longer still by solitude, for time is swift when one
...alks hand in the hand with another. The trees were taller, the
...dergrowth thicker, though the clean stone ways led as always
... the height. There she found it little changed, the caribou
...oss crisping gray beneath the sun, aromatic juniper bushes
...rming their berries, and the view revealing the ultimate
...aces, north, north beyond the waters of the lake where God
...d rested, pressing his hand into the soft stone.

...Rose stretched out on the moss, shielded her eyes with her
...rearm, and gazed up into the highest blue where a white
...eck soared, gazing down upon her. It was a place of happiness
...d sorrow. She wept for loss and in gratitude for what had
...en. Her lips could still taste the wax colors and the slices
...f shortbread that melted on her tongue. She could feel the
...armth of wool tartan wrapping her in a mother's embrace.

...For the first time in several weeks she felt a desire to draw,
...ut this was not possible because she had neglected to bring her
...t materials with her on the hike. She remained in the hollow
...f the stone for several hours, dozing, remembering, thanking
...od for the gift of Euphrasia.

...The sun began to fall toward the earth. A yellow-green
...undog circled it. Rose watched it change colors and move.
...ed-winged soldier birds traded stories of war from their co-
...erts in the rushes. In the north a storm brewed. She got up and
...alked back to Crazyman River.

...ays passed, days of contentment. With her pastels, she painted
...e little warblers that trilled in the high leafy branches of
...irches. And the swallows that made their thousands of apart-
...ents in the clay banks by the river and drove away the
...ightier crows and ravens. The creek skinnied down into a
...in brook under the pulsing sun. The clearing broiled one day
...nd drank rain the next, turned as green as her landlady's Irish
...awl with mauve flowers woven into mint. Butterflies flew

round and round Rose's head and locked upside down in aeri
acts of lovemaking.

The boys from the village brought her more fish, some o
which she cooked fresh, and some of which she smoked, hop
ing to take it to the city with her in September. She paid the
for it, but began to worry a little about her money running o
too quickly, realizing that a third year at the Institute would b
impossible now unless she was able to find a city job ne
summer. This, then, might be her last summer in the north fo
years to come. Thus she drank deeply of all the things she sa
drank through her eyes the limitless colors and sounds ar
smells. She walked in many directions, but the walking co
much in terms of energy, and for that reason she accepted tl
gift of meat that one of the boys brought to her in early Augus
a big hare dangling over his shoulder, the blood already dryir
on the skin of his neck.

"No money", he said. "It's a present." And thumped his che
like the cartoon Indian in the movie. She smiled, but did n
have the heart to reject his gift, he was so exhilarated by h
conquest and his generosity. Though he was not in any wa
crazy, as Tchibi had been, his appearance was as wild and dirt
She felt a fondness for him, because he was so like her Nishim
her partridge. O to see him again! But this could not be, for tl
absence was part of the offering for him. The boy slit the brow
furry belly with a pocket knife, peeled the skin off, and pulle
out the steaming entrails. He flung the guts into the nearl
bushes where birds and insects might feed on them. That don
he led Rose to the trickle of creek, and sluiced the still-war
cavity of the hare's body. Then he skewered it on a stick and pu
it at an angle over the fire. She tried to force a dollar on him, b
he put his hands behind his back and ran away grinning into th
fiery weeds and disappeared through the shadows of the pines

One day she went again to the northeast, far beyond the ea
flank of Threefinger Lake. She walked for hours on the mean

ring highways of stone that cut through swamps and impen-
rable bush. In time she came to the pool where she had been
ansed of the hatred that had erupted briefly in her heart after
uphrasia's departure. She knew now that there had been no
ortal sin in the shredding of the woman's portrait, that it had
en no more than a cry of pain. Even so, she recalled the
tensity of her anger, her sense of abandonment, the few
conds when she had wanted to destroy, if not Euphrasia
rself, at least the memory of her. The water had washed the
ound clean, yet the memory remained.

It was a deserted place, the drip-drip of a spring deep in the
one feeding the circlet of the pool. She disrobed and bathed in
and emerged refreshed. Then she continued to walk, search-
g for a coffin under the weariless sky. She searched for it by all
e could remember of the way, but could not find it. The wind
tempted to speak to her, but she could not hear.

"Tchibi?" she asked, "Why am I alone and far from you?"

That night, asleep in her tent, she dreamed of the white bird
at hovered over the world. He swooped and soared. She
ached to take his wings to climb upon his back and ride the
ind with him. But he rose beyond her reach, speaking to her
ith his turquoise eyes, "Come."

She awoke, for it was impossible to go to him, she was held
the earth. Her feeling of loneliness was total, a knife cutting
to her breast. In the dark she reached for the lantern, but
nocked it to the ground. The glass chimney shattered. She got
from her blanket to clean the mess, and cut her heel on a
ard. It was not a severe cut, easily bound with a rag, but it
ieved her nonetheless, for she had lost her only light save that
ovided by the fire. The rain pelted the canvas roof, gusts of
ind made the tent cords groan, and the night was darker than
urial shroud, no moon, no stars.

And I said in the excesses of my mind, wailed the wind,
I am cast away from before thy sight.

On the following day the fox returned. He stopped in the high grass at the edge of the clearing. He jumped about on stiff legs, he pranced and bucked and then threw himself down on his back, wiggling about, opening his mouth wide as if he were laughing. Up he leaped again, prancing and bucking and turning in circles. Io, he was a crazy fox, a mad fox. Birds gathered around to watch. A brown rabbit appeared from nowhere, drawn by curiosity. The fox threw himself down again and wiggled all about on his back. The rabbit crept closer, her ears pricked straight up in astonishment.

Suddenly the fox ended his antics, shot like a red arrow at the rabbit, and seized her neck in his jaws.

"Ay, ay!" Rose cried, "Let her go!"

But the fox trotted off into the woods, his meal dangling from his sharp mouth.

"Io, you have charmed your prey!" Rose shouted angrily.

The weeks moved too swiftly. There was a single Mass in mid-August, and it was a joy, for Rose had been without Communion since her last day in the city. The Presence swelled within her like sweet-fire. O, he spoke to her in the words that were soundless. Yet he did not linger, and it seemed to her that he wished to return her to the aloneness in which he had placed her for a time. From it she must learn a thing, an important thing, he seemed to say. But Rose was unsure what it might be.

She continued to make pictures, trying now the small tubes of egg-paint on sheets of paper textured like canvas. At first the white surface permitted a little madder-green for summer leaves, and a blue-green for water. Then more colors found their place—gold for minnows, orange-yellow for fire, a bit of purple for the passionate flowers, and brighter reds for the raspberry and partridge berry and the other berries which were the fruitfulness of the earth, and its ornament, and its playful

ss. All this occurred as the actual berries sprang up in every
rection, familiar and consoling on the tongue, though the
rtridge-berry needed sugar when spread on a disk of hot
nnock. When the late summer sky turned deeper blue, burn-
g the blueberries bluer than scorched steel, she ate them as
ell and remembered.

More brilliant colors began to erupt in the forest. Even on
ose blustery overcast days when the lake appeared in its most
rbidding guise, all its waves aroused into gray fangs, the colors
uld not be dimmed—the birches showing their first brush
okes of yellow, the ground-hugging bushes sparking into
ange and scarlet. Not long after, wêwe the goose returned
om her Arctic feeding grounds, her long neck straining toward
e south, her bands of light feather, dark feather vibrating
avelets of air, dropping from the sky only for a brief rest at
areefinger Lake. In the mornings when a cool mist was on the
orld, she lifted from the water and cut the sky, honking,
rving her name in the wind.

uring the first week of September, Rose made another jour-
y into the northeast, intending a final good-bye to the
ull and its memories. When she passed through the village
d entered the Land of Little Trees, she began to think of
hibi with great intensity. Unsure of the rightness of it, she
tended a hand to him, and he clasped it, and together they
alked on.

"I may not come this way again in my life", she said. Was it to
rself that she spoke, or to Tchibi, or to Jesus? She did not
ow.

Turning to Jesus, she said, "O my Lord, may I walk with my
loved brother in the pretend way, which is the art-way of the
ind and heart?"

She was uncertain of the answer, but her desire did not feel
e darkness. It was a good-bye to him also, for this was the

place of the childhood they had shared, and neither of the[m] might see it again. It took them most of the morning to clin[b] to the skull, because Rose's back was aching badly and fr[e]quently she was forced to stop and rest. When they arrived, s[he] saw that nothing remained of the burned tree except bits [of] crumbled wood sinking beneath the encroaching moss. Pop[lar] saplings were fringing the socket.

They stood side by side on the crest and gazed across the la[ke] which was a sheet of steel under a blanket of cloud.

"Do you remember?" Rose asked.

He nodded. "It is the place where you brought me back [to] life, Ogini. This is the land we loved."

"We were together then. Always we were together."

"Do not return to the city, Ogini."

"I must go."

"It is a barren land, the city."

"There are many barren lands", she said. "In this place I a[m] now alone. It is not good to be so alone. Perhaps I will find y[ou] there in the city, for none here know of you or can tell m[e] where you have gone."

"We will find each other again, Nissime."

"I hope for this, Nishime."

Tchibi's eyes became fierce. "In our world, the one wh[o] strives to find a separate path is called strange", he said, looki[ng] off toward the trees. "But we must not heed them, the on[es] who mock."

Rose took his hand and said, "Come, I want to show yo[u] something."

An hour of walking brought them to the high, glacier-wor[n] plateau of granite where the Land of Little Trees tumbled ov[er] the edge of the escarpment. Rose stopped at the brink an[d] her eyes plunged down into the vast plain below, filled wit[h] swamps drained by innumerable creeks threading northward t[o] the Arctic sea.

310

In the rock crannies where a little soil had collected, the wild blueberries were dusky ripe. She and Tchibi picked and ate them. When they were content they lay down in a pocket of moss and let their faces bake in the sun, while there lingered behind their eyes a hallucination of berries burned upon the retina by long looking.

When Rose sat up again, she gazed farther east along the table of rock in search of the memory she had desired. But the square of white light was no longer there. She lurched to her feet, her heart feeling a moment of disquiet. Tchibi followed. As she walked along the edge of the cliff, Rose wondered what had happened to this final, this most strange memory. Perhaps the angle of the sun was wrong, or it might have been that the box had grown unreflective with the passage of years.

By the time she reached it and stood a dozen feet away, its true condition was revealed. Only splinters of wood and bits of bone remained. An arch of vertebrae rose and fell into the waves of moss, tinted by lichen, bleached white where the sun touched.

She bent down and picked up the intricate carving. Pieces fell away, leaving only three in the palm of her hand.

"What is it, Ogini?" said Tchibi. "What have you found?"

"The past", she said. "And the future."

He was silent.

At that moment Rose saw the brevity of life. She understood, as well, that within her own span of time she could create nothing beyond what was given. Words or embraces, cries or chants, drawings and paintings and carved stones, all burst like a clutch of birds from the open fingers, all fell back into the soil. But it was not, in fact, a falling into nothingness, for the speaking of words sent waves throughout the world.

She put the vertebrae back into their hollows in the moss.

"We are but dust and ashes", she whispered.

"Ogini," said Tchibi, so quietly she almost did not hear, "what will you do?"

She looked at him trying to fathom his words.

"Will you leave this land and forget the memory we made together?" he asked.

"I must leave, Nishime."

"Why must you?"

"I must leave, but never will I forget. There are pictures I must make, the many faces where Christ hides. The many faces of mankind, the known and the unknown— my grandmother's face, which is the face of a mother, and the face of the boy who is my brother."

"Me?"

"Yes."

He gave a warbling cry—the sad song of the solitary loon.

She listened carefully now to his breathing and felt the heat of his hand in hers. Io, it was sweet-fire!

"You must carry me, Ogini", Tchibi said. "You must carry my pain, and your own besides, for I do not lift on my own wings."

Now he turned to her and spoke with great earnestness: "I am thirsty."

"Drink from the many waters, Nishime", she said, pointing to a pool of rainwater cradled in a bowl of rock.

"I am thirsty with a thirst that cannot be quenched", he said.

"Do you not know?" she said. "Do you not know there is quenching!"

"I cannot see it. I cannot taste it", he answered.

"You are thirsty for God, my Nishime. It is he who fills our thirst. Open your mouth and drink!"

"But I cannot!" he cried.

"Why can't you?"

"I cannot see the love you speak of."

"I see it for both of us."

312

He fell silent, and the form of him and his colors faded away.

On the morning of her departure, Rose wandered disconsolately around the clearing. She stood within the charred remains of the cabin, and stirred the ashes with her foot. It struck a solid thing buried in the wet ash mud. She knelt and tugged it loose. It was the partridge stone that Tchibi had given to her as a Christmas gift many years ago. It was no longer green. It was black, yet the shape and the speckles of the feathers, or the torture, were unmistakable. She wrapped it in leaves and put it carefully into the deer-hide bag that Oldmary had made for her. Feeling that she was now bringing part of him with her, she turned and walked in the direction of the village, and the airplane, and the many paths that would take her to the barren lands of the south.

12

Rose surprised herself by the pleasure she felt unlockin[g] the door of her little room on King Street. When she entere[d,] turned on the light, and gazed about, the joy of shelter greete[d] her. Though she had lost all those whom she loved, this dwel[l]ing place was her own, if only for a while.

The roll of drawings leaned undisturbed against the wall i[n] her closet. She undid the string that bound it and spread sever[al] around the room, on the floor, on the table, on the be[d.] Instantly the dingy room burst into flames, and she smile[d.] Then she unwrapped the binemin stone and placed it at the fe[et] of the Sacred Heart.

The past comes with you, she thought, *the inner garden cannot b[e] taken from you.*

Rose counted her pennies, trying not to hold them too close t[o] her eye, reminding herself that they could blot out the sun.

Trust what is happening, she whispered. *For in all places he [is] with you and cares for your every need.*

Fifteen hundred dollars remained, barely enough to make [it] through the second year. Indeed, if she paid both the rent an[d] the tuition, there would be little left for food, in fact no mor[e] than a few weeks worth. She asked at the corner store if ther[e] was part-time work, but the Lebanese man said there was non[e;] he had a family for that. What was she to do? She asked a[t] several stores up and down the street, but her color and th[e] strange shape of her body made people uneasy.

She returned to the practice of daily Mass with great relie[f.]

d during the first thanksgiving after Communion she asked
e Lord to help her make ends meet.

We must ask, she said to herself. It is good to ask, for he is the
ther-King and he is love. Within us is not only the seed of the
shiwed, but the worse seed, which is to make a god of oneself.
hus it is good to need God, and in our need be reminded that
e are not God.

I do not have enough money for the year, Kije-Manito, she said to
m. *Beloved, Beating Heart, is there a way?*

After the first Sunday Mass, the landlady walked home with
er.

"Yer a godly child", she said. "I can see that, Rose. If you
ke, you can pay me by the month. The lump sum'd be nice, to
e sure, but my conscience pricks me on it."

Rejoicing at how quickly the Beating Heart answered her
ayers, she thanked the landlady, and told her it would be a
eat help.

On the day of registration, Rose searched for Deirdre in
e hallways of the Institute, hoping to warm the city with a
iendly face. The leotard lady greeted her with large smiles and
ninterruptible chatter and long languorous strides, but was
sily distracted by the many other students swarming in the
lls. The new students, the first-years, were noisy and great in
umber, for there was a continuous supply of young artists,
ose saw. Several of those who had been with her last year were
issing, though at least half of them had returned. The third-
ears were the fewest, and among them, Rose found Deirdre.

She was telling jokes and tossing her copper curls in a ring of
rls who were eating their lunches in the basement.

"Rosy", Deirdre said. "Great t'see you. Back for more of the
me?"

"Yes. I am eager for this year, Deirdre," Rose said. "There is
ways so much to learn."

"Yeah, ain't it the truth."

Deirdre crumpled wax paper into a ball, which made Ro
feel at ease, it was so familiar and friendly. Deirdre shot the b:
across the room, where it landed inside a wastepaper basket.

"Score!" she shouted, making the other girls laugh and som
long-haired boys look at her with interest.

Rose stood beside the girls' table, merely enjoying the
company, saying nothing. Deirdre glanced up at her, then looke
wryly at her other friends.

"Don't mind our Rosy", she said in her joking style. "Ros'
not the talkative type."

Everyone grinned, looked away, and began conversatio
with each other. Deirdre began telling a story to another gi
Rose listened for a while, then left.

It was disappointing, because she had wanted to tell Deird
just a little about her trip to Threefinger Lake and to ask abo
her friend's summer experiences. But she understood th
Deirdre was a popular person, and that it was selfish to want
keep her for herself. It was good to be reminded that she d
not own people, that she could not make them act as sl
would like them to. This was a small sacrifice. It was a kind
poorness, and to be poor was to be rich.

The next morning classes commenced, and the study
painting began in earnest. Much of what was taught to h
she already had learned from her experience with the sm:
tubes of egg paints, and from the pastel sticks. The spectru
that shattered into its many colors, the mixing of colors—tl
was like breathing. She did not need to think about it, f
her eye and hand knew what to do. But the oil paints that ooze
from the large metal tubes when she squeezed them onto
palette—Io!—these were a different substance altogether. The
colors were strong, but the material of them was difficult
control. She had to think about every act, every stroke of tl
brush, each blending, each application. They did not obe
They had minds of their own. Yet, whenever she was able

aster them to a degree, the results were startling. It was a new
way of seeing, and thus it was a new way of speaking.

The many languages of man were so different from each
other, she thought. They all issued from human mouths, and
they all said much the same things, though the sounds were
different. Thus they pointed beyond themselves to something
deeper that was linked to something higher. It was to the
thinking-way that all spoken words pointed, to the meaning-
way, which pointed in turn to the being-way. The differences
between languages were a remnant of the Tower of Babel,
Rose saw. With paint she could leap across the ravines that
separated the many peoples, speaking in a tongue that was
known to all.

Rose liked the studio classes best, for in these she just
worked. She painted. There were three studio classes for painting, taught by professors who were older people, polite and
distant, dressed casually, but neatly. There was a single art history class taught by the leotard lady, and a life-drawing class
taught by a bearded young man who wore tattered clothing and
sandals, even in winter, and smoked cigarettes incessantly. He
lived upstairs with the leotard lady.

In the life-drawing class, the students continued to use charcoal, studying a thing called "form", which was the outer shapes
of objects and their masses and the spaces that they displaced.
During the first month, they concentrated on rendering each
other's faces, replicating the plaster busts of horses, cornucopias
of plastic fruit, and the wooden mannikins that gestured on
swiveling joints. Most of the professors liked realism, which was
the reproduction of a subject as close to its visible form as
possible. This was necessary training, they said, and of course it
was. The leotard lady disagreed strongly, but this did not affect
the studios, for she merely showed slides and talked. She was a
great admirer of Picasso, who broke all the rules, who dismantled life and reassembled it, she said, and Marcel Duchamp,

who made art from anything. A urinal of his and a bicyc
wheel were in the National Gallery.

One elderly professor, Dr. Ganze, a man who had come fro
a distant land called Schleswig-Holstein, told his students th
could become geniuses later, after they mastered the basics. N
one laughed at his joke, for his voice was full of anger, and th
did not like him. Rose liked him for the true things he sa
about art and for the warnings he gave to the students abo
pride—he was the only teacher who spoke of such things.

"Observe *The Raft of the Medusa*", he said, pinning a print
the wall of the studio. "Appreciate the drama of the raft: th
writhing torsos, the pathos, the convulsing waves, the scream
ing wind, the thirst, the desperation of the survivors as th
rescue ship appears on the horizon."

"Is it arriving or disappearing?" a student asked in an arg
mentative tone.

"An excellent question", the professor said. "A litmus test
the psyche. The viewer is invited to discover whether he is
optimist or a pessimist, *ja*?"

This reduced everyone to silence as each examined his ow
psyche.

"Now, you have skimmed the surface of the drama,
the vicarious experience. Below is the ocean of meaning in
which Géricault asks you to plunge. Go deep. Try, if you can,
see more."

Silence reigned for long minutes as students strained the
eyes toward the picture, glanced surreptitiously at their wr
watches, or dreamed as they stared out at the red leaves beyor
the studio window, hoping for rescue.

"Anyone?"

No one offered.

Scanning the room with his cool, though sympathetic eye
the professor lit upon the introverted Indian girl hiding behir
her easel in the corner.

"Miss Wâbos, can you tell us what is beneath the waves?"

Rose felt certain now that he did not like her, that he had ⸢sin⸣gled her out for embarrassment. Unable to speak, she blinked ⸢rap⸣idly.

"Sharks?" someone said.

"U-boats?" someone else suggested, dangerously, for every⸢on⸣e knew that the professor had come from a tainted race. He ⸢sh⸣ot an amused glance at the satirist.

"Deeper", he said without taking offense. "Deeper than the ⸢sh⸣arks and the U-boats. Come, Miss Wâbos, I sense a depth in ⸢yo⸣u."

Clearing her throat she said in a small voice. "It is the being ⸢un⸣der the waters, a presence as old as the world."

The professor looked at her curiously.

"Please, continue, articulate it for the rest of us, if you will", ⸢he⸣ said in a quiet voice.

"I do not know for certain", she said tremulously. "It seems ⸢to⸣ me that it is about losing and finding. And losing again. ⸢T⸣hen everything depends on the finding."

He mused on that. "A good answer, deeper than the sharks. ⸢B⸣ut you are offering me a crumb, so that you might swiftly ⸢es⸣cape public scrutiny. You are capable of more. Do not be ⸢af⸣raid."

"It is as if the whole world is the sea," she said, "and the raft ⸢is⸣ the wreckage of a great ship that went down at the beginning ⸢of⸣ the world."

The professor's eyebrows raised.

"Continue."

"We are the survivors."

He nodded, his eyes fixed on her, his face unreadable. Rose ⸢bl⸣ushed mightily and stared at her hands folded on her lap. The ⸢pr⸣ofessor looked out the window, lost in thought. Without ⸢re⸣sponding to her last comment, he said, "Draw the structure of ⸢th⸣e image, all of you. You need not overfocus on detail. Seek

the sculptural form of the two dimensions you see before yo
Then, over the entire drawing, a sepia wash, yellow och
mixed with a little brown and a drop or two of linseed o
Tomorrow we will begin the copying, if it does not offend t
geniuses in the class. To copy is to learn from what has go
before. We do not create *ex nihilo*, out of nothing. We are n
God."

This last comment was greeted by sardonic glances amo
the students, who had evolved beyond such antiquated co
cepts. One of the few who were not repelled, Rose felt a th
of recognition wash through her. She took a sharpened pen
from the tray at the base of the easel and began to copy.

Two weeks later, after the trees had stripped down to th
bare limbs and sleet had become not uncommon, mixed wi
snow flurries and the screech and bang of minor car accider
outside on King Street, the studio copies were close to compl
tion. Many of the students' works were impressive in th
exactness. A few were interpretive, displaying various wea
nesses of perception or technical skill. One was a blurry ca
toon, produced by a girl who burst into tears and fled from t
classroom never to return.

"Ach, poor child", the professor murmured.

Rose also felt like fleeing. She struggled valiantly to fini
her copy, but it continued to surge and dip beneath her brush
It was so unlike the original that it reeked of failure.

Life-drawing class was the most troubling of all Rose's studi
for after the first month the drawing professor—the your
bearded man—moved on from plastic fruit and wooden torso
He informed the students that henceforth they would concer
trate on the human form.

"*Live* human form?" someone asked.

"Of course live human form", the instructor replied. "Eve
Monday, we will have a nude model. Those who cannot disti

_ish between nudity and nakedness may absent themselves. _rudes may especially absent themselves."

At Sunday Mass, Rose asked the Lord to guide her on this _atter. She had seen plenty of nakedness in the shower room at _er old school, though there had been no attraction in this. Her _nly experience of the unclothed male form had been a set of _rms and ankles decorated with burn holes. And the nudes in _useums, in books, in parks, in a few paintings, the drowned _ilors in *The Raft of the Medusa*. But such nakedness had elicited _ty. She had avoided the Greek sculptures after the initial _lance and the very first stirrings of emotion.

She hoped that the model would be a woman, which was _ufficiently human to instruct, to arouse empathy and nothing _ore. Indeed, the first model was a woman. She was about _rty years of age, her teasly hair canary yellow, her lipstick and _ascara laid on thickly, and her very red fingernails much in _se, splaying and unsplaying like the fan on the Japanese ki-_ono covering her overfull form. As she entered the studio, she _eemed to be pouting. But Rose soon learned that the woman _as not unhappy about her job. The model made jokes and _sked if she could smoke while posing. The instructor said of _ourse she could smoke. He lit one also, and together they _eiled her in a miasma of exhalations.

When it came time for her to mount the pedestal, she did so _onchalantly, in much the same way that other people climb _nto buses. Elevated above the ring of drawing boards and _asels, she sat on a high stool, then dropped the kimono from _er shoulders. She was rather overweight, her manner breezy _nd talkative. She kept asking the professor for cigarette after _igarette. She crossed her legs and bounced them. She seemed _ored, but not uncomfortable.

"Can I get one of those pictures when you guys are fin-_hed?" she asked.

"Could you ask her to keep still, sir", a student begged.

"Sorry, kid", the model crowed, laughing. "Mum's th word."

The professor took up his own sketch pad and made a draw ing of her in no time at all. He tore it from the pad and showe it to her.

"Geeze, that's good!" she said.

"It's yours", he said.

"Sir—lady!" students complained.

"Sorry, kids, I won't move a muscle. I promise."

She stood, she curved, she sat, changing her position ever twenty minutes.

Rose did not enjoy the session, for the human form seeme too vulnerable without its hide or its plumage. She recalled th sudsy baths in the cabin at Crazyman River, and the care th Grandma had always taken to guard her dignity, though th guarding became apparent only in hindsight.

She drew the woman's body, struggling for precision, but he heart was not in it. Sketch after sketch, she felt increasingl defeated by the subject and her inability to transfer it to pape

"See first the form", she said to herself. "Understand i Absorb it as a word. The shape, the volume, the mass whic displaces air. Then see the shape of the air around it. Draw th air, leaving the hole in space", said her eye.

It helped, but the drawings remained lifeless. Only when sh switched from charcoal pencil to the thicker charcoal sticks, di the drawings begin to move. In the end she remained dissatis fied with them all, for it was obvious that her hand and eye wer running without the engine of the heart. You could draw an paint only what was within you, it seemed.

"Only love creates", she said to herself. "I am ashamed, for do not love this woman. Nor do I pity her, for she is stronge than all of us. What, then, am I to do?"

She resolved to complete the tasks that the drawing professo demanded of the class, and no more than that. There would b

322

investment of heart. She would obey and endure, and at the end of the year would destroy the drawings with relief, for they were dead.

"Excellent", said the professor breathing smoke over her shoulder. "But try not to overemphasize the character. You're concentrating too much on the face. We're not after her individuality here. We're after the architecture of the flesh."

At lunch time, the woman pulled a dress over her body, slipped her feet into high-heel shoes, and went off to the cafeteria joking and chatting with the students. Rose left also, and went out onto the wet streets where she desired to find a tree and listen to the wind raking its rattling branches, which were also nude. She found one in a nearby park and listened to its complaints until she felt a little better.

On Monday of the following week, she prepared herself to endure another session of "dead-drawing" as she had come to think of it. She was the last to arrive in the studio, a minute after the hour. Of the twenty students in the class none were absent, and a current of excitement hung in the atmosphere. A different model was seated on the platform.

The model was a black man. He was robed in a white bedsheet draped about his shoulders. His large bare feet stuck out from beneath its hem. He sat with hands clasped between his knees, bending forward, his head lowered as if in shame, as if he were receiving a scolding. While the students bustled at their easels, arranging pencils and charcoal, flipping pads of blank newsprint paper, the professor stood by the platform giving the model instructions: where to stand or sit, how to pose, and for how long. The man nodded, but he did not cease staring at the floor.

Rose slid into her chair at the back of the room.

"Okay, class", the teacher barked, clapping his hands for attention. "Loosen up, zip those lips, time for serious work."

He nodded at the model, who got slowly to his feet, his

chin on his chest. He pulled the sheet from his shoulders and dropped it to the floor at his feet.

Rose looked away from him. Not because there was a temptation in it, but because her heart was stricken with the waves of anguish that emanated from him. He, the model, did not know the difference between nudity and nakedness. For that matter, neither did she. She was beginning to wonder if there was a difference.

A small scrap of privacy was left to him, for he wore a pair of white underbriefs. He was about thirty years of age. His body was of great size and strength, without any fat, and from its muscles one could read a history of arduous physical labor. Who was this strong man here, she wondered. What had brought him to this, if he so hated it?

Io! He is afraid, she thought. *He feels himself small in our eyes.*

Now the engines of her heart ignited, for empathy is a fire that can surpass the stirring of desire. Desire was not the issue of the moment. She glanced at his face, which was like stone, the lids of his eyes lowered, almost closed, the body standing square.

"Turn the upper torso, would you?" the instructor asked. The man did not at first understand.

"Like this", said the instructor, swiveling his slender frame. The students laughed.

The eyes of the model began to blink rapidly, and Rose realized that he thought the laughter was at his expense. He did not know his own dignity. He thought it had been stripped from him; she could see it in the tightening of his lips and the blinking that did not cease. She tried to draw the magnificent torso, but her hands would not do it, for that would be an act of reduction, of pushing him deeper into the realm of things. For a thing to be a thing was good. For a man to be a thing was to be degraded into less than a thing, into a no-thing.

"I cannot", she said to herself. She put the charcoal onto the

sk and sat woodenly, staring at the blank paper on her draw-
g board.

Then she thought that she could at least pray for him. In the
ty, she had noticed that it was harder for her to pray. How
sily it slipped away. How easily the unceasing flow of faces
came less real, and in the end not real until they spoke or one
oke to them, making them real.

She closed her eyes.

*Jesus, Beating Heart, see him there, that man. He feels himself alone.
dark thing claws his heart, pulling him down. Let it not be so. Give
n courage. Give him hope.*

"Break!" said the instructor. An exhalation of tension es-
ped from many mouths throughout the room. The model sat
wn on the stool and hung his head.

"Miss Wâbos, how come no drawing?" the instructor asked
he frowned at her empty paper.

"Today I cannot", she said, nodding in the direction of the
odel. "He is suffering."

The instructor shrugged and walked away.

After the break the model was told to strike a running pose,
t leg behind, right leg forward, arms thrust for counter-
lance. It was a difficult position, and as the man held it for
ve, then ten, then fifteen minutes, his limbs begin to tremble
d shine with sweat.

She prayed for strength for him.

Why does he endure it? she wondered.

By eleven o'clock heaps of papers lay on the floor beside
ery easel except Rose's.

She sat and prayed.

At eleven-fifteen, a group of students put their heads
gether, nodded to each other, and walked over to the instruc-
r's desk.

"Uh, sir, we were wondering if, uh, he needs the under-
ear."

The instructor smiled and leaned back, hands clasped behin his head.

"In pursuit of professional excellence, are we?"

"Yeah, something like that. I mean, we paid our tuition. Yc said nude. This guy's not exactly nude."

"Why don't you go ask him to strip", the instructor said wi a small smile.

"No, thanks."

"I will", proclaimed a bold young woman. She strode to tl platform and spoke to the model in a low voice, her fa straining for an attitude of professional courtesy. The mod stared at her for a few seconds, then looked back at the floc The entire class watched in anticipation. Rose alone plead with him silently: *No*, she said, *no*.

He stood, his chest heaving, folding his arms, unfoldi them, and folding them again. His lips trembling, hands sha ing, he turned away from the students and removed the last his clothing. Rose instantly stared at her blank paper. Tl other students scrambled for their desks and the instruments their art.

"A side view first", the instructor suggested into the echoi silence. The model turned. Charcoal began to scratch throug out the room.

"Front view now, upper torso pivot to the left."

The model obeyed. The room inflated with the sound of l agonized breaths.

"Now the runner", said the instructor after ten minutes.

"Now, take a rest. Try an exhausted boxer pose, seate elbows on knees."

This too the model obeyed.

Mercifully, the bell rang for lunch. With mutterings a groans and the flipping of paper on the many pads, the sessic ended. The model looked up, saw the students rising to leav He pulled the sheet from the floor and covered his body.

The instructor barked loudly, "Back at one o'clock, every-body."

He went over to the model and said in a cheery voice, "Hey, you were great, buddy. You're the best. Think you can take a few more hours of this?"

The model ignored him. He rested his forehead in his hand, like Rodin's thinker, and closed his eyes. When the room was empty, save for Rose and the model, she got up and went to him, carrying her lunch box with the Scottish girl on its lid. She sat down on the edge of the platform. Close to him now, she saw that he was very tall and powerful, a black mountain, like a mountain that had been burned by forest fires. She opened the box. Inside there were two sandwiches, an orange, a banana, and a thermos of lukewarm tea. She offered the open box to the man. He did not seem to notice.

"Excuse me, sir", Rose said in a small voice, for she was a little frightened of him. He looked up with a start. His eyes, she saw, were wet. He stared at her, and she looked back, feeling the gentle pull of falling-into-seeing. She sensed warm winds blowing through him from a very distant and calm blue sea, and silver fish flapping in a net beside a beach of white, white sand. A black man dancing and laughing as he emptied his nets, watching his children running beside the rhythmic chant of waves, beneath a high blue mountain.

"Would you like some lunch?" Rose asked.

His voice, when he spoke at last, was deep, though broken. "No, thank you", he said.

"Do you mind if I sit by you?"

He shook his head, staring at the floor.

"What is your name?" she asked.

"Cletus."

"That is a beautiful name, like the martyr."

He made no reply.

"My name is Oginiwâbigon Wâbos, which is a strange name."

A flicker of interest stirred in his eyes.

"Don't you want to know what it means?"

"What it mean?" he asked in a voice as solemn as the sea.

"It means roseflower rabbit."

A smile twitched on the edges of his lips.

"You right, little girl. Dat a strange name."

The accent in his English was unusual. It had music in it.

"Where are you from?"

"Jamaica."

"Where is that?"

"In the West Indies."

"I am an Indian too," she said.

He straightened and pulled the sheet tighter about himself. "I can see dat, little girl."

Curiosity was growing in him, she could feel it.

"I am not a girl, sir. I am twenty-three years old."

"I want to be alone", he said. "Please go away."

"I will go away, if you wish."

She stood. But for some reason, he seemed to regret what he had said. Eyeing her lunch box he pointed at it.

"I wouldn't mind a bite o' dat orange."

She handed it to him. He glanced at her suspiciously and closed his large white teeth over it, peel and all.

"Do you like tea?"

He nodded.

She scurried to the wash sink and found a clean mug. She poured some tea into it and brought it to him. He drank it in a single gulp.

"Would you like a sandwich? I cannot eat them all."

"If you insist."

Insist was a thinker's word, she knew.

"Have you moved to this land recently?" she asked.

He nodded.

"You must miss your country very much."

328

"I do", he nodded and nodded.

"The warm winds blowing from the calm blue sea, and silver ish flapping in a net beside a beach of white, white sand? And hildren running along it beside the singing waves."

He took a sandwich and looked at her more closely as he ate.

"The waves do not sing", he said. "They cry."

"Ah," she said, "I did not know. I have never seen the sea.)id you work very hard in your life?"

He nodded. "Very hard."

"At what did you work?"

"Cutting cane."

"What is cane?"

"Sugar cane."

"That is why you are strong."

"It must be."

"I am sorry you feel sad."

"I'm not sad."

"I'm sorry you felt so alone when they drew you."

He did not respond. He dropped his eyes and took another ite of the sandwich.

"It is wrong to force you to do a thing that is so hard for ou."

"They ask. They pay. I need the money."

"Do you want to work here for more hours?"

He shook his head. "Got no choice."

"Why do you have no choice?"

"Got to eat. Got to send money back to my babies and my vife at Morant Bay."

"Beneath the blue mountain?"

"How you know such a thing, girl?" he exclaimed in a high-itched tone that belied his deeper voice. "How you know hat?"

"I saw it."

"You been southside Jamaica way?" he said, astonished.

"No."

He shook his head again. "You a strange girl."

Rose smiled at him. She opened her deer-hide bag and rummaged and withdrew whatever fell into her hand. She held it out to him and dropped it on the sheet stretched across his knees.

"What dis?" he said staring at it.

"It's for you, from the Beating Heart."

"What dis beating heart, you say?"

"You will know him. He is by the many waters, and on all shores, and he stands upon the blue mountains and all mountains, and there he shall stand on the last day."

The man's skin rose up in goose pimples. He stared at the money in his hand.

"Dis two hundred dollars. Don't be foolish, girl."

"It is for you, so that you will know."

"Know what?"

"You will know you are not a thing, you are not a no-thing, you are a good man, a father, a husband, a man who went naked for his babies."

"You stop talkin' like dat!" he said gruffly. Rose could see that he was not angry, that he was disturbed and in his great strength did not want to show tears before a girl.

"I have to go now", she said. She offered her hand. He put the money into his left hand and shook her small fingers with his massive right hand. His skin was as black as a summer night and as warm, as trembling as the sky when the *tchibekana* shimmers the speckles on its necklace. The palms were as pink as conch shells.

"You a crazy girl."

"I am not crazy. You know who gives this to you."

His face crumpled. In a child's voice he said, "I know him. I know him." Then he turned away and hid his face. She left the room and did not return to it until one o'clock. When she

330

rrived, she found that the man from Jamaica had gone and the tudents and instructor were stomping about, irritated by the nodel's unreliability.

ater in the month, the old painting professor removed the Géricault and pinned a Goya to the wall of his studio.

"Those who are ready may copy this", he said, and stood back.

It was a large print of an etching that Rose recognized: *The Sleep of Reason Produces Monsters*. It depicted a man with his head in his arms, perhaps sleeping, perhaps hiding, while bats nd demons fluttered about his head.

"An experiment", said the professor. "Obviously not a painting. An etching, black and white, two dimensions, no ttempt to make the illusion of a third dimension. See the orm. Reproduce it, and translate it into a painting. Mutate the wo fields into three. This time you are free to play. The work s the play and the play is the work. The form is not yours, the original word is not yours, but you may interpret with color nd chiaroscuro."

Ripples of excitement ran through the class, for the new project offered a trace of creativity. Rose was not ready to begin he Goya, for she was still struggling with the Géricault. Her copy was the last to be completed. She was not happy with it. The form was close, but the figures were a disaster! The ones hat arched upward, beseeching the disappearing or arriving escue ship, stretched toward the sky as if pulled by a power of nverse gravity. The ones that dangled into the sea were sucked lown by it. The waves were a cacophony of visual sound. The color was all wrong, brass terror and magenta despair. There was too much black in the water. Frustrated, convinced that it was impossible to finish the work, she groaned and fought a emptation to cry. Her hands were completely covered in oily mears. Her face was dabbed with turpentine, her eyes stung by ts pine perfume.

331

"You are finished?" the professor said. She looked up to find him standing behind her, peering over her shoulder. Startled she jumped.

"I cannot finish it. It will never be finished", she said miserably.

To her astonishment he smiled knowingly.

"Of course it will never be finished. No true painting is ever finished."

"It is a failure. It is a terrible copy."

He smiled again, murmuring little German niceties, his eye flickering all over her canvas.

"In this regard I will agree with you, Miss Wâbos. It is a *terrible* copy. Though it is technically sufficient, it is undistin guished as draftsmanship. Nevertheless, it is the other dimen sion that makes it a success."

"What do you mean?" she asked.

"The dimension of the inner eye. The interpretation which has conveyed the angst, the *Weltschrecken*—the world-terror— the great ship that went down in the beginning." He gestured to the other students, who were huddled over their Goya copies. In a voice that could not be overheard, he confided, "Some have replicated perfectly, others not so well, and all are compe tent. Yet none of them have expressed the world-terror. Only you."

"But it is the worst!" she argued.

"It is the best", he said and went away.

During the first two weeks of December, the cold weather rattled the windows of the Institute, the shortening days threatened the death of light, and heavy overcast brooded above the smog-ridden city. Rose began to copy the Goya with trepidation, for it was a horrible work, containing the faces of evil that she had seen in gnarled firewood during childhood sickness.

To draw evil? she wondered. *Is it good to do such a thing?* After

332

prayer and thought, she decided that it was permissible, for it made a word of warning. As with the Géricault copy, she fell into the canvas, and plunged, losing consciousness of the noise in the studio. There were moments when she despaired of the stubborn brushes, threw them into the pot of turp, scooped up pods of cool paint in her fingers and smeared it on the canvas and rubbed and nudged and scratched the shapes into an illusion of three dimensional form. Sepias and browns and blacks and purples and greens—bile green, shrieking green, chaotic green, backlit by the sallow light of madness. It was ugly. It was a frightening image. It was a frightening experience.

With greater frequency the professor strolled, as if casually, to her corner during his rounds of the studio. He always paused behind her, watched her dig into the paint as if she were crushing a handful of berries and cramming them into the waiting mouth of the canvas. He said nothing. He went away and came again.

On the last day of classes before the Christmas holidays, Rose felt that she had executed a second failure. As the other students jostled through the doorway at a quarter past four, hastening to the party in the basement cafeteria, Rose stayed behind, seated at her easel, frowning, an ache in her throat.

The clock above the professor's desk ticked loudly. Far away the waves of laughter and music broke upon the shores of hearing. The professor cleared his throat. Rose looked up and saw him seated behind his desk, eyebrows raised, tapping his wristwatch with an index finger.

"It is time", he said. "Now you will make a stop."

"But it isn't finished!" she said.

"So soon you forget: *Never* is the best work finished."

"And the worst", she replied, realizing too late that she had contradicted a professor. Strangely, he smiled.

"*Ja*, it is so. But in your case, it is a best. Another best."

Rose blushed.

333

"Please, Miss Wâbos, you will put away the paints and wash your hands. It is Christmas."

He looked at her with much kindness. A falling-into-seeing began, but the seeing was without inner pictures, it showed her only a *sense*, an old man who had known many losings and who was feeling at this moment singularly happy. It came and went in an instant. He stood and shoved back his chair. He picked up a Christmas gift from the desk and held it out to her. It was wrapped in green foil, tied with red ribbon, and decorated with a star made of braided straw.

"With your permission", he said bowing to her slightly, "I make a presentation for you."

Rose was dumbfounded. A gift from the sisters, yes; or from the beloveds whom she had carried on her back, yes. But a stranger? Then she realized that during the previous four months he had in a mysterious way ceased to be a stranger.

"Please to come here", he said. "I will not bite you."

He smiled and offered her the package

"You may open it", he said placing it into her hands with great politeness.

She undid the wrappings carefully and put them aside for saving. It was a book. An art book. A collection of paintings by Henri Rousseau.

"Thank you, sir", Rose breathed.

"Do you know him? Are you familiar with Rousseau?"

She shook her head.

The professor cocked his head in serious amusement. "You will, I think, find in him a mentor. Like you, he was not—how shall we say it—was not distinguished as a draftsman. You understand that I value precision in drawing most highly. It is of great importance. Yet, it is secondary to the depth of perception. Here", the professor reached and flipped a page. "Here is a heart all on fire for the world. The beautiful world."

"The world is so beautiful", Rose said.

334

"Precisely. And when you one day leave this institution, I [be]lieve you will go on to do as he did, though in a language of [yo]ur own."

In the first image that her eye fell upon, a man slept on the [san]ds of the desert in a multicolored robe. Beside him was a [sle]eping lute, its strings vibrating. A golden lion sniffed his body [as] he dreamed unheeding beneath a full moon.

Rose's eyes lit up. She turned a page.

A rabbit nibbled herbs in a forest glade.

In another, an angel blew a trumpet over a city where people [ma]rched and shouted and waved banners and weapons.

In another, a tiger clawed the body of the dying antelope that [it] had felled, its jaws devouring the living flesh.

In another, a mad child bearing a sword and a flaming torch [ro]de a leaping black horse over a field of naked corpses.

"*Der Krieg*", sighed the professor.

In another, a naked woman played a flute beside a fruit-laden [tre]e in a tropical garden; a snake hung from its branches yearn[in]g toward her.

"*La Charmeuse de Serpent*", said the professor. "Does it [sh]ock?"

"It is very beautiful", said Rose. "As beautiful and dangerous [as] a black pearl clutched to the heart."

He glanced swiftly at her. "You are an unusual person", he [sai]d shaking his head. "To produce such images! It is the lan[gu]age of poets."

This puzzled Rose, for the language of images was her native [to]ngue. It was ordinary. As the world thawed, the melted words [flo]wed out as rivulets.

"Tell me, Miss Wâbos, what is Rousseau's intention here? Is [th]e woman charming the serpent or the serpent charming the [w]oman?"

"Perhaps they seek to charm each other, and both are [de]ceived."

335

"An excellent answer."

"A litmus of the psyche", she said, smiling, though it wa great liberty to make a joke of a professor's words.

He chuckled. "Yes, a litmus. Exactly. The eye interprets, a in the interpretation the viewer is revealed to himself."

Rose turned a page. In the next picture, a child danced w a puppet.

In the one that followed, a dirigible balloon floated pas garden where two children played, oblivious to its presence.

Finally, a spotted leopard attacked a man in a jungle, clawi the naked black torso, pulling him down. Or were they da ing? It was hard to tell, because over all the horror, or the p hovered a disk of red sun, bathing the exploding flowers w gaiety.

Rose closed the book.

"Thank you, sir."

"Do not mention it", he said with a bow. "*Fröhliche We nachten*, Miss Wâbos. A happy Christmas. I will see you again January."

They bid each other good night, and the professor left t room whistling to himself, tying a long scarf about his ne Rose left a few moments later, after a last glance at her painti of the Goya.

Christmas was silence. It was snow falling through the qu streets. It was an empty house full of creakings and groanin but heated at the core by the presence who was with h Whenever she lay down on her bed and closed her eyes, s could hear him within and without. This flow of words-wit out-words was mixed with the faint carols that wafted in fro neighboring houses, the new softness of traffic in the street, a trolley sounds that were hushed as at no other time of the ye Most enjoyable were the chirpings of sparrows that pecked t bread crumbs she put on the window ledge. If she left the wi

w open an inch or two, the warmth attracted dozens of
em, huddling, jostling for position, too shy to enter the room
t inspecting her sideways with the little brown seeds of their
es.

How happy she was this Christmas. She knew that her joy
is purely a gift from the Beating Heart because it was the first
ne in her life that she was completely without the many *ningâs*
ho had mothered her. The sisters were gone across the ocean,
e landlady had gone away until after the New Year, Deirdre
is—well, doubtless she had her own life, her own family.
ose had expected to be lonely and to weep during the holi-
ys, but it was not so. Each day increased her solitude, and with
came each day's measure of joy. At morning Masses she felt a
owing anticipation for the great feast that was approaching.
ne Lord was pouring out an unusual amount of consolation,
 if she were crossing the last stretches of the desolate land, and
 the near distance an inn of refuge now appeared.

Christmas Eve Mass was the most glorious. Oh, the many
ildren who attended with their mothers and fathers. Io, the
ve that came from him when she prayed, *My life is yours. I am
urs.* And the ceasing of pain in her back—also his gift. On her
meward walk at one o'clock in the morning, the many bells,
d the soft, slow-dancing snow! How quiet the city, how
mforting the blanket that covered the sky, how safe and warm
r little room with its clanking radiator, and its whispering tea
ttle, and the jeweled fruitcake that Rashid, the Lebanese man,
d given her for Merry Christmas. She sat for hours in the
illness, watching the snow fall in the alley, listening to the
arrows, the graces of the birth of Manito washing her beyond
ne and space, into the sea of being. It was warm as a cabin. It
as sweet as strawberries in winter. It was the embrace of love,
s, at times she almost smelled the permanent smells of wood
noke and tobacco and moose hide. And felt the arms of a
other around her, and the high faint honking of Wêwe or the

night-warble of Mang. When the image of Tchibi appeared
the center of her inner eye, swimming in the river of souls,
did not disturb her or dispel her peace, for he was part of t
sweet-fire. His face was untroubled, as he was intended to
from the beginning, before the great shipwreck.

"Io, this is you, Binemin Edzo, this is the word that sleeps
the heart of you, it is the man you are in the eyes of Go
Wherever you may be in this world, I am with you."

As dusk fell on the afternoon of Christmas Day, she walk
in deep and quiet happiness to the parish hall of Holy Fam
church, and there she ate a splendid dinner, served by the Sa
Vincent de Paul Society. The meal was turkey with cranber
sauce—this was a special treat, for the bog-berry was a favor
of hers—and bread stuffing with onions, steaming and full
juices. The potatoes and golden yams dribbled with real butt
The apple pie was topped with slices of orange cheese a
round white orbs of vanilla ice cream. In bowls by each pla
there were salted walnuts, cashews, and hazelnuts. The ma
guests, the old people and the homeless people, were gratef
They said little to each other. They ate large quantities of foo
and some of them slipped the uneaten portions into plastic ba
that they pulled from their pockets—the Saint Vincent peop
did not mind; they offered plates of candies and hot minceme
tarts and encouraged people to take those along as well.

Rose embarrassed herself by eating too much, but it was
feast day, it was the Birthday. She could not resist taking a fe
candies home in her pocket. And two tarts that warmed h
hands for the journey.

That night she fell asleep praying for Tchibi. And rested
her sleep. And listened to the cries of children running beside
beach of white sand, dancing, laughing, teaching the solem
waves to sing with joy. And mused in her dreams on the ma
surprises the Lord had waiting for her.

338

13

On New Year's Eve, a loud banging on the front door of the house roused Rose from a letter she had been writing to Sister Madeleine. Trying not to trip on the staircase, she hurried down to answer it, fully expecting to see a stranger. Great was her surprise when she found her friend Deirdre standing there, puffing her cheeks, stomping her feet from the cold, hands thrust into the pockets of her jeans.

"Rosy, girl! Howarya? Can I come in?"

"Of course you can, Deirdre", Rose replied with beaming eyes.

"Can't stay long. Just wanted to wish you Happy New Year."

"Happy New Year to you too, Deirdre."

Deirdre stepped inside the front hall, and Rose closed the door behind her, shutting out the wind and the street noises that had returned to normal after Christmas.

As Rose led Deirdre up the staircase to her room, the visitor stared at the décor, whistling a tune under her breath, bouncing as if a suppressed dance was inside her limbs.

"Wow", she said, on entering Rose's room.

"This is where I live," Rose smiled. "Isn't it wonderful?"

"Wow", Deirdre said again, looking uncomfortably at the green walls and the many strange pictures taped to them and the little altar with the statue of the Sacred Heart.

"How much d'you pay for this place?"

"Eighty dollars a month."

"Eighty dollars a month! You're being robbed."

"Oh, no, Deirdre. The landlady is very generous."

Deirdre snorted.

"Would you like a cup of tea?"

"Sure, sure, that'd be fab."

While Rose got the kettle steaming on the hot plate, Deirdre sat down on a chair by the window, chafing her hands, blowing in them, bobbing to an inaudible tune.

"What are you doing tonight, Rosy? Goin' to a party?"

"No, I will stay here and think about the new year."

"Me too, I'm thinkin' about the new year. 1963! It's gonna be a great year, a really great year. I can feel it. I'm gonna blow this bandstand for good."

"What do you mean, Deirdre?"

"Movin' up in the world, movin' up", the visitor replied.

"You graduate this year, don't you? Are you going on become a designer of clothes? I hope you do, Deirdre. I believe you would be very good at it."

"Yeah," Deirdre said, "I'd be famous in no time flat."

Rose poured the tea and sat down on the other chair. Deirdre put three tablespoons of sugar into her cup. Rose brought a pint bottle of milk inside from the window ledge. Deirdre took it and topped off her cup, spilling some.

"Oops, clumsy me!"

While Rose searched for a rag to wipe it up, Deirdre lit a Pall Mall cigarette and blew smoke at the ceiling in a long thin jet.

"Rosy, can you do me a favor?"

"A favor? Of course, I will, Deirdre. What is it?"

"I'm in a bit of a bind at the moment. Caught a bit short. Can you spot me a twenty?"

"Twenty dollars?"

"Yeah. Twenty'd be fine. I'll pay you back. I promise."

Every natural instinct within Rose now surged forward, willing to offer what she could. Then a doubt entered.

"I want to lend you the money very much. But I do not have enough for my school year. I would need to be repaid soon."

340

'Hey, don't worry, I'll get it back to you. You won't lose any
ep over it. Deirdre always pays her dues."

"I hate to mention it, Deirdre, but you have often asked me
lend you money. It has been a year and a half now since you
gan to ask me for help." (Oh, how painful it was to say such
ngs!) "I know it is easy to forget. I forget things all the time.
ish I could say the debt does not need to be repaid, but I will
in much difficulty if I do not have the money back."

Rose said the foregoing in a tone of extreme tact and regret.
wever, just as she feared, Deirdre took it the wrong way. Her
s snapped and her mouth scowled.

"I paid you back. I know I did."

Rose shook her head.

"I'm sure I did. Okay, maybe I lost track and forgot some of
But look, Rosy, it's not nice t'weasel money out of people,
ecially your friends, try t'get more than what's owed you."

"I'm not—" Rose rushed to explain.

"Yeah, I know. I know you didn't mean it the way it
nded. But, look, it's water off a duck. You didn't hurt my
lings any."

This was a relief.

"I think I can spare twenty dollars", Rose said, going to the
set. Lighting another cigarette, Deirdre watched Rose take
deer-hide bag from the hook, remove a twenty dollar bill
m it, and hand it over. She accepted it with a wink, pocketed
and said, "Thanks a mill, Rosy, you're a lifesaver."

"How soon can you return it? Next week I must pay my
ing tuition and my rent."

"Cheeze, you're really up against, aren't you?" Deirdre said
itably. "Look, didn't I tell you not to worry. When Dee-dee
s don't worry, she means don't worry."

"All right, Deirdre, I know you are a dependable person."

"Hey, dependable is my middle name."

At that moment the doorbell rang. Rose jumped to her feet.

341

"I'll be right back", she said as she went out into the hallw
At the head of the stairs she paused and turned. "Have sor
more tea," she called. "There's Christmas cake too. Take ar
thing you like."

"Take your time, Rosy," Deirdre called back.

Downstairs, Rose opened the door on the second une
pected visitor of the evening. Slouching on the porch wa
young man in jeans and a canvas jacket. Despite his youth
thin mustache grew on his upper lip. A cigarette dangled fro
the corner of his mouth.

"Dee-dee here?"

"Deirdre? Yes, she is. Would you like to come in?"

"Nah. Tell Dee-dee I gotta get goin'. Ask her is she com
or isn't she."

Rose was about to do as he suggested, when Deirdre car
skipping down the staircase.

"Hold your horses, Skye, I was just havin' a little chat w
my friend here."

"Yeah, you and your little chats. I been sittin' out there in t
cruiser for half an hour waitin' for you, burnin' gas. Let's go

Deirdre breezed past Rose and went through the door wit
out saying good-bye. The young man put an arm about h
shoulder and together they hurried down the walkway tc
waiting car, rumbling at the curb. It was an older car, covered
rust spots, its back end tilted higher than the front, and a fox t
on the aerial. They jumped inside, and Skye drove away with
screech of tires and a honk.

At Mass the next morning, Rose prayed for Deirdre and Sky
After Communion she experienced a long consolation, fro
which she stirred only as the last parishioners left the churc
Outside, the day was sunny, warmer than it had been for weel
and icicles dripped from the eaves of the apartment blocks ar

d brownstone houses. Sparrows chipped in the melting gut-
rs, pecking at salt crystals. Children rolled sodden snowmen
small front yards.

Because it was the Feast of the Mother of God, Rose rested
bed all day, slept off and on, grateful that the pain in her back
eclined to almost nothing, as it always did on major feasts. She
ad Grandma's Bible, a passage about Our Lady fleeing into
gypt. Next she read the Beatitudes, lingering over what the
ord said about the blessedness of poverty. She loved this part
pecially, because it gave her so much comfort. She was poor,
e belonged to him, she was blessed. Even so, she knew that a
erson could possess a secret pride in this—yes, the spirit-pride,
e most dangerous of all, for it was the realm where the *matchi-
anito* moved with great subtlety.

"Do not be proud that the Beating Heart has blessed you so,
)giniwâbigon," she chided gently, "for what is good in you has
een given to you—it is no merit of your own."

On January second, Rose awoke to the normal pain in her
ack. It was a little worse than usual, which she attributed to the
eather, a mixture of severe cold and high humidity, the north-
n front and the great lake warring for supremacy over the city.
he house was no longer empty, for a few of the other tenants
ad returned from their holidays, and she could hear them
lking in the halls or moving about in the flat above her. It
as good to have company again, though she would miss the
olitude.

Remembering that her corner of the refrigerator contained
o groceries, she got up, dressed, found her deer-hide bag in
e closet, and went out. At Rashid's store, she gathered milk,
read, cheese, jam, white lard (a treat to spread on the bread),
ranges, and apples. And a tub of strawberry ice cream.

"Ice-a-creama? At this time-a-year?" Rashid scolded as he
imbly fingered the cash register beneath the icon of the Mother
f God. He was a heavy, olive-colored man, whose skin was

343

darker than her own. "Don't freeze you-self, Miss Rose. Whe**
you mittens, silly-lady?"

"In my pockets, see, Rashid!" She smiled at him. It fe**
childlike, daughterlike, it was a lovely sensation.

"Okay, okay, that's good. Now you pay. Today is nine dolla**
and ninety-five cents you own me."

While she rummaged in her deer-hide sack, he slipped a b**
of marzipan into her shopping bag, gold Arabic letters shinin**
on the cellophane. An almond tree on the blue mountains **
Lebanon.

"You shouldn't, Rashid. You have babies to feed."

"No argamint. Very sweet. Eat it, keep you warm when yo**
walk to art school."

"Thank you, Rashid."

Where was the money? Perplexed, Rose, emptied the con**
tents of the sack onto the counter: Rosary, birth certificate,
package of Kleenex, three drawing pencils, the Rousseau book**
a box of fine charcoal sticks, a subway token, a bus ticket, a**
envelope containing the unraveling rose that Grandma ha**
made for the sack. A packet of new red and white seed-bead**
a needle, and thread. And much more.

But where was the roll of paper bills, the tens, the twentie**
the fifties?

"I am sorry, Rashid, but I forgot to bring my money. I wi**
go home and get it. Will you keep the groceries for me?"

He waved his hand dismissively. "Take. Take with you. Com**
back, pay later."

"Oh, thank you so much. I'm sorry for the inconvenience.**

"What inconvinion?! Get outa here, Miss Rose." He place**
the paper bag in her arms. "And put on mittens," he growled **
she left.

Back in her room, she picked through her belongings. Surel**
it was in the room somewhere. Perhaps it had fallen from th**
deer-hide sack and rolled into a corner. Inch by inch she wen**

rough the room. The pockets of the studio smock in the
)set were empty. The pockets of her special dress were too
.all for a roll, but she checked anyway. Peeking under the bed
e found only a stack of old pastel drawings. She looked
erywhere. Under the table. Between the mattress and the
.ll. Under the mattress. Under the pillow. Nothing.

She checked the communal bathroom, knowing she would
•t find it, for there would have been no reason to take it there.
.e top of the refrigerator. The hall. Had it fallen out of the
g on the way downstairs? If so, perhaps one of the tenants had
ven it to the landlady for safekeeping until the owner was
.ind.

The landlady told her no one had turned in lost money.

"There's some finders are mighty good keepers", she sug-
sted with a suspicious look. "I'll keep an eye open for any
.ilt on the boarders' faces. I'm good at that sort o' thing. Don't
)rry, if they got it, it'll show."

"I hope we find it, because I would feel very bad if I couldn't
•y the rent", Rose said in a distracted way.

"I would too", said the landlady.

Rose returned to her room and sat down on the kitchen
.air, feeling agitated, fighting a growing fear.

"It must have dropped from the bag in the street", she said
.ially. "And none will know who it belongs to."

Then she began to tremble, for she saw how easily a life can
se its way in the world. She buried her face in her hands. "Io,
sus, I have lost the money you gave to me. What shall I do?
'hat shall I do!"

How foolish she was! Oh, yes, more than foolish, for she had
.own full well that people were not always honest. She had
ken care to guard the money, for it was her legacy, it was the
.ture, it was her learning. The coin was not to be buried or
asted. It was to increase. Now she had lost it!

She tried to calm herself, to pray and pray, but the danger of

her situation loomed very large, like a thundercloud appeari
on the north end of Threefinger Lake, ascending in a clear sl
rising, rising, thickening.

Rose cried muted, frightened tears. After some time, si
dried her eyes, looking bleakly at the floor, hoping to spot t
missing roll. What was she going to do? Just before Christm.
she had gone to her bank and withdrawn enough for the spri
tuition, for the rent until next June, and for food and
materials if she was extremely careful. Only thirty dollars i
mained in the account.

Sighing, she returned to prayer, went inward to the he.
within the heart, the silence within the silence, and there s.
what had happened. Io! this falling-into-seeing was brief a
bitter, and when it was completed the wrestling with ang
against Deirdre was not a small one. She urged herself not
hate Deirdre, to pray for her, to offer the back pain for h
because she was a lost-girl, a darkness-inside-girl, who cou
not love. Deirdre was poorer than Rose, poorer even than t
homeless people, because she was an empty shell; she h.
sought to cram it full of the pleasures money could buy in ord
not to feel her emptiness. She had food and shelter and clothi
and health and intelligence and a talent for design and a futu
of her own. Yet she had stolen.

Rose prayed a rosary for Deirdre, asking Our Lady for t
special grace of mercy and for the right words to speak to t
girl when they met. It was important that the truth be spoke
because Deirdre must become aware of what the sin had co
Doubtless, Deirdre had mistakenly believed that Rose was ri
in money. Rose now saw her own foolishness in the matte
how she had made it more difficult for Deirdre by rolling ar
unrolling the large sums in front of her eyes. She had done
unthinkingly, because money was not really important to her,
was just a tool. But she had overlooked what money meant
other people. For some, it was the most important thing of al

346

"When I tell her what she has done, I will not be harsh,"
ose said to herself, though she did not know precisely how to
 harsh, even if she had wanted to be so. "I will tell her I
give her. I will ask her to return what she has not spent.
ten, as a reparation, she must repay the missing part. I will
ak of it to no one else, for I do not want to shame her."

This resolve infused Rose with a certain energy. She got up,
refully locked the door of her room, and walked to the art
iool. Though classes were not scheduled to begin until the
lowing day, the secretary was in the office. Rose rapped at
r open door and went in.

"I'm trying to contact a friend of mine", Rose said. "She is a
dent here."

"What's her name?"

"Deirdre."

"What's her last name?"

Rose realized suddenly that she did not know. She shook her
ad.

"Well?" said the irritated secretary, who had been inter-
pted. "Doesn't your friend have a last name?"

Rose shook her head again. "I need to find where she lives.
ase, it's very important."

"That desperate, eh?"

Rose nodded. She reminded herself to offer no explanation,
protect Deirdre's reputation, for all of us make mistakes and
e least said is soonest mended, as Mère Jean always pointed
t to the sisters.

"Well, there can't be many Deirdres in the world," the sec-
ary murmured with a frown, scanning a card file. When she
und what she was looking for, she scratched the information
 a slip of paper and handed it to Rose. "That's all we've
t. Deirdre S. Carmody. The address is Spadina Avenue—no
mber, no phone. Why we didn't get a street number is
ybody's guess. Registration days are a nightmare. Probably

347

she told us she'd drop off the missing info later and then forg
to do it."

"Deirdre is sometimes forgetful," Rose said.

The secretary checked the thick city phone book. "Nobo
listed under that name. Not even a D. Carmody. Sorry."

"Thank you for your help," Rose said.

"No problem. Well, good luck. Hope you find your frien

Rose walked the several blocks to Spadina Avenue, whi
stretched for miles from south to north. Much of it was ru
down tenements and old store fronts that had been built in t
last century. It was a busy street, filled with traffic and thousar
of people, many of whom appeared to be poorly dressed. Hea
ing north, she searched along it for three hours, her rosa
swinging in her right hand, praying, drawing many glanc
bumped aside or squeezed to the curb, and sometimes off t
curb by the pedestrians hurrying to escape the cold. Her n
stung in the wind, even the mitts ceased to keep her fing
from aching, and her ears were overwhelmed by the roar
traffic. She knew it was an impossible task, but she held on t
small hope that Divine Providence would arrange a meetin
She walked throughout the afternoon, going ever slower,
the ache in her back became a continuous beating, as if a *mate
manito* were striking her again and again with a willow switc

With the remaining coins in her pocket she bought an ap
and a muffin. She ate them on a bus stop bench, observing t
chickadees at her feet. She fed them a few crumbs from t
muffin.

"Dee-dee-dee!" they chirped, squabbling among themselv

"It is a beautiful name she has", Rose said. "Like music
dee-dee-car-mo-dee. Dee-dee-car-mo-dee! How gifted she
yet she does not know it."

Rose got up and walked on. As night fell, she began to s
that it was the will of Manito that she not meet Deirdre in su
circumstances. Tomorrow at the Institute she would take h

348

de and speak to her. Possibly, Deirdre would deny that she had
ken the money. She might make a loud scene that would invite
teners and watchers. Yes, Rose saw this now, saw that Deirdre
as weak in her conscience and might add sin to sin in order to
otect herself. It would be better to invite her for a walk; per-
ps they could go after classes to the museum and speak of
e trouble between them as they stood before a beautiful paint-
g, for paintings were about truth. Before such mastery all lies
uld die upon the lips. Deirdre would be ashamed, but Rose
uld swiftly reassure her that the act was forgiven.

The journey back to King Street was a long and arduous one.
 the time she arrived at her room, Rose's toes were frostbit-
n inside her rubber galoshes, and her fingers, which she had
pt unfrozen only by thrusting her mittens under her armpits,
hed with chilblains. Her back was a torment. She went down
e hall to the bathroom, hoping to soak in a tub of steaming
ater, but the shower was running, and a tenant within was
histling. She returned to her room and threw herself down on
e bed. Without removing her parka, she wept and finally fell
leep.

In the morning she awoke feeling sore and depressed, but
ady to face the ordeal of confrontation. She went to Mass,
cepted the brief consolation after Communion, worried
 how easily it was washed aside by anxiety, and prayed for
ength. Then she walked to the Institute. She searched every-
here in the halls, the basement cafeteria, and the third-year
dios, but she did not see Deirdre. Speaking with third-year
dents was a puzzling experience because none of them knew
here Deirdre was, none offered help, and at the mention of
eirdre's name their faces seemed to tighten, their eyes grew
utious.

Rose's first class of the term was taught by the leotard lady. It
as a lecture on the Cubists, with a slide show of their work.
ose did not focus overlong on the teaching or the images.

More than a few of the latter portrayed men and women empty shells broken into pieces. "And reassembled", enthus the leotard lady.

"Like God", Rose said aloud, without planning to. Thou no one seemed to notice.

"Cubism is the future", said the teacher in tones that a usually reserved for sacred things.

"Really?" said a brash student. "Don't you think po Modernist abstraction is the cutting edge?"

"No, it's an offshoot", the leotard lady replied coolly. "Cu ism will always remain the foundation of everything that fo lowed—and is yet to follow. Observe, for example, Picasso's *I Demoiselles d'Avignon*."

She clicked the manual switch of the slide projector. Fi nude women appeared on the screen, their beast faces affixed the broken pottery of their bodies. Rose looked away.

"Magnificent!" exclaimed the leotard lady as the Indonesi bell-gong sounded far below.

Rose got up and left the room. During lunch hour s waited in the cafeteria, hoping that Deirdre would enter some point, but she did not appear. When the bell-gong reve berated throughout the building, calling the students to class she went upstairs to her first painting studio of the new ter She looked forward to a reunion with the old professor, hop to tell him a little of her woes, if he would listen, and to eli some advice. I have lost my money, she would say, not telli him how. What am I to do?

Surprised to see a young woman pacing the teacher's pla form, reading from a sheet of paper, and chalking notations the blackboard, Rose sat down at her easel and waited.

"*All art is a lie—Picasso*" was printed in bold letters across t top of the blackboard.

Printed beneath: "*Man now realizes that he is an accident, that is a completely futile being—Francis Bacon.*"

And a final epigram: "*He who would be a creator, both in good
1 in evil, must first of all know how to destroy and wreck values—
etzsche.*"

Rose approached the young woman.

"Why are you writing those words?" she asked politely.

The young woman removed her wire-rim glasses and fixed
appraising look at Rose. Her unblinking eyes slowly took in
: bent form.

"Because they are true", she replied casually.

"They are not true", Rose answered with as much kindness
possible. "I know they are not true."

"You *know* they are not true? *How* do you know this?"

"They are a lie."

"*All* of them are a lie?" the woman smiled unpleasantly. "All
them, you say? Have you read Descartes?"

"No."

"We'll be reading passages from his writings this term. He
: a lot to teach about how much we can *know*."

"Where is the painting professor?"

"Dr. Ganze has had a heart attack. He's recovering, but he
•n't be back until next September. I'm your painting instruc-
: for this term."

Rose now wrestled with a dilemma. The words on the
.ckboard were lies. *I am your teacher*, the woman had said.
ould one be taught by a bearer of lies? The structure of the
>blem spun past her in a few seconds. She gathered her
longings and left the class.

Down at the secretary's office she knocked and entered. The
>man looked up.

"Find your friend?"

"No."

"You look worried."

"I am, Miss. I have a serious problem. I was supposed to pay
: my spring term this week but my money has been lost."

351

"Your money has been lost. Well, that's not very good ne[w] is it. You know that checks have to be on my desk by the end [of] this week."

"If I don't find it right away, is it possible to continue [my] studies until I do. I *will* pay you later. I promise I will."

"I'm sure you intend to pay us, dear, but we can't do [it.] We've had a lot of abuse of our patience over the years, stude[nts] saying they have no money when they have plenty for mov[ies] and new clothes and the like. We can't make exceptions. Y[ou] understand, don't you?"

"Perhaps if I took fewer classes. I have already decided [to] drop out of some."

"Now we've got two problems instead of one. Look, d[ear,] this is an accredited institution. We just can't do things haph[az]ard. If you want to graduate—"

"I do not need to graduate. I need to learn."

"Yes, but—"

The remainder of the conversation went in smaller circ[les] and failed.

"I'm sorry", the woman said as her final word. "The end [of] the week and no later."

Unable to bear this additional bad news, Rose left the bui[ld]ing and walked toward home. Halfway there she remember[ed] that she had not yet paid Rashid for the groceries, revers[ed] direction, and went back downtown to her bank. There s[he] closed her account and pocketed the thirty dollars and chan[ge.]

By then it was late afternoon, and the sun was already rolli[ng] low in the southern sky, preparing to plunge into the lake, a d[isk] as red as tropical flowers in the forests where beasts claw[ed] naked men and pulled them to ground. It was after sev[en] o'clock by the time she reached Rashid's Grocery and paid [her] bill. This left about twenty dollars. She walked on to the chur[ch] and attended an evening Mass, but the fear gnawing in h[er] prevented any sense of consolation. Still, a little strength e[…]

352

red. This would be badly needed, she soon discovered, for on returning to her room, she found a note pinned to the door.

Rose, please pay the January rent. It is overdue a week.

She went out onto the streets again, praying all the way, begging God to arrange a meeting with Deirdre. It was not impossible. He could do it. Surely he could do it. It seemed to take much longer to reach Spadina Avenue than it had the day before. It took hours to make her way north along it and back south again to King. Nothing. Not a sign of her, not even a hint from heaven, no words in her heart, no knowings saying, *this is the way, you must follow it, stop here, up these stairs, knock, this is where she lives.*

No, just the opposite happened. As if all grace had become an abstract painting, its figures distant, drained of meaning. She found herself thinking *about* faith, as if it were a thing outside of her. She knew it was real, but she walked around and around it, inspecting it and analyzing it, not living it as fire lives within a stove, or a flower lives sleeping within its seed. This was the most frightening feeling of all—to be outside. As if it were not enough that all human strengths were falling away from her, now the supernatural ones were fleeing from her as well.

Why?

What had she done wrong?

Why had he not warned her?

Why had he not protected her from the darkness in Deirdre?

And if he had not, did this mean that she had been mistaken all along about his purpose in her life? Was it her own dream, or Sister Madeleine's, or Mère Jean's, that she become an artist and go out into the world? How could she ignore this question? Their dreams for her were well intentioned, but was it possible they were mistaken? Surely this could not be discounted, for people were often mistaken about many things, and even the best were so.

Io! it was so confusing.

At midnight she arrived at her room and slept. At dawn, she got up and went to the parish, where Mass once again gave her strength, though like yesterday's it seemed to fade quickly, pushed from her heart by the fear that licked and burned and spread through the undergrowth.

All that day she walked Spadina Avenue back and forth. Three and a half times. Stopping once to drink a cup of tepid chocolate in a café, to bite from the marzipan bar, to catch her breath. But Deirdre seemed to have disappeared from the face of the earth. Arriving at her room after eight o'clock, she saw a fresh note pinned to the door.

Rent must be paid promptly by tenants. This room overdue eight days.

She went down to the landlady's suite to explain that she was doing everything in her power to recover the lost money, but the landlady's face was colder than it had ever been. A television program played in the background; she kept casting an eye over her shoulder so as not to miss anything.

"I'll give you another week", she said. "I'm a patient woman and a charitable one, but I'll not be made a fool of. I been burned before."

As Rose well knew.

On the third day of the search, she thought she saw Skye's car pulling away from a curb near the intersection of Spadina and Bloor Street. It had the same fins and rusty spots and the fox tail on the aerial. A blur of coppery red hair filled the front seat. Shouting inarticulately, Rose forced her body to break into a trot, which set off shrieks of pain in every joint of her back. Faster and faster she went, hoping impossibly to catch up. But they sped away, and she stumbled, gasping, crying, losing her balance. An old bearded man caught her by the arm and held her upright. Seeing that she was steadied on her feet, he passed quickly on and disappeared into the crowd.

Rose went to sleep that night feeling hot all over, a cough sping in the bottom of her throat. From time to time she voke and spat small bits of green phlegm into a handkerchief. the morning she awoke to the sound of rapping on the door. was the landlady. She was perturbed, a no-nonsense mood s upon her.

"There are some that says they had money and lost it. There some that says they had money and lost it, but didn't. Which the two are you? Eh?"

"I'm sorry", Rose tried to explain. "I have been trying—"

"Tryin' is the word. I'm feeling sorely tried myself, my fine ung miss. I hate to be hard on the matter, but a person must e. You have twenty-four hours to pay me the rent, or I'll be king you to leave."

Rose lay in bed another hour, her eyes hot, and her flesh rning.

Io, my Lord, I do not understand your will in this. Do you wish me leave? Is my learning over? If you wish me to go, I will go, but where all I go? And how?

She fell back to sleep and dreamed of many things, sad, dark sings with no findings, and the angels bending over her, rrowing for the hardness of man that was leading her farther the suffering way. In the strange manner of dreams, the old inting professor came before her and said, *It is the best.* Rose sagreed, saying, "Dr. Ganze, it is the worst." *No,* he an- ered, *it is the best way, it is the finding-way hidden within the ing-way, for no work of art is ever completed without it.* Then the d bearded man who had kept her from stumbling came be- re her. His hair was as yellow-white as antler bones and his es were purple velvet, watery and wise with experience, and said to another, a shadow who could not be seen: *You see is one, this little heart that regards all wounded untamed things. She ll go farther, she will go very far and see much, but first she must be rified.*

Then the shadow voice said, *By such cruel paths you lead y*
beloved.

And the old man replied, *Your way is short and in appearance*
manner of pleasure, yet it bears the fruit of darkness. The way of l
beloved is the long way, for it is hard and narrow and bears a harvest
joy. She knows its meaning. She knows, though for a time it sle
beneath the great waters.

She is dying, said the shadow. *You have let her die. It does not lo*
like love to me.

You are correct. It does not look like love—to you.

This, said the shadow with a sneer, *is your concept of greatne*

Then the old man looked long at the shadow; it fell silent a*
fled.

Rose awoke in the night gasping for breath.

"Ay, ay, I do *not* know, I do *not* understand! I cannot see t
great truth which is hidden, for I cannot breathe. I am a sm
bird; I am *bineshi* and I am dying."

Then she broke into wails and loud coughs, which we
greeted by thumping on the walls and the ceiling.

In the morning, the landlady used her passkey and came in
the room unannounced.

"What is this?" she muttered, fists on hips, staring at Ros
body wrapped like a slug on the bed. "Is it the drink, then? Su
it is. I knew well enough I'd see this day. Doin' what all yer ki
does eventually, never pay a mind to a widow's plight when
quick sip is for the taking."

But when Rose hacked up a gout of green phlegm on t
sheets and rolled over in delirium, clutching a small crucifix
her hand, the landlady's face was stricken, and she hurried
the bed and knelt.

"Glory be t' Jesus, Mary 'n' Joseph, she's sicker than a dog
Jumping up, she scurried about the room in a tizzy. "O
fergive me, dear Lord, where's the towel, where's the kettle
The old woman stomped along the hallway and returned with

356

t cloth with which to slake the fever, only to find that Rose
1 begun to shake with chill. Tossing the rag aside, the land-
y went downstairs to her apartment and returned in a mont with a bottle of cough syrup and a spoon.

"Dear God, girl, drink this."

Down it went, two spoonsful. Which Rose blasted across the
ets in a mighty onslaught of unstoppable coughing.

"Tsk", said the landlady, who hated waste. She shook her
d, her mouth tight. Death in the house was a landlady's worst
htmare. As if she didn't have enough worries. She would call
octor. No, the girl had no money. Well, the charity hospital
n. She ran to the phone.

Rose concentrated on breathing, or else the flesh did the
centrating for her while she floated in the half sleep of those
o, one way or another, are rendered powerless. Everything
rt—inside and outside, inside the inside, and inside that as
ll. To live was to feel pain. Well, if this was his wish, so be it.
it was not the way she would have made the world, but she
1 not made the world, nothing was possible for her except
at he had given. To love was to create, to create was to love!
is she knew. This alone she knew. The lies on the blackboard
ined and barked and cooed and purred in contradiction. The
ks of students fell swooning before them, the shadow words,
weasel words, the *kinoje* words. The old painting professor
red his protest: *Awake, Rose! Do not listen to the words! Cling to*
raft! Do not sink! And Mère Jean leaned over the bed,
king the wet hair from Rose's forehead. *Ma petite, it is the*
e of desolation. Do not fear, for it is a great gift. You will know, you
understand.

e remained a month or more in a hospital run by the Salva-
n Army, among the many others of the city who were with-
t means. Much of her time there was spent drifting in and
t of dreams or remembrance, or quietly listening to the

beating of her own heart. Or reading the landlady's note o
card decorated with pink roses, in the solemn words that
reserved for funerals and other notices of termination.

*Dear Rose, I am grieved you are sick. I pray for your recovery. It
is my regret, however, that I am forced to let your room, for I
need the income badly. I am a widow and childless and have no
other means. Yours sincerely.*

Underneath the bed was a cardboard box containing her thin
some clothes, a roll of drawings, the deer-hide sack, the leath
saddlebag with K. B. on it, the yellowy-stained photograp
the binemin stone, the tin box, and charcoal sticks, wh
snapped in her fingers when the nurses brought them to h
releasing the memory-smell of the old cabin and the orig
of her art. The very last scrap of her legacy, the twenty doll
was missing. If the landlady had taken it, this was only rig
because the money was owed to her.

The ward was cleaner than any room she recalled since I
with the sisters. The beds were stainless steel and covered w
crisp white sheets. The only decoration on the walls wa
single picture of Jesus, or Jesus as some imagine him to be: lc
curling blond hair, a girl-boy face, a thin wisp of beard, tre
bling purple lips, and blue watery eyes. She turned from it, fo
was not the Jesus she knew, the hidden face within her hea
Still, the room was a place claimed by him, and cleansed
him. There was no Communion, but three ladies in purple a
blue uniforms took turns singing Gospel songs and readi
aloud from the Holy Scriptures. The words were as stars flo
ing like the *tchibekana*, and Rose rested in its light, listening
the call of Mang the bridegroom.

Though memory was now fractured, and some of it d
persed in the way that stars from time to time are flung from t
loon's necklace and lost among the fields of infinity, Rose clu

358

the images that remained. As she fell through space—up or own, she did not know—she pulled a long umbilicus behind er. Connected to her heart, it uncoiled into the shadows of me, dwindling to a thread as it receded. At the other end of ae thread—back or forward, she did not know—was Oldmary, er fierce black eyes fixed on the flickering red vigil light in the arkened mission chapel, rocking as she uttered her rosary eside a little girl.

Asleep or awake, or floating between the two, Rose fluttered er wings and tried to open her mouth, but she could not eak. Mang was gone. Gissis was gone. Aloneness, aloneness, ae stillness when the creator of everything seemed silent, when was his time to sleep, permitting the wind to speak for him. torms cracked the sky and stabbed the water and shook the arth. Ay, ay, small loons quivered in their coves and partridges id under logs and the *bineshi* trembled in her nest.

I am a small bird, yet he sees the sparrow fall and he sees the sparrow se, and in no matter of its small life is he unaware. But was his eye n *all* winged creatures without exception? Did his eye some- mes turn elsewhere?

On occasion, human arms went around her shoulders and ently pulled her upright, made her sip from a bowl of warm ilty broth. She tried not to hack it out, to spray, to make a mess aat others must toil to clean. Io, she was a burden!

Slowly the medicine began to push, push the *neshiwed* from er flesh. Little by little, her breathing eased. Time flowed ontinually through the windows and out again, sometimes ushing in on sun-raving rivers, at other times drifting on gray ddies, or coagulating in motionless violet pools in the safe ark.

She sat up during the third week. In the fourth her lungs eased to wheeze, bubble, and ache. She was very weak and eeded help to get up for the walk to the bathroom. There vere bedsores too. And embarrassment, for the doctors

359

brought student doctors to point out the deformation of he
spine and the dents in her ribs that the braces had left. Bu
they spoke to her as if she was a person, for which she wa
grateful.

In the fifth week, she sat in the recreation room and stitche
the rose back onto the deer-hide sack, replacing the missin
beads with new reds and whites and pinks. This task brought
touch of happiness, for it was so like returning to the garde
she and Tchibi had made at Crazyman River that she almo
could hear the singing bells and smell the scent of fryin
bannock wafting toward them from the cabin. Often, she fe
asleep holding the partridge stone in her two hands, pressed t
her chest, warming it. It warming her.

In the sixth week, a man in a blue and purple uniform visite
her and said that she was recovering, she could soon leave th
hospital, was there any place she would like to go?

"To France", she said.

"That is a long way. Don't you have family among your ow
people in the north?"

"None are living," she said.

"Are there any friends you could go to?"

"All are gone."

"Rose, if you could choose, where in all the world woul
you go?"

She could see that this was a loving question, only ha
serious, for he was a kind man, and when all real ways wer
closed he liked to dream a little. And because she too liked t
play in this fashion, his playing lifted her heart.

"I would go to the island of the blue mountain, where th
children splash the waves as they run along the white san
beneath the sun, and they sing, and their father and mothe
listen to the singing as they hold the fish nets billowing in th
wind."

"Is it far? Is it a native place?"

"It is far. It is not the place of my people, but another people."

"It sounds like heaven", said the man.

"It is like heaven in a way, but it is not, for fathers must leave, going out into cold and barren places, seeking a way to feed their babies. And sometimes they are naked, and the eyes of people claw them, or the panthers pull them down beneath the bursting flowers that are as red as the sun, and devour them."

His eyes grew troubled. "Rose, do you know where you are?"

"A hospital."

"Yes, that's right. Which hospital?"

"In the cold barren land."

"Can you tell me your family name?"

"My name is Bineshi", she said, though not with great certainty. "I think it is. Yes, it is one of my names."

"It's Wâbos", he said gently.

So she remained there for another week, growing in strength, eating regularly again, spitting the last bits of the bile-green meshiwed germ from her body, until it was all gone.

At the end of February the man, and a lady who also wore the uniform, drove her to a shelter for homeless women. They said they hoped to see her again, that she could visit the place where they met for prayer whenever she liked. The lady gave her a pocket-size New Testament. Rose thanked them, and they went away.

The shelter was a former school building far to the east of the downtown core, in a neighborhood of crumbling buildings even older than the place where she had once lived on King Street. There were women of many kinds staying in the two big dormitories. It was much like the dorm at the school in Thunder Bay had been, though more silent, for many of the women were ill or confused, or withdrawn deep into the caves of themselves. Less silent women came and went, sometimes with small children. It was not a place of great happiness, though was without fear.

Rose lived there three days. Throughout most of that tim she rested on her bed and read the Bible, pondering the way th Father-Manito so often sent his servants into cold barren plac with little to guide them or feed them except his light goir before them and within them. And a bit of bread. Weaker an weaker they became until he was stronger and stronger withi them. It did not seem like love, though it was, and its harve was frequently great.

On the next Sunday afternoon she went to Mass, followir the directions of the social worker who managed the shelter. A always she carried her deer-hide sack with her, containing h most precious possessions, for the fear of theft had not yet le her. The weight of the *binemin* stone in the bottom of it w heavy that day. The roll of drawings poked high above th top of the leather saddlebag slung over her shoulder. It took ha an hour to walk to the church, the journey exhausting, th weather still cold. When she arrived, she slid into the back pe behind an organ that no one played. The Mass was swift, an Communion sweet. But it all blurred in her mind after tha and she stumbled out of the church because she thought sh had slept through the ending and another Mass had begun.

Then she turned and walked back in the direction of th shelter. An hour passed, during which time the roaring of th turbulent streets increased in her ears, and dizziness cam upon her, and faded, and came again. She stopped once c twice to bite a piece from the marzipan bar that she found i the deer-hide sack. It was stale but very sweet, and it revived he strength. At other times she looked about her, trying to recog nize the buildings that flowed by, but they all seemed th same—reddish-brown, crumbling, and covered with man signs, their windows containing solitary faces that looked ou solemnly at the world. They did not speak to her for they wer

362

behind glass; their eyes did not swivel to follow her because there were so many like her passing to and fro. She was not real, because they could not make her real, and she could not make them real.

I am tired, she said. *I can go no farther. Where is the place I am going?*

Surely it was close, only a block or two ahead. She continued onward, crossing block after block, distracted sometimes by the crowds of gray pigeons strutting along as if they were small people, or the sparrows lining up on the telephone wires, chirping their concerns to each other, gossiping about Rose.

"She is lost", they said one to the other.

"She is not lost. A little farther, and she will arrive."

Because it was now late winter, and the spring was only a month or two away, and the inland sea was warmer than the old barren land, there was less bitterness in the air, and the mist, though cold, hinted at rainy days to come and the uncovering of the nakedness of the earth as the white sheet is slowly pulled from it. Yet it was an illusion, for winter was never as easily defeated as people hoped. Snow now began to drift down in shimmers, miniature grains dusting Rose's shoulders, covering the sidewalk with baking sugar, making the footprints of people appear out of nothing, as the tracks of wolves and deer and mice and rabbits press remembrances of themselves onto the rag paper of the earth.

"Surely she is lost", said one sparrow to another.

"She is not lost", said a bolder chickadee, who was practicing his end-of-winter song. *Chick-a-dee-dee-dee-dee! Chick-a-dee-dee-dee-dee! He's coming! He's coming!*

This made Rose pause, for it seemed to her that the birds knew something the people did not.

Stopping at a large wastebasket by the curb, she pulled from it a green plastic garbage bag, and wrapped the roll of drawings in it. The journey to the shelter was stretching long

ahead, and she did not want her pictures ruined by th
weather. She went on.

Now the light in the sky began to fade, and it came to h
that the sparrows were right and the chickadees wrong. Th
trolleys and buses increased, and the people packed with
them clung to metal bars and swayed and pressed their bodi
together in clumps, and all eyes looked outward, or inward, b
not at each other.

The snow fell more heavily now, and the harsh green ar
amber and red lights at intersections softened as they change
for the veil of snow muted everything.

"Wâbos", Rose said to the people who passed. "My name
Wâbos, yes, that is it. I am a rabbit. Or a roseflower, I think.'

Addressing the many little birds who had abandoned th
wires and were chittering and fluttering under the eaves of th
buildings, she said, "Sometimes I, too, am a bird like you,
am a *bineshi*, though silver, a sliver of the moon, whom I ca
ningâ."

"She is not your mother," argued a chickadee, "for she
only a reflection."

"This is true", said Rose. "This is true. Yet it is a thought th
comforts me."

Into the early evening she walked, until the city thinned ar
fields of rail yards and factories appeared on both sides of th
streets. Still the city did not cease, for outcroppings of reddis
brown leaped up in front of her, and fell behind again. Cease
lessly the baying of horns, the thumping of motors, the whistl
and the roarings, continued in all directions. The chimney
belched their black smoke, and beneath them the spinnin
blades screamed or spewed out newborn metal, and unthink
able weights fell and pressed useless scraps of old metal into soli
cubes, because Cubism was the future.

Now the city fell behind, and towns appeared, all linked b
the chain of the road. Stopping beneath the light post of a g

364

tation, Rose looked around. The birds were gone. None of them had been willing to leave the city.

"I am lost", she said. "I am finished. Io! It seems to me that once again I have fallen through your fingers, and I drop into the abyss. Why did you not hold me?"

She cried ugly tears that became soundless wails.

What did she have to show for her going forth into the world? She had lost her legacy, and now she wondered if she were losing herself. Perhaps she had lost the Beating Heart as well, for he was silent when she came to him in the churches and in the prayer of the night. In every station that was his, a red lamp said he was there, but she felt nothing, not even the deeper feeling that is the presence within the silence. It too was absent.

"Wait!" she cried. "This cannot be true, for only this morning I felt him. What is wrong with my mind? Is it the sickness that has pushed the memory-way from me? See, he is near. He is always near. He is sleeping within me, as the flower sleeps within the seed, or the fire within the ember, or the great truth breathing beneath the waves. Io, I wish he would awake!"

Please, please, speak to me, or show me!

Where did he want her to go? Why did he not speak? Was it because he wanted her to guess? But guessing was a foolish way, was it not? It led thisway and thatway and she easily might miss the path that he most desired for her.

Why did he hide from her?

Was it because there were so many like her, so many, many people, millions of beloveds, billions of them, even the unheeding? How could he keep track of them all? And why should he keep track of one so small and useless as herself? Had she become a shell, an empty-thing? Had he held her too tightly in his hands and now her wings were tearing, and he knew he must let her go? Or was he holding her so close no words of reassurance were necessary?

When she had rested a little, and eaten another bite of the

stale marzipan, there were seconds of peace. She felt that he wa
longing for her to trust him, that he was taking her farther o
the darkness-way, where all treasures but him are dropped on
by one along the path, the forest grows more dense, the ligh
fails, and the love that walks with you—within you—looks a
you and says with his eyes *I am here, do you not trust in our love*
But she was afraid now, more afraid than she had ever been i
her life, for in the dark a person cannot see the eyes of love, an
there is only silence.

"I will go home", she said to herself, hoping that, perhaps, h
was listening. "If you will not speak to me, what else am
to do?"

Still he did not speak.

"I will go home, then, north where *wêwe* the wild goose flie
each spring, for it is home to her. I will walk, to show that it i
not a running-from, but a going-to. It will be hard, the hardes
thing that I have ever done, for the north is far. I will offer it.'

14

e windblown snowy pavement curved up steadily into the
er of souls. As Rose walked along the gravel shoulder, she
certain that eventually it would take her there, or at least
the true north which is the place where the river touches
earth. Toward midnight a station wagon pulled over to the
oulder ahead of her. Its red signal light winked on and off,
l its smoking exhaust pipe idled, until she had plodded as far
ts window. The window rolled down, and a young woman
ked out at her.

"Do you need a ride?" she asked.

"No, thank you", Rose replied.

"Going far?"

"Yes. To the north, which is my home."

"Well, I don't think you're going in the right direction ex-
ly. You're heading east on number seven. Is that where you
nt to go?"

"I do not know", Rose answered, her eyes blinking with
nfusion, realizing that the compass in her mind was broken.

"You're miles from nowhere, and it's an awfully cold night.
hy don't you get in, and I'll give you a lift as far as Peter-
rough. There's a bus station there. You can get a ticket for
erever you want to go."

"It would, perhaps, not be right", Rose said. "I must walk, to
ow that it is not a running-from, it is a going-to. It is hard, but
ch is his way with me." She turned to walk on.

"Who?" the lady called. "Whose way with you?"

"The Beating Heart."

The woman's face was open and kind, but she frowned,

thinking. She opened the passenger door. "Listen, Miss
don't think the Beating Heart would want you to freeze
death. I think he wants you to have a rest and get warm. Ok
So why don't you hop in and I'll take you where you n
to go."

It was very difficult to resist this offer. It grieved Rose
take a lesser way, the way of smallness, the way of weakn
when she had so recently resolved to prove her willingness
go the darkness-way. But perhaps even in the darkness-v
there were supposed to be moments of relief. She got into
passenger side of the vehicle and closed the door. The won
drove on. The heat inside the car was very high. Three cl
dren slept in the back, covered with blankets. A small wh
dog groaned, shifted its body between two of the children, a
closed its eyes.

"We're going to Ottawa", the woman said.

"Is it in the north?" Rose asked.

"Kind of. Sort of northeast of here. Where did you say y
were going?"

"I do not know. For the compass is broken. And the memo
is blurring. Because I am ill, my thoughts do not flow in
straight-way."

The woman glanced sideways at Rose with a worried loo
"I'm sorry to hear that," she said in a sympathetic voice. "Wo
you like to come with us?"

"Where are you going?"

"Uh, to Ottawa."

"In the north?"

"In the northeast", the woman said again, both hands gr
ping the top of the wheel.

Five minutes passed. "Are you hungry?"

"Yes."

"I have a snack box for the kids, but they're out like ligl
Here, why don't you open it and see if there's anything left."

There was a peanut butter sandwich, a bruised apple, a bundle of carrot sticks, and a little box of raisins.

"It's all yours", the woman smiled.

Rose ate it all and fell asleep.

Four hours later the glow of a city appeared on the distant skyline. The woods thinned on both sides of the highway and the dark cubes of farms appeared, black against the blue-black night, solitary lights winking on here and there, men going out in the dark to milk cows. The woman let Rose sleep, worrying about the whimpers that came from her, the twitching of her hands, the way she slept sideways, guarding the deformation of her spine. The woman felt an ache in her throat, and a helplessness.

"I'll ask her to stay with us", she thought. "But what will Jake say if I bring her home without so much as a phone call to warn him? She's obviously a little unbalanced. How unbalanced? Would she hurt the kids? I don't think so, but—"

The woman stopped at a gas station on the outskirts of the city and bought bread and eggs and a carton of milk at the all-night grocery attached to the station. While the attendant was filling the tank, she continued to muse on the problem, staring ahead through the windshield, swallowing the ache from time to time.

"There are so many of them, more and more every day. Why do people suffer so much? Why does this poor girl have it so hard when I've got it so good?" She shook her head. "Life! I'll never figure it out."

When she had paid for the gas, she turned the ignition key and drove on.

"But what can I do? It's hard enough raising three kids in these times, maybe another one on the way."

She glanced quickly at the passenger, removed a rosary from the pocket of her dress, and prayed it for Rose as she drove into the heart of the city. Around six in the morning the woman

369

parked in front of a restaurant in the downtown area south
the Parliament buildings. She reached over and gently sho
Rose's shoulder.

"We're here", the woman said. "End of the line."

Rose rubbed her eyes.

"Decision time, Miss. I'd like to make you an offer. I w
wondering if you'd like to stay with us for a while, just un
you're feeling better. My husband and I have a spare room
our basement. Our place is a wreck, but it's home. You cou
say it's my kind of north."

"I cannot," Rose said, "for he has not told me where I a
to go."

"Right", the lady nodded. "Exactly right. That's why may
you need a stopping place until he tells you where you ne
to go."

Rose thought about the offer, or took it deep into her hea
She closed her eyes. The woman waited patiently.

"I cannot hear him as I should," Rose said at last, "for
darkness-way is upon me. But if he were to speak, I think
would say I am free to go thisway or thatway, but his preferen
is a way that is certain."

"Who is this *he* you've mentioned a couple of times?"

Rose looked into the woman's eyes.

"You know him."

Choking back tears, the woman nodded. "Yes, I know him
know the one you mean. I know him."

"The choosing is a road which branches", Rose said. "Bo
paths lead on to different futures. Both are good, but one is
lesser good."

"Why don't you think of our place as a house at the fork
the road? Stay with us a few days, get well and strong, then yo
can continue your journey. He would understand. I know I
would."

"It is so. He would understand", Rose replied solemnly. "Y

370

the delay, the road would change and arrive at other stations
our dream. And from it many branches spread. Each choos-
; changes all other choosings."

"Do you really believe that?" the woman said with quiet in-
isity. "I don't. I believe that some of the roads would change,
t not the big ones. Why don't you come home with us?"

"I cannot. I cannot, though the reason for it is hidden from
/ eyes!"

The woman blinked and shook her head sadly. She sighed.

Rose opened the door. "Is this Ottawa?"

The woman nodded. Rose stepped out.

"Good-bye. Thank you."

"Wait", cried the woman. She reached into her pocket, with-
w a rosary and a ten-dollar bill, and gave them to Rose.
lease. Please take them."

Rose accepted the gifts. "Thank you, lady. I will think about
u for a very long time. I will carry you and bring you in my
art on the offering-way. I will ask that you may be strong to
ar whatever burdens he gives to you."

The woman's eyes spilled tears, and she looked away. Rose
ised the door and walked in any direction that the wind cared
blow. It blew south down the canyon of a long street called
nk. The route was deserted, the dawn breaking over stop-
hts that changed colors continuously, and street lamps that lit
e storefronts and sidewalks. Pieces of paper trash blew along
side her, racing her, pulling ahead, falling behind, tumbling
d looping as if they had a will of their own. A clock in a
urch tower struck six o'clock. A bus passed with no passen-
rs. A car rolled in the other direction. Two, then three more
rs pulled onto Bank from side streets. The traffic increased
adily, people appeared, hurrying this way and that on foot,
ddled inside their coat collars, blowing clouds of soul-breath
m their mouths. By eight o'clock Rose had reached a bridge
er a frozen canal that wound through the city. She left the

371

street and descended to a park that bordered the canal. Sic
walks followed beside its railings, disappearing back in the
rection of the north as the canal bent in a wide curve. As Ro
walked along, she passed men with shovels scraping the sic
walk clean of snow. They were smoking cigarettes and jokin

The sun came up bright and clean over the city. It wa
beautiful place, she saw, full of parks and waterways. Childr
skated to school on the canal ice, red or blue or green tuqu
flying out behind them, book satchels strapped to their sho
ders. Here and there, hockey sticks clacked among small gat
erings of boys who were stealing the last free minutes. An o
man passed her, walking a Scottie dog. It looked at her a
bowed.

By noon, Rose reached the end of the canal, near a castleli
hotel, a large train station, and the spires of the Parliame
buildings. She stopped and ate the last of the marzipan. She v
thirsty also, and ate a mittful of snow scooped from a cle
snowbank. Without knowing where she was going, she climb
the steps from the canal park and reentered the bustling stree
Uncertain about why she had been brought to this city, s
tried to pray in the words-without-words, clutching the rosa
inside her mitt, but there was no sensation of union, and all th
she could find was a yearning for the empty space where s
must go to fill it with herself. She went to the west—it was w
because the morning sun was warming her back a little, and t
north wind beat at her right cheek, stinging it with frostbi
She held a mitt to the dead spot as she walked.

She came to an alley a few blocks from Bank Street. On o
side of the narrow passageway was an ancient stone building
many floors. On the other was a new one of steel and gl
soaring twice as high as the old, as a crystal of quartz v
sometimes jut from granite, squeezed out of the cracks by t
weight of its age. Deeper in the alley was an alcove in the wa
of the quartz building that offered some protection from t

372

ıd. There she found a square of metal, covered with rungs,
into the concrete pavement. Warm wind blew up from it.
Rose tested the rungs with an outstretched foot. It held. It
s strong. The smells of paper and coffee and a thousand clean
ıgs blew out with the air. She sat down on the grate, then
lay down and closed her eyes, intending to rest for a few
ıutes before resuming her search for the word of Manito that
s waiting for her somewhere in the many streets. She fell
ep.

Later she awoke feeling a little chilled, but not cold. The
rm air continued to rise all around her. She was stiff from
•ping on the hard surface, but her thoughts had regained a
rtion of their clarity. The sun now arched downward from
west, the borderline between light and shadow slipping
ng the tower walls at sharp angles. As Rose gathered the
•ngth to stand up, the form of a man stopped at the entrance
he alley and looked inside. He did not move for a moment
:wo, then rising suddenly on his toes, he pitched forward and
•de toward her with great deliberation. As he approached, he
ered a slice of bronze light reflecting off the glass walls. Io!
His face ignited, his hair radiated spokes of gold. His coun-
ance held her spellbound. He was perhaps an *anjeni* of the
rd.

He stopped a few feet away and gazed down upon her.

'Is it fallen from the heavens?" he said in a voice as melodi-
s as the wind, as golden as the rivers of paradise.

Rose swallowed hard, for an anjeni is an awesome being and
r people in this world are privileged to see one.

"Cannot speak, brown *Sperling*?" he said.

"I can speak", she breathed, still shaken by the immense
ıuty of his presence.

"Tell me, then, what is your name?"

"I am Rose. I think Bineshi, or Wâbigon."

He laughed gently. "Woebegone is appropriate."

373

"What is your name?" she asked in a trembling whisper.

"Wolfgang Amadeus von Falkenstein, with a small v", answered and sat down beside her.

His back to the wall, he seemed to be looking through solid stone of the building opposite, meditating on the m human scenes that were within it.

"You are, perhaps, a wanderer?" he said.

"Yes."

"I, too, am a wanderer."

"I thought you were", she answered carefully, for she did want to let him know she suspected his identity. It was unusual name for an angel, but she had heard they often tr elled in disguise.

They sat in silence for several minutes.

Then he did a surprising thing. He removed a plastic from the side pocket of his jean jacket and pulled threads tobacco from it. Flipping a tiny rectangle of white paper fr his chest pocket, he licked it and rolled the tobacco into a tu twisting the end of it into a point. He lit it with a woo match.

The smell of the burning fiber was rich and nauseating was different from Grandma's tobacco. As he sucked it w half-lidded eyes, staring at the wall opposite, or perhaps celestial visions, Rose permitted herself a swift examination his face. It was the face of the Greek sculptures she had seen the museum, the perfection was the same, the skin as pure polished marble, the shock of platinum hair resembling it al The eyes, of course, were alive, and they were the most ange thing about him for they were crystalline blue, like the rarest quartz. Of course an angel cannot disguise his eyes, for the e are, as Mère Jean once said, the windows of the soul. Eve thing else about him was ingeniously camouflaged.

His name, the first part of which he pronounced *Voolf-go* was the cleverest touch. The accent in his words was like

374

rgling of brooks. The second part, *amad-deus*, perplexed her tally, but the final part, *falcon*, conjured up images of a young night treading the alpen crags above his castle, a hunter bird on s extended right arm, its bells tinkling in the high wind, wacking on the leather hood—she remembered the picture om a story Euphrasia had read to her many years ago.

"You are alone?" he asked after the passage of unmeasured ne, when he had flicked the tiny butt of his cigarette into the ottomless pit beneath the vent.

"Yes. As he well knows", Rose said. "And I thank him for nding me a guardian and guide, for I do not know the way."

The *anjeni* turned sideways with a curious smile and said, What?"

A doubt entered Rose's heart—and an uneasiness. But she smissed it, realizing that Voolf-gong needed to preserve his sumed identity, for he knew better than she the fragility of umans in the presence of the divine.

"It is all right", Rose said daringly. "We do not need to speak f it, for I understand."

"Ah", he said, nodding emphatically. "You do understand. I ought you would."

"Where will we go?" she asked.

"Wherever you like", he replied. "But why not stay here for while? It is warm. Tell me, Rose, what are you doing in this ace, without visible explanation?"

Rose decided to play the game with him. "I am resting until find the station of my dream. Or the place where I am led."

"You are, perhaps, a clairvoyant?" he asked with interest.

"I am an artist", she replied, though it felt strange to present erself as such. Instantly she wanted to retract the statement, for was no longer true, if it ever had been.

"An artist!" he laughed with great jolliness, the thicket of atinum flipping upward, defying the laws of gravity. "Yes, of ourse. Of course you had to be. For I, too, am an artist."

He pointed at the paper roll poking from the top of the saddlebag. "You are a painter, I presume?"

"With pastels. I am not very good with oils. Would you like to see them?"

He frowned and pursed his lips. "Later, I think. Yes, later would be better."

"You said that you, too, are an artist. Are you a painter?"

"No", he replied with much self-effacement. "I am poet."

"To be a poet is a wonderful calling. It is to see the thawing out of creation into the words of the spirit. But you already know this."

"Of course, of course, that is elementary." He jumped to his feet and strode back and forth in front of her. "Rose Woebegone, would you like for me to recite my poems?"

"Yes, oh, yes."

"The following is a short one, merely a sampling."

He crossed the alley and leaned against the stone wall. Closing his eyes he recited from memory:

> "Little Adolphus Hitler
> Come don't be so bold!
> Let Mama put your mittens on
> or you'll catch your death of cold."

Voolf-gong opened his eyes and waited for her reaction. He parted his lips and showed his perfect teeth. She did not know what to think. Hitler, she recalled, was a bad man who had lived a long time ago. Was it in Germany? Possibly she had misunderstood the meaning of the poem.

"Did you like it?" he asked with a mischievous smile as charming as a fox.

"It is simple, Voolf-gong, but it made me feel the love a mother has for her child."

He laughed. "Exactly. But it is not the best, I admit it myself. o much like the greeting card."

Rose did not grasp his meaning but had read enough poetry know that it sometimes takes a while for the music to be wed in the heart of the listener.

"Another?" he said with an eager grin.

"Oh, yes, please."

He withdrew a sheaf of papers from the back pocket of his nts.

"I warn you, it is more difficult. You do not know me well t, Rose, but in time you will understand that there is—how ll we delicately express it—a Faustian side to my rather mplex character. This is the downswing of the Hegelian rwerk. Tick-tock, tick-tock. *Und das Glockenspiel.* Bing-ng, bing-bong."

Rose smiled at his joking manner, though the meaning was scure. He smiled with her, abruptly terminating it with a wn.

"Perhaps you will not like it. Perhaps you will not under-nd it."

"I will try. I will listen carefully. "

"*Und zo*, I begin," he said. And read the following aloud with eat feeling:

I am too large for this world
I am too old to join the sneer parade,
Too young to dress up in black death's-head costumes
and revel in the pleasure-feasts of violation.
I scream with the razor voice of frustration
for bodies (a plentiful commodity) are beyond my
     reach,
their tumbling forms familiarized by photographs of
     burial pits,
Though I am good at flags

377

and I can sing Horst Wessel songs
imbibed at Opa's knee with *schnitzel und strudel.*
I spray with shot the weeping fowl,
in my imagination,
laughing, laughing my Zarathustra laugh,
more fearful than the bleeding hole
in the skull of a priest.

I observe the wagon-lits depart with a freight of
　　　children
grateful that I am not among the *Kindertransport,*
relieved that I belong to the masters and the guards,
hearing only insects resume their gossip in sunny
　　　playgrounds
where the ash falls down to cover the prints of small
　　　feet,
and soldiers' boots
and droplets of blood,
while the wasps quarrel
about their clay monuments in the tool shed.

At night I am a body wrestling in a glandular
　　　mind,
a heap of oily rags, waiting for a match,
my various lusts are nothing new.
It is a bad day.
It is a bad century.
Nothing left for me to do. It has all been done.
My lines are memorized
from the vocabulary of Oldspeech
which is the language of amber dragon-poets,
by which we golden boys tell lies with truth,
growing larger with the practice of our art;
upon the many stages.

Now comes my part,
all lights are on me and the crowd is hushed.
I become,
I am forever,
I am the great shrieking of creation.

olf-gong looked up.

'Well, what do you think?"

'Oh", said Rose, a little overcome. "I didn't understand it.
t it's very strong."

"*Ja*, strong. It is strong," Voolf-gong admitted. "But perhaps
s too much *der Blitzschlag, der Bombenerfolg*. A smash hit!
ash! Crash! Like the black lightning, no?"

'I, uh, well", Rose murmured.

"Tsk! But tell me you liked it."

"I'm not sure."

He sighed. "You are forgiven for your lack of faith. It is not
possible for you to believe, because we are only at the
ginning."

"The beginning of what, Voolf-gong?"

"The beginning of the dialogue-decalogue-decayalogue.
til then, I endure the Dichter's fate. To compose his art, the
chter must suffer alone. It was ever thus. Oft is he misunder-
od, as misunderstood as the Himalayan black bear who roams
: heights. He is called the moon-bear by the sherpas because
the white crescent on his chest. When surprised by hunters,
rolls down the mountain in a ball. They think he is insane,
t it is a higher sanity, for they are charmed by his escape and
nnot throw a spear from sheer amazement. Rose, dear, have
u observed the moon-bear rolling down a slope?"

"No. It must be a beautiful thing to see."

"It is. I have seen it. And what I have not seen, I know. All
ngs I know."

Rose puzzled for a moment over this last statement. "I think

379

you may be wrong in this, Voolf-gong, for it seems to me t
only God knows all things."

"Ach, let us not quarrel. You are young. You have much
learn. But the poem is the issue here. The Faustian and the an
Faustian zones are in dialectic tension, you see. Please help
admit that you liked it."

"I didn't understand much of it."

"Ach! But this is only the crude English translation. If
could hear this in Cherman! In Cherman it is a chem,
rhyming, the meter, the structure! You will pardon me if I
it . . . I am a master."

Voolf-gong then proceeded to read aloud in German
original version of the poem. The sound of his words gurg
like spring meltwater over a series of evenly spaced stor
When he was finished, he said, "You hear it? The flow?
internal music?"

"I think so."

"Ah, Rosebud", he smiled, slapping his knee with the
pers. "You are a prize. Did you know that these stupid, stup
stupid North Americans do not *hear* poetry. They are
interested. They will not listen. *Und zo*, I am condemned
wander in this naked city, sleep on the sidewalk like the cr
street-peoples."

"Maybe we *are* crazy street-people, Voolf-gong."

He laughed. "*Ja!* Maybe we are that."

"But we are not alone."

"That is correct. We are not alone. We have each other!"

For *other* he said *uzzarh*. His face twitched, and his
dribbled a few pearls of spittle. His fingers, the nails bitt
down to the quick, trembled. The paper rattled. Rose felt t
the *anjeni*—if he were indeed such—was perhaps overdoing
disguise.

He knelt beside Rose. "Is it possible? Is it possible that at
I have found her, she whom my heart seeks?" He shifted

dy close to her and put an arm around her shoulders. He
zed down tenderly into her face.

"Rosebud, Rosebud!"

Rose began to feel nervous.

"Rosebud, let us never be separated."

Although this thought was in accordance with the ways of
n and angels, Rose began to think he might not be an angel
er all.

"Let us be . . . *married!*" he breathed with great warmth into
r ear.

Rose jumped and pulled away from him. This was clearly not
accordance with the ways of men and angels. The image of
ors and a screaming universe began to thaw in her mind. She
gan to doubt in earnest.

Their faces were inches apart. Gazing obsessively into her
es, he whispered, "Rosebud, do not torture me; give me your
swer."

"I . . . I would have to think about it," she said. "We have
t met."

His face crumpled in disappointment.

"But we know each other! We are both *artists!*"

"Yes, but we might not be the right ones for each other."

He looked offended. "But I am a *von*, with a small *v*! Do you
ow what this means? No? This means aristocracy."

She shook her head obliquely.

"Am I not handsome enough?"

"You are very handsome."

"Am I insufficient?"

But that was obscure. "No, I don't think so", she said shaking
r head again, shifting her body an inch or two away.

"Do you not admire my style? Is it not original: Prussian
st-Mondrian baroque? And the color of my eyes? Are they
t unique: prussic acid blue, most effective when spilled
ainst a background of cement-gray in subdued light?"

381

She did not understand that at all.

"Ach, I know what is the problem! It is because of ▮ parents!"

"Your parents? But I haven't met them. I don't know a▮ thing about them."

He laughed bitterly and hung his head.

"*Ja! Ja!* You are very kind. Always it is so! Always my disgu▮ is *kaputt machen*! I am unmasked."

"What do you mean, Voolf-gong?"

"Is it not clear?! Does not my lineage go ahead of me l▮ the leper's bells? You have heard the bells. You can see. Y▮ know."

"No, I don't see. I don't know."

Turning his eyes slowly upon her, he sighed heavily.

"I," he said in a low voice, pausing for dramatic effect, "▮ the illegitimate son of Adolph Hitler and Eva Braun."

"Oh", she replied. She was fairly certain who Hitler was. F▮ who was Eva Braun?

"It is true", he stated in a fatalistic tone. "It is my lot. Mu▮ *und* Vati gave me to a woodcutter's family, to avoid embarra▮ ment, to be raised by them until such time as the Reic▮ destiny was fulfilled. I grew to manhood in a village near Ber▮ tesgaden. The rest, as they say, is history."

"Oh, that is sad, Voolf-gong. Did you ever see your mot▮ and father again?"

"*Nein.* They were gone, psssht! Like smoke, like gazoli▮ fumes."

He tipped his head back against the alley wall and closed ▮ eyes. A gust of plastic-scented air suddenly blew upward fr▮ the rungs of the vents, enveloping them both in warmth.

"Now you know everything. Or at least the worst", he sa▮

"That's all right", she said gently, patting his arm. "None ▮ us emerges from a perfect past."

He laughed hysterically. Then cut it off in midstream. R▮

382

not sure whether she should say something to comfort him,
keep silent, respecting his pain.

"*Und zo*," he said at last, "I can see that you do not wish to
try me. This I understand. But can we at least be friends,
spite this sinister knowledge which hangs between us?"

"Oh, yes, yes, Voolf-gong," she reassured him fervently. "Of
course we can be friends. We *are* friends."

He smiled sadly. "You are too kind, Rosebud. You are a
phenomenon of forbearance."

She returned the smile reassuringly.

"Are you hungry?" he asked with an abruptness that startled

"Yes, a little."

"I, myself, am also hungry. But I have no money."

"Oh", she said, groping in her pocket. "I have some."

She showed him the ten dollar bill.

"Is that all you have?" he said miserably.

"Yes."

"It is enough. Now we eat", he said plucking the bill from
fingers. "I shall go back unto Bank Street, and there I shall
find a food store. Soon I return with nourishment."

"I will go with you."

"*Nein, nein.* It is a considerable distance, and I can see that
you are fatigued. Besides, it is very cold."

"Thank you, Voolf-gong. You think of people's feelings."

"Yes, it has always been so with me," he admitted. "I am, as
they say, too sensitive."

"I will wait here for you."

He stood and pushed back the hair from his brow. Smiling
strangely, casting his eyes about the alleyway, he said, "Guard
this *Opernhaus* for me, Rosebud. The play is not quite over."

"Please come back quickly", she stammered. "And be careful. There are bad people on the streets."

He laughed again.

383

"*Auf Wiedersehen*, little *Fledermaus!*"

He strode toward the street, turned onto it without look
back, and disappeared.

Rose lay down on the vents, luxuriating in the warm gust
ventilation. Though the hunger in her belly was intense,
was filled with gladness. She had found a friend. If he was
an angel, as was now obvious, and if he was also a little crazy
was at least a decent person who was capable of concern f
stranger. She was no longer alone in the world. He was a k
person, though troubled, she could see. But of course his
was difficult, the two unhappy parents, for instance.

Some of what he had told her did not make sense, beca
when she had briefly fallen into his interior she had found
woodcutter's log chalet, only an apartment block in a city
boys roaming the streets like wolf cubs and a stage upon wh
he shouted lines from a book while other young people
plauded. Never mind, she thought, he would return soon.
would tell her more. He would explain.

Rose dozed for a while, keeping an ear open for his retu
ing footsteps. Then, despite herself, she fell asleep. When
awoke some hours later, she saw that night had fallen and
was buried in the deep shadow of the alley. She wondered if
had lost his way or had been accosted by the many bad pec
who roamed the streets, sometimes in packs. She waited a
longer, then decided to go searching for him.

Bank Street was practically deserted. A city bus rumbled p
empty of passengers, its sign proclaiming *Out of Service*.
stores up and down the street had extinguished their advert
ments. All doors were locked. Closed signs on each. Two blo
north she spotted a brightly lit entrance from which a man
woman emerged—an all-night convenience store. The cou
crossed the pavement and walked quickly down a side str
Rose went in.

A heavyset man looked up from his newspaper and rota

a cigar across his lips. He stared at Rose from behind thick glasses.

"Help you?"

"I'm looking for a man", Rose said timidly.

"Aren't you all?"

Rose did not understand that.

"Any particular man?"

"His hair is gold, and he is a poet."

"Oh, that narrows it down."

"He is German."

The shopkeeper smiled crookedly.

"His name wouldn't by any chance be Wolfgang?"

"Yes, yes, it is!" Rose stepped forward. "Have you seen him?"

"Every night I see him."

"Oh! You know him! Is he a friend of yours?"

"Yeah, we're real close."

"Did he buy food?"

"Yeeees, he bought some chips. And smokes."

"Did he say anything? Did he tell you about me?"

"Nah, he didn't tell me nothin' about nobody."

Rose looked at the floor, thinking hard.

"Perhaps he is looking for me", she said.

"I doubt it, kid."

"Oh, I'm sure he is looking for me. Did he say which way he was going? He is probably worried."

"He ain't worried, believe me."

"But he must be." Rose's voice ascended steeply from the key of doubt to the key of fear.

The man looked down at his paper and shook his head.

"Tough luck", he grumbled. "Tough luck."

Rose stood without moving in front of the cash register.

The man looked up again. "Still here?"

"Where can I find him?"

"Couldn't say. Look, did he give you that line about being Hitler's son?"

She nodded slowly.

"Did he, by any chance, ask you to marry him?"

Rose stared at the floor.

"Uh-huh", said the man. "Wolfie strikes again. Well, don't take it to heart. You aren't the first. Or the last."

Frozen into immobility, feeling the ache in her stomach and her back and a black stone expanding in her chest, Rose said nothing.

"Got any money?" the man asked, knowing the answer.

"No."

"Figures. Well, sorry I can't help. Time to move on, kid."

She turned toward the door.

"Time to move on", he said again, as she went out. Without giving her another thought, he returned to the sports section of his paper.

Out on the sidewalk Rose did not know where to turn. The wind whistled down the street, twisting snow flurries and litter into devil's dances. A bell struck solemnly in the distance. She turned and walked toward the sound. Fifteen minutes later she stood on Wellington Street, facing the Peace Tower of the Parliament buildings.

The clock said midnight. The wind shrieked.

Dizzy, she stumbled to the shelter of an alcove in a building where an American flag snapped above bronze doors. She rapped on the doors, but no one came to answer. Crouching down and huddling on the steps, she began to moan. She closed her eyes and rocked her body.

Some time later footsteps klick-klocked along the sidewalk. Rose looked up and saw a lady approaching from the east. The lady looked young from a distance, but as she came closer she looked older. She wore a short fur jacket and a black plastic miniskirt. Her bowlegs moved along with casual determination upon spiked heels. As she passed the alcove, she spotted Rose and stopped. She stared for a minute, saying nothing. Rose stared back. The woman's face was heavily painted.

"Hey!" the woman said in a raspy voice. "That ain't a smart idea, kid. Embassy's closed."

Silence.

"Cat got your tongue?"

Rose shook her head.

"You're gonna freeze to death if you stay there."

With the sleeve of her dirty parka, Rose wiped her face.

"No place to go?"

Rose shook her head again.

"Broke, I'll bet. Not a penny to your name?"

Rose nodded.

The woman opened her purse, and for an instant Rose thought she would remove money from it and give it to her. Instead, the woman took out a package of cigarettes and lit one with the click of a metal lighter. The wind tore the smoke from her mouth, which was also chewing a wad of gum.

The woman looked vaguely sympathetic.

"No home? No moolah? No pals? No job?"

"Yes. I mean no."

"Down on your luck, aren't you? And you ain't a likely candidate for my line o' work."

Rose wondered what that might be.

"I'd take you home with me, put you up for the night, if I could. But I share the place with a couple other workin' girls. We work at night, see, and you might scare off the customers."

The woman dragged hard on her cigarette and squinted her eyes.

"Still, the ways and means committee never sleeps. I guess I can give you a break."

The woman took a few steps closer, reached down, and

pulled Rose to her feet. Rose drew back from the heavy scent of perfume and the clutching hands in black leather gloves.

"Don't worry, don't worry, I ain't gonna hurt ya. C'mere."

She dragged Rose to the curb, and a minute later a taxi pulled out of the front gates of the grounds of the Parliament Buildings across the street. The woman flagged it down.

She pushed Rose into the back seat and barked at the cabbie, "Take her to the Good Shepherd Mission down on the market. Here's a twenty, buddy, and it's worth your life if you try any funny business. Got it?"

"Gotcha, Ma'am", he said, giving her a salute.

"Now, don't you worry, honey", the woman said to Rose. "They're good folks down there at the woman's shelter. Bible thumpers, but sort of all right, if you know what I mean. Clean beds, big breakfast. No fee. Kick the door in if they're asleep."

She threw another ten at the cabbie.

"Hell, on second thought, she's too little to kick the door in. You wake 'em up, buddy, willya?"

"Sure thing", he said. "It's a slow night."

Ten minutes later, the cab pulled to the curb in front of an old building in the labyrinth of the market area east of Parliament Hill. The cabbie banged on the door while Rose waited in the car. A light went on upstairs, and a moment later the door opened, revealing a young woman with a shiny face, clutching the lapels of her housecoat.

The cabbie explained everything, and the woman beckoned to Rose.

She asked no questions, took her in, and led her up to the second floor on a rickety staircase. In a small kitchen she made a pot of tea and a sandwich, both of which Rose gulped down. The woman sat opposite her at the kitchen table, observing Rose with thoughtful eyes. After a trip to the toilet, Rose followed her to a dark dormitory smelling of disinfectant and old clothing. There were twelve cots in the room. Snoring lumps occupied eleven of them. Rose lay down on the empty cot and fell asleep.

In the night she had a dream. It had been many years since such a dream had come to her. The white wings hovering over the world extended from horizon to horizon. The turquoise eye turned and looked down at Rose huddled under the rough wool blankets and did not withdraw his gaze. He saw the black stone that was crushing her heart and took it from her. In its place he left a silver stone. But the stone was not hard and cold because it breathed, because it inhaled and exhaled. Still, there was a wound in it.

"From this city you must go tomorrow", the white bird sang, "to other appointed stations."

"Why?" Rose cried.

"Because you must see."

"*Why* must I see?" she protested.

"Because it is the labor which has been given to you."

"I do not want it!"

"What, then, do you desire?"

"I want to go home!"

"You are always home."

"I want to see Oldmary."

"She is with you."

"I do not understand", Rose wailed. "What do you want of me?"

"A life is a word. Its meaning and its shape are the answer you seek. It must be lived in order to be spoken."

"But where do I go?"

"To the royal mountain, to a place where the hand of the Father has touched the earth in this land."

Then the wings flexed and disappeared above the turbulent dark.

When Rose awoke, she wondered where she was to go. There was only one place she knew of where God had touched the earth in this land: Threefinger Lake, which he had pressed into the warm stone as a sign of the Three-in-One. But it was far. Somewhere in the north, on the border between the Land of Little Trees and the ultimate barrens. How could she go there?

Over breakfast the young woman with the shining face asked for her name.

"I am Rose, or maybe Bineshi. Rabbit too."

"Do you have a home, Rose?"

"I had a home, once, a long time ago."

"Where was that?" the woman asked as she fed her.

"North, somewhere", Rose said. "I can't remember. I could remember if I tried. But the bird said no."

The woman looked at her anxiously.

"A bird?"

"Who hovers over the world, with his eye upon us."

"What kind of bird is it?"

"I knew once, a long time ago. I think he had a name, but I forget. No, I remember—it is Winijishid-Manito. A white bird that said the words you couldn't hear, and the words took the shape of tongues of fire, Grandma said. You sat in the back, which was the place you liked best because you could see everything from there and were not seen, because you were very small. You could hear the words which Jesus sent by the messenger bird and feel the fire which did not hurt."

The woman asked if she could say a prayer. Rose nodded. The woman bowed her head.

"Dearest Lord," she said, "I do not know who this daughter is. I think she is yours. But she is terribly alone. Be with her. Guide her. Protect her from the wolf."

Rose looked up. "I have to go now", she said.

"Wouldn't you like to stay with us for a while?"

"No, I can't."

The woman gave her more food, which Rose put into the saddlebag. She also gave her a little money and asked where she would like to go.

"I don't know."

The woman's eyes saddened. "You mean you're going to just wander? That's not safe. Winter is—"

"The bird said to the royal mountain, where the hand of the Father touched the earth in this land."

"The royal mountain?" The woman repeated the words slowly and sipped her tea, pondering. Finally she looked up. "Ah, I think I see."

So she drove Rose to the train station, bought a ticket for her, and put her on the train, and cried a little as it drew out of the station. But she dried her eyes and went back to her own place, because there were so many, many in need of help.

From the window of the train Rose watched the passing farms and the roads and byways that branched in all directions, reshaping the many futures constantly. Her heart was a fluttering thing, and the wound in it grew and grew until it filled her entirely and seized her thoughts, and a shadow that hovered above the train, fighting with the many soaring *anjeni* who also accompanied her, said to her a false thing. It said that nothing existed outside the wound. And because she listened to it, because the pain was very great, she asked for release, saying, "I would be better off dead than alive."

But the ways of the Lord are mysterious. He does not grant every wish. The wishes for escape are most carefully weighed in his hands.

In this way did Rose of the Ojibwe come to the great and terrible city of Montreal.

15

"*Mont Royal, la prochaine gare!* " the conductor called as he strolled through the carriage. "Mount Royal, next station!"

Rose sat up straight in her seat and stared out the window at the passing factories. So it was true! There was a royal mountain. It was real, the bird had not lied, which was a reassurance, for dreams will sometimes lie. Yet she was disappointed to learn that the royal mountain, the second place where God had touched the earth in this land, was surrounded by a city.

The train rolled to a stop, and Rose stepped out onto a cement platform. People embraced arriving passengers or climbed onto the train. All of them ignored Rose or did not see her, for stations are a complex tangle of leavings and takings, beginnings and endings. The train rolled on, the people departed, and Rose stood alone blinking at the sun.

Where am I to go?

On the street outside the main entrance of the station, Rose stopped. Where was the mountain? All about her there were houses and the fingertops of trees and many walls of stone and brick. Countless cars zipped thisway and thatway. Squirrels ran along the airways, and pigeons walked on the ground. But none of these could speak. She searched for a sparrow or chickadee, but even the small birds of this city were unable to speak. And so she tried to ask directions from the human passersby. Two people brushed her aside when she approached them—ay, ay, they did not see her, for she was not real. The third stopped; he was an old man carrying a newspaper under his arm. He did not respond to her English, so she asked him in the imperfect French that she remembered from her life with the sisters.

"Is the royal mountain in this place?" she began.

"Yes, it is", he replied patiently.

"It does not look like a mountain to me."

"The mountain is beyond, a little to the south. See that corner over there? Go to it and turn to the right. Follow it for a long way, and you will arrive at the mountain."

"Is it the place where God touched the earth in this land?"

His face wrinkled. "Some say it is so. Many go there. If you go there, you can decide for yourself."

"Thank you, sir."

He tipped his hat and shuffled on, staring at the sidewalk, for he was very old, and the old must watch the surface beneath their feet.

During the walk to the mountain, Rose felt a strength enter her, for to move upon the earth without direction was a dissolving thing, a not-arriving thing that left one exhausted. But to move with purpose, even when the purpose was obscure, was to feel a wind from home, promising, promising. Always the mountain had been there, always it had waited for her, and now she was coming. It knew she was coming.

On Queen Mary Street, the mountain swelled above the office towers and the miles of homes and apartment blocks. It was an island of forest in the heart of the city. And on its crest was the greatest church Rose had ever seen. It was capped by a green copper dome, and on top of that was a cross of such size that giants would have run from it. The building was so high that museums and the ramparts of government would shrink before it. If the black totem were to be placed beside it, the totem would be a little stick. A bell rang as Rose began to climb toward the entrance. In the melting slush of the steps, several people knelt and prayed. They ascended a single step with each prayer. Rose felt a sudden longing to do the same. She knelt and prayed the word prayers, the thanking prayers, and the praise prayers in a river flowing from the heart. Yet when she

393

tried to stand to take the next step, it cost her an enormous effort. When she knelt again, her knees trembled and gave way beneath her.

"Io, I cannot! See, even here I am smaller and smaller and have nothing to give him."

She struggled to her feet and wiped the slush from the deer-hide sack and the saddlebag. She gripped the iron railing and began to climb slowly, pulling herself upward toward the dome that shook with the song of mighty bells. When at last she arrived, she pushed the great brass door open and went inside. At first she could see nothing of the interior, for her eyes had not yet adjusted.

"It is dark inside the Lord's mountain", she whispered. But this thought was instantly swept aside by the infusion of presence that was thick in the air—that she inhaled and exhaled. Joy burst upon her like a wave, and washed through her, and carried her deeper into the radiance hidden within the church. Slowly the light of her eyes increased, and everywhere she looked were glowing wood, and marble floors, and gold. Then she saw a giant statue of Saint Joseph above the altar and the tabernacle, where the Beating Heart pounded with a love so great that Rose fell to her knees and pressed her face to the floor.

"Io, it has been so long, so long", she sighed. "You, you", she cried, slipping so swiftly and deeply into words-without-words that the few people scattered throughout the pews wondered for a moment if she had fainted. But they reminded themselves of the many times they had seen such things in this place. For all men fell in this place, a holy falling, as they were pulled gently from the birth canal and fell into the hands of God.

The air burned sweetly. The river of love flowed in all directions, dissolving the upness and downness of things, the thisness and thatness, consuming, creating, in the fire of love that did not destroy. The throngs of angels swam in the liquid air, singing as they swam. *Sanctus, sanctus, sanctus! Kije, kije, kije-*

Manito, you are all light, you are all love, you are the Sea of the Ojibwe, you are the sea of all peoples, you are the sea of being in which we live and move and have our smaller being!

Io, rivers of tears poured from her eyes onto the floor, tears without sound or grief, tears of spirit joy. When she unbent and stumbled to a pew, she knew that what the Spirit had told her in the dream was true, that the hand of God had touched the earth here and continued to touch.

"I thank you, I thank you, for you have not let me fall through your fingers."

Then there came *Anamessikewin* and Holy Communion, when the sweet-fire entered her flesh and radiated through all layers of her being. It was too much, it was too generous. But she drank and drank of it and let him warm her through and through.

Later, when most worshippers had left the chapel, she opened her eyes, got up, and went deeper into the shrine. By a series of corridors she arrived at a large inner hall where thousands of vigil lamps trembled in ranks along the walls, the watching-lights of paradise. So full of silence was the room, the eternal peace whispered among uncountable tongues of fire. Here was the heart of the world at last, the hidden spring that poured from the stone of the mountain.

Rose peered into the shadowed areas between the pillars and the images, and in the ruby light she saw hanging upon the walls hundreds of crutches, misshapen boots, and braces. On some there were little messages inked onto the leather and chrome: *Merci, Seigneur*, thank you, Lord, thank you for my healed leg, *mon nouveau pied*, my child, *mon enfant*, my eyes, my heart, *ma vie*, my life! On and on, hundreds of large miracles and countless smaller ones. Thus, a knowing came upon her, though it seemed to arise from within, as if it were a word that had always slept there, and she had not until this moment known of it.

The little father is a sign of the great Father, and the world is in need of him, for the eyes of fathers have looked elsewhere than upon their children.

"Oh, give me a father," Rose prayed, "as once you gave to me a little brother."

She returned to the immense chapel within the shrine and rested in its light for many hours. It was not necessary to stir from it. She was home at last and need never go from it. But it was not so, for the ways of heaven and the ways of men are mixed and confused in the fallen world, and though no harm was meant by it, the servants of the house of God came to her in the deep night and said that she must leave, for the doors were about to be locked.

"May I remain here?" she asked. "With him."

But they said it was not possible, there were rules, she would have to go. So she obeyed with a sinking heart, feeling that even in her one true home she was not at home. Twice over it hurt, ten times more than an eviction from a rented room, for this was the center of the world and the sanctuary of her beloved. They led her gently to the doors.

"Come back tomorrow", one said to her. "*Saint-Jo* is always here. He never takes a vacation."

The mountainside was very dark, though all around the height the lights of the city spread toward the horizon. Rose saw for the first time in her life how great in number were the branches of the tree of man. And greater in number the human lives that lived upon each branch, making their many choosings, changing pathways with each choice. It was so complex that she reeled from the thought of it and sat down upon a curb to silence her mind and hide her eyes.

"I must not fear", she admonished herself. "A father has been given to me. He too was cast out from a place that was his home and went at night into the place of exile."

He is with you, he is with you, sang the wind.

Still, the fact remained that there was no place to go. She walked slowly about the upper levels of the mountain, circling the shrine. The dome was illuminated by spotlights; it was a word lifted up over the city at all times. "I will not depart from it," she said, "for this is the station of my dream." In an undergrowth of shrubs and small trees to the left of the shrine, she found a pathway. At its entrance was a carving of the first station of the cross. And behind it a large marble statue of Saint Joseph holding the Christ Child. She went to this and sat down on a mound of last year's leaves; heaps of them had drifted up against the pedestal, covered with a fine dusting of snow. She brushed it away and sat down on the crackling brown blanket. Within minutes the warmth of her body was reflected back to her. She pulled more leaves across her legs. This too was warmer.

With a smile of peace, Rose laid the deer-hide sack, the K. B. saddlebag, and the roll of drawings carefully beside her, pulled more leaves over her body, and fell asleep.

In the night she had a dream.

It was no longer winter. It was autumn. A small oginiwâbigon wandered on a mountain among the trees. Her legs blurred against a russet of leaves that had fallen all about. Her arm angled into the air, jerking the string of a kite that skipped and failed, then dipped and sailed, a large white bird shape humming on its dowels. It went up at last, and she was tied to the sky. Though the afternoon was far gone, the sun blazed on the copper dome, the mountain upon a mountain, against which the light washed green-blue.

Now the hush fell, and the night laid itself over the earth. The mountain was deserted. Saint Joseph was finally able to climb down from his marble height and wander without being noticed. He carried a little boy through the shadows, rustling the leaves with his sandalled feet, searching, searching for the kite-girl who had lost her way. As he approached she heard his steps and, in a moment of distraction, let go of the string. Her toy now caught in the upper branches of the trees. It was trapped and torn. She looked up at it, her tears running down, arms reaching in the timeless gesture of those who seek to rise.

"Where are you going?" asked the man. The girl stepped back, afraid. But his voice was soft, his skin as brown as a father's hands, calluses thick, and hairs curled upon the blue veins. His hands reached up and a gust of wind unraveled the kite from its trap. It sliced gently down, now this way, now that, until it settled at their feet. The girl looked at him. He looked at her. The babe in his arms looked too.

"It is night," the man said, "and every child on earth is sleeping now, save you. Every child belongs somewhere."

"No", she said. "Not me." She looked away from him.

"Rose of the Ojibwe," he whispered, "for you there is everything. It is coming."

But Rose saw only the coming of winter. Down through the long bold beeches the wind wailed, the kite flipped and tumbled on the ground, and the many little ribbons tied to the tail became birds fluttering in anxiety, crying *Ningâ, Ningâ!* My mother, my mother!

"I must go alone", she said.

"You are not alone, though you feel alone", he replied.

"But who is with me!" she cried.

"I am with you", he said.

"It is broken", the girl said, pointing to her kite.

"It is torn", he said.

"It will never fly again", she said.

"You cannot know", he smiled, "what will and will not fly."

He put his free hand into his pocket and removed a needle and thread. He offered the baby to her. "Will you hold him?"

"I am too small," she said. "I might drop him."

"It is he who holds you," the man said.

The girl took the baby into her arms. He was warm and roly-poly. He curled into the crook of her arm. In his eyes she saw the reflection of many stars and a far wheeling galaxy.

Now the man's needle stung the cloth, again and again it stung as it pulled together the severed weave.

"There," he said, "your bird is healed. It will fly again. Let's go climb the mountain."

They walked together around the bronze dome, leaving behind the squabbling cars, the siren wails, and the jubilance of discotheques and bars. The baby was serene within the girl's embrace. He did not mind her ugly hump, he saw only her encircling arms, felt her warmth, and heard the thumping of her heart against his ear.

At the height, in an opening among the scrawling trees, the man unrolled the silk. The wind took it. Then against the dowel-cross the fabric arched, the line whipped and sang, and the kite rose, yearning toward the farthest breaking point. It rose higher, beyond the limitations of natural belief.

"Higher!" laughed the girl.

"Higher!" laughed the man.

"Higher!" laughed the eyes of the baby.

The man offered the string to the girl. She offered the child to the man. The exchange was complete. Now the wind was harnessed in her hand, and she was pulled by it. Her feet left the ground. She rose higher. Onto the mountain slowly fell the pinwheels of snow, mixed with the hot melted tears of angels, and the cheers of saints. Higher. Below her feet the city shrank.

Higher!

Then she flew up into the river of souls.

A policeman found Rose in the morning, a lump half buried in a drift of leaves. He frowned. He shook the shoulder that poked from the heap. The shape stirred, alive. A brown gnome appeared, grabbed its possessions, and bolted away into the woods.

In St. Henri, a slum of Montreal, there lived tens of thousands of people in tipsy tenements made of clapboard and tar paper and toppling brick, underneath an undulating sea of flat roofs crowned by the spires of old churches. The mountain towered above it to the north, though the dome of the shrine was hidden on the far side. Rose walked along Rue Sainte Philomène, a confine misted with sewer steam and littered with garbage, listening to the French children laughing and chattering in their rapid tongue. These were human sounds. These were the sounds of a village. Little boys clacked their hockey sticks, shooting pucks made of frozen dog droppings. Their cheeks flamed red, their hockey sweaters were tattered, their mitts made of old wool-darned socks. As Rose passed them they stopped their game and stared at her. But she was a momentary distraction, of no great importance, for St. Henri was home to many strange people. They resumed their play among the rusting parked cars tilted thisway and thatway with tires on the sidewalks.

"Where am I going?" she asked of the narrow strip of sky, for the river wind was blowing westward along its frozen course, bearing the scent of a distant sea. The street was strange to her, yet familiar. It was not the one true home of the shrine, yet it felt closer to homeness than the other part of the city where rich people lived. It was to be expected that in this lowest place the sparrows and other small birds would again begin to speak.

"A little farther", they chipped and pipped. "There you shall find the station of your dream."

"The dream is behind me," she cried, "for I was cast out from the place which is my one true home."

"That is not so", they protested. "It is always waiting for you. You shall return."

"But I do not know the way!"

"See, the way opens before you. She comes."

From the east, which was the direction of the sea, a woman walked. At first she seemed to be a snowbird puffed with the cold, for her coat was a round ball of white feathers, her thin legs were garbed in tight black stockings, and upon her feet were white boots. She jingled as she approached along the sidewalk, tossing her merry head under a white fur cap. It was a woman, of course, Rose was sure of that. Not a bird. She was bopping as Deirdre did. Her arms pressed a shiny red purse to her chest. As the woman swerved to pass by, Rose flashed a glance at her face. She was young, about twenty-five years of age, heavily decorated with mascara, lipstick, and rouge. The ringlets of hair falling from underneath her cap were yellow.

"I believe you wish to speak with me", Rose said in French to the woman's back, for she moved too quickly for a more cordial introduction. "I am the one who seeks an opening-way."

The woman stopped in her tracks and turned around. "Say again?"

Rose repeated it in English. The woman looked regretful. "Sorry, honey. Don't have time today. Take care. Bye. Don't catch cold."

She turned to go.

"There is, perhaps, a mistake", Rose said, following the woman, clutching her arm. The woman stopped and looked down at the little brown hand. Then she looked at Rose, her eyes still friendly, but cautious. She took in the face, the baggage, and the bent form.

"Need a dime?"

"I am looking for a place to live, and a labor, that I might remain in this place, which is nested beneath the mountain of the Beating Heart."

The woman laughed whimsically. "A place to live, huh?"

"Yes," Rose nodded. "I believe you can lead me to it. I believe you were sent to me."

"Sent? By who?"

"You know him."

The woman shook her head. "Sorry, honey, don't know what you're talking about. Look, gotta go. I'm late for work."

"May I walk with you?"

The woman shrugged. "Okay, if you like."

Side by side they proceeded west along Sainte Philomène.

"My name is Rose Wâbos. Yes, now I remember. My thoughts have been unclear because of the illness, but now it returns, as rivers melt in springtime and flow again. Though sometimes I am called Bineshi, or Nissime, which is his joke with me, because I am smaller and younger."

"No place to go?" the woman asked without pausing in her stride. Rose hurried to keep up.

"Yes, I need such a place. I believe it is waiting for me, but I do not yet know of it."

"Hey, you speak kind of classy for an Indian—no offense I hope. Where'd you learn to talk like that?"

"At the sisters' school. They have gone away to France, and it is certain they will not return. I do not know exactly where I am to go, yet I am on a journey to the river of milk, the river of souls which some call the *tchibekana*, the river of stars."

The woman laughed. "Hey, me too. I'm kind of a star myself."

"I sensed this about you", Rose nodded solemnly. "What is your name?"

"Carlotta Fishbein. Course that's not my stage name. I'm an actress. The public knows me as Carmella Fabian."

"By what name shall I call you?"

"Might as well stick with Carlotta for now." The woman stopped again and looked at Rose. She laughed and shook her head. "Well, well, I should've had a second cup of coffee. What's wrong with my head? You're perfect."

"What do you mean, Carlotta?"

"Just perfect."

Carlotta resumed her brisk walk, and Rose followed her until they arrived at an intersection. From there they turned left and entered a warehouse district close to the banks of the river. Down an alleyway they went for half a block and arrived at a set of steps leading into a lopsided building.

"Here's home", Carlotta said. "Follow me."

With an old-fashioned bar key, she unlocked the red door at the top of the steps and pushed it open, Rose close behind her. Inside they strode down a dark hallway and entered a large high-ceilinged hall. The sound of shouting echoed from the rafters.

"Where the hell are the fairies?" roared a lion.

"How the hell should I know?" shrieked a lioness. "I told them to be here by nine."

"That's the director and the choreographer having a difference of opinion", Carlotta whispered. "Act smart. I'll introduce you to them."

Proceeding across the wide floor of the warehouse, they rounded the corner of a pile of packing crates stacked eight feet high. Behind it, Carlotta and Rose found a young man and a middle-aged woman glaring at each other, shaking empty coffee cups at each other.

"Ahem", Carlotta said.

The director and the choreographer spun around and faced the interlopers.

"What do you want, bloody Hippo?" the lion growled.

"Don't call me Hippo, bloody Marco. My name is Hippolyta, Queen of the Amazons."

Rose was totally confused by this exchange, for she had supposed that Carlotta had only two names. Still more confusing, the director, the choreographer, and the star withdrew into a conspiracy of sardonic laughter.

The young man, whom Carlotta had called Marco, was in his late twenties, lean and tall, with hunched shoulders and a face that had grimaced, shouted, and snarled very often during its short life. Barefooted despite the chill, he was clothed in a pair of jeans torn at the knees and a gray sweatshirt on which the letters OLD VIC were printed in faded white letters. His hair was black, tumbling in every direction. He wiped it off his forehead, but it instantly fell back in place. The older woman was very handsome, her hair bunched to the side like a thicket of brittle kindling, silver threads entwined with the brown twigs. Like the director, she wore jeans and a sweatshirt, though her feet were bound in thick socks and pink running shoes.

Their laughter wound down as they inspected Rose from top to bottom with their eyes.

"Who, pray tell, is this?" the woman asked.

"This, Isadora, is a fairy that came out of the woods."

"If you call me Isadora one more time, Carlotta," snapped the woman in a low voice, "you will become a fairy yourself."

"Sorry, Mrs. Brocklehurst, won't happen again", Carlotta drawled, leaving no doubt as to how faithfully she would honor this promise.

"Now", the woman said all businesslike. "Who is this?"

"This is Rose", Carlotta said. "She wants to be a star."

The man named Marco grimaced. "A star? I see. Is she willing to start at the bottom?"

"You'll have to ask her yourself. By the way, where is Bottom? I need that script he borrowed yesterday."

"Late", said the lioness.

"Late", said the lion.

"And Cobweb and Moth and Mustard Seed? Late too, I suppose."

404

"They had a party last night. You know what gin does to Moth's little brain."

"We'll never be ready", Carlotta groaned. "Three weeks, three bloody weeks before dress, and they must have their parties. Did anyone phone them?"

The director reached out and took the choreographer's hand in both of his. "Come, my Queen, take hands with me, and rock the ground whereon these sleepers be."

"Do it yourself, idiot!" the choreographer sneered at him, throwing his hands away and stomping off.

"Dear, dear", said Marco.

Rose, completely disoriented by the conversation, was beginning to suspect that she had made a mistake or that the sparrows had tried to mislead her for a bit of sport.

"Thank you, Carlotta", Rose said when she could catch the star's eye. "I have to go now."

"Wait a minute, wait a minute. Where're you off to? I thought you said—"

"I must have been mistaken", Rose explained, edging away. "This is not the station of my dream."

Strangely, the star and the director both smiled in unison. The director stepped forward, went down on one knee, took Rose's hand in both of his, kissed it, and said with great and gentle passion, "Oh, my dear, that is where you are wrong. For this, you see, *is* the *Dream*."

Carlotta led Rose to a row of stacking chairs lining one wall of the warehouse, and sat down with her. She pointed to a make-shift stage constructed of plywood sheets and cinder blocks at the far end of the room, where men on stepladders were rigging spotlights.

"This is the home of Cirque de la Lune", she said. "Sometimes known as Cirque des Lunatiques. We're a company of actors. Most of us are amateurs, but a few of us, like me, have

405

some training—I took drama at McGill. Marco and Isadora are professionals. They both acted Shakespeare for years, Isadora in England and Oregon, Marco at Stratford. Marco is actually the world-renowned Mark Chandler-Ross. We call him Marco the Magnificent. As you can see, he's a charm boy, but don't let that fool you, he's a crackerjack, smart as a whip when it comes to the comedies. Not so hot on tragedies. Isadora's another cup of tea altogether. Thinks she's a genius, wants to be famous again. She was, sort of, in the fifties, but that's past history. She's a pill, avoid her like the plague."

"Why was she so angry at you for using her first name?" Rose asked.

"Because her first name's really Margaret. She thinks she's another Isadora Duncan, the famous dancer-choreographer. Drives her crazy when I call her that."

"Carlotta, I am unsure about all of this. I am not an actress."

"Hey, hardly anybody in this troupe can act. Lack of talent never stopped me, girl. So why don't you give us a try. Just for a day. With first night only weeks away we're getting a little desperate. One of the fairies ran off with her boyfriend, you see, and we need a stand-in."

"I . . . I do not think I am suitable, Carlotta. My appearance—"

"Your appearance is fantastic!" Carlotta said, grabbing her arm and putting her face close to Rose's. "You're shorter than the average person, right? And you're kind of a forest person too, just like the real fairies, right?"

Rose shook her head. "I would be too shy."

"Shy? Hey, who was it stopped me in the street with some great lines? Who was it, eh? Eh?"

"That was not acting, Carlotta, and besides, there was only one person listening—you."

"Yeah, and it's entirely possible that on opening night there'll be only one person in the audience—my Mum. Maybe nobody.

We have a reputation we're trying to overcome. This is our last chance. We did Ionesco two years ago and bombed, like I mean *totally* bombed. I told them that dancing *The Rhinoceros* was an idiotic idea, but Marco and Isadora wouldn't listen. Last year they tried this completely nutty singing version of *Crap's Last Tapes*—you ever read Beckett? No?—anyway, it was an even bigger bomb, as you can imagine. So Marco says to Isadora we have to do something straight this year, like a Shakespeare comedy or something. And here we are doing it." Carlotta looked about the room in disgust. "Yeah, here we are. Half of these jerks don't have their lines memorized, Bottom's a moron, the fairies are completely out to lunch—I mean figuratively and literally—and anybody else you see here in Athens is a neurotic with psychotic tendencies. Whaddaya say? Want to give it a whirl?"

"Are you a neurotic with psychotic tenden . . . tenden . . . ?" Rose asked without intending to offend, merely for clarification.

"Tendencies—me? No. I'm the exception that proves the rule. So, whaddaya say, Rose? We need a fairy, and you're perfect for the part."

"But I have never acted. Oh—that is not exactly true, for once I was a flower in the sisters' May pageant. The words I had to say were simple, but I did not do very well."

"What were the words—the lines?"

"I said, 'I am a Forget-me-not, Our Lady's eyes so blue. Plant me in the spring, and I rise up ever true'."

"Gee", Carlotta said, nodding repeatedly. "That was terrific. What do you mean you can't act?"

At that moment a portly young man dragged his feet into the room and crossed it in the direction of Carlotta and Rose. His eyes were puffy, he wheezed, his chin and upper lip bristled with several days growth of blond beard.

"Hi, Hippo", he mumbled.

407

"You're still alive, Bobby. That's a blessing to us all. Did you bring my script?"

"Yeah, here it is." He threw it at Carlotta and ambled slowly toward the stage.

"That was our Bottom", said Carlotta, rolling her eyes at the ceiling. "A very gifted young actor, destined for great things."

She shuffled through the pages of script and shoved it into Rose's hands. "Here, read this."

Rose peered at the lines beneath Carlotta's index finger. Gathering her courage, clearing her throat, she said aloud:

"Get your weapons in your hand, and kill me a red-hipped humble-bee on the top of a thistle; and good monsieur, bring me the honey bag."

"Oh, wow, that was perfect! Except it's *mounsieur*, not *monsieur*. That's Shakespeare's little joke, you see."

"It cannot be correct, Carlotta, for I know from experience that it should be *monsieur*."

"Trust me, it's *mounsieur*."

Rose looked at her dubiously. Carlotta was about to say more when a terrible shouting erupted from beyond the stack of boxes. Another voice joined it, then another, lions and lionesses and cubs roaring and screaming at each other.

"It's awful early in the morning for this sort of thing", Carlotta said to herself. "Bloody prima donnas. Sounds like a bottom's getting kicked."

Shortly after, the portly young man rounded the corner of the boxes, his face red, though his pace was in no way amended. He shuffled in the direction of the door.

"Bye, Bobby!" Carlotta called.

He dismissed her with a flick of his hand and was seen no more.

"Looks like another great career just bit the dust," Carlotta mused. "What a pity."

The director and the choreographer stomped into the center of the room, arms tightly crossed, faces flashing with anger.

"You said—"

"No, Marco, *you* said—"

"I merely said, 'So what if he's your nephew! He can't act!' "

"Oh, that's all you said, is it? Well, let me tell you—"

"Yeah, that's what I said. And I'll say anything I like until this company starts to work like professionals. The real issue here, I mean the *real* issue, is where can we get a good Bottom—"

"Don't ask me," the choreographer replied, "ask your fairy friends."

"Cheap shot, Margaret. Cheap shot. One more crack like that and out you go."

"Please, give me the pleasure. You fire me, and I'll smear your name all over the guild, all over the map, Marco, as far as Stratford—*both* Stratfords. I can ruin you if I want."

Carlotta grinned. "Oh-oh, looks like the shadows have offended each other. Never mind, it's easily mended. Happens all the time."

The director and choreographer stomped off to another part of the building, head to head, still squabbling.

Carlotta sighed. "As you can see, Rose, we need help. Serious help. Please consider my offer."

"I . . . I will try it for a day, Carlotta, to test the path that is before me, for I see no other at the moment."

"Fabulous!" Carlotta said, jumping to her feet. "Wait right here." She hurried off in the direction of Marco and Mrs. Brocklehurst.

What happened next was torturous. Rose was put on a chair in the center of the stage, a spotlight trained on her. The theater company gathered round to listen.

"Right, let's get started, Miss . . ." Marco said, as the audition was about to begin. "Miss what?"

"My name is Rose Wâbos, yes, that is what it is, not Bineshi, though sometimes I am called by this name. And Nissime."

"Okay. Miss Wâbos it is."

"You may call me Rose, if you wish."

"Right, Rose. Now read the lines beginning halfway down the page where Bottom says, 'I see their knavery'."

With much hesitation Rose began:

"I see their knavery", she whispered.

"Louder!" the director said.

" 'I see their knavery: this is to make an ass of me; to fright me, if they could. But I will not stir from this place, do what they can: I will walk up and down here, and I will sing, that they shall hear I am not afraid'."

When she had finished delivering the lines, Rose stared at the trembling papers in her hands.

Mrs. Brocklehurst, arms folded, scowling, tapping the toe of her right foot, said in a threatening voice, "Mark . . . don't be ridiculous. This is a serious comedy, not a farce."

"Wrong, Margaret, it *is* a farce."

"But not a farce within a farce within a farce."

"Come on, Margaret, give her a chance."

"I think she'd make a good Moth", Carlotta interjected. "Or maybe Pease-Blossom. Yeah, Blossom just has a couple of lines."

"Absolutely not", Margaret snorted. "*Absolutely* not. Can you see this poor girl leaping about the stage with—well, with her handicap? It's ludicrous. It's mockery."

"The audience would never know", Marco argued. "They'd think it was part of the costume."

"What audience?" Carlotta said.

"Shut up, Hippo", Marco snapped.

"What costume?" Margaret said, tapping her other foot. "And as for her playing Bottom, she's—how shall we delicately put it—she's completely devoid of all thespian graces."

"Nonsense", Marco shouted leaping onto the stage. "Rose, Rose, you did just fine. But it needs more expressiveness, more life. Now watch me. I'll play Bottom playing a character named Pyramus—a play within the play. He's supposed to be comic, so I have to overdo it."

Gesturing wildly with his arms and many extravagant facial expressions, Marco recited the following:

"Sweet moon, I thank thee for thy sunny beams;
I thank thee, moon, for shining now so bright,
For, by thy gracious, golden, glittering beams,
I trust to taste of truest Thisby's sight.
　　But stay, O spite!
　　But mark, poor knight,
What dreadful dole is here!
　　Eyes, do you see?
　　How can it be?
O dainty duck! O dear!"

With a flourish he jumped from the stage and bowed to the company. They erupted in applause; even Margaret joined in.

"Well done, Priapus," she said.

"*Pyramus*, Isadora. *Pyramus*."

"If the cod fits, wear it", Margaret said.

The company burst out laughing. Flushing red, Marco turned quickly to Rose.

"Do you see what I mean? What did you think?"

"It is a beautiful poem, Mr. Chandler-Ross. I was moved by the way the author speaks of the moon."

There was a moment of stunned silence, followed by snorts of laughter. Confused by this reaction, Rose hastily reread the lines, wondering if she had misunderstood their meaning. But no, the meaning was clear.

"Break!" Carlotta cried. "Let's have a break."

Marco and Margaret wandered off together, and the rest of the actors and actresses dispersed in several directions. Carlotta remained, staring at Rose with a glumness that contained a touch of sympathy.

"I have failed, Carlotta. I have ruined the lines."

"Ah, don't worry about that. We all flub lines. Besides, Bottom's too big a part for a beginner. It would have been hell to learn him in three weeks. I still say you're perfect for Moth or Blossom."

"But Mrs. Brocklehurst said—"

"Ah, don't listen to that old hornet. She just likes to make people feel rotten."

"Perhaps she was right about me. My handicap would make a problem for the audience. It would distract from the play."

"Nah, I don't think so." But Carlotta's eyes said otherwise. "Hey, I'm gonna get some coffee and wake up. Want one?"

"No, thank you."

"Okay. Sit tight, I'll be back in five."

When Rose was alone in the great echoing room, she bent forward, face in hands, and began to weep silently to herself. *Io, all that I touch comes to nothing. Why did you bring me here?*

Then a voice like soft thunder spoke to her from behind and above her head.

"Dost thou feel small and despised among men, poor child?"

Io! Io! It was a voice like God's! Rose looked up and all around. There was no one else in the room.

"I do not understand your way with me," she cried aloud, "for I go where I am led, yet at each station I become more lost than ever. See how the legacy you gave to me has been lost because of my foolishness. Sick and weak of mind have I become because of it. And I do not know where you are taking me. The sparrows lied to me, and if they can so easily deceive me, if I cannot discern between the false and the true, what hope is there for me?"

"Untrammeled hope!" boomed the voice, "For because thou art small and guileless thou hast escaped the pitiful fate of the much-endowed. Behold their egos strutting before the spotlights. Behold their ambitions and their crass assumptions. See how they take the genius of the bard and make themselves superior to it, bending it to their purpose."

"Who speaks to me? Is it you, my Lord, or an angel, or a devil?"

"I know not which to tell you, for at various times I have been all three."

A loud crash sounded behind Rose, and she turned in her seat to see a hammer rattling down the steps of a towering ladder at the back of the stage. She started, for seated on a wide wooden beam above the top step was an elderly man, gazing down at her with a look of affection. He was heavy of build, his face brown and wrinkled. His long hair and beard were silver-white. He wore overalls and T-shirt, and on his head a black beret.

"Do not be alarmed", said the old man, smiling. "I am human—fully and lamentably so."

Rose got to her feet. "Who are you?" she stammered.

"I am the past straining to be the future. Or more precisely, an audience of one."

"I am Rose."

"I know. For I am the unseen witness to the comedy below. Good day to thee, Rose. Neither Thisby, nor Hermia nor Hippolyta nor Blossom shall you ever be. And certainly not the clown. Yet thou art a Rose is a rose is a rose and shall not depart from your intended form."

"Are you a prophet?" Rose asked timidly, for she knew that prophets looked very much like this man and often spoke in riddles.

"A prophet?" he guffawed. "Good heavens, no! Though I be, in a manner of speaking, a voice crying in the wilderness, I am

413

as much a prophet as you are Bottom. I am, in fact, the scene painter."

"You are a painter!" Rose exclaimed. "You are an artist!"

"Unfortunately", the old man said and began to climb slowly down the ladder.

After pondering this a moment, Rose said, "It seems, sir, that you are without happiness in your work?"

"Happiness? What is happiness?" he muttered as he reached the floor of the stage. "I paint, therefore I am!"

Rose gazed at him with sympathy. As he stood before her catching his breath, she saw that his clothes and his forearms were spattered with so many colored dots, small and large, that he resembled a pointillist painting by Seurat. His face was speckled by them, too. It struck her that despite his pompous statements, there was kindness in his eyes.

"Behold!" he declared, extending his left arm in a wide sweep of the room. "Behold the harvest of my years, the ruins of my ambition, my ego tempered by the vertigo of soft-impending death, and the ironies of fate, with which I am overly familiar."

"There is no feast of arrogance in you", Rose said meekly.

"On the contrary, my dear. I am a veritable infestation of arrogance. Even so, I try never to eat fellow members of my species, I do admit."

"I do not understand, sir."

He smiled sadly. "No. Of course, you wouldn't. What I mean to say is, the arrogance of this troupe of *lunatiques* grows hungrier the more it is fed. Such is the nature of cannibalism."

"What were you doing up there?" Rose asked, glancing at the rafters.

"I had just nailed a roll of canvas to the beams when you entered stage left with fair Hippolyta."

"Is the canvas a painting?"

"Indeed it is. A backdrop for the fairies."

"May I see it?" Rose asked.

"Later", the man replied. "Though I love the perspective of the heights, it costs me something to ascend. I am old and the blood grows thin within my veins. No longer do I sail with gallant Odysseus."

"You were a sailor!" Rose exclaimed with admiration.

He chuckled, eyeing her fondly. "Yes, I was. Many ships have I crewed, plying the seven seas that are known and some yet undiscovered. The *Argo*, of course, whose name is on all men's tongues. And *Hispaniola*, which bore poor mad Ben Gunn away from his island of unthinkable treasures."

"I am glad to meet you, Mr. Gunn."

"Glad to meet *you*", he said with a courtly bow, lifting the beret from the top of his head. "Actually my name is not Gunn. Allow me to present myself. I am Hugo Dyson. And may I say how very antiquated and delightful I find your diction? How pleasant your self-effacing and maidenly demeanor. Did you hie thee from a nunnery and fly across the vast mysterium of time to join this feast of fools?"

"I was raised by nuns", Rose said uncertainly. "And by my grandmother."

"What tribe are you?"

"I have no tribe, though in part I am from the Anishinâbe people who live far to the northwest of here."

"Ah," he nodded sagely, "I have heard of them."

He turned suddenly and looked up at the roll of canvas suspended above them. A long cord dangled down from it. He took its end and dragged it toward Rose.

"Would you like to do the honors?"

"What do you mean?"

"Simply pull. Tug, tug. I lied to you about loving the perspective of the heights. I no longer believe in ascension, except when it cannot be avoided."

Rose tugged on the cord. The roll of canvas on the ceiling

slowly unwound on pulleys, dragged downward by its own weight. A forest scene appeared before Rose's eyes, containing thick dark trees, a pink sun, a Greek acropolis on the horizon, and pools of water so deep that she could almost see her reflection in their violet depths.

"Oh, it is beautiful!" Rose gasped.

"It is decoration only, dear girl. It is fluff and nonsense, for which I receive a desperately needed pittance. *Deus ex machina*, Rose. *Deus ex machina*. God—however you conceive him to be—is always lowered from the rafters by devices of fantastical engineering, as in Leonardo's notebooks." He paused, eyeing her with some concern. "Of course you haven't the vaguest idea what I'm talking about, do you?"

"No. I'm afraid I don't. I am not an artist, though I once studied to be one. In the past I painted—"

His grizzled eyebrows shot up. "You are *not* an artist? How delightful. Everyone and his uncle is an artist these days, and rare is the person who disclaims the title. Yet you paint, you say."

She nodded.

"Any evidence upon your person?"

She cocked an uncomprehending eye at him.

"Uh, do you have any of your paintings with you?"

"I have some pastel drawings. But they are very poor works. I would be ashamed to show them to you."

He grinned broadly. "Even better. Show me, lass, show me, quickly now before the thespians return and whisk you away into an alternative future."

With some reluctance, Rose climbed down from the stage and went to the doorway where her belongings were leaning against the wall. The old man shuffled after her. She knelt and removed the roll of color drawings from the saddlebag, stripped off the plastic garbage bag, and untied the string that bound them. One by one she peeled away the layers:

Forests seething with fertility.

Lakes grinding their steel fangs.

Euphrasia sleeping on the edge of the void, while demons and lovers called to her, a black pearl clutched to her heart.

A copy of the black man wrestling-dancing with a leopard.

"I see you admire Rousseau", Hugo said. "Interesting."

A cabin in flames, a silver bird ascending to the burning stars. Tchibi crucified.

There were dozens more, most of them smaller and older.

Finished, Rose looked up. Gone was the sardonic and knowing look in the old man's eyes. Silent his mouth, which only minutes before had been full to overflowing. Gone his learning and his talent. Gone his ironic wit. He was, she saw, merely an old man with sad eyes.

"They are not very good", Rose apologized, her heart aching in tune with her back, every part of herself aching from the total failure that was the sum of her life.

Hugo continued to gaze at her with a solemnity that seemed the breaking wave of a deep and dark sea. He inhaled heavily. And exhaled.

"I am sorry", Rose said, rolling the drawings. "I told you they were poor."

When he spoke at last, he said simply, "Dear child, how wrong you were. The sparrows did not lie."

16

Hugo invited Rose to take a cup of tea with him. He called it a glass of tea. His house was on Rue St. Benoît at the base of the mountain, in a once respectable area that St. Henri had long ago invaded and taken over as its own. The narrow Victorian brownstone was squeezed between identical copies of itself, with only a few feet of alleyway between. It sagged in rather disturbing places, but it faced south toward the sun and thus caught whatever light there was. The view from the front porch was uninspiring, or more accurately it was bleak, for in no direction was there to be seen anything other than the rooftops of the large undeniable slum.

Inside, the walls of the hallway were covered with moody crackled paintings and sepia photographs of ancient monuments. Deer antlers served as a hat rack. Draped above a doorway at the far end of the hall was a blue and white flag with a star in its center. Flanking it were photographs of scowling bearded men.

Hugo led Rose down the hall past stacks of newspapers that lined both walls to a dimly lit kitchen. The air was musty with long-dissolved coal smoke, burnt toast, congealed grease, and the musk of cat. A sickly potted cactus sat on the window sill overlooking the alley, and ceramic plates hung on the stained paisley wallpaper. A kitty-litter box overflowed beneath an open sink, and upon the table stood a heap of unwashed dishes and empty tins. An orange cat sat in the middle of the clutter, licking something out of the bottom of a tea cup, the tips of its ears showing.

"This is Golda", Hugo said. "She does not converse with

ordinary mortals, though of course she is very political. She has an argot of her own by which she makes her wants known. It has taken my wife and me many a year to decode it. Do you like cats?"

"I have never known a cat", Rose said.

"Then let me introduce you to one. Mouse, Goldie? Mouse?"

The cat extracted its head, leaped off the table, coiled around Hugo's leg, and shot through the crack in a dark cellar door.

"She doesn't see people", said Hugo. Pausing, he added, "That's if you discount my wife and me." He laughed a deep woolly laugh, hoar, hoar, hoar. Rose smiled.

Hugo banged a kettle onto an element of the electric stove, turned a knob, pushed aside the frying pan, shoving it and other things with a clatter onto a heaped drainboard.

"Goldie!" came a high pitched cry from somewhere in the interior of the house. "What are you doing?"

Hugo squinted at the ceiling. "There she is, there she is, that Stradivarius of a woman, that fine peach, that golden princess of Israel, slayer of bad kings and art critics—my Esther."

Rose followed Hugo up a narrow creaking staircase to the third floor, which was a winterized attic. The sun poured in from the southern wall that was almost all window and from a skylight. She basked in it while the man shouted the name of his wife into other rooms. Rose looked about the attic, realizing that it was Hugo's studio. Its unvarnished hardwood floors were pebbled with spinning galaxies of paint droppings. The walls were white plaster, much of their surfaces blocked by huge canvases filled with slabs of color. More paintings leaned in piles against the walls. Art postcards and reproductions of the masters were pinned or taped on the few remaining spaces. Rose noted Van Gogh's sunflowers, Rembrandt's *The Jewish Bride*, Chagall's *Samson Overturning the Columns*, and an intaglio print of a Persian lion-warrior.

"Esther! Where are you?" Hugo cried.

"Where are *you*, Huggo?" answered a woman's voice.

"I'm *here*!"

"But *where* is here?" The woman's voice was accented with a European flavor similar to that of the sisters, but not French. "Do not make me search for you, you silly old man. I am in the studio."

"So am I, Esther!"

"Where?"

As if on cue, husband and wife emerged from alcoves at opposite ends of the room and glared at each other. The woman was not much taller than Rose. A careless observer would have thought her a girl in her early teens, if not for the silver hair, slightly disarrayed, sweeping upward from her temples in two wings. Her white blouse was embroidered, Rose saw, though she revised this observation as Hugo took his wife's arm and drew her slowly across the room. The decoration on the blouse was not embroidery; it was paint. Her charcoal gray skirt was also smeared with it, as was everything else, except the olive skin of her face, down to the shin bones and slippers. The woman's piercing black eyes made Rose want to straighten her spine, as did her pursed and beaklike lips.

The woman was not a person to be taken lightly, Rose saw. As she stepped forward to meet Hugo's wife, it struck her that here was the actual ruler of the house.

"Who is this?" the woman asked abruptly.

"This, dear Queen, is Rose—a child found wandering in the storm. She stumbled by chance into that den of confusion known as the Cirque de la Lune."

"An actress?" the woman asked coldly, eyeing Rose's mis-shapen form.

"No, an artist", Hugo said.

"An artist?" The eyes did not cease to examine.

"A glass of tea for a waif is the purpose of this visit."

"Is she from Cognawaga?" Esther asked.

Hugo turned to Rose and explained, "That's the Indian reserve across the river." Then to his wife, "No, my dear, our guest is from another tribe and another place, west of the sun and east of the moon. Notice, if you will, the clear and disingenuous eye of this child; does it not indicate that she is from another era entirely?"

"I am Esther, wife of Huggo", the woman said, cracking half a smile, her hand out-thrust for a shake.

"Hugo", Hugo corrected.

"Huggo", Esther insisted.

Hugo shrugged, "It is an old joke, Rose, a repartee between two misanthropic prodigies. We tease because we love. We spar because it makes the heart continue to beat. *Sparito ergo sum.* Between us there is a great bond, the like of which has not been seen since Dante and Beatrice."

"Pablo and Dora."

"Now, now, stop that."

"You started it", said Esther. "Rose, you come sit with me on this charming packing crate. Huggo likes to create a Bohemian atmosphere about himself. Huggo, go get the tea. The kettle is whistling."

When Hugo had left for the regions below, Esther guided Rose to a set of wooden boxes beside an empty easel of immense proportions. They sat down facing each other. For both, it was one of those rare occasions when they need not crane their necks to meet the eyes of another adult.

"So, you come to visit the scene painter."

"Yes, it was kind of him to offer. I am sorry to interrupt your work. I am uncertain of my destination. I thought—well, I had thought that the theater company was the station of my dream, for the sparrows told me to follow the woman."

"The sparrows told you? My, my, do all Indians speak like Hiawatha?"

"Like who?"

"Never mind. Who is this woman the sparrows told you to follow?"

"Carlotta."

"Carlotta Fishbein?"

"Yes, though she is better known as Carmella Fabian, the famous actress."

Esther began to heave with suppressed, though somewhat mirthless, laughter. She shook her head. "Oy!" she said.

"They wanted me to act a part in their play, but when I read the lines they were not pleased. I am afraid I could not do it. It seemed to me that the sparrows had misled me. But your husband said they told me the truth. He must be a wise person to know such things. Still, I do not understand where I am to go."

"Huggo is a very astute judge of character," Esther said, "except his own. All right, you have passed the first hurdle. You may stay for tea."

"Thank you, Mrs.—"

"Dyson. But you may call me Esther. Should I call you Rose?"

"Yes, please."

"The relationship will be temporary, Rose, so we need not strain for an excess of formality. Tell me, why did you not remain with the Cirque? Very few young people would choose a glass of tea with Huggo over a single minute with Marco the Magnificent. Rare is the one not fatally attracted. Little moths burned to a crisp."

"Do you know Mr. Chandler-Ross?"

Esther rolled her eyes. "Do I know him? Do I know him? Let me tell you: Huggo has painted scenery for that man for quite a few years. Did he tell you about the *Rhinoceros*? No? What a fiasco! Huggo nearly had a nervous breakdown trying to come up with drops that would work. Marco was never satisfied.

Never! Huggo is so sensitive. I do not wish to parody him, for the sensitive artist is an exhausted cliché, as you must know. But Huggo is, well, he is a real one—"

Rose listened with sincere attentiveness. Esther had the gift of words. Many had such a talent, but not the prudence to control it. Clearly, she was one who sought the pulse, diagnosed, cut with a scalpel.

"—so you see, Rose, the forgers of public taste are in essence selfish children playing their grown-up games. They have not suffered. They are incapable of philosophical reflection. One survives in their company only by playing the tiny fool on high heels. So can one be blamed for looking for an occasion to toss a grenade, to disturb, to raise a question or two in their tragically stunted minds? If you had seen what I've seen—ach!—the Cirque's idiotic and easily deceived board of directors, who tremble in worship as they bow before their *enfants terribles*. Do you know, Rose, why wealthy robber barons like to fund the pretty dancers and the pretty actors? It is because they need to salve their conscience. The culture is sucked dry by their materialism, and we are supposed to kiss their hands whenever they pump a drop of juice back into it. They are swamp adders, the lot of them—"

Esther paused to catch breath, and to shake a wing of hair from her face.

"Whatever you do, do not—I mean do *not*—go back to that cirque. You will be absorbed, you will be digested, you will cease to be whatever it is you are. By the way, what are you exactly? Oh, yes, Huggo said you are an artist. Is this true?"

"No, Esther. I once studied art, but I have little talent. I am not an artist."

All residue of suspicion suddenly drained from Esther's face, replaced by a lovely look of affection. She said nothing for a moment, then went on with her lecture:

"I'm relieved to hear that you're not an artist. Marco has a peculiar affection for artists. He is also a collector of the un-usual—forgive me—those like you, like me, who do not fit into the pattern of the norm, if you understand my meaning."

Rose shook her head.

"Marco the Magnificent possesses, or is possessed by, a qual-ity that draws both men and women to him. They all want love, of course, but they all end up as the carrion of one insatiable appetite. During the years Huggo and I have known him, Marco has devoured and discarded many little devotees. I see that you are a young and naïve girl, and so it is to be expected that you cannot yet see through his disguise. I myself suffered a brief intoxication, though thankfully during the twenty or thirty seconds of its duration, before the mask became transpar-ent, he was distracted by someone else, and I escaped unscathed. Once inoculated one is fairly safe, but it would be unwise to presume upon immunity. Those who work with Marco must learn to step carefully around the hole he makes in the tropo-sphere. I am one of the few who are now safe. He loathes me and tolerates Huggo."

"Why does Hugo work for him?" Rose asked.

"Huggo continues to work for the Cirque only because he is willing to accept the coolie wages. Huggo is a fool—a dear fool. But Marco is an oily and odious fool, and he knows what I think of him. You are another matter. You are a bush-baby whose marrow might hide some answers for Marco, if the bones could just be split. He will want to try. What is not drawn irresistibly to him, he will sooner or later set out to pursue. There, now you have been warned."

Esther sat back with a look of satisfaction, just as Hugo entered the studio bearing a tray loaded with glasses, a teapot, and various other items.

"Having a little chat?" he asked with good humor.

"Yes", Esther answered, winking at Rose.

Hugo muttered and fussed as he laid the tea things out on a

424

packing crate. Esther bossed and scolded him all the while. He ignored her instructions and bantered back without concern. While the old couple were getting things arranged, Rose struggled to absorb what Esther had told her. How strange the ways of the human heart, she thought, how odd that Esther should be so certain she was in danger from the director. There was no danger of that, for she too had found him pitiful and unattractive. Earlier that morning, during the brief moment when she had veered in the direction of falling-into-seeing, a child had appeared before the eye of her heart, a small, frightened child clamoring for attention. Falling-into-seeing was almost entirely a thing of the past now. During her early years it had taken the form of detailed color films flashing across her mind, showing her things that she could not have imagined on her own. It had faded steadily with time, if fading it was. Perhaps it had merely changed, the vivid pictures subsiding into a deeper kind of knowing.

As Esther reached forward to take a biscuit from the chipped plate, Rose noticed a line of purple letters on her forearm. Or numbers. To her surprise she experienced a sudden eruption of the older version of the gift. She fell-into-seeing with an intensity that had been denied her for years.

A naked woman stood in an open square of ground surrounded by low sheds. Countless naked women stood silently all around her. The woman was as tiny as a child. The soldiers smirked and pointed at the new arrivals. One, merely a youth, broke wooden matches in his teeth and spit them out. She endured his cold eyes only for a second as the shorn fuzz on the back of her neck began to rise, the bristles of her scalp lifted in terror. She examined the earth at her bare feet. She hoped she was modestly clothed in the universal nakedness. As they waited for the shouts and whistles, the soldier's eyes passed on, wondering at the joke of five hundred naked women standing at attention before him. He too was dressed for the occasion, a greedy boy lost in a uniform, the costume of power.

If there is a heaven, the woman whispered, *Shema, shema, shema. . . .*

"Io!" Rose cried aloud, jumping to her feet, tears running down her face.

Startled, Hugo and Esther looked up from their glasses of tea.

"Io!" Rose cried again. "I understand!"

"What's that you said?" Hugo smiled crookedly.

"What do you understand?" Esther asked.

"I see that I have come among the Hebrews. I am blessed to meet the firstborn of the Lord!"

Hugo and Esther stared at her in astonishment.

Esther chuckled. "Hebrews?"

"I did not know you were of the chosen, for fatigue and distress blinded my eyes. The flag with the blue star, and the bearded men. And your name, Esther. And the wounding upon your arm."

Esther glanced at her tattoo and frowned. She cocked her head sideways and observed Rose carefully.

"The wounding, you call it. Do you know what this is?"

"It is a mark the *kinoje* made upon you—the biter, the devil, he who would turn all men into things bound for destruction. Yet you have survived, Esther. You have escaped from his jaws, and this is a sign of hope for me, for it is a promise."

"A promise? What are you talking about? Why is it a promise?"

"It says that his power is limited and brief. He is restrained. He cannot do all that he wills."

"My dear girl," Hugo interrupted, "do you know what you're saying? Do you know what this little row of numbers means?"

"I do not know, for I am ignorant of many things. I sense its

426

deeper meaning, though the colors and the shapes of all that happened to you, Esther, are unclear before my eyes. Yet I saw you pray, *If there is a heaven. Shema, shema, shema.* And the soldier with the eyes of a devil-fish cleaning his teeth with a wooden match."

Esther struggled to her feet, a shaken look upon her face. She glanced at Hugo, he glanced at her. He put a hand on her arm.

"This young woman, Esther . . . she . . . it's in her paintings too. It's something new. I wanted to tell you——"

Esther walked from the room without a word. Her footsteps echoed on the staircase.

Hugo sighed and stared at the floor.

"I have offended your wife", Rose said. "I am sorry."

Hugo shook his head. But he was only half listening.

Rose turned toward the door. "Thank you for tea, Mr. Dyson. I will go now."

Shaking himself, Hugo stood and put a hand on her shoulder. "Please wait. It's not what it seems."

"I do not understand."

"Maybe none of us do. In any event, would you like to see Esther's paintings? Come on, I'll show you."

Without waiting for Rose's reply, he shuffled to the end of the room and went through a doorway. Rose followed him into a smaller section of the attic. This room was darker, lacking a skylight, but the flick of a switch lit up the interior, revealing a single easel and several dozen small paintings.

"This is where she works."

An unfinished painting rested on the easel. It was a red-haired woman selling crated pigeons in a marketplace. The agony of the captive was in the woman's face. Rose knew without thinking that it was a self-portrait. The face bore no resemblance to the artist, yet it was her, it was her heart—this was immediately visible.

Rose looked a long time. It was deep waters and into it she

could plunge as she had not plunged since Dr. Ganze had introduced her to Géricault.

A second portrait, leaning on the wall to the right of the easel, was a white-haired bearded man standing in snow with a striped shawl over his head, his face lifted in a tenderness of praise to the slate-colored sky. It was Hugo's face. In his hands were diamonds that spilled like stars flowing from the *tchibekana*.

"Transference", Hugo explained. "It's really her father, holding the symbol of his profession."

In another, a medieval city was in flames while hundreds of birds rose in the vortex of the firestorm.

"Antwerp. Esther is Belgian. This one is called *The Souls of the Just*. She is not a believer, you understand. It's merely a cultural reference point."

"Are you a believer, Hugo?" Rose asked.

"That depends on what you mean by believer. I believe in painting. I believe in Esther's love. I believe in the predictable selfishness of human nature with even greater certainty. This is the material of a rather broad faith."

"Though you no longer believe in ascension."

His eyebrows raised. "That is correct, I no longer believe in ascension. The souls of the just do not fly up like little birds. This world is all there is."

"But that is so sad, Hugo. It is grievous to me that a person as fine as you would believe such a lie."

"So? You believe that sparrows lie. I believe old legends lie."

"But the sparrows did not lie."

He laughed ruefully. "Let us hope they didn't."

He turned to a stack of paintings and lined them up along one wall. For the most part the images were of birds, though there were a few portrayals of children, whose faces were as plain as white flowers, playing in acid-green swirls of air and sulphur-yellow water. Stripped of any hint of sentimentality, any prettiness, they were nonetheless beautiful to the eye. Over

428

and over, the faces of mankind were revealed, expressing awareness and yearning, and rendered with skill such as Rose had only attempted in her drawings.

"She is a very great artist", Rose whispered.

"Yes, she is", Hugo murmured. "She won't admit it, but she is."

He led her back into his own studio, which was at least twice the size of Esther's.

"My work is ten times larger than hers and one tenth as good", he said. "Don't you agree?"

Rose thought about the question before answering. "Yes, this is true, Hugo."

He roared with laughter.

"I think you are a humble man to see it", Rose added.

Still laughing, he waved for her to stop, "Say no more, say no more!"

"Oh, now I have offended you as well. And after all your kindness—"

"Stop, stop. Is there no end to your guilelessness? It is refreshing, but one might hyperventilate from too much oxygen. My, my, all this truth in one day! Now listen, you have not offended me, and I doubt you have offended my wife. She is just a little overcome with memories. She is resilient and will come bouncing back in a moment, probably to offer a stinging comment about my latest painting."

He pointed at a giant slab of stretched canvas. There was little on it except streaks of gray over bare white. Rose kept silent.

"Its title is *Ratio*", Hugo said proudly.

"What does rat-see-oh mean?"

"The febrile product of the seething human brain imprisoned in mortality. So you see, Rose, what a picture must have in common with reality in order to depict it—implicitly or explicitly—in the way it does, is its pictorial form." He peered at her with a sly smile. "Now, repeat what I just said back to me."

429

"I do not think I am able to, Hugo."

He guffawed. "That's a sign of a healthy mind. All art is a lie, Rose."

"Do you believe that?"

"Well, not always a *bad* lie. Not always a *malicious* lie. But certainly it is always illusion."

Uncomfortably, Rose dared to engage in a contradiction. "If what you say is true, then every word is a lie."

He frowned and tried to see her point, but, because he could find no reply, he shrugged.

"I mean," Rose went on, "the word *bird* is not actually a bird, and in that way it is an illusion, yet it carries the truth from your mind to my mind. Is that a lie?"

"No, not in that sense. But—"

"Art is a language. Sometimes it speaks truth and sometimes untruth. Is this not so?"

"Maybe it was at one time, but I maintain that in our times all art has become a lie because we have nothing left to say."

"Surely truth is always truth, and a lie is always a lie?"

"You *are* a surprise, dear girl. Are you sure you're from this planet? Only an alien would dare to make a case for truth in these times. As if truth could be bolted down to the floor of the universe. Immovable, foundational. Ha! That's optimism talking. You're a mere slip of a girl, a fledgling. You believe in the inexhaustible splendor, the flowing sap, the restorative elements of life that you think you see at the root and branch of existence. I do not fault you for it. Nay, nay, optimism is understandable and even delightful to observe in the young. But, come, tell me more. Tell me why you think a lie is a lie is a lie—with apologies to Gertrude Stein."

Rose fell silent, struggling unsuccessfully to absorb his meaning. She stared at the floor. No answers came to mind.

Hugo chuckled and let her be.

Esther reentered the room as if nothing had happened and

430

said with a confident demeanor, "Would you like some supper, young lady?"

The smell of broiling fish floated up from below. And hot toast. And tea.

"Yes, please", Rose answered, scarcely believing her good fortune.

They took their meal together on folding card tables in a little parlor on the ground floor. The ratty armchairs were comfortable. Golda the cat draped herself along the headrest of Esther's chair, licking paws and purring into the woman's ear. Hugo lit a coal fire in the shallow well of the fireplace and turned out the electric lights, leaving only a single antique oil lamp burning. The gentle light was so much like that of a winter evening in the cabin of her birthplace that Rose ate more fish than she had intended to, unable to stop her hand from reaching again and again to the serving dish. Hugo and Esther observed her closely as they picked at their food. They refrained from glancing at each other as she crunched the fish heads and the crispy tail fins and swallowed them with obvious pleasure. When Rose realized how much she had eaten, she flushed red.

"Did you receive the ten-dollar explanation of pictorial form?" Esther asked by way of distraction.

Rose nodded, chewing steadily, eyes bulging like those of Thisdog and Thatdog.

"Do you understand it?"

Rose shook her head.

Esther smiled. "Good. Neither do I. After *years* of his explanations, still I do not understand. Either his thoughts are in a realm far above our heads, or it's a case of the emperor refusing to admit he is naked."

"It's an old quarrel, Rose", Hugo said. "She says I haven't suffered enough."

"But are you not also a Hebrew, Hugo?" Rose asked earnestly. "Did you not suffer under the Germans, like Esther?"

"No. I suffered in another branch of the diaspora. We were once the Daseins of Rotterdam, but somewhere back there in history an ancestor of mine chose to assimilate, and we became the Dysons of Birmingham."

"The Germans, eh?" Esther probed Rose's eyes. "What could you possibly know about the Germans? Have you been to school?"

"Yes. The nuns who taught me were from France. They, too, suffered under the Germans."

"A little food rationing?" Esther murmured dryly.

"Their sisters were killed", Rose said.

Hugo and Esther looked at her uneasily.

"The Germans are not all bad", Rose blurted, worrying that she might have encouraged an old bitterness in her hosts. There was Voolf-gong, but there was also Dr. Ganze. One was an amber dragon–poet who told lies. The other clung to the raft of the great shipwreck and told the truth.

"Of course they are not all bad", Esther said. "Do you think they're so different from people here? Take away our security, pssst! Collapse the economy, psssst! Then you will see how fast all our nice countrymen will trot to the nearest platform, hungry for a sanitized de-Nazified demagogue, a democratic *Führer*, and of course, a scapegoat or two—"

Hugo interrupted. "Esther. Not at supper."

Ignoring him she went on. "Do you think it will be easy to choose? He will come disguised in the beginning. And what if you have children to feed? What if you are terribly alone? It becomes so complicated. It becomes so hard to breathe and harder to think. That is why we must work now. Pull the masks off the little demagogues while they are still in the larva stage. Squash them."

Rose looked down into her hands.

"But Esther," she said at last, "is it not possible to change their hearts? What if we were to love them?"

"Love them?" Hugo said. "Goodness, girl! They would merely interpret your love as adulation. Then the masks would grow bigger."

"I think you are wrong in this, Hugo, for I do not mean the love of the surface waves, but the love that sleeps under the waters, that moves on currents of sacrifice."

He stared at her, uncomprehending.

"Huggo! Huggo, stop your lecturing!" Esther said.

Hugo frowned at his wife. "Me? *Me* stop lecturing! Darling, no one surpasses you in that department."

"Ha!" she said.

They fell silent. Hugo picked flecks of paint from the back of his hand, momentarily lost in thought, his eyes heavy, wrinkled pockets of fatigue. He stroked his beard and adjusted the beret on the crown of his head. His appearance and attitude seemed a caricature of the quaint old-world artist. If there was a little deliberate cultivation of the image, he could hardly be faulted, because for many decades he had paid a high price for it. He was dedicated to his way of life. Moreover, he was conscious of the things that mattered, even as he denied that they did.

Hugo turned to Rose. "When Esther lectures, she believes she's illuminating her listeners. When I lecture she believes I'm tormenting them. My Stradivarius cannot stand the sound of the tuneless catgut that I am. Esther, my dear, I'm not doing anything but telling this girl the facts of life. It isn't just millions who have perished since the turn of this century. It is hundreds of millions."

"There are times and places, Huggo. Now is not the time."

"Any place is the right place, my peach-wife. Any time is the right time. Your right time never comes, for you do not like to remember."

Esther's face grew as cold as stone. "I remember very well", she said in a dangerous voice. "But I do not yammer about it."

She was breathing hard and shooting a beam of something dark at her husband. He folded his arms in self-defense. This was followed by a brief locking of eyes, then a silent reconciliation.

Hugo, his temperament somewhat softer and more capable of deferring, mumbled, "Well, you're probably right, my love. I just don't want this girl to be a slave."

Rose, looking at them both, said, "I am not a slave."

Strangely, Hugo and Esther laughed.

"No," they said. "Of course you aren't."

Then they all grew quiet. The sun seemed to have set. The parlor window was black. The day's events were definitely coming to a close. Rose began to think about moving on—to where, she did not know. She shrank at the thought of it. Esther offered more tea. Rose accepted another cup and sipped it slowly.

"Rose," said Esther abruptly, "you must think we are crank people. It is true. Huggo especially is a crank person. He is a fussy old English lapsed Jew, a rundown humanist who treats himself inhumanely. He needs constant watching. He will not take care of himself."

This was followed by more of their jokes, but Rose did not push for explanations.

"He must paint or he will die", said Esther, stopping the cycle of banter.

Hugo wrinkled his brow as if to say, you are being melodramatic, my dear, a little extreme again. He changed the subject.

"Really, Esther, you must see Rose's pictures."

Rose said, "I cannot paint or draw any more, for I do not know the choosing-way that he asks of me."

"Who?" Hugo and Esther replied in unison.

But Rose did not answer, for the pain of their disbelief would have been unbearable. She was beginning to love them, and love will inevitably drop the final veil, and behind the veil was total vulnerability. The conversation became thick with spaces and unreadable gestures.

434

The old man said, "You cannot paint, you say? Good, that's a beginning. Yes, a very good place to start. It means you are ready to learn."

"Rose, let me see your pictures", Esther pressed.

Reluctantly, Rose unwrapped the roll of her pastels and began to spread them out on the floor. Hugo knelt and held back the curling edges of paper. Esther leaned forward in her chair. Frowning, then scowling, and finally allowing a slight trembling of her lips, she said, simply, "Yes."

"You see what I mean?" Hugo said.

Esther nodded. "How is it possible? The sources are almost invisibly embedded. A little Rousseau maybe. See this one, perhaps Géricault had a trace of influence. This one owes a debt to Goya. But it seems to me that the influences only deepen the original voice. She absorbs it all and translates it into her own unique language."

"Not unlike the Fauves and Expressionists—not to mention a touch of the Symbolists—but in no way has she become ensnared by any of them. It's all grounded in a passionate reality suffused with some kind of metaphysics. Marvelous! Simply marvelous!"

"And so full of fire", Esther mused. "The moons and stars. The cosmic sense is highly developed. The draftsmanship leaves something to be desired."

"That's true of some of the great painters of the century. Draftsmanship can be improved, but no one can seize this gift as his own, this thing she has . . . this seeing."

Esther looked up suddenly. "Rose, where are you living?"

This was unanswerable. Rose opened her mouth but nothing came out of it.

"She is of no fixed address at the moment, dear", Hugo murmured in an undertone. "Do you think—?"

"My thought precisely."

"The back room. I'll clean it out."

435

"No, not enough light. She needs light."

"All right. But how will we—? You know there's barely enough to pay the—"

"Never mind that. We'll find a way. I'll sell the *Pigeon Seller*."

"No, Esther, that's your—"

But Esther was no longer listening to him.

"Rose. We are both moved by what you have shown us. You are very gifted. Huggo and I would like to help you. Would you let us help you?"

Rose closed her mouth.

"It would give us great pleasure if you would consider staying with us for a while. We have plenty of space. It won't cost you a penny. Perhaps you can do the dishes from time to time or take Huggo for his walk and clean his brushes. In exchange, we offer studio space and a little bedroom and all the food you can eat, such as it is."

The old couple looked at her, waiting for a response.

Rose sighed. "I thank you for your kindness, Esther and Hugo. It would be an honor to live with you, for I greatly respect the Hebrews, and I am moved by your art. Your paintings are beautiful, Esther. And Hugo, yours are brave, though puzzling."

Hugo laughed. Rose began to roll up her drawings and pack them into her K. B. saddlebag. As she did so, she continued to speak:

"Yet I feel that I cannot accept. You do not know me, and what good am I to you? I am a burden, and all that I touch seems to turn to the losing-way. The sacrifice-way. You have suffered, and it is not my part to ask more suffering of you."

"It would be a joy, *Liebchen*!" Esther said.

Rose stood and bowed to them. "Thank you for your kindness. He is leading me. He will show me to the station of my dream."

"Who?" they said in unison.

"Rose," Hugo said, frowning over a thought, "isn't it possible that *he* has already led you to the station of your dream? Could it be that *we*, such as we are, are the final destination?"

"I do not know, I do not know", Rose shook her head in confusion. The confusion lasted all the way down the hall to the front door, all through the process of getting her dirty parka onto her body, and all the way down the porch steps. Hugo and Esther followed her out into the cold night air. Rose stopped and looked back at them. They resembled two old groundhogs peering cautiously from their hole. She heard a whisper perhaps, or was it the shadows of the night street, the length of the journey ahead? Something in its loneliness repelled her so utterly, seemed so murderous, that she turned and said quietly, "Yes, I will stay."

The little household of the soul was, for Rose, not a crumbling, sagging thing. It was the most solid place she had experienced since the sisters' cloister. Within three days, it was completely and irrevocably home. Her bedroom and studio were on the second floor. Both were small rooms, the latter slightly larger and facing south for the light. She spent an entire day ridding them of the heaped debris accumulated during years of neglect. Stacks of newspapers and art magazines were moved out to the corridor. Picture frames and rolls of canvas went up to the attic studios. A mummified mouse was disentombed from a bucket of glazier's pins, heaps of dust and cobwebs were gathered and discarded, a faded print of Picasso's *Portrait of Dora Maar* was torn from the wall, crumpled (secretly by Rose), and burned in the parlor fireplace. She felt guilty about this act, but reasoned that it was within the boundaries of honesty because Hugo had told her to throw into the garbage anything she did not want for her own use. She did not like the way Picasso had chopped the woman into pieces and shoved the parts back into wrong places.

Hugo helped Rose turn the old mattress on the bed, examine it for parasites, and beat clouds of dust out of it. The vacuum cleaner whined in the room for an hour, sucking the air clean. Rose washed the squeaking window with vinegar and water and wiped it so crystal clear that the light burst in with a passion grown frantic after long denial. She mopped the wood floors of both rooms with soapy water that wrung out black in the toilet. Then she scrubbed them again until it washed out brown. And finally clear. Like absolution. Like new beginnings.

She pinned a few of her own color drawings to the walls, reserving a special place for the *Nativity in the Northern Woods*. It brightened the wall at the foot of her bed so that she could see it first thing each morning. The medal of Kateri was pinned above the pillow, alongside a crucifix that Mère Jean had given to her. She placed the *binemin* stone on the windowsill and the portrait of Tchibi's crucifixion above the washstand, where she would remember to pray for him and offer the day's portion of suffering for him. The hurt of absence was not so sharp in this room, for it was contained within a sense of shelter that she had experienced only in two other places during her life. It was as if she had always known Hugo and Esther; though not everything about them was understandable, she was united to them at the heart. This was more than a confraternity of art, or a commonwealth of failure. Each of them had suffered from the ripping and shredding that the spirit of *kinoje* or the spirit of the *neshiwed* had done to them.

Rose sighed to herself: Io! Io, whatever it had done to Esther and Hugo was like a bad work of art! It was not creating, no, for only love creates. The *kinoje-neshiwed* had tried to destroy them while dressing itself in the costume of creating. Now they were being put together again. The artist who was repairing the three of them was not like Picasso; he would not glue them like shattered mismatched pottery. No, it was more like the end of winter; it was melting ice; it was the thawing of three rivers of poetry; it was the flowing of three *ones* into one *three*, so that a greater flowing might become possible. And the end was the sea.

The kitchen was the worst aspect of their life together. Rose took an entire day to clean it and put it into a semblance of order. Much of the food at the back of the refrigerator was spoiled by mold. One particularly bad item was a lump of cheese that smelled like rotting flesh. She threw it out, though Hugo scolded her affectionately over this missing delicacy, which he called Limburger. Meals were irregular. Esther gave Rose money to purchase a stock of soup cans, sardines, vegetables, and boxes of crackers. Rose used some of the money to buy flour, lard, and a jar of strawberry jam.

On the seventh day of their life together, a Sunday, Rose found a church four blocks way. Few were the worshippers in it; sad and old was the priest. Yet the presence of the Beating Heart was very powerful. So great was her gratitude that Rose remained for an hour after the *Anamessikewin* had ended, pouring a river of love toward the Presence. And he returned it in kind. Upon her arrival at the house on Rue St. Benoît, she found Hugo reading a novel aloud to Esther in the parlor. They greeted her with smiles, but said nothing, for Hugo was in mid-sentence. Rose went to the kitchen and fried bannock for them. When it was ready, she brought a plate of it to the parlor, steaming and glistening with melted grease and dribbling red sweetness. They drank tea together and gorged on the bannock, and her two hosts, no, her two friends, exclaimed that it was a feast and wondered aloud why this treat was unknown in Europe and perhaps in the Americas as well. Contented, they went off to their bedroom for an afternoon nap.

The cat was self-indulgent, its habits so very unlike the dogness of dogs that Rose found it difficult at first to feel affection for the creature. Yet, one night during the second week, Golda scratched at the door of Rose's room begging for

439

permission to come in. The cat jumped onto the end of her bed, promptly curled up, and went to sleep. It purred and wheezed with a comforting rumble, giving off so much heat that Rose's cold toes were warmed all night long. If Hugo and Esther had one fault, it was that they turned down the heat each night to near-freezing, in order to conserve pennies. Yet this too was familiar, for Rose and Grandma had lived the same way, by necessity or weakness, unable to rise from deep sleep beneath the fur blankets to put another log into the firebox of the wood stove. Now, years later, buried under three wool blankets, Rose found it even more difficult to arise in the night. Her body was aging, so much so that it ached all over when she woke in the mornings, her breath making frost clouds in the glassy angular light.

Each night Golda came to her without fail. Smiling, Rose welcomed her and savored again and again the small joke that God had placed inside the cat. In her cat dreams Golda was voyaging upon the great waters in search of fish, a little motor inside of her, rumbling for all to hear. She was so safe that she could sleep on the bed of a stranger; she was a queen in her small realm, selfish and spoiled and willful, yet she was curiously humble, for she too served in her own way. Rose began to see that catness had its purposes in the vast and very complicated canvas of creation.

Rose's studio was bare. It echoed. The light in it flowed from east to west. Silence fell slowly through the beams and settled on the hardwood floors, so old they were dark brown, etched with the feet of absent furniture that had been arranged and rearranged according to the generations that had lived here.

Rose stood in front of the drawing table Hugo had found in a back room and dragged in for her. She had a few sheets of heavy paper left from her days as an art student, and Hugo had found more. It was tinted as pale gray as the pigeons roosting under the eaves, with small flecks of pink and brown. This was good. The earth too was speckled, and its imperfection was its texture.

One whole morning in the second week Rose sat on the wooden stool in the studio, watching dust motes fall to the floor, like time. Esther had given her a set of pastels to use, but whenever she picked up one of the color-sticks it seemed to say nothing to her. It was not connected to what she could see with her eyes. Until this moment all seeing, even the most symbolic, had been drawn in part from the riot of imagery thrown up by the physical world and by the familiar movements of man upon it. She had been able to draw Tchibi's agony, for example, only because the living Tchibi was before her, as well as cabin logs, nails, ropes, and the ever-presence of fire in its many forms. Though these images lived within her still, they seemed to have faded. Or else they had been pushed to the background by more recent events. Now dominating the foreground of her mind were walls, a floor, a ceiling, and a surrounding city.

She picked a red stick from the box of colors and scraped it across the paper. Red contained fire and released it. Yet it did nothing for her. No feeling arose when the streak cut through the sheet of tranquillity. Because a great deal of her experience had been losings, she worried that her gift was being withdrawn. Yet she sensed that it was merely sleeping. It had been many months since the sickness overtook her, since she had been lifted up and taken to this new land, and during that time she had created nothing. She could not expect to do so instantaneously. She was safe, she was home, as safe and at home as Golda, but it would take time for the head-knowledge to trickle down into the heart-knowledge and bind together the eye-and-hand-knowledge, permitting the river to flow.

She remembered the mountain where God had touched the earth in this land and with a start recalled that it was close. Indeed the house was built upon its lower slope. She would go there and pray for the grace to draw and paint again. If this was the station of her dream, as she now felt sure it was, then he would not withhold the grace she needed in order to do her work.

Because it was a mild day, hovering near the freezing mark, she walked around the base of the royal mountain to its far side where the shrine arose slowly in front of her eyes. As she went along the sidewalks, enjoying the sights and sounds of mothers walking small children, the shouts of boys on their lunch hour playing hockey in the side streets, she felt that once again her life was beginning.

All her former strength had fallen away during the journey here, but it had been replaced by better things. It was the losing-way that taught the trusting-way. At certain moments she had weakened, had let the darkness of discouragement into her heart, and a trickle of bitterness, feeling that God had let her go, dropped her into an abyss. She had wondered why love would do such a thing. Now she understood. Now she saw that he had been drawing her more closely to himself with every step. Her health was returning, and the solider words of reality were again God's instrument for speaking to her. As she prayed in thanksgiving, it seemed to her that he said, *See, I have given you a place of shelter, food and warmth, and a space to work. I have given you two people who have need of you, and you of them. Though they do not know me, they are within my eye and within my own suffering. And with all these riches I have given you the great gift.*

"Which gift is this, my Lord?" she whispered, eyeing the many sparrows twittering in the gutters. "Do you speak of the seeing which is for the offering-way?"

This also, said the word. *And with it the pictures that you make, which are words for the blind to see and understand.*

"Will they understand, my Lord?"

Many will look without seeing, hear without understanding. Some will see and hear, yet it is not for you to know.

Then the word grew still, for the holy place was near.

Her second visit to the shrine of Saint Joseph was like the first, and she was as overcome as she had been before. The Beating Heart pounded with so great a love that it even exceeded what she had felt during her first visit. Or perhaps she was better able to receive it. She fell to her knees once again and pressed her face to the floor.

"Io, Beloved whom I cannot see", she sighed. "You, you", she sighed again.

In the heart of her soul she saw his wounded feet, bare and battered and bleeding, and she reverenced them so deeply that the entire world slowly shifted in a great turning, and she was no longer a deformed woman but a small child dancing on a crest, while the forest burned all around her. "Death is the last of enemies, but soon, soon, soon," cried the many souls of the just rising upward in the fire, "soon the final enemy, death, shall be hurled into the Lake of Fire."

As she danced around him, her small hand in his great wounded hand, smiling up into his smiling eyes, she cried out, though the cry was a song that issued from her lips:

"I thank you, I thank you, for you have not let me fall through your fingers."

After that there was *Anamessikewin*, and Holy Communion, and in the resting time, in the thanking-without-words-time, as the many worshippers departed, Rose's hands fell open on her lap. Then it seemed to her that Saint Joseph came down to her from his marble height, and he placed into her hands colorsticks and paintbrushes. The child in his arms reached for her, and she reached for him, for he was warm and roly-poly. But they withdrew from her because the time was not yet ripe for that embrace.

When Rose returned home, she found Hugo and Esther napping in the parlor. Even Golda was asleep, stretched out in a puddle of gold on the back of an armchair. A coal fire glowed in the hearth. Upstairs, she gently closed the door of her studio.

It was clean and warm inside. The colors sang in the little box of memories, greeting her. The lid opened, and the grace poured in rivulets from it, mingling with the river in her heart. She sat down at her drawing table. She took a stick of blue, which is the color of the sky. And she made a sky. In it she made a white bird with the open space of uncolored paper. Then she made an eye with the turquoise stick. The eye blazed with blue wisdom-fire above the weary world. Above the anguished tangled quarrels of mankind, above the turbulent lakes and writhing forests, and the burning which is everywhere, the sweet burning of creation and the dark burning of destruction.

17

On March nineteenth, there was a festival of Masses and processions at the shrine, and Rose spent all day there, returning home in a state of great joy. She had several times tried to tell Hugo and Esther about the wonder of Mount Royal and about what was occurring in her soul because of it. This day was no exception. As usual, they could not comprehend. They listened, looked thoughtfully at each other, and murmured learned comments about "cultural reference points", "points of departure", and "the need for a pantheon of symbols".

"Every religion is a prism that allows one a look into the spectrum, Rose", Esther told her. "The prism is like a palette of solid colors. The manufacturer and the chemical components of paint will vary, but the sun strikes upon them in a similar way. In the hands of an artist who understands their qualities—and their limitations—each brand may produce a masterpiece."

"Esther, I am confused by a thing. Did you not tell me that I must not trust the words 'tempera paint'?"

"Yes, but what does that have to do with anything?"

"The labels in the art stores use the word 'tempera' for both the cheap poster colors and for the egg-paints that are the most brilliant and durable of all. The expensive paint and the imitation both have the same name."

"I see your point, Rose", Hugo chuckled, eyeing his wife mischievously. "Do you see her point, my dear? Rather a good point, don't you think?"

"What point?" Esther gestured irritably. "All analogies are imperfect."

"Don't be testy, dear, don't be testy."

"I am not being testy!" Esther snapped.

"Let us judiciously change the subject," Hugo coughed, humming to himself. "It's time to get ready for the theater."

"The theater of the absurd", grumbled Esther. "I had hoped they would fold. I had *so* hoped the building would be condemned. I had hoped, insanely, that the government of the Cirque would be overthrown in a revolt and its leaders executed."

"*Nu, nu,* darling. No need for extremism." Hugo turned to Rose with a look of jolly enthusiasm. "Tonight we are going to see *A Midsummer Night's Dream.*"

Esther, despite her lack of enthusiasm, dressed herself in an emerald-green evening gown with rhinestone earrings and tiny high-heeled shoes. Over her shoulders she draped a black fur coat that smelled of moth balls, after tucking and pinning the frayed cuffs and sewing on a missing button. Hugo scraped as much speckling as possible from his hands, passively endured a stiff brushing of his hair and beard, and donned a tweed greatcoat over his blue flannel shirt and corduroy pants, none of which had really escaped the universal decoration. His shoes were scuffed, but he managed to leave the house without Esther's noticing this detail. Rose went as she was, though she did squeeze into the green jumper that Sister Clothilde had made for her one Christmas. It split at the seams, but Rose had no time to sew it up, because the taxi had arrived and was honking its horn.

At seven-thirty, it dropped them eight blocks away, deep in the heart of St. Henri, at the front entrance of the Cirque de la Lune. A small crowd gathered by the door, chatting and smoking and laughing. All were dressed in fine attire; many glanced at the newcomers with interest. From inside the open double doors came the sound of stringed instruments tuning up, loud bangs and a roar or two.

446

"Hugo! Hugo, old pal," shouted a round bald man who came striding over in a tuxedo. "Great to see you." He shook hands with Hugo and Esther and eyed Rose curiously. Hugo made the introduction.

"This is Clive. He's the drama critic for the *Montreal Gazette.* Clive, this is a friend of ours, Miss Rose Wâbos, an artist."

"Glad to meet you, Rose", he said, squeezing her fingers briefly. "Hello, Esther. Still trying to keep the old boy alive?"

"It's a job."

"Yeah, a dirty job but somebody's gotta do it."

"He's worth more dead than alive," Esther replied, "but then, so am I. It's a standoff. We have an agreement. I don't murder him if he doesn't murder me."

Clive roared his appreciation. "Hoo! That's a good one. You never change, Essie."

"Don't call me Essie. Did I give you permission to endow me with a diminutive? Did I?"

Clive roared again, then switched to another mode. "Look, Hugo, there's Trevor Marlowe, the art critic. Maybe he's here to see your sets."

"Not likely, Clive."

"A torturous evening lies ahead, Huggo", said Esther. "Let us enter and abandon all hope."

They entered the building arm in arm, Rose trailing behind. In the lobby Hugo handed three tickets to a doorman and led the way into the theater. Rose was surprised to see that the interior of the warehouse had been completely transformed. Seats for the audience were arranged in clusters of ten and twenty, like islands, between thickets of paper foliage that filled the entire space.

"Oh, dear", Esther groaned. "Marco has gone creative again. We are all, no doubt, to be ensnared in his plot. Well, there's nothing we can do about it now. Let's sit as close to the rear as possible."

"My sentiments exactly", said Clive.

"We have our choice of seats, it appears", Hugo said. "Not much of an audience yet."

"Maybe they heard it's a new work by Marco the Magnificent", Clive replied archly. "Did you see his *rhino*-saurus?"

"See it?" growled Hugo. "I was trampled by it."

"Sit down, sit down here", Esther commanded. The four guests sat and stared at the stage. It was a low acropolis of canvas rock, a purple curtain drawn across its crest. Fairies peeked through a crack in it, then tittered noisily and fled.

"Oy, oy", Esther groaned.

The lighting was muted, the ceiling spots covered with green filters. Beyond the front row on the right, musicians tuned their instruments, flipping through the scores on their stands.

"What will they perform, I wonder?" Esther grumbled. "The *Nutcracker Suite*? Maybe the *Flight of the Bumblebee*? Maybe we will all need an aspirin by the end."

The men chuckled.

"Well, a good stiff drink, to be sure", Clive said, *sotto voce*, because Mrs. Brocklehurst was swooping down between clumps of paper fern in the direction of the foursome.

"She's coming, Clive."

"For you, Hugo."

"No, for you, Clive. I'll enjoy watching her try to melt you. Ambitious and insatiable, that woman. She wants a good review tomorrow."

Clive stood, extending his hand to the choreographer.

"Margaret, darling."

"Clive," she said coldly. "Did you bring your anti-sneer medicine?"

"Haven't needed it yet, Margaret."

"Ha! Hello, Hugo, Esther."

"Good evening, Mrs. Brocklehurst", Esther nodded. She gestured at the paper jungle. "This is Marco's handiwork, no

448

doubt. Huggo would never have consented to such a travesty."

"Travesty? I think it's quaint and daring. Listen, I haven't come to quibble about aesthetics. I know you will attempt your usual hasty departure, so I wanted to catch you before the play begins. We're having a big party afterward. Cast and backstage staff and funders too. It's at the Ritz. You're all welcome. You come too, Clive. It's not a bribe because you're going to write a devastatingly nasty review no matter what we do. In fact, you could have stayed home and written it, saving yourself the unnecessary task of seeing the actual play."

Mrs. Brocklehurst wheeled and returned backstage.

"The Ritz!" Clive whistled. "Wow. How on earth will they pay for it? The audience better get here fast."

"Audience or no audience, the tab isn't a problem tonight", Hugo explained. "One of the benefactors is paying. She hired the orchestra, too."

"What! That'll cost a small fortune."

"It's just for tonight. From tomorrow onward—if there is a tomorrow—it's recorded music only."

"Who's the rich benefactor?"

"Mrs. Morgan."

"Mrs. Who?"

"Come on, Clive, don't pretend. The great lady who's got her fingers into every cultural pie in the city."

"Oh, *that* Mrs. Morgan. Well, it figures. So, Marco doesn't have a worry. Even if no paying customers show up, he's achieved what he wanted—an opus dedicated to his meteoric rise in the world of high drama."

"*Canadian* high drama," Hugo corrected.

"Come, come, don't forget Stratford. And the Shaw Festival. And the. . . ."

The two men then proceeded to chew together on an old bone of contention—the existence or nonexistence of a

449

national culture, adding the inflammatory spice of whether or not it was right for the government to fund said culture. Hugo took the negative position. The debate continued with a certain vehemence and indignation on both sides, though without rancor, for both men were in fact enjoying themselves, filling the long-drawn-out minutes before an opening that had been deliberately delayed for effect. The debaters dropped their argument instantly when the lights were finally dimmed and the musicians struck up the opening notes of the score.

"Oh, no", Esther wailed in a stage whisper. "I don't believe it. Marco's using *The Rites of Spring*! I *hate* Stravinsky!"

"Pathetically transparent, isn't it, my dear," Hugo whispered back, "the barbarian themes, carnality, the dreary obviousness of it all—"

"Shhh, you two", said Clive.

The curtain opened. Hugo's pink moon began to glow above the acropolis.

"Lovely, dear, lovely", said Esther patting her husband's hand and holding it.

"Fluff", said Hugo in a gruff voice. "Fluff and nonsense."

Rose was mesmerized by the beauty of the scene and the genius of the various actors and actresses who now began to appear in the foliage, some to the right and to the left of her. But she became disturbed by the lack of clothing, for most of the troupe, human and fairy alike, wore little more than gossamer veils. The light continued to be subdued, however, and modestly robed the semi-nakedness, except whenever a human or fairy form leaped in front of colored spotlights for a second or two. The fairies were the closest to nudity, wearing nothing but minuscule cloth leaves affixed to strategic spots.

"How grateful I am that I did not become a fairy", thought Rose.

"The fairies are drama students Marco shanghaied at the last minute", Hugo whispered to Clive behind his hand. "Can't you just feel their exultation in being so daring and artistically progressive?"

"High-class pornography", Clive shot back.

"Shush", said Hugo. "Are you completely devoid of culture, man?" And both began to chuckle too loudly.

As the story unfolded, it seemed to Rose that a person of tremendous imagination had written the tale and filled it with the poetry of thawed ice. The performance was also an act of great imagination, though it seemed to her that the two imaginations were not the same, for one was a wide and deep and swiftly flowing river, and the other was like a runaway torrent in rapacious spring, full of mud and debris. The music was both awesome and frightening, for there was a darkness in it. Rose tried to focus on the splendid canvas Hugo had painted; how dear it was to her, for it had been the backdrop to an important part of her own story.

Carlotta began to recite her lines.

> Four days will quickly steep themselves in night;
> Four nights will quickly dream away the time;
> and then the moon, like to a silver bow
> New-bent in heaven, shall behold the night
> Of our solemnities.

How greatly gifted Carlotta was! It was a little disappointing that she was forced to shout, but that was no fault of her own, for she was high upon the acropolis with Theseus, and the fifteen or twenty people in the audience were clustered at the very back of the theater. It was distracting, also, that the fan behind the curtain was a bit too noisy for simulating the wind and plastered Carlotta's violet gauze against the contours of her body and Marco's purple silk to his, an unfortunate detail of which both actors seemed oblivious.

And there was Bottom. Oh, she was glad the director had

asked Bobby to return. He was perfect, so round and clownish. So mumbley and slow. So funny. It was strange the way people laughed at all the wrong spots whenever he spoke. The way he flushed red. He recited the lines about knavery very clearly and with a ferocious look on his face that made the entire cast fall silent and forget their lines for a moment and Clive the critic erupt in a single loud bark of a laugh. And he did not stumble when he came to the lines about killing a red-hipped humblebee on top of a thistle, about gathering the honey bag. He did pronounce *monsieur* improperly—*mounsieur*, he said—but then, nothing in this life was perfect.

Finally, toward the end of the play, Marco and Carlotta mounted the acropolis together, hand in hand. Long white tubes of pillars were lowered from the rafters all about them and hung suspended.

"A nice touch", Clive said.

"That was Huggo's idea", Esther said.

As Marco-Theseus began to recite, the wind increased, plastering his body with regal purple, the gold wire of his coronet clamping the sweating black hair to the skull. The spotlights whirred noisily, revolving, throwing a spectrum of alternating colors upon the sinewy form that moved like a ballet dancer this way and that way, flourishing his form like a rapier's blade, the legs flashing like scissors, the neck arching like a swan, forcing Rose to look away and Esther to snort in disgust and the two old men to struggle mightily to suppress their humor.

"Nijinsky!" Esther hissed. "This week he is Nijinsky. Now he will leap and try to hang suspended in space."

She was right. Theseus leapt, though he did not hang suspended. He landed with a loud thump on the groaning boards. Hugo and Clive looked at Esther.

"How did you know, Essie?" Clive asked.

Esther shrugged. "Fauns are always predictable."

Rose did not hear this, for she was entranced by the slow

sweet pulling of a violin bow across a string, and the arching of Theseus' long neck. As he began to trumpet his famous lines, a great blow fell upon her heart, a stricture or blaze of memory. She closed her eyes and fell back in time, or was it that the ocean of memory swelled up from within.

She was curled in a lap on a mountain under a burning blue sky, the arms of a mother wrapped around her in the heather. And as Theseus spoke, Euphrasia Gorrel whispered the lines in unison, her lips to Ogini's ear, tearing open the long-forgotten wound.

"Ay, ay!" Rose gasped. Esther, Hugo, and Clive glanced at her.

> "Such shaping fantasies, that apprehend
> More than cool reason ever comprehends—"

"Ay, ay!" Rose sobbed.

"Dear, dear", Esther muttered in a soothing voice, patting Rose's hand. "It's only a play."

> "And, as imagination bodies forth
> The forms of things unknown, the poet's pen
> Turns them to shapes, and gives to airy nothing
> A local habitation and a name."

"What's the matter, luv?" Hugo asked Rose. "Are you all right?"

"It's the melancholy", Esther suggested. "Or else the blasted hormones. In any event, let her be, Huggo. Watch the play."

Esther continued to hold the hand and pat it. Rose buried her head in Esther's fur shoulder.

"Names have a power", she groaned.

"Yes, yes. Shhh, shhh!"

"And they are lost, they are lost!"

453

"Did you say you've lost something, dear?" Esther asked sympathetically, as the fairies popped from the bushes all around them and rushed en masse toward the stage.

"They are gone, they are gone!"

"Now, now, Rose, what is this raving? Calm yourself. The idiotic play is almost over. Soon we shall go home. I will make you a glass of tea."

"Oh, Esther, it is the sacrifice-way. I thought I could carry it, but it is too heavy."

"She is distraught," Esther whispered to Hugo, who was staring at the two women with male perplexity.

Rose continued to sob: "Where is he? Where is he?"

"Where is who, *Liebchen*?"

"My beloved, my Beating Heart, my Binemin, my Tchibi, Euphrasia of the flowers, Oldmary—Ay! Ay! The many, many souls of the just who go up in the flames—"

"The souls of the just go up in flames. . . ." Esther murmured with a look of pain. Her eyebrows arched in the direction of Hugo. Hugo shook his head as if to say, Don't look at me for an explanation.

Fortunately, the final lines of the play were now rolling toward completion, as Puck, a fetching adolescent with fangs, bleated to the audience:

> If we shadows have offended,
> think but this, and all is mended—
> That you have but slumb'red here
> While these visions did appear.
> And this weak and idle theme,
> No more yielding but a dream,
> Gentles, do not reprehend.
> If you pardon, we will mend.
> And, as I am an honest Puck,
> If we have unearnèd luck

Now to scape the serpent's tongue,
We will make amends ere long;
Else the Puck a liar call.
So, good night unto you all. . . .

Stravinsky roared in for the finale, circular fairy dances broke out in many parts of the warehouse, the lights flashed with dizzying randomness. The major cast members linked hands and coiled down from the mountain acropolis, entering the lowlands of the forest, entangling the patches of audience, kissing their cheeks, foreheads, lips, tossing cloth leaves left and right, squealing and darting naked through the foliage, enmeshing the whole world in their overheated chorale, chanting, leaping, their gossamer flying behind them in the cavorting wind, the veils falling to the floor as the sweating forms thumped away into the shadowed wings.

The lights went up. Esther, her arms still around Rose, cast a sarcastic look at her husband. "Oy", she said. Hugo rubbed his face with a speckled hand. Clive chuckled to himself and penned studiously in a notebook.

"Let's go home", Esther said. "I need an aspirin."

But it was not to be. Outside, on the sidewalk, Esther and Rose stood side by side waiting for a taxi. Hugo and Clive stood a few paces away tearing the play to pieces, laughing conspiratorially, trading accounts of other failed theatrical ventures involving the Cirque de la Lune.

When the taxi pulled up to the curb, Clive said, "Listen, folks, it's too early to turn in. Why don't we all go to the Ritz for a nightcap?"

"Well, it *is* free". Hugo mused. "What do you say, Esther?"

"No. Rose and I need to go home."

Clive frowned and folded his arms. "What, and spoil all the fun! Come on, girls, it won't hurt you. Dry your eyes, Miss.

455

Shakespeare is a magician. He can make you cry, but he really wants to make you laugh after you've had a good cry. What say?"

Rose shook her head, "No, thank you. Please go without me."

Clive and Hugo looked so disappointed, and Esther so undecided, that Rose relented. "Perhaps we could go to the party for a little while."

"Excellent!" Hugo said all smiles. "Rose, I'm sure Carlotta will be glad to see you again."

They squeezed into the taxi and were taken around the base of the mountain to the downtown core of the city. Within minutes they arrived at the ornate canopy of the Ritz-Champlain on St. Catherine Street. The lights of the chandeliers in the lobby were blinding. A liveried footman led them down a corridor so wide it was almost a street, paved with Persian carpeting. At the entrance of a banquet hall, one of a dozen on the block-long corridor, they were met by Bottom, munching a sandwich and trying not to spill a glass of wine.

" 'Lo, Hugo."

"Hello, Bobby. Are you all right? Butterflies all gone?"

"Yeah, all gone. Did we bomb?"

"As usual, Bobby, but you were among the redeeming qualities."

"Oh, good. 'Lo, Mrs. Dyson."

"Good evening, Bobby. You were brilliant."

"Thanks. Want a sandwich? There's wine too. If you want some, you gotta go in there."

They went in there and found that several members of the cast had arrived before them. Members of the audience seemed to have been invited as well, though this did not swell the crowd appreciably. The major actors and actresses had yet to arrive. A buffet table stretched along one wall. At the far end of the room footmen were lighting candles and making last-minute adjustments to the orchids on the head table.

"Sumptuous", Hugo said. "May Mrs. Morgan live a long and happy life."

"It's so pretentious", Esther snapped in a low voice. "Where is this famous Mrs. Morgan? Did she attend the play?"

Clive nodded. "She was there in the front row with some of her friends, other wealthy old crones. Hey-ho, there's Trevor Marlowe! I'm going to go have a word with him about your scenery, Hugo."

"Don't bother, Clive."

After Clive departed, Hugo, Esther, and Rose sat at a round table in the corner of the room most distant from the head table. A waiter brought a tray full of wine glasses. Hugo took three from him.

"No, thank you", said Rose.

"May I drink yours, then?"

"Huggo, behave!" Esther slapped his hand.

There were about eighty people in the hall now, a fair portion of whom had not attended the play.

"Who are all these unpleasant people?" Esther asked.

"Funders, board members, and camp followers. A critic or two."

"Critics!" Esther snorted. "All critics should be flogged—publicly."

"Darling, you are in an uncommonly vitriolic mood tonight. You behave yourself."

"Let's have a bite to eat and get out of here, Huggo. It's always the same. I am so disgusted with the banality of it, the endless prancing of their egos. I want to go home. Did you feed Goldie before we left?"

"I did. Listen, doveling, I hate this as much as you do, but it is our bread and butter."

"It's not *my* bread and butter."

"Well, to tell the truth, bread and butter is not our fare here this evening. I fear we have come among the lotus-eaters.

457

Beware, Esther, beware, Rose, for the effect of this food is such that those who partake of it lose all thought of home and wish to remain forever in this land."

"Let one of those fauns and satyrs near me, and I will speak my mind."

"I expect they've heard you speak your mind before, darling. Which is why none of them approaches our table, though we sit perched on the edges of our seats eyeing the crowd hungrily."

"I am hungry only for the sandwiches. And perhaps a little of the caviar. I do smell it in the air."

"Yes, there is indeed caviar, and I suspect it is real. Red and black. Shall I get you some?"

"In a while. For the moment, I wish to look. I wish to memorize all those silly faces containing nothing but their false images of themselves. I will replicate them in a painting."

"Now, now, keep calm."

Esther instantaneously switched from sour to sweet, turned to Rose and asked, "Feeling a little better, Rose-*Liebchen*?"

"Yes", Rose nodded, though the inrush of fabulous imagery and sounds and smells was overwhelming.

At that moment the leading roles swept into the room. Fortunately, they were all fully clothed. Applause erupted in every direction, except from the corner. First came Carmella Fabian and the youth who had played Puck. Behind them came Marco.

"There is the King of the Night People", Esther murmured.

Marco was arm in arm with a mauve-haired woman of undefinable age. It was obvious even from a distance that she had once been beautiful. Her bearing was graceful and regal, though it was without a hint of haughtiness. She rustled in pale jade silk, and around her well-exposed collarbone hung a diamond pendant.

"Is that your Mrs. Morgan?" Esther asked with distaste.

Hugo nodded.

People crowded around the lady and Marco, pummeling them with bravos and more applause. Marco led the woman to the head table, where he pulled out the central chair for her. Mrs. Brocklehurst sat down on the other side, as did many of the leading cast members and a few gentlemen in evening jackets.

The chandeliers dimmed, the candelabra flickered on each table. The music of a synthetic Viennese waltz oozed from the loudspeakers, careful not to drown the tides of exuberant chatter. Catching Marco's eye, Hugo waved and lifted his glass. Marco looked away. Rose hoped that Carmella would notice her, but the actress did not turn her head.

The guests streamed toward the buffet, filled their china plates with various hors d'ouvres, and took their seats, choosing from among the dozens of tables arranged in widening rings around the head table. Those closest to the head filled quickly. Hugo, Esther, and Rose sat alone in the outermost orbit, ringed by a wide empty no-man's-land, as if an antipersonnel bomb had exploded in their vicinity.

Esther sighed, "I'll have that caviar now." Hugo went away and returned shortly carrying a plate heaped with slices of buttered black bread and gobbets of roe. The three abandoned guests began to eat, Rose most enthusiastically, for the fish smell was irresistible. She kept eating throughout the speech that Marco made thanking the benefactors, the board members, and the cast. Through the joking and the tittering of fairies, through the jests that were hurled from the crowd, and through the uproarious laughter cast back by those seated above.

Rose's attention was caught only when a great silence fell. She looked up to see Mrs. Morgan rising to her feet and all eyes fixed upon her with beams of appreciation.

"—to render Shakespeare in new forms intelligible to modern man. Mark Chandler-Ross has done this, I believe, with a mastery rarely seen in contemporary theater."

"Bosh", Esther muttered. "Fig pie and lollipops."

"That he demurs the praise surely due him is a mark of his humility as an artist", Mrs. Morgan went on, undaunted by a loud belch from Bottom, who was stationed close to the food table. "It is my hope—nay, it shall be my most urgent project—to interest the director of the Stratford Festival in hosting the Chandler-Ross *Dream* as the centerpiece of this coming season."

Mrs. Morgan smiled graciously and sat down as gasps and thunderous applause broke out in every direction. Marco stood and, bowing from the waist, kissed her cheek. Mrs. Brocklehurst did the same from the opposite direction.

The music swelled loudly, and the waiters swarmed into the hall with fresh trays of drinks for everyone. Laughter and convivial discussion broke out in all directions, save for the dead zone in the corner.

Esther reached for a glass of red wine.

"Darling, that's your third", Hugo frowned. "You wouldn't want to get tipsy. You know what you're like. You say things that are better left unsaid."

Esther downed the drink in two swallows and reached for another.

"Esther—"

"Leave me alone, Huggo. I am beginning to enjoy myself."

"Uh-oh." Hugo gazed at his wife analytically for a moment, then stood up. "Rose, please keep an eye on her. I have to go talk to Clive." He crossed the room and found the drama critic deep in a heated discussion about Harold Pinter, the bright new American playwright. Clive extracted himself without difficulty, and both men left the room.

"There they go," Esther said. "The great escape. They will now proceed to the bar in the lobby, where they will consume more whiskey than is good for Huggo's blood pressure. Clive will pay, of course—this is understood. They will talk and commiserate about their respective failed careers. They will get drunk. Clive will pay for a taxi to take Huggo home. I will meet him at the front door about, oh, say one o'clock in the morning and put him to bed on the sofa, where he will awake tomorrow morning completely depressed. In a week from now, when he has overcome his suicidal thoughts, he will ask me to make a big pan of scrambled eggs and will go upstairs to the studio, get out his paint rollers, and make silly tire tracks on the canvas. Poor man, he cannot accept his failure."

"But Hugo is famous, is he not?" Rose asked.

"No, my dear, not quite. He had some local fame for a time. Once he was a gifted realist. His paintings are in a number of museums in England. But he had this little nervous breakdown about ten years ago and has never been the same since. During the recovery, someone convinced him that the passion he was pouring into his work was killing him. He embraced abstraction as therapy. Nothing I say to the contrary will dissuade him. The critics all moo and bray the same message: 'Abstraction is the future! Realism is dead!' What a lie. It's the abstraction that's killing him. He thinks he is escaping his pain, but in reality he merely buries his heart."

"He loves you, Esther."

"Oh, yes, he loves me. He loves me very well, Rose. But I am not his first love."

"Oh?" Rose said uneasily.

Esther laughed. "His first love has always been, and always will be, painting. For him, to paint is to live. He thinks it doesn't matter what he paints as long as he paints. Thus, he chooses a field that has the least emotional content. He thinks he can have his cake and eat it too. In fact he is losing everything, but slowly, slowly."

"Yet he has not lost you."

"In the end, I will die and be lost to him. Poor man. I love him so much, Rose, but he is a pig-headed fool. He seeks

461

to escape the suffering, and in the end he suffers more than anyone."

"And you, Esther. Do you suffer? Surely you do, for I see it in your paintings, and I saw it—"

Esther swallowed her fifth glass of wine and turned a slightly unsteady eye upon Rose.

"*Shema, shema, shema?*"

"Yes", Rose nodded.

Gazing at Rose thoughtfully, Esther remained silent for a few moments. Then, sighing deeply, she said, "To suffer is to live. To live is to suffer. This I have accepted. This is the price of the paintings."

"Then for you, also, to paint is to live?"

"Of course."

Suddenly Esther bristled with hostility. Looking up, Rose saw that Marco was working his way around the hall, shaking hands at each table, gathering compliments, his face glowing, his eyes flashing repeatedly at Mrs. Morgan, who accompanied him.

"Oy, preserve me!" Esther groaned.

Arriving finally at the table where Rose and Esther sat, Marco reached across Rose with a hand extended toward Esther.

"How nice of you to come, Esther. I won't ask how you enjoyed the play, because I can guess your thoughts on the matter already. Ha-ha-ha! But didn't you think Hugo's set was fantastic?"

"Fantastic it was", Esther replied glumly, giving the hand a single shake and dropping it. "Fluffy and puerile, nineteenth-century pastoral romanticism, with a heavy dose of Puvis de Chavannes. Hugo is a great artist. He deserves better than a third-rate warehouse, a third-rate version of a great play, and a third-rate company of jesters, *un cirque des fou fous*."

Astonished by the sheer nastiness of Esther's response, an attack that struck more deeply in the atmosphere of universal adulation, Marco took a step back, flushing with a conflation of humiliation and anger. He cast a hasty glance over his shoulder, grateful that Mrs. Morgan had been delayed at another table. Huffing with stung pride he quickly mustered a response. In a low voice he said, "From you, that is a compliment, dear little old-world fossil. You come into my party as a nonpaying guest and you have the gall to sit in the corner dressed in that ridiculous fur coat looking for all the world like a dowager empress with piles, or a vulture with tatty feathers, waiting for something to devour. Don't you ever get tired of being yourself?"

Esther smiled—a dangerous sign, which Marco would have recognized if he had not been so young.

"You are right, Magnifico. I am a vulture. I sit and wait for dead things. That is why my eye is always upon you."

"Ha! Can't you be more creative than that?"

"If you like. Let me at least say that your version of the *Dream* was not Shakespeare. It was not about Shakespeare at all. It was about Marco Chandler-Ross. It was about the ego that tried to eat the world. You speak of vultures. Just because you are a pretty boy, snapping up the little moths left and right, you think you are not a vulture. You are a vulture surpassing all vultures, and soon you will be an old vulture like me. Soon you will sit in corners at parties where greater talents are honored, trying to remember the praise that was once heaped on you, but you will not remember it because your besotted brain will have become riddled like Swiss cheese, any smidgen of talent it once contained long ago dribbled out with the other fluids."

"Swiss cheese?" Marco laughed. "Truly insulting, Esther. You sure put me in my place." He laughed again, a loud hollow sound.

Esther was not dissuaded. "In my long and complicated life, I have met many like you, male and female, people for whom the rest of the human race are just things, props that you move about on your stage, extensions of your monumental self-absorption, food for your senses or sensibilities."

"Now it's Jane Austen. Now you're the *literary* vulture."

"Who is Jane Austen?" Esther snapped. "One of your moths?" Marco laughed and shook his head.

"Please", Rose interjected timidly, touching Esther's arms with her trembling hand. "You do not need to be angry with each other. You do not need such hard words."

Marco smirked and turned his gaze upon Rose, his brow furrowing in curiosity.

"Thank you, Miss whoever you are", he said. "Now just tie Esther to her leash and take her away, would you?"

"I'm not going anywhere", Esther said in a voice as cold as the grave. "I'm staying till they turn off the lights and sweep up. I have a mind to ruin your party, Marco."

A burble of gentle laughter swept across the table. All three combatants looked up to see Mrs. Morgan standing a few paces behind Marco, a smile playing on her lips.

"Hello, everyone. I always say that creative tension must out. I see it so frequently at these get-togethers. There are such tremendous strains in putting together a theatrical production, or an *oeuvre* of any kind, that we sometimes say things we later regret." She stepped forward and extended a hand to Esther. "You're Hugo's wife, aren't you. I'm Estelle Morgan."

"Charmed, I'm sure", Esther said with a furtive look at the woman, shaking the hand and letting it go as soon as was decently possible.

"And who is this?" Mrs. Morgan asked, offering her hand to the little shadow-girl sitting beside the formidable Mrs. Dyson.

"This is Rose", Esther said coldly. "She's a friend of ours."

"It's a pleasure to meet you both", Mrs. Morgan said with a winning smile, taking Marco's arm. "I hope you stay as long as you can. Is Hugo here tonight? I did so want to congratulate him on the fabulous painting of Athens. It stirred the soul, it was so haunting and majestic."

"Puerile", Marco mouthed silently at Esther.

"Please give him my regards, won't you", Mrs. Morgan said. "And pass on to him my thanks for his outstanding sets. Have a *wonderful* evening."

Mrs. Morgan deftly swept Marco away in the direction of the next table.

"Oy", Esther breathed and finished her sixth glass of wine.

Rose felt bad about the whole situation. She knew that all those involved in the misunderstanding were basically good people. She would try to explain Marco to Esther on the way home.

"Perhaps we should go", she suggested.

"Go? Who said anything about go? I'm staying. That was just the opening round."

"We must not fight people, Esther."

"Wrong! We *must* fight them."

"But why? What good would it do?"

"I hate them", Esther seethed. "All of them! If you could have seen the way he treated my Huggo—a great man—like a stagehand, like a serving boy. Scrapping one design and demanding another, again and again and again, year after year. Not because there was anything wrong with the designs, but merely because he enjoyed his power over Huggo. It amused him to treat an old man that way. He used Huggo like a tool."

Rose kept silent, worrying over the dark malice in Esther's eyes, puzzled too, for beneath the malice was a grief so profound that Rose sensed she could never understand it.

"I've had it with those privileged spoiled brats!" Esther went on. "Someone must stop them." Esther's diction was beginning to degenerate into a distinctly old-world accent. "I will slaughter them. I will decimate them."

"Oh, please, Esther, let's go. We must not repay their blindness with unkindness."

Esther snorted and signaled to a waiter.

True to her word, Esther waited and watched. One by one the tuxedos made their exits, followed shortly by the lesser classes. Mrs. Morgan departed about midnight, with many pecks and hugs from the cast. After that, Mrs. Brocklehurst glided from the room at the head of a covey of dancers. A few moths flew out the exits. Bottom left with a doggie bag under one arm and a bottle under the other. Puck threw up and was carried out by the waiters. Marco slouched at the high table, grinning, glowing with success. The gold coronet sat askew on his brow. His eyes shone with triumph. If from time to time he threw a worried look in the direction of the far corner, where a black shadow and a lesser shadow sat waiting and watching, these were only minor relapses. After each, he forced himself to drink and eat and laugh the more, and romp and gather in his arms a number of fluttering moths, who kissed him with self-induced abandon.

"Act five begins", Esther said. "Now is the moment. Come!" She stood and tottered unsteadily toward a vacated table close to the head. Rose followed with trepidation.

At half past midnight, the waiters began to blow out the guttering stubs of candles and glance at their wrist watches. Their faces lost all semblance of hospitality and they leaned against the walls with dish cloths dangling from their forearms. About two dozen people remained in the room, huddled in small groups around the high table, talking, entering the phase of serious drinking, girls on boys' laps, boys on girls' laps.

Marco suddenly stood, scraped back his chair, and turned a smirking eye on Esther Dyson, who was sitting front row center staring at him without expression.

"Speak!" he barked.

This evoked the intended laughter from the audience.

466

"Are you plotting a tragedy?" he said, with sweeping gestures.

Esther said nothing. She continued to stare at him until he flinched and began to stride back and forth upon the stage. Wheeling on her, he said, "Did you not know that Rosencrantz and Guildenstern are dead? Shylock too?"

Still Esther did not speak.

"Art thou the banquet's ghost?" he cried. The audience chuckled in appreciation. He resumed his pacing.

"If it were done, 'twere well it were done quickly", he growled, switching to a strong English accent.

> If th'assassination
> Could trammel up the consequence, and catch
> With his surcease success, that but this blow
> Might be the be-all and the end-all—; here,
> But here upon this bank and shoal of time,
> We'ld jump the life to come. But in these cases
> We still have judgment here, that we but teach
> Bloody instructions, which, being taught, return
> To plague th'inventor. This even-handed justice
> Commends th'ingredient of our poisoned chalice
> To our own lips.

Marco paused. Slamming the palms of his hands on the table, he leaned toward Esther.

"To *your* own lips," he said in a hoarse stage whisper.

Murmurs of amusement rolled to him from the audience.

Throwing himself erect he grabbed a butter knife and began to pace again, loudly declaiming.

> Is this a dagger which I see before me,
> The handle toward my hand? Come, let me clutch thee!
> I have thee not, and yet I see thee still.

Art thou not, fatal vision, sensible
To feeling as to sight? or art thou but
A dagger of the mind, a false creation,
Proceeding from the heat-oppressèd brain?

Marco threw himself down into his chair and craned his neck, laughing with delight at his own performance. The audience applauded.

"Observe carefully, Rose", Esther said, loudly enough for all to hear. "See the thyroid glances of the pub-crawlers, the eyes of bullfrogs poking above the green slime of the swamp, croaking the poetry of higher realms."

"Oooh!" groaned the crowd in admiration, for they loved an articulate conflict.

Rose tugged on Esther's coat sleeve. "I think we should go", she said.

"Not yet, not yet", Esther said in a small and very dangerous voice. "As you know, my Rose, faces have texture and form and content because human beings are not abstractions. They are real." Esther paused. "*We* are real", she corrected. "You and I."

"Appearances can lie!" Marco shouted.

"That is why the expressionists distort," Esther continued without acknowledging the interruption, "for the purpose of revealing the truth of the subject matter. The truly wicked are those who distort for the sake of distortion."

Marco feigned shock: "The truly wicked, she says! Hark, a moralist is among us. Fie! To the barricades! Man your weapons before she unmans us!"

Laughter volleyed about the room. The waiters eyed the guests with awakening interest, half smiling to each other.

Esther tottered toward the stage and pointed a finger straight at Marco.

"This man", she cried, "is an *automatiste*. He paints with *you*, pathetic actors and actresses. You are his tools. His inspiration, I tell you, is from the darkest of muses. He trusts in ghosts more than he trusts in human beings."

"Oooh! Oooh!"

"Dear Lady Vulture," Marco said, bowing in a dramatic act of self-deprecation, "do you not recognize genius when you see it?"

"I do", Esther replied coolly. "Though its handle is not before my eyes."

"Oooh! Oooh!"

Suddenly, as if to distract, Marco, throwing his arms wide, opened his mouth and burst into song, his well-modulated voice booming the lyrics of a Gilbert and Sullivan opera. As he weaved back and forth before Esther's eyes, he grabbed another glass of wine, grinning at her, bouncing his body in time to the music, as the audience joined in the singing. When it was done, he pointed at Esther.

"Your turn, Lady Vulture."

Esther shook her feathers and snarled, "I do not sing. I have not sung since the gas chambers."

"Oooh-oooh!"

Momentarily taken aback, Marco shrugged, for really there was no reply for this. A few of the unsatisfied cast their eyes about the room, searching for lesser artists.

"Hey, what about the girl? Give us a song, girl—you, the one with the Vulture Lady!"

Rose shrank into her seat.

"Come on, be a good sport", someone shouted. "Sing us a native song!"

Cries of encouragement broke out from every direction. Esther shot Rose a warning look, then shook her head at the others, threatening them with the direst punishment. Marco jumped from the stage, grabbed Rose's arm, and pulled her to her feet.

"Pay your dues, Blossom. Sing us a song the Indians sing."

Face red, unable to meet their eyes, Rose tried to fall back into her chair. But Marco would not let her.

"Please", she whispered. "I can't. I don't want to."

"Just one, *ma petite*, for me." He kissed her cheek, a lingering, insinuative kiss that was rewarded by the snickering it was intended to elicit.

"No, no", Rose pleaded, flaming a deeper red.

"Up you go, up you go", Marco grinned, lifting her onto the chair. Until she found her feet, he held her by the arm.

"That is enough!" Esther roared with amazing volume.

"Be quiet!" Marco growled, "You old fake!"

Eyes flaring with rage, Esther went eyeball to eyeball with Marco.

"Let her go", she hissed. *"Satyre syphilitique!"*

His upper lip curling back from the teeth, Marco raised his right arm to strike her.

"Go ahead, hit me. It will give me such satisfaction to read about it in tomorrow's headlines: *Fascist Shakespearean Beats up Holocaust Survivor.* Beautiful!"

"Please, please", Rose wailed. "Don't fight. Don't fight. I'll sing."

Esther and Marco broke their hate-stares and stepped back, both of them aghast at what had almost happened. Marco dropped into a chair, barked an ugly laugh, lit a cigarette, tilted his muscular neck upward, drawing many admiring glances, and exhaled.

"So", he said with a wave of his hand. "Sing!"

Esther grabbed Rose's arm. "Get down from there. Let's go. I've been a fool to think I could win this battle."

"Esther, you do not understand."

"I understand perfectly. It was my self-indulgence. I caused this ridiculous fight. Let's go!"

Rose paused, wondering how she could explain it to Esther. Her role seemed clearer now. She would fling herself between

470

the two hatreds as a sacrifice. If she did not, Esther and Marco would surely meet again in a worse conflict.

"They are sad and far from God, Esther. A sacrifice is needed."

"Do not be insane. Come! Now!"

"Please," Rose pleaded, "don't be angry with each other. I will sing."

"An Indian song!" someone shouted.

The audience began to pound the table tops rhythmically in imitation of native war drums. When the pounding subsided, replaced only by the pounding of blood in her ear drums, Rose sighed and looked at her feet perched on the edge of the chair.

"Well, come on, do it", someone shouted.

"I do not know what to sing", she said.

"Anything. So long as it's Indian."

Cheers, more war drums.

Gradually the room quieted, the chatter died, the glasses stopped clinking, a waiter turned off the canned music.

"*Nind anishinâbe-nagam*," Rose whispered, "I will sing an Indian song."

Lowering her eyes, flushing again, she opened her mouth and released a faint warble. She stopped and cleared her throat. Now all eyes and ears were on her. Someone laughed nervously. Someone else shut it off with a curse. Rose practiced the warble again, then the clumsy sound thinned and steadied. Remembering an Ojibwe song that honored the holy souls, she slowly sang its verses in her native tongue. Her listeners, greedy for what they assumed was something darkly pagan, would have been disappointed to know it was a Christian hymn. When she was finished, a smattering of applause came from the audience.

"That was kinda short", someone shouted. "Give us another!"

"Enough, Rose!" Esther said.

"More, more!" shouted others.

Rose inhaled and exhaled. She ignored the voices of the audience, but listened attentively to their breathing souls. Then, opening her mouth once more, her voice climbed to a high pitched chant. And in that way she finally sang the song that had been sleeping within her for many years.

> On the high rocks,
> in the Land of Little Trees,
> under the soaring sky,
> I found in the swallow moss
> a broken box of tea-wood.
>
> I was a child,
> not familiar with the holy wind,
> and ignorant of age.
> I found an old woman's memory
> in a casket sitting on the stones.
> It was not the darkness of windigo,
> it did not frighten me like devil masks,
> there were no dead birds falling like rain,
> so I looked within.
> She wore bits of parka fur,
> and a green rusting cross
> on ragged calico,
> as blue as sky,
> as flowered as Arctic June.
>
> But I was young
> and there were moons
> rising full of milk in the south
> calling for the little birds to drink.
> Homeward, I returned,
> to the place which was my dream,
> for spilling from the river's mouth
> were spawning fish.

I jumped in with buckets,
there were too many of them in the shallows
to flee.
I filled my flesh fish-full,
broiled on twig fires
the silver glut,
swelled my sinew;
my skin was young and brown
over whiter bone.

The heap of fish gorged
the dogs for a day,
Thisdog and Thatdog
ate the rotting heads and spines
that lay among the grass.
When it was done,
I walked the miles out into nothingness again.

I found her as I had left her,
for even the wolves had been kind,
and the ground squirrels (*sik-sik*) too.
Mice and lemming had stripped the flesh
gracefully,
leaving only the bare message of bone
and the grey ropes of braided hair.
I would kneel.
I would kneel,
offering what I had.
And what I had was this:
my listening
to what she had to say.

By this point Rose had ascended completely above her timidity,
and was no longer fully in the room. She closed her eyes and
raised her voice even higher.

I too was once a girl, the woman said,
I too ran free and full
of fish
out upon the ice
of Threefinger Lake or Crazyman River,
as under a growing sun
it chimed and broke
and moved beyond, slipping into the sea
by the many veins of water.

I too nursed the grass dollies,
and played the string games,
and stomped my little feet
in many dances,
and sang the many songs,
Ay, ay! O, o! Ay, ay! O, o!

Then to a man
the woman-child was joined,
his heart a begging bowl.
And I unborn,
remembered the sound I had not heard,
her young laughter
as she tossed her black braid,
then her cries as a child was born,
and her smile
as she suckled live brown boy flesh,
and watched it grow,
watched it go
out beyond the fracture line
of land and sky
to hunt *atik* the deer.

I did not know her,
though I knew her,
and I ask now,

474

did her eyes grow dim,
did she tell the village tales,
then lose her whole self
under pox and TB?
Or was it simple age
that left her out there in the wind,
left her out there in a box stamped Tea?

I was ignorant and from a lesser age
yet I heard her soundless music,
I learned her silent speech,
and came in time to sing
for her spirit
in sacred, fragile,
summer.

Rose heaved a great sigh, opened her eyes slowly, and climbed down from the chair. She sat and remained without moving, staring at the table top. Esther took her hand. For a minute there was not a sound in the house. Then, Marco grunted, put his cigarette into his mouth, squinted from the smoke, and began to applaud with loud, slow claps. One by one the others copied him. The applause was not an enthusiastic outburst. Neither was it mockery. It was a perplexed but appreciative act of respect for what the listeners could not understand. An unprecedented mood had come upon them. It was awe. And because awe is a form of powerlessness, they were forced eventually to shake it off.

"Wow!" someone shouted. "Existential!"

Which made the hall shake with laughter.

"Brilliant! An absolutely brilliant performance!" Marco boomed. "You are Titania! You are the Queen of the Fairies. You have completely possessed a band of cynics with your craft. See, look about you, not one of them realizes that you have just entertained us with the story of a coffin full of bones."

He began to laugh hysterically, and it was obvious that he was drunk.

"Here's to death!" he shouted, raising his glass.

"To death!" many of the guests shouted gleefully.

The lights seemed to go up at that moment, the canned music resumed, and the several beautiful young women in the room began to distract. The moment was over.

"Rose," Esther whispered, "let's go."

And so, the two friends departed unaccompanied, unnoticed, bearing their tragedies and their knowledge into the streets of the great city.

18

The next morning Rose awoke to a household situation that was exactly as Esther had predicted. Hugo lay asleep on the parlor sofa, under a blanket, snoring. The smell of whiskey was strong in the air, and the unmistakable odor of commiserated failure—the rotten luxury in which the two men had indulged to excess the night before. Hugo awoke depressed. He did not speak to the women. He did not acknowledge their presence other than to accept the single cup of black coffee that Esther brought to him. When he had swallowed it in a gulp, he stumbled wearily down the hall to their bedroom, closed the door, and remained inside. He did not eat any food that day, nor the next. Three days passed, during which Esther did not go up to her studio on the third floor, but puttered about on the ground floor, dusting furniture, straightening toppled stacks of newspaper, grumbling, sitting in the parlor reading a thick book, muttering over it, underlining passages, wiping her bifocal lenses, scowling, throwing the book down—and throughout all of this keeping an ear cocked to every creak and groan emanating from their bedroom. Each night she slept on the sofa.

"Is he ill?" Rose asked, as she washed dishes after a supper of boiled cabbage and fried fish.

"In his mind, which is wrestling with demons of his own making. Stubborn man, whenever he is like this, he always increases the dose of the drug that is killing him."

"What drug is that, Esther?"

"Philosophy."

"A friend of mine, Mère Jean, used to read philosophy. I did not know it was bad for you."

477

Esther scowled. "A drug", she said, wobbling her head sideways for emphasis, "can be a medicine. Yet the wrong dose will sicken the patient. Too high a dose kills him. Huggo thinks he is taking medicine. But this medicine was made by deranged chemists."

"Who are they."

"Dr. Kandinsky, Dr. Picasso, and Dr. Duchamp—all of them liars and madmen."

"Is all their work falsehood, Esther? I do remember seeing a beautiful little painting by Picasso in the Art Gallery of Ontario."

"A woman's face?"

"Yes. It was deep and sad."

Esther snorted. "Sometimes the insane have relapses into health. The minotaur was never consistent; the insanity took over completely as he became an old crazed bull, besotted with his many lusts and his colossal pride."

"Is Hugo besotted, Esther?" Rose asked nervously, scrubbing carbonated fish from the frying pan.

Esther shook with sudden amusement. "No, my dear. He is that genre of man known as normal. He loves as most men do. And his pride is also within the range of normal. It is the heroes of the revolution who have misled him. Because of them, he is infected with the *Zeitgeist*."

"What is *Zeitgeist*?"

"The spirit of the age. He is haunted and seduced, for he does not like to grow old and cannot bear to be forgotten." She sighed. "If only he would relapse into Fauvism or some little tributary of cognitive Expressionism. Perhaps then we could lure him still farther into the zone of the reactionary. Ha! We might even reverse the tide of art history. In the end he might even return to realism and become a happy man again."

But Esther realized she was throwing too many technical terms at Rose.

"Did anyone feed Golda today?" she asked.

"No one, as far as I know."

"Well, we needn't bother about Goldie, Rose. She will not go hungry. The mice have been increasing."

"She is getting so fat."

"You, too, are putting on weight. It is good to see, *Liebchen*. Your cheeks are rosy. Your eyes are shiny. What cheer you bring into a gloomy house of two old people."

"Thank you, Esther, but it is you and Hugo who give me joy. You are so kind. Yet I feel I am a burden. Can you give me other jobs to do? The walls need washing, and the cupboards and drawers should be cleaned of mouse droppings."

"Forget the mouse droppings. We did not bring you here to make a maid of you. When will you paint? Three weeks you are with us and still you do not paint."

Rose pondered the question before answering. "I have made my papers flat and washed them with water. They are drying now. I have set out the box of oil pastels. I sit in the beautiful light of my studio window and wait. It will come. I know it will come, for the thawing time is close."

Esther looked out the kitchen window at the brick wall. Rain was falling in the alley.

"Yes, spring is close. Soon you will paint. I will paint. But who will make that silly old man paint?"

As predicted, Hugo came into the kitchen on the seventh day after the *Midsummer Night's Dream*, and sat himself blearily at the table. He was thinner, needed a bath, and his eyes were haggard.

"Esther, dear, would you be so kind as to make me a big pan of scrambled eggs? I have such an appetite today."

After a hearty breakfast and three cups of strong coffee, he went upstairs to his studio to resume his career. At about ten-thirty in the morning Rose and Esther heard a loud crash and ran up to the attic to find a dripping roller dangling from a hole in the center of a canvas that lay shattered on the floor.

"Huggo? Where are you, Huggo?" Esther cried shrilly.

Another crash echoed.

"Are you on the back staircase or the front staircase? Answer me!"

Another crash.

"He is destroying his paintings in the storage room", Esther said, shaking her head. "Look at this mess! He has stabbed the painting. He is really stabbing himself."

"Perhaps he is stabbing his weakness", Rose suggested.

Behind them a heavy tread thumped down the front staircase to the ground floor. The door of Hugo's and Esther's bedroom slammed shut.

"Oy", Esther said. "There is nothing to be done. Go back to your work, Rose. Paint if you can. I cannot. Perhaps tomorrow."

Rose returned to her second–floor studio and closed the door without a sound. She sat in front of her drawing table and prayed. She asked God to give grace to Hugo, even though he was not a believer. She begged him to drive the *Zeitgeist* from the house and to rescue Hugo's mind from its slavery. Then she prayed for her own work.

She pinned a sheet of pale gray paper onto the board and stared at it. It was an emptiness darker than black. Taking white and blue pastel sticks, she made a moon upon it, the tiny strokes working together to create an impression of silver. Below that, she planted a forest of black pines, stippling their tops with green. Below the wall of trees she swathed a field of snow with palest mauve. Across the field three figures walked hand in hand. The central figure was the smallest, like a child, though its back was hunched as if bearing a great burden. Around them she painted a ring of amber light, and in the corona three small silver birds. The sky was darkened with cobalt, then curtains of green fire began to dance on it. After that, the speckles of the *tchibekana*, and the diagonal tangent of a plunging loon.

Io! it was flowing!

Throughout the remainder of the morning she worked, and when Esther yelled up the staircase, calling her to lunch, Rose took the picture down to the kitchen. Esther smiled with pleasure when she saw it.

"Good", she said. "At last it comes back to you. Now you begin again."

Rose hastily gobbled a cucumber sandwich and swallowed a glass of milk. Then, without thinking of the dishes, she trotted along the hallway to the bedroom beside the parlor and knocked.

"Go away," said an old tired voice within.

Rose rattled the door handle but it was locked. She knelt, slipped the drawing under the door, and returned to her studio. All afternoon she labored over a second drawing, this time expanding the fields of snow and sky, adding three comets that plummeted into the earth. Upon an expanse of blue snow three white horses bucked and bolted, for they did not understand the shower of light. The moon was full, and the river of stars poured across the field of night.

As the studio window grew dark, Rose began work on a third picture. This was a more personal one, deeper in the heart, and more dangerous. It was a portrait of Tchibi as she imagined he must now be. He stood against a background of swirling fire. His bare feet were balanced upon a solid globe of white quartz. He was a tall, brown Indian man with wide green eyes beneath a spray of red-brown spikes, the dome of his forehead shining with grace. His mouth firm and confident. His shoulders arched high, for there remained a little tension in his body, as a memory of the suffering-time of his childhood, as a small cross to carry, though its burden was no longer heavy, for the suffering had been converted into

481

wisdom. He was strong beneath the tan deer-hide of his shirt and trousers. In his large hands he held a speckled stone, and a knife with which to carve the stone, which was himself. The self, and the grace that infused the self, flowed together and formed a single artist. On one shoulder a partridge perched. On the other a silver bird. And over the whole figure a large white bird hovered with wings extended, always containing him, always protecting.

"Io, my Nishime, where are you?" Rose whispered, and felt the tears rise within her, and spill, though it was a mingled joy and sadness flowing together. Now hope thawed in great force, rushing through the fractures in the rock of the world, filling the empty places, winding through countless channels, over-spilling basins, making the bells chime and the gardens bloom, making all the scattered pieces of the world return to their intended order, as they were in the beginning, before the great and terrible falling which was the history of man. The oceans sang within her, and the skies sang too, and the earth, for each element remembered its place and its purpose.

Rose did not show this image to Esther. It was not secret, no. But it was a private thing, too deep for exposure. In time she would show it to her friends. In time. Not yet.

Hugo remained locked inside the bedroom. Not even Esther's spicy *latkes*, and the irresistible aroma of frying bannock sizzling with melted lard and dribbling with hot raspberry jam, could lure him out. After supper, Rose and Esther drank a pot of tea in the parlor, Rose reading her Bible, Esther flipping through her own thick book, underlining with a pen, muttering impreca-tions. As the evening wore on, they heard Hugo stirring on the other side of the wall. From time to time he coughed and grumbled incomprehensible things. Around eight-thirty he came out, and entered the parlor with a sheet of paper in one hand. He plunked himself down on the footstool in front of the hearth and glanced at Rose. He tapped the paper with a forefinger.

"So," he began, "so—"

Esther peered at him over the top of her bifocals. "You wish to say something, Huggo?"

He cleared his rheumy throat. "So, Rose, you're making the little pictures again."

"Yes, Hugo", Rose smiled. "I have made two others today."

"Three in one day! Rather overproductive of you. Well, aren't you going to show them to me?"

"If you wish", Rose replied uncertainly. She went upstairs to her studio and stood there for a few minutes, deliberating. She felt no timidity in showing the comets and white horses. When it came to the portrait of Tchibi, however, she hesitated, for it was so close to the heart of her soul that it was total exposure. "Still," she thought, "to show it is to walk the dying-way, the sacrifice-way. They are good people. Though they will not understand it, neither will they mock. I will offer my heart's nakedness for Tchibi."

When the two old people bent to examine the drawings, they did not linger long over Tchibi.

"Who is this lad?" Hugo asked.

"He is my brother."

"So, you have a family", Esther said curiously.

"I am alone in the world. I have not seen my little brother in many years. He was a boy when we last met. Where he is I do not know. The picture is how I think of him."

Hugo put the drawing aside and peered closely at the horses bolting under the rain of comets. Esther continued to regard Rose's eyes thoughtfully.

"I like this one", Hugo said. "Here's your old cosmological sense loud and clear. Drama, movement, mystery, darkness, and light. Eloquent complexification, yet fetchingly restrained."

"Please with the baroque praises, Huggo. Rose, it is as strong as a blow. Will these comets destroy the earth?"

"I do not know, Esther. It is merely how the thought came

483

to me, in pictures, without words, without an end to the story."

"You know," Hugo mused sitting back, the lines of his face easing, "you know, when I was a boy, I used to walk out in the hills beyond Birmingham. Out as far as Kingstanding." He chuckled to himself. "I always thought someday I would meet a king standing out there. I was a romantic in those days; at fourteen years of age I was a romantic. The Americans were preparing to inflate the economy of the West with their greed, Wilson was making speeches at Versailles, the war to end all wars was over, and the streets were full of lads with missing limbs. My father was out of work that year. There wasn't enough money for coal. My mother was feeding us three times a day on porridge. Yet I was never happier. Spent too much time in the Museum, I suppose, looking at too many Pre-Raphaelites. One Saturday I walked and walked till the leather was falling off my boots, and the hobs began to dig into the soles of my feet. I didn't care. I was looking for a king standing, and I knew I would find him that very day. As dusk came on, my heart began to sink. The day was ending and I had not found him. A black cloud descended on me. I'm a fool, I said to myself. I'm a dreamer, just like Dad says. I turned to walk back to the city, and suddenly I saw a sight that stopped me dead in my tracks. Beside the road, lights were coming on in an old brick manor house. In a great round window I saw the king. He was standing with one arm reaching for me, and the other touching his chest. Below him in the field three white horses were grazing."

Hugo shook his head. "When you're a kid, everything's bigger than life. The king was a stained-glass window, of course. Some kind of chapel. The horses weren't bucking or galloping. They were as quiet as a boneyard, just lifted their heads and watched me pass. There weren't any stars falling. But it was like a glorious sign, like happiness that comes out of nowhere at the very moment when everything seems most dark."

"So, did you go in and meet the king?" Esther asked.

"Of course not. I went home. I drew the scene with a stub of pencil on lined paper. Biggest mistake I ever made."

"Why do you say that, Hugo?" Rose asked.

"Because once I started drawing I couldn't stop. It took over my life. It made me what I am."

"But that is a wonderful thing, Hugo!" Rose exclaimed. "You are a wonderful man!"

Hugo and Esther chuckled simultaneously.

"Thank you", Hugo said. "I shall survive a few days longer on that gratuitous and entirely inaccurate observation."

Esther peered at him over the top of her bifocals.

"Huggo, there's bannock on the stove, and that raspberry jam you're addicted to. I made the bannock myself. Rose taught me."

"A splendid idea", he said slapping his knees and creaking to an upright position. As he went out the door, Esther called to him. "Make us another pot of tea, will you?"

"Coming right up, my love!"

The two women smiled at each other as they listened to the sound of a banging kettle, water faucets, and squeaking cupboard doors. Suddenly Esther grew serious and pointed to the drawing of Tchibi.

"You love him, whoever he is. I do not think he is your brother."

Embarrassed, Rose nodded. "Yes, I love him. He is the brother of my heart, not of my blood. He was given to me."

"It is a powerful work of art, Rose. It is the best of the three."

"Hugo did not seem to like it."

"Huggo is distracted by the lovely dramas you made in the first two. He is seeing only his memories. This is a gift to us, because your pictures have spoken to something long buried in him. It may even awaken him."

"I prayed for this."

"You prayed, did you?" Esther said, cocking a dubious eye. "More important, you painted."

To the many souls Rose carried on her back, including Marco, Carlotta, Bobby, Mrs. Morgan, Deirdre, Voolf-gong, and all the others, Hugo and Esther were now added. It surprised her that she had not thought to do so before. The old couple had seemed so much in love, so kind, so creative. Now their hidden pain was emerging, and Hugo's especially needed the sacrifice-way. The medicine-drug he had imbibed for many years was indeed killing him, she saw, yet she was encouraged by the way he had responded so quickly to the three horses.

Rose's back ached more than ever, though her spirits were steadily lifting. Most mornings she went to Mass at the local parish, accepting with a certain resignation that the sweetness after Communion was again declining in frequency and strength, as if the Beating Heart were telling her to go back into the world with him resting inside of her. It seemed that he was asking her to live as other people did, with little consolation, for to feed on consolations alone was to remain a pampered child who wanted nothing but jam, jam without bannock, jam without the labor of baking and washing, jam without waiting in hunger. As the consolations came and went, it seemed to Rose that she could not read a consistent pattern in them. He embraced her whenever he knew it was right to do so.

She did notice, however, that they were more frequent just before particular sufferings or humiliations. Lesser when the ordinary things of life were going well, when there was little pain in her body. When she suffered with him, he blessed her, though on Fridays it was *only* suffering and darkness, especially at the third hour, a single hour in which all colors drained from the world and she knelt on the bare floorboards of her studio or bedroom and held on, held on, held on to the memory of his constant returnings while a *kinoje* spirit seemed to strike her on the back again and again with a willow switch. Or perhaps it was the *Zeitgeist* punishing her for its expulsion. On Sundays there was little or no pain, and no darkness; there was always a touch of sweetness, her heart and mind light, without worries, without regrets. It was the only day of the week that she refrained from entering her studio. Instead, she developed the habit of making a fine dinner for Hugo and Esther because they were toiling in their studios, as if all days were alike.

"Are you painting again, Esther?" Rose asked one evening as they puttered about the kitchen.

"Yes, of course."

"Are they pictures of birds?"

"Yes."

"Did you sell your painting of the pigeon seller?"

"Yes."

"You sold it to feed us, didn't you?"

Esther shrugged. "I sold it to feed myself as well. And Huggo."

"Has Hugo returned to his roller-painting?"

"I do not know. I am no longer permitted to enter his studio. It is my guess that he is still wrestling with the *Zeitgeist*."

"I do not think so, Esther. For the *Zeitgeist* has been banned from this house, though its marks are still upon Hugo's mind."

Esther shot a puzzled look at her, frowned, shrugged, and went on chopping rancid liver into Goldie's dish. Later that evening, Hugo entered the parlor with a large sheet of blue Ingres paper in his hand.

"Ahem", he said.

"Why do you disturb us, Huggo? Can't you see we're reading?"

"Important announcement, ladies: Joycean ineluctable modalities become eluctable. In a word, end of era, beginning of new one. Behold!"

487

He spread the sheet of paper and held it open in his spattered fingers.

"Oh, Huggo", Esther sighed, clasping her face between both hands.

"Oh, Hugo!" Rose said, beaming.

"I know, I know, it's retrograde and derivative, but it has given me a perverse pleasure."

Three human figures wrestled with a wild horse prancing on a field. The turf was blood red, the sky a chaos of cobalt, the humans black and bronze, the horse a muscular unleashing of titanium and silver.

Hugo tried to look humble. "Géricault's *Horse Reined In by Slaves* had something to do with it, of course. And Miss Wâbos, our resident alien."

"Yes, yes, Huggo, all of that is visible, yet it is your own. It is magnificent!"

"Io, that horse frightens me, Hugo, with its great power and beauty, but it is a happy fright."

Hugo gave a belly laugh. "You think so? Well, it's outdated, of course. But who cares if it's outdated? Who the hell cares about all that? I enjoyed making it."

Esther did something that Rose had not yet seen during the weeks she had lived in the house. Esther tottered to her feet and embraced Hugo, stood on tiptoes, and kissed him full on the lips.

He blushed. "Ah, my Stradivarius-woman, my peach-wife, my droll and lovely. What a numbskull I am. What a dreaming ninny and boiled Bohemian balderdash I have been. Give me another of those kisses."

Rose considered it the right moment to go to the kitchen to make a pot of tea. When she returned to the parlor she found Hugo and Esther seated side by side on the sofa, holding hands, gazing without words at the picture of the horse.

"So, Rose," Hugo said. "Are you offended that I copy you?"

"No, Hugo, for to copy is to learn. It is to love what one sees. It is to pass on the seeing to another."

"What about originality? What about creativity and—"

"To create is to love, Hugo. To love is to create."

The old couple looked at their strange little boarder and nodded.

After they had consumed a pot of tea and a plateful of bannock, they all sat back smiling to themselves, musing on their own thoughts, casting glances from time to time at the amazing horse that had bucked and bolted out of Hugo after such a long sterility.

"I decline to accept the end of man", Hugo pronounced grandly, solemnly, into the comfortable silence.

"And I decline to accept the degradation of man", Esther replied.

"There *is* a difference", Hugo countered.

"They are the same", said Esther in a stringent tone that allowed no contradiction.

"Tch, tch, tch, not at all the same, my dear, though there is some overlapping of intention in the beginning stages of resistance. I, for example, decline to accept the end of man, yet I do not presume to prohibit the degradation of man."

"Well I, for one, certainly do. At least in my work."

"That you do. That you do very well indeed."

"Yes, I do", Esther said sharply. "And so should you!"

The exchange now spiraled upward into a stratosphere which would remain forever beyond Rose's ability to fly. Astonished by the dramatic shift from marital affection to ferocious debate, she wondered if it would end in a frenzy of mutual interruption, the torn flesh of ideas floating in a pool of bloody emotion.

"Color is the test, Huggo. Like a diabetic's strip dipped in urine. The world-catastrophe is gray, steel and slate, and ash, and iron. When the world is finally rendered down to a limited palette, to *argent taupe*, then we will know it has arrived."

"No, no, no, Esther! That is where you are so wrong. The world-catastrophe—the visual field—will always appear in bright colors, but ordinary. So that when the retina of the eye registers a normal spectrum, it prompts the voice of reason to say: 'You see, all is fundamentally intact, all is well, complete with ordinary difficulties, which is life!' And all the while you are choking on the ashes."

"Of course, on this we agree. We have always agreed on this. Why do you tell me what I already know?"

"For elucidation, for the sake of our guest. Remember, in the ashen world there is always disorientation and denial, no matter how bright the colors."

"Are you blind? She may be a little disoriented, but in her, life affirms itself. Did you not look closely at the three pictures she made?"

"Of course, of course, but all of us distract ourselves, in one way or another, from the charnel house of man."

"She does not hide, she does not distract herself."

"It is a matter of degree. The whole world is in denial."

"Some, not all, Huggo. Denial is for those who do not value life—until it is their turn to be escorted to the place of execution. Or to the station of betrayal."

"My dear, *I* am the family pessimist, not you. Do not usurp my rights. You must not pester your wounds."

"I will pester if I so wish, for they are my own wounds, not yours. And I say large betrayals have their roots in the myriad small betrayals. It begins with one. However small."

"Why do you speak of betrayal?" Hugo said defensively. "Do you think these ten abstract years have been a betrayal?"

"I did not say that. Everything becomes useful, as long as one *returns* from his journey into absurdity. As long as he is not *swallowed* by delusions of grandeur."

"But those—the delusions—can be reversed."

"If recognized for what they are."

"But *who* ever accomplishes *that*?"

Esther pointed to the horse. "You did, Huggo. You did."

Stopping in mid-sentence, Esther turned to Rose and said in a voice as paper-thin as Belgian pastries, though not as sweet:

"Don't you agree, Rose?"

Caught and shamed by her inattention, she replied, "I don't know. I don't understand."

Which satisfied them. The old couple laughed sympathetically, held hands again, and gazed at her fondly.

"Don't worry, Rose", Hugo said. "We spar because we love."

One morning over breakfast, Esther said to Rose, "When will you paint?—I mean *real* paint?"

"I do not know, Esther. There is an emptiness in me. A waiting."

"Well, don't wait too long."

"May I visit you in your studio today? May I watch while you paint?"

"Ordinarily I do not like company in my studio. Do you think it will help you get started on your own work?"

"It might."

Remembering how inspired she had been by Sister Madeleine, with her bonbons and her enthusiasm, Rose sat on a three-legged stool in the corner of Esther's studio and made herself invisible. She watched closely while the woman worked on a portrait of an elderly lady boiling red water in a washtub.

"Are you still there?" Esther asked after an hour.

"Yes. Is my presence disturbing you? I will leave if you wish."

Esther gave her a wry smile. "Stay. The company is nice, as long as it doesn't say too much. But you needn't be entirely mute. You can shift on the seat and scratch your nose if you wish."

"Thank you, Esther. May I ask a question?"

"Ask."

"Who is the woman in the painting?"

"Why do you want to know?"

"Because she resembles my grandmother. Many times have I seen her washing laundry in a tub over a fire, just like that. The burning logs are the same, her black coat is the same. The snow upon the ground is the same."

"That is my grandmother. She died in a punishment camp by the name of Breendonk, south of Antwerp."

"Oh, I am so sorry, Esther."

"It was, I suppose, a mercy. She could easily have survived long enough to be shipped to Auschwitz with the other Belgian Jews."

"Were you among them?"

"Of course."

"Can you tell me about your grandmother?"

"What do you want to know?"

"Anything."

"Why do you want to know?"

"Because I too have lost my grandmother. Because I have no family now."

Moved, trying not to show it, Esther put her brush into a jar of turpentine. She sighed. She looked out the window and began to speak.

"So much I remember. It all comes back to me. If I could paint every detail I would, but must be content with small pictures that capture only a little of the beauty of our life. I remember watching my grandmother labor over the laundry in the back yard of our apartment block. That day she was tossing an armload of sheets into a tub of cold water, scrubbing them with salt—her hands were so red and chapped. The sheets were saturated in blood, the horror of my mother's blood making pink froth. My grandmother turned to me and said, 'How

492

wonderful, Esther, to have a new baby sister.' When the blood was out of the cloth, she wrung the sheets and put them into a cauldron boiling on a fire of crackling chestnut branches from the tree we had trimmed the previous winter. As she stirred it with a paddle, Grandmother made it seem so ordinary, so happy a labor, yet it was the spilled blood of my mother.

"The blood connected all living things to each other, connecting them also through the chain of time, spilling or melting from all things in time—I can see it in other memories. Blood sprayed across the cobblestones of the Antwerp market where peasants hooked the wire-bound feet of hares dangling upside down, with ruby droplets on the amber noses. Grandmother, adjusting her waxed wig and the lace shawl she had made, purchased one from the kosher butcher for the Shabbos stew pot. Blood spilled in a thousand different ways. But that was later.

"Before the Germans came, there were good memories, because the world was beginning for me. I was young and strong. I was a stubborn child, very rebellious. I can still see Papa storming up and down the parlor of the apartment. Oh, he was angry. 'A vase painter is not desirable, not desirable in the least, Esther. But it is *permissible*, the flowers, the curlicues, the lines and decorations that the Most High has written into the earth, and the artisans of old placed within the Temple. But not the faces, Esther, not the idols! Never the art school, like the goyim! Never, Esther, never!'

"Because Papa was a liberal Hasid, a very rare creature indeed, he relented, after much soul-searching and pain. He and my grandfather had lost their positions in the street of diamond merchants. There was no income; we needed to eat. And so, I went to work in a china factory.

"After that, the dark times came. I saw other fires, so many, many fires, the roaring logs on which the human bodies were thrown.

"And the *Shema* prayer?" Rose asked.

"And the *Shema*, for all my family was taken, and all of them perished except for me, even my baby sister was taken. And where they are buried I do not know, except I think that their ashes were taken up, not so much as the souls of the just—though they were just—but as ashes that went up, up, higher, higher until they hit the emptiness of space and drifted down through the skies of Europe and enriched the many gardens and fields that survived."

"When did you meet Hugo?"

"In autumn of 1945. In a Red Cross camp for survivors. The first time I saw him, I was opening a package on my cot when he came into the dormitory with a mop. At first I was frightened; I thought he was a German, he was so tall and blond. But the face was all wrong for a German. And the way his body moved, bent as if he were afraid of *us*, or ashamed of what he saw spread out before him, the rows of skeleton women. Not a trace of the Aryan Cain in him. But what kind of Abel was this! He was so shy, with a wild, sad look in his dreamer's eyes, as if all his life he had longed for the sight of galloping horses and was denied it. I had not seen a face like it in years. I did not look at him for more than a second or two because a nurse had placed something more interesting in my lap. The package contained socks and a bar of chocolate, a needle and thread, and women's things, sent by an American relief society.

"The amazing young man mopped his way along the cement floor of the hut, stepping carefully around the skeleton women whose eyes swiveled to observe his passage. As he came closer to me, I saw that his eyes were blinking with horror and trying not to show it.

" 'We are alive,' I said to him in French, for I did not yet know he was an Englishman. In his inimitably bad French he replied, 'I know, Madame.'

" 'We will not hurt you,' I said.

" 'This, also, I know, Madame.'

" 'Then why do you stare at us?'

"Of course he could not reply to this. So I said, 'Speak with me, for I have spoken only with evil men for three years.' Tears filled his eyes and he sat down at the foot of the bed.

" 'Are you a coward?' I asked scornfully. I was angry at all men and wished to punish one.

" 'I am a conscience-objector,' he answered. Of course, he meant conscientious objector. A pacifist.

" 'Conscience-objector? What is that?' I said to him.

" 'It is to refuse to do harm for any reason', he said.

" 'You', I declared, 'are an imbecile!'

"Without taking offense he replied, 'I am an artist, which is probably the same thing.'

"Pity or love, who can say what brought us together? Perhaps the fact that I told him I, too, was an artist, a painter; or perhaps because my hair had not yet grown in again and there were no wigs to be found at that early stage, and because, I suppose, I had passed through fire into a world where the demands of the Most High had become, to a certain extent, rather abstract.

"He told me he was from England, that he believed in Peace and in Art.

" 'What do you paint?' he asked.

" 'Flowers', I said, 'and lines and curlicues—and the structure of a demented universe.' As soon as I said this, I shocked both him and myself by bursting into wails and screeches for the first time since my capture. Most people would have been repulsed. I suppose he found me fascinating in a macabre sort of way. He was ridiculously handsome. For a skeleton woman, this was an impossible situation. I was utterly humiliated on every level.

" 'Leave me', I screamed at him. But he did not leave. He sat and looked into my eyes. He said nothing, merely looked. When finally I controlled myself, I said,

" 'Go find someone fat and English and definitely not Jewish.'

"'I am Jewish", he said in that rusty voice of his. 'I am constitutionally unable to fall in love with any woman who is not Jewish. Moreover, Madame, I am fatefully attracted to slender women.'

"I began to laugh hysterically. He took my hand. I slapped it away. He took it again, and I let it stay there. How warm and gentle his hands. Hands that had never struck another person. Hands that had never killed.

"'I am no longer a believer', he said. 'Does it matter to you that I am not?'

"I was dumbstruck. I could not reply to this.

"'Would it ruin my chances?' he asked.

"This was so ridiculously alien to my recent experience, so replete with the sentiment of cheap romantic theater, that I shook my head in disbelief. He mistook it as an answer to his question. Yes, Rose, always we have misunderstood each other's meanings, even from the beginning. He smiled at me. I smiled at him. It really hurt my face, that smile. My first smile in years. That did it. We were in love. We have not fallen out of it. Don't ask me why. We're an insanely improbable pair."

As the last scraps of snow disappeared beneath the April light, Rose walked again in the unfolding world, and rediscovered her love for it—all of it. Everywhere in the streets meltwater ran into oily backyard puddles, and in the brave little front gardens crocuses pushed pink-white-yellow-mauve through the slime to trumpet victory once again. Cats soaked in the sun on fire escapes, and in the alleyway the clothesline was loaded with dozens of Hugo's long black socks, curling and looping in a light breeze, like mysterious Hebrew letters.

Rose took her pastel box and drawing pad outside most days and would sit sideways on bus-stop benches looking down the streets at the neighborhood children. She sketched their coats of many colors in splashes of red and blue and brown. Her hands were numbed from drawing in that cold of almost-spring, when the day's puddles still froze at night. Sometimes she gripped the instruments of light and darkness so tightly they would snap.

As the weeks passed and the grass grew again through the greasy winter film, she would take out a box of watercolors and some heavier paper. She tried to capture the rolling spring clouds, the boats on the harbor water, the rust and oxide and blood tints of the aging tenements. If the memory of the forest was fading just a little, she was compensated by a sharpened attention to the natural geometry and the decorations that the Most High had smuggled into the city. Hugo and Esther were careful not to overpower her with praise for her new work, but they were pleased by it. As much as they were able, they refrained from lectures. They had become protective of that shoot which, like all flowering things in the urban field, was both potent and frail.

One day Rose took a little pastel drawing that she had done and showed it to Hugo in his studio. She noticed with a certain disappointment that he had taken his image of the horses and stored it behind some boxes of trash in a corner. He had begun a huge canvas full of undefined blocks of lifeless form. Or absence of form. Her heart sank when she saw it. She said nothing.

"What's that you've got clutched in your hot little mitt?" he asked.

"Something I made today on the street. Is this good, do you think?"

"What do I think, you ask? What I think doesn't really matter, does it?" He peered at her ferociously. "Do *you* think it's good?"

"Well . . . yes, I do, Hugo."

"Then it's good."

"Thank you, Hugo."

497

"Don't thank me. Thank yourself. Now, answer me this: When are you going to do *real* painting?"

"What is *real* painting?"

"Oils, girl! Oils!"

Hugo and Esther gave Rose old half-tubes of oils that neither of them wanted anymore. And she would try, oh, she would go out with a portable easel into the parks and try to make small mirrors of the greenery she found there. And wondered why she dried up, could not do it. She cried in frustration and once went so far as to pitch the box into the mud beside the walkway. Then quickly retrieved it, shamefaced. Whenever she tried to make herself quiet inside, to go back to the feelings she had once known in the solitary places on the skull at Threefinger Lake, or the pool of cleansing, or the edge of the barrens by the box full of a dead woman, it seemed that she could, if she tried, paint. But the feelings had become weaker since her arrival in Montreal. No matter what she did, the towering geological formations of tenements and office towers, the rumbling within it, *l'arrogance* on its gaudy face, blocked the flow of creation that only pastels and pencils were capable of opening. Yet she sometimes took the portable easel to Mount Royal, the little green mountain rising like virtue from the standing ruins. It was quiet there, the air full of flowing. She would draw it, and sometimes succeeded in splotching oil color onto the drawing, but the end result was always lifeless.

As months went by and autumn began, a small collection of drawings, pastels and watercolor sketches accumulated in her room. She was proud of them, happy that patience could achieve so much. But she did not consider herself a real artist. Her concept of such a calling was defined by the exotic romance of the grizzled old man and the mysterious old woman, and further enlarged by the intense young people who came in gypsy clothes and beads to sell their own art in the square of Place d'Armes or along narrow Dickens Street in the Old City, where the tourists roamed throughout summer and into the autumn.

One Saturday morning, Rose went down to Place d'Armes and sat against the wall of a stone building, with a stack of her pastels and water colors at her feet. On either side of her, artists were selling their pictures, their works fixed by clothespins to strings or mounted on mobile display boards. Browsers strolled along looking at the images, some stopping to buy. Many paintings and drawings were being sold that day, but no one seemed interested in Rose's pastels. They always moved quickly on, after no more than a superficial glance at her pile, after one look at the hunched girl in grubby clothing, the Indian face, the eyes so shy that they mistook her expression for furtiveness. The artist to the left of Rose advised that she should spread the pictures out along the five feet of wall allotted to her. The wind tried to scatter the papers, so Rose weighted them with small pieces of brick that she found in an alley. And the *binemin* stone that she always carried with her in the deer-hide bag. Even so, the tourists continued to take a single look and pass on swiftly.

Rose knew that her work was rather poor in comparison to that of the art students and the professionals. As she listened to them socializing on either side of her, she began to sense what their culture was all about. To be an artist was to love candlelight and agony, chianti and ecstasy. Art was Paris and New York and London. It was pressurized and mercurial. Painting was heroic struggle, the quest to tear spirit from the elements and reassemble it in better shapes. And to sell the product.

"I am not like them. Io, what a mistake I have made", she said to herself at the end of the day, gathering her pathetic bundle of papers together as she made ready for the escape.

That night she described her attempt at marketing to Hugo and Esther. They frowned as they listened—which she misinterpreted.

"I'm sorry I wasn't able to sell any", Rose apologized. "I wanted so much to contribute to the household expenses and to pay a little rent."

They rolled their eyes. "Oy, oy", Esther said. "Huggo, will you *please* explain a few things to this child! It is not the rent, Rose. That is not our motivation. When, *when* will you understand us?"

"Easy, Esther, easy. We hardly understand each other, you and I, so how can we expect our guest to——"

If they had been gentle at first, they now become firm. They told her in no uncertain terms never to repeat the foolishness of becoming a street artist.

"You must go *inward*, Rose", Esther said with great severity. "Not outward. If you go to the market streets, you will look too much at what sells, then you will come home and paint what sells. The pretty mementos for tourists. Then you will become a prostitute."

Horror crossed Rose's face.

"The prostitution of art is what Esther means", Hugo mumbled. "You become a machine, you sell your gift for a few dollars, and in the end the gift dies. Sooner or later it dies."

One day Rose showed them her most recent work, a pastel drawing of a scene she had witnessed in a cul-de-sac on Rue St. Benoît. It depicted children wheedling candy from each other in front of the *épicerie*.

"It is charming", said Esther doubtfully. "It has flavor, and you are learning to be more free with your strokes." But there was something not entirely happy in her voice. "All right, I hope you keep up with this. It is a step forward."

"You mean, you think people would like these, would buy them?"

"Again! Again with the buying and selling! We are going to have to protect you from yourself, young lady. There are galleries downtown, just a notch above the street trade, that would be happy to buy these pretty things and sell them. They would give you some money—not much, you understand, because you're an unknown. Then you could say, see Huggo and Esther, I'm a real artist, just like you. Is that what you want, Rose?"

"I do not know, Esther."

"You want to become a little factory?"

"Not so fast, Esther", Hugo cut in. "Rose, Rose, don't look so crushed. By now you should be accustomed to Esther's adamantine approach to everything. Try to overlook her style of speech. Consider the content of what she's saying. On this, I think I agree with her. You have something good here. You could be a successful painter. Yes, you really could. By successful I mean you'd be able to have your own place and pay the bills and eat properly and buy materials. But not much more. I don't know how long you'd last, mind you."

Rose was busy consuming with exhilaration the idea that they believed she was good at the thing she most loved to do. She was, however, taken aback by what Hugo said next.

"You would never be happy. It would never be enough. These are very nice, yes, but you would be trapped in them. You must not become a painter of pretty things for parlors and board rooms."

"An artist is a *disturber*," said Esther, "one who upsets the comfortable people. Not to punish but to open the eyes."

This is confusing, Rose thought.

"Give it time, give it time", said Hugo, holding her small painting up to the light. When he returned it to Rose's hand, he said, "I'm worried about you. When you first came to us, you brought a roll of drawings that was full of fire and strength. It was unique. When was the last time you made something like those early ones, eh? Eh?" Fixing her with an accusing eye, he growled, "Push to the outer limits!"

"Is that where you are, Hugo?" Rose asked, "Are you at the outer limits?"

501

He thought for a second or two, took a deep breath, and scowled at her like a thundering cloud on Sinai. Esther snorted, "Style, Huggo, watch your style."

"I am approaching the limits always", he declared. "And if I should fail, it means nothing. Nothing! Because your outer limits will be different than mine."

To Rose it had seemed at first that the world of art was divided into realists and nonrealists. But the longer she lived in the city, the more she saw that the spectrum of reality extended from horizon to horizon. The borderline was not clear. She could scarcely find her own position in this range, except to see herself grouped vaguely with Esther and the other realists. And she could no more specifically place Hugo, who was over there in the distance with an equally hazy band of nonrealists. It became a source of continual puzzlement for Rose, one that she would never completely resolve, for everyone was seeking essences, developing private languages, proclaiming sincerity.

There were dozens of galleries in the city and many of them, including the large public institutes and museums, were very supportive of the kind of art Hugo believed in. One day, Rose wandered into a commercial gallery on St. Catherine Street, not far from the Ritz. When she saw that it was full of empty canvasses, she thought for a moment that it was an art supply shop. But each canvas was signed by an artist, priced at thousands of dollars, and labeled with titles such as *White Interior #12*. Rose stood back a little upset, for it seemed to her that the painting was a lie, and that the lie was being offered for sale. The canvas had no pigment on it at all. It was an emptiness offered as a something, a nothingness offered as a word. There were whole rooms full of such things: string dangling from a ceiling—*String*—and pictures of printed alphabets—*Cosmobet*—and a plastic pool with live quacking ducks in it—*Pond*. As if the role of disturber had here been liberated from the artist's traditional submission to the objectivity of appearance. As if he were set free to disturb in limitless ways.

Rose left the gallery in a daze. As she rode the city bus back to St. Henri, she stared out the window, wondering if Hugo knew something that she did not. There was so much intelligence in his theorizing. He had put his life's energy into his work. Perhaps he was speaking a visual language that was too advanced for her to comprehend.

"Is he seeking his own words-without-words?" she mused.

She prayed for him, and for herself, asking God to shed light upon her ignorance.

"Hugo?" she asked one day as she sat on a box watching him paint an abstract. It was gray and black. She disliked it greatly. She wished he would paint another horse.

"I believe you wish to interrupt me," he said gruffly, "but without taking upon yourself the weight of honest guilt."

"I don't want to bother you, but—"

"*But*—?" he said with a dramatic arching of a single eyebrow.

"But, may I ask you a question?"

"When have you ever hesitated to ask me a question? Ask away."

"Is modern art . . . a lie?"

"What do you mean by modern? That term is a big enough bag to hold all kinds of wriggling beasties."

"I mean, is abstract art a lie?"

"A lie?" He paused, eyeing her with cool appraisal.

She frowned.

"You're really asking if abstract art is *evil*, aren't you", he went on without waiting for a reply. "Your question reveals your subconscious judgment on the matter. Evil is not a word I would use. Is abstract art bad? No, not in itself. But what do we mean by bad, eh? Eh? Bad taste, bad aesthetics? Bad intention? Bad skill? Bad this and bad that? The answers to those questions are as varied as the artists."

"But is there not something wrong with throwing away life?"

"What do you mean, throwing away life? Colors are part of life, aren't they?"

"Yes", she said, knowing he was right about this, but straining for a missing thought.

"Maybe you're upset by the revolution?" he murmured, squinting at his palette.

"What revolution, Hugo?"

"The cultural revolution. The soft Maoists."

"Who?"

"My friends and mentors, the culture terrorists, the chaps who've done the coup d'état."

"I'm sorry, Hugo, I don't understand."

"The revolution has become the establishment, you see. Hierarchy cannot be avoided in human affairs, dear girl, and now that we've all become equal, the revolutionaries are in charge in a big way."

Seeing Rose's confusion, Hugo patted her shoulder.

"Don't worry overmuch about it. Tomorrow they'll be gone and another revolution will sweep through town. Your job is to do what you have to do, and pay 'em no mind."

"But, Hugo—"

His other eyebrow went up.

"But what will they destroy while they're in charge?" she asked.

He did not answer. He grimaced and went back to his painting. She saw that he was a man who painted one thing today, a conflicting thing tomorrow, and back to its opposite the day after that.

The doubt injected into Rose by the reign of abstract art was not easily dispelled. She knew that she was a simple person, barely educated, easily fooled, and thus she wondered if she had, as Hugo suggested, judged it too hastily. This was a possibility, but she could not shake the nausea that afflicted her whenever she encountered it.

Surely, Esther could explain. When Rose raised the subject in Esther's studio the next day, the older woman threw her brush into a pot of turpentine, straightened her spine, and lifted her chin in preparation for a quarrel. The quarrel was not with Rose, that was soon plain to see, for Esther began to pace back and forth, her eyes snapping, staring at the floor.

"You ask me if abstract art is a lie?" she fumed. "You ask me this! This you should not ask me, because if I start I will not stop, and then I will go and tear strips off that man in the attic!"

"Oh, Esther, I'm sorry. I shouldn't have asked."

Esther snorted. "No, you should ask. This you should ask, because if Huggo gets you painting the tire tracks, I will kill him. Simply, I will *kill* him!"

"He won't, Esther. I won't—"

"You ask if abstract art is a lie? Ha! Tell me what you see in those Nietzsche parlors funded by the government! Gashes of color, splatters of randomness, heaps of plastic, wriggling electronics, and photographs of nothingness. Where there is anything recognizable in them it is meaning mixed with meaninglessness. Absurdity and darkness and destruction dissolving into one lie—that there is nothing but death."

Esther paused for breath, her face flushed, mouth twisting bitterly.

"Thank you, Esther", Rose murmured. "I will let you get back to your painting now."

"Stay!" Esther barked. "It is the dismantled universe, sold as trash. The demolition of language itself, the empty petty egos trying to liberate spirit from matter through violation of the material of language. It is the *Endlösung*, the aristocracy of a camp! Ideas ripped to shreds so that all the world becomes Guernica, everything reduced to the screaming horse, the screaming mother, the screaming flesh, the screaming *shema*—"

Trembling, Esther stopped, turned away from Rose, and picked up her brush. Without another word she began to slap bits of color onto her canvas.

Rose got up and left.

19

Late one afternoon, as she was walking home, Rose turned a corner just in time to see a dozen children gathered around a small figure collapsed on a snowbank. They were throwing ice and gravel at him. One, the tallest, stood on tiptoes, arms thrust high bearing a large chunk of ice that he was about to hurl onto the victim's face.

"Stop!" screamed Rose and rushed forward, knocking the ice from his hands. Most of the children scattered, terrified by the black gnome that had appeared out of nowhere, but a few of the older ones remained and stared belligerently at Rose from a few paces away. They shouted accusing things in *patois* French but she did not understand them.

The victim—a boy no more than eight years of age—sat upright in the snow with his face in his hands, a trickle of blood coming down over his brow, mixing with the slush on his cheeks. Rose helped him to his feet and brushed the filth from his clothes. She turned to the others who were still shouting at her.

"Why do you do this?" she said.

They hopped around her like dogs circling their prey, mimicking her words, braying forced laughter, calling her names that the ignorant use for native people. Then, seeing that she was immovable and somewhat frightening, they went away to other games, hurling behind them mockeries and curses.

The boy sobbed quietly, his face aflame with tears and blood, snow and mud. With her handkerchief, Rose wiped his face clean. She asked him why this had happened, but he understood no English, and Rose's French was locked into the classical accent of nineteenth-century Gallic convents. Moreover, she was alarming on every level, except for the fact that she had saved him. He could only mumble brokenly the little bleats of wounded dignity.

Articulating slowly and with great care, she asked in French where he lived. He answered by pointing a finger down the street. As they walked along together, he did not speak, but kept his eyes to the ground, sniffing clots of blood from time to time. When they neared the boy's tenement, he gave Rose a quick look and said sadly, "Merci." With heavy steps he mounted a spiral staircase that wound up the exterior of the building to the third floor. Rose watched him arrive at the door, noting the darkened windows of what appeared to be an empty apartment. He let himself in with a key.

Rose sat on the step stool in Hugo's studio and told him about it. The old man grimaced without interrupting the series of strokes he was laying onto the canvas. On the easel there was a picture of men struggling to tie down a galloping red horse. Four other pictures of horses now hung on the wall, all galloping, under various weathers and moods. She was pleased to see that he had shifted again toward the world of the figurative, and realized that her prayers for him had not gone unanswered. The single return to abstraction now leaned against a far wall.

"I do not understand those children", she sighed.

"Well, Rose, I hate to bring it up, but may I ask you why such little dramas are so common in a Christian nation? Hmmm? A supposedly Christian nation?"

"I do not know", Rose said. "It seems to me that many who call themselves Christian are not so."

"An honest answer, girl, as always." He grimaced. "But two thousand years of *your* palette and the predominant color is still sanguinary. They are still stoning each other!"

"Why are they like that?" said Rose.

"You ask me? I simply do not know. The wolf in man, I suppose. Maybe somebody bloodied their pride this morning.

508

Maybe some ancestor taught them to spill blood when they don't get their way. Tell me, Rose, now that you're getting to know them, what do you think of the pretty children you put into your drawings?"

"Inside their hearts, Hugo, I do not believe they want to be as they are. They do not know the better way."

"You're an optimist, Rose. When are you going to paint the truth in those streets? Why don't you make a pastel of those cruel little faces you saw today?"

"Because I cannot believe that cruelty is the whole truth, Hugo."

"Aha!" said the old man, turning an accusing eye on her. "*Badratio* is at work here. Blasted *badratio*!"

It sounded to Rose as if he were saying something about a bad rat. She frowned and struggled to understand.

"What is a *bad-rat-see-oh*, Hugo?"

He put down his brush, wiped his nose with the back of his hand, and tapped his head with a forefinger, leaving paint on his hair.

"*Ratio* is Reason. Intellect. Mind-power. Most of us have a measure of it. Some of us try to pursue reasoned trains of thought. But sometimes all of us—and I mean *all* of us—devise seemingly rational reasons for our actions without being aware of our true motives."

Rose frowned.

"No? Then let me put it another way: There's a bad rat in the mind."

Rose shuddered.

"Nibbling, nibbling, nibbling at the core of reason", Hugo added.

"Hugo, is it not more correct to say that a bad rat is in the heart?"

"Whatever", he shrugged. "You get the idea."

She nodded.

He pointed to her picture of happy children that she had given him weeks ago, and which he had pinned to the wall by his easel.

"Pretty, pretty, pretty", he said.

"What do you mean, Hugo?"

"You make these pretty scenes because methinks you are subconsciously worried that no one is going to buy a picture of children brutalizing other children. Who wants to hang that over a living room sofa, eh? Eh?"

"But, Hugo, it seems to me a better thing to show what is most true and beautiful in man. Why should I show what is false in us?"

"That's where you're wrong! You have already painted it all, the true and the untrue within us. Look at that native man you drew, the one with the birds on his shoulders. It's not a pretty picture, but it's a true one. So take that eye of yours and apply it to our charming young neighbors here in Saint Henri. We are *all*, every one of us, those little monsters in the streets. There's no denying it. We are children hurling ice into each other's faces. When are you going to face the fact that you can't paint beauty until you have a good hard look at the ugliness?"

"But I do see it. Why must I paint it?"

"Because to paint is to protest! And in the protest you ask the only real question: Where is the one who designed this patched-up old motor of a universe—the one you think runs like a sterling Rolls-Royce in the eye of God? Tell me, Rose, why does he not tinker, eh? Why does he not rev the engine, eh? And clean the spark plugs, eh? Or is it all a bad joke? Maybe it's just the smiling Buddha of time moving toward the moment when each two-legged, no-legged soul will face the eternal night and walk into it with no trail back, his past rolling up behind him like a filthy rug. Or is it a carpetbag of personal history that will contain his dirty laundry for eternity? Answer me that, eh?"

Whenever Hugo was both poetic and bitter, Rose knew that creativity was upon him. She felt it best to leave him with his galloping horses, for she understood that they were his particular way of asking questions, or simply loving what could have been, and might yet come to pass. Before leaving, she could not resist one little question.

"Why do you not paint the cruelty, Hugo?"

"Because, because. . . .", he sputtered. "Because I would paint it too black, and all that black paint would kill me. The black would cover the whole canvas of life, you see, and there wouldn't be enough whisky to wash it off. And if I did that, it would kill Esther too."

"You paint the horses for Esther?"

"Yes, for her. So she won't worry over me."

She liked to do menial tasks for Esther and Hugo, especially for Hugo, because he was so much like a clumsy harmless bear who did not know how to care for himself. Esther had often been ill during the previous months, short of breath and low on energy, and for that reason the responsibility for much of the cooking had fallen to Rose. She was glad of this, for it was a good excuse to abstain from learning to use oil paints. In addition, she helped in Hugo's studio, spreading white gesso basecoats upon his canvases with a paint roller. "Ah, here is the origin of his speckles", she exclaimed to herself, discovering how rollers would spray colored confetti on everything around, but mostly on her own arm and face. She also liked to tack the creases of stretched canvases across their frames. And sand into fuzz the large rectangles of hardboard on which Hugo would sometimes paint. She washed his brushes daily so that they would not become bent and gummy in the tin cans of solvent. She was sent off to the hardware store on numerous errands: "More turpentine, Rose. I'm all out of bloody turps." He would always be missing something—nails or framer's tacks, eyelets, rags, charcoal, varnish, wire, or tea . . . or patience. She would watch the old man's steady, stooping concentration, how he agonized over hues and tones, roughing up texture to match his mood, almost weeping into his palette at times from helpless dissatisfaction, as he wrestled with stallions on turbulent fields of blood.

One afternoon, as Rose sat in Hugo's studio tearing up threadbare sheets into rags, she felt the air electrify with his frustration. The artist, with a stomp and a roar, hurled a wide, wet brush across the room to smack against the far wall. It stuck for a moment before sliding down slowly onto a pile of magazines. Rose hopped over and retrieved it quickly, handing it back to him when he finally lifted his face from his hands. She could say nothing to Hugo that would be of any use, but looked at him sympathetically, trying to comfort him with her eyes.

He took her by the arm and pointed at his canvas saying, "Look, Rose, look. How could I be so stupid? I have boxed myself into a corner."

Rose stared at it without comprehension: A tiny human form riding a giant horse leaping into the sky. Blue and green were the only colors.

"You see?" he demanded.

"No", Rose said, for it seemed to her that Hugo was not boxed in at all, that he was moving beyond the forms he had learned from Géricault. Now his own language was building upon the foundation. Clearly, he was afraid of the new power emerging from himself.

"I think it is beautiful, Hugo. It is growing. *You* are growing."

"Beautiful? I am *so* sick of that word! Please do not use that expletive again in my presence. Its meaning is utterly unreliable."

"Of course, Hugo. Though the painting *is* very beautiful."

"Arrrgh!"

He went back to work, shaking his head, groaning as he gave

birth to his galloping children. By the end of the day he called Rose up to the attic to see what he had done. He was now beaming with pleasure, he had conquered some problem that was still elusive to Rose. She could see no dramatic difference in the painting, yet to him it had become a new creation. Upon looking again, however, she saw that the form was now more fluid, as if the horse and rider were swimming in the air. The air was a deeper blue, a blush of blood was coursing just beneath the horse's dappled skin, and the face of the rider was exultant with fear and hope inextricably combined. A single hind hoof touched a field of incandescent green. Throughout the work, sparks of silver and orange brought it to life.

It was all so interesting, all so puzzling.

Beyond room and board they could pay her nothing for her small labors. She felt she should be paying them, but no, they liked the situation just as it was. She was not a servant, she was more an apprentice, their young friend, and, though none of the three would openly admit it, a daughter.

Esther would hint at Rose's training now and then, saying that canvas was still cheap and remnants could be had for nothing at the chandler factory. The old brushes could be revived. There were always unused tubes of oil color lying about that she could have.

"You cannot stay with pastels and watercolors forever, Rose."

"Why is that, Esther?"

"Because the medium itself expands the powers of the eye."

"But both are colors."

"Of course, in the same way that some words are common to all languages. But certain thoughts are impossible in certain languages."

"Yes, I think I see what you mean, Esther."

"Are you too proud to ask us for oil paints, for canvas, for a little training? Are you too much the genius to be the humble beggar?"

Io, Esther's tongue could sting!

"No, it is just that I am already a burden. I do not wish to take more of your time, for you are a great artist."

"A burden, she says! A burden!" Esther rolled her eyes and slapped her own forehead. "Huggo, help me with this poor child. She is beyond me, simply beyond my ability to convince. She thinks she is the fringe people and must pick through the trash cans of an unwelcoming world."

"My darling," Hugo replied, "so soon you forget. Did you not feel that way yourself, once upon a time?"

"Stop lecturing, Huggo. Convince this child that she is not a burden."

"You are not a burden, Rose."

"You heard him, Rose. You heard what he said. Now, no more nonsense."

And so, she promised to try oil paints again. But how? Her copies of *The Raft of the Medusa* and *The Sleep of Reason* had been her only serious attempts, and the memory of them was saturated in the pain of those half-remembered days, more than a year ago. Or was it two years? A lifetime seemed to have passed, as if she had always lived with Hugo and Esther.

One Monday morning, after the old couple had gone upstairs to their studios, Rose locked the door of her small studio and prayed. She asked again for the painting-grace. There was peace in the silence that followed. She took a ragged-edged square of canvas and tacked it to her drawing board. Upon it she drew a copy of Tchibi's portrait with a dark pencil. The lines were more fine than charcoal. It did not feel the same, it did not feel quite right. Yet as she worked on the eyes she saw that precision carried its own power. The eyes leaped out at her and pulled her inside, until she *became* Tchibi as she drew, and erased, and blew away the rubber debris, and redrew, and expanded, and added details, the little holes upon his skin, the vibrations of wings in the background sky, stroke after stroke of the pencil eliciting the sensation of loon songs, for all song is but a vibration of waves in the air, and visible lines are the outer edges of a wave.

Then the actual paint. The bare palette was terrifying. If she chose one path it eliminated other paths. And if she added a second color—burnt umber for instance, or red oxide—this also changed the course of things. But you must choose, she admonished herself. God chose first, she explained. You are not making yourself into God, no, if you are placing your little choosing within his great choosing. Has he not put a little of himself in you, a reflection of the light, in order to share the power of his love?

Yes, so the choosing is love, it is creating *with* God, and it is good!

Bravely, she laid a row of tubes on the tray beside her palette. After a deep breath she set to work, choosing echoing strokes of black and white and sweet-green fire. The shattering of paralysis stirred memory, led to other colors. A mix of raw sienna, ocher, and titanium buff for the skin. Red oxide alternating with burnt umber for the hair. Experimenting with blending, applying it, scraping it off. Io, it was hard to do this painting! When she took a break from it and stepped back a few paces to see what she had done, she burst into tears. It was very ugly. It was a soup of mud.

Esther rapped at the door. "What is the matter, Rose? Why do you cry? The whole house can hear you!"

Rose let her into the room and showed her the disaster.

Esther pursed her lips and furrowed her brow. "Now, now, it's not so bad that you must cry about it. Here, look at this." Esther stepped forward, and with a rag deftly wiped some of the paint from Tchibi's forehead, cheeks, nose, upper lip, chin.

"See how the light beneath appears. See the three dimensions?"

And yes, a face had emerged, not precisely Tchibi's, but strong.

"Esther, it is wonderful. But I thought a painter only put paint *onto* a canvas."

"You put it on, you take some off, you mess with your fingers if you like, you fix, you putter, you clean the baby and dress him, no? Like that. You start with the baby and soon you have a big strapping man."

Esther took a tube of paint, squeezed some bright ocher onto the palette, and with a fine-haired brush dashed a few thin strokes of light around the nostrils and under the pouches of the eyes. After that, a touch of red mixed with purple. She thinned it with a drop of linseed oil and blended it. Then a sheen of blood washed over the cheeks and the lips. Olive green under the ridges of the brow. Titanium white, with hair strokes of grey and blue in it, and one of the birds became silver. Brown with black speckles turned the other into a partridge.

"This ball he stands on—what color should it be?"

"It is a globe of white quartz."

"So—maybe white?"

"White with silver and blue in it, for it is a loon-star, it is a fire that fell from the heavens, from the river of souls."

"The river of souls? All right, here, you do it, Rose, for the image is in your mind's eye. It's beyond me."

Rose obeyed Esther, and was pleased with what she accomplished. Then she experimented with other parts of the image, the tan deer-hide clothing, the flecks of brilliant hot color for emphasis, as sparks that would bring it to life, just as Hugo had brought his flying horse to life. Esther sat on a wooden crate and observed. Time flowed without measure. It was nightfall when Rose finished the painting. The two woman stood back and examined it. It was not Tchibi exactly, but it was a powerful portrait of someone.

"So, you want to have a big cry now?"

"No, Esther", Rose smiled. "It is good. I learned much from you today."

"You will promise to keep painting?"

"Yes, I promise."

But Rose abandoned her promise after that single painting. It was so unlike Tchibi that it dismayed her. Painting was too large for her. It was too large for the world inside her, which was already filled with preoccupations. She returned to pastels, and answered vaguely whenever Esther or Hugo asked if she was painting. They understood perfectly the truth behind her small and rather innocent evasions. They did not probe, they did not pressure. They respected the mysterious processes of growth; above all they revered her freedom.

Esther spoke often of the need for perseverance, the necessity of small steady paces of effort and a continuous renewal of dedication. Yet it seemed that her strength was not infectious, she could not inject it into Hugo, who was easily discouraged.

"He is afraid", Esther once explained when the old man was not in the room. "It was not always so. Before his breakdown he was the prince and darling of the dealers. The markets of commercial cunning have rescued me from the garbage cans, painting by painting, dollar by dollar, but he has sold nothing in years—nothing. It is a heavy burden on him, for his confidence was broken, and even now it has not recovered."

It bothered Rose that Hugo had slipped into obscurity. One day, when Esther was sick in bed, Rose spent a whole morning sitting on a packing crate in Hugo's studio, praying silently for him, and studying the way he painted. At one point he dropped his brush into the turp-jar and agreed to share with her a pot of tea. As he slurped from his cup, she asked him why some artists were popular and some were not, even when their works re-sembled each other.

"I would prefer to believe", he said in his most didactic tone, "that there is in the honest painter a subconscious power that is revealed subtly in his work. There is always something missing in the work of an imitator, or those who paint for money. Even if he's brilliant technically, even if it's not immediately apparent, it will reveal itself soon enough. You develop an odd feeling, an inner sense of something not being right."

"What is it that tells you a painting is good or bad?" asked Rose.

"Again with the good and bad, eh? Well, I can't really tell you what it is, but if it's not there the painting is dead, even if it's as realistic as a photograph."

"You mean if it's there, then people will buy it?"

"If only that were so. People buy paintings to match the color of their carpets."

Rose laughed, for she knew that Hugo liked to joke.

"Ah, my Rose, such a nice young lady you are." He sighed. "What will become of you? What will become of us all?"

"Esther told me you were once famous in England, Hugo. I know that your paintings will be well known and loved again."

"Will they? While it is true that my little green landscapes of the Midlands were popular, over the years my brush developed this tendency to stretch the depth and light into dimensions that were hard to identify. Result—loss of popularity, at least with the ordinary folk."

"Did you like your new work? Were you happy?"

"Happy? Well, for a time it satisfied, as an empty room will satisfy the overloaded senses. But one cannot remain there forever. However, the critics, and the poor deluded souls beguiled by them, purchased a few of my empty rooms and said lovely things about them. Thus I, too, was deceived. How easily I was deceived."

Rose's heart quickened. Had he admitted that his abstractions were deceptions?

He gave her a sad smile of resignation. "So now I am consigned to be a hidden genius. My wife feeds me like an aging inmate who has lost his senses—such is the grandeur and the pathos of her fidelity."

"You have not lost your senses, Hugo. It seems to me that you have regained them."

"I'm not sure it is possible to regain them. I was entranced by the concept of pure abstraction, its simplicity. I said to myself that we must become liberated from slavery to how things look or are expected to look. That the world of things was illusory and that we must see with our minds beyond it."

"But is it not the heart that sees?"

He sighed. "I always assumed it was the eye. And the brain. I jumped to an enormous conclusion and abandoned language itself, you see, in pursuit of pure perception. It was a lie, Rose. Moreover it was a boring lie. But I wanted the lie, you see. Always watch out for the bad rats. Bad rats will tell you anything. The splendor of creation is rich, and it's the doorkeeper of a mystery. Be patient and it will let you through. But this is the age of Cyclopean impatience, isn't it. I was disillusioned by the madness of the world, lost my patience, lost my taste for life's magnificence."

"And now you are finding it again!" she burst out.

"Fair child," he chuckled. "Don't presume too much. I'm giving it a last shot, that's all."

"You must give it everything, Hugo, you must."

"Well, I'll try. I'm not sure it's possible to sustain it after all this time. A horse now and then, maybe. The problem is, I painted the surface of closed doors for too long. Nothing but closed doors. When you've spent too many years ignoring whatever it is that breathes softly behind closed doors. . . ."

They both fell silent for a time as Hugo squeezed a spiral of white onto his palette.

"What is it that breathes softly behind the closed doors?" Rose asked.

"Don't know. Don't presume to know."

"How wonderful that after all this time the door is opening now", Rose said. "After your long walk, just when your heart was sinking and you were abandoning hope, the lights appeared in a house in the night, above a field of horses. And a man appeared in a window. You looked and saw and remembered, for they were words spoken to you."

"Were they?" Hugo said rubbing his nose, dabbing white onto a shank of flesh straining toward the breaking point as its hoofs left the earth. "Who spoke, do you think? No, don't answer that; I know what you think."

"He spoke and though you did not go to his door, you listened, and now these many years later. . . ."

"Quiet now, I'm concentrating", Hugo interrupted. And Rose left him to his horses.

One summer day, she ventured farther east, to the edges of St. Henri, where blocks of decaying tenements had been flattened in preparation for the construction of new office buildings. In a wide, empty square a traveling circus had erected a few tents and carnival rides. There was a ferris wheel, and a water tank into which a black boy would fall whenever people threw a baseball and hit a target. There were stalls where stuffed animals and plastic trinkets could be bought. The smell of popcorn and spun-sugar cones was in the air, and the wonderful scent of frying onions. In one tent there was a petting zoo with donkeys, midget goats, rabbits, and a single swaybacked horse. In another, little dogs wearing clown hats danced on their hind legs, and three ladies in pink leotards swung on wires and bounced on trampolines. In a third, a depressed elephant walked slowly round and round carrying giggling, wide-eyed children on its back, their hands stroking the bristles on its neck.

In the center of the midway, a sign over the doorway of another large tent advertised MADAME COQUINE'S HOUSE OF

MYSTERY. Because the word *mystery* was of great importance to Rose, she bought a ticket from a man in a striped suit and straw hat. He pointed to the entrance with his cane. Rose went in, unable to see anything at first, for the light inside was dim. During the seconds when her eyes adjusted she felt a desire to leave, for the air was thick with wrongness; it was the opposite of the golden liquid air of the shrine on Mount Royal.

A voice cried from a loudspeaker, "Welcome, welcome, welcome to the Royal Family of Freaks, past, present, and to come! Step right up, step right up, ladies and gentlemen, take a look and don't be shy! Welcome, welcome, welcome—"

Presently there emerged under the glare of light bulbs a scene of milling bodies and displays. Against the curving walls of the tent were cattle stalls, and parked in each was a human being. At first, Rose wondered if she had made a great mistake, and turned to go. Then she stopped and asked herself if the Lord wished to show her something in this place, perhaps a person she must pray for, take upon her back. There were many candidates. The fat lady, the tattooed people, the limbless men, and those with hideous cancerous growths. Rose's eyes reached for the eyes of the people in these displays. But her look was returned by only a few lifeless glances, staring at the lump, the *thing*, of her. She could not stand the feeling this brought upon her, as if she were struggling weakly within a burlap sack. Worst of all were the onlookers, for their naked curiosity contained no compassion. Their eyes were deformed, for they had paid money for the strange privilege of looking at other human souls in this way.

I cannot bear it, these eyes, all human spirit flattened down into the world of things. I must go! I must go! Terror rose in her heart, as if she were running in a nightmare, slower and slower, her feet sucked into sinking mud as a beast chased her, faster and faster.

At the exit, she halted and stared at the final display. It was a ten-gallon glass jar. Floating upright in a womb of formaldehyde sat a little naked girl, a baby with its umbilical cord still attached, though the mother was severed from it. Rose's heart fell frozen and burning through the floor of the tent and the earth, and all her being was now a seeing only. The small form was a brown leathery deformity, a frog of a body, except where a head and delicate limbs defined it female and human. Its hair was wispy black. Its eyes—for the eyes were open—were dark black orbs, reflecting points of light from some far-wheeling galaxy.

"Io! It is me!" Rose cried, running from the tent.

It was impossible to exorcise the image without the help of her gift. Vomiting was not enough, nor telling, nor weeping a private complaint to God. On canvas, secretly, she made a drawing of a little girl in formaldehyde, then painted it. As she did so, both in the drawing and the painting, an unleashing of love poured from her, and passionate anger. And grief. First she made the image true to what she had seen. Then she painted over it in stages, making the child as beautiful as possible, put color into her skin and joy into her eyes and a small bird into her hand, a silver bird that could leave or stay as it wished, for the holding was not in any sense a grasping. The bird chose to stay. The child no longer floated in chemicals. She rested in a crib of wild flowers, a circlet of white birds flew about her head, and in the background a distant mountain rose, green and holy.

This is what I would have given you if I were your mother, Rose said to the girl, *yet I cannot be your mother. Even so, a mother of the spirit I will be. And I will carry you, and I will not forget you. And if it is his will, the one who made us will give to you the dream I painted.*

So, in this way Rose learned that it is possible to recreate the broken world and to help redeem it.

She showed it to Esther and explained it.

"I see", Esther mused. "Yet there is a problem. Before my eyes, I see only a beautiful sweet arcadia, a bower for your beloved baby. Hidden from my eyes is the horror that you saw. In this sense the painting is only for yourself. Is there not a duty to tell the entire story? Because the story would shift the balance of the world, if it were known. Even if only a little. As does every true word."

"But what can I do?"

"Go back. Go to your studio now and paint a second image. The horror, the death, the negation of the child's humanity. Go no further than what you saw with your eyes. Then, when you are finished, put the two side by side."

"If I did that, there would be not one, but two words."

"No, you would have three words: The word that shows the evil of turning a person into a thing, the second word that shows what should be given to every child. The third word is the understanding created in the mind of the viewer by the juxtaposition of the two. Each is made stronger by contrast with the other."

"I do not know", Rose said, choking a little. "It would be too hard to do it again."

"Would it? Not even for the girl's sake? Do it for her."

And so she did. But the new painting did not evolve as Esther had suggested. Instead of a single image of the baby in the bottle, Rose made a larger work on a piece of gessoed hardboard that she begged from Hugo. On it she drew two human forms, twins floating within an amniotic sea. One was happy and smiling, though she was deformed. The other, also deformed, was dying. She wailed with a mouth open wide in terrified incomprehension. The cords braided about the two figures, entwining both. They clung to each other with their small arms and with their eyes. The dying child was dropping down through the entrance of the birth canal as if sinking into a downness that was really an upness, or an outwardness, where the happy child was to follow. At the base of the work two large brown hands, as brown as the hands of God, were waiting to receive them. In the breast of the dying girl was a silver bird. In the breast of the living girl was one like it. Within both birds were small flames.

"Good", Esther said. "Not what I suggested, but still, very good. The sentimentality is gone, the cupid card is gone. Now it is real. It is a story and an icon all together."

Esther put a hard finger to the center of Rose's chest. "And it came from there. Never forget. It's all in there. Inside."

Hugo took one look at the image and wheeled, returning to his own studio without comment.

"It's too intimate for him, that big strapping fellow", Esther explained. "There are certain things he cannot face, death and birth being two of them."

That evening, however, Hugo, attended supper as if nothing had happened. Over tea, he proposed an outing.

"There's an interesting show down at the Metropol Gallery", he declared. "I read about it in the paper this morning. Grand opening tonight. Shall we go?"

"What is it, Huggo? Do not drag us out to another tedious performance of the strident egos. Please, no more strident egos."

"Not at all, my dear, not at all. This is actually something more in Rose's line. A rather surprising new development in Canadian art. It's a group show of native artists, expressing themselves, so says the advertisement, in uniquely native style. The critic who previewed the show says it's going to be an earth shatterer."

"That pathetic Trevor Marlowe again?"

"To be sure, Trevor suffers from a tendency to hyperbole, but he has on occasion been known to get something right. What say? Shall we go?"

"Rose, you want to go?"

"Yes, I would like to go", she said, for it had been a long time since she had any contact with native people. And she had not known until now that there were other native artists like herself.

They immediately got on their coats and took the next bus for downtown.

The Metropol was crowded. Wine was being served by waiters, cameras flashed, a journalist or two scribbled in notebooks. Important people were present. Women in gowns and jewelry, older men in tailored suits. A few native men stood in a self-protective ring in a corner—the artists. Dressed uncomfortably in Woolworth suits and ties, they stared at the floor as they answered the questions that charming women chattered at them. Moneyed men prodded them with unanswerable commentary, thrusting their ample bellies forward as evidence of their business acumen. The natives retreated, preparing to make a stand. A waiter brought them drinks on a tray. They shot looks at each other. They reached, took, and drank. And mumbled, and laughed at one another.

"Hugo! Esther!" a voice cried from across the room.

"Preserve us, Huggo! Preserve us! It's Chloe Templeton."

Esther stiffened, Hugo snorted.

"Courage, my dear, courage", he murmured.

A woman about thirty years of age swept toward them, glass in hand, navigating the crowds adeptly, stopping to kiss here, comment there, now touching an arm with long fingers that were employed artfully, now laughing at a bit of repartee. Her chin pointing at the perfect angle, her brindle brown hair chopped short for effect, she arrived at Hugo and Esther and kissed each of them on both cheeks.

"Darling!" she cried. "And you too, darling old Huggo!"

Hugo wagged his finger. "Only Esther is permitted to call me Huggo."

"Of course, Huggo, of course. You troglodyte, you charming old neo-Fauvian. How lovely to see you."

Chloe Templeton's catlike eyes glittered with the pure pleasure of such an outstanding evening and the surprise of meeting old friends.

"It's been simply ages, hasn't it. We must get together. Any shows planned for the near future?"

"None", Esther shook her head, looking more vulturelike and tiny than she had since the *Midsummer Night's Dream*.

"Well, that's easily mended. Let me talk to Favio and see if we can't arrange something." She placed a hand on Esther's arm. "Still painting the delightful bird scenes, Esther?"

"Yes", Esther croaked without a hint of warmth.

"And you, Huggo, still out-abstracting Willem de Kooning and Kenzo Okada?" She twinkled and added mischievously, "Or is it Roger de la Fresnaye?"

"Nah", Hugo snarled. "Can't stand dem bums."

Chloe recovered quickly. "You joker! Now, who is this?" she said turning her eyes upon Rose.

"This is Rose Wâbos, a real artist", Esther said icily. Chloe ignored the chill. She bent over, offering her hand as if Rose were a small shy child. "Hello, Rose. I do hope you enjoy your visit with us. As you know, this is a very important night for your people. Well, for all of us, really. It is the launching of a new era of perception in the West."

"Hello", Rose said a bit uncertainly and shook the hand. Too distracted for communication, she eyed the native men in the corner, wondering who they were, trying to resist a stronger urge to head straight for the paintings. She noted only that there was a great deal of bright color.

Chloe turned to Esther and whispered excitedly, "Favio's over there squiring around Herr Something from the state museum in Bonn, and some collectors from Amsterdam—connected with Shell Oil, I think, or is it someone else in the petroleum club. I can never tell them apart. I wonder if they'll be able to understand the real meaning of these paintings."

"What," said Esther in a tone calculated to sting, "what do *you* say is the real meaning of these paintings?"

"The real meaning?" Chloe repeated, her face instantly grave. "Why, I think these artists have developed a kind of Sanskrit of the soul!"

"Sanskrit?" Esther said in tones of extreme sarcasm. "Perhaps you mean Swahili?"

"Oh, yes, that too."

"Esperanto", Hugo contributed with feigned seriousness. "More like Esperanto."

"Exactly, Huggo, exactly!" Chloe said. "A universal language, the Rosetta stone of the visual plane. Oh, look, there's Mrs. Morgan. I must go welcome her! Estelle darling!"

Chloe launched for the far side of the gallery, where she engaged in a rather public ritual of embracing Mrs. Morgan.

Esther groaned. "That, Rose, is probably your first encounter with a millionairess. Not a bad woman, really, just shallow. She is an *artiste*. No door stands closed to her, no matter how trivial the little works of art that she makes."

"Now, now, Esther. Remember what you once said? All critics should be flogged—publicly. Aren't you being ever so slightly critical?"

"Be quiet, Huggo. Imagine, Rose, the pretty collages clipped from the pages of fashion magazines, glued with expensive rabbit-skin gesso and imported Burmese sizing to the finest mahogany boards, and decorated—nay, dressed up like little girls' cutout dollies—in real lace."

"Don't sneer, Esther, maybe she's pushing back the frontiers of the infinite."

"Be quiet, Huggo. Lace art, I tell you. Lace art! What next! My grandmother was a *real* lace artist—she *made* the lace. This woman—"

"Tut, tut, you're just jealous because she has an annual solo exhibit. It's the caste system, darling. You can't defy the laws of caste, so you might as well get used to them."

"I will never get used to them!" Esther huffed. "It is ridiculous! It is a little Frau Hitler."

"Nonsense. She's a perfectly ordinary, white Anglo-Saxon agnostic. Now be quiet and enjoy the show."

Esther ignored him and took Rose's arm. "Chloe Templeton", she said too loudly, "is the significant relationship of Favio Ontolli, the owner-curator of this gallery."

Fortunately, these comments were drowned by the tides of conversation rising in every direction, and the clinking of glasses, and the artists who were beginning to unwind, joking with each other in their native tongues and stilted English. Lionized at every turn but unable to play the elaborate games of the gallery crowd, they shook hands with the dazzling guests and answered rather obscure questions with single words, yes, no, maybe. Then grinned at each other. Intelligence was in their eyes, Rose saw, and various kinds of suffering. They were not exactly enjoying themselves, but they were grateful for each other and for the serious attention people were paying to their work.

"Little red stickers, Esther. Lots of little red stickers", Hugo announced cheerily.

Indeed, gallery employees were busy scurrying here and there putting red dots at the base of the frames.

"A sellout show, to be sure, Huggo. I'm glad for them. Look at those brooding faces, so uncomfortable among us. They deserve better than this."

"I expect so. That one with the ponytail is like a portrait by Bronzino, don't you think, the ferocious dignity of him. Watch, I guarantee they'll make a cultural icon of him within the year, poor fellow. We're starved for heroes, Esther."

"A jaded and creatively exhausted nation will turn to any spiritual source, don't you think?" said a deeply cynical voice belonging to a shoulder that bumped Hugo's elbow, spilling a drop or two of wine onto his jacket. The spots disappeared instantly among the other colors.

"Trevor, old lad!" Hugo said.

"But will it last?" said the art critic for the *Gazette*.

"Absolutely", Hugo replied. "Guarantee it." And emptied his wine glass down his throat. "Rather an infusion of blood, don't you think."

"Blood, Hugo? Maybe. Or bread and circuses. The imported Nubians in the Roman Colosseum is my guess. Lots to write about here."

The art critic went off to interview the natives. Arm in arm, Esther and Rose went off in another direction to view the paintings. There were at least sixty works. Esther led, stopping for a minute or so before each work, ignoring the greetings that occasionally were offered to her, turning to Rose from time to time: "What do you think? What are they about?"

What were they about? The catalogue provided an answer in twelve pages of script and as many pages of illustration. The works in the show were by a group of twelve painters, all members of the Cree, Ojibwe, and Odawa tribes of the northern Ontario woodlands. Most were young men in their twenties or thirties. Two were women. The subject matter varied. A few blended native and Christian themes. The overwhelming majority portrayed the mythology of the Old Religion.

"Io, I am not at peace", Rose said quietly into Esther's ear. "This is the voice of the spirit world where good and evil are confused."

"How do you know this? Are you familiar with the native iconography?"

"I feel it in my soul", Rose said. "Here, in this one, for example, is a shaking tent, which my grandmother warned me against, for it is the shaman-way, the way of opening to the demon spirits which the magicians say are good. They are not good. For it is the realm of the people who frightened me when I was a child; they cursed my family, invoking the darkness against us. Even so, the grace of our baptism and our prayers was with us, and we were not harmed. In these times, I wonder how many are guarded as we were. Few, I think. The shamans are people without holiness. Power they seek, not humility. Vengeance they want, not mercy."

Esther digested this, but made no comment. They entered a side gallery that was filled with animal figures performing many wonders and mysterious gestures.

"The colors!" Esther exclaimed. "So vibrant, so vital. There *is* power here, Rose. Why do you say it is not good? I am very impressed."

"Beware, Esther. Its beauty beguiles the eye and confuses the thoughts—"

"Perhaps it seeks to teach, to enlarge us—"

"That is why it is dangerous, because it promises what it cannot give."

"Dangerous, you say? You, an artist! You, a native person yourself. Rose, you confound me utterly. Are you perhaps a little jealous?" Esther squeezed Rose's arm affectionately to show that she intended no hurt by the question.

"I do not envy them", Rose replied. "No, I fear for them."

At that moment they were interrupted.

"Mrs. Dyson," said a voice behind them, "and Rose, I believe. How lovely to see you here."

"Good evening," Esther replied with characteristic coolness.

As on the evening of the *Dream*, Mrs. Morgan was beautiful for a woman her age. The flawless skin of her face and bare shoulders, the subtle jewels, a dress of shimmering velvet that was now dark green, now black, now richest burgundy.

"This is a breakthrough, don't you think?" the lady asked Esther.

"Possibly. Yes, almost certainly. A new language."

"Precisely", Mrs. Morgan replied with a gentle air of thoughtfulness. "We are much in need of a larger vision. In their proximity to the primeval forces of nature, these twelve apostles, if you will, are returning us to the foundations, and thereby reorienting us to the infinite—don't you think, Rose?"

After a pause for thought, Rose replied haltingly. "In a way, Mrs. Morgan. But life is full of struggle and confusion. It is a war between good and evil. These images confuse the lines between the two."

"*If* there are lines", Mrs. Morgan said in an academic tone. "At the very least they raise some important questions. Look at this work by Morrisseau: *Man Changing into Thunderbird*. Primitive, yet curiously sophisticated. The anthropologist would see it as a replica of antiquated cosmology. The ethnologist would view it as a piece suitable for a museum of dead culture. Yet it is alive!"

Esther murmured agreement. "You are right, Mrs. Morgan. It is very much alive."

"Ultimately this is not about native society. This work and many like it here this evening approach the level of universal human myth. This painting is about metamorphosis. From Ovid to Warhol, man is ever seeking metamorphosis."

"What is metamorphosis?" Rose asked.

"Change", Esther explained in a quick aside.

"Change, yes, but more than change", Mrs. Morgan explained. "Metamorphosis is the transformation of a being from one state into another. All things *change*, but not everything *rises* above the laws of entropy—of decline and corruption."

"That is true", Esther nodded, glancing at Mrs. Morgan with interest, her hostility melting away.

The two older women smiled at each other. Mrs. Morgan continued. "The thunderbird is a frequently repeated iconic figure, have you noticed?"

"I have", Esther nodded.

"It occupies an interesting position of domination, and it even seems to coordinate the other themes. Is this not the native version of the universal hero-martyr? It is my guess—a conjecture only, of course—that here is their Christ-figure. Many religions have a hero-king who battles the forces of darkness, is killed and goes down into the underworld, then rises again to life."

"A fascinating conjecture, Mrs. Morgan. Fascinating."

"Please call me Estelle."

"Please call me Esther."

When the two women plunged deeper into a discussion both fascinating and esoteric—and impenetrable—Rose wandered off to see more paintings. She passed by the artists once or twice, hoping to meet them, but they were still surrounded. The one or two who spotted her in the crowd looked away, for there were several native guests, and Rose was not one of the more attractive representatives of their race.

She overheard one of the artists say, "—at the World's Fair in Montreal, we'll be painting the mural for the Canadian Pavilion. Expo 67 they're calling it. After that comes Osaka, Japan."

Another broke in, "Maybe Morrisseau'll do the mural, maybe Carl Ray. Daphne Odjig too, I hope."

"Is Miss Odjig here tonight?" asked a critic.

"No, but there's some of her work here. She's great, mixes Picasso with her own vision."

"How about Morrisseau and Ray?"

"Couldn't come. Busy."

"And Ben Thunder-eagle?"

Laughter erupted all round, but no explanation was forthcoming.

"No, Ben's busy too", said one of the artists.

In her route about the large gallery, Rose had been struck especially by the work of both Morrisseau and Ben Thunder-eagle. Where Morrisseau's work was striking in form and brilliantly colored, though often unbalanced in composition, Thunder-eagle was subdued, subtle in his color palette, and yet strangely the most powerful of all. If any of the art in the room merited the title of sophisticated, it was his. There was no hint of the cartoon in his work, as there was in several of the others.

Rose circuited the room once more, seeking a closer look at the works of the man called Thunder-eagle. The first she came to was *Thunderbird Warrior.* In this painting an eagle stood upon the crest of a giant rock. Its neck was stretched back, its beak open. A spirit-thunderbird in the sky above plunged toward it, spitting fire into the eagle's mouth. The sky was a torment of red-black shreds of cloud.

Next was *The Beast beneath the Waters.* Here the canvas was divided into two horizontal planes. Above was a murky brown sky, below was black water. A white canoe floated upon the line where they met. It was filled with men paddling furiously for shore. In its wake, a second canoe was going down, the tip of its stern disappearing as it sank, the canoe plummeting and all the little men on board spilling out, falling into the open jaws of a giant monster that awaited them.

Windigo Dancing portrayed a crazed man-beast holding human captives in its claws, opening its jaws and eating them as its legs cavorted above a village. A small church burned at the *windigo's* feet, a toe crushing one half of it.

Riding the Wind portrayed a stylized Indian sitting astride a thunderbird, riding it as a man would ride a horse. Straddling his back was a spirit shape in the form of a feathered serpent. From its mouth spirit-lines (lines of power) emanated, circling the man, holding him as if with reins.

In *Bang-wa-jusk, the Man-eater,* a wolverine devoured a child, and because it had violated the law of protection, it was flayed and burned by spirit-lines emanating from the divine power of the cosmos. It screeched in protest against the worst punishment: a white slash of fur that henceforth all of its offspring would bear upon their backs as a mark of shame and warning to others.

In *Serpent Tale,* seven snakes entangled a man, coiling about every limb. One snake opened its jaws over his head (his thoughts), one bit into his chest (his heart), and a third coiled between his legs (his potency); the remaining four bound his arms and legs. An eighth serpent, smaller than the others, but more frightening, coiled about the man's neck and pressed its nose to his, whispering into his mouth.

Rose could bear no more. She located Esther, and extracted her with much difficulty from the profound discussion that she was still conducting with Estelle Morgan.

"—of course, all religions are merely misunderstood mythologies—"

"I have always thought so myself, Estelle. It is not a widely understood insight—"

"Though I believe it will not always be so. When anthropology and spirituality one day integrate their visions, then we will see a birthing of—"

"We must leave, Esther", Rose whispered intensely.

"Is there a problem?" Esther asked.

"I have seen all that I want to see. Please."

"Rose, dear," Esther admonished, "I haven't seen everything yet. And I don't know if Huggo has either. Patience, now, we'll be going before too long."

"I need to leave now", Rose said firmly, so completely out of character that Esther acquiesced.

"All right. Let's go, then. I'll find Huggo. I enjoyed our discussion, Estelle."

"We must continue it at your convenience, Esther. I have always longed to see your work, but hesitated to interrupt you in your studio. I know very well what people such as myself represent to the authentic artist, and I am mortified to find that I am such a person."

"Nonsense. You're not at all like the rest of them. You are, if I may say it, something of an artist yourself—in temperament."

"That is a high compliment coming from you, Esther. Thank you."

"Come to my studio any time. We don't have a telephone, so just come whenever you like."

Mrs. Morgan seemed overwhelmed with emotion.

"This, from the woman who painted *Birds in Wartime*. I am speechless."

"How do you know about *Birds in Wartime*?" Esther asked with amazement.

"I travel a great deal, expanding my collection. Last year I was in Antwerp with my husband—he is in the field of international finance, you understand, so we do get around. I especially wanted to see the Rubens in the cathedral, but the Flemish masters in the Royal Museum of Fine Arts could not be resisted. There, I stumbled by accident upon the contemporary art collection. When I saw your painting, it instantly leapt out at me from a crowd of modernists." Estelle Morgan placed a trembling hand on the string of emeralds on her collarbone. "My heart ceased to beat for a few moments. The symbol of all martyred lives, the universal embodied in the particular, the caged birds released by catastrophe—it was the apotheosis of myth. Genuine myth, not legend. I marked the artist's name in my memory and bought a print of it. How could I have known that one day I would be privileged to meet you face to face."

Blushing scarlet, Esther murmured small deprecations which everyone ignored for various reasons. Estelle embraced Esther, who returned the embrace with tears in her eyes. Rose tugged at her arm for a few moments while the two older women exchanged parting comments. Then she and Esther went to find Hugo. They made a relatively efficient escape and went home together on the bus, Hugo and Rose flanking Esther, who remained completely silent during the journey.

Mrs. Morgan arrived one Saturday morning in a black limousine, driven by her personal chauffeur. She came to the front door by herself and knocked with a certain timidity. When Esther opened to her, the two women embraced like old friends, and Estelle entered the house as a visiting queen—a queen, it should be noted, who had no airs of superiority or condescension, who seemed to radiate a genuine gratitude for the privilege of visiting their home.

Esther insisted, over Hugo's protests, on a visit to the old man's studio. Estelle spent tactfully silent minutes examining Hugo's abandoned abstractions, but enthused over his new creative tangent of galloping horses.

"They are powerful, Hugo, though I must admit I am an amateur, and you should not pay the least attention to anything I say. But I know what I like, as the cliché goes. And I am in love with these horses. As archetypal as Marino Marini's, as fluid as Franz Marc's, yet better I think, for there is a unique passion in yours, dark and light passion, and the music of the spheres. The horses leap toward the hidden sound that emanates from beyond the overcast skies, sensing its presence before the slaves do—if they ever do."

"Why, I hadn't thought of that", Hugo murmured, furrowing his brow, bending at the waist to stare intently at his own offspring. "Yes, it's there all right." And looked at Mrs. Morgan with sudden appreciation.

After that, they proceeded to Esther's studio, where the two women remained for an hour discussing Esther's work. Close to noon, Hugo called for a tea break. As they made their way downstairs, Mrs. Morgan inquired about Rose, asking if she might see the young woman's studio. They paused on the second floor, and Hugo rapped on Rose's door.

"Come out, come out, wherever you are!" he teased.

"I am working", Rose said politely without opening the door.

"Mrs. Morgan is here", Esther said. "She would love to see your paintings."

"Only if you wish to let me see them, Rose", Mrs. Morgan said, raising her voice slightly in order to be heard by the shadow on the other side.

Rose considered the request. She did not like Mrs. Morgan, perhaps because the woman was sympathetic to pagan themes, or else because she had so swiftly penetrated the defenses of the impenetrable Esther Dyson, and this sort of power was both mysterious and dangerous.

"Another day would be better", Rose said at last. "I am in the middle of work, and it would distract me."

The three people waiting in the hall chuckled to each other with understanding and went downstairs for their tea.

Rose sat at the drawing board staring at a white sheet of paper. Her fists were clenched between her knees, her mouth firm.

What is wrong with me? Why do I dislike her? Am I jealous?

But this was unanswerable. It was a feeling, she knew, and feelings alone were not trustworthy. She took her pastels and began to draw. At first she did not know what she intended. Curiously, the streaks of red took a shape disturbingly similar to the forms of the paintings she had seen at the exhibit of native art. A dancing man-shape in the very center. All about him was red air. On either side of him trees burst out in full leaf, deep green, with orange and yellow fruit upon them. In the sky hovered a distant white bird, its eye turquoise. The line of the earth on which the man-shape danced was a steeply curving ellipse. Below the earth, a great black beast waited, its jaws open wide, spewing spirit-lines upward, its fingers seeking the down-seeking roots of the trees. The claws and the roots met and entwined in a struggle that was utterly silent but expressed by strokes of sickly green and bruised purple and the red of drying blood. The beast's eyes were yellow, the spirit-lines of falsehood and malice spewed from it in jagged spears of gentian violet, lancing the earth at the man's feet, entering him through his soles and rising to his head, filling him. As he reached up to the bird, the earth sucked him down, and he lost hope in the bird, for it seemed too far from him and his eyes were now blinded by weeping yellow matter, the liquid of decaying thought.

It was ugly and frightening.

"Ay, ay, I have made an evil thing!" Rose cried, stepping back so suddenly that her chair fell over, banging the window sill, knocking the *binemin* stone to the floor.

Standing perfectly still, Rose closed her eyes and prayed.

"Ay, ay, is the evil within me, that I make such a word of evil?"

Yet peace returned to her swiftly as she prayed, her heart steadied, and she looked more closely at the work. Was it, after all, a word of evil? Perhaps it was a word of warning. And if it warned against evil and spoke of man's need for the Holy Spirit, was it not a word of good? Yes, this was so!

Still, there had been a cost to make it. It cost her a struggle against something in the atmosphere that did not like it, though its power was weakened in the room because of prayer, and because of the crucifix and the other holy things. Present in the room, as well, were the many words of love that had come from her over the years, the pastels and drawings, and of course the *binemin* stone, which was the word of love that Tchibi had given to her for safekeeping, yes, it had been himself that he had placed into her hands.

She glanced at the floor, remembering that it had fallen. With a cry of anguish, she saw that it was broken. She dropped to her knees and picked up the two pieces, pressing them back together. But they would not hold together. She burst into wails.

Ay, ay, what had she done! Was this the cost of the image? Had the enemy struck her most precious possession because she had dared to utter a word against him? Or was it only an accident? Were there any accidents in this world? She did not know the answers to these questions. She sat down on the floor of the studio, her back to the wall, and held the pieces of stone against her chest, warming them, wetting them with her tears.

Later, after the limousine drove away, Rose went down to help Esther make supper. Esther was in the kitchen humming to herself, light on her feet, doing little elfin dances between the stove, the refrigerator, and the sink.

"Rose, Rose, we have news! A wonderful day! A day of new beginnings! Mrs. Morgan has purchased the painting of my grandmother and the washtub. She wrote a large check, more than I could have asked for. We will live for months on it! Moreover, she will speak to Favio Ontolli about the possibility of a show next year. It was her own idea. And she insists on asking for a separate show for Huggo as well. Can you believe it?"

Fighting back tears, Rose said, "It is wonderful news, Esther. I am happy for you."

Hugo entered the room at that moment, whistling, smiling to himself. Stopping in his tracks, he inspected Rose's face.

"If you're so happy, girl, why are you crying?"

"I have broken a thing that is precious to me", she explained, showing them the two halves of the *binemin* stone.

"Oh, ah", they said, coming close, patting her shoulders in sympathy, revealing their very good hearts.

"Not to worry, little bird. We'll fix it in a jiffy", Hugo declared. He banged about in the cupboards and found some glue.

"This epoxy is magical stuff. Give me that stone."

As Rose watched closely, he applied the glue to the exposed interior. She trembled, yearning for him to avoid any mistakes with it. The fracture ran from beak to tail, straight through the center of the partridge heart. There was, of course, no heart inside, for it was solid gray stone. Hugo squeezed the two pieces together, bound the whole with several elastic bands, and handed it back to her.

"There, quickly mended. Let it sit for twenty-four hours, and it'll be as solid as a rock again."

"Thank you, Hugo, thank you", she said, hurrying upstairs to place it on the windowsill.

Then, like the collapse of everything, Esther was dead.

The evening before, Esther's chest had felt heavy, and she had gone to bed early. In the middle of the night, Rose was awakened by an ambulance's siren and its red lights flashing through her bedroom window. She stumbled downstairs and found a frantic-eyed Hugo bending over a stretcher that two men in white were carrying along the hallway to the front door.

"I'm all right! I'm all right!" cried a small bird voice. "Stop that fussing, Huggo, get ahold of yourself. It's just a little pain in the chest."

Hours later, Hugo dragged himself into the house, leaving the front door wide open. His eyes were a landscape in which giants devoured what remained of human habitation and scattered the human names as carnivores will scatter the bones.

She is dead, thought Rose.

Hugo did not need to speak the actual words, for his face said everything. He went to his bedroom and closed the door with a terrifying gentleness. Rose closed the front door. She went to the kitchen and made tea. She fed Goldie. She cried silently. She beat back fear. She went upstairs to Esther's studio and felt its emptiness.

There was a new painting on the easel, a depiction of a woman selling crated pigeons. Similar to the earlier work, it was different in that the woman gazed at the birds with great love, her hand resting on the open doorway of the cage. The birds, ruffling their wings, took flight.

20

After the memorial service and the interment in the Jewish cemetery on Mount Royal, Hugo refused to be consoled. He wanted to be alone. He told Rose to go home, he needed a solitary walk, to remember Esther. Rose went to her parish church and sat in the subdued light of the whispering candles for several hours, praying for Esther's soul, praying that Hugo would not let himself be consumed by despair. Praying, also, for guidance regarding her future. Esther was dead, and it would not be proper for a young woman to live with a lonely man, alone together in a great echoing house.

Hugo, for his part, trudged through the grubby night streets, the dripping of gutters and drainpipes a requiem in his ears. Following nothing in the mist save his own dim feet and bleak beckonings, he went into the side lanes among houses of crumbling stucco and old automobiles disintegrating in heaps of rust like abandoned dreams. Cutting across a demolished industrial lot, he came to the edge of the river, the big movement of water that split the nation, carrying ships from the sea almost to her center, and back again.

Is all this effort and groaning nothing more than a preparation for death? he asked. Is the world one immense extermination camp? For what, Esther, for what, my queen, did you escape the bombings, the nasty little plans the Nazis had for you, the suction of suicide? Did we come hand in hand to old age only to find that in the end there is nothing but death?

"Esther?" he roared, the sound of his voice terrifying him. "Where are you?" He would kick something in rage, would smash and kill death, but there was only the sighing of snow as it gave way humbly beneath his boot. "To hell with you, Charon!" he shouted across the river. But there was no answer from the water, no dip and lap of the bargeman's pole, only the deep boom of an ice-breaker smashing its way up the St. Lawrence.

Back in his studio, he sat staring at the blank of canvas on his easel, its whiteness a cruel joke. What could the thundering horses do against the pale rider, the death-bringer? Run away? Ha! The horses ran, chased by slaves, the slaves freer than the wildly free horse, yet still slaves. It was all illusion. Eventually the slaves faltered, exhausted, tripping, tumbling flat on their faces. The horses too eventually fell, their wind broken, all horses fell, broke their legs, were shot. Merciful death was the only escape from death. Irrational! Yes, he was being irrational all right, but he had every right to be, didn't he?

"Show your face, Death, and I'll shoot you! Or I'll draw your smirking face."

After anger there was emptiness and numbness, followed by fear. Then the cycle repeated itself. He thought long about doing what he had so often threatened, but could not, seeing in one black surge of guilt what it would do to the little deformed woman who lived under the same roof with him. It would leave her with nothing—then Death would rack up three victims in one shot. *I'll kill myself later,* he said to himself.

In the meantime, Rose gently reminded him that he should eat something. She stuffed bannock into him. He chewed the mealy sawdust, spat it out, and told her he was not interested in food.

She told him to work, to make images. "That is the way to defeat it", she said.

"Defeat what?" he demanded.

"The lie", she said in a small voice, as humbly as only she could.

"What lie?" her threw back at her, knowing what she would reply.

But she merely looked at him and said nothing. He knew what she meant all right. If he wanted to live, he must paint. Yet he had no strength. He would force his attention onto the canvas and lift the brush, only to feel it drop from his hand in a sagging glut of fatigue, a daze of futility. He had nothing to create, neither could he copy what was already there. Was not art merely the groaning of that poor dumb beast of burden, man? Even mules pretend to gallop. Even slaves imagine they are free.

In time, of course, he began to shuffle through the dutiful human things, and the more he exercised these atrophied movements, the more free he became of the imminent victory of Death. *Later*, he often repeated, *later*. Rose pushed tea and plates of food at him. He ignored the food. He did permit a little tea. She supposed it was keeping him alive. But he could not draw or paint. He felt that his presence in the house, in the world actually, was absurd. He slept a great deal and sometimes wept to himself in the middle of the night, unable to lie down without a lamp burning beside the bed, staring for hours at the moth-eaten fur coat hanging from the door hook. He was quarantined by an unseen virus of soul but not yet dead of it, knowing no cure.

Rose's grief was not as deep as his and was healed more swiftly by the rivers of grace that he refused to believe in. Still, it was very hard. She too cried in the night, sometimes sobbed, for Esther had been a mother to her. Feeling trapped in a wire cage by an old man going slightly mad, fearing that she might wake one morning to find blood running out from under the bathroom door, she sometimes succumbed to the temptation of discouragement. Just when life begins to swell with golden light and fruitfulness, she thought, an axe falls, a body is split open and the offspring dropped into a pot of boiling water.

Whenever she prayed the rosary, her hopelessness receded somewhat.

On a certain Friday, when the pain in her back was unusually severe, Rose felt that her life was now over. She crumpled the magazine illustrations and posters of art exhibits that adorned her walls and threw all the cones and seeds and brave organic things into the street, where they were crushed by the wheels of the passing traffic. She was no artist, she told herself. She had no gift to give to the world. She barely mustered the will to attend Sunday Mass, and even the house of supplication seemed to have been emptied. There were no consolations, only plodding obedience and pain. Yet, she forced herself to return to the practice of daily Mass, to confess her moments of black thinking to the old priest.

In April the rains began washing the world again. Crocus flowers popped through the grass in the parks. Rose went out one morning at the hour when the streets thronged with children on their way to school, filling the echoing canyons of high-rise and brownstone with the sounds of swarming birds. As she passed a school yard, she saw a boy leaning against the chain-link fence, watching a game of stick hockey in the playground. Despite herself, she stopped to look at him, for there was longing in the stance of his body. He turned toward her, and she saw that his face was horribly scarred, all its features melted like dirty wax. Only the eyes seemed human, and they burned with a bright intensity.

Ay! she gasped. *It is not right! It is not right!* she screamed silently. *I will give him my face! Give me his face!*

She turned away from the scandal of disfigurement and fixed her attention on the consoling presence of the ordinary, but the image came with her. As she continued to walk she saw the question being endlessly, mutely, raised: Why so much suffering, why was it everywhere? Why did it seem to strike with particular cruelty against the innocent? Perhaps it was the clarity of the boy's eyes flashing with courage, perhaps it was Rose's own recent loss, but it came to her that within man's suffering there might be a mysterious nobility—a glimmer of who he might become.

At Mass that evening she pleaded with God.

Io, my Lord! If I cannot take his pain from him, may I at least lessen it for him? In this way, may I be a small mother to his soul, even though we do not meet again in this world?

And it seemed to her that the Beating Heart gave his consent.

Encouraged by this, daring to go further, opening the deepest well of her heart, she cried:

Io, my Lord! Is it possible for me to become a mother of the soul and a mother of the flesh? For I long to have a child of my own.

But in this he was silent.

Throughout that spring and summer, Rose painted and drew very little. Mostly she walked about the city, always looking at its complex textures. The many faces, staring at her, or averting their eyes from the disfigurement of her. The creeks and rivers of traffic. The steeples pointing to the *tchibekana*. The alleys where the humblest side of existence could not hide itself— garbage cans, laundry on the wash lines, dogs establishing their territories, and sparrows puffed out on the naked backyard elms. Quiet trees, the elms formed the arches and apses of some great cathedral, echoing with the vibration of human lives passing within it.

In the gutter, a cat pawed the skeleton of a herring. Am I useless, Rose sighed to herself. Am I a cat picking old bits of flesh from a skeleton? Or am I the throwaway part? Am I a bundle of bones spit out by an owl when it has dissolved the meat from its victim?

In her childhood she had asked, would it not have been easier for the baby rabbit to step out of its pelt and hand it over to the predator to save all the fright and squeaking and ripping, and the beating of terrible wings in the darkness. Grandma had told her that her question was thinking with little girl thoughts. No creature lightly surrendered what was its own, Grandma had said. Only with struggle is a life overcome, and whenever possible it cries its protests into the listening leaves or across the reaches of countless rivers.

The boy with no face was captive in his ruined flesh, yet he had chosen to live. Could she do less? She could not exchange his tragedy for hers, but she could at least paint the dignity of his soul. Was this possible? Perhaps that was the reason Esther had urged her to paint the horror of the girl in the bottle. If only Esther were here, they could discuss this difficult question.

What was this abyss Rose now felt between herself and the many who had become eternally absent? If only she could have touched the cold silken hands crossed on Esther's belly, in the emerald dress, the fingernails that not even the embalmers could entirely rid of paint. But she had not dared to touch, and the casket had been opened only for a moment while the wedding ring was removed. Other hands, other losses. Old-mary's hands as brown as tanned hide, hands that had gutted fish and coddled babies. If Rose could have touched those hands, death would not have been a mere letter of termination. It might have been disarmed of its strangeness and terror, and she would have understood the proper proportion between the living and the dead, between time and eternity, a geometry that was as fixed and without malice as the principles of linear perspective in Leonardo's notebooks.

As Rose turned to the crumbling house on Rue St. Benoît, she saw that a pink moon hung opalescent in the sky, like one of Hugo's theater backdrops. It beckoned, and she strained forward to some far celebration of light, realizing that for now she could only yearn across the gulf of time and space, across the solitude that existed between all people, between the living and the dead, a void that was too broad for the frail bridgework of

546

words. Until that distant consummation she would ever fall short of union, would remain outside the singing-dancing of mankind, inside her mysterious self, waiting, waiting to know and be known, to love and be loved.

In late August, a man came to the house and spent two hours with Hugo upstairs in the attic. Rose, hiding in her studio, did not see him. After he left, she ventured downstairs to find that Hugo seemed less dazed than usual. At supper, he even ate a little cracker with his tea.

"Who was that visiting you today, Hugo?" Rose asked.

"A predator", he replied cryptically. "But one who will feed us."

"What is his name?"

"Favio Ontolli."

"Oh, how wonderful, Hugo! Does this mean that he will give you a show?"

"No. I suspect it means that Mrs. Morgan paid him to come on an errand of mercy, to buy a painting of mine, so that she will not have to read about my suicide in the *Gazette*."

"Oh, Hugo," Rose said in a scolding tone that was disturbingly like Esther's, "please do not say such things."

Hugo returned to his studio the next day and made a tiny horse, a blue horse galloping on a field of total black. That evening, when Rose went upstairs to tell him that it was after nine and that his tea was getting cold, he mumbled something and grunted at the canvas.

"You are painting again, Hugo. I am so happy to see it."

"How about you, Rose? Are you painting?" It was the first time in months that he asked anything about herself.

"No, Hugo. I have been walking and thinking. I go to museums a lot. I find it hard to paint since—"

"Since she left us."

"Yes, since she left—us."

"What do you think?" he asked, pointing at the painting.

"It is dark and sad and true, Hugo. It is a word from your heart. You have painted the word that is in both of our hearts."

Then his face crumpled, and she left him alone with his feelings for a while. He came downstairs to the kitchen later and said, "Rose, dear, would you make me a big pan of scrambled eggs. I have such an appetite."

She smiled and did as he asked, feeling that at last they were emerging from the great shroud that death had cast over them. The next day she went searching on the holy mountain for pine cones and small bits of twig and shrubbery and abandoned bird feathers to bring back to her room, to replace what she had so foolishly thrown out. Upon her arrival at the shrine she noticed a bulletin announcing a three o'clock Mass. She went inside, gasping as she penetrated the liquid, grace-filled air, wondering why she had stayed away from the shrine so long. She drank deeply. And at Communion there was a consolation. Her ability to pray returned at that moment, the barren land prayer giving way after a bitter winter to the prayer of spring. She saw how far she had gone into the desolation. Then, as never before, did her poverty and crudeness leap out at her, her hands small and grubby as she opened them on a pew scarred by generations hungry for God. An ugly person she was. It was a good thing, she thought, that God did not love according to appearances.

From then on life wobbled back in the direction of normal. They tried to read a stream of books far into each night, Hugo on the sofa reading poisoned philosophy, she in the ratty armchair reading books of art history, soaking up thousands upon thousands of color prints of painting and sculpture made during millennia of creativity. These were like bits of bark floating by in the foam of the deep waters. If they were too frail to cling to for life, at least they were a sign that somewhere there was solid land. Rose began to draw more often, but still could not muster the will to paint.

In the drowsy sun of an autumn afternoon, she sat sketching the brightly colored trees in a little park not far from the house. The walkways were temporarily deserted, and at the moment when she felt most grateful for this haven of peace, a noise of galloping hoofs thundered around a curve in the path. A rushing shape approached through piles of red leaves, scattering them left and right. As if one of Hugo's paintings was breaking forth from the slavery of two dimensions.

Rose tore her eyes from her drawing to see two gasping little girls running hand in hand. They went past at a tremendous clip, leaving in their wake a whirr of whipped air, spiraling leaves, and a stream of sound like a long pure note, as if they were humming together.

One child was blind. Her eyes were gouged and scarred, her head nodding in a sightless headlong plunge, her face intent on nothing save the grip of her companion's hand, the unsuspected thickness of air, and the taste of utter exhilaration. On the face of her seeing friend were other ecstasies—large, open, racehorse eyes, the panting thoroughbred power of giving the impossible thing. The seeing girl had bestowed upon her blind friend a different form of sight, the feeling of wind on skin, of small unused muscles pumping at catastrophic speed, the awesome pitch through treacherous air that always contained within it the threat of collision, and the promise of soaring.

There is my soul, thought Rose. *O, O, ay, ay, that I might trust what you are doing with me in this rushing darkness!*

Rose returned home with a feeling of intense purpose, went straight to her studio and stared at the piles of pine cones, maple keys, wasp nests, and other treasures she had retrieved from the parks throughout the city. The pine cones spiraled inviolate on their stems. Some of the seed wings were broken, and the hive was ripped a little. Each life is like this, she said to herself. Some are burned and some are blind, and some see, and some do not see, but all are part of the texture, and the texture is beloved, for it is part of the form that the Beating Heart has made.

Then she inscribed on the canvas a drawing of the blind girl and her friend. And on another canvas the burned boy who had only eyes. She worked all night, alternating between both, and as the colors flowed, and the darkness and light wrestled, or danced: once again she discovered that the flow of making had not been taken from her. As she painted her children she spoke to them, for in a sense they were now within her, they were connected to her and to each other in the rivers of life that cannot be separated from all living waters.

Throughout that autumn, Rose painted steadily. In late October, the cold settled into the city. In November, winter fell in earnest. On the second day of that month, because it was the feast of All Souls, she attended an early morning Mass and offered it for those who had died among the people she had known. Esther was foremost in her thoughts. She also recalled that somewhere on the earth there was a woman she had once called Youngmary-the-mother-of-my-flesh. With a pang of regret she realized that seldom were the times she had prayed for her mother. Why was it so? Were they not connected? Surely there was no soul as important to her own life as this faceless one? And why had she come to mind on the feast of all souls? Had she died? Rose tried to pray for her, but could force nothing from her heart, though she sensed that God accepted the offering of her will.

After Communion, the face of Tchibi came to her with a great urgency. This was puzzling, for she was certain he lived.

That night she and Hugo read as usual in the parlor. He sat by the fire, muttering over a magazine article.

"It's a bad comedy, Rose, a farce within a farce—within a farce. They're using your people, just like they use us. Mad

550

puppeteer jiggles the strings of the little wooden protagonist. The audience applauds, the puppeteer pockets the coins, and life goes on as usual. Does anyone ever bother to ask the puppet how he feels about it? How will this one end, I wonder?"

"How will what end, Hugo?"

"This fellow here, this artist. I think we saw some of his work at that show we went to last year."

"What are you reading, Hugo?"

"A piece about native art. Here, read it yourself."

He thrust it at her and went off to make a pot of tea.

The arrival of the white man's civilization in North America ushered in a struggle between two cultures—one mystical and intuitive, the other rational and pragmatic, the product of scientific revolution.

The aboriginal peoples have no word for art. Nor can they conceive of creativity apart from ordinary life. Among them there are no discussions on high art or low art, nor have they established their own galleries in which to enshrine culture, for culture *is* life to the aboriginal peoples. Art-as-art is a foreign notion, but in recent years a synthesis of western European art forms, such as painting, and aboriginal symbolism has been under way.

The article went on to describe the growing reputations of a dozen woodland Indian artists, members of the indigenous peoples of the vast wilderness which stretched from the Great Lakes to the Arctic.

Ben Thunder-eagle is among the greatest of the woodland artists. He learned the old legends from the medicine men and the tribal elders of the Anishinâbe people and believed he had to risk everything to record his heritage before it was swept away by white civilization.

During the past ten years his original work has attracted growing attention, even in the closed circles of the government galleries. Collectors in Europe and the United States have thronged to his exhibits in Toronto, Montreal, and New York, lining up for hours on opening nights. Last year he sold over $50,000 worth of prints and paintings.

A success by modern standards, it seems that he is not immune from the epidemic of violence plaguing native communities. Described by friends as a member of the Grand Medicine Lodge, as a shaman of great power, Thunder-eagle was arrested in Thunder Bay, Ontario, last week, and charged with malicious destruction of public property.

A spokesman for an Anishinâbe band outside Thunder Bay maintains that Thunder-eagle is a man of peace, one who dedicates himself to preserving the native way of life. A controversial figure in the politically divided community, the artist was born Binemin Edzo in a remote fishing-trapping village of northern Ontario. He has been released in his own custody until trial next month.

A sociologist at Laurentian University, professor Marleena Crombie-Collingwood, blames the agony of many native artists on the "dysfunctionality of patriarchal European religion and the imperialist white culture which has violated the natural purity of aboriginal societies".

Rose could read no more. She saw only Tchibi's eyes.

Ogini, he said, placing into her hand a sphere of perfect white. *Come to me. I am dying.*

She had learned to listen to that small voice. In the past, whenever she had ignored it, she had regretted her inattention. Whenever she had listened to it, she had later discovered how right it was to do so. Thus, she had gradually come to trust it. It was the *anjeni* guardian, she supposed, or the Holy Spirit.

"This man is my brother", she explained to Hugo, pointing at the paragraph. There was no photo of the artist, only a reproduction of one of his paintings—the eight snakes entangling him.

Hugo gave her more money than she needed—they were both too distraught to make measurements of such things. He took her by bus to the railway station and put her on the next train departing for the northwest.

The journey was long and troubled by a desperate feeling that the train was going too slowly. The snow began to fall as the rails turned toward the hills above Lake Superior. Winter fell early in this region. Io, how long it had been since she had felt it, how pampered she had become in the long summers of Montreal. How quickly she had forgotten the darkness and coldness of the north. Hour by hour her anxiety grew.

Upon arriving in Thunder Bay, she took a taxi to the reserve outside the city and inquired of various people where she could find Ben Thunder-eagle.

"Did you not know?" one after another informed her. "Ben's place burned down last night. He's in the hospital."

Alarmed, she asked, "Is he badly hurt?"

People shrugged. "Maybe. Maybe not. It's not the first time. Whenever he drinks, there's trouble."

How odd it felt to meet so many who knew him, who spoke of him intimately. It made a strangeness come upon her, and a fear, not only a fear of what the fire had done to him, but a fear that he might no longer know her, and she him. Yet the small voice had spoken. *Ogini, come to me, I am dying.*

But how could it be? For the words had come days before the fire. Was his cry about another kind of dying?

Directed to the site of his cabin, she stood before it, staring in disbelief at the black cavernous hole still poising the fangs of a few dangling boards, frothing with ice, like the jaws of a devil-fish opening onto an eternal devouring.

"Ben fell asleep", said an old man who was passing by. "He was drinking again. He was mad about the trial and the lawyer's fees. He knocked over a lantern. Or maybe one of the drunken ones kicked it over as he slept. That's what the cops think, anyway."

"Io," said an old woman, "those warriors, those medicine men, they are all crazy. He ran out into the night with his clothing on fire."

"Like a torch he flared", said the old man shaking his head. "He ran about the street. It took many of us to throw him to the ground and cover him with snow. The screams of eagles came from his throat."

Rose's legs began to shake. She felt now the engorging of a cloud more vast than the sky, a thunder-terror-cloud. As she traveled by taxi to the hospital, pictures raced before her eyes, the paintings she had seen in the exhibit of native art. How strange that she had looked at them unheeding of their maker, not knowing that her own Tchibi was Ben Thunder-eagle. Now she recalled the odd sensation of recognition she had felt when looking at them, though they were not much different from those of the other artists. The over-brimming tension in them, the playing with fire and spirit-lines, the dancing with demons disguised in the shapes of animal and bird spirits, pushing always toward the dangerous edge. She remembered Tchibi running in the cold weather in his shirtsleeves, as if his over-heated frame had more than enough fire to thaw the winter landscape. Leaping over cliff banks or into ravenous water, without care for where his feet landed because he was young and indestructible, or else sought destruction.

Rose passed unchallenged into the corridors of the hospital, stopping only for a moment at the deserted reception desk in the lobby where a small radio played to itself. A sign beside the elevator door told her that on the top floor there was a "Burn Unit." She entered the elevator and pushed a button. As the metal box hummed and clanked, rising with lurches, her skin felt clammy and her heart beat wildly. When the doors opened she stepped out into the military gaze of a middle-aged woman behind the counter of the ward station.

"Yes?" the woman said.

"I would like to see Binemin Edzo", Rose said.

"There is no one by that name here."

"He is called Ben Thunder-eagle."

"Only family are permitted. Are you a family member?"

"I am his sister."

"Even so, it's long past hospital visiting hours."

"He is dying. I must see him."

"I'm sorry, there's too much risk of infection with burn victims. And as for dying, no one really can tell yet. The doctor says—"

"He is dying", said Rose forcefully.

The hall was deserted, and the nurse was quiet for a moment. Her shoulders moved into gentler shapes, and she said, "Come with me."

She led Rose down the corridor on her soft white shoes and stopped finally at the doorway of a room. The nurse turned to her and whispered, "I don't know why I'm doing this. But—"

"He is dying, and it will be tonight", Rose said with finality.

The nurse nodded toward the interior of the darkened room and walked away down the hall. Rose entered with dread. The air inside was thick with the sickening odor of burnt flesh and disinfectant. Only a dim white light burned on a far wall, casting a glow on a hospital bed, massive and shining beneath a bank of machines. Plastic tubing coiled like spirit lines around a shadow form on the bed. Jars of liquid dripped life into it. Rose could barely breathe, and her legs almost gave way beneath her as she moved slowly toward it, terrified of what she would see.

She had not thought about what he would look like. Whenever he had come to mind he had been the Tchibi of the past, the wild boy cavorting in the trees, warbling loon songs, eating minnows, cramming berry mash into his wide grinning mouth, eyes flashing green sweet-fire. She had expected to see only a slightly larger version of the memory, and was unprepared for the man lying before her. The naked body was stretched in utter abandonment, arms and legs spread wide, a band of white cloth suspended untouching across the blades of his hips, someone's afterthought of modesty. The head was covered in raw patches, all hair singed from it, the face unrecognizable. Red or charred islands of skin covered his frame, separated by yellowish seeping matter.

As Rose stood gazing down into the bed she ceased to breathe. The objective horror of the man's state was shocking enough, but beneath this was an undertow of deeper horror—the realization that the brother she had loved throughout all these many years had not remained the image in her mind, nor had he become the man she had painted in her portrait. It was now very clear that he had lived his own life, and that it had taken a direction beyond her knowledge and given to his flesh a form that had never been an extension of her love for him. Over no part of him, it seemed, had her prayers and offerings exercised an influence. Perhaps a little at the beginning, but if his art and his accident indicated anything, it was that her endless sacrifice had been futile.

Though he was still alive.

"It cannot be him", she said. "No, it is someone else. Surely it is a mistake. It is another man who burned in his cabin." She turned to the window, wondering if he was roaming about outside, hoping that it was so. Yet she knew it was not, for the largest patches of skin—along the inside of one calf, on the belly, and another on the inside of an upper arm—all bore the holes of his more ancient torture.

Rose began to pray without words, without thoughts.

Io! Io! Ay, ay!

She came closer and clung to the steel bars of the bed rail. "Tchibi", she whispered. "Nishime, it is Ogini. I have come."

She did the irrational, forbidden thing; she took his ravaged hand into her own, holding it, infecting it, begging that she might not be causing him any pain. The hand was hot.

Silent tears dropped. Then, sobbing burst like the first creation of sound and poured over the irreversible damage. As she wept, the remembrance of the poor bush chapel of their childhood came into her mind. *Jesus our King is born, Jesus our King, Kije-kije-kije-Manito*, she and Tchibi kneeling side by side as they gazed at the crib and the crucifix hanging above it.

Then the partridge stone he placed into her hand that Christmas eve. His eyes saying, *This is me, Ogini. To you, I give myself.*

Ay, ay! Was the fire in the loon-boy's heart now a nothing, a throwaway?

Tchibi had not moved, could not move, but the fingers of his hand twitched, the membranes weeping fluid. The lids of his eyes cracked open, the white half-exposed and bloodshot. The dull green irises swam in their sockets, fixed for a moment on her face, and could move no more. Then closed.

"Tchibi, it is me."

Rose suddenly felt the shadow shapes of seven serpents all around her, then an eighth, smaller and deadlier than the others. She prayed the name of Jesus against them, and they coiled back as if stung, withdrawing into the corners of the room.

His lips trembled and split.

The air whistled from his throat: "O-ghi-ni-niss-i—"

"It is me, Nishime. I am with you."

Again his breath whistled, though it formed no words.

"Does my hand hurt your hand?"

"Rose?" the lips whispered.

"Yes, it is Rose."

"Bread."

Bread? she wondered, fearing for his mind. They had given him medicine to deaden the pain, and it had confused his thoughts.

"Gor–don?"

Who was Gordon?

"Kin–oj–e?" the lips quivered, the whistle rising to a low moan.

At the name of Kinoje, the serpents hissed and crept closer to the bed.

Rose prayed again and they withdrew.

"Fa–ther?" Tchibi said. But the father had long ago disappeared after the torture. This was the most torturous thought of all.

"An–drei?"

Father Andrei? So that was who his spirit sought! Io, where was the priest? Gone, as so many others had gone. Where in all this wide world could he be found? West of the mountains, far, far, too far.

"Bread," Tchibi moaned.

"Yes, my brother, we ate the bread and jam together with Father Andrei, and Oldmary too. Do you remember how we laughed and played?"

"Gor–don!" After this word his lips curled back from his rotting teeth and a deep thump-thump burbled forth—wailing incomprehensible words: "That-is-not-my-name."

"Binemin is your name, my Tchibi."

"White-man-is-not-my-name. *Oma-ka-ki.* Frog. Flies. Eat. Straw-berr-ee. Win-ter."

His chest began to heave more rapidly, tears slipped from the corners of both eyes.

"Gor–don!"

Gordon? Though he might have said *garden.*

"Do you remember, Tchibi? The garden we made, you and

I? It was the joy-time. We were together. Now, in the suffering-time, we are again together."

"Ningâ?"

This made Rose weep anew. Was he crying out for his own mother, the one who had helped torture him, or the mother she had been when he was a baby, before the motherness in her was disfigured? Or was he crying to her, Rose, as if she were his mother, he the child? The agony flowed through her heart, piercing and burning at once, splitting open the image of the partridge that she had held inside her all these years, it broke from beak to tail, its small thumping heart exposed, despised, corrupted, encoiled by the many serpents that had promised it eagle-flight, and pulled it down beneath the earth. *Soon, soon,* they hissed, *beneath, beneath you go, into the jaws of the kinoje serpent, the Great Neshiwed which is forever devouring.*

"Not forever!" Rose cried aloud.

"Ogini?"

Once more his eyes opened and swam, seeking her face.

"It is me, Nishime, Binemin, Tchibi, my loon-boy, my beloved. I am with you."

The fingers curled slightly around her own. There was nothing weaker on the earth, yet it sought to hold her.

His eyes found her, green eyes that were filled with neither sweet-green nor bile-green, but with fear and confusion. He did not understand anything that had happened to him, not since the first burning many years ago, when the world had reversed its colors from light to dark.

"My Tchibi, I will speak unto your heart now. If your ears can hear me, squeeze my fingers."

For a second only, the stems of his fingers curled more tightly around hers.

"Now I speak, for I am certain that your heart hears me. If your thoughts are confused, it does not matter, for the heart of the soul hears. My Tchibi, you will live, for I will ask it of the

559

One who made you, for nothing will he deny me. Little have I asked of him in my life, but I ask him now. This I ask of him, that he bring you back to life."

Rose let go of his fingers and extended her hands over his upper body, the left suspended above his head, the right above his heart. First she grew silent inside, then all motion ceased within her. She closed her eyes and waited. Time slowed still further. At the trembling edge of all cessation, she opened the tabernacle of her heart wherein the Beating Heart seemed to sleep and spoke with him.

"Io, Jesus, *nintessinindjitawa*—I stretch my hand over him."

Though there was peace, there was also silence.

"*Nin gegea,* Jesus—heal his wounds, Jesus, in your name, if it is your will, Manito."

Still the silence. Yet the peace increased, and the serpents hissed as they withdrew still farther.

"*Nin pikwawigan*—I am hunchbacked. I am small and ugly, as you made me to be. All my life have I borne this without complaint, for I have offered it to you for the one who lies before us. Io, my Lord, do not let it be a waste. Do not let him fall."

She waited and prayed for many minutes. Yet the silence did not answer. Tchibi's chest continued to rise and fall, but weakly now, like a stone forgetting to breathe. His eyes were closed, his lips open, cracked, bleeding, his hands curled like the claws of a dying animal pinned on its back by a predator.

Why was his body failing? Why was God not healing him?

Then she began to fear, for it seemed that the Beating Heart must surely have turned away from her and that all her years of the sacrifice-way had meant nothing to him.

"O my brother, where are you?" she cried loudly.

With this the serpents began to approach again, hissing in her ears.

Sssoon, sssoon, they hissed, *beneath, beneath you go, into the jaws of the kinoje serpent, the Great Nesssshiwed which is forever devouring.*

"Help me, help me, Winijishid-Manito!—Holy Spirit, why do you not heal him!"

Then she heard a beating heart. It was Tchibi's heart hammering with sudden wildness, and it was her own barely keeping time with it, yet beyond and beneath and above and around them both was the great drum-throb of a heart so immense that nothing could contain it. Rose did not understand. She knew only one thing: Tchibi was dying, he was going from her forever, he would no longer walk upon this earth, he would be absent not only from her eyes but also from the wind and the light and the many waters that all men shared.

"Tchibi, Tchibi, do not fall into the abyss", she pleaded, for he was a small burnt mannikin suspended in the cruel hands of the universe. The savage universe-god gazed at her—Io, was it *anjeni* or devil?

The thought struck her like a fist. Was *this* the hidden face of God?

"No! No! *Matchi aiiwishiwan!*—It is a wicked thing!"

Never would she believe that this was the hidden face! Never, no matter what her senses told her! Never!

"Eee-ay! Eee-ay!" she wailed.

Now her voice raised to a mighty cry:

"O Jesus, *O nin ishkidee!* My heart is tired of sorrow and grief!" she wailed. "Speak to me! Speak to me! Why are you silent? See your little brother before you on this cross, see him. Though he has fallen back into the *enamiassig*-way, the pagan-way, still he is a child. So much was taken from him, so little was given, less did he understand. Have mercy, Lord, have mercy upon the one you gave to me. For if you gave, then he belonged to you; and if I yet belong to you, he is in my hands, and you are in me, and so he too is in your hands. I hold him! Ay, ay! I hold him, and so you too are holding him! Io, Jesus, do not let him drop from your wounded hands into the darkness where the mouth of the beast opens to take him. Ay, ay, Jesus, carry him up with you, for he has nothing, and he is nothing without you, as I am nothing without you! Hear me, hear me, O my God, for my heart is broken over him, and he is broken within me, and within you, for you are within me, within *you*, O Beating Heart!"

Then there came to her suddenly, as a word is sometimes read on the wide extended firmament of the sky, a promise. A promise that only his flesh was falling, falling down through the dark waters into the mouth of the beast that is under the waters, the *kinoje-neshiwed* spirit, the jack-fish, devil-fish, death-fish spirit. And the man-spirit of Binemin Edzo was washed clean of the false names that clung to him, entangling his heart and mind, the serpents were pried from him and cast down, he was cleansed in the waters of the Great Mercy and bathed in the waters of her tears flowing as creeks flow to rivers, and rivers to lakes, and lakes by many waters unto the sea. And then she knew that his spirit was becoming as silver as *atikameg*, though the washing was like a fire of purification, it was a terrible burning yet within the burning was the joy, for he was going up, up, up into the hands of God. And one day, too, his flesh would rise with the rising of all flesh and be restored and the last of the enemies would be hurled into the Lake of Fire.

Then the stone exhaled slowly. After that, it did not inhale. It was still.

Rose wept bitterly into the hand she held, crying not for the sins, which had been scarlet, but for the orb of quartz which once had been whiter than snow, the prism of Christ which had been within him from the beginning and was now gone.

The following morning, after the death certificate was signed, a secretary at the hospital handed Rose the possessions that had been brought with Binemin to the hospital on the night of the fire. The large manila envelope contained two items: a spherical soot-blackened stone that had been found in the charred pocket of his pants and a scorched aluminum medallion. All his other possessions had been destroyed by the fire.

Rose stayed at a motel in Thunder Bay for three days, until he was buried. She said to every official person who inquired that she was his sister. She signed the documents that were necessary—he had no other family to do this task. No one seemed to notice or care that the names were wrong. She endured the lawyer who stopped her in the hospital corridor and said that Ben Thunder-eagle was bankrupt, there was no legacy, she needn't think any inheritance was coming to her, there was no legal will, he had wasted everything on parties and gifts to his friends in the movement. Moreover, there were unpaid legal fees. . . .

She did not know what the movement was and did not ask. She looked at the lawyer with great pity, for it seemed to her that many were the souls who appear at funerals with money in their thoughts. Just as she had once desired a red shoe and a brass dog, they did not understand what was gain and what was loss. It was the fallen part of human nature that sought to gain by another's loss. How pitiful they were, how pitiful she was, yes, even within her own heart the seed of the *neshiwed* had once, long ago, almost taken root. Yet here was one in whom that seed had become a twisted tree, its roots clawing deep into the soil of his heart, entangling and encircling and possessing everything, for he assumed that all men were like himself, that all men desired to profit in this way.

Rose paid for the coffin and the stipend for the priest who said the funeral Mass. She tried not to resent the medicine men who stood scowling outside the church and chanting at the graveyard. She prayed for their conversions. She prayed also for the Toronto businessman who owned an art gallery and whom she overheard telling a newspaper reporter that the country had lost its greatest native painter. And she overheard him again at the reception held in the Native Friendship Center, saying to another whiteman, someone from the National Gallery, *tragic* and *alcohol* and *genius* and many such words, as his eyes flitted across the sea of the Ojibwe and Odawa and Cree in search of new genius. And the whiteman from the National Gallery said to the whiteman from the Toronto gallery, "The real problem is you've lost your major source of income, haven't you?"

No one spoke to Rose, not even the university professor whom everyone called Marleena. Seeing the golden curls across the room, Rose went forward to introduce herself to her old friend because she felt sure that her very first falling-into-seeing had intimately and permanently connected them. But when Marleena's eyes glanced off her as if she were invisible, Rose held back. For a moment she experienced a brief return of the old gift, fell for a few seconds inside those blue eyes and understood what had happened to the woman during the ensuing years: the hardening of her heart, the anger and intelligence and willfulness that had grown side by side. Marleena was powerful. Marleena was strong. She was of great importance in the room. And Rose was just one of the many small people who had come to lament; yes, she was in Marleena's eyes a nothing-person.

Before leaving on the train to Montreal, she paid one last visit to the grave, knelt upon the frozen dirt, kissed it, and said, "I will see you on the Last Day, Nishime, and until then I will pray for you always, as you rise in the great purifying unto the place of forever-singing."

And she took from that place only the small scorched medallion of Kateri and the globe of quartz which was no longer white, but covered with many stains.

Hugo was very considerate. He did not ask, did not probe, though eventually she told enough for him to discern that she had suffered the greatest loss of her life. They continued to live together as they had from the beginning. Both of them were grieving, both adjusting to different kinds of absence. Both were grateful for each other. They painted in their studios most days, Rose fitfully and without much vigor, Hugo with a certain solitary intensity. In his many new horse paintings, lonely riders searched the heavens with their blind eyes. The horses continued to gallop, but the landscapes were sometimes indefinite; at other times the old strong chiaroscuro of reds and cobalts and blacks returned. He was not greatly depressed, but neither was he happy. Perhaps he had never been happy unless Esther was by his side.

"Am I happy or unhappy now that Tchibi is no longer by my side?" Rose asked herself. What a strange thought! He had not been by her side since her thirteenth year, and now she was twenty-five. Or maybe twenty-six. Possibly she was thirty and didn't know it. Threads of gray had appeared in her hair. Her face was spreading like a pudding. Tiny wrinkles had crept around her eyes. The years were blending into each other.

Winter passed, then summer, then autumn, then the cycle repeated itself. With the passage of time the edge of her grief grew duller. There was a lingering sadness that did not contain the glint of a black blade, no, it contained a hint of joy, for she had received the promise that Tchibi was rising through a purifying fire, as Grandma had risen, toward the place of Great Singing. He was alive, he had not gone out of existence, he had merely been carried to another station of the journey, beyond the reach of the eyes but not beyond the reach of the heart. In her heart she carried him still, and her love for him continued and grew. So the heart's loss was also, strangely, the heart's gain.

21

During the summer of 1967 a World's Fair came to Montreal. There, a giant pavilion was built, dedicated to the native peoples of the country, and on its outer walls were murals painted in the styles Rose had seen at the exhibit of native art the Ontolli Gallery had hosted three years before. She was thrilled to see that art by native people was now considered significant, and that millions of visitors were looking at it with interest. Yet she was disturbed by the pagan themes of the murals. Where was it leading her people?

Hugo took her to see the fair several times. He was growing older, fighting arthritis in his hands and knees. He walked more slowly than he once had, but this was not unwelcome to Rose, who, as the years rolled by, was moving ever more slowly. She seldom thought about her back because for some years now its continuous ache had become part of ordinary existence. Only when she foolishly went without food or sleep, or bent for too many hours over her drawing table, did she remember it, for then it made its loudest complaints.

She remained unconcerned that her own work had received no public attention: not a single purchase, nor an offer of a show from the people who did occasionally drop by Hugo's studio. From time to time he sold one of his horses, and this was only to be expected, for his paintings were becoming exceptionally beautiful, always changing and developing according to his moods and impulses. The sales were infrequent, however, and thus their life continued hand-to-mouth, as it had been from the beginning.

"Only enough manna for one day at a time", Rose liked to

remind herself. Of course, there were those rare events that brought in enough money to support them for longer periods. More of Esther's paintings were sold during the spring of 1968, and the income paid for six-months' worth of rent, food, and art materials. Hugo kept only his wife's last painting, the untitled portrait of the pigeon seller releasing her captives. He titled it *Freedom*.

If, from time to time, Rose felt a qualm about living entirely upon Hugo's generosity, she accepted the state of dependency as a gift from God, which he gave in order to keep her trusting in him. That she stood as a bulwark against Hugo's loneliness and temptation to despair was not unknown to her, but so, too, was he a bulwark for her. He was, although not a Christian man, at least a man of great kindness. He would harm no one, and surely this was noticed by God. He was, she supposed, the father she had never known. Like a Hebrew before the coming of Christ, perhaps a little like St. Joseph.

"Did you paint today?" he would ask her each evening when they shared their pot of tea in the parlor.

"No, Hugo, I did not. I was very tired today."

Sometimes it was, "No, Hugo, today is Sunday. I do not work on Sunday."

"Sunday? Are you serious? Is it Sunday? I thought it was Wednesday!"

"No, Hugo, it is Sunday."

At other times it was, "Yes, Hugo, I made a picture of a tree I once saw many years ago."

"May I see it?"

But they were both rather too tired to climb the stairs again.

"On second thought, maybe you can show me tomorrow."

"Hugo," Rose once asked, "when you paint, do you remember the horses in the field where the king was standing?"

"You mean Birmingham?"

"Yes."

"Absolutely", he nodded. "Absolutely. As fresh in my mind as if I had seen them this morning."

"Do you remember the king too?"

"The king? Oh, you mean the stained glass. No, he's faded. Rather vague now, though I suppose I could recall the details if I really tried."

"Have you ever thought of painting him?"

Hugo peered at her. "No, my dear. And may I say, without hurting your feelings, please do not try your little missionary tricks on this old sinner."

"I wasn't, Hugo."

"Weren't you? All right, I believe you. I will grant that Rose Wâbos is incapable of deceit. But it's suspicious, girl, very suspicious, when a fervent young Christian suggests, ever so delicately, that an old lost Jew should paint a picture of Christ."

He laughed. She laughed also, though her laughter contained an undercurrent of sadness.

Then it happened. The unthinkable. The knife edge upon which the past and the future balanced.

In late autumn of 1968, a visitor came to visit Hugo in his studio. As usual, Rose made herself invisible, but she did say a prayer that Hugo would sell a painting because the larder was growing empty again.

Goldie sat by her feet, cleaning her fur, extending her legs elegantly to reach the most difficult parts. Rose scratched Goldie's ears, smiled at her, and returned to her work. Around eleven o'clock, heavy footsteps sounded on the stairs and thundered along the hallway.

"Oh, no", Rose thought to herself. "Hugo wants to introduce me to someone. Io, I wish he would not!"

The raps on the studio door were lighthearted but insistent.

"Rose, my *savante sauvage*. Destiny knocks."

"I am occupied, Hugo. It is not a good time to leave this painting."

"If you open, my dear, I think you will not regret it."

Sighing, Rose went to the door to let destiny in. It took the form of a tall, fine-looking man in his early fifties, dressed in a suit that shimmered like black silver. A red handkerchief puffed from his jacket pocket, a red tie hooked the eye immediately. His face came later. It was a darkly tinted face surmounted by a full head of silver hair. His eyes were brown. At first Rose thought he must be a native person; then, examining the features, she realized that he was not.

"This is Rose, Favio", Hugo said.

"Ah, the elusive Rose", Favio Ontolli said in a voice as rich and fluid as olive oil. He entered the studio, his lips shaping and reshaping themselves into variations of a smile, his eyes half-lidded like Goldie's—with self-contentment or amusement, it was not clear.

He offered his hand for a shake. Rose shook it.

"This is the owner and chief curator of the Ontolli-Metropol, Rose. Head nabob of the *Kulturkampf*. A very important poobah. He wants to see your work."

"Only if Miss Wâbos permits", said Favio Ontolli with gracious deference, bowing slightly.

"If you like", Rose murmured, though she was not happy about it. She felt certain—no, she knew—that he was merely curious, that he wished to see the hunchback in Madame Coquine's House of Mystery. Doubtless Hugo had urged him to waste a few minutes examining her drawings and paintings, Hugo's loyalty and affection for her outweighing his judgment. The curator would take a look and make some suitably encouraging comments, then leave, never to come again.

She was wrong. He glanced at the uncompleted painting on the drawing table, looked elsewhere, then returned to it.

"What do you think, Favio?" Hugo asked.

The curator's face assumed a mask of critical objectivity, though it was possibly not a mask; possibly it was himself.

"In all honesty, Hugo, I thought for a moment that it was more of the same. Every street corner is packed with enterprising young wildlife artists. Then, a moment ago, something happened. This painting drags you in. It's not the cliché it seemed at first glance. Look at those dogs. They are killers. Moreover, I think they're metaphors." He turned to Rose and asked with great seriousness, "Are they metaphors, Miss Wâbos?"

"I do not know, sir. It is a scene I once saw with my eyes."

"It is a metaphor", the curator said to himself. "The dogs are human nature. The owl, it's also human nature. See the owl's outraged dignity. And its courage. The refusal to flinch or to fly away."

"It could not fly away", Rose explained. "It was sick."

Without responding, Favio Ontolli tugged up the creases of his trouser knees and bent on his haunches to peer at several paintings lined against the wall.

"Who is this man?" he asked pointing at an old portrait of Tchibi.

"My brother."

"Your brother. What's the meaning of the two birds on his shoulders and the globe he's standing on?"

Rose felt that it was rude of the visitor so instantly to demand nakedness of her. She did not reply. Regardless, he moved on to the next picture. The twin girls in the womb.

"Again with the small birds, and the flames." He glanced up at Hugo. "She has her own lexicon, I see, sign of authentic generative powers."

"We used to call it inspiration, Favio", Hugo said with a wry smile.

The curator's face deflected the comment.

One after another he went through Rose's paintings, growing more and more silent as he progressed. Then Hugo directed him to three large cardboard boxes in the corner. The curator went through the first with slow deliberation, his eyes reading each work, analyzing, frowning, smiling.

"Strange. Very strange, yet haunting. Some of these more primitive works are completely original." He sniffed a brown sheet. "*Ecco!* Is this a paper shopping bag?"

"I expect it is", Hugo replied grinning. "The solvent, I believe, is kerosene."

The curator's face convulsed in agony. "You monster, Hugo! Why don't you give this woman some turpentine?"

"I did, Favio. And canvas. Esther gave her oils. The primitive work was before our time, the homemade charcoal, the coal oil, the lamentable paper. Part of the mythos, wouldn't you say? Rather good details for a catalogue."

"Yes, indeed."

The discomfort of standing by as others discussed her life and her most intimate works was too much for Rose.

"I will go and make us some tea, Hugo", she murmured.

"Fine, Rose, fine", the old man said distractedly as she left.

When she returned with a tray of cups and saucers some minutes later, she interrupted the two men, who were head to head in an animated discussion, the nature of which she could not begin to guess, the subject of which, she supposed, was herself.

"Rose," said Hugo, "this gentleman and I have just been negotiating. He is now quite prepared to lead you away in chains." Hugo fixed the other man with a cold smile. The visitor arched his brows slightly as if to say, *Ah, these artists! What one must endure to make a living!*

"Miss Wâbos," he said, "I am willing to let you have a show at my gallery in the spring of next year. Somebody has dropped out of my stable, and a gap in our schedule of exhibitions has appeared. A show of subject matter both unusual and diverting would help to fill in for a few weeks."

"Favio likes the equestrian imagery that is currently popular among the cultured set, Rose. It is a compliment. It implies that you are a thoroughbred. It also implies that he wishes to own you."

"Tut-tut, Hugo, not at all. It implies that I wish to give the young lady's work some exposure. I can promise nothing, of course, in terms of the market."

"He means cash sales, Rose."

"An indelicate expression. What I mean to say is that she's an unknown, with some rather anachronistic themes. It's hard to predict how the public will respond."

"She speaks fairly good English, Favio. You might want to try addressing her directly."

"Of course. I'm sorry. What I mean to say, Miss, is that you shouldn't get your hopes up. I think your work is interesting. The style is primitive, autodidactic—self-taught. There is a growing interest in this genre. However, certain themes in your work are counterproductive, and thus I—"

"In what sense counterproductive, old boy?" Hugo interjected.

"The rather simplistic and exhausted image bank of, well, Christian symbolism."

"Ah", Hugo said with a flourish of melodrama. "What you really mean to say, Favio, is that you are so far ahead of the times, so very avant-garde, and so very, very brave and daring in your revolutionary shows, that you cannot afford a loss of your reputation as an iconoclast. Am I correct?"

"Don't be nasty, Hugo, or should I say *Huggo*. You sounded just like Esther when you said that."

"Who's being nasty, Favio?"

"You are. You would like to think, wouldn't you, that I am a cardboard cutout capitalist who milks the poor suffering artists

572

for all they're worth, a nasty fellow with a big cigar, asking the price of this little innocent's soul. Am I correct?"

"Correct. Let me ask you, Favio old chum, old *paesáno*: Who lives in the million-dollar mansion in Outremont, and who lives in the rented slum dwelling in Saint Henri?"

"I live in Outremont now, Hugo, but I once lived in a hole deeper and smellier than this. It was in Napoli. My father was a pig butcher. So please do not inflict your inverse snobbery on me."

Hugo laughed. Favio suddenly laughed as well and slapped Hugo on the arm.

"That's why I like you so much, Hugo. You tell it like it is."

"Does that change anything?"

"No."

"I see. It's just part of my color, my mythos."

"Do we need to pretend with each other? You are too old for that, Hugo, and I am too busy. Let me at least say that you and Esther enjoyed a reputation as characters. This assists in sales. Collectors do not buy art; they buy reputations in art history."

"I know, Favio, and it stinks worse than your father's apron."

"If the world were different, I would not play these games. Nor would you."

"My personality is not a game. It is my own. How I wish it were otherwise."

"Really?" the curator smiled. "Well, I'll take your word for it." Turning to Rose, he said, "In the meantime we are faced with the question of Miss Wâbos, whether or not she wishes to accept the invitation."

Behind Favio Ontolli's back, Hugo nodded vigorously.

"Thank you for your invitation, Mr. Ontolli, but I am not interested."

573

Hugo's eyes popped. Favio Ontolli simply stared at her as if he did not believe his ears.

"Thank you for your interest", Rose said. "I must return to my work now."

Hugo squeezed out a rather artificial chuckle. "Uh, just a moment, Rose, I don't think you understand—"

"But I do understand, Hugo. I thank you for trying to help me, but it is not his way with me."

"Who?" asked Favio Ontolli.

"Uh, she means, uh, God", Hugo explained.

"Yes, Our Lord gave me to understand that I must be prepared at every moment to lose everything."

The two men stared at her uncomprehendingly.

"Thank you. Good-bye", Rose said politely.

"Just a moment more of your time, Miss Wâbos," Favio Ontolli said with a strained note of humility. "Are there any conditions under which you *would* accept the invitation?"

"Yes. I would consider it, if I were free to select the images for the show."

"Some innocent!" Ontolli murmured under his voice. Then, more loudly, "There are far too many images for that. Far, far too many. Hundreds here, I think."

"Then I'm sorry."

"You don't understand, my dear", Hugo interjected. "It's the gallery's right to select what goes into the show."

"Then I do not need the show."

Perplexed, Ontolli shook his head. Finally, he was struck by an inspiration.

"Would you agree to a show in which you had the right to select six pieces of your own choosing?"

"Six is very few."

"I foresee a show of about forty works. Six is a considerable portion."

"I would have freedom to choose any six?"

Obviously Ontolli was not happy about the terms, but for some reason he exhaled loudly and said, "Yes, you have my word. Do we have a deal?"

Hugo looked sideways at the curator, marveling at what Rose had done. Judiciously, he kept silent.

Rose looked out over the rooftops of the slum, watching the sun punch holes in the tin sheet of sky. She was not peaceful about what was happening. Then again she was not unpeaceful. What was this strange feeling? Where was she? Was she adrift on a new part of the ocean?

"Yes, I agree", she said with finality.

When the curator had departed, Hugo threw his arms about her and kissed the top of her head. Then he let her go and gave a great belly laugh.

"Unbelievable, Rose, unbelievable! That—and I tell you without any doubts whatsoever—*that* was a first in the life of Favio Ontolli. It means that he senses the worth of your work, and moreover he suspects that it's going to make him a good deal of money. He's willing to bend a little on the images that—well, how shall we delicately put it—that might undermine his credentials in the avant-garde establishment. He's willing to take a risk on you, a very big risk in fact."

"Perhaps I am taking a risk on him, Hugo."

The old man's face sobered. "That's true. That's quite right. And we shouldn't forget it."

"Hugo, I hope he offered you a show as well."

"Yes, vaguely, for some time in the future, he says. He likes my horses. But there are too many of them, and the canvases are too big. He says I have to get busy and make a mixture of small, medium, and large. The large for public galleries and museums, the medium for pretentious private collections, and the small for the carriage trade."

"Does he offend you, Hugo, with such requests?"

"Absolutely. He knows it, and I know it."

"What did you decide?"

"I told him to come back and see me when he's ready to examine the work as a good in itself, not as an object for marketing strategies."

Rose smiled. "Then this was a day of *two* firsts for him."

"Why, that's true, isn't it. Thank you, bright lass, I didn't even see it."

"You suggested my work instead?"

"Of course I did. You're more gifted than I am. And I think you're ready."

"Hugo, I am not more gifted, merely different. And I am not ready."

"Ah, Rose, you will never be ready according to those obscure and entirely tyrannical standards that you impose upon yourself. You are ready. And I think the world is ready for you, whether they know it or not."

"I am not completely at peace about it."

"Not at peace about it? My girl, you're going to be the envy of thousands of artists in this country."

"No, no, that is unimportant. Only the *work* is important."

He roared with laughter and stomped back and forth through the studio, rubbing his hands with glee.

"Yes, yes, I can see it all now! The world-famous artist, Rose Wâbos, plodding through life, suffering from delusions of obscurity, absolutely convinced that no one knows her, stalked by paparazzi."

Ignoring this foolery, Rose scolded him. "Hugo, I think you sacrificed yourself for me."

"Nonsense."

"Yes, you did."

"We'll say no more on the matter. Now, he's coming back tomorrow with an assistant to select the pieces for the show. Is that acceptable to you?"

"Yes."

Favio Ontolli arrived at ten the next morning with a young woman who was introduced as the assistant curator of the Ontolli-Metropol Gallery. They all went up to Rose's studio, Hugo included, and began the long process of going through several cardboard boxes of pastels, a large roll of older drawings, and the piles of paintings—more than three dozen of the latter.

By lunch time they had made only a little progress in the selection of pieces that would go into the exhibition. Ontolli seemed to take a lot of time deciding. His assistant even more.

"Look, Rose, this is all new to you, isn't it?" Ontolli said. "Why don't you let us proceed on our own. My assistant and I can discuss things without you standing there feeling as if you're being dissected. The exhibition will be controversial. That means Ms. Pannenburg and I will be arguing with each other for hours. You really don't need to be here."

"The managing has begun, Rose", Hugo said dryly. "Why don't we go for a long walk? I'll buy you lunch."

Throughout the following winter, a great silence reigned over her life. A waiting, a hibernation, a sleeping of creation. She drew and painted each day, and this labor forced her to be attentive to the core of her life's meaning. She often admonished herself that life was not about exposure, or shows, or people's opinions. Life was faithfulness to the word that surfaced within you. Regardless of whether you were making a picture of birds and animals, the more mysterious scenes of the heart, or the struggle between good and evil, life was speaking a word, and your task was to repeat it as closely as possible.

Yet the passage of minutes, hours, days, and weeks became oppressive. Time was experienced as mass and weight. Whenever she tried to measure it (*three more months to go, and then my show begins*), it slowed, slowed, slowed to a dead stop.

"Hugo?" she would ask more often than his patience could endure, "Do you think he has lost my paintings?"

"No, my dear, I'm quite certain that he hasn't."

"How can we be sure?"

"I was in the Metropol this morning and was taken on a conducted tour through the framing department. I saw your brother being dressed."

"What do you mean?"

"Favio Ontolli is a creative genius when it comes to the perfect frame. He has chosen for all the works a simple box frame of basswood, a natural wood with a faint glow of matte varnish, as pale gold as sunshine. The pastels are also matted with an ivory-colored conservation board and non-glare glass. His judgment is perfection itself. The pieces I saw were so tasteful in their simplicity that no jarring contradictions were evident. The unadorned wood, the mat boards—it's all consistent with the native ethos, you see. Yet the elegance of the entire effect is undeniable. Elegance without ostentation. Not a hint of the baroque. He has respected the subject matter utterly."

"I am glad, Hugo. Still—"

"Please, Rose, I'm reading!"

"What are you reading, Hugo?"

"An antique fable, a shaping fantasy, called *Pamela: or Virtue Rewarded*, by an eighteenth-century English novelist. A rather optimistic vision of human nature, but diverting. A tale painted in rosy tints. Shall I read it to you?"

"No, thank you, Hugo. Did you see any of the six that I chose?"

"The six? What are you talking about? Oh, yes, the 'reactionary and counterproductive' works, to quote a certain nabob of culture known to us both. The 'simplistic and exhausted image bank of'—how shall we delicately put it—'Christian symbolism'."

"Yes, those six."

"I saw the crucifixion and also the forest nativity. Not yet framed, but soon to be. The others? Well, it was rather a busy place, hundreds of things happening all at once. Now, please, stop your infernal worrying, my girl. I want to get back to virtue rewarded."

"Yes, Hugo. I am sorry to interrupt you. You're sure they're all right?"

Hot air escaped through Hugo's nostrils.

"Slowly but surely, each of your children is being dressed in his finery. Not one of them shall be neglected. All shall be equally respected. If they aren't, I will personally throttle Favio Ontolli. Or publicly flog him. There, does that set your mind at rest?"

"Not exactly, Hugo. When is opening night?"

"Seeing as how this is only the third or fourth time you've asked, I will tell you again. It is scheduled for May the first."

"The first of May? Io, Hugo, this is a blessed thing, for it is the feast of Saint Joseph the Worker!"

"Fabulous. I hope he will be free to attend."

"He will, Hugo. I am sure he will."

During the month of March, time speeded up again. She worked with renewed energy, restraining herself from beginning two, four, five paintings a day, struggling to keep the current on one canvas at a time. It seemed the high sunny wind was in her always, the joy of expectation, the kindling of hope and faith in a future where she now might find her place. The small bird toiling below, the large white bird singing above, watching over every detail. When she went to church or the grocery store, she passed through the exhilarating streets smiling at everyone. Many returned her smile. There was a bounce in her step that would not be repressed. She waved up at steeplejacks working on the iron girders of the tall buildings that were going up on the borders of St. Henri, and some waved back down.

"Are you all right? Do you have a fever?" Hugo would ask on such days. "Let me make you a little soup."

"I am fine, Hugo. I am trying not to be excited about the show. Only five weeks to go."

"Five weeks and counting. Relax, girl. Fame is a siren, and many sailors have been brought to shipwreck listening to her song."

She was grounded only by those moments of stillness in church and by a habit she had developed of sitting in her bedroom at night with the loon-star and the *binemin* stone in the palms of her hands, her eyes closed, feeling time slowly dissolve, praying for Tchibi's soul.

The night of the opening came. When Rose returned from noon Mass at the shrine on Mount Royal, she found Hugo whistling and preening in front of the hall mirror. Dressed in his personal concept of splendor, complete with cravat and starched shirt and his speckled tweed suit, he seemed every bit the man of the world. He had even brushed his hair and beard, all by himself, something he had rarely been moved to do since Esther's death. Moreover, his shoes were polished and shined. She saw how much he wished to celebrate for her. She felt indeed a daughter to him, and it increased her joy greatly. She hugged him.

"Now, now, control yourself, girl", he chuckled patting her head. "There's still five hours to go."

He beamed continually throughout the afternoon. He read *Pamela* for a couple of hours in the parlor, spilled a cup of tea on his white shirt, and had to change it for a blue one. Rose made fish and chips for supper, but neither she nor Hugo did anything more than pick at their plates.

"Care for a smear of Limburger on toast?" he asked.

"No, thank you, Hugo."

At six o'clock, Rose went upstairs to her bedroom to dress.

She found the old green jumper that Sister Clothilde had made for her many years ago and shook the dust from it. The shoulder straps were a little frayed, and some of the tiny *bineshis* and flowers were unraveling. She repaired what she could with needle and thread and let out the expandable waist a few more inches. She put on a clean white blouse, then the jumper, and over all an undamaged cardigan sweater of Esther's. Then came brown wool stockings for warmth. And finally, a pair of low-heeled pumps that she had purchased from the thrift store a few days before. In the mirror over her dresser, she noticed the disorder of her hair and was a little surprised to see that it was now almost entirely gray. She brushed it back and fixed it behind her ears with bobby pins. She washed and dried her face.

"Ogini, what a sight you are! Who would recognize you?"

She thought suddenly of the many souls who had poured their love and their labors into her life: Oldmary and Tchibi, Euphrasia of the Flowers and Mère Jean, Father Andrei and Mrs. Boyle, Sister Madeleine and Esther. Yes, and Youngmary-the-mother-of-her-flesh. And her grandfather K. B., yes, even he, for his poetry was perhaps a part of the river of creation within her. Yes, so many souls. It was more their day than hers. She was only a little charcoal stick in the hands of the Beloved. If not her, then another twig would have been sufficient for his purposes.

"Io, Beating Heart, I thank you that you have blessed me to follow you and to be held within your hands suspended over the abyss. You did not let me fall in the falling that is without end, and the little fallings you permitted were only to teach me to fly. Yes, I am a *bineshi*, and you have not let me drop into the jaws of your enemy. In the open air between your hands at last I am learning to fly."

She knelt on the floor, kissed the bare planks, and asked the Beating Heart to use her pictures, if he so wished, to touch the souls who looked at them this evening and during the weeks to come. When a taxi arrived at the curb outside and tooted its horn, she got up, kissed the crucifix Mère Jean had given her, and went downstairs.

"I thought we were going by bus, Hugo!"

"Bus? On a night like this! Aaargh! How I long to give you a gilded carriage and four. But all I can afford is a lowly motorized sedan. Come on, girl, into that parka. We should have been there half an hour ago. We mustn't keep the guests waiting."

"Oh, I am sorry, Hugo."

"Women!" he said in jolly exasperation. "Always fussing over their appearance. Well, never mind, we'll be fashionably late, which is only befitting on such a dazzling eve."

As the taxi began to plunge into the canyons of the wealthy downtown area, Rose told Hugo that she wanted to walk the final few blocks.

"Butterflies in the tummy?" he asked.

"A little. I want to have a moment of silence before the opening."

When the cab turned onto St. Catherine Street, Hugo told the driver to pull over to the curb.

"All right, Rose, let's walk."

"Would you mind if I go alone, Hugo?"

"Are you sure?" he said hesitantly. "You could get lost."

"I won't", she smiled at him.

"All right. I'll see you at the gallery. You can't miss it. It's four blocks down thataway. Big lights, crowds of people. Noise, music, and a painting by Rose Wâbos in the window."

As the taxi pulled away, Rose stood without moving on the sidewalk, gazing up at the crest of the royal mountain. She breathed the chill night air, listened to the traffic, surveyed the lights of the city as if it were a surprise party that was about to break open for her. Yet a curious stillness expanded between the steps of her shoes, the noise of the traffic faded, and the sweet ancient fullness swelled in the deepest part of herself.

Theatergoers streamed around her, eyeing the deformed little woman, a red orchid pinned to the collar of her parka, gray-haired, a broad featureless brown face, the black agate eyes gazing into space, seeing what no others could see.

"Grandmother?" she said quietly. "Tchibi?"

She had seen nothing, merely a presence. Two presences, really, and also the *anjeni*, whose quiet presence had grown stronger in recent weeks. She pulled herself back to the task at hand and hurried on.

The Ontolli-Metropol was just as Hugo had described it. The music of stringed instruments burst from it as the front door kept opening and closing to admit a stream of guests. As Rose peered through the plate-glass display window, she saw many people moving about in the blinding light within. One of her paintings partly blocked the view. It was her portrait of Tchibi standing on the quartz globe, the two birds on his shoulders.

Io, how different it looked! The frame was so beautiful, as if it were a door that he had just stepped through, or a window in time that she could peer through. It hurt to see it, though she could not explain why. *Perhaps*, she told herself, *it is because he no longer belongs to you alone.*

A doorman examined her attire and did not want to let her in.

"I am the artist", she explained shyly. "I painted the pictures in the show."

His frown implied that he did not believe her.

"Is Mr. Ontolli here?" she asked. "If I could speak with him, I know he would want me to be here."

"Oh, you know Mr. Ontolli?" the man said uneasily. "Well, I guess it's all right."

Because she was small and had not dressed in a fashion that would attract eyes, few if any of the hundreds of people in the gallery seemed to notice that she was among them. This was good, for she was happy to be invisible. Across a sea of heads she saw Hugo laughing and gesturing dramatically with the man named Clive and another of his friends, the man named Trevor. They were drinking wine. Everyone in the room was drinking wine, laughing, talking, swarming back and forth. The noise was deafening.

Fragments of conversation tossed along the current:

"—as I said, primitive, yet—"

"—not what we've come to expect from the aboriginal community—"

"—unknown—"

"—a protégée of Hugo Dyson's. You know Hugo, the English painter—"

"—oh, yes, the painted beard, slightly mad—"

"—Esther passed away three —"

"—Guggenheim—"

"—but nothing is signed—"

"—is she one of those prodigies—"

"—mentally handicapped, I hear—"

"—no, physically—"

"—gifted—"

"—haunting—"

"—sensual—"

"—sublimated libido—"

"—savage innocence, don't you think—"

"—what is a *Bineshi*—"

"—catalogue says it's Ojibwe for small bird—"

"—pseudonym—"

"—is she here yet—"

"—I don't think so—"

"—though there are a few natives—"

How wonderful this invisibility. Rose knew that it offered her the freedom to move about the gallery as if she were not herself. For a little while she would be granted the strange perspective of seeing her own works as if they had been made by someone else.

A patch of crowd cleared near the left of the entrance, exposing Oldmary kneeling, gutting fish, looking up at a little girl who was telling her what Kinoje had said about K. B. The face of Oldmary stricken, the girl rubbing her left arm.

Beside it was the painting of the two sisters in the womb, clinging to each other.

To its right a little naked boy was nailed to a cabin wall, his body covered with burn holes, his mouth open in a scream that had no end.

The faces in the paintings seemed to stare at Rose, as if all of them were stripped and nailed to a cabin wall. Were their eyes reproaching her for exposing them? She suddenly felt ashamed. Her face burned as many people walked past commenting, analyzing.

Now do your labors and your sacrifices become visible, said the voice. *Words for the blind to see.*

"Will they understand, my Lord?" Rose asked aloud, though she did not realize how loudly she had spoken.

Many will look without seeing, hear without understanding. Some will see and hear, but it is not for you to know.

"—that one's a shocker—the kid on the wall—"

"—one nude in a show this size?—"

"—yeah, but it's the most prudish nude I've ever seen—totally symbolic—"

"—it's her metaphor for existential vulnerability—"

"—cliché nativity—"

"—but translated into her milieu—"

"—of course everyone knows how the Jesuits brainwashed them—"

"—a flock of nuns—is the artist joking?—"

"—doubt it—"

"—remember the show we saw here three years ago—"

"—oh, yes, man changing into thunderbird—"

"—think of it—nuns changing into flying geese—"

"—either she's incredibly naïve or she's incredibly mad at them—"

"—let's go; it's depressing—"

"—Favio says some of it's a throwback—"

"—why are you crying—"

"—I don't know why—it's very moving—"

"—more wine—"

"—artist is late—on Indian time, no doubt—"

"—catalogue says she's young—twenty-nine—"

"—do you see her—"

"—a few natives here tonight—"

"—not that poor old woman—with gray hair—the hunch-back—"

Although Rose was unable to discern how far her work penetrated into the hearts of the guests, she prayed that some were changed by it, lifted beyond the cold dark barren land into the freedom of the open skies. As she moved slowly from room to room, peering at pastels and paintings between shifting bodies, and probing into suddenly vacated spaces, she felt a growing joy inexplicably mixed with fear. She understood now the power of the painted word. She also began to know the peculiar pain when it was misunderstood, or worse, understood and rejected.

Unnoticed, she came upon a cluster of finely dressed men and women gathered around the portrait of Euphrasia sleeping on the skull by Threefinger Lake, clutching a black pearl to her heart.

"What's it about, Favio?"

"The artist wouldn't tell. Someone she once knew, she said. But I think that's a cover story. It's highly symbolic, and my guess is it represents a struggle between the archetypes in her own psyche. As you can see, the central figure is a tall white European female. You don't have to stretch your analytical skills too far to see that it's an idealization of what the artist would like to be—and never can be."

"Come on, Favio, are you telling us all native people want to be white?"

"Not quite so cut-and-dried, Trevor. Racial envy is a two-edged sword. I, for example, have always wanted to be a white Anglo-Saxon Protestant apostate who writes art reviews for the papers, yet when my Mama presents me with a bowl of *polenta*, I instantly abandon that futile dream."

Much laughter erupted all around.

"On my part, Favio, for many years I longed to become a Mediterranean Catholic apostate and womanizer, but whenever my Mothah presents me with a gift of blue-chip shares in Seagrams, I instantly abandon that futile dream."

More laughter.

"You are amused", said a woman's voice, gentle but commanding attention, "because you believe yourselves suspended above the darkness of the abandoned. Would any of you accept to be a child nailed to a cabin wall?"

Instant silence.

"Or this woman torn between demons and angels?"

"Mrs. Morgan is right", said another female voice. "Male pathology infects male exegesis to the core."

"That might be going too far, Ms. Pannenburg. I merely meant to say that our analysis may be infected by our immunity."

"Are we immune, Estelle?" Ms. Pannenburg replied, her eyes flickering at Favio Ontolli. "Are we not all, at every moment, about to lose everything?"

"Only when the tax man cometh!" Favio said. "Estelle, as usual, is the voice of moderation and probity."

With her hawk's eye Ms. Pannenburg spotted Rose hiding at the back of the crowd and bustled toward her.

"Here she is now. The artist. Come this way, Bineshi. We were just admiring your painting."

Suddenly, out of nowhere, Chloe Templeton burst onto the scene. Bending at the waist, she took Rose's other arm and kissed her cheek.

"Bineshi, darling! The show is fabulous! Simply fabulous!"

Hugo overheard the commotion and elbowed his way through a swiftly expanding ring of guests, spilling droplets of wine on a few.

"Bloody good show!" he roared, beaming. "Now leave her alone, you idiots, robber barons, and swashbucklers. Can't you see she's feeling shy. Come with me, Rose, come with me."

He grabbed her arm and drew her away, though a few guests tagged along. Favio Ontolli and Ms. Pannenburg followed with proprietary interest. Favio took over from Hugo and began a series of introductions. To all and sundry he explained that *Bineshi* was a *nom de plume*, actually a *nom de pinceau*, and that the artist had insisted on her right to remain anonymous.

"Sort of a traditional thing", Favio said. "Artist as channel of the earth spirits."

"Actually, no, Mr. Ontolli", Rose spoke up. "I am not a channel. The shaman is a channel or a hollow tube through which the wicked spirits speak. My way is to be a beloved twig in the hands of the Creator. We make the pictures together."

That reduced everyone to perplexed silence.

By way of distraction, Hugo said in a too loud voice, "Favio, old chap, where's Chloe? I want to say hello."

"Chloe", Favio replied with great seriousness, "is over by the anchovies conversing with the president of CP Rail."

An uncomfortable silence spread, and one by one the guests drifted off to other conversations, for it seemed that, having uttered her cryptic self-explanation, the little Indian artist had no more to say.

Hugo, Rose, Favio, and Ms. Pannenburg stood alone.

"Chloe and I are no longer an event", Favio said to Hugo in a low voice. He put an arm around Ms. Pannenburg. "Clarissa and I—"

"Clarissa? Oh, right, I heard about you from Sam Richardson."

"*Who* is Sam Richardson?" Ms. Pannenburg said haughtily.

"A gossip columnist", Hugo replied in a friendly tone.

Favio and Clarissa exchanged looks.

His face exhibiting an offended dignity, Favio Ontolli said in a dangerous voice: "Who does this Richardson write for? Tell me, Hugo. I am quite prepared to sue—"

"Actually, Favio, he did his best work in the seventeen hundreds. Haven't you read *Clarissa: The History of a Young Lady*?"

"Hugo," Favio fumed, "you are impossible!"

Ms. Pannenburg, for her part, fixed Hugo with a withering look and walked away. Favio hurried after her.

Hugo sighed. "Dear me, it's so discouraging trying to name-drop with these people. They never recognize the names."

"Neither did I, Hugo", Rose ventured.

"Never mind, we've successfully cleared the decks. Now, as a special favor to me, will you walk me around this astoundingly unique and thought-provoking exhibit? If you do, I promise not to reveal your secret identity."

"All right, Hugo. Where would you like to begin?"

"Anywhere."

They got past the owl and the dogs, an Ojibwe mother nursing her child, and a black winged creature plunging into a lake of fire, before Mr. This, a bank president, and Mr. That, head of a university department, interrupted them. The exchange was predictable, reeking of money dangled as bait, but neither Hugo nor Rose bit at it, and the men went away.

Hugo and Rose had time to look at two more paintings, the woman in the barrens coffin and the girl in formaldehyde (two of Rose's six), before they were interrupted again. This time it was a critic from the influential journal *Vie des Arts*.

"I'm going to do a story on you", said this gentleman. "I'll call you after the show."

"Actually, sir," Rose replied, "I would rather that you do not call me."

Astonished, he took a step back, alternating between amusement and nursing an insult.

"Do you know who I am?" he asked in self-parody.

"She does. That's why", Hugo replied.

"Are you her keeper, Dyson?"

"No, a friend."

"Ah, a *friend*."

"The work speaks for itself. She doesn't need to play the hyped-up self-promotion games that you carnivores prey upon."

"Then you can forget the review, *friend*."

Small tides ebbed and flowed about them, containing faces that popped to the surface, listening for clues to the meaning of the paintings. No one stayed very long in Hugo's vicinity. He was both tactless and, despite his attempt at dressing up, rather shabby.

Far across the gallery, Mrs. Morgan stood at the center of a group of admirers, nodding at a painting, explaining it—Rose thought it was her pastel of the blind girls running through the autumn leaves. Or perhaps a bird-kite pulling a girl into the *tchibekana*.

The front door blew open and several people in the crowd gasped and flocked toward the personages who now entered.

"Dear heavens above", Hugo muttered. "Hide yourself, Rose, hide yourself. It's Marco the Magnificent." Because all eyes in the house were turned to the actor-director, and the almost equally famous Karla Fabienne, and the fascinating entourage that always accompanied them, Hugo and Rose were able to navigate unseen through the crowd in the direction of a small alcove, Rose marveling over her friend's new name.

Marco and Karla embraced many people, saving intimate endearments and lingering embraces for Favio and Clarissa, a less definitive hug for Chloe, who had slipped a little in the hierarchy, and especially for Mrs. Morgan.

"What a gorgeous dress!" Marco cried so loudly that not a person in the gallery failed to hear.

Mrs. Morgan escorted Marco through the exhibit, picture by picture. They stopped now and then, whenever Mrs. Morgan tried to make a point, though it was obvious that Marco was only making a pretense of attention. His eyes darted this way and that, mouthing kisses at various people, nodding with forced agreement as his guide pointed to a detail in a painting, embracing whoever approached, drinking their adulation as his proper due. Before they had completed half the circuit, he was pulled into a crowd of people who wanted to hear about his latest play. And within a minute, he had become the entire show.

"It wouldn't be an exaggeration to say that *Equinox* will be the centerpiece of the new season at Stratford. We've even borrowed the lead male dancer from the National Ballet for the scene where the naiads and dryads rise up and kill the sun-god. It's brilliant! Absolutely brilliant. The scenes are being painted right now in Italy and will arrive by ship within the month. In the meantime, rehearsals are a torture—sheer torture."

"How do you like the exhibit?" asked one of the more impetuous or thoughtless onlookers.

"The exhibit?" Marco asked, looking about as if he were so accustomed to finding himself on constantly changing sets that he could not always focus properly. "Oh, yes, interesting. I adore *les primitifs*. Oh, look, there's Favio! Favio, you old

Saturnalian, give me your hand, and let's hope there's gold in it. When are we getting that grant money?"

"Not so loud, not so bleeding loud", said Favio Ontolli laughing, blushing, rather enjoying the unexpected treat of a world-famous dramatist calling him by his first name, in public.

"Where is Esther when I need her?" Hugo whispered to Rose.

Shortly after, the troupe of actors departed like a receding summer storm, many water sprites and wood nymphs fluttering out after them. Sighs of deflation emanated from many quarters.

There were among the guests a small number of diffident and homely people. One, an old man in an ill-fitting suit, timidly approached Rose. His hands were large, dirt was under his fingernails. He addressed her in French.

"You are the artist?"

"Yes."

"You love the mountain of Saint Joseph."

"Yes, I do, for it is the place where God touched the earth in this land."

"I think so too", he said. Taking her right hand in both of his, he kissed it, and with head bowed, he turned swiftly away and shuffled out the front door.

Hugo was dumbfounded. "What on earth was that all about!"

But Rose felt it unnecessary to reply.

Next, an older woman arrived, writing on a notepad.

"You're the guilty party, I assume?" she said with a twist of her lips, as if she and Rose shared an embarrassing secret. She pointed to the portrait of Tchibi in the window. She smiled crookedly and her eyes brittled, her teeth glittered, and she said, "Who is that divine young beast? The partridge, you call him. Is he your lover?"

Rose stared at the woman.

"Ahem—" Hugo cleared his voice, preparing for battle.

"And these landscapes! Those small grassy stretches for instance, they're absolutely erotic!" The woman balanced on one leg, crossed her ankles, and smirked. Enjoying herself, she observed Rose's reaction. Rose reacted by walking away.

A moment later, an elderly native woman came to Rose and stood in front of her, blocking the way. Without introducing herself, she said, "May I bless you, Bineshi?"

"With what blessing?" Rose replied cautiously.

"With the blessing of him who died for us, by the merits of his five wounds and the greatest of these, the wound in his heart."

Recognizing the spirit in these words, Rose bowed her head. The old woman, immensely fat and wrinkled, smelling slightly of fish and wood smoke, closed her eyes and placed both hands on the crown of Rose's head.

"Uh, just a moment—" Hugo said, but stopped in midsentence.

Very beautiful and powerful people gathered round to catch a glimpse of native ritual. In a quiet voice, the woman began to pray in a language Rose did not recognize. Peace flooded through her, a calm that she sorely needed after the lady with the notebook.

Finished, the old woman nodded abruptly and stood back. "You call yourself Bineshi. The Spirit says otherwise, though it is true you are a small one. You are the flower of his Heart, though you are hidden. He says that you must not cease to trust him in all that is about to happen. Do not be afraid."

Worried by these words, Rose asked, "What is to happen?"

"I do not know, for the Beating Heart has hidden it from my eyes. Much have you suffered for him, and much more will you suffer. Even so, it is for the good of souls. Stand firm. In the end all things will be revealed, the good and the evil, and the fruit of each man's work."

"I will stand firm, if his grace is there to fill me."

"No grace will he deny you, yet he does not promise you happiness in this world. In the next—"

"What's going on here?" Favio Ontolli demanded, strolling into their midst.

"Be quiet", Hugo hushed him.

"Is she making a disturbance?" Ms. Pannenburg asked.

"Not at all", Hugo said.

The old woman stepped forward once more and whispered into Rose's ear.

"Your sister awaits you, across the river."

"My sister?" Rose asked.

"She who is the firstborn of the Lord among our peoples. She the lily, and you a rose. In our time there are many roses blooming in the garden of the Lord. They are hidden among the peoples. Some will do a greater work than yours, some a lesser. Some will be known and others unknown, yet all give fragrance. He has given the lily to you and you to the lily. Pray to her."

"Io, old mother, what is your name?"

"My name is not important. Yet I will tell you—I am Elizabeth. I am Iroquois from Auriesville in New York. The Spirit took me while in prayer three days ago and told me that I must go to the great city of Montreal and speak to the heart of a woman he would lead me to. He said she is called the small silver bird who is a rose among the many roses."

Rose put her arms around the old woman and they rocked their bodies gently as one.

The gallery personnel and the many guests looked away.

Rose kissed Elizabeth's cheek.

"Io, I thank you, Elizabeth. For this word from him strengthens me greatly."

"Pray for me as I pray for you."

"I will."

Favio Ontolli looked irritated. He took Rose's arm and pulled her away, and never again on this earth did Rose meet Elizabeth. Hugo was drawn aside by Clive, and together they headed toward the bar, where stronger spirits were being sold.

"There are important people here I want you to meet", Favio said to Rose.

"That woman was very important, Mr. Ontolli."

"Was she? Listen, Rose, I know that type. They come for the wine and cheese and never buy a thing. She's a window-shopper. You shouldn't waste your time. Come over here and meet—"

A lady from a television station asked Rose if she would be interested in having an interview in conjunction with a documentary on her life and work.

"With the surge of interest in the land rights of native peoples, Bineshi, the documentary would highlight their plight and their demands for a political voice in this country."

Rose declined.

"Don't you owe it to your own people? Surely, now that you're a success, you won't forget the downtrodden."

Rose said nothing.

A success? Little red stickers were going up under many of her paintings. She was beginning to feel dizzy, though she was drinking no wine. The orchids swirled hysterically in their vases.

A man approached, a man whom earlier in the evening Favio had introduced as a member of an arts council that handed out grants of money to impoverished artists. During the former conversation he had been lavish with his promises. Now, alone with Rose, he stood sideways, talking out of the corner of his mouth, not really looking at her.

"You young painters have it easy", he said. "You don't know what it means to struggle. I wanted to be an artist when I was young, but I had to get a job to keep my family going." He sipped his wine, his eyes tired, strained, his years used up, his mouth bitter. "You're all spoiled", he said. "And besides, representational art is dead in this country!" His coup delivered, he wandered away with his head in the air.

Whatever was being said to her now was not overly painful, for the words that Elizabeth had delivered were a comfort so deep that even the feeling of nakedness which had overcome her earlier in the evening was now clothed. She nodded amicably at the roaring, humming mass that was nibbling, gobbling, devouring her heart's blood smeared out in colors for them to weigh and analyze and handle with cold fingers. She wished Esther were here.

She wanted to leave now, to go home to the silent little bedroom, and sit in it, kneel in it, praise and thank God for his generosity. How far he had taken her, far from the beginnings, far from the fingernails scratching in window frost, from the twigs pulled from the firebox, scraping lines across the cabin logs. He had accomplished it through the many years and many friends, the *ningâs* and the *kinojes* and the *anjenis* blending in the river of time, flowing into her present and sweeping her into the future. Io, to kneel in silence and thank and praise, and gaze in awe at what he had done. To weep privately in gratitude for the word he had sent by the Iroquois woman. And to think about what she had said. About her sister, the lily. Across the river. What did this mean exactly? What lay across the river? Hugo might be able to tell her. She would ask him tomorrow.

"Rose!"

She looked up to see Hugo smiling down at her.

"Shall we call it an evening, *savante sauvage*? It's after eleven and the throng is thinning, leaving only the thrifty and thieving. You look like you need some fresh air."

He took her arm and guided her out into the street under the mantle of the jumping city and the distant stars fading in the glow of the street lights. Her ears were ringing with the clamor and car horns and the continual wail of ambulances lamenting over the fallen.

Her arm was only vaguely part of her now, yet she must obey it and the warm fingers which pulled her away down the telescoping streets. A taxi arrived. It took them across town to the house where it seemed she lived with an old man and an orange cat, and the orange cat meowed and said, "Well, how do you like success? Did you see the mouse I caught while you were out enjoying yourself? Now *this* is success." The mouse was gummed and mangled, but Goldie had laid it delicately in the center of the kitchen floor as her contribution to the family larder.

"Now, now, Rose, don't cry, it's just a mouse", Hugo said, pushing her up the staircase past the whirr of color, the wall paintings singing, especially the pigeon lady smiling at her captives as they fluttered their wings and took flight.

He opened the door for her and gave her a light push.

"Get to bed, Rose. Knit up the unraveled sleeve of care. 'To sleep, to sleep, perchance to dream'—"

"Good night, Hugo", Rose sobbed. "Thank you for everything."

"Not at all, not at all. It was a truly delightful evening. I fended off five mythical beasts, sustained flesh wounds from two or three, demolished another, drank an inordinate amount of free wine, evaded Marco and Carlotta, lectured to Clive and Trevor, humiliated Favio and Clarissa. But most important of all, I drank deep of the pure spring water of your glorious night. Your unprecedented and singular triumph over this great city."

"This great and wicked city, Hugo, in which three million people live, not knowing their left hand from their right."

"My sentiments exactly. Now to sleep, to sleep."

As Rose drifted away into the world of dreams, she saw a dance of turquoise light in the eyes of the white bird, eyes that grew and grew until they were enormous silver-blue crystal comets hurtling toward the earth at great speed. She could almost reach out and touch the twirl and weave, the elongated tails fanning behind in ten thousand spokes of light.

The last thing she remembered was the ice-blue comet fire expanding in her vision until it flared and burnt her, yet the burning was love, it was purifying fire. It called to her like a summons, but she could not reach it, and she fell beyond consciousness into sleep.

22

The first weekend after the opening, reviews appeared in the *Gazette*, *Le Devoir*, and *Arts Montreal*. Hugo read them to Rose in the parlor.

"Here's Trevor's, Rose. Are you ready?"

"I am ready, Hugo."

"'Self-taught, the artist has developed through her strong but delicate works an awareness and sympathy with her subject that are transmitted very easily to the viewer. She walks the narrow line between labored overemphasis and studied vagueness with admirable confidence.' The rest is just descriptions and titles." Hugo looked up, beaming. "Not bad, not bad."

"What does he mean?" asked Rose.

"Kulturbabble. Now here's another. Uh-oh, it's by your good friend and mine, the critic with the fixation."

Hugo read the review aloud, sparing Rose nothing:

The current show at the Favio Ontolli gallery is a display of sentiment that collectors and students of anthropological painting will find disappointing. Defying all normative symbols of the rebirth of a truly vital indigenous culture, the artist has reverted to the banal platitudes of a borrowed culture. The subject matter is anachronistic, quaint, and unrelievedly narrative. Bineshi (the artist's pseudonym) is first and foremost a storyteller. To this reviewer's mind there is all too much of this type of work flooding the market these days, drawing the public away from the real purposes of fine art. The exhibit is not Art in any permanent or universal sense. It is illustration.

599

Bineshi is self-taught, an autodidact (emphasis on the didact), a realist of shifting allegiance, and though her subject matter is derived from a reality worth considering—the native experience—she paints it with the eyes of a yet immature vision. There is no evidence in any of the works of a sensitivity to the political and social crises of her own people, a regrettable omission guaranteeing that she will be at best only a footnote in any future history of the restoration of aboriginal culture—a rebirth, I might add, that is desperately needed.

A few portraits have been included in the exhibition, most of which lack the erotic freedom of the landscapes, yet the sexually loaded *Partridge*, a portrait of the artist's lover, is an exception, an example of lust and archetypal sublimation at its best. Indeed, the entire show is a complex self-examination of the psyche, digging deep into unresolved conflicts and unfulfilled passions. The small number of Christian works hint at the sources of the artist's pain, as does her insistence on anonymity. The self-flagellation, the misidentification of fulfillment as sin, and the overwhelming pessimistic ethos reveal her unacknowledged conflicts, especially her anger at organized religion. Furthermore, there is a wholly subconscious effort to throw off these alien encumbrances.

Artistically, there is promise here. This may not be the last we see of this artist's work, if in the years to come she is able to wrestle with her personal demons and defeat them. If she finds her own voice, an authentic woman and visionary may emerge from the rubble heap of European patriarchy.

Hugo looked up. "Well, what do you think of that?"

"*Kinoje*," Rose whispered.

"I beg your pardon?"

"She is clever but lacks wisdom."

"Clever? I think you're being generous."

"Hugo, do you think I should write a letter to her and correct the mistakes she made?"

"Don't waste your time, Rose. I suggest flogging. Public flogging always has a meritorious effect on such people."

"Oh, Hugo, you cannot mean that. It is cruel."

"My dear, recall that I am a pacifist. I did not mean *physical* violence. Dear me, no." He paused and gazed at the ceiling, twiddling his thumbs, musing aloud. "I envisage clamping her into a set of antique stocks in the Place d'Armes. Her past and present victims will stream before her wearing the scarlet letter—A for artist. She too will bear a mark of shame, the letter N for nitpicker, or C for caviler, B for belittler, P for pettifogger, et cetera, et cetera. It will happen on a lovely summer afternoon. Mild. Sunny. She will be immobilized and muted, painlessly, for ten to twelve hours, while the many victims sacrificed on the altar of her ego will stand before her reciting passages from her collected articles. Any artist in the city, or the country for that matter, can come and deliver his analysis of her writing, her pathetically arrogant and stunted worldview, her ambitions, her psychological projection, her revisionist history, her unresolved conflicts, her lusts, her ambitions, her patently false public persona. At no point will she be handled with anything other than gentleness. No invective, no fisticuffs—I can't stand fisticuffs—merely a reasoned and exhaustive dissection of her self-deceptions, which are many, or as you would say in your religion, legion. Then, when that's completed, she will be unlocked from the stocks. She will, of course, desire to scream at her tormentors, to call a lawyer, to repair to her typewriter and dash off the most scathing article in the history of criticism. But we shall not let her go immediately. No, first she will be led to an easel set up in the square, surrounded by hundreds of artists, tourists, media representatives, federal and provincial culture commissars, and many small gifted children who might otherwise have become her victims in the coming generation. We will have an 'art happening'. She will be invited to paint a picture. If she succeeds, we will let her go. If she fails, we will also let her go, but we will write reviews of her life and work which we will send to the most influential periodicals in this country."

"Hugo," Rose said doubtfully, "that is a failure in charity."

"I know", he said, pleased with himself.

"Esther would not like it."

"On the contrary, Esther would have loved it. She always told me we have to stop the Hitlers in this world."

"Is this writer a Nazi, Hugo?"

"Oh, yes, my dear, she is a Nazi. The very worst kind of Nazi, the kind that thinks she isn't. Public humiliation, I say, is the best corrective for that kind of person."

"You are joking."

"I admit it. But wouldn't it be nice—"

"No. It would merely spread the hatred."

He sighed. "Ah, well, one can dream. Rose, why don't I make us a bowl of soup?"

"Yes, please, Hugo."

"Crackers?"

"Mmm, mmm", she nodded.

"A few slices of Limburger on it?"

"No, thank you", she said, laughing.

During the following week the words of Elizabeth from Auriesville continued to surface in her mind. *Your sister awaits you across the river.*

"But I have no sister."

She who is the firstborn of the Lord among our peoples.

"Could it be—?"

She the lily and you the rose.

"Kateri!" Rose cried in excitement. From the little altar in her bedroom she retrieved the scorched medallion that had been saved from Tchibi's pocket. She rubbed it until the face of Kateri appeared.

How easily her beloved sister had slipped away from her thoughts during the years she had lived in cities. Ay, ay, how the memory of her had faded, how swiftly Kateri had become just one of many saints in the litany of prayers, a word, a name, an ancient tale, lost among the growing number of tales that filled her mind.

That Sunday, after Communion at the shrine on the Royal Mountain, it came to Rose that she must seek her sister beyond the waters of the great river. But how? Where in all of the vast lands to the south would she find her? Perhaps she lived near Auriesville, which was the home of Elizabeth. Perhaps elsewhere. But where?

"Hugo?" she said over a lunch of sardines and tomato soup in the kitchen. "Have you ever heard of a person named Kateri?"

"Kateri? No."

"She is my sister. She lives across the river."

"You have a sister, Rose? Will wonders never cease! Why didn't you tell me?"

"She is an adopted sister. I have never seen her with my eyes."

"Oh. Maybe she lives on the reserve across the river. It's about half an hour from here by car, maybe an hour by bus. Want to go this afternoon?"

"Yes.

"Well, let's go. I'll pay the fare. My treat."

"No, Hugo. I need to go alone."

Slightly hurt, he murmured that he understood, but insisted on giving her ten dollars, in case the bus times were bad and she needed to take a taxi home.

By midafternoon, Rose was climbing down the steps of a bus on a street of ramshackle houses close to the south shore of the St. Lawrence. The village of Kahnawake, which the white people called Cognawaga, was home to hundreds of native people, a place almost as poor as St. Henri. To the northeast, across the waters of the river, the spires of Montreal rose like a celestial city in the mists. It was a cold day, but sunny. Native boys knocked a hockey puck about in the streets. A little girl ran along the sidewalk, dragging a kite. Old people sauntered. Young men and women stood at corners talking, joking, smoking cigarettes, and pretending to fight. Dogs scavenged in overturned trash cans. The atmosphere was very familiar to Rose, though the people's faces were a little different than those of the Ojibwe. So, too, their language, though a few of its sounds were similar to her own tongue.

Speaking in English, she asked some teenagers if they knew where she could find Kateri, but they only stared at her, not knowing what she meant. She walked on, realizing that even she did not fully know what she meant. Who exactly was she looking for? Kateri had gone to heaven. Perhaps she was supposed to meet a person *like* Kateri, possibly a girl who lived as the saint had once lived, in prayer and self-sacrifice. Or perhaps a memorial of some kind. Possibly a person who could tell her more about her sister's life.

Rose stopped an elderly woman and asked if she knew Kateri.

"There are many Kateris", the woman answered.

"I seek the first Kateri", Rose explained. "The Blessed Tekakwitha."

"Ah, *that* Kateri. Her shrine is down by the river, in the church of the Jesuit Fathers. Go that way. Turn left. It is five minutes by foot."

Shortly after, Rose found herself standing with a thumping heart in front of a poor old mission church. It was badly in need of paint, and a window beside the front door was cracked. The building was very old, older than the houses surrounding it. She opened the front door and went inside.

Of the many churches and shrines where Rose had prayed during her life, this was the one that seemed most saturated in holiness. Older than the shrine of St. Joseph, poorer than any church she had ever seen, save for the chapel at Threefinger Lake, yet it was the richest. The air was thick with the presence of the Holy Spirit. Rose fell to her knees on the floor and worshipped the Beating Heart in the tabernacle. In two streams his love reached out to her, one from the Sacrament and one rising up within her, flowing together into one pouring— pouring in and pouring out until time ceased altogether and everything became a sweet burning, without pain of any kind, without fear of any kind, without the need to know anything, for everything was contained within the mystery.

When at last the force of his love was veiled once more, she struggled up from the floor and slid into a creaking wooden pew. The flow of tears that spilled from her eyes was soft and filled with gladness.

"I am home", she whispered.

For an hour she sat like this, eyes closed, without moving, without thinking. Possibly two hours. Breathing love in, breathing love out. Finally, voices roused her from this deep water. Whispering voices. What they said she could not hear, yet they were good voices, a man, a woman, and the tiny mewings of a baby the woman held in her arms. The man and the woman were natives, poorly dressed, the man a few years older than the woman. They knelt in an alcove to the right of the sanctuary.

Rose longed to go to them, to beg them to let her hold their child for a few moments. But she could not make herself do so, for she was ashamed of her deformity, her ugliness. She knew they would see her as a strange person. They would be protective of their child, and though these young Christians might try to hide their fear, it would show in their eyes. This would hurt her too much.

They were praying with their foreheads pressed to the side of a large white box in the center of the alcove. Rose got up and moved closer, hoping they would not notice her presence. She knelt a few feet behind the couple and waited while they completed their prayers. She pondered the box and thought that perhaps an old missionary was entombed in it. If so, she would ask him to intercede, to guide her to her beloved sister, or to a place where once Kateri had stood upon this land.

"She is yours, Kateri", said the young woman. "Pray for her."

Then Rose understood. This was her sister's tomb. The bones of Kateri herself rested here, awaiting the Last Day.

"Io!" she cried aloud.

The couple turned and looked at her. They smiled and resumed their prayers. Then they made the sign of the Cross on their foreheads, lips, and chests—and also on their child. They got up and went away. When the door of the church closed behind them, leaving Rose alone in the echoing space, she edged forward on her knees and put both of her hands on the tomb. It was made of chiseled white stone. The light that came from it was part of the great river of light that poured from the springs of the tabernacle, swelling into a river so wide that none could cross it, and, flowing into the sea, it made its waters wholesome.

"I have come to you, Kateri. It is me, it is Bineshi. It is Rose."

No answering words came from the tomb, yet a knowing within Rose's heart grew and grew until she felt the presence of her sister gazing down upon her from paradise. Though they were separated by Rose's mortality, they were united within the waters of life. Who could explain this!

Kateri smiled at her. Rose kissed the cool surface of the stone.

Then the words of the Lord came to Rose's heart: *Soon*, he said to her, *you will go farther. You will go very far, but first you must be purified. Three journeys do I give you. Three journeys lie before you, for the good of many souls and for the good of your own soul.*

Then the knowing receded, and all sensation of flowing waters ceased, and thus she was left with herself.

On the day following the closing of the show, Rose went down to the gallery to collect her unsold paintings. She was amazed when Ms. Pannenburg announced with a hollow smile that the show had been a complete success. Everything had been sold.

The woman handed her an envelope. "Here is your payment, Bineshi. I hope it's satisfactory. The statement is enclosed."

"Thank you. I am very grateful for all you have done for me and for my work. Do you think I may have another exhibit one day?"

"Well, that depends . . ."

"Next year?"

"Possibly. We might be willing to offer you a show in a year or two from now." Ms. Panneburg hesitated, then forged on. "I don't know how to say this exactly, but both Mr. Ontolli and I feel it would not be to your advantage to pursue the line of subject matter that was included in this show."

"What do you mean?"

"Native art is on the brink of a great explosion. It has already begun to burst into the world market."

"Then I—"

"Our problem, you see, is that you don't really fit into any category that private and public collectors are presently interested in."

"But my work was completely sold—"

"Yes, but this wasn't an ordinary situation. Mr. Ontolli made an exception for you out of respect for Esther Dyson, and, well, for Hugo too. But the subject matter—"

"Do you not like my work?"

"It's not a matter of liking or disliking. The public is no longer interested in this subject matter."

Utterly confused, Rose replied, "But they do seem to be interested."

"A private collector bought the problematic works, the, uh, Christian works. Ordinarily we would not have exhibited them because there is really no demand for this subject."

"Who is the private collector?"

"That person wishes to remain anonymous. I'm sure that you, more than anyone else, understand the advantages of anonymity."

Rose shook her head. "For myself, it is to remain hidden so that the pride-way will not—"

"Yes, well, you see the person in question purchased the unpopular pieces as an act of kindness, in memory of Esther. But it is not the sort of work that this person usually collects. No serious collector is interested in Christian work. And it would be unfair to our other artists, people of dedication and vision, if we were to cater to a special interest group." Ms. Pannenburg seemed suddenly uncomfortable and began to shuffle papers around her desk, her face and body signaling that it was now time for Rose to leave. But Rose would not leave and the woman looked up vexed.

"That about concludes it", she said.

"Please, I do not understand what you are telling me."

Ms. Pannenburg's lips tightened. "If you must know, your work is counterproductive to the development of art history and to the renaissance of genuine aboriginal culture."

"You mean I don't fit."

"In crude terms, yes. Perhaps if you were to examine your own motives. Are you not still the little Indian girl trying to remain in a protected institution, trying to please the nuns?"

"No", Rose shook her head. "I make pictures of what is in my heart. I paint what I love."

"Then you do not understand what you love. The Church is a necrotic tumor on the social body. It will either be removed or it will continue to sicken the body."

As if hit by a blow, Rose took a step back.

"If you wish to have another show here, you will have to drop the Christian themes. Try to find your own voice, Bineshi, like the true native artists. Every authentic woman and visionary arrives at the moment of illumination when she recognizes that she has been buried by the rubble heap of European patriarchy. When you find yourself, you will climb out from under it. Then you will become a genuine artist."

Rose turned to leave.

"Best of luck", said Ms. Pannenburg, and shut the office door.

Rose walked downstairs slowly, passing gallery employees who were hanging a new show: abstracts—paint flung and dribbled at random across each canvas. Stung, disoriented, she saw that this art testified to her total foolishness, her enormous presumption in trying to attend the festival of culture. She emerged into the street to discover herself strangely lost, belonging nowhere.

When Rose recounted to Hugo her conversation with Ms. Pannenburg, his face soured.

"Do you mind showing me the check and the statement?" he asked.

Rose passed the envelope to him.

"I do not understand that woman, Hugo. The show was a success."

"I agree with you, a resounding success. Well, well, well—isn't this interesting. Here you have a check for fifteen hundred dollars. Not bad. Not bad. That's nothing to scoff at. Yet in my estimation over thirty thousand dollars worth of your work was sold. They took their commission, of course. Forty percent. That's standard in the business. But what's this! They charged you for half the costs of the reception and the advertisements. And it looks like they charged you retail prices for the framing." Hugo's eyes slitted and his voice fell. "Those voracious, cadaverous, insidious, perfidious—"

He concluded with a very crude word.

"Well, Rose, it seems Favio and Clarissa have squeezed every last possible penny from you. It's all strictly legal, of course. But I expected better of them. I'm sorry."

"It does not matter, Hugo."

"Yes, it does matter", he mumbled, reading the itemized invoice for the second time. "I should have known, I should have known. Certainly about the frames. We could have done them ourselves for a quarter of the cost."

"Still, Hugo, I have received a great deal of money. It will enable me to work for almost a year."

"*Almost* a year? Maybe, if you live on cat food and crackers."

"Also, I have many drawings that were not in the show. With these and the new works I make, I should have enough pictures for a show next year."

"Maybe", he said. "But I wouldn't count on it. It sounds very much to me as though they were interested in you only because you're native and it sounds good in the ads. But they weren't at all happy about the religious work. And they just told you that, from now on, that subject is *persona non grata*." He eyed her puzzled expression. "They're saying, don't call us, we'll call you."

"You mean—?"

"They mean to tell you, my dear, that if you don't bend to their will, you can just get lost."

"I do not understand. They seemed to be nice people—"

Hugo gave her a look of pity. "Oh, yes, nice people. Good breeding runs from every orifice. But you have to understand one thing: They live in a jungle, and they've made themselves masters of it. They have their weapons and maps and native bearers. And whenever it comes to a choice between them and you, guess who gets thrown to the lions."

"To the leopards", Rose corrected.

For a month after that, Rose tried to draw and paint, but the heaviness of her heart stood in the way of every attempt. She walked to the shrine of St. Joseph and back most days, feeling little or no consolation, entering a time of desolation that had no explanation. She did not really credit the feeling to the setback that she had recently suffered at the hands of the art world, for the art world had also rewarded her to some extent. No, it was somehow connected to the knowing that she had experienced while praying at Kateri's tomb. *You will go very far, but first you must be purified.* She examined her conscience scrupulously, but could find nothing marring it that would invite a purification. Perhaps she had misunderstood.

On the other hand, there was a danger in success—*la fête de l'orgeuil, la fière arrogante.* The small wounding had shown her that a thread of pride-root had indeed taken hold in her heart, without her knowing it, like a trickle of pollution secretly entering a stream of clear water. She had hoped, had she not, for an end to the privations caused by lack of money. She had hoped for the means to contribute to the household expenses in order to ease Hugo's burdens, and also to relieve herself of the feeling of dependency. Most of all she had wanted her work to do good in the world, and was it not reasonable to suppose that the better known her work became, the more good would come of it? But she had also wanted the world to speak well of her, to say she was not a nothing-person. Io, it was all mixed, the wholesome water and the unwholesome. And though the greater part was good, the presence of the trickle of pollution could infect the whole.

"So, Ogini," she said to herself, "see the great kindness of Our Lord in this, that he does not permit you to drink from soiled springs. He desires the best for you. The pain of it is hard, but it is because he loves you so much."

Acceptance came, and peace.

She continued to struggle to make new pictures, but it seemed that all creative flow had now ceased within her. No matter how much she asked for it, regardless of how many prayers and sacrifices she offered, it would not return. What was happening to her?

Other words surfaced in her memory. *Three journeys lie before you, for the good of many souls and for the good of your own soul.*

She fell asleep one night in early August asking many questions of the silent darkness above: What kind of journeys? When would she go? How would she know where to go? But the silence did not answer her.

Strangely, it was Hugo who brought a word of guidance.

"Rose, my girl, I've had a thought regarding your good self. You're fretting and fussing, and wasting weeks of your time trying to get blood from stone. Not that you're a stone, mind you. Figure of speech, don't look so shocked."

"I am trying to paint, Hugo. Really I am. Also, I want to give you half of my money for the rent and heat. The winter will be upon us within three months and—"

"No, no, no. You misunderstand my motives! How many times have we had this discussion? Not a penny do I ask. Your good company and your endlessly patient housekeeping are ample payment for what I provide. After all, if the truth be known, what exactly *do* I provide? A roof (leaking), a space to work (dusty and dark), heat (intermittent), and company (unstable). It is *I* who am indebted to *you*. But I have not become so entirely selfish that I fail to notice your needs."

"My needs?"

"Yes, your needs. You're becoming cramped and frustrated. You're not able to create. It's time."

"Time for what, Hugo?"

"Time for you to see the larger world. My advice is this: 'Go forth with one equal temper of heroic hearts, made weak by time and fate, but strong in will, to strive, to seek, to find, and not to yield.'"

"I do not understand, Hugo."

"A journey, fair Ulyssia. A journey."

"Where would I go, Hugo?"

"Wherever you like. There lies the port; the vessel puffs her sail."

"I do not want to go anywhere."

"Want is not the same as need."

"Still, Hugo, where would I go?"

"Why not a sojourn to the Old World? Europe. See the Louvre in Paris. The British Museum in London. Many a happy hour, nay, happy day and week, did I dally in both places. Also, the Prado in Madrid. Yes, yes, the marrow quickens within me even as we speak. You must go to Antwerp and see *Birds in Wartime*. Also New York, where Meister Guggenheim has enthroned an Esther Dyson. Oh, Rose, why didn't I think of this before? Foolish old woollybear that I am!"

"I suppose there is much I could learn", she said with mixed emotions.

"The eye expands. The heart expands also."

"If I go, you must come with me."

"Nonsense. You must go alone."

"But I cannot go alone!"

He shook his head. "You must."

"Why must I?"

"So that the eye will gaze without distraction, free of another's interpretation. So that solitude will age the vintage. You will look, you will absorb, you will reflect. You will return a changed person. You will make great paintings upon your return."

"There is no guarantee of that, Hugo."

"Agreed. But I wager that a great artist—not a great *native* artist, not a great *Canadian* artist, not a great *woman* artist—but a great world's artist will come from this journey."

Scenting a whiff of the pride-way, Rose withdrew her momentary enthusiasm.

"I do not know. Perhaps it is arrogant."

"Arrogant! Good heavens, girl, I shall never understand you. No, it's settled. Go you will, and return you will, and we shall all be the better for your journey."

"Even so, Hugo, it would cost too much money."

Scowling, he rubbed his bushy chin with a speckled hand. "Hmmm, that is so. What to do, then? What to do? Let me think on it."

Rose continued in some discontent during the following days, walking, praying, questioning the silence. Then, on a Thursday evening during the first week of September, a visitor came to the house unannounced. It was Estelle Morgan.

"Hello, Rose", Mrs. Morgan said at the front door. She offered her hand. Rose shook it.

"Hugo is not in, Mrs. Morgan. He has gone with Clive and Trevor to a concert."

"I know. It is you, you see, with whom I wish to speak. May I come in?"

Rose led her to the parlor and scurried to the kitchen to make a pot of tea. She also filled a plate with dry bannock and a jar of jam, hoping that Mrs. Morgan liked such treats. When they were settled before the fire, sipping their tea, Mrs. Morgan leaned forward and said, "I was very impressed by your display last spring at the Ontolli-Metropol. I hope they treated you well."

Rose kept silent, guarding herself against even minor lapses of charity.

"You needn't say a word", Mrs. Morgan said after a studied appraisal of the silence. "The world of business is utterly ruthless, and never more so than when it purports to be the valiant defender of culture. Let us say no more on the matter. With your permission, I would like to see your studio and any unsold works you might wish to show me."

Reluctantly, Rose agreed. As she climbed the stairs ahead of Mrs. Morgan, she tried to understand the reluctance, attributing it to her old mistrust of the woman's power and her flirtations with the pagan-way. Still, Mrs. Morgan was not an evil person, that was clear. She meant well, and Esther had liked her very much, and that was saying a great deal because it took a lot to win Esther's heart. Perhaps it was the old jealousy. She did not like this woman, no, not at all. And she was a little frightened of her as well—why, she could not say.

In the studio, Rose opened the cardboard boxes of pastel drawings and began to rummage through them. One by one she sorted them, laying aside the best, a mixture of styles and scenes, most of them landscapes, a few strongly Christian themes, and a few intimate memories both symbolic and literal. Mrs. Morgan sat down on the painting stool and observed with so complete a silence that on occasion Rose looked up to see if the woman was still in the room. Once or twice it seemed that she caught sight of tears in Mrs. Morgan's eyes, but it was perhaps a trick of the light. The beautiful face was perfectly composed, and the perfect mouth smiled a little whenever Rose turned in her direction.

Finished, Rose carried a stack of about sixty pastels to a table beneath the studio window. Mrs. Morgan stood beside her. One by one Rose slowly placed each image before the visitor. Neither she nor Mrs. Morgan said a word. From time to time, the woman put out a hand and touched the edge of a sheet of paper and, asking permission with her eyes, set it aside. Rose nodded in agreement. The number of these grew steadily. When eight had been chosen, all landscapes, Rose's excitement reached the level of trembling. When the number reached ten, the trembling tipped over into numbness. And by the time it was twenty, she was beyond all speech.

The twenty-first was an older work, an early pastel that she had done at Threefinger Lake. The paper was wrinkled and creased in several places, and some of the wax smudged.

"This is an interesting piece", Mrs. Morgan said. "Similar to that larger work you had in the exhibit. This is its prototype, isn't it?"

Rose gave her a puzzled look.

"I mean to say, this is the original work from which the more developed painting derived. The style is simpler, more hastily executed. Yet the subject is the same. An anguished woman sleeping on the crest of a rock beside a lake, a man bending over her with love, opposed by some sort of monster, am I correct?"

"Yes."

"And the bird—such a very large white bird. Is it symbolic?"

Rose nodded.

"May I purchase it as well, Rose?"

Again Rose nodded.

"Can you tell me the prices of each? Before you answer, I do encourage you to value your work. Yes, you should value it highly."

"I—I do not know what price to ask."

"May I suggest, then, that you ask twice the value placed on your pastels by Favio Ontolli?"

"I do not understand—"

"The gallery seriously undervalued them. These are very important works of art, and they will long survive most of the reputations that Favio inflates and peddles. Your work contains genuine insight and a harsh beauty. It is presently considered of little account in the world of commercial and public art. Those worlds are dominated by politics, influence, and greed. But my sense is that it will not always be so."

"I—"

Mrs. Morgan withdrew a red calfskin checkbook and a gold pen from her purse and bent to write. She handed a slip of paper to Rose.

"I hope I have not been illiberal. Is four hundred dollars per image sufficient?"

"I—"

Mrs. Morgan gave Rose more than enough time to answer. As she stared at the script on the check, Rose's mouth hung open. Eighty-four hundred dollars. The visitor, recognizing the artist's discomfort, turned away and began to browse among a few half-finished paintings that leaned against the wall. She made a circuit of the room and returned finally to Rose's side.

"Is the exchange agreeable to you? Is it fair?"

Rose nodded and pocketed the check, feeling a sickly mood as she did so, as if she were cheating Mrs. Morgan. Her mind told her that it was not so, yet the overwhelming riches that had just been dropped into her hands seemed inconsistent with the worth of the work, which she felt was minimal.

Mrs. Morgan, to distract them both from the uncomfortable situation, let her eyes wander toward the collection of natural objects on the window sill: the pine cones, maple keys, bits of fluted driftwood, and the loon-star.

"A perfect sphere", she mused. "How lovely it is."

Then, catching sight of the *binemin* stone, she seemed for no accountable reason to be mesmerized by this dull misshapen object.

"An interesting form. May I touch it?"

"Yes."

Mrs. Morgan picked up the stone and held it in both hands. She closed her eyes and let its weight speak.

"It's quite beautiful. Like a bird."

"It is a partridge."

"Ah, a partridge. Yes, I see the shape now, the little beak, the speckles."

Rose kept silent, watching with a guarded expression, for no other person save herself and Tchibi had ever touched the *binemin* in this manner. Hugo had also touched it, but only for a moment as he repaired a neutral object. Neither he nor Mrs. Morgan knew that it was a part of Tchibi's self, that it was the word of love he had given into her hands so many years ago.

In an abstracted tone of voice, Mrs. Morgan said "I love stones. I am quite a collector of oddities. I have a slab of red sandstone from Prince Edward Island that the sea carved into the shape of a fish, as if the sea were dreaming of its children. And an extensive set of chrysolite, tiger's eye, and geodes. Are you familiar with geodes? No? Ugly round stones which, when split, reveal an astonishing microcosm within, symmetrical caves of multicolored crystal. I also have a marble plinth from the Roman Forum. And a fossilized giant snail from the Seychelles. Perhaps my most precious stone is from the mountains of northern Turkey. In a village that lies at the base of Mount Ararat, there is a gargantuan anchor regarded by the villagers as a relic from the Ark. I was able to purchase a small ballast stone, which has no resemblance to any geological formations in the surrounding area. Indeed, it is stone from Mesopotamia, hewn into rounded shapes by the hands, I am told, of Noah and his sons."

Mrs. Morgan smiled deprecatingly, to allow a little space for healthy disbelief. Withdrawing into her own thoughts she stroked the *binemin* stone, her eyes closed, her chest swelling slowly, inhaling and exhaling.

Rose resisted a strong desire to grab the *binemin* from Mrs. Morgan's hands. Despite the woman's extraordinary kindness, the dislike Rose felt for her seemed to increase with every passing moment. Yet she rebuked the rush of negative emotion, admonished herself for her lack of charity, her jealousy, her fear.

"Io," she said in her thoughts, "ay, ay, Ogini, what is the matter with you? She is a poor lonely woman. If you desire mercy for yourself, would you withhold mercy from her?"

Mrs. Morgan opened her eyes suddenly.

"Rose, I hesitate to ask." She swallowed noticeably. "You will think it grasping of me, I'm sure. But it would please me greatly if you would consider making a little gift of this stone to me. You must feel free to say no, of course."

Ay-ay-ay! Rose reeled with the shock of this request. Her face betrayed nothing.

"I—"

"Perhaps the stone is meaningful to you. Yes, of course, how silly of me not to see it. Surely it is meaningful to you. I am sorry. I have been insensitive."

She handed the *binemin* back to Rose. Rose took it and felt the heat of the stone burning in her hands. It was the heat of Mrs. Morgan.

In the few seconds of silence that ensued, a silence in which the visitor would not have been able to discern the slightest disturbance on Rose's face, a great struggle began.

See how she desires this thing, Rose said in the privacy of her own thoughts. *This thing which is the most precious of my possessions. It is my heart and his heart that she asks for, yet she does not realize. How could this woman ever value it? How could she know what it cost? Never, never will this blind person understand what she asks for.*

Io, see her beauty and her wealth, see her health and her power. She possesses all that human beings strive for, yet she asks for more. And she asks of me the very thing I cannot give.

Even so, Ogini, see that the Great Heart has given to you the love that this woman lacks. See how he has poured out his gifts upon you. And your sins he has washed away, both the sin of your humanity in the Great Waters, and the sin of your own choosing, the seeds of hatred and envy that have been in your heart. See how great is his mercy for you, yet you would withhold mercy from her.

Rose stared at the floor, feeling the heat drain slowly from the *binemin.*

Ogini, she said to herself, *have you made of this remembrance and this beloved word an idol? Have you? Have you clung to it more than you cling to the will of the Father?*

Looking up at Mrs. Morgan, she smiled at her and said, "I would be happy to give it to you. Please take it."

She placed it gently into the woman's open hands. The trembling hands closed over the stone.

"Why, thank you, Rose. That is very thoughtful of you."

Realizing that she was still holding something back, still clinging to a shred of idolatry, Rose took the loon-star and offered it as well. Mrs. Morgan accepted it without a word.

Shortly afterward, her chauffeur came up to the studio and under the woman's direction carefully gathered the twenty-one pastels and drawings and took them downstairs to the white limousine.

At the front door, Mrs. Morgan surprised Rose by suddenly embracing her, taking care not to harm her back, and kissing her cheek. Leaving the lingering perfume of violet talcum, she left.

Rose went up to her bedroom, threw herself onto the cot, and wept as she had not done since Tchibi's death.

Mrs. Morgan's check was good. Hugo proclaimed that it was not rubber, perplexing Rose with his inexhaustible storehouse of expressions, but she knew by this that he was happy for her; he was always poetic in such a mood. He made a little party just for the two of them, baked a whole salmon for her, compiled a list of paintings that she must see in Europe, filled pages of directions to museums in various countries, advice for airports and railways, and many more details that she knew she would never use. It was his way of sending his care after her.

Alternating between elation and doubt, Rose held onto the possibility that she might be spared the trip at the last moment. Yet the day finally came when Hugo arrived home from a visit to the travel agent, bearing an airline ticket to London. He gave it to her with a broad grin.

"This is a mistake, Hugo", she said.

"It's no mistake. You're going."

"Are you evicting me?"

"Yes, absolutely."

"Then it seems I must go. But Hugo, if I go, who will cook for you?"

"I will cook for myself."

Feeling a surge of maternal anxiety, Rose frowned. "If I go, would you promise to feed yourself properly?"

"Absolutely. I'll even feed Goldie too, if you insist."

"You would not drink whiskey, would you?"

"Whiskey? What is whiskey?"

"You would promise?"

"Of course. Need I say more?"

On the evening of her departure, Hugo went with her by taxi to the airport. At the security gate, he shed a gruff tear and patted her hand. Then he handed her a little package that had arrived in the morning's mail, and which he had forgotten to give her. She slipped it into her deer-hide sack and promptly forgot it, as the dizzying complexity of events swept her through a series of gates and into the aircraft. It was half full, and Rose had a good selection of seats to choose from. She sat at the back, by a window. Night was falling as the roar of the engines shook every cell of her body, and she lifted from the earth and climbed into the *tchibekana* which the white people call the river of milk, but which is in fact the river of souls.

She was frightened and thrilled. As the plane leveled off above the silver moonstruck clouds, the fear declined and left in its wake a joy that was wholly human in origin, yet not without its touches of grace, the little reminders that she was not alone, that her sister and the Beating Heart were with her. She prayed the rosary on the beads that the woman had given her several years ago in Ottawa, prayed for that woman, prayed for her own safety and Hugo's protection from his dark moods and for guidance, that she might see what the Lord wished her to see, that the words she had heard at Kateri's tomb would be accomplished.

Three journeys do I give you. Three journeys lie before you, for the good of many souls, and for the good of your own soul.

How this would come to pass she could not guess. There would be a purification. The inner knowing had informed her of this, she supposed, because the Lord did not want her to be unprepared. She prayed another rosary, and as usual felt a little regret that she did not know the Mother as well as she knew the Son. She longed to know her and wondered why there was a distance between them. She trusted in her intercession and understood her role but puzzled anew over why she did not feel her presence.

After that came a meal. Then the lights were dimmed and blankets distributed. Rose dozed for a time, then awoke to see the night outside blazing with millions of stars. She remembered that there was a package for her in the deer-hide sack. She rummaged and found it.

The package contained a small jeweler's box and a letter. The envelope was addressed to Miss Rose Wâbos, Rue St. Benoît, St. Henri, Montreal, Québec. Written in gold ink in the upper left hand corner was a name without a return address. The letter was from Mrs. Morgan. Rose supposed that it was a note of thanks, a courteous response to the gift of the loon-star and the *binemin* stone.

Dearest Rose,
Long have I watched your progress as an artist, from the moment I learned of you. Do you remember our first

622

meeting, can you still see that lady whom you met at the banquet after the *Midsummer Night's Dream*? How shy you were, how very afraid of us all you were—the powerful and the wealthy—and perhaps you had good reason to be. I am sometimes gifted with the ability to transpose myself into another's eyes, to see how I must appear to other people, gazing at—O strangest of dislocations—at me. Yes, the powerful and the wealthy exist on plateaus that most people do not dream of seeing, let alone live upon. Metamorphosed from ordinary beings, we assume our roles upon a stage where only professionals are permitted to remain for long.

Do not envy us, Rose. Please, do not. For as we rise in this world, so do many things fall from us. With our success we are given a lethal dose of insecurity. Ever after we doubt the motives of all. Never again can we assume that we are being valued or disvalued for ourselves. It is always a case of are we useful or not useful, and in this manner we rich are degraded into the world of objects.

In you, there was no such guile. In you, I saw no avarice or ambition. I read your eyes rightly, for they saw rightly. You pitied me, yet you did not despise me (a rare conjunction). You love, Rose. Why is it that you love, when you have received so little from life and have been given instead so many difficulties that would have crushed lesser persons, such as me?

I remember a little girl I once knew, small and clear of eye. How clearly she penetrated my own fragility, intending no offense as she portrayed with little sticks of color the exact state of my soul. I remember you in my arms, trembling with a child's natural longing for its mother, with the first hint of a curve in your spine. I remember the happy hours that we passed in the sun and the wind. And Binemin forcing mashed berries upon us both. I remember your love for him. I remember the shaman who split us all apart.

My enduring shame is that I ran from you. I ran because I was afraid, not so much afraid of the tricks of the medicine man, but from the fragility of my own mind and the shattering revelation of my self-delusions. The edifice of the self is a frail household easily demolished.

Yes, I ran, and I knew that I could never forgive myself for this. Yet here you are; like a miracle in a mediaeval morality play, you appear out of nowhere. You have survived, you have become what you were intended to be. Who, then, has sustained you over all these years? Who has taught you the wonders that flow from your eye and hand?

I know that you will ask yourself why I did not identify myself to you from the beginning. When I heard that the Dysons had taken in a houseguest, a native woman named Rose, an artist, I wondered if it was you. But it couldn't be, I told myself. There are so many native women, so many "Roses", so many who suffer a physical disability. Then on the night of the *Dream* I realized that it was you. I saw that you were in Esther's and Hugo's capable hands.

Yet I tried to help. I purchased several of the works at the Ontolli show anonymously. The religious works. Do not infer from this that it was an act of pity on my part, for those six pastels and paintings were among the best in the show, and I could not bear to see them ignored, unrespected, or purchased by those who could never understand them. The six and the twenty-one are in safe-keeping. I will respect your anonymity if you will respect mine. However, because they are unsigned they might one day present a problem for art historians. In the event of either your death or mine, the identity of their creator will be revealed through my estate. For now, the time is not yet ripe. I cannot name a single collection that is not dominated by the spirit of the times. The emperor insists upon his wardrobe, but it will not always be so. In the meantime you must travel and look and probe into the roots of this dark world, so afire with beauty and dread. You must paint what you see, Rose, and you must not hold back your honesty. Our times are ill. Indeed, I am ill. We all are infected with the desire to see only what we want to see.

For so many years as you toiled in pain and under the weight of failure, I longed to swoop down and come to the rescue like the grande dame, scattering money and security like a wealthy old aunt. Would it have helped? Perhaps a little. You cannot guess the anguish I experienced as I wrestled with this question. Yet never was I far from you. If there had been the slightest hint of starvation or eviction from Esther or Hugo, I would have arrived on the scene, in spite of the risk of ruining everything with what my personality does to people and situations, yet totally unable to prevent it. I was there in the background during a few tight scrapes. Esther's death was the worst, for I was certain that Hugo would plunge irrevocably, leaving you lost and without resources. But to everyone's surprise he survived. Still, he is a man adrift, and he needs you now more than ever. You are his spiritual heir, the child he never had.

Perhaps you are angry with me. Of course you are, how could you not be? I would not blame you in the least. I abandoned you twenty years ago, and, in this second extended abandonment, I could have come forward at any moment, but did not. Will you forgive me? Please forgive me, Rose. Please let us begin again when you return from Europe. My husband is taking a position with the International Monetary Fund, an agency of the United

Nations. When we are resettled, I will send along our new address. Then, if you wish, you can contact me.

You will wonder at the name: Estelle. It was my own attempt at rebirth, for it is true that names have power. Names and words. They change us forever if we would permit and if we would understand. Yet a name can also be an object that is collected in a box with other names, like shells from the sea, old coins, stones, and pearls that are held too closely to the heart.

I know what it is you gave to me. I know what it cost you to give those two precious stones to a strange wealthy woman who you believed could never treasure them. I saw what you tried to hide from me—your dismay and your sacrifice. Be assured that your partridge is safe, so too the little globe on which he stands with birds upon his shoulders. Yes, it was all there in the painting, your wonderful portrait of Binemin as a man. Soon I will return the stones to you.

In the interim, I send you a gift that you must dispose of as you see fit. It is torn from my heart. I never want to see it again. Now I am empty, waiting to be filled.

Please do not abandon me, as I abandoned you.

Euphrasia Morgan

Rose opened the jeweler's box and found within it a small black pearl.

23

In late September of that year, a solitary walker appeared on the crest of a hill cloven by two hedgerows. Between these dark green walls a bridle path wound down into a trough in the hills through which flowed a slip of river. Small brick houses with thatch or slate roofs clustered at the bottom, close by a narrow bridge made of stone and heavy timber. Smoke rose from chimney pots. Sheep dotted the meadows that rose on every side.

The traveler paused for a moment and shifted her backpack, so that its aluminum frame would not dig into her arching spine.

"Io, it is beautiful", said Rose Wâbos to herself.

Of the many images of fabulous art and architecture which had so enriched her mind during recent weeks, none had moved her as did this scene of tranquillity, for here it seemed man had dwelled for thousands of years, in peace with nature and with neighbor.

In the Tate Gallery in London she had seen a painting of a similar landscape; indeed there were many such portraits of the English countryside, though when she had viewed them they had seemed more mythical than literal. Yet here was such a valley, as real as a picture.

Rose smiled in delight, then resumed her journey down into the village, which announced its name on a little sign nailed to the bridge post: *Thatch Upping*. Seating herself on a stone wall beneath the sign, she sighed with relief, glad to have arrived at a habitation of human proportions. She recalled her three weeks in the great city as a plunge into an unceasing roar and the disorienting turbulence of millions of people moving in all directions at once. She shook away the thought of it, retaining only the fading memories of several museums and galleries, all of which blended into each other, leaving only a few painted images on the surface of her mind, as hemorrhaging northern rivers will, after spring gives way to summer, recede to their proper levels depositing shining stones on the shores.

She unfolded a map of the lower half of England and pored over the section depicting the shires of the southwest part of the country. Thatch Upping was not on the map, though the town of Wantage, five miles back, was there, a tiny black dot. Rose now saw that the heights of land that she had climbed during the previous two and a half hours were the escarpment of a line of hills that cut across several shires from southeast to northwest. There were few villages in the region, and those that existed were, for the most part, farming communities of various sizes. This was the smallest she had yet encountered.

She was very hungry. The walk had invigorated her, and her brown cheeks glowed with a flush of blood beneath the surface. Her eyes sparkled with enthusiasm, for it seemed to her that she was inside a great work of art, a canvas so broad that she could not see its frame in any direction.

The village contained only a single street of cobblestones, along which the dozen or so houses and shops were lined. Here the bridle path ended, and a narrow road began, running through the center of the village and beyond, disappearing over a hill to the west. Across from the bridge there stood a small brick church, its steeple hardly higher than the peak of an old grist mill that flanked it. The mill's wooden wheel spun slowly under the force of a sluice pouring over a low dam. Nowhere was there a person to be seen, though a jaunty Scottish terrier approached, sniffed her ankles, wagged its tail, and proceeded about its business.

On the other side of the church was a nondescript frame and

wattle building with a sagging thatched roof. Above its front door a shingle-sign said, *Three Penny Inn, ales and meals.* Rose pushed open the heavy oak door and went inside, startled by the clink-clank of a copper sheep bell that swung from the upper frame. The interior was dimly lit by two leaded windows and a dull electric light in the center of the ceiling. There were no customers; neither, apparently, was there a proprietor. Rose unshouldered her baggage, sat down at the table closest to the entrance, and looked about the room, noting that it contained little decoration, only dark wood tables and chairs, and a service counter with pump handles and trays of drinking glasses, above which were suspended shelves of clay tankards.

Presently a door opened behind the counter, and a little man of about sixty years emerged, wiping his hands on a dish cloth. His cheeks were the kind of jolly hue that inspire both amusement and affection in observers, and his eyes were small blue buttons that shone with a mixture of caution and wry humor. When he saw the rather unprecedented shape of Rose, his hands ceased to wring the cloth and his mouth opened a little as if he were at a loss for what to say. Then he quickly found his professional face and smiled pleasantly enough.

"Help you?"

"Yes, please, sir. I am a traveler and have need of a meal."

"'Ave need of a meal, d'you? Well, we're good at that sort of thing. What d'ye fancy?"

"What do you cook?"

"A frightful lot o' things. I can tell you're not from these parts. Can I make suggestions? For the meal, I mean."

He came around from behind the counter and approached her with a small chalkboard menu. All the while he eyed her with something like amazement. To be sure, during his many years of living, he had not, until this moment, seen a four-foot-high, brown-skinned, hunchbacked woman whose hair was completely gray but whose eyes and expression were those of a child.

"I can recommend the steak and kidney pie, depending on your budget, if you don't mind me being bold about the matter."

"Do you have toast?"

"Aye, we're masters of the toast-making here. Bit of jam with it too, I'll venture, and the five-peel marmalade? Like a sip of beer to go with it?"

"No, thank you. Do you serve tea?"

"We do. Black and English or the herbals?"

"Strong tea, please. Yes, black."

"White?"

"I'm sorry—?" she replied in a puzzled tone.

"With milk, I mean", he said in the nick of time. "We call it white here. And sugar too?"

"Yes, please."

He kept hovering and staring, as if he could not see enough of the phenomenon.

"Where are you from?" he asked in a tone that really meant, What exactly are you, for though I mean you no ill, I am quite perplexed as to where you are situated on the spectrum of humanity.

She told him. Shaking his head, he inquired why a person such as she (though he did not elaborate on what *she* was) would take it into her head to go tromping through this remote region.

"I have been in London, visiting galleries, seeing paintings", she explained.

"Oh, that's a lovely thing to do", he said sincerely, but obviously straining to find the connection between his question and her answer. He sat down opposite her, perhaps wondering if she was as real as his senses seemed to suggest.

"The city of London was very draining", she went on. "My eyes were blurred by it, and my ears deafened."

"Aye, I know the feeling. Hate the place myself. Went to the

Coronation in '53 and that was more than enough o' London for this old lad. Thatch Upping is busy enough for me."

"It does not seem busy, sir."

He laughed. "Middle of the afternoon t'is quiet enough. By four or five the *Three Pennies* will be needin' the riot police. Always like that, six days a week, 'cept on the Lord's Day, when we're closed."

"Oh, it is good of you to close on the Lord's Day. He who sees all things will not forget your sacrifice, nor fail to reward you for your obedience."

The man raised his eyebrows and shook his head again. He nodded to the menu.

"Make what sense you can of it, Miss, but I do suggest the kidney pie to go with the toast and tea."

"Yes, I would like the pie. I am very grateful for your kindness, sir."

He took the chalkboard from her and stood, blinking, smiling, and shaking his head. Then he went to make her meal. A minute later a large round woman emerged from the kitchen, flicked a curious look in Rose's direction, wiped the counter top with a rag, and disappeared behind the door from which she had come. Shortly thereafter, two teenage boys squeezed together through the doors, stared at Rose without any effort to hide their raw curiosity, and went back into the secret chambers of the pub. This was followed by a burst of giggling—small children who could be heard but not seen, for evidently they had crawled on hands and knees through the door and remained hidden behind the counter. Presently, two thatched roofs, two brows, and two sets of blue eyes appeared over the rim, stared at Rose for a few seconds, then sank in a whirlpool of mirth. The door opened again as if by ghosts, and the giggles withdrew into the kitchen.

Rose smiled. She suspected that she was as exotic to them as they were to her.

A steaming hot meal was delivered by the innkeeper, who hovered a minute over the table as she made the sign of the cross and said a silent grace. Shaking his head again, he went away without another word.

Later, when the meal was concluded, and Rose felt the tea beginning to work in her blood, she unfolded her map and inspected it without any idea of where she wanted to go.

"Need some directions?" asked the innkeeper, who had returned unnoticed. "Little lost are we?"

"No, not lost, sir. I am on a holiday and merely wish to ramble wherever the wind takes me."

"Well, the wind's prevailing to the west this time of year. Not much to see out that way till you get over the Berkshires. It's a fair hike before you come to the old carriageway that swings south to the M4. That's the Bristol to London motorway. About ten or twelve miles from here. A long way for a lady to walk."

"I like to walk", Rose explained.

"Well, Miss, if you like to walk it's a lovely one. Mostly sheep farms and moors till you get close to the M4."

"It sounds perfect."

When Rose stood to make her departure, the whole family crowded out of the kitchen, gazing shyly at her, and followed her to the door.

"That way?" Rose asked pointing to the left end of the street.

"Righty-ho", said the pub keeper, nodding and pointing. "That way." His wife and children also nodded and pointed in perfect imitation, but failed to speak. They went outside onto the cobblestones as she drew away and watched her until she had proceeded up the street and disappeared over a rise.

The road wound slowly upward across the escarpment, spilling over swells in the body of the earth, dipping into glens, and rising again. Rose began to groan with the pain in her spine.

She always felt it, yet the dull ache was so completely ordinary that she rarely thought about it and in fact usually failed to notice it. Now, however, the increased exertion of climbing, added to the weight of the backpack, was demanding effort of muscles that were seldom used to this extent and were loudly protesting. She rested from time to time, sitting down on tussocks of grass beside the hedgerows, turning her thoughts to matters more interesting than her physical ailments.

She remembered the paintings she had seen in London at the National Gallery, the Tate, and the British Museum. She had explored those collections with growing amazement, awed by the seemingly infinite creativity of man, yet also dismayed, for in comparison her own little accumulation of artworks seemed pathetically small in number and poor in quality. Room after room, gallery after gallery, century after century, the genius of human creativity spilled over from an inexhaustible reservoir. Moreover, in every city of Europe there were museums containing many more marvels than these. As she had looked and pondered, Rose had felt herself simultaneously shrinking and growing—growing in awareness of the central role played by art in bridging the gulf between peoples. Shrinking before the immense volume of painted words that had come from the heart of mankind.

With a great effort of sympathetic imagination, she had greeted her fellow artists across the millennia, had closed her eyes, had seen them toiling in a thousand places and conditions, had heard their tears and laughter, their groanings and longings, and had felt keenly their passion to make beauty. Through beauty they had sought to wring meaning from the raw material of experience, just as she did in her own primitive efforts. In the end she had been overwhelmed by it all and had sought some wild and beautiful place of natural creation.

"How small I am", she now said to herself. "Still, *he* is near. And nothing shall I fear."

She struggled to her feet and continued on, wherever the wind would take her.

The road began to wind downward, entering a broader valley through which another small river meandered. The barren moors were replaced by sheep pastures quilted with the darker green of countless hedgerows. In the bottom land, the route swerved around an increasing number of thorn-brakes and hummocks of smooth white stone jutting from under the earth like broken bones. Flocks of small black birds wheeled in unison, broke in midair, for no apparent reason, and scattered, only to rejoin in aerial choreography and settle in the fields, as if on signal. Their little chorus filled the air while meadowlarks, fewer in number, contributed their piercing solitary notes.

The road curved around the flank of a hill and climbed a gentle grade toward an old stone farmhouse. In the front yard stood an elderly woman in a house dress and rubber boots beating a rug that hung from a wire. She stopped to watch Rose pass. Her face, though pleasant, gazed at the stranger with a mixture of incredulity and alarm. Rose approached the slat-wood gate and was the first to speak.

"Excuse me, Ma'am, can you tell me how far it is to the nearest inn?"

The woman said nothing for a moment, frowned, her eyebrows knit as if deliberating on the correct response to this difficult question.

"For eating or sleeping?" she asked in a thick accent.

"For both."

"On foot are you?"

"Yes."

"'Tis a long way to the junction of M4, where there be an inn."

"Is it many miles?"

"Aye, it might be six. Then again, it might be ten. We go that

634

way naught. You might try Thatch Upping, t'other way." She pointed to the direction from which Rose had just come.

Rose did not want to retrace her steps, but estimated that even at a brisk pace it would take three or four hours to reach the inn at the M4, and by then it would be night, with the autumn chill coming down hard.

"You might try Bradon's place, a mile or so down the road", the woman offered with a guarded look. "They sometimes take travelers for the bed and breakfast."

Rose thanked her and moved on into the west.

An hour later the road took a sudden swerve to the north and entered a ravine where stands of holly and oak vied for the water of a creek that ran down from the high places between cut-stone banks. A hundred yards farther along she heard the bleating of sheep and saw a flock flowing like a land-bound cloud over the undulations of the hillside. Beyond them was a stone barn and house. A dog barked faintly in the distance. Smoke slid sideways from the chimney of the house. As Rose approached, a trace of recognition grew within her that she supposed was no more than the sense that often comes upon a traveler in a strange land, when at nightfall, after a long day of exertion and unusual experiences, he arrives at a station which promises shelter.

Rose paused by the stone fence that separated the front yard from the road and put her hand to the rusty iron latch of the gate. A metal plate on the hinge post said *Bradon, Registered Purebred Cheviot, Merino, Blackface.*

Wrinkling her brow, feeling her heart begin to hammer for no reason whatsoever, she remained as if frozen, unable to proceed down the walkway to the front door, unable to retreat. Inexplicably, she felt that she knew this place as she had known only one other in her life, the cabin at Threefinger Lake.

A thirteen- or fourteen-year-old boy ran around the corner of the house, chased by a black and white dog. Unaware that they were being watched, the boy and dog fell to the ground and wrestled. The dog nipped the boy's ankle, the boy rolled and pulled the dog's tail, the dog grinned and bolted away out of reach, then darted in close to nip the other ankle.

"Aye, Rip, not fair, not fair!" shouted the boy, his laughter pealing upward in the cold air, his breath turning to white puffs, the sheep and the birds all laughing with the great sport that does erupt, from time to time, in creation.

The front door opened, and orange-gold light spilled out onto the front step. A man emerged. He was about thirty-five or forty years of age, lean and strong, in baggy wool pants and a white shirt open at the neck, sleeves rolled up to the elbows. His black hair needed cutting, his shoulders stooped a little, but it was obvious that this dishevelment was the result of hearty and long labors. As the man watched the antics of the boy and dog, he seemed to be both amused and irritated.

"Here, lad, that's enough", he said in a sharp voice. "Your mother has tea ready."

"Oh, Pa!" the boy cried in mock dismay.

"Leave Rip be. She needs t'go nurse her puppies. Come in and wash yer hands."

The boy tried to squeeze out a few more seconds of play.

"You heard me. No more lollygagging. Get in here, now!"

The boy was about to obey when the dog scented Rose, pricked up its ears, and charged toward the gate. It leaped onto the stone wall and began to bark at her.

The man and the boy stood still for a moment or two, then strode side by side toward the fence. When they spotted Rose, they stopped abruptly and stared.

"Good evening", Rose said trying to make herself heard above the dog. The man quieted the animal and stepped forward.

"Good evening", he said noncommittally, though his eyes flickered all over her with the now familiar mixture of curiosity and caution.

636

"The lady down the road said that you take in travelers", Rose said timidly.

"Aye, we do sometimes", he said, without any hint of warmth. "Are you looking for a meal?"

"Yes, sir. And a bed for the night, if that is possible."

He regarded her doubtfully. A bed, his expression implied, meant that this strange visitor would remain under his roof, and he might not be able to sleep easily because of it, for who knows what trouble will blow in the door with the unidentified, and the unidentifiable.

"I'm not sure we have a bed for you", the man said after an uncomfortable delay. "But a meal now——"

"But, Dad," said the boy, looking at his father, "we have the spare room for the B and B's."

The man silenced him with a gesture.

"It's getting dark. Are you on foot?" the man asked.

"Yes", Rose replied, wishing that she had not stopped, for it was obvious that she was unwelcome.

"There's no way you can walk to the next inn. I could drive you to the M4 or Thatch Upping—at either place you'll find a stopping place for the night."

"Whatever you wish, sir. I don't want to be an inconvenience."

As he mused on her reply, his face continued to wrestle with itself. Then, having arrived at some decision, he said, "Well, you might as well come in."

Turning abruptly, the man headed toward the house. The boy opened the gate for Rose and walked ahead of her in the footsteps of his father, glancing over his shoulder to see if she were following.

Inside, the front hall smelled of baking bread and roast meat. The light of the electric lamps lifted Rose's heart despite her discomfort. The man pointed her into a small parlor where she seated herself on a chair before a mound of peat bricks glowing in an open hearth. While he went off to another room to speak with his wife, the boy sat down opposite Rose on a fender stool and stirred the embers with a poker. The dog flopped onto a tattered rug and began to pull tufts of fur from between its paws.

"My name's Kyle Bradon", said the boy, looking at her without a trace of shyness. "What's yours?"

She told him.

"Where are you from?" he asked.

She told him that as well.

"Why are you out this way?"

"I am on a holiday. I like walking."

"Lots of people come hiking through this way, but mostly in summer. Aren't you cold?"

"A little."

"Can I take your gear and store it for you?" he offered, jumping up. She handed it to him. He left the room, and through the arched passageway she saw him hanging the backpack and the saddlebag on a wall hook, where they remained in view.

"Do you like living here?" she asked.

"Yes", he said, though she sensed immediately that he did not, in fact, like living here.

"Have you ever been away from this place?"

"Never. I was born upstairs", he pointed to the ceiling. "Dad's been away. He was in the army for a while. We went to Blackpool when I was a kid, for a holiday. But I don't remember it."

"Where do you go to school?"

"Thatch Upping. There're eight of us in the school. It's boring. I don't go much."

"You don't go much?"

"That's right. Dad had an argument with the teacher last month. The teacher quit. They haven't got a new one yet, so I'm on holidays now. Suits me fine."

"What do you do when you're not at school?"

"I look after the sheep with Dad. I read books, too."

"What kind of books?"

"Robert Louis Stevenson. *Kidnapped* is my favorite. Well, no, *Treasure Island* is my favorite now. And *Robinson Crusoe*. Mum reads Shakespeare plays to me, too, though they're pretty boring."

"Shakespeare?"

"Have you heard of 'im?"

"Yes", Rose smiled.

They were interrupted at that moment by an apple-cheeked woman with wispy hair who entered the parlor wiping her hands on an apron.

"Good evening", she said to Rose. "Tea's served, if you'd care to join us now."

Rose followed the woman and the boy down the hallway to a bright country kitchen dominated by a rough plank table set with four places. Platters of meat and steaming bowls of vegetables were arranged on it. Rose sat where the woman directed her, across from the boy, between the mother and the father. The hosts bowed their heads and said a Protestant grace. The boy bowed his as well, though he looked up from under his brows to see what Rose would do. She closed her eyes, bowed her head, and prayed silently. Feeling the precariousness of her situation, she made the sign on the cross invisibly, in her heart, and added a silent thanks to God for the hospitality of these strangers, however reluctant they might be. She realized that in appearance she was not an attractive member of the human species, that her skin color, her features, and her deformity all spelled strangeness, and for most people strangeness suggested danger. Their reserve was evident, and yet they had overcome it with an act of kindness. This revealed much about their characters, and for that reason Rose began to like them on some level that was apart from natural affinity.

They ate in silence for several minutes, a sense of tension growing steadily, until the dog began to snuffle and snort as it continued to preen itself. The boy laughed. Then the mother offered Rose some chutney to spread on the meat. Rose said thanks and took it. Their fingers brushed, electric with the potential of human contact. The woman's cool appraising glance lingered on Rose's eyes and softened a little.

The man began to speak of the weather, the threat of an early winter.

Then the boy spoke up and announced all he had learned about the little woman who had come to visit.

"She's an Indian", he grinned in conclusion, and began whooping, imitating native war-cries.

"Enough of that, now", his mother remonstrated with a severe glance. The man smiled faintly.

"It's all right", Rose said. "I do not mind. Many who have not met my people think of us in the images from films."

"Please don't be offended by the lad", said the woman. "He's a bundle of energy and no place to put it. He'd like nothing better than to see your country. Where is it you say you live? Canada?"

"Yes, in the great city of Montreal." Rose, who habitually thought of it as the great and wicked city of Montreal, dropped the second adjective. "Though I am from a place much farther north, in the forest below the Arctic lands."

The boy grinned mischievously and whooped again.

"Kyle, stop!" said his mother.

"I had an ancestor went to Canada", the man said, chewing his meat, his eyes distant and musing. "He went there after the Great War, and no one ever heard from him again."

Rose put her utensils down on the plate.

"I know", she said and burst into tears. Hiding her face in her hands she tried to stop herself, but the water poured out as if from a ruptured dam, breaking down the restraining edifice piece by piece. Under the force of the increasing volume everything shattered. She sobbed uncontrollably. She saw the past and the present simultaneously, also the insideness and outsideness of what was happening, saw especially herself as they must see her—hideous and irrational—trapped within her ugly, homeless body. The dog sat up on its haunches and began to whine. The three Bradons remained frozen in their chairs, staring at her in amazement. Many thoughts passed through their minds, many fears, and anger and disgust. The possibility of a telephone call to the constable at Thatch Upping or to the hospital at Wantage did not go unexamined. Nor did they omit consideration of a quick drive down the road, delivering the deranged woman to an inn or a highway or any place other than their home.

Mrs. Bradon worked through the process more quickly than the others. She got up from her seat, came over, and stuffed a linen handkerchief into Rose's convulsing hands. Standing beside the little hunched form, she patted the heaving shoulders and murmured consoling words.

"There, there, now. It's all right, it's all right. Not to worry. Can't be helped."

Slowly, Rose lifted her eyes and wiped the tears from them, though the enormous ache in her heart remained.

"I—", she murmured and broke into fresh sobs.

"No need to talk just yet", said Mrs. Bradon. "Just let it all out, and then you'll feel better." She glanced authoritatively at the two males. "Kyle, would you take Rip up to the north pasture. There's that ewe that's taken to wandering. See if she got into the paddock all right. Ned, you might want to fetch me that buttermilk jug that needs washing. It's in the milk shed."

Man and boy scraped back their chairs and went quickly outside through the kitchen door. Mrs. Bradon sat down beside Rose and put a hand on her arm.

"Are you in trouble, dear?"

Rose shook her head. "No", she murmured. "Not at all. It is life."

"Life?"

"The mysterious currents of Divine Providence."

"Divine Providence?"

"Which brings the soul back to its beginnings, to the place where the great wounding occurred."

"What do you mean?"

"Those places and times when small choices lead to great errors. Where fear and unforgiveness launch a terrible suffering. Though in the beginning it does not seem so."

Mrs. Bradon, making no sense of this, stood and went to her stove where a kettle was steaming.

"I'll make us a nice pot of tea", she said.

When it became apparent that Rose had more or less succeeded in controlling herself, and when a brown teapot was set down on the table with chipped mugs and a porcelain jar of sugar, the two women sat face-to-face, daring to look each other in the eye.

"Now, tell me your trouble", said Mrs. Bradon in a firm motherly voice that brooked no refusal.

"I know this place", Rose said in a trembling voice.

Mrs. Bradon wrinkled her brow, trying to assess the nature of the visitor's derangement.

"You say you know this place?" she prompted. "Why is that? Have you been here before?"

"No, this is my first time in England. I know it in my soul, for it is the place of my forefathers."

Mrs. Bradon resisted a temptation to smile, for the statement was so incredible that not even the speaker, surely, believed it.

"My grandfather was born here", said Rose.

In a voice radiating doubt, Mrs. Bradon said, "Your grandfather? What on earth do you mean? Who, do you think, was your grandfather?"

"His name was Kyle—and now I know that it was Kyle Bradon."

The woman stiffened and sat back in her chair, eyeing Rose with open distrust.

"Kyle Bradon is my son. There was no Kyle Bradon among that generation."

"Was there a Ned Bradon," Rose said timidly, "who died at Passchendaele in 1917?"

Mrs. Bradon's face went white with shock and confusion. "Yes, there was a Ned Bradon", she murmured. "He died in the war. My husband is named for him. But how would you know such a thing?"

"Because Kyle Bradon was my grandfather."

Mrs. Bradon's face twisted into an expression that looked very much like fear—fear of the unknown, fear of the irrational. Yet as the thoughts raced through her mind, her expression altered, as if what Rose had said now began to make sense. Or at least was no longer strictly impossible.

The woman cleared her throat and took a sip of tea from her mug. Rose did likewise.

"If what you say is true, why have you come here?"

"I did not mean to come here. I was simply hiking in the hills. It was an accident that I found you."

An accident. All my life is an accident. I am an accident.

Tears welled up again in Rose's eyes, followed by the stab of anguish known only to the unwanted.

"An accident", the woman repeated in a toneless whisper.

"I am sorry. I did not mean to come here."

"What is it, exactly, that you want?"

"Nothing. I want nothing from you. I did not mean to disturb you, nor did I wish to see what God has shown me here—my past."

"*Your* past?"

"A part of it. But a part of it that has always been hidden from me, and silent, as memories locked inside a trunk."

"A trunk?"

"Of the mind."

But Mrs. Bradon no longer seemed to be concentrating.

Rose stood up. "I'm sorry. I will go now. And I will not bother you again."

The woman stared at her, shaking her head. Suddenly her eyes cleared, and, as if arriving at a decision, she reached out her hand and held Rose by the arm.

"Don't go yet. I'm sorry if I seemed, well, to doubt you. It was such a surprise. A part of Ned's past is missing too, you see. Like a gap in his memory, a hole that no one admits is there. Something dark that his parents would never talk about. Something painful they tried to push out of mind, but never really succeeded in doing. His grandparents were worse, the old man and the old woman, bitter people they were. Maybe—"

But Rose was already going down the hallway in search of her parka.

Mrs. Bradon followed. "Please stay", she said, her face softer now, though still puzzled.

At that moment, the boy and his father came in the front door, glancing at the two women uneasily. The man held a jug in his hand. The woman took it from him and said, "Come to the kitchen, Ned. The tea's ready and there's something I have to tell you." She glanced at Rose. "Please."

Rose bowed her head, and they all filed back into the kitchen.

"What's this?" Ned Bradon said, his voice hard, his eyes suspicious. "What's the trouble, then?"

"No trouble", said his wife. "But an answer to prayer."

"Prayer?" said the man. "What prayer?"

Ignoring the question, she sat down at the table and poured tea into four mugs.

"This lady is a relation of ours, Ned", said Mrs. Bradon, not looking at her husband.

He snorted in a sarcastic manner and said, "A relation?"

"Yes, Ned. She is the granddaughter of Kyle Bradon."

"But *I'm* Kyle Bradon", piped the boy.

"I believe there was another", his mother said, looking at the man. "Wasn't there, Ned?"

He did not answer.

"Is he the one who went to Canada and was never heard from again?"

He nodded.

"Well, the past is come home, it seems", said his wife.

"What's that supposed to mean?" he snapped, though it was plain that his ill temper was due more to some undefined apprehension than to irritation.

"Dad?" said the boy, fascinated. "Was there another Kyle besides me?"

"Lots of Kyles in our family", Ned replied, "if you go back far enough."

"There are some in the graveyard too", said his wife.

"The graveyard's full of Bradons," he admitted, "and I suppose a few of them were Kyles."

"There was a knight, wasn't there, Dad?"

The man's face soured. "Now let's not get onto *that* subject. I've had quite enough of your daydreaming about the knight who maybe never existed."

"But people say an old knight built a castle in this region, hundreds of years ago."

"What people?" the man snorted, his lips twisting unpleasantly. "People will say anything when they've got nothing better to do."

"He came over with the Normans, didn't he, Dad?"

"That's a legend. There's no castle to be found in any quarter, not that I've seen."

Rose wondered at the bitterness of his tone.

Mrs. Bradon proceeded to repeat to Ned and Kyle the little that Rose had told her. When she mentioned the Ned who had died at Passchendaele, the living Ned started.

"Aye", he muttered. "That would be Great Uncle Ned." He eyed Rose with suspicion. "You say you know all this. You come here out of the blue and tell us things that any snooper could pick up in the books at Thatch Upping. What do you want from us?"

Humiliated, Rose stood to make her final effort at departure.

"Please", Mrs. Bradon said, once again taking Rose by the arm and pleading with her eyes. "She is what she says she is, Ned. She's a relation of ours, though how and why I cannot say. Perhaps she could tell us more, if you'd give her a chance."

The man glanced at Rose. "What for?" he said in a low voice. "What good would it do?"

Mrs. Bradon paused before answering. When she spoke at last it was with a fierce calm that no one dared to interrupt.

"I will tell you why. Because there's a dungeon in your minds—all you Bradons, so harsh and proud. There have been times, Ned, yes, there have been times when I wondered if I could take it any longer. . . ."

"Mum!" the boy cried, but said no more, glancing back and forth between his parents.

"There's a hardness in you, Ned. And I speak of it because I love you. I'm not putting up with it any more. And I'm not stomaching you teaching it to Kyle. Hard, sneering, and unforgiving your folks were, with nothing good to say about anyone who wasn't just like them. You're not a bad man, Ned, I'll grant you that. And you've treated me well, but there's something not right."

The boy got up and left the room.

"Tell me, then, after all these years, Fern, just what you think is not right about me."

"Are there words for it? I don't know. But it's there, like a dark thing that's always making its presence felt, but quietly, so quietly you can't ever catch it and throw it out."

"What are you talkin' about?"

"It was worse in your father, and it was even more terrible in your grandfather. If anything the old woman was worse than he was—it nearly killed me those two years she lingered on, with her endless judgments and her foul temper. The way she punished people. The way she kept everything under her control. Nothing could satisfy that woman. Nothing. Just a great black hole in her heart into which she nearly sucked everything that was good and beautiful about her family. I—"

"Stop it, Fern. You don't know what you're saying."

"I know very well what I'm saying. The way you and your family just throw people away. Cut them out, discard them as if they weren't real. You've infected me with it, and. . . ." Her lips quivered and tears sprang to her eyes. "And I've started to see whiffs of it in the boy. Now we have a chance to break out of it. This woman is bringing us something, a gift, I think. And what it is I cannot say, but you're a fool, Ned, if you don't listen to her."

The man folded his arms and looked angrily at Rose.

"A gift?" he huffed. "This was a peaceable evening before she turned up."

"That's what I mean about the Bradons. You want peace. You'd rather somebody didn't exist than have them disturb your evening, wouldn't you. Remember the kids from London during the Blitz. Remember the one your Mum and Dad adopted. Then, after the war, when he had some problems, they just took him to an orphanage and tossed him back. Ha!" she snorted, crying now. "Threw him away they did. I remember that boy. He was troubled because he'd seen his world blow up. He'd seen his family die. He was lower class, wasn't he? Couldn't learn our rules, could he? Sinned too, didn't he? Shamed the great Bradons, famous throughout the shire for their stiff spines and their righteous ways and their superior farming. Juvenile court was too much for the Bradon reputation. Back he goes into the dustbin. Sorry, we made a mistake about you, you aren't our son after all. You didn't work out. Disposable people, Ned. That's what I'm talking about. Disposable people."

Ned Bradon scraped back his chair. He stood, and the chair tipped over, clattering to the floor.

"Shut up", he snarled.

Fern Bradon stood and faced her husband, fearless, her character as strong as his.

"No shutting up from now on. No lies, Ned. The great secret poisoned your family for three generations. And no one even knows why any more. It's just the way we are—mean and suspicious and not a merciful word for anyone who's less than perfect. And why? Because back somewhere around the First War a miserable old couple, as proud as Satan, decided they couldn't forgive some weakness—"

"What are you gabblin' about? I don't know what you mean."

"It's taken me years to see it, to admit that it's more than just a quirk in your family's way of dealing with the world. It's wrong, and I hate it. I hate it so much, at times I want to scream. And it's so crazy, Ned, so crazy and needless. It was all so long ago no one even remembers, no one still alive that is. I've tried to get at the truth of it, tried and tried, years of careful conversations with any neighbors who'll still talk to a Bradon— precious few, I might add. No one remembers. All that remains is how much we're disliked. Not because of *it*, whatever *it* may have been, but because we're hard and have no mercy, and we always have been it seems. Years of looking at tombstones and dusty parish records haven't told me a thing, just a big shadow, neither good nor bad. Just like most of the families in the region. Why, then, are we so different? Why do people hate us, but never let on that they hate us? What did we do?"

"We didn't do nothing."

648

"But *something* happened back then that turned you all inward. What was it? I want to know, and I want to know now, because I won't allow it to kill my son's heart the way it—"

Ned Bradon sat down, shaking his head, his eyes dark and brooding. "I always hated it too, but it's *inside* us and it won't get out. It's the way Bradons are, that's all."

"No, it's not the way Bradons are. At least they weren't always like that. It doesn't have to be this way. What was it, Ned? What was the skeleton in the closet? An axe murderer? Insanity? Treason?"

"I don't know", he mumbled. "I don't know what it was."

"I do", Rose said.

The Bradons stared at her with trepidation.

Rose got up and went to the hallway to find her baggage. She returned to the kitchen with the leather saddlebag and set it on the table.

"K. B.", said Fern Bradon, feeling the letters with her index finger.

"Aye, so it is", breathed the man, bending over to look closely. He drew back and glanced sideways at Rose.

"This was my grandfather's", she said. "His name was Kyle."

Slowly, item by item, she took out the fragments of memory. The man and the women slid their chairs close beside Rose, unconsciously narrowing the great abyss between themselves and the visitor. Fascination overruled everything, even the anger that had filled the room only moments before. Rose showed them the photographs one by one, beginning with the portrait of a man and woman standing in front of a stone house on a hillside surrounded by rows of trees and fields in which there were many sheep.

"That's our place all right", Ned murmured. "My father took down those trees in the late forties, sold them for quite a pretty penny he did. And that's them, sure enough, the old folks, my father's parents. How young they are."

"Ned, look at Nana's face. The date says 1913. That's before the war. She was a different person then, it's plain to see."

"Must have been. She looks pleasant enough. And the old man, Granddad, I can't ever remember him smiling, but look at him here with a grin as broad as the meadow."

"Before the war", his wife repeated. "Before *it*. Whatever *it* was." She turned to Rose. "What was it?"

Slowly, as if assembling a crude mosaic or a picture puzzle, Rose told the story of her grandfather. At one point she removed from the saddlebag the old documents, the birth and marriage certificates.

"A Catholic?" Ned said with discomfort, "You say he became a Catholic?"

"Yes, and died one. In 1926, he was taken by influenza. He was a suffering man."

"But what happened? Why did he leave England?" Fern asked.

Rose showed them the medal that her grandfather had won in the war.

"He was brave, you see," she explained, "and he did what he was supposed to do. But then it all went black for him. His brother Ned was killed, and he grew sick of killing in a war that seemed to have no explanation, only madness and carnage. He ran away from the war. I do not know any details about this part of his story. I can tell you only what he told my grandmother, his wife."

"She was an Indian?" Fern asked disingenuously, for several photographs of Oldmary Wâbos had already been shown.

"She was a native person of the Anishinâbe, the Ojibwe of the northern woodlands."

"That's a tribe?"

"Yes, it is a tribe. Though we call ourselves a people, not a tribe."

It was a very great deal for the Bradons to take in at once, so at a certain saturation point Fern got up to make another pot of tea. Ned went out to find the boy. A few minutes later he brought him back to the kitchen, his hand resting on his son's shoulder.

"It's our past, Kyle, a part of it we never knew. Come and see. It's very interesting."

The boy glanced up, surprised at the uncommon gentleness in his father's voice.

"He ran away from the war, you say?" Ned asked.

"That is what my grandmother once told me. He hated killing. He was angry at God and at the war and the men who caused it and at the Old World. He wanted to forget everything that had happened. So he came to a land that had few memories, and no memories for him. To begin again."

"Oh, that is sad", said Fern Bradon, her hand on her chest. "But why didn't he contact his parents?"

"I don't know for sure", Rose replied hesitantly. "He said they were ashamed of him and despised him. They had said hard words to him, they said he should have died with Ned. I think it broke his heart. The medal was not enough, you see— not for him, not for them."

Ned Bradon inhaled loudly, sighing, permitting a low groan to escape his lips.

"Pride", Fern whispered, as if to herself. "Devilish pride. Disposable people. A disposable son."

"But how can we know what they felt?" Rose pleaded, for she knew that the merciless were the ones in greatest need of mercy. "How can we understand what they endured! How dreadful were their sufferings. To lose a son. Then to feel as if they had lost another! Perhaps they were only confused by their grief and said things they did not really mean."

"You are too kind", Ned said coldly. "Perhaps they would rather have had two dead heroes than a live deserter. Yes, it was pride all right. That hard thing in them." He swallowed audibly. "And in me."

He looked at his son, and his face sagged under the weight of controlling his emotions.

"But why is the Bradon name scratched from all the documents?" Fern asked.

"I think my grandfather did it because he wanted to forget. He told Oldmary that you could wipe out the past and start again."

"Not that way", Fern said, glancing at a photograph of two old people in an antique frame under the ticking wall clock.

"That is why I never learned my name. Not until a few hours ago. Because I am mostly a native person, and my grandmother all native, we returned to our original name."

"What is it again?" the boy asked.

"Wâbos. I am Oginiwâbigon Wâbos."

The boy smiled. "Oo that's super! Og-ni-wa—?"

To Rose's surprise, Ned said, "Ogini-wâbigon Wâbos."

For a few minutes, the three Bradons practiced aloud the curious words, stumbling over the syllables. Then suddenly they all smiled shyly at their guest.

Fern suggested they go into the parlor. Ned told Kyle to fetch more peat for the fire. Later, when they were comfortably settled around the glow of heat in the hearth, Rose read to them the poems her grandfather had written more than fifty years before. The words brought tears to Fern's eyes. Ned kept his face reposed in a manly sternness, but his eyes reddened as he stared at the floor, listening carefully. The boy sat on the hearth rug, legs crossed like an Indian, gazing into Rose's face, his mouth open, drinking in every word.

Fern and Ned asked for the brittle yellow snippets of poems clipped from newspapers. They reread them silently, passing them back and forth. For a time they seemed lost in their private thoughts. Eventually Fern said, "Would you tell us about your life, Rose?"

652

And so Rose did.

The hall clock was chiming eleven by the time she had given them a brief account and, though no one wanted the evening to end, yawning erupted all around.

"I have to be up in six hours", Ned said apologetically.

"Yes, and I must go now", Rose said standing. "I thank you for your kindness, for the time you have spent with me."

The three Bradons looked shocked.

"You're not going anywhere at this time of night!" Fern exclaimed.

The boy was speechless with anxiety.

The man stood and approached with a bowed head.

"Rose," he said, "we would be pleased if you could—"

"If you would drive me to the inn at the M4, Mr. Bradon, I would be grateful. I'm sorry for the bother—"

"There's no way you're going to an inn", he said gruffly, still staring at the floor. "Fern?"

"I'll go make up the spare room, Ned."

"But I—" the visitor stammered.

"Nonsense", said Ned Bradon, looking her full in the eyes. "You're staying with us. You're family."

She remained with the Bradons for a week. Though their habits and manners did not cease to be perplexing at times, engendering a mild discomfort that prevailed throughout the entire visit, a sense of kinship deepened with every passing day. The boy, especially, became dear to her, for he bore the name of a man who was a missing part of her past, in fact, a missing part of her self. Many were the conversations they shared, yet after the first day the subject matter switched from Kyle's mysterious great-great-uncle to the more interesting subjects of native life and the wilderness of North America.

He showed her the perimeters of the Bradon land, a considerable holding of more than three hundred acres, including a small stand of oaks no larger than an acre, which they called "the Forest", the little stream that wound through the bottom of their property, which they called "the River", and the high moors where the boy especially liked to wander alone, with his dog and a walking stick.

On a sunny afternoon three days after her arrival, he led Rose to the highest point of land in the region. From a mound of green turf shaped somewhat like a broken ring, they could see for many miles in all directions, the rolling waves of the Berkshires to the west, and to the southeast, the distant blue field of England's lower counties.

The wind was cold, but not so much that it brought them anything other than invigoration. Kyle's cheeks flushed red, and his eyes danced. It came to Rose that her grandfather surely must have stood on this spot more than seventy years ago, looking much like this boy, the same wise innocence, the same enthusiasm emanating from every cell of his young body. Each movement spelled energy and hope, and the beginning of new life. The past—the past was the soil laid down by untold generations, the dark loam from which he had grown. Was it true that nearly a thousand years of his ancestors—*her* ancestors—had lived in this one fixed point on the planet? Was this, then, the true center of the world?

She watched the boy as he gamboled up and down the turf, ran circles with the dog, chased birds, and leaped into the air. His abandon resembled that of Tchibi at his most free, during the hot summers when fleeting happiness had returned to him and pushed back the darkness.

She sat on the hump of the ring and let him run. It was enough to close her eyes, to lift her face to the sun, to savor his joy, the purity of the air, the music of the many birds.

He returned to her, red-faced and out of breath.

"We're cousins, aren't we, Rose?" he gasped, grinning. "Dad says we're second or third cousins or something."

654

"I guess we are, Kyle", she said.

"Can you keep a secret?"

"Oh, yes, I am very good at secrets."

"If I show you something, do you promise you won't tell?"

"What is it?"

"It's something nobody but me knows." He indulged in a few more breaths, hands on hips, chest inhaling and exhaling, blond hair flailing about in the breeze.

"All right, I promise not to tell."

"I found the keep", he announced.

"The keep?" she said, puzzled.

"You know. The castle. The one made by the knight who first settled here. The first English Bradon."

"Oh, that is wonderful, Kyle. Where is the keep?"

He laughed loudly. "You're sitting on it."

He bounded up the slope to its top, two or three feet above the level of the pasture, and threw himself down beside her. Rose looked all around. There did not appear to be a trace of an ancient edifice, not even the ruins of a foundation. The ring was not a true ring; it appeared to be no more than a natural formation in the surface of the hilltop.

Gesturing with his outflung arm in a wide semicircle, Kyle launched into a romantic soliloquy regarding the history of what surrounded them.

"All that you see before you, Rose, was once a forest of great oaks. Huge they were, greater than any trees now known in England." He patted the turf and looked at her with grave sincerity. "In this very spot the first Bradon built a castle. I know what you think. You're thinking, where are the stones? Where are the towers?"

He tilted his chin up, smiling into the sky.

"Can you hear them? The trumpets? The shouts of the men, the neighing of war horses? The clanging of armor?"

"I think I do", Rose said, and though she was not convinced

of the existence of a castle, it did seem to her that on this windy height time dissolved without effort, and the past became present and solid, and alive.

"First he built an earthwork", the boy declared.

"What is an earthwork?"

"A wall of soil and rubble, just a pile. It was a very primitive kind of fort. They lived inside it for a while, keeping watch at night against the bands of Anglo-Saxons that wouldn't come to heel. He and his men had longbows, great swords, and shields. They had sharp axes to bring down the trees that they hewed into mighty beams. Blocks of cut stone were brought on carts from near and far. Up went the castle, month after month, year after year. It was a small castle, but it *was* a castle."

Rose chuckled. This was a new concept indeed; she had never considered herself a princess in a castle.

"You don't believe me!" he said. "Come on, I'll show you!"

He reached out, took her hand in his, and helped her down the few feet into the center of the earth ring. Like the surrounding pastures its surface was smooth, well-grazed turf, littered with the countless black pebbles of sheep droppings.

"Where are the stones of the castle?" Rose asked, daring to insert a little realism into the fantasy.

"Hundreds of years ago, three hundred, maybe five hundred, maybe six or seven hundred years ago, somebody had a battle here. No one remembers it. It's not in any book. They dismantled the castle. The stones were carried away. Maybe they became the stones of our house and barn, and the stones of the watercourse down by the bridge on the road."

Rose recalled the fine gray cut stone of that tumbling race, the sturdy bridge that carried the road over the stream—an unusual amount of hewn stone in a land that was all soft green.

"But they didn't take everything away", the boy said, his face flushing with excitement. "Nobody realizes. Nobody knows. It's been forgotten for hundreds of years. I found it."

"What did you find?" she asked curiously.

"The cellar." He pointed to a spot twenty feet away on the inside wall of the ring, near the cliff edge. There was nothing there besides uninterrupted, unmarked turf.

He led the way. When they arrived at the spot, he crouched down on his haunches and pointed to lines that had been scratched in the grass, forming a rectangle approximately two feet by three.

"I made that a few weeks ago."

"What is it?"

He smiled secretively and did not answer.

"You said a cellar, Kyle. Is there a staircase underneath?"

"Not exactly. There's an opening."

"How did you find it?"

"I was bored one day. I came up here. I thought, maybe if this was a castle once, a long time ago, I might find an arrow-head or something. So I cut into the dirt with my pocket knife, peeled back a square of sod, and saw nothing but more dirt underneath. My knife blade's only three inches long, and I figured maybe it takes a hundred years to make an inch of soil. So I said to myself, you're down about three hundred years, Kyle, why not go deeper? I cut into the dirt under the spot I'd cleared off. Still no arrowheads or swords or helmets or anything. I kept digging, down five or six hundred years, give or take a century. Suddenly my knife hit stone. I cut around the edge of this square you see here. Stone, all the way. So I went back to the barn and got a shovel. I cleaned it off expecting to find just the chalk that's under these hills. But, no, it was hewn stone. Well, Kyle, I said to myself, that's interesting, but there's no way you can cut through stone. Just when I'd decided to cover it all in again, I saw the crack."

"A crack in the stone?"

"That's right. A joint where it met another stone. It was a fine joint I can tell you. Here, let me show you."

He knelt, peeled back the layer of sod, and rolled it off. Then he scooped out dirt with his bare hands. It took several minutes to uncover the ancient man-made block. He had brought along a short iron pry bar in his knapsack, and he now proceeded to insert its sharp end into the crack at the side closest to himself. Straining, his cheeks puffing, he managed to lever the stone up a few inches; it vibrated and boomed with the deep resonance of stone rumbling against stone. Contributing her minimal strength, Rose grabbed the edge of the block and pushed. Kyle shifted the bar for a better footing, threw his entire weight into it, and the stone fell sideways onto the turf.

Before them was a hole from which cool air wafted, bearing an odor of freshly dug potatoes. Kyle grinned at Rose in triumph.

24

"It's very dark down there", Rose said, peering over the edge.

"Don't worry, I've brought a torch", the boy replied, pulling a small flashlight from his jacket pocket. He dropped his legs into the hole and followed them, his head disappearing entirely from view as he plunged. Half-expecting to hear a long tapering wail and a distant splash, Rose peeped anxiously over the edge, only to see his grinning face looking up at her, inches away.

"Come on in, Rose", he said.

"I'm shorter than you, Kyle. Is it safe?"

"Sure, it's safe! Try it."

Against her better judgement, she slid her legs over the edge. Rolling onto her stomach, she nervously gripped each side of the hole with her hands and lowered herself slowly. As her head went underground, she felt her feet hit a solid object. Kyle's light flashed about her ankles, showing her the way. "You're on a step-stone", he said. "One foot farther down and you're on the floor.

When they were safely planted on what appeared to be a subfloor of flat, undressed yellow-white rock, the natural chalk of the region, Rose and Kyle stood upright. This presented no problem for Rose, for the chamber was about five feet in height, but Kyle's hair brushed the upper ceiling, bringing down a shower of dust.

"What is this place?" Rose asked wonderingly.

The room was about ten feet square, a cavity hewn out of the escarpment by natural forces or human will, it was not clear, though the walls were scored in places by the marks of ancient tool work.

"It's the dungeon", Kyle said.

"Why is the room so small?" Rose said turning slowly in a circle.

"It would've been too much work to make a cellar under the whole ring. Would've taken years and years, and for what purpose? It was easier to build with stone above ground. But they cut this under the tower, maybe as a hiding hole if the tower fell under a siege. Maybe for storing things."

"There is nothing stored here, it seems."

"Maybe", he said. "They were pretty good at hiding. The tower was pulled down at one point, maybe it was destroyed in a battle. Of course it might have just fallen apart. But somehow I don't think so."

"It seems a small castle."

"No, the ring was just the tower. Most of the castle was wood and stockades outside the tower. This was a last resort, you see, where the defenders would retreat if all other defenses failed."

"Do you think that happened, Kyle?"

He nodded soberly. "Yes. Brave men died here. Why they died and at whose hands they died is long forgotten. Their names are gone too, except I'm sure one of them was a Bradon. Last week when I was down at Thatch Upping, I checked in the old records at the church. Our pastor let me see an archive they've been putting together. The building we use is only a couple of hundred years old. It was built on the site of an older church, and we inherited some of the records from those days. The records don't go back as far as the Norman invasion, but in a fourteenth-century entry there's mention of a marriage between Kayol Bredon and the daughter of a neighboring lord. It says only that Kayol was a descendant of somebody named Sir Karolus le Breton. But it doesn't say anything about who Karolus was, or where he lived. I guess they just assumed in those days that everybody knew. I think Karolus le Breton built this castle."

The batteries of the flashlight began to dim. Kyle went topside again and dropped back down with his knapsack. He removed from it a paraffin barn lantern, matches, a packet of sandwiches, and a thermos of tea. After consuming a brief lunch, they sat with their backs against the wall, each lost in his own thoughts.

By the diffuse light of the lamp, Rose saw that centuries of sifting dust, and the dirt that had washed into the cellar, had accumulated over a third of the floor space, largely in the direction of the edge of the hill on which the tower stood. The floor was tilted either by natural incline or by artful stone cutting. At various times in the past, water had flowed here, dripping through the cracks of the ceiling, or soaking through the porous rock during years of unusually heavy rainfall. On the upslope side, the deposit thinned to nothing; on the downslope, it looked as if it was several inches deep. Rose crossed the room toward the area where most of the sediment had settled. Kneeling, she rubbed a pinch of it through her fingers. It was as fine as sand, though darker.

"I wonder if there is anything buried in this?" she said.

"I've been wondering too", Kyle said. "In fact I've been planning to excavate the dirt. What do you think? Want to try it?"

"Of course I do!" Rose exclaimed. "But what will we use for tools?"

He jumped up. "I'm going back to the house and get some." He frowned as he glanced down at Rose's little body. "Uh, I guess I'd better get a stepladder too."

Rose laughed. "Yes, we didn't think about that. I doubt I could get back up without it."

"See you later, Rose."

Without undue effort he jumped onto the step-stone, raised his hands to the opening, and with a combination of leap and pull was out in an instant. Before Rose knew it, he was back again.

661

"Look out below!" he shouted, then lowered a short stepladder, two shovels, a bucket, and a leather pouch of tools.

They set to digging the dirt, carrying pailful by pailful to a corner of the room that was bare, dumping it into a pile that rose steadily higher. Kyle took care to empty each pail slowly, watching unblinking as the soft grains spilled, hoping that artifacts would appear. None did.

When they had cleared most of the dirt from the floor, they took a break. Kyle's enthusiasm seemed no less dampened by the lack of treasure. Though a treasure would have been a fabulous crown to his efforts, he seemed to take the entire excavation project as a great adventure in itself.

"The thing we have to figure out is why the castle fell. I've been trying to find out about it, but there's no mention of the place in any history books I've been able to track down. The churches around here have loads of records of births and deaths and marriages, but they're a bit short on the big picture, the whole history of the region. A book I got at the library says that after the Normans came, parchment documents were used far more than during the Saxon era. There are tens of thousands of 'writs and charters' as they called them, just from Kayol Bredon's century alone. I'm going to try to learn the story of this place, but I've a feeling it's going to be a long search."

"What do you think happened here, Kyle? What is your guess?"

"My best guess is that Bradon Castle—let's call it that for now—was built sometime in the century after the Norman invasion of 1066. We have to be careful here, because it could have been built on the site of a Saxon fort. But for now, unless you're an archaeologist, Rose, maybe we should start with the assumption that it's Norman."

Rose looked at Kyle with new respect. He was eloquent for a fourteen-year-old boy. The English schooling, she supposed.

"Now let's suppose a certain Karolus le Breton, who lived in

662

the century following the invasion, was given the castle and its lands by the king as a reward for some service. Maybe the old Saxon lord of the region had died with all his family—famine or war or plague, for example—leaving the land without a lord to govern it. Along comes brave Karolus, the knight. He's not a Norman exactly, though he is from the French side of the channel. So they don't hand over to him a big earldom or make him a baron or anything. But they do give him this lonely little fort in the high downs. That's one way it might have happened. The other way, and this is the likeliest, he was given this land when it was wild and empty, too high for crop farming, off the beaten track, but good enough in its own way. And he built the castle himself."

"That's our guess about the beginning, Kyle, but what about the end? How did the end come?"

"The end. Hmmm. Now we're closer to our own times. Maybe six hundred years ago, maybe five, or maybe seven. That puts it between A.D. 1250, let's say, and the late fourteen hundreds. Somewhere in there the castle fell."

"Much could have happened in between."

"But what? That's the real question: What?"

By then the oil was burning low in the lamp and the square hole of the entrance was deepening from dark blue to black. Kyle squinted at his wristwatch.

"Oh-oh", he said. "We're going to be late for tea. Let's pack up and come back tomorrow."

They arrived at the farmhouse by a quarter to six, earning Kyle a scolding from his mother and a cursory interrogation from his father.

"We were up on the moors", the boy explained, red-faced and a little shifty-eyed. "Lost track of the time."

"Well, you should know better than that, Kyle", said the mother. "Besides, we don't want to wear our guest out."

Rose smiled her appreciation, defusing the situation still

further by putting her small brown hand on the boy's shoulder and saying. "He's an excellent guide, Mrs. Bradon. I can't remember when I've had a more interesting day."

"Fern", said Mrs. Bradon. "Please call me Fern."

Rose went to bed early that night. In the morning, after breakfast and barn chores, Kyle asked his mother's permission to stay out all day. Reluctantly, she gave it. When he and Rose arrived at the castle ring, they hastily rolled back the sod and within minutes were down inside the cellar—or was it really a dungeon, Rose wondered. Kyle had brought along an extra oil lamp and a heavy flashlight with a broad beam. The room seemed flooded with light now, and many of its features that had been invisible the day before now stood out. Two of the walls, forming the ell corner farthest from the opening, appeared to have been mortared in patches, the cracks of the joints disguised by shadows and by irregularities in the chalkstone. If Kyle and Rose had noticed this the day before, it would not have made an impression on them, but in the increased light it was apparent that the configuration of the wall was not entirely natural. It was a measure of how artfully the work had been done by some anonymous mason that even now they merely noted it in passing and turned to the remaining dirt by the cliff side wall.

It took about an hour to clean away the last of the dirt, and when the stone floor was completely exposed, it had not offered a single artifact. But something interesting had appeared at the base of the wall. A hole measuring about six inches high by eight inches wide.

"What is this?" Rose asked.

"I don't know, but from the way the dirt all seems to flow down to this spot, I'd say it's a drain hole. It's on the cliff side of the ring and at the bottom of the floor's slope, so it could be an underground sewer or—"

"You mean to say—?"

"No, I don't think it was the castle septic. But I'll bet that drain's a runoff for any water that seeps in." He paused, staring at the hole. "I wonder", he murmured. "I wonder."

He lay down and reached into the drain hole and scooped out more dirt. Again and again he pulled dirt from the hole, until his arm went in as far as his shoulder. His face contorted in concentration, the wiggling of his torso indicating some effort that his hand was making deep inside. His eyes lit up and he withdrew his hand clenched around an object. Though they both had entertained the possibility that a little treasure box full of jewels might emerge, or at least a rusty sword, the object itself did not entirely disappoint them. It was a smooth oval stone as large as the boy's fist.

Rose knelt beside him and together they inspected it. It was coated with long-dried sediment which was easily brushed from its surface.

"Look, Rose, there are hieroglyphics."

"What are hieroglyphics?"

"Old letters." He blew the rock clear of dust and rubbed it on the front of his jacket. Squinting his eyes, he read the following aloud:

ABSCONDITA AB OCULIS

E L XIX

Beneath this was scratched a tiny hieratic flower:

The letters were cut with rough precision, not scratched, on the rounded surface. He turned the stone over and read an inscription on the reverse, mouthing the letters in a faltering voice:

EVANGELIUM S LUCAM

XIX

LAPIDES CLAMABUNT

"*Evangelium S Lucam. Lapides clamabunt.* What does that mean?" he murmured. "Any ideas, Rose?"

She shook her head. "It might be Latin."

"Latin? How would you know that? I mean——"

"It sounds like the Latin we use at Mass. *Evangelium* is the word for Gospel."

Kyle flashed an excited look at her. "Then Lucam——"

"Yes, I think it means the Gospel of Saint Luke."

"Then the letters underneath are probably Roman numerals. Maybe it's a date."

"It could be the number of a chapter", Rose suggested.

"I'm pretty rusty on Roman numerals, but Dad might be able to figure it out. What about the other words?"

"*Abscondita ab oculis* and *Lapides clamabunt*—I don't know. Does your father read Latin?"

"Just on medicine bottles for the sheep. That's about it. Mum doesn't either."

"This is a wonderful find, Kyle. Something you will treasure all your life."

He nodded solemnly. "Yes. It is. The builders must have put it under the wall as a memorial. Some kind of religious blessing maybe."

"Do you have a Latin dictionary at home?"

"Unfortunately, yes."

"Why do you say unfortunately?"

He laughed. "Mum's been after me to get started on it. She bought it at a church sale in Thatch Upping last year. She's always trying to get me into books."

"It seems she's made a good start, Kyle. You seem to have read a great deal. You know more history than I do."

"That's because history's really interesting. Not like dead languages."

"Perhaps this language is not as dead as we thought", Rose mused. "I wonder what it will tell us?"

That evening after supper, Fern left the house for an hour's work in the milk shed, where she intended to churn butter. Ned made his apologies and drove off for a farmers' meeting at the nearby town of Shevret. Kyle brought the Latin dictionary down from his bedroom and opened it on the kitchen table. From his pocket he pulled the "keep-stone", as he called it, and set it beside the dictionary. Rose pulled up a chair beside him and observed silently as he copied the inscription onto a sheet of paper.

"Shouldn't we tell your parents about this, Kyle?" she said.

"We will. Soon. But just for a few days I want it to be our secret. Do you mind, Rose?"

"If it's only for a few days. But they do have a right to know."

"Yes, that's true", he said in a voice straining to sound mature and reasonable. "The problem is, once the news is out the place will be swarming with experts, and you can be sure we won't be allowed inside again. The National Trust will declare it out of bounds until the archaeologists have a go at it, and it could be years before we get another look."

"Still—"

"Please, Rose. Please don't say a word just yet. After all, it's *our* ancestors who lived up there. And *we* found it."

"All right, Kyle, I did promise to keep the secret. You have my word."

The dictionary was nearly a century old and beginning to crack with age. The stone seemed incongruously young in comparison. The book contained, in addition to the ample lexicon, a section explaining Roman numerals. It took close to half an hour before they were reasonably sure of their translation.

On one side of the stone the words said *The Gospel S Luke 19*.

"This has got to mean Luke, chapter nineteen", Kyle said. "But what does the S stand for?"

"Saint, maybe."

The words below it were roughly translated as *Stones cry out.*
On the other side was written *Hidden from eyes. E L* (an abbreviation of *Evangelium Lucam*?) *19.* Followed by the flower.

"What on earth does it all mean?" the boy exclaimed.

"Why don't we check the Gospel itself?" Rose suggested. She went off in search of her knapsack and returned shortly with Oldmary's Bible in her hands. She sat and began to flip earnestly through the pages until she arrived at the nineteenth chapter of Luke. Kyle bent over her, their arms touching. Rose read the entire chapter to him. When they arrived at the thirty-ninth and fortieth verses, a light went on behind the boy's eyes.

And some of the Pharisees in the multitude said to him, "Teacher, rebuke your disciples." He answered, "I tell you, if these were silent, the very stones would cry out."

"Rose, you hear that? *Stones cry out!*" She nodded and proceeded to read further:

As he drew near, he saw the city and wept over it, saying, "If this day you only knew what makes for peace—but now it is hidden from your eyes. For the days are coming upon you when your enemies will raise a palisade against you; they will encircle you and hem you in on all sides. They will smash you to the ground and your children within you, and they will not leave one stone upon another within you because you did not recognize the time of your visitation."

"There it is, Kyle—*Hidden from eyes.*"

"You're right! The Scripture says *now it is hidden from your eyes.*"

"It is a puzzle. Why did our ancestor have this particular passage inscribed in the stone?"

"It's not a blessing. It's a—" He paused, thinking intensely. His brow furrowed. "It's like a warning."

"Or a lament."

"Maybe. If it *is* a warning, or even if it's only some kind of dark saying about his own era, in either case he was trying to leave a message. To whom, I wonder?"

"To his children. To those who would come after the time of trial."

"Time of trial? What do you mean?"

"He has put the first verse on one side of the stone and the second verse on the other. In the first, he tells us that the stones cry out. In the second, he says that not one stone will be left upon another."

"Yes, and the two passages are also back-to-back in the Bible. One flows into the other."

"They seem to be two separate incidents in the life of Our Lord, yet they are connected. Jesus is approaching Jerusalem where he is about to be crucified; the Pharisees try to silence the people who are acclaiming him as the Messiah. In the next breath Jesus is weeping over Jerusalem, prophesying that it will be completely destroyed, and all within it."

A profound silence took hold of Kyle and Rose, and it seemed to both that they were floating down through time to the moment these very words had been spoken. Remembering all that had occurred from the entry into Jerusalem to the Resurrection, recalling also the subsequent destruction of the city, they were transfixed by the mysteries of time, of knowledge, and of human blindness.

The boy was the first to shake off the mood. "I still don't get it. Why did he put these passages on a stone and hide it under the wall of the tower?"

"I'm not sure, but perhaps the man who made this stone was surrounded by enemies. Maybe the castle was under siege."

"Encircled, hemmed in on all sides?"

"Perhaps he knew that he was about to be smashed to the ground and his children within, and that not one stone would be left upon another."

Again Kyle seemed lost in thought. He looked at Rose and said, "But why the flower?"

"I don't know."

"The castle knows", the boy whispered. "The castle knows."

Next day was a Sunday, and the Bradons offered to drive Rose to Shevret, where there was a Catholic Mass. Ned informed Rose, not without a certain abashment, that after his farmers' meeting the night before he had taken pains to find out the time of Mass.

"Unless you want to go with us to Thatch Upping and become a Methodist", he quipped.

A half-hour drive brought them to the village of Shevret, a hamlet slightly larger than Thatch Upping. Ned told Rose that he and his family would circle back to their own service in Thatch Upping and return to pick her up within a couple of hours. Did she mind waiting? Not at all, she reassured him. It would give her a chance to look at the old architecture of the village. They dropped her at the door of a small stone building of very great age.

The Mass was celebrated reverently, but stiffly, by a gaunt, elderly priest. Perhaps he was still trying to adjust to the vernacular and the discomfort of facing the congregation. The parishioners were few in number, no more than two dozen, most of them older people. After Mass, they departed quickly, leaving Rose alone with the Blessed Sacrament. The sweet-fire was quietly present. She prayed for the Bradons, for the healing of their past—the great wounding, as she called it. The words of her tearful confession to Mrs. Bradon on the night of her arrival now came back to her: *the small choices that led to great errors, when fear and unforgiveness launched the terrible suffering, though in the beginning it did not seem so.*

In the light of her growing familiarity with English history, and the discovery of her ancestor's castle, she now began to wonder if *the great wounding* had its roots farther back than she had supposed. Moreover, it struck her as acutely strange that she, a woman from a shack by Crazyman River in a savage and dangerous land, an almost-nothing person, a brown bottom-of-the-world person, should have aristocratic ancestors. She laughed. The laugh was greeted by a small cough. Startled from her reverie, she saw that the priest was standing beside her, looking at her with puzzled friendliness.

"Good morrow, Madam", he said in an accent so thickly English that Rose had to replay it in her mind before his meaning became clear.

"Good morning, Father", she replied, rising.

"You're a visitor", he said, his eyes twinkling. "We don't get many visitors out this way. Care for a cup of tea?"

Rose very much wanted a cup of tea. She followed him into the sacristy and beyond it through a low doorway (the priest had to bend his neck to go through) into a small kitchen. He introduced himself as Fr. Benedict, a curate of the local diocese. Rose introduced herself and briefly explained her presence in the country.

"An artist, is it?" he said with interest. "Then you'll be wanting to know about these old stones, won't you?" He launched into a lengthy description of the building's history. Until recently it had been a parish of the Church of England, he said, but dwindling attendance had forced the local Anglicans to sell it back to the Catholics.

"Yes, God writes in centuries. We're in a new chapter now, though even our parishioners are few and far between. But we're growing, we are, two baptisms and a marriage last year. Before Henry and Elizabeth it was always Catholic, of course.

The sacristy and this lodge are Norman. The older section, the nave and sanctuary, is Saxon. Saint Edward's we've been called for centuries, but the original name was Saint Austin of Canterbury. We've a holy well, too, somewhere out there in the fields, where it's said miracles were regular in days past, before the coming of the bad years."

"Where is the holy well, do you know?" Rose asked.

"It's lost now. But no doubt we'll find it again, and then the miracles'll be flowing once more. Four hundred years or so—what's that to us? Just an interruption."

"You say the church was Saxon. Do you have old records from those years?"

"Records? Oh, lots of them. Writs and charters and the parish records. Not many from the Saxon era, because they weren't as keen on parchment as the Normans. The French, now, they were regular fanatics about the documents."

"It is all so fascinating. History is long here."

"Or short, depending on how one looks at it."

"There is so much to learn. An ancestor of mine once lived in the region."

He flicked a curious glance at her face, his thoughts loud with the effort to connect her appearance to what she had told him.

"What was the ancestor's name?"

"Kayol Bredon, a descendant of Sir Karolus le Breton."

"Kayol Bredon", he digested the name. "Kayol Bredon. Not familiar to me, though I've only been here six years and not had time to go through all the old papers. But Karolus le Breton, his name I recognize very well. He's the one who commissioned the digging of the holy well, after he returned from Jerusalem. The Third Crusade that was. In 1190, he left, and returned with King Richard in the spring of the year 1194, if I remember correctly. It was an ill-fated expedition in many ways, though they came close to capturing the holy city."

"Do you know anything else about him?"

"Naught but what the parish records show. There is an old letter down in the cellar with the other things. The British Museum's been after the bishop to turn over all the ancient documents, but they're still hacking and cleaving each other at the bargaining table. In the meantime, I'm custodian. Want to see it?"

"Oh, yes", Rose breathed.

The priest led her back into the sacristy, and in a corner of that room, behind a wall of vestment drawers and shelves containing many chalices and reliquaries, he lifted a trapdoor and descended. Rose followed him down a staircase of rough foot-worn stones and entered an atmosphere that smelled so familiar she hesitated only an instant before recognizing it as the aroma of tanned deer hide. The scent was mixed with other odors: dust, earth, and the peculiarly pleasant perfume of ancient books. At the bottom, the priest flicked a wall switch and the buzz of a fluorescent light was added to the hum of an electric dehumidifier. The cellar was a long catacomb hewn from the white chalk of the region. On stone lintels lining both walls of this rectangular cavern sat yellow limestone caskets, each about three feet in length. Inscribed on the sides of a few were Roman numerals, and the letters A.D.

"One for each century, up to a certain period, then it gets rather busy", the priest said. "The volume of paper increases toward the time of Henry, then declines steadily. The Civil War is skimpy. As you see, about the year 1700 or so, things pick up again; now, these brass caskets contain that period. Then the steamer trunks take over in the 1800s—the documents in those are in poor condition. Moldy. A great pity."

He patted a modern plastic box, sealed with an airtight lid. "Now here's the biscuit. Good archives from about 1880 to the present. These bins are my idea. Had them put in last year. They do lack aesthetics, I admit, but they're very effective for preservation."

673

"Could we see the twelfth century?"

"Of course, of course", he said and went down the aisle toward the far end of the room.

"Here we are", he said, lifting a metal lid from a stone casket. Inside was a wooden box and within that a layer of dark brown, oiled cloth. It smelled like old moose hide. Unfolding the wrapper carefully, Fr. Benedict extracted a plastic garbage bag, which was taped carefully around the innermost material.

"Tsk-tsk, I'm not much of an archivist, but the people from the Museum will see to this when I'm gone."

With some effort he lifted the mound from the box and took it to a wooden refectory table in the center of the room. When the bag was off, he began to separate the contents into several little piles.

"Here we are", he said, peering over his bifocals at Rose, tapping a pile. "Latter end of the twelfth century. Karolus begins in here. He ends up somewhere in the thirteenth century. That's in the next casket, so I'll see what I can find over there and leave you with this for now." He twinkled at her like a cheery host and drew up a rickety wooden chair to the table, gesturing that she should sit on it.

While he rummaged in the thirteenth century, Rose went through a large number of baptismal and marriage certificates. Among these were occasional letters from bishops and secular authorities, mostly written in an older form of English and a script that Rose found torturously difficult to decipher. There were some Latin documents as well, and on most of them was a profusion of wax seals and ribbons. It was such a wealth of unintelligibility, that Rose felt dismayed by it all. The priest was preoccupied with some distraction of his own in the other casket, so she continued to pick through the documents without much hope of finding anything that would shed light on the mystery of Bradon's keep. Starting at the top of the pile a second time, she worked her way through it more

674

carefully, her eyes scanning blindly, hoping that Karolus' name would leap out at her. Half way down she came upon a document that was ocher brown with age, a thick parchment from the bottom of which dangled several ribbons and wax coins.

Aside from the name *Karolus le Breton*, in bold calligraphy, she found the text impossible to read. The words could be Latin, French, or an older form of English. She turned to the priest and told him of her difficulty.

Standing beside her, he bent over the manuscript, peering closely at it through his glasses.

"It's French to be sure. A few words of Latin to boot. But mostly Old French. Quite a stew it is. Anyway, here's what it says. I translate roughly, Miss, but as close to the original as these old eyes can manage."

He read:

Karolus le Breton does hereby grant the land and pay the moneys for the digging of a holy well at Chevreuil, in the parish of Saint Austin, for the purposes of devotion and supplication to the Saint and to the Holy Mother of God and Good Saint Joseph, with the intention that all manner of ills be cured by the Mercy of God. In memoriam of the siege of Jerusalem, where did fall three of the sons of Karolus, who himself was wounded by the Saracen, yet recovered. Pray for their souls. Pray for the remission of my sins that were abundant. Karolus le Breton, Feast of Saint Austin, Anno Domini 1195.

"Is Shevret the modern word for Chevreuil?" Rose asked.

"Yes, it would seem so. A *chevreuil* is the French word for stag. A *chevrette* is a doe or fawn. Perhaps the name of the town altered as the town shrank over these many years. Turned from a roebuck into a fawn." He chuckled. "There's only one Saint

Austin's in the region and only one holy well that I've ever heard of. Thus I think it safe to say that Shevret and Chevreuil are one and the same."

"Here is his name again", Rose said, pointing to the document beneath it.

"Ah, yes, this is the letter I told you about. It's in a finer Latin, so the writer was educated. There are a few French terms and even more English ones peppering the lot. He says this:

My Lord Bishop, here be a copy of the charter of Sir Karolus le Breton, writ by his clerk, an ancient document, one hundred six years past, for the contract with indentured servants for the construction of the holy well, famous now throughout the Bishopric and in diverse regions beyond. He it is who went with Richard to Jerusalem and returned sonless. Thane in this region, he fell in the Battle of Lincoln in 1217, leaving one newborn son. He was lord of the demesne held by charter, granted by King John, for lands west of the ridgeway south of Oxford, all lands from the Roman bridge at Chevreuil in the east as far as Rivière Sainte-Croix in the west, with the corner post at the Bishop's stone, in perpetuity to his descendants forever, God grant the grace. Copy of the Charter of Land rights is in keeping with you until the time of trouble passes. Let it also be remembered that moneys were paid by the present Lord of Sainte-Croix, Sir Kay Bredon, for the refurbishing of this church, in the fourth generation of the line of Karolus, and on condition that upon his death his natural remains be interred in the Yard, beside his ancestors. Upon his death the Lord Bredon further promises to bequeath certain books to you, in custody of the priest of Saint Austin's, notably the *Bréviaire* that his forefather brought from Anjou, the

Gospel copied by Eadui monk of Christchurch, Canterbury, and the *Epistolary* which was made at Padua.

Fr. Benedict paused and looked up. "It goes on for a good deal yet. Are you sure you want to hear it all?"

"Oh, yes, please", Rose replied.

The priest continued to read the titles of a series of holy books bequeathed to the local bishop through the parish priest of St. Austin's. Whatever was the significance of these entries, they were causing the present parish priest of St. Austin's to groan six hundred years after the fact.

"They're all gone now", sighed Fr. Benedict, shaking his head. "I wonder where they went." Clearing his throat he returned to the document and proceeded to read out a list of books that were to be passed on to the "new school" at Oxford upon the death of Sir Kayol Bredon.

The document concluded with: *Writ this Michaelmas Day, Year of Our Lord 1302, through the hand of Robert of Malmsbury, priest of Saint Austin's, Chevreuil. Witnessed, Aethelred, clerk of the parish. Witnessed, Walter, steward of Castle Sainte-Croix.*

Three wax seals were attached by ribbons to the base of the parchment.

Fr. Benedict looked up. "Where was Sainte-Croix, I wonder?" he mused, staring into the middle distance. "There's no place by that name in the region, at least not that any living man has heard of."

Rose trembled with suppressed knowledge.

"May I make a copy of this, Father?" she asked.

"A copy? Certainly you may make a copy."

Rose rummaged in her deer-hide sack in search of paper and pencil.

"Oh, my dear, that's the hard way. Why don't we get our scribe to make you a duplicate? The Canon of Saint Austin's is most efficient."

Taking both documents—Sir Karolus' and Robert of Malmsbury's—Fr. Benedict remounted the stairs and led Rose back into his rectory. In a room off his kitchen, which apparently was his office, he flicked the power switch on a photocopier, placed the first parchment face down, and waited for the machine to warm up.

"This is probably archivist heresy", he smiled sheepishly. He took twenty minutes to jot down translations onto separate sheets of paper. He made photocopies of these as well, a set for Rose and a set for himself.

"A morning well spent, Miss. I haven't enjoyed myself so much in years. You must come back again. My door is always open."

She thanked him, asked for his priestly blessing, and knelt. He appeared startled by the request, but recovered quickly and made the sign of the cross over her. They wished each other a happy Sunday, and Rose left. The Bradons arrived at the front steps of the church a few minutes later and drove with her back to the farm.

On Monday morning, Kyle declared to his parents that he and Rose were going to go walking in the hills again that day.

"Poor Rose", Fern exclaimed. "Aren't you exhausted? You don't have to traipse around with this gadabout every single day, you know. Are you sure you aren't being overly patient with him?"

"Not at all, Fern", Rose smiled. "I love it. Every part of it."

"Well, if you really want to", Fern said doubtfully. "In any event, I'm going to pack you a good lunch."

An hour later, Rose and Kyle were back in the dungeon of the castle. They sat down on the step-stone under the light, and Rose showed the boy the photocopies that she had obtained at St. Austin's. His eyes grew large, and his breathing quickened as he read them in entirety, uttering not a single word.

"Oh", he said at last, looking at her with a flushed face. "Oh, my word. This is—this is fantastic! Do you think—?"

"Yes, I'm certain, Kyle. We're sitting in Castle Sainte-Croix. It means Holy Cross."

"Castle Holy Cross", he repeated, leaning his head back against the wall, staring at the far wall. They remained in silence for a time, trying to absorb all that had happened during the previous two days.

Kyle was the first to stir from the reverie. Pointing to Robert of Malmsbury's letter, he said, "In perpetuity to his descendants forever, God grant the grace." He raised his eyebrows at Rose. "That's us. You and me. We're the descendants."

It suddenly struck them both as so humorous that they began to laugh simultaneously, Rose's small bird twitters and Kyle's robust guffaw.

"This is *our* castle", the boy said with such joy that Rose could not fail to be infected by it.

"Kyle, the places named—the forest and bishop stone and river—do you know them?"

He shook his head. "There's no forest near here, not any real forest, that is, except the little oak wood we call the forest. And it's too far west, unless it was once part of a huge forest that stretched away into the east. If *chevreuil* means roebuck in French, it must have been a place where they hunted stags. I don't know of any river called Sainte-Croix, but its name has probably changed. There's the Ock north of us, but that can't be it. In the west there's the river that drains the Lambourn Downs . . . maybe that's the one."

"What about your own stream, the one you call the River?"

"It might be, but it's pretty small. More than that, if it *is* the river the records refer to, it would mean the old knight's land stopped right here. Which can't be the case, you see, because he wouldn't have built a castle on the *edge* of his land. More likely he would've put it in the center. Besides, there's a village called Bishopstone about ten miles west of here. If it's the place where the boundary marker was, then our keep *is* right in the middle. Anyway it's all lost now, broken down into bits and pieces over the centuries."

"Even so, I feel it very close, Kyle, as if it happened yesterday."

"You feel it too?"

"Yes, and I can hear it also."

He nodded solemnly, looking at her with unaffected trust.

"Well", he said pulling the keep-stone from his pocket. "We haven't found treasure, but at least we have this. And we've learned a lot about our past. If only the man who cut the stone had put a date on it."

"The flower must mean something."

"Yes, the flower. I thought at first it was a rose, and then I wondered if maybe the castle was destroyed during the Wars of the Roses. But that's in the fifteenth century, and if the castle was leveled in those years, there'd probably be a lot more showing above ground."

"And probably the memory of this place would not have faded so completely."

"Right. There are lots of ruined castles all over England, some much older than this. Parts of them are still standing, and they're remembered. So why not this one?"

"That is a great mystery", Rose said. "And the meaning of this flower—"

"Also a mystery. And why those strange words above it: *Abscondita ab oculis*. Hidden from the eyes?"

He looked slowly around the room, straining his eyes. Abruptly he got to his feet and approached the far wall. As Rose watched, he began a strange sort of movement, as if he were doing knee bends in slow motion, with his flashlight pointing to the section of the wall where he stood. Up and

680

down went the light. He took a step to the right and repeated the curious ritual.

"What is it, Kyle? What are you doing?"

"I don't know," he muttered, his eyes inches from the wall, dropping and rising with the motion of his body as if the light and his eyes were a single apparatus that must work together if his intuition were to prove correct. Up and down went the light, so slowly that Rose began to wonder if the boy was going too far into the realm of fantasy.

"Kyle——"

He silenced her with a gesture. On and on he went, moving slowly in increments toward the corner of the room farthest from the light of the cellar opening, and which had, until this moment, remained in deepest shadow. At the juncture of two walls, he dropped slowly to the floor, following the beam of light, then froze as his face neared the floor. Lying down flat, he scratched the face of the stone with a fingernail, then tapped it gently with the edge of the flashlight.

Tap-tap, tap-tap.

"Come here, Rose", he whispered intensely. "Look at this."

Crouching down beside him, head beside his, inches from the wall, she saw a tiny configuration of ridges, no more than a wrinkle in the surface, the size of a large button. He pointed to it. It seemed a natural imperfection.

"Tell me what you see", he said.

"Nothing, really."

He moved the flashlight so that its beam shone on the wall at a sharp angle.

"Look again."

There, suddenly materializing before their eyes, was a faintly incised flower.

"*Abscondita ab oculis*", he whispered.

"Hidden from the eyes", Rose echoed.

Getting up, he went to find his tool sack and returned with a hammer and pry bar.

A few more taps, and the surface of the stone began to show fracture lines.

"This bit here isn't stone", he said. "It's the same color as the chalk, but it's mortar."

He chipped some more, going carefully around the incised flower. The fragment fell off, leaving the flower intact. Rose retrieved it and wrapped it carefully in a handkerchief which she laid for safekeeping on top of Kyle's knapsack.

The mortar was ancient, and thus it was harder than the surrounding natural stone. Piece by piece it gave way before the chiseling bar. Within half an hour, a small hole no larger than the bole of a pencil appeared, revealing that the mortar was more than three inches in thickness. Kyle worked to enlarge it. Another hour passed, and though the hole grew in size neither Kyle's large hand nor Rose's small one would fit through. They broke for lunch and ate their sandwiches in silence, guarding the hushed thrill of what was happening, thriving on the excitement of anticipation, not wanting to ruin it with words. After they had downed quick sips of tea from the thermos, they returned to work.

By midafternoon the hole was large enough for Rose's hand to go through.

Kyle signaled with his eyes that she should be the first to investigate. She put her hand slowly into the darkness. Nothing but empty space met her fingers. The air inside the secret chamber, if air it was, felt like black velvet vapor.

"Nothing", Rose said shaking her head at Kyle. She pushed her forearm as far as it would go, and still her fingers failed to make contact of any sort.

Kyle sighed and resumed his chipping. Another half-hour passed. Pausing to amass his strength at one point, he gave a mighty bang on the end of the bar, and its point suddenly cut deep into a section of more porous mortar. It fractured into several chunks. A few more blows with the hammer, and the entire covering fell away, exposing an opening about six inches square. Kyle cleared away the rubble from the entrance and shone his flashlight inside. His chest heaving, his face contracting with excitement, he pivoted the light this way and that, straining to see what fell under its beam. With a cry, he thrust his arm inside.

"Ah! Ah!" he cried. "Oh! Oh!"

"Io! Kyle, what is it? Are you hurt?"

"No! I've found something! It's heavy!"

He wiggled his body backward, the arm withdrawing, the hand locked on some as yet invisible object. Slowly his wrist appeared, white with dust. A faint scraping sound came from within. Then his fingers emerged, gripping a box as white as his fingers.

When it was fully out, he sat up and put it on his lap. His eyes blinked rapidly, his hands trembled.

"What is it?" Rose asked pressing close.

"A casket of some kind."

He rubbed the dust from it. Fashioned of green metal, it measured roughly five inches high by four wide, and its length was approximately a foot.

"It's brass, I think, or bronze", he whispered.

The hinged lid was embossed with figures: Two antlered stags facing a heart surmounted by a cross. The remainder of the box was without ornamentation.

Hardly daring to open it, Kyle handed it to Rose. "You do it", he said.

Stunned by this generosity, she took the casket in her hands and tried to open the lid, but the hinge bar running along one side refused to move. She braced the base in her hands, and Kyle gripped the lid in his. Straining with all his might, he managed to pry it upward a fraction at a time, until without warning it sprang wide open with a clink. He grabbed the flashlight and shone it within.

It contained three objects. One was a tube of some kind, a much oxidized metal cylinder sealed at both ends by lumps of dark wax. The scent of bees was still in it.

The second item was a ring wrapped in a cloth that disintegrated at the touch. It was untarnished gold, the band wide, containing at its apex an oval stone that refracted glints of amber-yellow. Cut into its surface was a tiny stag with a cross in its antlers.

The third item was a small ivory box with a lift-off lid. It was unornamented, badly yellowed, spotted randomly with green and black mold. Kyle opened it and stared in puzzlement at what it contained—a lump of wax. Like the wax plugs of the metal tube, it was reddish-brown in color, and it crumbled at the touch. Handing it to Rose, he went back to a close appraisal of the ring and the tube.

As Rose warmed the wax ball in her hands, it did not so much soften as continue to crumble. A glint of metal appeared, followed by another. Finally it all fell away, revealing a silver cross of unusual design. Its vertical bar was the same length as the horizontal, and in each of its four corners was a tiny cross.

"Look at this, Kyle."

"A cross", he said with cursory interest, then quickly returned to the more fabulous ring, which he now slipped onto his baby finger, the only finger onto which it would go. It looked out of place on the large farm-boy hand.

"A child's ring", he said. "Then again, maybe it isn't. You know, Rose, those suits of armor from the Middle Ages are all pretty short. We think of those mighty knights and kings as giants, but they were little guys. Poor vitamins and minerals, Mum says. So maybe this was Karolus' ring."

"Which means he must have been about my size", Rose offered.

Kyle laughed. "Well, maybe a little taller. But not as tall as me. It's strange to think of them like that, not what you'd expect. But then lots of things in life aren't what you'd—"

He eyed Rose's short stature and did not finish the thought.

"What are we going to do now, Kyle? Don't you think it's time to tell your parents?"

"Not yet. I was wondering if we could go back to Shevret tomorrow. I'd like to meet that old priest at the church. Maybe he could tell us what this stuff means."

"Yes, why don't we do that."

"Uh, do you think we can trust him? I mean, he could just call the National Trust, and then we'd lose everything."

"We can trust him. He has a few secrets of his own, I think."

"Do you know that for sure?"

"Not really, but I have a sense he doesn't think governments should have the right to swoop down and claim every piece of history as their own."

"They say they're claiming it for the people of England."

"They have a good argument, Kyle. We should at least consider it."

"I know", he said sadly. "I know. But just for a while I'd like to keep it to ourselves. To soak it in."

"To remember it?"

"Yes, that's right. To remember what was, because it's a part of us—you and me—and because when you forget the past there are holes in your mind, and you're walking blind."

That night, Rose and Kyle asked Ned to drive them to Shevret the following day, on the pretext of attending morning Mass at St. Austin's. Ned eyed the boy curiously and mumbled something to the effect that he hoped his son was not thinking of becoming a papist. Kyle laughed and assured his father that was impossible.

"I'll just go along for the ride, to keep Rose company."

"And how will you get home?" the man asked. "We're talking about a needless waste of petrol, and two round trips for me. I don't mind dropping you off, but I can't spare the time to go back and pick you up. I have to be in Newbury by ten to meet the people from the Ministry of Agriculture."

"We can walk home afterward", Kyle declared.

"Walk home! It's twelve, fifteen miles. What does Rose say about that?"

"Oh, I would love a long walk, Ned. Truly I would", she replied.

"You would? I must say you're made of hardier stuff than I am."

"And I want to pay for the petrol for driving us to Shevret."

Ashamed of his lapse into parsimony, he waved away her offer. "Now, now, you can just forget the idea of paying for a short drive like that. I can be as tight as bark on a tree, Rose, and it's a bad habit. We'll say no more about it. I'll have you there in time for your Mass."

Ned and Fern went upstairs to bed about nine o'clock that evening, leaving Kyle and Rose chatting, eating currant buns, and sipping warm milk in the kitchen. A mischievous look played on the boy's face as they ate. At about nine-thirty, he went to the bottom of the stairs and cocked an ear. He returned to the kitchen and whispered, "They're asleep."

Retrieving his knapsack from his bedroom, Kyle removed the three artifacts from it and laid them on the table.

"Oh", he breathed softly, staring at the treasure with large eyes for the hundredth time. "This is amazing. This is too wonderful."

"Kyle, is now the time to open the pipe and see what's inside?"

"Yes."

Using a cooking skewer, he picked with slow and careful movements at one end of the tube. Small bits of the wax plug

686

broke off, falling into a little pile on the table. When the opening was clear, Kyle shook the tube gently and a long cylinder slid out of it and fell into the palm of his right hand. It was animal hide of some kind, well-tanned and very thin, bound by a single ribbon that might have been red at one time, but was now dull brown with age. It was secured by a bow that had fused with the passing centuries. So tight was it that no attempts at undoing the knot would budge it.

"I hate to do this", Kyle murmured. Taking a set of nail clippers, he snipped the ribbon close to the knot and pulled it away. At first the hide did not want to relinquish the shape it had held for so long. It was brittle, almost like parchment. Yet the kitchen was humid with the weather, not to mention the kettle steaming on the stove. Rose and Kyle unrolled the outer wrapping with utmost care, exposing an inch or so every few minutes. The hide seemed to inhale the atmospheric moisture and relax bit by bit. Finally, it was open, its edges held apart by their four hands, revealing a small parchment scroll secured by a ribbon. This they opened in the same manner as they had the hide covering.

"Look", Kyle whispered intensely. "It's an old document of some kind."

"It does seem so", Rose answered. "I saw many like it at Saint Austin's. But this one has only a single seal."

Peering closely at the disk of rust-colored wax affixed to the bottom of the parchment, they saw that it was embossed with the image of a tiny stag with a cross in its antlers. Etched in the wax, in Roman capitals, were the letters BREDON STE CROIX.

"This must have been the seal of the Lord of Sainte-Croix", Kyle said. "Look, it's a perfect match for the ring. Can you read what's written on the parchment?"

Rose shook her head. "No."

"Neither can I. It looks like a funny sort of English. Very old. Do you think the priest at Shevret might be able to read it?"

"It's possible. He translated the older documents he showed me. So maybe this one will be simple for him."

"Yes, but he's going to wonder where we got this. That could blow everything wide open, and I don't want that to happen just yet."

"Why don't we make a copy?"

Kyle jumped up, rummaged in a kitchen drawer, and found paper and a fountain pen. Setting to work with dedication, he completed a fairly good facsimile within the hour. In addition, he copied the inscription on the keep-stone onto a separate sheet.

"We'll show him this also, Rose, and see what he makes of it."

"Isn't it clear, Kyle? Whoever put it in the drain hole intended it to be found—found by someone in the future, that is. I doubt if he wanted it found by whoever tore down the castle. My guess is that it was supposed to guide us to the hiding place where we found these treasures."

"That's my guess too. But there are a few details about the keep-stone that aren't so clear. I'll be interested to know what your old priest makes of them."

As promised, Ned dropped them at the door of St. Austin's shortly before the eight A.M. Mass and roared off on the road to Newbury. Kyle followed Rose inside the church, glancing about the interior with boyish interest. When Rose proceeded down the aisle to the front pew, he refrained from following and seated himself in the pew closest to the door. Spreading his arms along the backrest and crossing his legs, he settled himself in for a close analysis of the alien rites.

Rose, for her part, sighed with joy at coming into the physical presence of the Lord; she knelt and prayed with great fervor for Kyle and his family, daring to ask for what the boy had already declared to be impossible: their conversion to "papism" or, more accurately, their conversion to a fuller encounter with the living Christ in his Church and in his sacraments. Presently the priest entered the sanctuary, robed in white English vestments embroidered centuries ago, preceded by a little altar boy who was dressed in a white soutane, tinkling a hand bell from which he was deriving much pleasure. Rose and the three other parishioners present stood, and the Mass began. The Offertory and Communion were rich in consolation for her, as was her thanksgiving afterward. There were no interior *words* from the Holy Spirit regarding all that had so far occurred during her stay, and by this she concluded that whatever God's intention might be, it was proceeding as it should.

After Mass, the priest again approached her and invited her to tea. She glanced at Kyle, who was still riveted to his seat at the back of the church.

"My relative is with me. Can he join us?"

"Ah, our silent observer!" the priest smiled. "Of course he may, of course he may!" And beckoned to the boy with a bright smile and a come-hither gesture of the hands. Rose made the introductions, noting Kyle's uncharacteristic shyness—and the curiosity that was churning beneath it.

Over tea in his kitchen, Fr. Benedict said, "You know, I could have kicked myself the other day for not asking you where you're staying. You see, after you left I went back down to the archives and did some more poking about. I found something that might be of interest to you regarding your family history." He glanced at the boy. "And yours too. They're one and the same, I take it?"

Rose and Kyle nodded simultaneously.

The priest smiled knowingly and stood. "Come with me."

Downstairs in the vault, he went straight to a stone casket that they had not looked into on the day of Rose's first visit. The inscription on its side indicated that it contained records from the fifteenth century. He opened the lid and withdrew a document that was sitting on the top. Taking it to the refectory table, he laid it down carefully before him and straightened his reading glasses. Rose and Kyle stood on either side, bending over in anticipation.

"This is a letter I stumbled upon after you left. You certainly piqued my interest, young lady, and I could not stop myself from doing a little Sherlock Holmes, to see just what could be found relating to the line of Karolus le Breton. He died in 1217, as you recall. After 1302—the date of Robert of Malmsbury's letter regarding his descendant Sir Kayol Bredon—there is only the usual material, births, baptisms, deaths, marriages, et cetera, for over a hundred years. Then, after the year 1484 all Le Bretons or Bredons simply disappear from the records. I think I have discovered why that is the case."

Fr. Benedict tapped the parchment.

"Tell us, tell us", Kyle said with an urgency that seemed to cause the priest some amusement.

"Shall I read it to you? Yes? I should say in advance, however, that this letter was written right here inside these old walls by one of my predecessors. Moreover, it was never sent. For whatever reason—the extreme delicacy of the subject matter perhaps—it has remained here undelivered, and perhaps unread until this very day. It's written entirely in Middle English—clearly a later work written more than two centuries after the invasion, at a time when the English tongue had succeeded in overwhelming the French. All right, here it is, though for the sake of clarity I will update the language somewhat:

'My Lord Archbishop, I write in haste, as the countryside is dangerous with bands of the Usurper's men. They have not thought to touch the holy places nor to manhandle your servants in the surrounding parishes, yet their mood is bent to havoc and outrage. The tidings are ill. Sainte-Croix has fallen. Sir Roland Bredon and all his household put to the sword, the chapel priest also, Edmund Turner by name, a friar of the order of Saint Dominic.

'A woodcutter in Chevreuil Forest, happening to pass nearby the castle, heard the sound of sword on shield and drew close. With his own eyes he saw Richard's men sacking Sainte-Croix. Thereafter the timber portions were set aflame, and numerous men upon the battlement and tower dislodging stones. Unlettered and slow of wit, yet he knows the name of the new King and is loyal to him. Thus, I take as reliable his report, which he told to me this morning, for he does not understand the nature of the troubles, nor why Roland is in disfavor. He did not claim to see Richard, who is reputed to be with armed forces in York. He saw a captain commanding the destruction, and upon his banner the white rose.

'My Lord, the people are in distress, several faithful of the parish have lost kinsmen at Sainte-Croix, servants all, and are in much grief. My own heart is dark with foreboding. Red and white, when shall it cease? What has become of the rightful King? Rumors have it that the boy is in London Tower. Forgive my boldness, but I say this ungodly strife for a throne is not the Mind of Christ.

'I send this to you by Robert, a mercer of Chichester, my kinsman who is with me presently, a good son of the Church. Your obedient servant, Bede Mercier, priest, Church of Saint Austin, Chevreuil. Feast of All Souls, A.D. 1483.' "

Fr. Benedict looked up and exhaled. Rose and Kyle remained as if spellbound. They stared at the letter as if it was a window through which they were viewing roaring fire and flailing sword.

Rose was the first to break the silence. "Father, can you tell us what this means?"

She gave him the sheet of paper on which she had written the inscriptions from the keep-stone. The priest took it, sat down on the wooden chair, and read it slowly.

"Hmmm", he said to himself. "What is this, now? What is this? Very interesting, very interesting."

He looked briefly at Rose. "Where did you see the original of this, I wonder? No, don't tell me; it would color my exegesis. Let me guess, let me guess." He closed his eyes, removed his glasses, and sat back with folded arms. Arriving at some conclusion, he opened his eyes and leaned forward suddenly.

"Well, for so few words this message reveals rather a lot, I'd say. First of all, it was written sometime between the thirteenth and the sixteenth century."

"How do you know that?" Kyle asked.

"Because the scriptural references are without verses. Now, it's rather a cryptic fragment, so I'm presuming it was written in haste or on a limited space—a small piece of parchment perhaps."

"A stone", Rose corrected.

Kyle flashed her a reproving look.

"Stone, eh? A small stone?"

"Yes."

"Well, that cinches it, then. Obviously he was trying to conserve space. *Evangelium S Lucam*, for example. The S stands for *Secundum*—meaning *according to*. The Gospel according to Luke. Now why did he abbreviate that word, yet spell out the words below? Why is there a chapter reference and no verse reference? There's only one convincing explanation. You see, the system of numbering *chapters* of the Sacred Scripture gained widespread use only in the thirteenth century. It was Stephen Langton, bishop of Canterbury who did it, and he died in 1228 or thereabouts, if I recall correctly. Now, the *verse* numbering only came in around the 1550s, when a certain Robert Stephanus published an edition of the Latin Vulgate in

Geneva. 1555 that was, I believe." Fr. Benedict hummed again, as if this display of scholarship on his part was in no way out of the ordinary. "So there you have it, our two chronological bookends: Somewhere between 1228 and 1555, give or take a few years, your stone inscription was written."

He said no more and seemed content to stare down at Bede Mercier's letter, humming and thinking.

Kyle intruded. "So that's why the person who inscribed the stone wrote out the lines of those verses."

"Yes, a very good deduction, my lad. I would say certainly that's why. There's rather a lot in the nineteenth chapter of Luke, so if your author wanted to say something specific, he would have had to give the reader a clue, a prompting line, if you will. It appears that he has done so. *Stones cry out* and *Hidden from the eyes*. Very interesting." Turning the full force of his Sherlock Holmes look upon the boy, he said in a deceptively quiet voice, "I wonder what he was trying to tell us?" His eyes remained unblinking on Kyle's for several seconds. "And I do confess to wondering where you got this."

At which both Rose and Kyle began to stammer and blush in a blatantly guilty manner, causing the priest to chuckle. Rose looked at Kyle, asking him wordlessly if they should tell all. He hesitated then nodded once, emphatically.

"We have found the ruins of Castle Sainte-Croix," Rose said.

A stunned look crossed the old man's face, followed by a rush of excitement.

"Sainte-Croix? You're not serious. What makes you think you've found it?"

Kyle pointed to the inscription from the keep-stone. "We found this in the dungeon of a keep on our land, up near where it must have been in the old days."

"Must have been? What do you mean, must have been?"

Kyle explained the position of the Bradon farm, then compared it to certain details from the description of Sainte-Croix in the letter of Robert of Malmsbury. As he listened, the priest's face grew steadily more serious, more entranced, more moved. When Kyle had finished presenting his case, Fr. Benedict shook his head in wonder.

"The *donjon*!"

"*Donjon?*" Kyle queried.

"The castle-keep in Old French. *Dominium* in Latin, which evolved into *domnio*, the lord's tower. We think of dungeons as damp dark prison holes, but in old usage it meant the whole tower." He shook his head once more. "Well, this is splendid news. Splendid news. Tell me, did you find anything inside?"

"We found the stone", said Kyle. "Then the message on the stone led us to a secret chamber in the wall of the cellar. Inside we found this." Into the priest's hands he now placed the transcription of the scroll they had found in the metal tube.

"We don't know how to read it", Rose said. "Can you?"

Fr. Benedict put his glasses back on, peered down at the paper, and inhaled sharply.

"Oh, my", he muttered. "Oh, my, oh, my." He glanced up at Rose and Kyle. "Oh, my, I think we'd better go upstairs and have a cup of tea."

Frantic with impatience, they followed him back to his rectory and sat nervously waiting for the tea to arrive. As he pottered about his kitchen, Fr. Benedict resisted every attempt on their part to dig an explanation from him, and merely kept muttering oh, my, oh, my, to himself. When the steeping teapot, cups, milk, sugar, and a plate of biscuits were before them, the priest took up the document and read aloud:

"I, Roland Bredon, Lord of Sainte-Croix, set my hand to this writ for the purpose of the Truth, before God and the rightful King. Richard the Usurper has been crowned by an act of Parliament, even though there is a living and true descendent of the Plantagenets, which is Edward,

known as the Fifth. It bodes ill. Richard Duke of Gloucester I shall never call King. He is without remorse, as he
proved by his crushing of the Woodvilles. In this way
he has ceased to be Protector of the Realm whose duty it
was to guard the kingdom and its rightful prince until he
comes of age. He has become Destroyer of the Realm and
cast the prince into prison. The boy, it is rumored, is captive in London Tower, at the will of Richard, along with
the younger prince, also by name Richard.

"Yesterday at dawn, men in the service of the Usurper
came upon the castle by diverse routes and combined into
a Force, killed servants, field laborers, and gate guards.
My eldest son, Kyle, lies dying, fallen under the enemy's
sword at the ramp. My heart is full-broken. Priest Edmund, our chaplain, is dead by arrow. Coeur d'Hubert,
my youngest, is escaped. We are under siege, and though
the tower remains in our hands, little hope is there. The
attackers wear the white rose upon their garb and banner,
and thus we learned that Richard is indeed the cause of
our woe. How this has come to pass, I cannot say, yet I
suspect it is my connection to those Lancastrians who
mistrust Gloucester, or else my message to the Tudor in
France has been intercepted.

"Under flag of parlay, the captain of the enemy sent
word to me this morning that Richard demands the sur-
render of Sainte-Croix and my arrest by the Shire Reeve.
If I refuse, he must obey the Usurper's command to raze
us to the ground, no stone left upon another, and spare
none alive within. At sunrise my answer is due the Sheriff
and the captain of the siege. It is night, and we have
prayed. I know my answer, and by our deaths we shall
defend, where stone and sword no longer may defend, the
true Britain and the Crown. I die for truth, shriven in the
Holy Faith. To my descendants, be there any, I send my

promise that if God provide the Grace, from Paradise I shall pray for thee.

"I have not seen Jerusalem, nor pilgrimaged to Rome. Yet the treasure of my ancestor, the sign of the Holy Cross which he obtained in Jerusalem, my signet ring, and this writ shall endure in the place prepared for them. The stone is inscribed and set in place. I pray there be one to find it and take its meaning aright. Yea, though men of violence and deceit shall level us so that no memory of us remain, even so I pray by the Blood of the Lamb that these words will be read by eyes of my lineage, that they might turn to God in time of trial and ever remember who is Master of Times.

"My soul and all the souls of my household I commend into His hands.

"God have mercy on me, a Sinner.

"Roland Bredon, Lord of Sainte-Croix."

That night, after supper, Kyle announced to his parents that there was something he wanted to tell them. Everyone went into the parlor, and when the boy had his parents' attention, he stood in the middle of the room like a ringmaster and, with flushed face and somewhat dramatic rhetoric, told them he had found the ancient castle.

Ned and Fern smiled at first, as if they were more than familiar with their son's overactive imagination. But as he recounted step by step the discovery of the keep, they put their tea cups onto their saucers and listened in earnest.

"It's up on the crest, where the ridgeway turns northeast, above the lambing meadow. It was all under the turf ring."

"That old hump of dirt?" the man said. "You mean—?"

"Yes, that's where our ancestors once lived. And there are all kinds of documents to prove it."

Kyle stepped up to his father, knelt before him, and placed into the man's hands the scroll, the Jerusalem Cross, and the ring.

"They're yours, Dad. You're the present Lord of Sainte-Croix."

"The Lord of Sainte-Croix," Ned mumbled, eyebrows knitted, staring down at the objects as if they were not really there.

Fern hurried over and sat on the arm of Ned's chair.

"But Kyle—where—how—?" she murmured.

"I found them in the *donjon*", said the boy.

As Kyle went on with the tale, the Bradons kept shaking their heads, murmuring questions, alternately perplexed and stunned by the wonder of it.

"All these years", said Ned. "All these years and it was just sitting up there waiting for us."

"It's been there almost a thousand years, Dad. And so have we. Hard to believe, isn't it?"

"Yes, it's hard to believe, son. Who would have thought—"

Fern frowned. "But how do we know that the Bradon name came from Bredon, and before that from Breton? I mean, it could be just a coincidence, couldn't it?"

"Aye, it could be", her husband replied, still staring at the artifacts in his hand.

"If they destroyed the Bredons and all the people living within the castle, as this letter says, then how did the line continue?"

"Coeur d'Hubert", Kyle said. "Remember? *Coeur d'Hubert, my youngest, is escaped.* So he must have survived, got married, and returned to keep the Bredons going."

"But Richard the Third hated them—"

"Yes, Dad, but two years later Richard the Third was dead. Henry Tudor arrived from France and slew him at Bosworth Field. The twenty-second of August, 1485."

"So you're saying that maybe Coeur d'Hubert returned here sometime after that?"

"Yes, Mum."

"Then why wasn't the castle rebuilt?"

"I don't know. Maybe because the wealth of the Bredons had been stolen by Richard and it was impossible to get it back. Maybe the only thing he had left was a heap of rubble and some land. His whole family was destroyed. He was a Lord, but he had nothing in his pocket."

"If that was the case, he would have had to sell some of his land just to survive", Ned suggested. "Then maybe he built a smaller house, using the stones of the old castle. He might have carted them down here."

Everyone went silent and began looking about the room. Though its interior was timbered and plastered they were suddenly aware that the house was very old, erected in time out of mind by long-forgotten people. It was a stone building, composed of large gray blocks that were not native to the immediate region.

"And the barn", Ned said to himself.

"The bridge over the river too", Fern said. "I never gave it much thought."

They talked long into the night. Neither Ned nor Fern could decide what precisely they should do with the artifacts. Unfamiliar with laws regarding antiquities and archaeological finds on private property, they resolved to contact the authorities in the morning.

"Well, maybe not tomorrow morning", Ned said in a barely audible voice.

"Why don't we go have a visit with the pastor at Shevret, this man who helped with the translations?" Fern suggested.

"Yes!" Kyle exclaimed. "He's great, really a super old fellow. He knows so much, Dad, and besides, he's involved with the same problem as we are—what to do with this kind of treasure."

"A priest?" said Ned uneasily.

Kyle nodded with a big smile. "He reads about five languages, most of them dead."

"Not as dead as we thought", said the boy's mother with a small smile of her own.

It was by then one o'clock in the morning, and everyone was tired, though they were too excited to sleep. Ned stood abruptly, looked each of them in the eyes, and said, "Come with me."

They followed him up to the second floor, and from there into an unused storage room at the back of the house. He flicked a light switch, then climbed a rickety ladder nailed to the wall, lifted off a wood cover in the ceiling, and went up through the hole into the attic. A single electric bulb dangled from the massive roof beam, throwing dim light in every direction but hardly penetrating to the corners. It was a bare room, the floor rafters covered with planking. Clouds of dust arose as they crossed the creaking boards. He led them to a roof beam at the far end and pointed a small pocket flashlight at a spot above his head.

"I just remembered this", he said. "Haven't thought of it in thirty years or more. I saw it when I was a boy. Look."

The others crowded close, peering at the side of the huge beam, black with age—how much age it was impossible to guess. Incised deep into the wood were initials:

H. B.   K. B.   N. B.
AUG 1914

"Three brothers", Ned said. "They were young lads—hardly more than boys—when they cut these letters. Great Uncle Ned died in the First War. I never knew what happened to

K. B.—no one ever spoke about him; there wasn't a single photo of him in the old albums—just blank spaces here and there."

"Who was H. B.?" Rose asked.

"My grandfather—Hubert Bradon."

"The names, Ned", Fern said. "Kyle, Hubert—they're family names, reaching back into the dark of the past."

"More like coming out of the dark of the past", replied the man.

"A bridge", said the boy, "crossing the river of time, going backward and going forward."

Rose awoke in the guest room of Bradon farm, aware that to-day she must continue her journey. Where this certainty came from she did not know. It was a grace, surely, or a prompting from the Holy Spirit.

A bridge crossing the river of time, the boy had said the night before, *going backward and going forward.*

It was time to go forward.

She told them at breakfast that she would leave that morning and was surprised by their reactions. Ned's mouth opened wide and his eyes grew troubled, then he reddened and stared at the floor. Kyle burst out that she couldn't go now, she just *couldn't!* Fern's eyes filled with tears.

"But we're just getting to know you", the woman said. "No, that's not exactly true. It's more like we've always known you, and strangely, as if you've always been here. But how can that be?"

No one offered an answer. Rose fell silent, wondering what it was about her that seemed to repel people when they first laid eyes upon her, and then changed them so they took her deeply into their hearts.

Io, it is he inside me. It is his love that they sense. He is the one they seek. Thus I must go, that they may seek him in the place where he desires to give all of himself.

"Long will I remember you", Rose said at last. "Always, I will carry you. For you are my family. My only family."

"You'll come back again, won't you, Rose? And you will write to us?" Fern asked.

"Oh, yes. We must write to each other and think of each other."

She refrained from saying the most important thing—that they must pray for each other. In time, she knew, they would be able to say such things to each other.

While Ned was off trying to track down bus schedules on the phone and Fern was in the kitchen packing a lunch for Rose, Kyle asked for a private meeting. They walked out into the meadow above the barn and kept walking. Before long they both knew where they were going. It was a demanding climb, more so because of the fatigue caused by the short sleep after their marathon conversation the night before. Still, there was a sweet sadness in these last moments together, and the minutes flew swiftly. When they stood at last on the rim of Castle Sainte-Croix, neither Rose nor Kyle could find words to speak. The wind blew sharply out of the north, and it sounded much like the faffling of banners. By some quirk of sound, a distant train crossing the patchwork of lowland in the east sounded its horn, and trumpets blared all around them, swords clashed, fire crackled.

"You should stay", the boy said.

"I have to go, Kyle."

"I don't understand why you have to go."

"It is time."

He mumbled something, then stuck a hand into his jacket pocket and withdrew a lump wrapped in tissue paper. He thrust it into her hand.

"It's a present for you."

Hesitantly she opened it. Inside was the chip of mortar on which Roland Bredon had inscribed the tiny flower.

"It's a rose, I think", the boy said. "Maybe the Tudor rose. Anyway, it's a rose, and you're a rose, and you should have it."

She stared at the gift lying in her opened palm, hardly daring to look up at him. When at last she did, she noticed the expression on his face, a neutral look hiding deep emotion. Part of the emotion was the loneliness of an only child, a boy who had found a friend, moreover a friend with whom he had shared an adventure and a great secret. That she was leaving was causing him pain. This moved her greatly. She saw also the profound generosity of his nature, the confidence and kindness within him that seemed to have sprung full-grown from the millennium-long Bradon wound. Light was in him, and soon a greater light would come to him, and it would spread to the rest of his family and to others, and where it would end none could yet tell.

But his pain was not unmixed with other feelings. No doubt he knew that the treasure they had found could not remain in the hands of a single family, because it was a national heritage. It would go to a museum, probably. The site of the castle would become an attraction for lovers of history and for tourists; archaeologists would be unearthing its grounds for years to come. It would be taken from the hands of its discoverer and given to others. Only for a few fleeting moments would he be able to hold it as his own. And though he might have kept the small piece of mortar without guilt, might have freely possessed it as the memory-stone of his great adventure, he was now giving it away. This was costing him much, though not a trace of struggle could be seen on his face.

She put it back into his hand.

"It belongs with you, Kyle."

He flashed a somber look at her.

She put her hand on her chest. "I carry it, and you, here."

That night, she boarded the Dover-to-Calais ferry under a blanket of crystal stars. Throughout the voyage she remained on deck, bundled in her parka, as close to the bow as she could get. There was a passenger bench by the forecastle, and she sat down on it. The evening was chilly, with an east wind blowing off the coast of France, heaving the ship up and down. The decks were deserted, and she was glad of the solitude.

Slowly, slowly, she felt England shrinking behind, and with it the events of her visit assumed their place in memory. Neither dissipating nor declining, they withdrew into concentric levels, details merging into each other but not dissolving: first the shape of England, then the countryside, followed in sequence by the Berkshire hills, the lonely stretch of road past Bradon's property, the farm itself, the castle, the cellar, the secret chamber, the ivory box, the coating of wax, and at the core of it all— the cross. And in the heart of the cross, a *word*. And that word was connected to its source, the cry uttered on a Cross atop the place of the skull in Jerusalem. The place of death that became the place of life.

Ships passed to the west heading toward England, floating castles emitting sparks of fire and trumpet blasts, unfurling banners of faint music. The wind sang too, the holy and familiar wind, the wind that connected all places on earth, that flowed unceasingly throughout time, bearing the sounds of human song, and cries of agony and loss and longing, words of despair and words of hope.

At a point of the crossing where Rose estimated the ferry was halfway to Calais, she stood and went to the railing. Inhaling the sharp clean air, her heart full of peace, she reached into her deer-hide sack and withdrew a small object. Opening her hand, she rolled it around in the open palm for a few moments, watching the moonlight and starlight try to illuminate what she held. But it could not receive it, for its surface rejected the light. With all her strength, she closed her fist on the object and hurled it far and high over the sea. The black pearl hit the surface of the blacker waves and sank without a sound.

25

The sea heaved beneath her feet, as it had unceasingly for days. She clung to splintered boards beneath the mast, crying, though no tears would come because she was parched and her body had none to spare.

Ay, ay! The beast beneath the waters opened its mouth around the flimsy raft, the dead and dying slipped off the edge into its throat, the acid-yellow sky boiled with rotting cloud. She stared at the madness of her fellow survivors, recoiling from their furtive glances as their eyes recoiled from hers, for they had eaten human flesh.

The black man pulled himself to his feet on the upper edge of the groaning timbers, gripping the ropes, shouting to make himself heard above the wailing sheet tied to the crossbar. His arm raised to the heavens, he waved his shirt at a horizon that reshaped itself with continuous and violent randomness.

"Sails!" bellowed the black man. Rose scrambled to her hands and knees, her spine contorted in agony. Gathering her last scraps of strength, she crawled up the slope of the raft, then braced herself to resist the downward catapult as it slipped over the crest of a mountain wave and plunged again.

"Where?" she cried.

"There!" said the black man as the raft reached the bottom of a valley and began to rise again. He pointed to a dot of white in the distance.

Through the writhing torsos Rose continued to crawl forward, seeing in her passage all the states of man: the despairing, the self-sacrificing, the faces taken by insanity, the pleading, the whining, the hating, and the hoping. Now many bodies clawed forward on either side of her, rising to their knees, lifting their arms in gestures that no rescue ship could have seen.

"Is it going away from us?" she screamed at the black man. He looked down at her for a second or two. She thought she saw in his eyes, beneath the terror and hunger that none of them had escaped, a sea of crystalline blue, warm winds scudding delicate waves across its surface, and silver fish flapping in a net that a man and a woman were spreading on a beach of white sand, laughing as their children danced along the endless shore.

"Is it disappearing or arriving?" Rose cried again, but the black man, with rake-scars across his chest and back from an ancient wrestling match with a beast that had sought to pull him down into the devouring undergrowth, did not answer her.

"An excellent question", said the voice of Dr. Ganze, the painting professor.

Rose blinked and stepped back. As if awakening, she found herself standing on a marble floor, her heart thundering, lungs rapidly inhaling and exhaling, in a museum in Paris.

She read the information plate affixed to the wall beside the painting.

> *The Raft of the Medusa*, Théodore Géricault (1791–1824), completed 1819, oil on canvas, 16 feet × 23.5 feet.
>
> During the Bourbon monarchy, a vessel of the Government of France, the *Medusa*, foundered off the western coast of Africa, with hundreds of men on board. Only a handful survived, after drifting for days on a makeshift raft. The artist depicts the very moment when the rescue ship is sighted.

Io! Io, it was the triumph of hope, not despair!

Flooded with gratitude, Rose sighed with relief.

Sensing the threat of oversaturation, she left the Louvre with no more than a few images in her mind. The Géricault was the most important she had seen so far, or the one most important to her. The painting was enormous, and this, combined with its painterly skill and the dramatic power of its subject matter, enabled it to overwhelm consciousness in such a way that it lived in her memory as—a memory of experience.

As she had every day during the preceding week, she walked through the streets of Paris to the *Chambre de Bonne*, a rented room under the eaves of a five-story eighteenth-century build-ing on narrow Rue S.-Sauveur, six or seven blocks north of the Louvre, on the right bank of the Seine. Each night the con-cierge gave her a bowl of soup, a plate of cheese, and a baton of bread. After supper, Rose climbed the staircase to the attic, where she said her prayers, read the Bible, and slipped into an early sleep under a goose-down duvet embroidered with white flowers.

The next day, following the directions in a guidebook, Rose picked her way through the labyrinth of the Louvre and found some paintings by Henri Rousseau. They were charming, but they were not the ones she was looking for. Retrieving from her deer-hide sack the now tattered volume Dr. Ganze had given to her years before, she flipped through it searching for the names of other collections containing works by Rousseau. To her delight she found that many of the best were in the Musée du Jeu de Paume, a gallery located somewhere in Paris. A close appraisal of her street map revealed the information that this museum was just a short stroll across the Tuileries garden bordering the grounds of the Louvre. Within fifteen minutes, she found herself standing in front of *La Charmeuse de Serpent*. Then she fell inside it.

Eden was inhabited by the subtlest of shadows that rustled through the high grasses and entwined the thickly-fledged trees. And Rose, standing naked among the lascivious flowers and burgeoning fertility of root, branch, and leaf, was drawn by the allure of a whisperer. *Beauty, beauty, beauty,* he breathed, in a voice that vibrated on the fracture line between hearing and unhearing. Who was he? If he spoke of beauty with such power, with such passion, he must be beautiful indeed. Taking up her flute, Rose played for him. Beauty flowed from her heart and took wing in the air. The waves rippled and undulated, soared high and plunged and soared again, seeking him.

A long black serpent dangled from the branch above her, listening.

"You are beautiful beyond compare," he whispered, "as dark as rosy ebony. You could be free of the chains of the one who bent you and burdened you. Straight I shall make you, if you come to me, painless I shall make you, and rich in powers, knowing good and evil, so that you might paint the black and the white in their true order, for they are both waves of the eternal light. For darkness is light, the light which is the greatest, for it is above the limitations of the human eye."

"Is it not below?" Rose asked, her flute song faltering.

"Come to me, and I shall explain it to you. All things shall I explain to you."

"God forbids it", Rose said nervously, her thoughts clouding and her senses blurring by the pleasure of his voice.

"God?" said the serpent. "Who, really, is 'God'? Do you see God?"

"I do not see him with my eyes, but with the eyes of my soul."

The serpent smiled. "Many are the dreams which flow through the mind, the *anjeni* and the antique fables. Gone are they; never did they exist. Yet now you see before you, with the eyes of your flesh, the one who has existed from before the beginning of the world."

Rose lowered the flute and fell silent, for it seemed to her there was no reply to this. Still, he was a serpent, and serpents, no matter what they might tell you, were deceivers.

"I am always willing to discuss these matters", he said, after an appraisal of her silence. "Perhaps I have been wrong. Perhaps there is a God, and I am but a creature like you."

Looking up at him with surprise, and a flicker of awe, Rose wondered if it were possible to convert the serpents. Could it be that they would one day bow before the King of Heaven and Earth?

"Beauty is from him", she said. "Let me play upon this instrument and sing of his beauty so that you might understand and rejoice."

The serpent withdrew from her a little, so subtly she did not notice.

"Oh, yes", he hissed gently. "Come closer that I might hear you the better."

She took a step toward the tree. The flute at her lips blew the clear air of Eden into melodious notes. They dissolved into each other and reverberated throughout all matter, making the waters roll, the feathers of the strutting ibis vibrate, the podded flowers burst on their stems, exuding a perfume of such heavy sweetness that the fruit in the trees dropped to the earth and the spears of jungle growth shot upward. Black snakes lifted their heads from the grass all about her and began to dance. Their bobbing and weaving enchanted her, and she could not tear her eyes from them.

"What power you have", said the serpent in the tree. "What great power and knowledge are within you, that you shake Eden to the core and win the hearts of all things." He dropped closer. "Io, Io, Rose, you are *La Charmeuse de la Création*, you are the Queen and Concubine, you are worthy of worship. Come to me and together we shall rule all things. I am your missing part. I am the shadow that you have not loved within yourself, for you were made for me and I for you, and together we belong. When you love me, when I am in you and you in me, then we shall rule the light and the darkness, for they are one and the same."

"I . . . I do not know", she said uncertainly, taking another step toward him.

"A thousand Binemins shall I give to you," the serpent whispered, "each more handsome and more strong than the other, each intoxicated with your beauty, yes, each shall worship you. And a thousand praises shall come to you, as the pictures and the poems and the songs flow from you into the cold dark barren lands outside our garden. They will look to you, Rose, as the voice of light, and the path to light, and together we shall lead them to freedom."

The serpent waited.

And Rose wondered why she was a weeping person, a nothing-person, bearing constant grief within her heart. Why, if God was love, had he made her so ugly, when beauty was bursting forth in every other part of creation? Why was she always in pain? Perhaps she had misunderstood everything.

"God said no", she murmured uncertainly, unable to meet the little pin pricks of the serpent's eyes, fixed upon her.

"God said no?" the serpent smiled indulgently. "Did God say that? Did God really *mean* that? Surely he did not mean *that*?"

"I . . . I . . . do not know."

"You do not know", the serpent whispered pressing close again. "You do not know because *he* does not want you to know. Come to *me*, and then you will know."

Rose stepped so close that the glittering eyes were next to hers, his skin now purple, now silver, now black, now white.

Ay, ay! Kije-Manito! Kije, kije, kije! Holy, holy, holy Lord Jesus, save me!

"Tell me, Miss Wâbos", said the voice of Dr. Ganze, as the garden melted, all the colors running into muddy browns. "Tell me, what is the intention here? Is the woman charming the serpent or is the serpent charming the woman?"

"They seek to charm each other and are both deceived."

"An excellent answer", he replied.

Shaking, Rose stepped out of the garden.

"I am in France", she said. "Yes, that is where I am. I am *here*, not there."

Art lovers strolled this way and that.

"Wonderful colors——" said one.

"Sensual——" said another.

"I wish this woman—is it a woman or a circus midget?"

"Shhh, she can hear you——"

"I wish she would stand aside and let others look——"

Rose moved on, still frightened by her experience, alarmed most of all by the strange dialogue with the serpent into which she had so easily slipped.

In the next gallery she came upon another painting by Rousseau. Dr. Ganze had called it *Der Krieg*. Its French title was *La Guerre*; in English, *War*. Now the full impact burst from the imprisonment of the faded print in the art book. It roared, whinnied, and exploded in the echoing space. Approximately four feet high by six feet wide, it was the scene that she knew so well, yet had not truly seen until this moment: a child astride a black horse rode through the ruins of a bombed forest. The child held a blazing torch in one hand and a daggerlike sword in the other. Its mouth screeched, its eyes blazed. The horse's hoofs galloped over a field of naked dead soldiers. A flock of crows settled on the human carrion, and in the background beyond the forest were vistas of devastated lands.

Ned Bradon lay beneath the hoofs, mouth gaping.

"Ah, ah," said the blue eyes and the startled smile of the hollow human face, "I am a small thing. I am the powerless, I am the broken, I am become the food for lesser creatures. I am alone in the empty universe, where only the strong speak a final word."

And Kyle his brother, gazing at the empty eyes, was pierced by the dagger of reality and wished to lay himself down with all the other dead. He had been a tall youth running upon the frozen soil of Flanders, brandishing weapons without conviction, earning medals without meaning, confused and divided, pleading with the absent God that he might not be forced to shoot another boy coming at him. Thus was his heart torn. Thus his mind broken. Thus he ran from the killer arisen like a giant within himself.

He hated himself for escaping out into the broad earth, in search of the places where peace and mercy survived in islands of sanity. But the *neshiwed* stalked him, for it was within him. And he fired a bullet at the empty heavens, then wept in shame.

"Speak to me, speak to me, O my Father", he cried. "O my true Father, why am I so alone? Why do I live when all flesh is falling and my brother is dead, and even my family has taken up the sword, wishing me dead because I brought shame upon them?"

Then Oldmary spoke to him without words, and they embraced, and from their embrace came fruitfulness, and the fruitfulness restored his hope. Then came the death of his children, and this broke his heart utterly, and he came at last to a bed of sickness, where there was no more possibility of flight. She held his body as it was taken, and prayed with him, and he looked up, yes, he looked up into the sky, and the bullet he had fired fell to earth. Hands came down to him, and received him.

"I am your true Father", said the warm hands upon the cold and shuddering body. "I am your Father, and no longer shall you call yourself abandoned. For the path of desolation need not lead to eternal absence, but to the gate of eternal life. See, you have cried to me, and I have heard. Now do you enter the gate of purification, which is love."

"I am dying, Mary", he said to his wife, in the smoke-filled shack by Crazyman River.

"Kyle, Kyle", she cried, washing his face with the tears of her own abandonment, as he grew still within her arms.

Ninety kilometers south of Paris, on the banks of the river Loire, not far from the city of Orléans, there stood a grand château built during the seventeenth century. This was the motherhouse of a once-great Order of nuns that had sent certain of their sisters abroad to the mission fields of New France. Although the nuns had now returned from there, and from many other nations, withdrawing like an ebb tide and shrinking in number, the château was still home to hundreds of sisters.

The driveway wound upward through sloping geometrical greenways and gardens separated by wrought iron fences, ornamental fountains, and marble Stations of the Cross, all of them covered with verdigris and damp mold. As Rose progressed through this scene of elegant decay, she saw here and there about the grounds elderly nuns clipping bushes or scattering seeds to flocks of small brown birds or merely walking, fingering their rosaries. Some, though not all, were dressed in the habit that Rose remembered so well from her childhood. It was the apparel of love, and thus she could not help but feel the amplified presence of love as she remembered Mère Jean, Sister Madeleine, Sister Clothilde, and the others.

Because she had come unannounced, she felt trepidation when she rang the bell in the entrance foyer and stood nervously waiting for someone to come to the wicket. When the portress arrived, Rose asked to speak to Mère Jean de la Croix, but the woman was somewhat hard of hearing, and this, added to Rose's French, made for a rather protracted exercise. In the end the nun threw up her shoulders in consternation. "*Mère Jean de la Croix? Qui est-elle? Mais, nous n'avons pas des noms anciens. Ils sont démodés.*"

This was dismaying, because Rose knew her several *ningâs* only by their traditional religious names, which were now, apparently, "outmoded".

"Mère Jean was among the sisters who returned from Canada", she explained.

"Ah, yes, yes, yes, now I know the ones you mean. Unfortunately, several of them are deceased, I regret to say."

Rose's heart sank. Which ones were dead?

"What am I to do?" said the expression on the sister's face. Then she was struck by a thought.

"I know what we will do. There is a sister who was with the ones who went to Canada. I will ask her."

Rose's excitement increased as the portress spoke into a black telephone.

"She is in her studio", the nun said after hanging up. "She will be right down. Please wait over there."

Rose took a seat on one of the wooden chairs lined up along the wall. Five minutes passed, during which her heart began to beat with anticipation. Studio? Was it possible that Sister Madeleine—?

The question was answered by a figure emerging from an elevator at the end of the foyer. A woman in her sixties bustled out of it, solidly built but by no means fat. She wore a tan pantsuit and low-heeled shoes. Her hair was dyed a satin-gold that perfectly matched her clothing. On her chest was pinned a small bare cross of silver.

"*Bonjour*", said the woman approaching with an outstretched hand. "You are a visitor from Canada, I hear? I was once in Canada, many years ago. I am Sister Paulette Gagnon. Can I help you?"

Even as she asked the question, her eyes grew startled and began to blink rapidly.

Her hands fluttered on her chest. "*Quelle surprise!*" she cried. "Can it be? Can it be you?"

"I am Rose Wâbos, Sister. Do you remember me?"

Tears spurted from Sister Madeleine's eyes as she flung her arms about Rose and crushed her. The little hands stroked the tragic spine, the tears began to flow.

"*Ainsi, ma chérie, tu retournes enfin!* At last I see my little *fleur de la terre sauvage!*"

Standing back a pace, she held Rose by the shoulders and inspected her up and down.

"But you do not resemble yourself, my dear", Sister Madeleine said in English. Then she let her go and began to wipe her eyes. "*Pardon*. It is so many years. So long I have remember you, Rose, and ask *le Bon Dieu* to guide you."

"Thank you, Sister."

"Are you well?"

"I am well."

"But why are you here—in France?"

Rose explained that the purpose of her journey was to acquaint herself with the art of Europe.

"Ah, a pilgrimage of culture! Then it is as I had hoped. You are still the artist. But of course you are! When the letters ceased, we were so worried about you. But Mère Jean told us to be confident. Our Rose is in the hands of the Great Artist, she said. Thus, I am certain you are famous. Very, very famous. Is it not so?"

"Not at all famous", Rose smiled.

"No matter. You have come, and this is the only importance. Oh, my dear, what a *fête* we shall make of it."

Rose laughed. Yes, beneath her new attire, Sister Madeleine was still the same person. At any moment she might pop a chocolate bonbon into Rose's mouth or drop onto her chubby knees to scrub a floor. Or throw a lump of red clay onto a tabletop, where she would beat it into submission.

She laughed again, and Sister Madeleine began to giggle through her tears, though clearly she was analyzing the weary face before her, the broad brown flesh that had replaced the vanished prettiness, the wiry native hair completely gray and badly cut, the hunched body that had not ceased to contract over the years. A sadness crossed Sister Madeleine's face as she noted with dismay that the child had become a bent old woman while she, the elder, had become vivaciously young.

Sister Madeleine sighed. They sat down side by side, holding hands.

"Now, *ma petite*, you must tell me all. All!"

In her diffident way Rose described the events of recent years, culminating in a description of her art exhibit. She passed lightly over the rediscovery of her English family, trying to keep to the subject of art, which was her previous bond with the nun. As Rose talked, Sister beamed fondly at her, though she did not appear to be so much focusing on the contents of the visitor's remarks as she was simply enjoying an unsuspected resurrection. Of course, given enough time, they would have launched into a lengthy discussion of their favorite subject, and they were about to do so when a bell clanged.

Sister Madeleine got to her feet reluctantly. "Tsk-tsk, there is the call for prayer. I must go. You will remain with us, of course! We have the little *hôtellerie* for the pilgrims. You may stay as our guest."

"I would be grateful for this, Sister Madeleine."

"Ah, *non, non, non*, you should call me Paulette", said her friend. "Those days are gone now. But I am the same." She thumped her chest, grinned, then fumbled in a pocket. Holding out her hand like an officious mother awarding a treat for good behavior, she dropped three cellophane-wrapped candies into Rose's open palm.

"*Les bonbons, sans sucre. Ce sont pour les diabétiques.* Now, I will take you to the guest house; then we shall see each other again after the supper."

As they proceeded down the waxed hallways, Rose asked, "Sister—Paulette—is Mère Jean—?"

"Mère Jean? Oh, you mean Sister Jeanne. *Oui*, Jeanne Blé is alive. Yes, very much alive, but not strong. You will see her too."

"And Sister Clothilde?"

"Alas, Clothilde is buried these five years. The other ones whom you knew—some have died, some have left the order,

716

some have left religious life altogether. It is regrettable. But—*tiens, alors*—it is new times for us all. The Spirit blows fresh air into the Church, does he not?"

No reply was possible because they had arrived at the door of the guest wing, and the nun in charge had begun to inquire of Sister Madeleine who the unusual visitor was and how long she would be staying. Sister Madeleine departed with promises of a reunion after supper. The guest mistress took over, and within minutes Rose was shown to the chapel, the refectory, and finally her room, where she was left alone with her thoughts.

That evening, after a small repast of bread, wine, and *omelette*, which she ate alone in the guest refectory, Rose went to the chapel to pray. It was larger and grander than any church she had seen in the New World, save for the shrine of St. Joseph, yet the atmosphere contained a haunting melancholy. So much did this contrast with the fabulous baroque ornamentation that she was greatly puzzled. There was a darkness, it seemed, brooding amid all the splendor. It was difficult to identify its source. Were the unseen angels lamenting in this space, or had the walls absorbed the private groans of countless nuns? If the former was the case, what precisely was wrong? If the latter, why had the cries of consecrated souls not risen to heaven and their residue been dissipated by grace? She did not attempt to analyze the situation, merely wondered at it, for it was inexplicable that in this place, the very source of the love which the sisters had brought to her as a child, there would be anything other than peace.

The Beating Heart was present in the tabernacle—she felt it. She knelt in the back pew and worshipped him. She prayed both heart words and mind words. But a certain knowledge came to her that while these were good, the Lord now desired something more of her. Going deeper inside herself she came to the center of stillness, to the place of emptiness, to the solid ground of her poverty. She rested there for a while, trusting that in the emptiness is the true listening.

He said nothing, merely smiled at her with the invisible radiance of his love. Acknowledging that everything—everything—was his gift, she smiled back.

"O my Lord," her heart said at last, "you know how small my love is! Io, how quickly I would abandon you, how easily I am confused and afraid. Ay, ay, my love is a tiny thing. How can I give you the love that your great heart deserves when I am so poor! Even so, this I give, this little scrap which is all of me."

Bells echoed in the chapel, and electric chandeliers hanging from the high ceiling suddenly lit up with a sharpness that hurt the eyes. Nuns dressed like Sister Madeleine arrived at random through different doorways and sat down in the front pews without bowing or genuflecting. There were about two dozen of these. A few minutes later more such nuns entered from a side door, and among them were three pushed in wheelchairs. The women in the wheelchairs wore their traditional habit, their backs were bent with age and their faces stared with rapt senility. They were parked in the wide marble space between the pews and the sanctuary. None of the women was younger than forty years of age.

After evening prayers, all the nuns exited quickly, save for a single black form in a wheelchair who remained motionless facing the altar. Sister Madeleine remained also. Standing, she scanned the empty pews of the chapel and spotted Rose in the shadows at the back. A cheerful grin lit her face, and she beckoned that Rose should come forward.

Contrary to Rose's expectation, the nun in the wheelchair was not Mère Jean. She was a small hunchbacked woman of very great age. Her neck was permanently bent so that her entire upper body was folded over the lower half. The woman turned her head sideways and peered up at Rose with eyes as clouded and watery as wet pearls.

"You come to us at last", she said in French.

"This is Sister Brigitte", Sister Madeleine explained in a low voice. "She has the disease of the mind and is not rational. But she demands to see the visitor."

Bending over the old woman, Sister Madeleine shouted into her ear, "She is here, the one you wanted to meet."

"Eh?" the nun croaked.

"The one you asked for."

Confusion crossed the face of Sister Brigitte.

"She is rather deaf", Sister Madeleine explained in a low voice. "And blind. Alas, it is the cataracts. The doctor says she is too old to have them removed. She is ninety-three years old. She was once the Superior General of the Order."

Rose knelt in front of the old nun and took her cool parchment hands in her own.

"*Bonsoir, ma Mère*", she said.

Slowly the nun's head moved to face Rose. Though she was sightless, something in her quickened. Her eyes watered.

"*Il m'avait dit que tu viendrais*", she mumbled.

"We don't quite know what she means," Sister Madeleine explained. "She thinks she knows you. She's being saying this for three days, and none can interpret her meaning. *Tiens*, tsk-tsk, it is a cross to grow old this way."

Putting her lips to Sister Brigitte's ear, Rose said, *"Oui, ma Soeur, je suis arrivée, comme le Bon Dieu L'avait promis."*

Standing back, Sister Madeleine folded her arms and observed with an expression of amused pity.

"She cannot hear you, Rose."

"I hear", said Sister Brigitte. "I hear you, though my ears do not hear you. I see you, though my eyes do not see you. For three days, he tells me you are coming."

To which no one could think of a reply.

"*Petite légionnaire*", said Sister Brigitte. "The refusal that I gave many years ago was a suffering for me and for you and for Mère Jean. It was the Lord's will."

Rose kissed the ancient hands.

"It was the Lord's will", Sister Brigitte repeated.

"Yes, it was the Lord's will", Rose replied, though she could detect no sign that the old nun had heard.

"*Le château de l'âme*," the quavering voice went on, "the interior castle, cannot rise unless the bastion of pride is leveled. The stones crumble, and only weakness is left. Then he comes. He comes to you, this I know, for he has told me so."

Rose squeezed the hands gently in affirmation. Sister Brigitte smiled.

"When all is taken away, nothing remains that is of you." Sister Brigitte's words stumbled. Her eyes began to wander. Her hands trembled.

Then the voice resumed: "When it is all gone, only *he* remains. He in you and you in him."

"Yes", Rose whispered into the deaf ear. "For he is love. He is all love."

"He is *sweet-fire*", the ancient voice whispered.

At the utterance of this expression, which until this moment she had thought was known only to herself, Rose fell into a deeper silence. She closed her eyes and it seemed to her that she floated down into the realm where souls perceive each other, and there she rested beside the soul of Sister Brigitte. Though it was a great soul, and though it had once been gifted with unusual powers of intellect and feeling, it was now that of a child. It was a small white bird with a flame flickering gently in its heart. It fluttered its wings, preparing to rise into the boundless sky. The two souls greeted each other and embraced.

"It is time to go back to the infirmary, Sister Brigitte", Sister Madeleine shouted.

Sister Brigitte said no more. Sister Madeleine looked significantly at Rose, frowned with sympathy, and wheeled the old nun away through a door into the cloister.

Ten minutes later, she bustled back into the chapel and said in a cheerful voice, "Now, we go to see an old friend."

Like Sister Brigitte, Mère Jean resided in the infirmary, in a section reserved for the bedridden. From the moment Rose crossed the threshold, she knew that Mère Jean had lost neither her reason nor her heart. The eyes sparkled in recognition, the expression on the shrunken face was one of profound joy steeped in patience and wisdom.

As Rose arrived at the bed and reached for the two hands lifted toward her, Sister Madeleine beamed and said, "I will leave you two alone. Jeanne Blé, Rose, have a lovely visit. As long as you like. I will return later."

For several minutes Rose and Mère Jean said nothing, contenting themselves with the reunion of hands and eyes. Whenever Rose attempted to say a few words, they died in her throat.

At last Mère Jean spoke. "My daughter."

"*Ma Mère.*"

"The years fly swiftly, Rose."

"Too swiftly, Mère Jean. I am no longer young."

"Nor I", Mère Jean said, amusement shining in her eyes. "Perhaps you have not yet noticed?"

They laughed softly.

"Oh, so many wonderful things has the Lord given to you, my Rose of the Ojibwe. Always I pray for you. Not a day has passed since we left Canada that I have failed to think of my children. Your letters told me much about your life, and after they stopped I listened for word of you in the silence. Now I read many more things in your face."

"What do you read?"

"That which I sensed from the beginning, from the very day

you came to us as a girl: that God's hand was upon you for a special purpose. That he would write a beautiful story with your life, if you agreed. It seems to me that you did agree."

"As much as I was able, *ma Mère*. I have understood little of it. I am often perplexed. I am not intelligent."

Mère Jean smiled. "The world has more than enough intelligence."

"What is the meaning of the story?"

"It is a hidden tale, Rose. Hidden even from your own understanding. If we were to know, would we not try to seize the pen from the author's hand?"

"Yet part of it becomes clear, year after year it grows, moving through the forest like a foot path, sometimes this way, sometimes that way. It is a long trail, always changing. I journey, journey, but have not yet arrived. And where I am to arrive is uncertain. Paradise? Yes, I believe in it, but I have not seen it. I tire, doubt grows, and I ask, Will I ever arrive? Then winter comes and the way is shrouded in snow, and all signs of the trail disappear."

"And you continue to walk."

"Yes, but I stumble over roots and branches, my foot slips into holes."

"What holes are these?"

"In my heart. There is a thing which worries me."

"Can you tell me what it is?"

"When the night grows deeper and the snow falls heavily, I cannot see. I lose my way."

"This is to be expected, my child."

"I know, *ma Mère*, and I understand that it is his way of leading me on the path of trust. Despite knowing this, and despite knowing about the many souls who have traveled this path before me, even so I begin to doubt. I bury myself in a dark insideness place like a rabbit in a burrow, and I begin to think he has left me alone in the forest. Then the wolf approaches. All warmth bleeds from the world, all colors are as nothing—only a dim memory of color. I love him. Yes, I love him, but in those moments our love too becomes a memory, it fades. And this is the most terrible thing of all, for I *know* that he is love, yet I feel helpless to love him. I am left alone with my fear."

Mère Jean gazed at her with affection.

"This too is the path."

"O Mère Jean, for you it is easy to understand!" Rose stammered. "You are surrounded by holy women, and you are always with him, but I—"

"You also are with him, and he with you. Always he is with you."

"But you are holy!" Rose burst out. "You are like the great saints, like the martyrs!"

Mère Jean shook her head. "Rose of the Ojibwe, do you not recall that we had this discussion many years ago?"

Rose shook her head.

Tears filled the old woman's eyes. "You call me holy because I am a nun? Ah, Rose. Little by little sanctity declines. Many are the voices that whisper in the ears of my sisters. Learned teachers come to us claiming superior knowledge. Yet they do not love the truth, for they do not love the Father. Pride. Subtle pride, the subtlest and most dangerous of all, for it is done in the name of God."

Mère Jean sighed so deeply that it came close to being a groan.

"My desires for holiness have been of little account—in fact they mean nothing. This is not what God finds pleasing in my soul. What pleases him is seeing me love my weakness."

"Love your weakness?"

"Yes, *love* my weakness, Rose. Love it—all of it, my littleness, my poverty, my blind hope in his mercy. Do not think this is a sad thing. No, it is a joyful thing—to consent always to remain without strength."

"I do not understand. Should we not be strong in order to do Our Lord's work?"

"We are to be strong with *his* strength, which is greatest when we are most weak. Surely you know this."

"At times I seem to know it, but when the light fails and he is silent, and deadly cold falls upon my heart, then I—"

"The strength he asks of us is the decision to trust him in all things, especially in the moments of greatest abandonment. Saint Thérèse of Lisieux says that true holiness consists in a disposition of the heart which allows us to remain small and humble in the arms of God, knowing our weakness and trusting to the point of rashness in his Fatherly goodness."

"Oh, that is so beautiful. It is especially beautiful for people like me, who are small from the start and are nothing but weakness."

Mère Jean smiled. "Precisely, my daughter. Thus, you swiftly drew near to the One who is always near to us. When I was young, I desired to be an outstanding saint. Of course, I was certain it would be for the glory of God. I was unusual in my generation because I was granted the opportunity to pursue advanced studies at the Sorbonne. During that period of my life, I admired immensely the Great Teresa of Avila, the Doctor of the Church, the gifted leader of souls. I thought that I would emulate her. Instead, our Savior gave me a humble task in a distant land, where my ambition and my degrees were of little importance. Thus, he brought me to live with his beloved children. It was Mère Brigitte who sent me to that dark forest— to the place I would rather not have gone. And there for the first time in my life I felt the taste of death—death to all that I had thought was myself."

"Did you regret coming to us?" Rose asked.

"In the beginning I did. But, little by little, it became the joy of my life. For he taught me the greatest and most scandalous lesson a soul can learn: that in losing everything, we find everything. In the dying I was reborn. In place of the Great Teresa he gave me his Little Thérèse. And he gave me you."

"Ay, ay, *ma Mère, ma Mère*", Rose sighed, stroking the old hands. "And he gave you to us. Where would I be without you? Where? I dread to think of it."

"So you see, Rose, he has held both of us all the while: me with my brilliant folly he has humbled, and you with your simple fidelity he has raised up."

"Am I raised up?" Rose said sadly. "I feel that I have failed him. For many years I have tried to paint the things of God, and still my work is poor."

"Poor? Even if what you say is true, Rose, it does not matter, for in your failure you may bring about a greater harvest for souls than if your work is praised throughout your nation and beyond. Perhaps the failure is a necessary sacrifice. Will there be a soul one day, I wonder, who happens to stop before a painting of yours and is struck a gentle blow in his heart? Will the Holy Spirit then speak to him, because of the word you have made flesh for his eyes to see? Will he perhaps turn to God and consider the impossible question?"

"What question, *ma Mère*?"

"Is God, after all, what he says he is? If he does ask this, God will answer him. This I believe. You must not doubt it. You may never see it; you may never know for certain; it may occur far from where you live or long after your death. But, because you existed, it will occur. You came into being, and you stood firm in the cold dark places of the world, you continued to walk through the forest in winter even when all bearings seemed lost."

"Do you really believe this?"

"I believe it."

"Trusting blindly—?"

"Yes, trusting that your abundant tears make the wilderness bloom, and your love makes your labors fruitful a hundredfold."

Sister Madeleine returned soon after, and inaugurated cheery repartee with Rose and Mère Jean, complete with dips into nostalgia. She chided the bedridden nun that it was not wise to exhaust herself with too much excitement. Mère Jean agreed (with a conspiratorial wink at Rose) that this was so. Sister Madeleine feigned a wounded heart, saying that she too had a right to some of Rose's time, and that a tour of the studio was next on the agenda. Agreement was reached all round that Rose and Mère Jean would meet again the following morning.

Rose was whisked off to a distant wing of the château, one whole floor of which had been set aside for Sister Madeleine's studio. There, Rose enjoyed seeing her old mentor's new art-work, which included semi-abstract clay sculptures of religious subjects. In addition, the nun had recently taken up arc welding and displayed her metalwork with particular pride. These items were of great size and entirely abstract. The tour completed, Sister Madeleine and Rose sat down and began a discussion on the nature of sacred art, a considerable traffic in *les bonbons sans sucre, pour les diabétiques,* and a trade of old memories from the school at Thunder Bay.

Sister Madeleine's laughter pealed loudly and frequently.

"Ah *oui, oui, oui,* and do you recall how Madame Boyle threatened me with the meat cleaver and the sherry bottle and mocked my French—I mean my English?"

"And Long-John, Sister? Do you remember Long-John?"

Guffawing, Sister held her belly and rocked. "How could I forget? The three-legged terror! *Le pauvre chien!* With the little knitted booties on his three feet so the ice would not make his paws bleed?"

"And the strawberry ice cream?"

"Yes, yes", Sister Madeleine cried, rocking back and forth, her hands fluttering on her chest. "The big tub of *crème-glacée* for Madame Boyle. She call me—" Sister Madeleine collapsed in a fit of hysterical giggles, face bright red, tears dripping out

726

of her eyes, "—she call me the *blimp*, she call me the *bleating great noon!*"

It took some minutes for Sister to quiet herself, for whenever she seemed to bring herself under control a fresh fit of giggling broke out.

"Ah, those were fine days, were they not, Rose? So much fun we had. So many beautiful *fêtes*! Mmmm, *la peinture*, *le chocolat*, the red clay. The winter blizzard outside, warm cocoa and *les Beaux-Arts* inside. Happy were those days—gone forever those days."

A shadow slipped across the sister's face. Jovial as always, filling every space with her big personality, she was still a child at heart, and thus she now experienced a small sadness as she meditated on the transitoriness of time. The mood quickly passed.

They talked long into the evening. Sister Madeleine asked about various aspects of Rose's life, but she could not seem to focus on detailed descriptions. The smallest scraps of information were sufficient. Nothing more was desired. She asked about the *bête*, Monsieur McKenna, but Rose knew nothing. She asked about girls whose names she remembered, but Rose had lost contact with them all and could not say what had become of them.

When Rose attempted a brief account of Tchibi's life, Sister Madeleine's attention visibly wandered, for she did not remember the boy. Interrupting the tale with sighs of resignation over the fate of *les pauvres sauvages*, she turned the subject to the wonderful changes in the Church, to its newfound "creativity", and to the freedom she had enjoyed in obtaining her master's degree in theology. Rose understood little of what Sister tried to convey in this regard and found her own mind wandering. At eleven o'clock they both agreed that it was getting late and that tomorrow they would have plenty of time to catch up on old news. Sister Madeleine walked her back to the guest wing, kissed her on both cheeks, and said good night. Rose entered her room, prayed, and drifted off to sleep gazing at a full moon that edged through the black lace trees outside her window.

Rose remained at the château for a week. During that time she enjoyed several visits with Sister Madeleine and Mère Jean. Only once did they meet all together, for the levels of communication between Rose and the two nuns were somewhat at odds. With Sister Madeleine there was affection, a mild distance, and the mutual exchange of information that evoked old memories, memories that had altered in Sister Madeleine's mind like aging wine in which the impurities had settled and any hint of sharpness evaporated. It was primarily nostalgia; moreover, it was plain that the nun was not so much interested in Rose's life as she was in the recapture of a portion of her own past. Clearly, the woman felt that she had gone on to greater things, such as theology and a position of some influence in the Order. The part of her personality that was most childlike revived in Rose's presence and seemed to give her much pleasure.

With Mère Jean, however, Rose's discussions were of a different kind. There was little reminiscence. There seemed no need for it because the past was immediately accessible for Mère Jean. Whenever she inquired about people known to them both, the nun always penetrated to the core of the issue: their unique characters and what had become of their lives.

She asked about Binemin Edzo. Did Rose know what had become of him? Rose told Tchibi's story in entirety, a tale that took most of one long afternoon. Mère Jean did not once interrupt, though from time to time she sighed, or her eyes grew moist, or she closed them for a moment of silent prayer.

"I remember him so well, Rose", she said at last. "Such a very little boy in some ways, with no one to care for him. No protection from the ones without conscience. To this day I see his face, fighting back tears as he told me about the sin of the man who ruled the senior boys. Oh, the pain of those little ones! It is a grief that does not depart. And grief mounts upon grief as sin spreads in the world. Without our Savior, how quickly we would despair over the state of man."

"After all these years, *ma Mère*, the question still haunts me. Why did God permit it? Why?"

"This question can be answered only by a man dying on a cross. And the man is God himself. He is suffering in us. And with us. And for us. He is in agony until the end of the world. We are not abandoned, Rose, never are we abandoned. Binemin Edzo was not abandoned. The Father sent you to him at the end."

"And the Father sent him to me."

"He loved you, that boy."

"I think this is so. It was a broken, imperfect love, as all human love is. It was not the love between man and woman. It was like brother and sister, though—"

"Though in your heart", Mère Jean said gently, "it was more than that."

"Yes. But my ugliness made a wall around me. Marriage was impossible."

"But the language of the heart, heart speaking to heart, this was not impossible."

Rose, feeling that there was nothing she could hide from Mère Jean, put her face in her hands, her throat swelling with sobs.

"To be fruitful is the deepest desire of the heart, is it not?" said Mère Jean.

Rose nodded blindly.

"The fertility of the soul was created in us for a holy purpose—for the generation of life. All souls desire children, even when they know it not, even when they vehemently deny it."

"I longed for children, *ma Mère*. To hold them in my arms.

To feed them. To love them. To give them strength and joy. To send them into the world with grace in their hearts."

Now she wept.

"When I was a child, I longed for a mother, and in time God gave me many mothers. I asked for a brother, and he gave me Tchibi. I asked for a father, and he gave me Hugo."

"You see how generous is the Lord, my Rose?"

"Yet in the secret places of my heart I have asked for a child of my own. Over and over again I have asked this of him. But he has given me none."

"Ah, Rose, *ma petite rose*. All is coming to you, full measure, pressed down, and running over."

"My life, *ma Mère*, my life. What is my life? It is cold and dark. It is barren."

Stroking Rose's head, the old nun whispered, "No, this is not true. Light and warmth are ever in you—in you more than anyone I have ever known. As for barrenness—yes, your womb has never held a child, and now it seems it never will. Yet how many are the ones you have carried in your heart, never to depart. You *are* a mother, Rose. You are a mother to them and perhaps to more people than you guess. Countless souls whom you will never meet, *en l'esprit et en la fécundité de l'art*. The word of love sows life in the world. And in this you are very fruitful."

Drying her eyes, Rose murmured, "You think too much of me. It is your own heart that is fruitful."

Mère Jean smiled at her and said nothing.

On the day of her departure, the sun broke through the late autumn overcast, a warm wind blew up from the south, and the château's park was filled with a great variety of singing birds. Through the hallways and in the chapel an atmosphere of energetic enthusiasm prevailed. Windows were thrown open, laundry flapped on lines, the convent cats sat in puddles of light on stone walls, cleaning their fur. In the gardens sisters laughed as they chatted to one another, pruned apple trees, planted flower bulbs, raked leaves.

The nursing sister in charge of the infirmary agreed that Rose could take Mère Jean for an outing on the walkways of the convent grounds. Mère Jean was lifted into her wheelchair by a hefty nun and bundled in blankets and scarves. Her weary eyes danced with the adventure. As Rose pushed the chair out into the back garden, the wheels rolling and bumping over the uneven flagstones, color appeared in Mère Jean's cheeks.

Neither of them said a word. Rose sensed that she would probably never again see Mère Jean on this earth and supposed that the nun was not unaware of this.

Passing a dry fountain, Mère Jean made a gesture that they should stop for a moment. The green residue in the marble basin was evidence that the water had only recently been shut off to avoid the risk of a winter freeze. In the center a statue of the Virgin Mary stood on a marble globe atop a fluted base. Around her head was a crown of twelve stars. Her foot crushed the head of a serpent.

"Before I went to Canada, I came to this spot to pray", Mère Jean said. "I was upset. I was disappointed. I washed my hands and my face in the beautiful spring water that flows here. I asked our Blessed Mother for a spirit of obedience. I asked her to cleanse me of my pride—and O how great and subtle was my pride, Rose, far greater than I imagined at the time. Of course, I had a correct distaste for human pride, and I acknowledged that like all men I was tainted with it. However, I was certain that it was only a minor flaw in me, a whiff that I could scarcely detect in myself. Little did I know what she would accomplish. Little did I know how much she would teach me. Ah, my Mother", breathed Mère Jean gazing up at the statue.

"Ningâ", Rose whispered.

"I did not know her in those early years. But in the years that followed, she took me in her arms and held me. Slowly, slowly I came to know her. Do you know her, Rose?"

"In my thoughts I know about her and revere her and pray to her. Yes, with faith I know her. But not in my heart. Why this is, I cannot say. I do not understand."

Mère Jean made no reply.

The dinner bell rang, faint and hospitable, from an open window of the château. The time was growing short, for Rose's train would depart at one o'clock in the afternoon. They returned to the convent by another path. When they reached the ramp leading to the infirmary wing, Rose paused.

"Mother—"

"Now we part, Rose. But not forever."

"Mother, do you have a word for me."

"A word?"

"A word I might carry with me through the cold dark barren lands, that I might warm myself by it in the darkest nights, in the depths of winter."

Mère Jean grew thoughtful. "So many things I would say to you, my child. . . ." Her voice trailed off.

"Will our Father not speak to me through you? Will he not give me a word from his ocean of silence?"

"I will give you what is in my heart, Rose of the Ojibwe. This poor heart, this poor, poor heart that has loved so little. I am drowning in his ocean. I am dying, and as I die I know less and less. Yet I believe I am drowning in the mystery of his love. This is my faith. On this my whole life is based."

"What is in your heart for me?"

"Take my hand, child."

Rose knelt beside the old woman and took both hands in her own.

"I will tell you, Rose. You alone will test the truth of it. Life teaches us what we need to know, if we will accept it.

And in life we must always trust, even when death seems triumphant."

"Still I do not understand."

"We have spoken many words to each other since you were a child. Of my words little was important. Indeed, you may forget them all if you wish. Remember only this—remember that when everything is taken from you, then shall everything be given to you."

Rose drew back. Though she understood the principle involved in the comment, and though it was a spiritual insight that she had meditated upon not infrequently, it now spoke to her with an immediacy that was absolutely personal. She felt a moment of dread.

Mère Jean leaned over and kissed her on both cheeks.

"Let us go, Rose. We do not want to be late for lunch."

With Mère Jean's words echoing in her heart, Rose desired to visit Lisieux. She spent three days there, residing in a pilgrim's hostel, spending much of her time in the cathedral and the chapel of the Carmelite convent in which Thérèse had lived and died. Hungrily did she gaze upon the enclosure, longing to enter, knowing that she could never do so. Still, she bathed in the grace of it and learned afresh that God had forever affirmed the path of little ways.

A pilgrim she was now, and the pilgrim-way led her on to other sacred places of the land. In each shrine she prostrated herself on the floor, kissing the ancient foot-worn stones, feeling the presence of the many holy men and women who had trod this path before her. The sea of God was vast and deep, and no monster lurked beneath its surface. If one drowned in it, as had countless saints down through the ages, this was not a plunge into annihilation, but a sinking into the arms of fathomless love.

At Lourdes, she bathed in the cold waters of the miraculous spring and prayed many rosaries in the place where the Mother of God had appeared to Bernadette Soubirous. Rose's back was not healed, nor did the pain in it decrease, though near-intolerable sweetness enveloped her.

On the way back to Paris, she visited the incorrupt body of Saint Bernadette at Nevers. There she read the words of the Blessed Virgin: "I do not promise you happiness in this world, but in the next."

Rose had planned to see many more works of art, to travel to Spain and Italy as well. But she felt a sense of completeness and an urge to return home. Only one more painting did she desire to see, Esther's *Birds in Wartime*. At the Paris station, she boarded a train for Antwerp.

She spent three days in the old Hanseatic city, wandering about the streets. She splurged on a handmade lace kerchief that she purchased in a Jewish shop. She stared at the dangling hares, dripping blood in the market, straining to explain to herself why the scene was so familiar. And at last she found the museum where Esther's painting hung.

Birds in Wartime was approximately three feet square. In the foreground of the image, medieval Antwerp was on fire. Small dive bombers plunged like flies among the conflagration. Birds of all kinds rose through the flames into the sky. Dozens of birds, darting and weaving, all straining toward the pale blue serenity above. Children were standing in the streets below, engulfed by flames, buildings falling upon them, their mouths open wide, their hands raised to the departing birds, beseeching. The birds were the souls of the dying children.

Rose remained paralyzed in front of the work. When she fell inside, screams erupted from many small throats, screams like air raid sirens, the most terrible sound in the world, the cries of burning children. She pulled herself back, fighting the hallucination of smoke in her nostrils. The crackling flames and the roar of crumbling monuments faded too slowly.

Ay, ay, Rose gasped. *Esther, Esther, this was inside you! Did you see it with your eyes?*

Rose returned to the painting the following day, and the day after that. Finally, she could bear it no more and returned to France.

She thought that before returning to Canada she would like to visit England a second time. A reunion with the Bradons would undoubtedly be a joy to her, but this was not foremost in her mind. She felt that she should go to Birmingham and try to find the place called Kingstanding. Why she had not done so while traveling in England several months before was inexplicable. Now, however, she decided to cross the channel once more, in order to find the place where Hugo's path had nearly brought him face to face with the true King. She would go up to the door of the manor house where the picture of Christ had once beckoned to Hugo, and she would knock on it. The door would open and she would go inside to find what he had failed to find. God willing, she would bring it back inside her heart and transmit it to him at last.

As she prepared to buy a train ticket for the port of Calais, an invisible hand seemed to stop her. It did not command, but neither would it retreat. It merely imparted a mysterious knowledge that she should not go to Birmingham, and that if she insisted on doing so, exercising her free will, something important would be lost. This made no sense at all. In fact it seemed the opposite of what she presumed God would want from her. She wondered if it was a temptation. But there was a quality to the knowing that was without beguilement or pressure. In fact it was suffused with peace. It was a quiet thing, without emotion or drama, and she simply obeyed. The next day, she boarded a transatlantic jet bound for Montreal.

26

As she rode the municipal bus to St. Henri, she absorbed the atmosphere that surrounded her, appreciating its familiarity, yet suffering the disorientation of those who have traveled afar only to arrive home with changed eyes.

Hugo had not met her at the airport because he did not know when she was returning. She had not written of her arrival; she wanted to surprise him.

Dear Hugo. How she loved him. He had been a good father to her.

Rue St. Benoît was already bound in winter, ice slicking the streets, sidewalks speckled with salt crystals and dirty gravel. Boys clacked their hockey sticks under a street lamp at the end of the block. The air was biting cold, perfumed with a low-lying cloud of automobile exhaust and the smoke of burning furnace oil. The impending reunion converted all of it into pleasure.

Rose felt momentarily deflated when upon arriving at the house she found that the windows were dark. She thought at first that Hugo must be out at a cultural event or visiting friends. Climbing the front steps she saw that a square of plywood had been nailed across a glass door panel. The spare key was no longer under the mat. Thinking that perhaps Hugo was sleeping, she twirled the bell, rapped loudly, and waited. No lights went on inside the house.

She walked down the steps to the street and stood there a few minutes, at a loss for what to do. Then on a whim she went to the house next door and knocked. The neighbor, an ever-smiling Chinese woman with whom she had enjoyed a long relationship of courtesies, opened her door and nodded without undue surprise.

"You come back", she said. "Nice to see you."

"It is very nice to see you, too, Mrs. Li. I have just returned from my journey. I see that Hugo is not home. Do you know where he is?"

Mrs. Li's face withdrew into an expression of formality that expressed both sympathy and reserve. She was dressed only in a cotton housedress and slippers. There was not much flesh on her bones. She shivered and beckoned Rose into her front hall.

"Very bad thing. You go, he no eat."

"How did you know he wasn't eating?" Rose asked.

"Skinny, skinny, no grocery bag, no grocery bag every time. Just bottle."

Rose now realized what the observant Mrs. Li was telling her: that her worst fears about Hugo had been realized.

"Is he drinking?" she whispered anxiously.

The woman nodded, embarrassed by what she had to tell. "He bring many bottle his house. Bag of bottle in alley. I find. I take food to him. He no want. He no eat."

Mrs. Li's son managed a Chinese restaurant four blocks away. Food was a major concern in her life, after the primary one of family.

"I'm sorry, Mrs. Li. I'm sorry for the worry he caused you."

"No worry for me. I worry for *him*!"

"Where is he now, do you know?"

"Not good. Not good news. He in hospital. Ambulance come take him. Policeman. Fireman. Not good. Not good."

Rose's heart sank. "Do you know which hospital he is in?"

"Not know. Maybe fireman know."

"Fireman? Why did a fireman come to the house?"

Mrs. Li's eyes grew wide with the pain of what she must tell.

"He make big fire in back. Burn many thing. Burn porch back there. Burn my fence."

"Oh, no, I'm very sorry."

"No worry, no worry", her hands fluttered. "Insurance okay. Nobody hurt."

"He didn't burn himself?"

"No. Nothing. He walk. He make big joke. Like horse. Hit policeman. Not good, not good."

Rose thanked her and left. Uncertain about what to do, she decided to find a hotel for the night. It was now close to ten o'clock; she was exhausted and not a little alarmed. By the light of day, she would be able to assess the damage to the house and hopefully find Hugo. Navigating the slippery sidewalks she headed north to the east-west artery of Rue Notre Dame, turned onto it, and a few blocks farther along came to an establishment by the name of Hôtel St. Henri. Letters were missing from the sign, and the lobby smelled of sin, but she needed a place to rest for the night. The room was inexpensive, quiet, and more or less clean, if she discounted the stains on the rug and the mold in the bathroom. She fell onto the bed of sagging springs, prayed a rosary for Hugo and, after accepting the fact that there was nothing she could do until morning, fell asleep.

The next day was an exercise in frustration. She found the landlord's number in the directory, called him from the phone booth in the lobby and listened to an irritable lecture about Hugo's neglect to pay the last three months' rent, not to mention the damage caused by the fire he had deliberately lit.

"Deliberately?" Rose asked in a small voice.

"Deliberately. Drunk out of his skull, he decides to burn a bunch of junk in the back yard. So the idiot builds the fire right beside the kitchen porch. The porch goes up, and he just stands there watching it spread to the fence next door. Whinnying like a horse. Laughing too. The neighbors put it out."

"No one was hurt?"

"No one but me. I'm plenty hurt. I'm *financially* hurt! What d'you think this is, a charity hospital for dingbat artists?"

Rose patiently endured the rest of the tirade, calmed him down, and arranged to meet him later in the morning at the small *Caisse Populaire* bank near Rue St. Benoît. He was not late for their appointment, and when the money was safely in his hands, he made rueful and vague apologies for his temper. Rose told him that she understood. He handed her a key to the house. Then he asked who was going to fix the damage—he certainly wasn't going to pay for it, he had no insurance against that kind of thing, he wasn't covered for arson.

"I will see to it", she replied.

"Well, you'd better see to it soon", he said, "because the fire marshal's coming at the end of the month to have a look. And the house has a lot of problems. He said it has to be done and done right, or they'll condemn the building. So you tell Dyson for me that if I lose my building he's in deep—"

"I will, sir, I will tell him. And I will pray that you do not lose your building."

The word *pray* startled the landlord. He blinked twice and walked away.

By early afternoon, Rose had made several attempts to contact people who knew Hugo. The Cirque de la Lune was touring in the United States. Trevor was out of town. A secretary at the Ontolli-Metropol told her that Mr. Ontolli was not taking calls that day. Yes, the gallery staff had heard about Mr. Dyson's accident but had no idea where he was. An obstacle course of policemen, firemen, and ambulance companies promised to check their records but could not say offhand just where he had been taken. They dealt with hundreds of episodes each day in a city of this size, and Hugo's event had occurred weeks ago. They promised to call back when they had something to tell her. She gave them the phone number of the lobby desk and asked them to leave a message. Then she tried phoning the information desks of every hospital in the Montreal region. There were rather a lot of them, and none had a patient named Hugo Dyson.

Finally, in a state of desperation, she telephoned the *Montreal Gazette* and asked for the drama critic. When Clive came on the line, Rose identified herself and asked if he knew where Hugo was. There was a long silence before the answer.

"Yes, I know where he is. I'm not sure *you* want to know."

"What do you mean?"

"He's in the Sunnybrook Institute—a mental rehab center. An asylum, as we used to say in the good old days."

Rose sighed. "Is he very ill?"

"I don't know. I haven't checked. And, frankly, I won't be checking."

"But you're his friend, Clive."

"I *was* his friend. The question is, was he ever *my* friend? You know, when you get right down to it, I think all I've ever been for him was a useful resource. Buy the drinks, commiserate, admire his iconoclasm, ooh and aah over his charming *bons mots*. I'm sick of it."

Rose wondered at the man's intensity, as if he were trying to convince himself, or to justify himself. She said nothing.

"Look, Rose, Hugo's a walking disaster zone. Can I give you some advice? You're the kind of sensitive, generous-hearted person he'd gladly use for the rest of his life. If you want to go through all that, it's your right to do so. But if you do, you'll be feeding the sickness and punishing yourself."

"What is his sickness?"

"In technical terms, I have no idea. But he's self-destructive. Now, I'm willing to grant that maybe part of it's genuine desperation of some kind. But a good deal of it is self-indulgent posturing. It's an act, a bloody irritating and insulting act it is too, because he wants us to believe the act."

"What act is that, Clive?"

"The tortured-artist-too-sensitive-for-his-times act. Well, I've had enough of that self-pitying bilge. When Hugo Dyson is ready to pull up his socks and get back to his studio and work, then maybe we can talk friendship. Then maybe we can talk respect. Until then, he's a user and a liar."

"Does he owe you money, Clive? I can pay what he owes you."

"Yes, he owes me money. But that's not my motivation here, Rose, not in the least. And I suggest you refrain from doing anything so stupid as paying his debts for him. It's time he started taking responsibility for his own life."

"I'm sure he will, as soon as he gets well and comes home. His paintings have become so beautiful during the past few years. I know he will begin to sell them."

A painful silence ensued.

"Don't you know?" Clive said in a subdued voice.

"I've just arrived home. I don't know much about what happened."

"Hugo burned his paintings—all of them."

She found him where the orderly said he would be, outside in the sun on a paved walkway scraped clean of snow. Bundled in a parka, a blanket over his shoulders, he was sitting in a wheel-chair staring at the parklike grounds of the asylum. His hair had been cut. He looked rather distinguished, except for his beard, which had grown halfway to his waist and had turned completely white.

She knelt in front of him and hugged him.

"Hugo, it is me."

"Oh, it's you", he said after a long assessment of her statement. "I know you, don't I?"

"Yes, Hugo. It's Rose."

"Ah. Are you going away again?"

"No, Hugo. I'm home to stay."

"There is no home. I burned it."

"No, you didn't burn it", she said, choking. "Only the paintings are gone."

"All the pretty little horses. Husha-bye, don't you cry, go to sleep, little baby."

Rose began to weep.

"Don't cry, girl; don't cry for them. They are happy as they go up, for they are riders of the wind, as horses were meant to be. No longer do they feed on mutilated pride. As I lay within my silent cage, looking through the prism, I saw that I was no longer a certifiable human. I was a committable human, led on a merry chase across more than half this dark century. I was a pussyfoot, an artful dodger, sidestepping abandoned children, waifs and strays, foundlings, castaways, and junk-people."

"That is not true, Hugo, for you found me and took me in when I had no place to go."

"Child of the secret garden! Child of the microclimate!"

"Oh, Hugo, what has happened to you?"

Looking up with what seemed sudden clarity in his eyes, he said, "Rose?"

"Yes, Hugo, it's me. I'm sorry I stayed away so long. I couldn't help it. I didn't know you were sick."

"I'm not sick", he said.

She buried her face in his chest. He patted the top of her head.

"Can't think. They buzzed the electronic route maps. Circuits down, girl."

She groaned and prayed and groaned again.

"Not anyone's fault, really. Pain in the head. Pain in the *memoria*. Got to thinking, got to looking into the black paint. Got to using it again. Whiskey solvent couldn't wipe it off. Ha. Ha. I saw the mangled blackbird of my youth, and the coalman's hands picking up the body. Bird smashing against glass—artist's blindness in youth. Metaphor. Spuds cooking,

742

Mum yelling, me watching knife fights in the alley, the bigger boys. No, I said. Peace, I said. We don't have to do it like this. Man lives by his dreams and art, his symbols unlock, they wash the slum of the spirit clean of blood. Oh, yes, I suffered for it. Nobody knows how much, except Esther, but hers was so much darker than my little gossamer prisons. Ha. You don't have to go to Auschwitz. It's all here, right now. There's lots of things come crawling out of civilization's woodwork—gangsters, speculators, investment brokers, bounty hunters, executioners. I remember catching rides on the back of the knacker's wagon, horse blood soaking your trousers, drying there, stinking me, riding with neighbor boys in old war jackets dreaming of killing men, soaking up men's blood, drying on the hands like paint, stinking us, never washing off. We were the hoplite warriors off to Thermopylae, destined to be borne home upon our shields. We didn't know it then, because we were immortal, didn't know *we* would become the old smoke-cadgers on Victoria Street with their stumps and their unshaven chins and their memories of courage. They frost the alleys with their breath, rattling the trash cans for a meal. At night they roll against the curb and sleep, their shadows barely breathing. They lost the war, Dad said. But we won the war, I said. Yes, but they lost it, Dad said. Clipped their wings, it did. I didn't believe him. Death, the myth of those who cannot fly. And Pegasus is boiled down into glue and fertilizer. The men too, their bodies plowed under the black soil of Belgium. So, I had to do it, had to burn it, had to stop the machinery, you see. Otherwise it sucks you in."

"Hugo, the doctor says maybe you can come home soon, as soon as you're better."

"Better? What is better? Is capitulation better? You understand, don't you?"

"No, Hugo, I don't."

Hugo laughed with his old mirth.

"*Badratio*, girl, beware the *badratio*. Bad rats gnawing in the maze of the mind. The flick of shadow, the calibration of silence, the syringe and the glass tube. To measure the drip of distillate anthropos, to weigh the pneumato-volume of the soul, to reduce and convert from gaseous form into liquid into solid, into dust—that is our lot. Nothing more."

"Hugo, Hugo, I do not understand!" she cried.

He smiled at her.

"It is a fancy of the doomed that golden-haired chrysalides become the incarnation of light."

Suddenly his vision cleared and his eyes focused on her face. He rubbed a hand over his eyes.

"Oh, I am not myself."

"You are *you*, Hugo. Your mind is tired. But soon you'll get well again. Soon you'll come home. I'll look after you. We'll paint again, you and me."

"Ah, ah," he sighed, smiling, "imagination is the flashpoint of intellect and flesh."

"Please speak to me in ordinary words."

He gave her a perplexed look. "What is ordinary?"

A nurse arrived with a tray of medicine. She gave Hugo two pills from a tiny plastic cup and another cup with water in it. He downed them both and smacked his lips.

"Soma," he said. "How I love my daily dose of Soma."

"It's not Soma, Mr. Dyson. It's called—"

"Literary allusion, my dear. Banbury T. Alphas, Betas, Gammas, and Epsilons. Dangling feet swinging in the wind."

The nurse shook her head and went away.

Rose and Hugo sat together in silence looking out across the rolling white lawns on which iron deer stood immobilized. A stiff breeze came up. Rose shivered.

"Blow, winds, and crack your cheeks! Rage! Blow!" Hugo shouted.

"Hugo", Rose said shaking his arm.

"Rats in the caged face or rats in the caged brain—it's the same thing!"

"Hugo, listen to me."

"Eh, what?" he said tearing his eyes away from a galloping herd of clouds.

"Hugo, Hugo, listen to me."

"What? What do you want to say, girl?"

"If Esther were here she would scold you."

"True, but she's *not* here. Explain that one."

"Her words are here, words she purchased in the fires."

"What words, girl? Speak up! Speak up!"

"I decline to accept the end of man."

He blinked, his chin fell onto his chest, and from then on he would no longer acknowledge her presence.

Rose returned to the house on Rue St. Benoît with a heart that had rarely been as heavy as it was now. She unlocked the front door and entered the house as an explorer, or as the first witness at the scene of a crime. The building was silent, except for the creaking of decaying wood and the faint scurries and squeaks that seemed to come from the heating vents.

The electric power was off, the house was an icebox, though water still gushed from the taps when she turned them on. The water was rusty, stinking of iron. The house reeked of cat smells, for it seemed that no one had thought to let Goldie out, to feed her, or to change her litter box. Rose found her in the basement. The creature looked a little crazed and terribly thin, but jumped into her arms eagerly, alternately purring and yowling complaints about what she had endured. The basement needed a major cleaning with pail and shovel.

Braving the kitchen, she found the refrigerator full of rotting food, the sink crowded with dirty pots and dishes that had become a nesting place for parasites. She tried to wash them in cold water, but gave up, because her hands turned blue and began to tremble. The potted cactus on the window sill was dead. She taped a piece of plastic over the smashed pane, shutting out the wind. A phone call to the Power Corporation elicited a promise that the electricity would be turned on the following day, if a portion of the outstanding balance on the account were paid. Rose walked to the nearest bank and put a deposit on the bill. The dregs of a coal heap in the cellar provided enough heat for survival that night; she slept on the sofa beside the fireplace in the parlor.

At around eleven o'clock the next morning, all the lights in the house suddenly went on. The radio screeched, elements on the stove sizzled and glowed, the refrigerator buzzed, the fans of the plug-in heaters began to blow warm air, acrid with the smell of burning dust. Rose went from room to room turning off whatever was not needed. As she made her way through a landscape of disaster, she collected empty whiskey bottles, tin cans, and cracker boxes.

After a few hours the taps ran with warm, musty water. She spent the remainder of the day washing pots and pans, scrubbing the toilet and bathtub, scraping sticky rings of sugary coffee from end tables and floors. By nightfall, she was exhausted, though not exactly depressed, for physical labor had always lifted her spirits. Even so, the extent of damage was considerable, revealing how far Hugo had gone into the realm of his black mood.

She cooked some fish and potatoes that she bought at the local *épicerie* and drank tea so hot, sweet, and charged with memory that she felt sufficiently buoyed to attempt an inspection of the upper floors. With great relief she found that her bedroom and studio were unaltered, though there was a layer of dust on everything. The boxes of her unsold drawings and pastels sat where she had left them. A few unfinished paintings still leaned against the walls. But on the attic level she found devastation, the hard evidence of Hugo's despair:

746

brushes locked in dry paint stuck to the walls, footprints criss-crossing the floor—red, black, green, white—empty canvases slashed, every tube of pigment squeezed of its contents, the worms of color flung at the white plaster walls. Scribbled in pencil on a gap was the puzzling message: *Chaos Triumphing over Kosmos: Homage à Pollock, Homage à Riopelle, Homage à Dionysos. Entire mural available at discount rates. Prices slashed for Fire Sale. Open for bids forbids opening.*

Across the longer adjacent wall another message had been applied in large black letters: *Equus bids you adieu.*

There was not a single horse painting to be found. The heap of ashes in the backyard was all that remained of them.

"Ay, ay!" Rose groaned.

Little by little, the house came alive again. She hired a man to scrape Hugo's studio and cart away the junk. Another reglazed the kitchen window. A third purchased an old door at a used building supply lot, cut it down, and replaced the kitchen door to the back yard. He also replaced the charred porch with scraps of lumber that he kindly contributed on his own. With the last of her money she paid the water and fuel bills, apologized and negotiated with other creditors. She cried to herself at times, wondering what it was that drove people to knowingly destroy all they had worked for. Overcome by little flashes of anger, she admonished Hugo, who was safely shielded in a mental institution, protected from her uncharacteristic impatience.

"Io, Hugo, this is a childish thing you have done! How selfish of you!" But such outbursts were always quickly overcome and spurred her on to renewed prayer for his recovery. The pain in her back was severe, doubtless because of the unusual amount of physical work required for the triumph of order over chaos. She offered it to God for him, reminding herself that she was not really angry at Hugo, but at the darkness which had assaulted him.

Once again, the problem of money remained to be solved. A

747

trip to the Ontolli Gallery was unproductive, for a secretary said that Mr. Ontolli and Ms. Pannenburg were traveling in Italy and would not return for several months. He handed Rose over to the assistant vice curator, who told her that he did not have the authority to make purchases until their return. No, there were no openings for shows, not for another two years at least, maybe three years. Those decisions were always Mr. Ontolli's department.

"Aren't you the artist named Bineshi?" he asked.

"Yes, I am."

"You live with Hugo Dyson, don't you?"

"Yes", she nodded.

"That was an unfortunate thing to happen", the assistant vice curator said. "Poor man. Is he recovering?"

"Yes, I think so. The doctor says it will be slow."

"Well," said the assistant vice curator, "if you would ask Mr. Dyson if he has any works he wants shown, the gallery would be happy to be his agent. The Museum of Modern Art called last week—"

"Would you be interested in being the agent for my work," Rose asked, "even though there are no shows available?"

But the assistant vice curator said, "I'm sorry, but that sort of decision can only be made by Mr. Ontolli."

"But I thought you said—"

"Oh, but Mr. Dyson is a special case", the assistant vice curator hastened to say. "He's famous now, and so is Esther Dyson."

"I see", said Rose.

Over a period of three weeks, Rose went from gallery to gallery in the city, walking to save money, toting along a roll of pastels in her old deer-hide sack. At each she asked for a show, or at least a place on a wall where a painting or pastel might be displayed. No one had space, no one had an opening for a show for at least two years, maybe three. Whenever Rose produced the catalogue from her exhibit at the Ontolli Gallery, they all seemed impressed but wanted to know why she had not remained in Mr. Ontolli's "stable".

"I am not a horse", Rose replied. It was said without rancor, but it effectively ended any future discussion. She did not mean to be impolite, but the maze of closed doors was beginning to take its toll. She was in constant pain and hungrier than she had been in years.

She thought of trying to contact Euphrasia Morgan, but she did not know how to find her. If she had written to Rose, the letter had disappeared. Perhaps Hugo had inadvertently used it as fire starter when he burned his horses. She would have to wait for another letter, hoping and praying that Euphrasia would not interpret the silence as rejection. A begging letter to Mère Jean might produce a little assistance, but a response would be weeks in coming, and, besides, Mère Jean had nothing to give but her prayers.

A letter to her English family might also be helpful, but she knew that they were only land-rich and probably had no money to spare. Besides, it would be too humiliating to fulfill every rediscovered family's nightmare: the long-lost relative who shows up only for the purpose of borrowing money. To become a parasite in the eyes of the only people left in the world who were connected to her by blood would be too hard. It was pride, she knew, and she admonished herself severely for it. But it could not be overcome. She wrote a postcard to Kyle and another to his parents, telling them that she had returned safely to Canada and thanking them again for their hospitality.

Rose went to the shrine of St. Joseph for Mass the next Sunday and soaked in the radiance of the invisible light. It lifted her spirits greatly and calmed her fears. Yet no practical solution to her problem seemed to present itself. Later that day, she was rummaging in Esther's old studio in search of a fresh stick of charcoal, anticipating that she must begin to do her own work again. There, behind a leaning stack of unused stretched canvas, she found a single painting by Hugo Dyson. It was small; it was very beautiful and strong; it was a horse. Or, more precisely, a man and woman riding on a horse. The reins drew the horse's head back, its flashing eyes pointing to a starry sky, all four hoofs leaving the earth in a leap that implied ascension. Affixed to the back was a note, dated a few months before Esther's death.

> Dearest One,
> A trifle for our anniversary.
> My love forever,
>   Huggo

Rose now wondered why she had not seen the painting before. Why had Esther not hung it on a wall? Why had it been kept here as if hidden? Who had she been hiding it from? From Hugo, perhaps? Or had it simply been forgotten during the months of illness preceding her death?

In any event, it still needed to be kept away from Hugo's hands. She wrapped it in newspaper and took the next bus downtown to the Ontolli Gallery. There she navigated through the bureaucracy of employees and reached the highest-ranking staff member, the now familiar assistant vice curator.

"I have a Hugo Dyson for sale", she informed him without preliminaries. "Are you interested?"

"We might be", he replied.

Rose unwrapped the painting and put it on his desk. When he looked at it, his eyes widened.

"Yes, you are interested", she said in a businesslike tone. "I do not have time to exchange complicated discussions with you, sir. I would not know how to do it, so I will speak plainly. An important museum is interested in Hugo's work. This is the only remaining painting that he did not destroy. I will sell it for three thousand dollars."

"I will have to consult Mr. Ontolli, and we'll get back to you when—"

"No, sir. You have the authority to purchase this."

"Actually, we don't purchase works, we only take individual pieces on consignment. You'll be paid—*if* it's sold."

"I am familiar with the policies of the gallery. You do not take risks. Artists take all the risks. They risk their lives, and you risk nothing. Therefore, I offer you a choice. You will write a check for three thousand dollars, payable to Mr. Hugo Dyson, and then you may have the painting. But you must do it now. If not, I will go to another gallery, possibly the Montreal Museum of Fine Arts, where the officials are well aware that the Museum of Modern Art in New York is interested in Mr. Dyson's work."

He stared at her with disbelief and dislike. "You're demanding rather a lot. Surely you realize that a thousand artists would kill for a chance to be handled by Favio Ontolli—"

Rose rewrapped the painting in newspaper.

"Good-bye, sir", she said politely and headed for the door.

"Whoa, whoa, whoa, Miss, uh, Bineshi. Hold on a moment, hold your horses, ha-ha, a minute. I think we can do a little business."

He whipped a checkbook from his desk drawer and began to write in it with smiling concentration. He tore the check from the book and handed it to her. She placed the painting on his desk.

Rose looked him in the eye. "You would have made me wait and suffer, merely to show that you are superior and powerful", she said without anger. "That is dangerous for your soul. You must examine your conscience, or else you may find yourself in a place of torment."

He laughed.

"Okay, okay, lady, I'll examine my conscience. Boy Scout's honor."

Rose departed with the check, returned home, found an old bank book of Hugo's, deciphered his account number, went to his bank, and deposited the money.

"There", she said and went home to make a pot of tea.

On the following Saturday she took the bus to the asylum and upon arrival was very surprised to see that Hugo was walking about in the hallway, chatting with the other patients, joking with them as much as suspension of reason and imagination would permit, and generally looking like his old self.

His eyes watered when he saw her. He embraced her heartily.

"Rose, Rose my voyaging lass, you have returned! Welcome home."

"Thank you, Hugo. I am glad to be home."

"I can't believe it's been eight months since I've seen you."

"I saw you last week, Hugo. Surely you remember. And the week before that."

He looked at her quizzically. "But that can't be! I—no, I—I was sure it was a dream. Or maybe hallucination. You were quite irrational, my dear, quite inappropriate in your behavior."

She let the subject be. In any event, he was looking much improved.

"How are you feeling now?" she asked.

"Not bad. Circuits connecting again. The little ride on the electric grid scrambles and unscrambles the wiring. Soma helps too. Soma always helps the moods, though there's a price to pay in lost focus, lost attention, so to speak. Sorting things out, if you know what I mean. What's real, what's not real, et cetera. Kind of a public humiliation. Laughingstock with real stocks. Let's go for a walk. Outside. I need fresh air."

They sat down on a bench in the park

"How is Esther?" he asked.

Rose burst into tears. "Hugo—"

"Oh. Oh, yes. She's gone, isn't she."

"Hugo, Hugo," Rose said drying her eyes, "I have some good news for you. The Ontolli Gallery has bought one of your paintings. Three thousand dollars."

"Oh, good", he said distracted by a sparrow fight on the lawn. "The deer are still staring, Rose. They keep waiting for us to make a move they can understand. They're great critics, deer are."

"Hugo, I need some help from you. You now have money in the bank. The rent is due. We must also pay for the electric bill, and I want to buy some art materials for you. Would that be all right?"

"And scrambled eggs, too, Rose. Scrambled for the scrambled. The doctor says I'm just suffering mild delusions, a roller coaster ride of disordered thoughts due to chemical imbalance. They're trying to pin down the cause. Once that's squared away, it's puff the sails and off to the seven labors of Hercules for this old boy."

"Did he say you could come home soon?"

"If the winds are fair from the east."

"That is good news, Hugo." Rose smiled. "I will make you a big pan of scrambled eggs. And bannock."

He grinned from ear to ear and slapped his hands together. "Wonderful, my girl. I have such an appetite."

After more disjointed conversation, Rose convinced Hugo to write out two checks, one for the rent and one for the outstanding balance of the electric bill. In a moment of lucidity, he peered at her and demanded to know if she was eating properly.

"I'm fine, Hugo. You left several things in the kitchen cupboard."

"Hmmm", he said. "Give me that checkbook."

He wrote a third check, payable to Rose Wâbos, carefully adding the circumflex over the *a*, she noted—a good sign, a very good sign. He stuffed the check into her deer-hide bag.

"Thank you, Hugo."

"Five hundred dollars. Enough to eat for a few weeks. More where that came from. Just ask. Time is liquidity squared at present. I need reminders, so don't be shy."

"Thank you, Hugo, but you shouldn't."

"Why not. Your situation is transparent to me. No one wants your work now, am I correct?"

"Yes."

"Dear Favio and dear Clarissa are inaccessible and have left discreet messages that your future is not to be encouraged, am I right?"

Rose nodded.

"And because of the nasty reviews and the ejection from the flagship Ontolli-Metropol, no other gallery in town will touch your work with a ten-foot pole, correct?"

Again she nodded.

"Mrs. Morgan's money is all used up, right?"

"Yes, Hugo."

"And your mentor has moved to that strange and exotic country of America, and where she is no one can tell?"

"Yes."

"Therefore, you will humbly accept a little money for food."

"Thank you, Hugo."

"If you thank me one more time I will have a psychotic episode. It gives me pleasure to be of some use. Now, not another word about it."

Life returned to an approximation of normal. She spent most mornings going to and from Mass at the shrine of St. Joseph and the afternoons trying to draw and paint again. Little was accomplished. No freshets of creativity burst forth. This was difficult to bear, but she reminded herself that for almost a year now her life had been thrown into disruption, and it would take some time to return to a regular schedule.

In an effort to clear the clogged springs, she turned to subjects that had been central to her heart since the beginning.

A face of Tchibi happy, a man flying in the stars. In another he was young again, running wild beneath the flying thatch of fire-hair, his green eyes as translucent as the sunstruck fern and balsam needles, his cheeks as red as the strawberry juice smeared across them. The bushes turning to the yellow-pink of September. And in the background three young men leaping in a holy dance within the flames of a fiery furnace.

Euphrasia sleeping in the sun beneath a bonnet, smiling, a tiny *kinoje* devil writhing down into a lake of fire in a shadow ravine, driven there by the sword held in the hand of a massive shepherd. His other hand was on Euphrasia's head, while above them the white bird gazed upon all things with his turquoise eyes. And a girl child curled in the woman's lap, sleeping, dreaming within the enfolding arms of the dreaming woman, as the man, the husband, the father, the shelterer, watched over them.

Oldmary's face, serene, with four babies in her arms, her embrace as wide as the earth's; she was held within the larger embrace of muscled arms that reached down from the heavens, drawing her upward.

Esther opening cages, white birds fluttering their wings as they bolted for the skies. Esther's hands holding a small white bird against her heart, and in the core of the bird a flame. To this image, and this alone, Rose gave a title. On the back of the canvas frame she penned, *Birds in Peacetime*.

On none of these works did she sign her name. None of them were completed; they were all rough color sketches, needing to be developed. Yet it was a good start. The rivulets were trickling again. It was a week of renewed hope.

On the following Saturday she took the bus to the asylum for her weekly visit with Hugo, anticipating that she would find him in good form as he continued his steady recuperation. It was not so. A nurse informed Rose that Mr. Dyson was very ill, he was in a coma.

"The doctors say he has had an aneurysm. That's a burst blood vessel in the brain. They're doing all they can."

She found him in a side ward containing eight metal beds, on each of which an inert human form lay under sheets, only their unconscious faces showing. Hugo was in the third on the left. She went to him and stood by the bed, looking down at the grizzled face, its great beard, its road map of creases and scars, the skin scored by more than seventy years of experience.

"Io, Hugo", she sighed, spilling silent tears.

She took his limp hand and held it. The nerves of his face twitched, and his limbs jerked this way and that without pattern. His breathing was shallow and irregular. From time to time small groans escaped from his lips, like the bleats of dying forest animals.

"My little father", she whispered in his ear. "Ay, ay, I come to you. See, you are not alone. Do not fear. Do not let your heart be troubled."

The twitching and groaning seemed to increase, and the face contorted without pattern. She removed the rosary beads from her pocket and began to pray. From the moment her supplications began, the twitching stopped and his body relaxed into a deep stillness. For two hours or more she remained standing by his side, holding the aged wrinkled hand, cleansed of all paint, stripped down to its bare self, the wind dying in its sails. At three in the afternoon according to the ward room clock, his breathing began to quicken and sharp little cries whistled from his throat. Rose pleaded for the mercy of God to enfold him and fill him.

"Ay! Ay! Out of the depths I cry unto you! Lord hear my prayer!"

His agitation ceased, and a few minutes later he took his last breath. When the body was perfectly still, she went and found a nurse.

"Hugo Dyson is dead", she said in a broken voice. "A great man is dead, though no one knew his stature. I hear his footsteps upon the earth, drumming, drumming, leaping and rising. I hear the horses, yes, I hear them, beating their hoofs and taking flight, yes, they rise, they rise. They ride upon the wind as horses were meant to ride. And now do the sweet songs reach down to meet his soul, and all those he loved come forth to meet him, and the many fragments of beauty that he gave to mankind, even in his blindness and his pain and his longing, yes, they continue to spread throughout the world."

The nurse made Rose sit down on a chair by the ward desk and hurried off to the body.

"Oh, Hugo," she wept, "your great heart saved me when I was without hope and guidance, and long did you shelter me, and little did I give you in return. You were my only family when I thought I was alone in the world, and I beseech the Beating Heart now to have mercy on you because of it. Nothing will he deny me, for he is love, and even though the gates of a human heart may be closed to him, mercy shall flood sweetly upon that heart and the gates will open. Io! Io, my family dwells in a golden city, my heart, it dwells there too. There is fire in the heavens below the abiding city, and through this fire you must pass, Hugo, as all souls must pass or turn away forever into darkness. Seek the things which are above, Hugo, ride higher and higher, yes, see the twelve gates into the city, see them approaching!"

Hundreds of people great and small attended the funeral service at the Shaar Hashomayim Synagogue on Kensington Street. According to his wishes, Hugo was buried with the rites of his tradition and his body interred beside Esther's in the Jewish cemetery. There were articles in the newspaper about his long and complicated career in art. Esther too was mentioned. Rose was not, though this did not matter to her.

A lawyer came to the house on Rue St. Benoît the day after the funeral and informed Rose that according to the stipulations in Hugo's will the contents of his and Esther's studios were to be donated to the National Gallery. A truck would arrive within a few days to collect all their works of art. It was an old will, unaccompanied by an inventory of paintings, he said. Would she be willing to compile a list of existing works, with titles and dates, to assist the gallery in documenting the artists' output?

"There are no works of art", she apologized. "They are all gone."

He stared at her with suspicion and left.

Later that afternoon she checked the mailbox on the front porch and found a letter in it.

Dearest little bird,

Thank you for your visit on Saturday. I was pleased by the news that the house has not been condemned by the fire marshal. So, too, the sale of a lone surviving painting by the pathetically anachronistic Dysonius Redux is, perhaps, a blessing in disguise. The money will pay for the miserable medicines upon which I now depend for my moments of lucidity. More important, it will keep you going until you are on your feet.

You visit me each week, obeying the impulses of your charitable heart and the laws of your inscrutable religion. Visit the prisoner. Console the madman. Be kind to the poor beggar. Bury the dead. Your eyes when you visit me are pools of love and sadness. You say such welcome lies to me: "You are going to be just fine, Hugo." With radiant confidence you pat my hand. You bring me your small drawings of birds, refraining to mention that you do it so I will remember Esther.

The reality is, I am in a psychiatric hospital with a failed mind. In this friendly home for Bedlamites I have nothing much to do. I listen to the brain's recordings, examine the pastel wallpaper, appreciate the smiles of competent young nurses, and assess with some amusement the limited psychological techniques of the husky orderlies who will manhandle me without malice if I act out my delusions.

In the air, I smell the astringent perfume of death. I will not live to see the spring. It is no sense of foreboding that tells me this, only an inner knowing: I am to die. Though the doctors assure me otherwise.

It is suddenly real, this thing, this lover-monster, death. I lie helpless and grinning at its face, asking who I was. Esther knew who she was. She who saw the face of death close up and thereafter never ceased to fight it. She was a guerrilla warrior, I a pacifist. (We were one of the countless role reversals that our century has so cleverly accomplished.) Neither of us have defeated it.

The territory through which we journey is thin glass suspended over depths of boundless mystery. It seems so firm as we begin to gallop across it, yet it always proves treacherous. Blindly we move, prancing and singing, neighing and naying upon this fine and ancient world, playing with her fire and air and water and stone as if they were our own. Yet they are not our own, and in the end everything is taken away.

A man struck down by his own mind must at least try to make some sense of this. That organ has often laid me low before, in other ways, and in such humbling moments I learned again the truth of our probings and gestures: we are small, yet from the center of the universe which is the

759

self, we write ourselves so large that a cosmos is too confined for our ambitions.

Now, this universe is shrinking. Only memory is left to me. *Memoria* the ancients called it—the fires of experience teaching the soul. In remembering, much is cast up which cries out for resolution.

I did not understand my father. He was never easily opened like a good book or a well-tilled field. Yet now, having arrived in my seventh decade, I begin to grasp a few small things. The differences between my father and myself were considerable. He was a workingman, and I an artist. He resigned himself to his lot in life. I sought restlessly something I could not explain. My own true face perhaps. Or a missing king, a hollow space in the air where I should have found him standing.

I was a blunderer from the start. I staggered my way through life, tripping at every turn. I sought to avoid the violence of our race by declaring an amnesty which everyone ignored. My father found me weeping over some injustice once, in boyhood. He placed a hand on my shoulder, a gesture I did not want. I was a dreamer and he mistrusted dreamers, for dreamers did not value real work. Thus, it was only one of two or three times in my life that he attempted a leap across the chasm between us. He said a little thing really, but it was to become utterly valuable to me. With his hand on my shoulder, his eyes on the pile of coal that needed shoveling into the cellar, he said, "Hugo, I think you will be a very different kind of man than me." I remember how I flinched, expecting a rebuke. But he went on: "The world needs many kinds of men. Else it's all coal and no sailing ships."

I recall my first painting. On a crisp November morning, I returned to the hills of Kingstanding in search of the king in the window. Before I reached it, however, I was slaughtered by a sword of beauty. A farmhouse on the edges of the city, a sun-spattered stone wall in the yard. The sleep of the earth outside the warm kitchen windows. Blue smoke rising from the chimney. Frost silvering everything. The only hot color came from the globes of fire in a basket tilting askew at the base of an apple tree. Leafless, the tree retained a few yellow winesaps, golden apples of the sun dancing upon the purple branches. I fell hopelessly in love. I drew it. I went home and began to paint it. Never again did I go as far as Kingstanding, for I believed the earth would always be enough for me.

If Esther had not come into my life, I would now be an eccentric grizzlebeard in a Birmingham slum, mad of course, painting nothingness and calling it genius. As it turns out, I have become a semi-respectable, semi-disreputable, public utility. Yet I am aware of my true stature: a plodder, a Fool, or as my Esther once called me, an Imbecile.

While you were in Europe, the strangest thing occurred. My reputation was poised upon the brink of a leap. My imaginings threatened to sell for thousands. The Museum of Modern Art sent an envoy, who made the first probes. And so it went, coiling about the mind: the sensual images of the self-as-success. It was seduction, Rose. It was siren songs. And since I was incapable of strapping myself to the mast like Odysseus, the paintings had to be burned. They were dangerous.

"Beauty is dangerous", you once said. "And so is holiness. But can we live without them?"

Did you say that, or did I only imagine you saying it? It's hard to know at this point. Dear child, with such cryptograms you so often sought to demolish my perverse logic. For my part, I always thought you were wrong, that you clung to your myth from a kind of desperate need, and (forgive me) not only clung to it but created it in the process. Yet in the home stretch I am willing to reconsider. Perhaps you are right. Maybe it is supposed to be this way, this inexplicable fragility of being, the not-knowingness of life, the beauty that can break your heart. Without it we would soon enough make ourselves into gods.

I still look into mirrors in hope of seeing there a hint of who I might be. The mirror is a reflection only and an inverted one at that. Yet if one looks into the depths where sight ends and seeing begins, into the bright dark glass of memory, there is much to be found. When I direct my rather unfocused eyes toward the image in the ward's bathroom mirror—a plastic mirror (we wouldn't want suicide in an asylum, would we)—I see a tousle-headed oaf of easy limb and mind, leaping across ditches and rails, climbing fences, traversing the warren of industrial man's habitation, seeking his true name, yearning toward a horizon where he might run and catch the laughing horses, and climb upon their backs, if they would let him, and ride the wind. There he is, within me yet.

How strange, at this late hour, that a lifetime of progress in painfully gleaned observation, of creative interpretation, of folly and tempered innocence, should be snuffed out at its highest point, before I have learned to ride. But if death is the last horizon, then we are in no way betrayed. I shall see my wife again. I shall take her hand and we shall spar, for old time's sake. Then together we will fly.

Tell me this is so, Rose. Tell me that I made a difference to at least two beloved people in this world, Esther and you. Do not try to reassure me with tales of how I fed you, for you could have been fed at a thousand other stations of your dream. Do not tell me that I taught you, for it was you who taught me. Do not tell me that I saved your mind when you were lost and wandering on the streets of this great and wicked city, speaking to birds, and worse, listening to their soliloquies. No, say rather that you saved me.

Believe me, this is not a lunatic's rant. Officially I am no longer a lunatic, neither suicidal nor depressed, only a little unstable. I am 'somewhat inappropriate', my psychiatrist says. He does not realize that I have always been somewhat inappropriate. To put it simply, I am old and tired. No longer can I chase the galloping horses like a strong, well-fed slave. I am a pigeon in a cage.

I know what you will say. You will, of course, tell me that few on this earth are as free as the painter, master of his own tools, captain of his destiny.

And of course I will refute you. He is a prisoner, I will argue, caged within his poverty, chained by his passion to create.

He is a prisoner of love, you will reply, and thus he is the only free man on the planet.

I hope you will visit me soon. I promise to behave as a perfectly rational man. We will discuss Art.

Hugo

27

After the death of Hugo Dyson, Rose's life entered a phase of deeper solitude. She took up residence in a rented two-room apartment on Rue Fauxjour, a few blocks from Rue St. Benoît. There, among the small of the earth, she blended in without notice. She made no friends, neither did anyone take it upon themselves to consider her an enemy. The other residents in her tar-paper apartment block were preoccupied with their own troubles and paid her no mind. If in rare moments they assessed her with a glance, they merely noted a stranger more burdened than themselves, insignificant and harmless.

Rose, for her part, was not unhappy. She continued to give what she could to those who crossed her path: the old people in the block who needed their garbage bags carried down to the curb. Small children on the street who needed their noses wiped. Beggars who asked for a dime. The desolate (there were many of these) who needed a smile or a word of kindness. Although at times people drew back from her gestures, she attributed this to their instinctive fear of the strange.

Was she strange? She supposed that she was. Her appearance, of course. And her nativeness. Perhaps there was also a problem with hygiene. The communal bathroom on her floor was always in use, and it was difficult to find a free ten minutes during which she could take a shower under the rusty nozzle that never managed to produce more than lukewarm water. She bathed once a week at the most, and then only in the predawn hours, whenever the ancient boiler in the basement was working. She made do with sponge baths and a quick laundry in a sink that no amount of vigilance on her part would keep clean. Her clothing, most of which she had obtained as a young woman, was now threadbare and patched. She tried to replace items that were no longer wearable by haunting the charity shops. From time to time she happened upon jumpers designed for short obese adolescents, or as a last resort she cut down dresses designed for taller women. Second-hand shoes and boots were always cracked or worn at the heel but were inexpensive. Socks were knitted with the wool she unraveled from ten-cent sweaters.

Rose did not apply for welfare, because she considered herself to be a working person. Once or twice a week she volunteered at shelters for the homeless, but restricted herself to a few hours at a time, because her energy seemed to have declined since the trip to Europe. She could manage little more than cutting vegetables into the giant soup pots, picking lice from children's hair, and listening to the stories of the abandoned. She prayed for them as they poured their pain through her ears, through her eyes, through her emotions, into the heart of God. She felt him near at those moments when she threw herself down across the void to become a bridge between earth and heaven, but the effort often left her exhausted.

Her painting occupied most of each day, and in the evenings she was employed part-time cleaning the offices of factories in the area. The other cleaning women were, like her, aliens. They were poor and spoke languages that Rose did not understand. The pay was low but sufficient to cover her rent, a simple diet, bus fare, and art supplies.

Because she was unable to obtain an exhibition of her art work, there was no income from that direction. The allure of Place D'Armes, where a new generation of hopeful young street artists was selling its work, never ceased entirely, but she clung to something Hugo had said to her before his death: his assurance that one day her images would be well known and that she must not scatter them for a pittance. Euphrasia had told her much the same thing, and thus, following the pattern of blind faith that she had established from her earliest years, she obeyed the voice of memory and merely added the new paintings, drawings, and pastels to a growing archive in her closet.

On Easter Sunday of Rose's thirty-third year, she attended the Vigil Mass at the shrine of St. Joseph. After Communion she experienced one of the deepest consolations of her life. The ecstasy seemed timeless, and when it was over she found herself in an empty basilica lit only by the flickering lights of votive candles.

At that moment the voice which had been long silent spoke again.

Three journeys have I given you. One journey you have taken, two are before you, for the good of many souls and for the good of your own soul. You will go very far, but first you must be purified.

Rose had forgotten these words from God that she had heard during her first visit to Kateri's tomb several years ago.

"Where do you want me to go?" she asked.

But he was silent.

"Here I am, Lord. I want only to do your will."

The silence continued until she understood that he would reveal in his own time and in his own way where she must go.

Months passed without any indication of what the Lord had meant. During that time she prayed more consistently for his will to be accomplished. In addition, the last words Mère Jean had spoken to her returned with a certain urgency, as if there were something in them she had not heard or accepted whole-heartedly.

When everything is taken from you, then everything shall be given to you.

A sliver of resistance made itself felt.

"Am I not poor enough?" she sighed.

General sadness and more specific regrets arose from memory. Her many losses. The way she had been surrounded by death for most of her life. So many, many of her beloveds had died, and those who had not died had disappeared from her life. Not least among her sorrows was her abiding desire to be a mother—impossible now.

"I am alone", she said with growing frequency, though she did not want to feel or think such things. "Why am I so alone?"

With an effort she renewed her willingness to abandon everything to Divine Providence; she offered her unruly sentiments to the Crucified Heart, begging him to transform them. They soon lost their power over her, but from then on they would not depart, and she wondered over this.

On the first day of October that year, an unexpected event occurred. Late one night, waiting for the bus after work, Rose noticed an old street person shuffling along the sidewalk toward her. He stopped a few paces away, motionless, and looked at her. She wondered if she had a few coins to spare. As she rummaged in her parka pocket, she said a prayer for him.

"Not necessary", he said in a rheumy voice, thick with age and experience. His eyes were brown, like old purple velvet that has been rubbed too long, as old as the world. He was dressed in rags, yet in his demeanor there was unaffected nobility. He smiled at her. It was a deep warm smile that contained a history of many losings and findings.

"Are you hungry?" Rose asked him.

"No", he said.

"Do you need a bus ticket? I have one I could give you."

"Thank you, I like to walk."

"Do you have a home?"

"Yes", he said in a soft voice, his eyes glowing.

Rose thought their conversation was concluded. But he

surprised her by pulling a folded newspaper from the pocket of his tattered coat and handing it to her. Without another word, he walked on.

Rose puzzled over this, for the man seemed purposeful in giving it to her. Usually she did not read newspapers. It was her habit to pray for the conversion of the world, and whenever volcanoes exploded, ships sank, or airplanes fell from the sky, she eventually heard about it and prayed for the victims. But she felt no need to know more. During the bus ride home, however, she obligingly turned the pages. At last, her eyes rested upon a photograph of two elderly women. They held a doll between them. The caption said that they were identical twin sisters who lived in St. Peter's-by-the-Sea, a fishing village on the Atlantic coast. The accompanying article was about the resurgence of folk art in the Maritime Provinces. The sisters made their living as doll makers. Their names were Winnifred and Minnifred McCaul.

Rose would never be able to understand how she knew that God wanted her to go to the McCaul sisters and meet them. It was simply a fact. Here, beyond all doubt, and beyond all explanation, was the second journey.

Rose fasted for a week, preparing spiritually, saving the money she would ordinarily have spent on food. She resigned from her cleaning job and was gratified to receive a severance check from her employer, something to do with provincial employment regulations. It was less than a hundred dollars, but this, added to the small amount she had scrimped into her bank account, paid for a bus ticket to Nova Scotia.

St. Peter's-by-the-Sea was an Acadian settlement that had stood firm on the rocky coast of Cape Breton Island for more than two hundred years. In its day it had been home to hundreds of people, but now it had shrunk to a few dozen houses perched on a slope that descended to a circular cove half a mile across.

The town was bereft of the young, most of whom went away to the mines at Sydney or to studies in Halifax. Few were the men who still fished for a living, and these were, on the whole, men of advancing years. Sagging boat houses lined the gravel beach below the main street, and upturned dories offered splashes of color in many a back yard. Stacks of lobster traps leaned against sheds by the waterfront.

Winter and summer, the north Atlantic pounded the outer arm of the cove which protected the town, its waves entering the small harbor with much diminished force. Rarely was the surface of the water placid, seldom the natural beauty of the rocky cliffs and grassy moors anything other than austere, the colors limited to the cool end of the spectrum. Yet when the sun shone and the wind dropped, St. Peter's was a place of great, if fugitive, cheer. It was on one such day that Rose arrived.

By the harbor front was a cluster of buildings that represented commerce and government: a grocery store, a gas station, a post office, and an outpost nursing station. Rose entered the grocery store, an antique building in need of repainting. It was dim inside, smelling of kerosene. Various chandlery and fishing items hung from the rafters. A large model of a schooner sat on a shelf above the cash register. A brass label beneath it read *Bluenose*. Beneath this, ferreting in a tin of Copenhagen snuff, sat a rotund man in a red checkered bush jacket. He was staring at Rose with his mouth open as if he had been quick-frozen.

There were several other people in the store, all men, gathered around a pot-bellied stove. The conversation they had been engaged upon in slow and easy tones ended abruptly. Turning in unison they too stared at Rose. No one said a word.

"Excuse me, please", she said. "Could you tell me where I can find Winnifred and Minnifred McCaul?"

Grins broke out on every face.

"You'd be a relation, I guess?" said the man at the cash register, which made the others grin more broadly.

"No. I merely wish to make their acquaintance", Rose explained. Then in a futile attempt at clarification she stammered, "We are the same sort of people."

This was greeted by laughter all around.

"I mean," Rose said, perplexed, "I am an artist, and they are artisans."

"That so?" said the man at the cash register with a dubious look. "Winnie and Minnie are famous now, with their pictures in the paper and everything. We don't want people pesterin' them. You're not a reporter, are you?"

"No", Rose said and waited.

The men in the store turned to each other and put their heads together, mumbling things that she could not hear.

"Please, sir, I have come a long way to see them."

"Well, I suppose I can tell you where they live. They're down by the water's edge on the far side of the fish-dryin' shed, in the lee of the stonegate."

He pointed to the right.

"What does their house look like?"

"Oh, you can't miss it," he said.

"It's big!" said a man at the stove.

"Biggest house in town", said another.

Rose departed with their chuckles echoing in her ears.

Outside, she turned right and proceeded down the road in the direction of a warehouse that seemed to be in the final stages of collapse. As she passed it, she noticed that its roof had caved in, and that high dead weeds encroached all about. On the far side of the building a narrow footpath curved off the road—indeed the road ended at that point—and descended toward the sea between hillocks of rock. As Rose passed through these natural gates she searched for a large house near the shore, but there was none to be seen in any direction.

770

The only building there was a small clapboard structure that she took at first to be a garden shed. It appeared to be two stories high, and, if this was so, each floor would be no more than four or five feet in height. Moreover, someone had spent a great deal of effort on it. It was painted bright yellow with white trim, the roof was covered with metal shingles embossed with gingerbread designs, and a stone chimney was puffing lazy wisps of smoke. The end of one roof gable was capped by a weather vane, a tin girl in a petticoat and umbrella turned inside out. There were curtains in the windows, shutters, flower boxes, and a ginger kitten licking its paws on a sill. A white picket fence surrounded the yard, in which flower beds were lying dormant for the season. It looked very much like a doll's house.

Rose thought that this perhaps was a little shop where the McCaul sisters sold their dolls and other handicrafts and that the structure was a clever illusion. No doubt she would find that there was a single floor inside, and that however small the building might appear to be when viewed from the exterior, its interior dimensions would be normal.

On the front porch sat two children's rocking chairs. The door, too, was miniature, so small, in fact, that even Rose would be forced to stoop to enter. She thought that the McCaul sisters must be fun-loving people who were fond of children, for they had tailored their place of business for the very young. She knocked.

An elderly lady opened the door and looked out at Rose. Her face was grandmotherish, wrinkled and sweet, capped by a blur of white hair. She was no more than three feet tall.

"Yes, can I help you?" she said in a tiny voice.

For a moment Rose was speechless, so astonished was she by the size of the woman, whom she recognized as one of the sisters from the newspaper photograph. Before she could respond, a second person appeared, no larger than the first.

"What is it, dear?" she asked, fumbling for a pair of bifocal glasses that dangled on a cord about her neck.

"A visitor, Minnie", said the other with a bright open smile.

"Can we help you?" said Minnifred.

"Oh, yes, please", Rose stammered. "I mean, I think you might. Though I don't know for sure. I came because he asked me to."

They looked at Rose curiously.

"Someone asked you to see us?" they said in unison.

"Yes—he—I mean—"

"Well, you'd better come inside, dear. The sun is shining quite nicely today, but it *is* chilly."

"Thank you very much", Rose said, bending her head to enter.

Once inside the building, she saw that it was a home. And contrary to her expectations, it was a two story dwelling, for the ceiling was only an inch or so above the top of her head. Standing in the entry hall with the two women, she could not help glancing around in wonder. Everything in it had been designed for very short people, and Rose, who had always perceived herself as the shortest of the short, now began to feel very large indeed.

The tiny parlor to the right of the hallway contained several pieces of furniture that, if not custom-made for children under the age of five, were handcrafted specifically for people the size of the McCauls. The electric lamps were of the smallest proportions, the woolen rugs on the shining hardwood floors were the size of place mats. Even the pictures on the walls were framed postcards of well-known artwork.

"I'm sorry. I didn't mean to stare", Rose said bringing her eyes back to the sisters.

They giggled. "Oh, all people stare when they come for the first time", said Winnifred.

"But they get used to it", said Minnifred.

"Though some people, the extra-large-size people, never can get as comfortable as they would like."

"Though we try to make people as cozy as possible."

"Oh, yes, we do try", said Winnifred.

"We have to keep them in the hallway," her sister tittered, "because they won't fit into the kitchen or the parlor."

"Would you like a cup of tea, Miss?"

"Yes, please", Rose said. "Though I don't want to intrude."

"But we like to be intruded!" exclaimed Winnifred.

"No, we *love* to be intruded!" Minnifred corrected. She turned and walked with an odd toddling gait toward a kitchen at the end of the hall. "I'll get the kettle boiling, Winnie."

"Thank you, Minnie."

Winnifred McCaul now turned to Rose, and with a businesslike clasping of her hands, inquired who, precisely, she was and why she was calling.

"I am Rose Wâbos, Miss McCaul. I am an artist. I read about you and your sister in the newspaper in Montreal, where I live. And I think I'm supposed to meet you."

"Oh, how lovely that you've come all this way—just to see us, you say?"

"Just to see you."

"Did you hear that, Minnie, our guest has come *just* to see *us*!"

"Yes, I overheard, Winnie", a voice from the kitchen called back "This *is* a treat. Should I get out the raisin pie or the shortbreads?"

"Why not both?"

"You're absolutely right. Is she a parlor person or a kitchen person?"

"A kitchen person, I think." She glanced at Rose inquiringly. "Am I right? A kitchen person is more neighborish, don't you think. Or familyish, or friendlyish."

"In that case," said Rose, "I would be honored to be a kitchen person."

"Good! I knew it the moment I saw you. There's a real kitchen person, I said to myself, the sort of woman you can sit and talk with for just hours and hours and pay no heed to the clock. It's in the eyes I always say. Pay no attention to the mouth, I say. Always give the eyes a good checking over. Anyway, we do love company. Not that we ever get lonely, mind you. We have each other. My Papa used to say that too. I expect I'm getting old, because I do find myself saying—and Minnie is even worse—saying the things he used to say. If he told us once, he told us a thousand times, 'Girls, you were born in your Mamma's tummy together and came into this world together and you growed up together. And you'll always have each other no matter what.' And hasn't he been proved right to the dotting of an *i* and the crossing of a *t*!"

Soon they were seated on little chairs around a low wooden table, beside a deep blue enamel stove which, though of miniature proportions, radiated ample heat.

The chamomile tea was sweetened with honey, the raisin pie seasoned with shreds of lemon peel and a scoop of maple walnut ice cream. The shortbreads were embossed with the shape of a sailing ship.

Rose found herself easily swept into the sisters' happy chatter and familiarity. Right from the start they insisted on being called Minnie and Winnie, and unlike many people in this world, they frequently used Rose's name when they addressed her. For it seemed they instinctively knew that names had power to bind and loose, to tame and soothe, that a name went straight to the heart.

They were heart people, that was clear enough. Ideas did not interest them. People did. And flowers, and the intricate personalities of small animals. And dolls.

Winnie was more talkative than Minnie, though this was

774

only a matter of minor degree, because they were both able to launch into lengthy descriptions of whatever they turned their minds to. They never interrupted each other, but they did complete each other's thoughts whenever a sentence presented itself as unfinished or inexact. Minnie was more of a doer than a talker. She boiled a second pot of tea and saw to the cutting of pie and watched to make sure Rose had everything she needed. It was she who toddled off to the parlor and returned with a cushion to put behind Rose's back. Moreover, she knelt and, without asking, peeled off Rose's cracked brown shoes and slipped a pair of hand-knit slippers over her feet.

During a lull in the conversation, Rose asked how they had come to live in such a beautiful house.

"Papa made it for us", said Winnie.

"Well, not exactly for us," corrected Minnie, "it was for our husbands, you see."

"There were supposed to be two," Winnie added.

"Husbands?" Rose asked.

"No, houses. For us and our husbands. Papa always planned to build a house for each of us. Yellow with white trim for me, and white with yellow trim for Minnie. When we were girls he promised that when we grew up, he would make homes for each of us when we were ready to start our families."

The sisters fell silent.

Minnie sighed. "We never found the right man."

"You mean *men*, dear", said Winnie.

"That's right, *men*. As you may have noticed, Rose, we are not . . . well, we are not *ordinary*."

"Not ordinary at all", her sister agreed. "There are so many over-large people in the world."

"Those poor people. How very uncomfortable they must be, don't you think, Rose? What it must take to feed them!"

"Oh, yes, and the trouble they have getting around", Winnie added. "It takes a lot of energy, you know."

Rose, sensing the delicacy of the subject, refrained from comment.

The sisters smiled at her.

"Rose, dear, aren't you glad that you're almost the perfect size?"

Rose nodded, then shook her head, mentally stumbling over their meaning. Were they saying she was too tall or too short?

"It's not often we meet someone of our stature", said Minnie, gazing at Rose with great affection.

"Someone so well *balanced*", Winnie put in.

"Did your father build two houses?" Rose asked, trying to change the subject.

"No, he didn't. Though he . . ."

"Though he wanted to very much. He had planned to build them side by side, you know."

"But he felt that building *two* houses before even *one* young man came along would be jumping the gun, you see. After Mama passed away, he just rattled around in the old house—"

"She means the big place."

"He didn't want us to rattle around like he did."

"It's gone now. It was torn down. The big hurricane of '36 damaged it so badly. Of course it was already falling apart, because Papa had put so much labor into building this place."

"He told us that if by chance a young man did *not* come to seek the hand of either Minnie or me, then we might find ourselves just rattling around in *two* houses. And where would we be then? He said we'd better wait until we knew for sure."

"A man of our stature did come to visit once, in the summer of 1944."

"No, dear, it was the spring of '44."

"Maybe you're right. Yes, I think you are. Oh, goodness, my memory is going."

"He was a Hungarian gentleman and quite refined."

"He had excellent manners."

"He was with a circus that passed through Halifax, and somehow he had heard about us. He came all the way from the city just to meet *us*. Imagine that."

"But he didn't stay", Winnie sighed.

"And after him there were . . ."

"After him there were no others. So you see, Rose, how wise Papa was? Now we are quite content in this place. There are days when it seems too large."

"Did your father make the furniture for you?"

"He made everything. He was very good with his hands."

"Papa was a shipwright."

"He built schooners. There never was a finer shipbuilder on Cape Breton."

"Nor a finer man", Winnie said.

"Nor a finer man", Minnie nodded solemnly.

"I can see that you miss him", Rose said.

The sisters' eyes moistened.

"Oh, yes. He loved us so much. He was so much fun. What a joker he was. And music! There was no end to the music in our house when we were small."

"Were you the only children?" Rose asked.

"We have a younger brother. Edgar's a manager at the Sydney mine", said Minnie.

"He worked underground for years and years", said Winnie.

"Unfortunately, he's very tall."

"But he makes the best of it."

"He brings us coal in his truck every autumn."

"He put in the electricity."

"And he built the kiln and potter's shed for us. It's a real tragedy, though—there's not a drop of Papa's music in his blood."

"Can't hold a tune."

"Minnie has all the music", Winnie explained.

"Such a lovely wife too. We like her a lot, but of course she's uncommonly tall."

"And the children—all tall."

"And the grandchildren too—not a small person among them. We had so hoped . . ."

"Yes, we had so hoped . . ."

"But, Winnie, we do have our own children."

"Oh, yes," Minnie smiled, "that's true. We have our own children."

Rose supposed that they were referring to their dolls. Homemade dolls of exquisite beauty were everywhere in the house, seated side by side on shelves, counter tops, kitchen cupboards, chairs, couches, and any other available space. On the window sill beside the sleeping ginger kitten, a wicker basket contained dozens of ceramic faces. Other baskets held tumbles of sewing material.

The conversation went on for several hours. Eventually, Rose noticed that the light was fading in the kitchen window. She now realized that the day was drawing to a close and that she had no more clear idea about why the Lord had brought her here than when she had first arrived. She stood and said, "Well, I've enjoyed meeting you very much. I should be going now."

The two old women looked surprised. Their mouths opened in consternation, their brows furrowed.

"But you haven't had supper", Winnie said.

"A guest has to have supper. And you'll stay overnight too, won't you?"

"We'll put her in the den, won't we, Minnie?"

"Yes, on the couch for the long people."

"There's so much we would love to tell you about."

"Our children."

"Yes, our children."

They stared at Rose expectantly, waiting for her reply.

Rose accepted gratefully, most of all because she had no idea where she might otherwise spend the night, and also because she was still puzzled about the reason for her visit.

The two old women slid from their chairs and sprang into action. Minnie began to bustle about in the kitchen and Winnie went off to the den to prepare a bed where Rose could sleep for the night.

"Now, you must be tired out from all our gibble-gabble, Rose", Minnie said as she placed three small frying pans on top of the stove. "Why don't you go into the parlor and relax. It'll take me a while to get supper on, and I like to concentrate. If there's company, I talk too much and can't concentrate, and then everybody goes hungry. So, toodle-oo, off you go."

Minnie's tiny bird laugh was quite infectious, and Rose chuckled as she made her way along the hallway toward the front parlor. There, she sat down in a diminutive armchair before an equally small fireplace that was flickering cherry red from a bank of electric heating elements. The kitten jumped onto her lap, curled up, and began to purr under Rose's caresses. Feeling the strangest mixture of contentment and perplexity, she fell into musing on the sisters' life. They had painted a simple picture for her, full of summer picnics with their brother and his growing clan, the kindness of neighbors who drove them here and there, and copious memories of "Papa and Mama". The ocean figured large in their discussions, as did sea shells, boats, the many species of birds they spotted in the dunes, and the flowers they liked to grow in their garden each summer.

They were happy people, content with themselves and well regarded in the community. Rose wondered at the laughter of the men in the grocery store, but in retrospect she saw hints of affection and a sense of irony about the vagaries of life. Doubtless, most if not all in that group had been born in St. Peter's, and thus the presence of the McCauls was completely normal to them. Visitors from the outside were the abnormality.

779

Given their fondness for their departed parents, Minnie and Winnie must have been very well loved from the moment of their entry into life. They did not consider themselves to be deformed or deprived and perhaps never had. They did not brood over or question their losses or imperfections.

"Rose! Winnie! Supper's ready", Minnie called. When Rose reentered the kitchen she saw that the table had been set as if for a grand dinner. A bowl of artificial roses sat in the center beside a tallow candle in a brass holder. The set of Dutch china had been arranged on a checkered blue tablecloth. The dinner plates were bread-and-butter plates, the cups and saucers from a child's tea set. In front of the three places were sherry glasses containing apple juice. On each plate was a sprig of broccoli, a lump of cauliflower, and a square fried egg.

A square egg? Rose raised her eyebrows at Minnie. Winnie and Minnie giggled. Minnie lifted one of the frying pans from the stove and showed her its shape—square.

"Round eggs are so dull", said Winnie. "Everyone has them."

"The nieces and nephews love the square ones."

"They never get bored by *our* eggs."

"They eat it all up without a scolding."

"The dears."

"Yes, the dears."

The meal, Minnie explained, was one of their favorites. They called it "Oaks and Clouds".

Because the sisters did not appear to have the custom of praying before meals, Rose said her grace silently, without being noticed. Then they all set to with enthusiasm.

"More wine?" said Winnie, tilting the can of apple juice to refill Rose's glass.

After supper there were raisin pie and shortbread again, followed by coffee served in the china cups. These were perfectly suited to the sisters' small fingers, but Rose found it difficult to manage. Noticing this, Winnie found a larger mug and poured Rose a fresh cup.

Later, when the table was cleared, Winnie glanced at Minnie and said mysteriously, "Do you think we could have . . . ?"

"Not on the first night, dear. It would be an imposition on our guest."

"She might like to join us."

"Well, I don't know. . . ."

The sisters shot an eager look at Rose.

"Do you like to sing?" they asked in unison.

"It has been many years since I've sung", Rose said. "I'm not sure I can any more. But I would love to hear *you* sing."

The sisters' faces lit up.

"The squeeze-box, Minnie!"

"Coming right up, Winnie!" said her sister, hastening out of the room.

A moment later, she came back carrying a concertina.

"This is Seraphina", she said, expanding the red bellows. "That's what we call her."

Minnie pressed buttons on one of the mother-of-pearl bases and contracted the bellows. A gust of notes issued from the reeds, then stopped.

"How about Ferlin Husky, Minnie?"

"Oh, yes, perfect. Rose, do you know Ferlin Husky's 'On the Wings of a Dove'?"

Rose shook her head.

Minnie began to coax from the instrument a soft and melancholy melody, the notes slipping and sliding now and then. She played the tune with fluttering eyelids. Winnie placed a hand above her chest and raised her eyes to heaven. Their voices joined in singing—high, atonal, permanently set in a vibrato.

> "On the wings of a snow-white dove
> he sends his pure sweet love,

on the wings of a dove . . .
o . . . o . . . o . . .
on the wings of a *doooove*. . . ."

Flushed with emotion, the sisters sang their way through several verses and then sang it all over again. If Rose had not been so moved by their guilessness, by their own pure sweet love, she might have laughed or at least permitted herself a smile. But in that situation of the bizarre rendered down to comforting homeliness and goodness, she could not. She caught the tune and hummed along with them.

After that came "The Ballad of the *Bluenose*", an epic in rousing tones recounting the adventures of the greatest of the Grand Banks schooners.

Other folk tunes and ballads followed, and concluded with "Fisherman's Alphabet", which set them all giggling. By then it was ten o'clock. Rose yawned, and her eyes drooped from exhaustion. The sisters noticed and led her to the "den", which was no more than an alcove off the parlor containing a love seat made up into a bed.

After the sisters had said good night and gone upstairs to their own rooms, Rose got into her nightgown and snuggled under the patchwork quilts. She felt slightly feverish, a sore throat was beginning to scratch, and there was a heaviness in her lungs. Even so, she felt very contented. It had been a long time since she had enjoyed such natural peace.

Before putting out the light, she let her eyes wander along the shelves, from which a crowd of little persons peered down at her. No one doll resembled another. Every detail, from the finely sewn garments to the hand-painted heads, was unique. The faces were composed of papier-mâché or cloth or unglazed bisque clay or high-glaze ceramic. Common to them all was a certain expression of innocence, cheer, and good will that was very much an extension of the McCauls' own hearts. Rose prayed for the sisters and fell asleep.

In the morning she awoke to a bubbling in her chest and shortness of breath. Her throat was raw. Winnie insisted that she stay in bed, brought her hot apple juice spiced with cloves, read to her from a book of poetry, then let her sleep. From time to time throughout the day, Rose awoke, listened to the surf pounding the beach below and the cries of sea gulls. In the shaded room with no one to see her, she cried quietly from weakness and from gratitude. She did not understand what was happening and had no energy left to think of an explanation.

In the evening, she felt more ill than ever. Minnie made her drink a steaming toddy which contained not only the now familiar apple juice, but also a dash of dark rum. Winnie spoon-fed her a bowl of something she called "hugger-in-buff", a hot soup of salt-cod chunks in a sauce of onions, potatoes, bacon bits, and sour cream. Then they serenaded her with more music. Rose clapped her hands at the finish of each song, laughed despite the stab in her throat, and croaked out an attempted apology for being a burden on them. They would not hear any of that and scolded her for trying. Overwhelmed by their kindness, Rose began to cry, covered her face with her hands, and buried her head in the pillow. They patted her shoulders and tiptoed out of the room.

Io, I do not understand! I do not understand!

The following several days were much the same. Then, one evening, after a piping hot soak in their pint-size bathtub, Rose felt almost fully recovered. She had not slipped back into the grip of her old enemy, pneumonia, and for this she was grateful. She dressed in clean clothing and went out to the kitchen, where she found the sisters sewing doll clothes. They looked up with homey smiles and greeted her as if she had always lived with them. Minnie popped her needle into a pincushion and made herself busy cooking a square egg for Rose.

On Saturday morning, after breakfast, the sisters glanced at each other conspiratorially and announced that they were going away for the day. They would not tell her where, but asked if she would like to accompany them. Rose was willing. Shortly after nine o'clock, a car horn beeped up above the stonegate, and the three women bundled into their coats. Winnie carried a large wicker basket, Minnie a round metal tin of the sort once used to store Christmas cakes. Its cover was a red plaid design, reminding Rose of another Scottish tin.

The car was waiting for them in the gravel lane. It was driven by a methodical and noncommunicative man who merely grunted, "Mornin', Min, mornin', Win", to the sisters and offered a more tentative "Mornin'", to Rose. His name was Earl. He was the postmaster and was heading to Sydney for supplies. The sisters sat in front as if they were Earl's two eager little daughters off on an outing, though they were old enough to be his mother. He said nothing throughout the journey, but Winnie and Minnie offered a running commentary on the weather and numerous items regarding the life of the people of St. Peter's-by-the-Sea. He replied with subtle variations on the grunt, also with shrugs, reflective tilts of the head, and by rubbing his chin or scratching the top of his graying brush cut.

After an hour's drive, the car pulled off the road onto a lane that went up over a barren moor in the direction of a massive building that rose on the crest of a hill. There was not a tree in sight, the wind was blowing the wild grasses flat, the sky was leaden. It was a scene of unrelieved bleakness, though the McCauls seemed in no way dispirited by it.

Agreeing to pick them up in three or four hours, Earl drove away, leaving the women standing by the steps of a red-brick building so large and so featureless that Rose was unable to guess what it was. The rows upon rows of windows were all barred.

Minnie and Winnie led the way into the main entrance. The smell inside was a troubling mixture of rankness and disinfectant chemicals.

"Is this a hospital?" Rose asked.

"No, dear, not exactly", Winnie replied over her shoulder as she led the way through a set of double doors into a wide hall that stretched away into the distance, almost to the vanishing point. The walls of this thoroughfare were painted olive green, its floor was battleship gray linoleum. The smell was stronger than in the outer foyer. Several doors could be seen on both sides, and from these there now appeared a number of curious faces. Some of the faces were very old and some very young, and all the ages in between were also represented. As the McCauls were spotted, squeals and shouts sprang from the mouths of these people, who were apparently residents of the building. Many threw their arms in the air and with cries of excitement ran, stumbled, or crawled toward the sisters. Within seconds they were surrounded by thirty or forty milling bodies, all vying for the places closest to the visitors. A tangle of arms enwrapped them, a chorus of gleeful nonsensical exclamations broke out, and beneath the discordant noise there was a harmonious feeling. There were many kisses and much handholding. Children jumped up and down tugging on the sisters' skirts. Old people clamped them in fierce embraces. On every face there was joy. Rose was pulled into the crowd, kissed, embraced, stroked, and gazed upon with amazement.

Rose was overwhelmed, not with the strangeness of their mental or physical deformities, but by the waves of unrestrained love that radiated from them all.

"Oh, Polly, not too tight, not too tight", laughed Minnie.

"Tod, you little scamp, get your paws out of the basket", Winnie giggled. "There's enough for everyone."

She opened the cake tin. It was full of chunks of saltwater taffy. The people crowded closer and bent their heads to look inside, but only the younger ones attempted to grab. Winnie gave the sweets to them first, then offered the tin to the others. Each of the residents selected a piece, without pushing or taking more than his share. Soon it was empty, the extra pieces handed out as seconds to the younger residents. All voices fell silent as everyone concentrated on chewing, their eyes glowing with pleasure. With that, Minnie and Winnie continued their stroll along the hall, trailing a number of bodies that clung to them, looped and bound by many arms, old and young heads leaning on their shoulders. Rose too was thus claimed. It was difficult to make much progress because of the entanglement of limbs, fresh kisses, and garbled questions that were put to her.

"Who you? Who you?"

"I'm Rose", she said.

"Wose! Wose! It's Wose!" cried several voices.

Her natural reticence was in no way affronted by this. Indeed, she found it so disarming and so comforting to be touched and caressed as if she were a kitten, that she wondered why this institution, whatever it was, was not mobbed by more people who, on the whole, were starved for human affection.

Presently, a man in a blue uniform emerged from the door of an office. Behind him came a woman dressed similarly.

"Hi, Min, hi, Win!" said the man. "Missed you last week. Where were you?"

"The craft show in Sydney", Winnie explained. "But, oh, how we missed our children!"

"They missed you too, or can't you tell", he laughed. "Come on, everybody, give the ladies a break. Make room, make room; they can't breathe."

He and the other staff worker helped to sort order out of the crowd, and Rose noticed that they did it gently enough, with only a little condescension.

"Thank heavens you came", said the woman. "Half the day shift's off with the flu. They're down to one staff on Chronic

Six, been callin' for help all morning. Think you could go give a hand later?"

"We'd love to", Minnie exclaimed. "Oh, my, we've been so remiss lately. I haven't seen them in weeks."

"Well, why don't you visit with these folks here, have lunch with them in the cafeteria, then go up to Chronic after. 'Course the elevator's broken down again. . . ."

"Oh, we don't mind. . . ."

"Yes, we'll be fine."

"Can our friend come along?"

"The more the merrier", said the blue man.

During the next two hours, Rose mustered every ounce of energy trying to meet the endless needs that popped up all around her. An old woman in a hospital gown needed her hair straightened and crooned to herself as Rose brushed and brushed the wispy tangle of white. For half an hour she rocked an eight- or nine-year-old boy who curled into the fetal position in her arms, sucking his thumb as he repeated incessantly the sound *oowah-oowah* until he fell asleep. A grossly overweight teenage girl begged for a game of checkers, which Rose played with her in a state of confusion until she realized that this version of the game had no rules whatsoever, and abandoned herself to the fun of pretending defeat and victory. Great hilarity ensued, both in the two players and a host of onlookers. After that, a girl of five or six years who lacked arms played bump-cars with Rose. *Bump-caw, bump-caw*, she cried, fluttering the little flaps of flesh that grew from her shoulders. Rose got the point and let the child crash into her a few times. The staff lady put a stop to this, but Rose consoled the girl by taking a walk with her up and down the hall. It was a very long hall. The girl chattered all the way, the words unintelligible. Only the eyes hinted at some meaning.

Not all the residents were as communicative. In some wards, television sets played in wire cages suspended from the ceilings, and in front of them withdrawn patients stared morosely without comprehension at black-and-white soap operas and cartoon shows. The scene would have been utterly demoralizing were it not for the fact that such individuals were few.

Alternately delighted, moved, horrified, and consoled, Rose was soon reeling. She detected in herself an urge to switch off her feelings. There was simply too much going on, and a great deal of it tore at the heart. Then, without warning, almost of their own volition, her eyes changed focus, and she saw each and every one of these people as an incarnation of a word. Theirs was physical poverty of the most abject and permanent kind. Yet within the flawed forms and limited minds there was something so eternal, so beautiful and holy, that at certain moments Rose was struck immobile with the wonder of it. They lived daily in their crucified flesh, and within their deprivation were the marks of crucified hearts. But they were free to love in their pain.

At every step of the way Rose continued to be surrounded by admirers, strokers, kissers, and huggers, a sea of eyes that reached out to her with longing. And she saw that the endless waves of their need was the converse of an endless fulfillment.

Over lunch—an extraordinarily noisy and messy affair—Winnie managed to tell Rose a few things about the institution.

"There are miles of wards, Rose. Hardly anybody ever visits the people who live here. We're just a drop in the bucket, Minnie and me. We've been coming for almost forty years now, and we really miss it when we aren't able to get here. Our children know us, you see. And we know them."

"They think *we're* children", Minnie whispered with a giggle. "Don't tell."

"I won't", said Rose.

788

"I sometimes wish we could take them home with us. But where would we put them all?"

"They're uncommonly large-sized people, most of them," Winnie said.

"Except for our babies."

"Yes, our babies are just about perfect. You'll meet them later, Rose."

"There are more than three thousand residents, you know", Winnie said on a suddenly serious note. "Most of them no one comes to see."

"It's impossible for us to get to know everyone, but we do our best."

"Yes, we do our best."

"Each week we spend time with our old friends here, then we add a new ward every month."

"Some of them are hard places. Very hard places, Rose."

"Like Melba."

"Yes, there's Melba. And Jimmy."

"But they're so . . ."

"Yes, so very . . ."

"Very what?" Rose asked.

"Well, you'll see. They steal you away."

"Oh, yes, quite away. You're never the same afterward."

"Never the same, ever again."

After lunch, the sisters and Rose made their way unaccompanied through the labyrinth of the institution. From time to time they passed staff members who greeted them in a friendly, if distracted, manner. Invariably they were recognized as Min and Win or Win and Min. Sometimes residents (or were they *patients*, Rose was not sure) recognized them, and then embraces and shouts of joy broke out afresh. The sisters never seemed to tire of it. They had all the time in the world, and knew the names of hundreds of people. From what wells of grace did they draw their love, Rose wondered. They did not appear to be people of religious faith, and thus she learned that love itself was a power of the soul, replenished from hidden springs even as it was poured out.

Penetrating deeper and deeper into the maze, they entered a wing in the farthest back corner of the building. Passing through another set of hall doors they came to an abrupt cul-de-sac by a staircase. There they began their ascent of six flights. All three found this an arduous task because of their infirmities, but in time they arrived at the end of their journey: a locked door and a sign that read:

Chronic Ward 6
NO ENTRY WITHOUT PERMISSION

Winnie pressed a buzzer, and the door clicked. Minnie pushed it open, and they walked through into a windowless room that was painted the uniform color of the rest of the building—olive green. It contained twelve stainless-steel hospital cribs crowded along the walls, six to each side. Before they could approach the beds, a nurse came out from a side door and greeted them.

"How's everybody today?" Minnie asked.

"Just fine, Min, just fine", said the woman. "A bit of bad news: When you were away we lost the little Jane Doe that came from Children's Aid."

Minnie and Winnie sighed. "Oh, dear."

"That poor child."

"Dear little Janey."

"She was blind and deaf, girls, not to mention all the other problems she had. Nature took its course. It was a mercy."

"But she had such a nice way about her", said Winnie.

"The way you could hear her feeling things inside, almost as if she were thinking", said Minnie.

"And the little smile when we held her!"

"Well, she's better off now", said the nurse.

The sisters fell silent.

"And who is this?" the nurse asked in a professional tone.

"This is our friend Rose. We wanted her to meet the children", said Winnie.

"The children would like her", said Minnie.

"Well, make yourself at home", said the nurse and disappeared back into her office.

"Come and meet the children", said Winnie.

"*Our* children", whispered Minnie.

At first glance it looked as if none of the patients were children, though most of them were small in size. All were mentally handicapped, all bore the added burden of severe physical deformities. The sisters led Rose from crib to crib. At each station they leaned over the person inside, touched hands or foreheads, smiled, cooed, and introduced Rose. The response from many of their children was minimal, almost unnoticeable.

Rose did her best to hide her shock. The compassion she felt for the crib people was great, yet this instinctive reaction was combined with a feeling of utter dismay. Her inability to help them in any way was the worst of it. But there was another reaction that welled up slowly within her, bubbling out from under the conflicting emotions. Anger. Raw outrage. It left her with an almost irrepressible desire to scream.

But what was she angry about? Confused thoughts ran through her mind, spatters of disconnected arguments, protests, explanations. Is this what had happened to Hugo? Had he been so overpowered by the debasement of the things he loved, that he succumbed to the temptation to believe there was no meaning whatsoever in the universe, that neither beauty nor ugliness mattered, and therefore neither love nor hatred, neither creation nor destruction? Had the burning of his horses been a scream of protest?

Rose too screamed, though it did not emerge as a sound that others could have heard.

"Rose, this is Melba. Melba, this is Rose."

Melba was a woman without eyes, only empty sockets. Her skull was covered with white hair cut short to bristles. Her hands were bound by leather restraints to the bars of her crib.

"She scratches herself", Winnie explained.

Winnie hoisted herself up onto a foot rail, bent over the top bar, and kissed Melba on the forehead. A high pitched sound like a piercing dog whistle burst from the woman's toothless mouth. She broke into a grin, and her head thrashed from side to side.

Minnie reached through the bars and stroked her hands and arms.

"She's deaf too, Rose. But she knows our touch. We have a special language for her."

"Yes, we made a special language. It took us years to teach her."

Minnie began to trace a pattern of dots across Melba's forehead with the tip of her finger. The whistle ceased, and Melba laughed. It was by no means an ordinary sort of laugh, but it was unmistakably an utterance of pure delight.

Winnie touched the palm of Melba's right hand, then the left, then the soles of her bare feet. A single dot on each.

Then she repeated the pattern. Followed by seven gentle dots on the forehead. Curiously the woman made seven click sounds immediately after.

Then a dot on each of her palms. Followed by two clicks.

Then a dot on each foot. Followed by two more clicks.

Then laughter.

"She's the loneliest", Minnie said. "Some of our children are deaf, and some are blind. But she's both. In the old days she just whistled."

"It hurt our ears."

792

"But we didn't give up", said Minnie, gazing at Melba with affection.

"You should never give up", Winnie added. "Never, ever."

For several more minutes they stroked, dotted, clicked, and laughed, seeking the common meeting place of the spirit that they had long ago agreed upon with Melba. When they were ready to leave for the next crib, Minnie kissed Melba's forehead, and made three dots in the center of the woman's chest. This was followed by three clicks.

Winnie reached into her basket and withdrew a doll made of cloth. It was a very odd looking toy, for it had little depressions where the eyes should have been. The hair was made of white wool, chopped short. She pushed it through the bars and gently tamped it against Melba's cheek. The woman nuzzled it. Winnie stroked her cheek with it, then her lips. The lips touched the various features of the doll, as if reading it, seeing it. Winnie snugged it into the crook between the woman's jaw and shoulder. Melba clamped it firmly to herself. She clicked three times, sighed, and remained still.

Winnie, Minnie, and Rose moved on.

In the next crib lay a middle-aged man. Like the McCaul sisters, he was a dwarf. Unlike them, his facial features were cretinous, and the cranium of his head was abnormally small. He was heavily bearded, barrel chested, with stubby arms and legs. A tube ran down into one of his nostrils. He too whistled. The sound did not come from his mouth but from a metal plug at the base of his neck.

The sisters engaged his eyes, which at one moment were scowling beneath their beetled brows, and the next melting with childish excitement. He clapped his gnarled little hands together.

"Good morning, Mr. Humbolt", said Minnie in a cheery voice.

Mr. Humbolt was neither deaf nor blind, and the ensuing

793

conversation, composed in terms of utmost simplicity, was a genuine exchange. He made answering sounds through the hole in his esophagus. Whenever he closed the hole with a fingertip he was able to make deeper grunts and chuckles. He smiled frequently, and Rose quickly grasped that what had appeared to be a fierce and possibly dangerous gnome was in fact a mild personality. Minnie refrained from kisses, but patted his cheek, which made his body shake with mirth. From her basket she withdrew a round cloth Santa Claus doll which looked very much like Mr. Humbolt himself. When she shook it, bells jingled inside. His eyes lit up, and he reached for it. When they said good-bye to him, he inclined his head in a courtly bow and offered his right hand to each of the visitors for a shake. They left him staring at the doll and shaking it.

"It doesn't take much", Winnie said. "A little goes a long way."

"They know they're not forgotten", said Minnie.

Although Rose was getting used to the ward, the effect of so many visual shocks and blows was taking its toll. She excused herself and left the ward for a few minutes. Outside on the landing of the stairwell, she stared through a barred window at the barren moor. Rain was falling.

She could not dispel the feeling of anger and struggled to understand it. At first she told herself that in a world full of beauty it was a strange thing that these people carried such a burden of unloveliness added to their weakness and pain.

Why had God, the creator of all things, allowed it?

Had he intended man—or at least some men—to be like this from the beginning?

And if it had not been his intention, why had he failed to correct it? If he was love, why did he continuously hover over this landscape of suffering and do nothing? Was this love? If it was love, then she did not understand what love was. No, not in the least!

Unable to solve any of these riddles, she returned to the ward.

Minnie and Winnie were leaning over a crib on the left side of the room. Minnie pointed to a crib on the other side of the aisle, in the corner by the far wall.

"Rose, why don't you go meet Jimmy?"

Rose approached the crib warily, wondering what new grief she would find. Looking down at the form inside, she saw what she supposed was approximately a boy. He was lying on his back, sound asleep. His arms were flung up beside his head. Bare hands and feet poked out from candy stripe pajamas. The fingers of the hands were curled slightly, tiny, perfectly proportioned. Judging by the size of his body he could be no more than six years old. His face bore an expression of profound repose, a presence emanating from a dignity that was compact and complete. The only disturbing aspect about him was the shape of his head. From the crest of his forehead upward, the right side of the cranium was caved in. Fringes of black hair fell in feathery bangs over his brow, but on the rest of the skull the hair was thinning to the point of partial baldness.

Rose tried to blind herself to all details above his forehead. Because he was asleep, she was free to gaze upon the little form without any demand to engage the person it unconsciously expressed. As she meditated on his face, she gradually came to see that he was a mote of pure presence, radiant as a beacon at land's end. There at the borderline between strength and the ultimate fragility of all flesh, he slept in the arms of forces beyond his control or understanding. Everything, simply everything, was above him in the hierarchy of power.

He inhaled and exhaled silently. Behind the membranes of his eyelids dreams were underway. If absolute fraility evoked in her a rush of desire to hold and protect and nurture, at the same time it instilled an agony that had its source in every loss she had experienced during her life. As she pondered, she realized that each person was unique, unrepeatable. How did God know which ones to bring together? By what unthinkable wisdom did he know that *this* life would inform *that* life with a word.

Rose understood that for many years she had survived on grace and by the repeated turning of her will toward conformity with the will of God. Until this moment she had always assumed that this submission had cost her everything. She now saw that it had not cost her everything, for in many aspects of her life she exercised her will freely. Moreover, in her attitude to the trials of her life—those which she had not chosen—she had retained a filament of resentment. There had been times when she had envied the strong and the whole and in rare moments had given in to sadness regarding the pain in her back and the greater pain in her heart.

Here was one before her who had been deprived of all choice. He simply existed. From the beginning, he had been reduced to absolute being in a way that she never had. Yet he slept in peace, and dreamed.

Without warning, his eyelids fluttered and opened. He inhaled sharply, a little breath. His lips parted, revealing a set of perfect miniature teeth. He did not move. As galaxies wheeled slowly through the depths of his brown eyes, he looked at her without blinking or showing any signs of surprise. Rose did not know if he was capable of thought or speech, but the consciousness in his glance was beyond question. The soul who now pondered her presence was so fully *there* that she was drawn by it into a mysterious current that began to flow between them. This flow was not a give and take, backward and forward, or up and down. Indeed, though she towered over him, all sense of dimension dissolved. Time ceased. Their eyes rested on each other without self-consciousness or curiosity.

No thoughts stirred in Rose's mind, and of emotion there was only awe. In this state of total presence, she experienced what until then she had known only in worship before the living God.

The child was not God. He was a creature, no more, no less. He was an eternal soul. And the beauty of the soul staggered her. Her heart began to drum with a sound that reverberated in ascending waves, booming across voids, through constellations, past the outermost stars on the edge of the expanding crystal sphere. His small heart beat in time with hers. Then they were one beating heart as they flew together through the *tchibekana* into the waiting hands that rushed down to greet them, the hands enfolding all ranks of creatures, containing them, holding them, drawing them upward.

The boy blinked. He smiled.

Shaking herself, Rose smiled back at him, wondering how it was that she could be both here with him and flying up the heights of the river of souls with him. Locked in their flesh, yet free.

Holding her with his eyes, he reached to her with both arms. The palms of his hands opened. She desired greatly to take him into her arms, to hold him and rock him like a mother with her child. But she knew that it was impossible—the weight of his body, the weakness of her arms and back, the depth of his steel cage.

Feeling more helpless than ever, Rose wanted to weep. But his eyes would not let her. His smile broadened, and, with his right hand, he reached up and took her fingers in his own. In the heat of his hand she could feel his pulse, as light as a bird sitting in her palm, its tiny heart thrumming in the cage of its delicate breast.

When at last the flow of union ceded to time's demands, and the room began to appear around them, the boy opened his mouth and made a sound.

"O", he said in a whisper.

Whether or not it was merely a sound, or an actual word, did not matter.

"O", Rose whispered back to him.

Io! her heart cried.

The little fingers curled more firmly around hers.

"I love you", he said.

The entire *tchibekana* exploded into song, the sweet-green fire blazed throughout the wide-extended firmament, the ten million times ten million times ten million stars rang with the holy laughter of measureless joy, all wild flowers opened their petals and poured out their perfumes, whales in the deep sported, all birds flew up into the skies, and for a single moment—the pause between one breath and another—light burst into every soul in the world.

When Minnie and Winnie arrived, Jimmy looked at the sisters and smiled at them. He spoke no more words. He did not seem able to move his head, but his eyes returned again and again to Rose.

"He likes you", Winnie said.

"Who is he?" Rose asked.

"He's Jimmy Doe", said Minnie twinkling at the boy. "He's our little Jimmy Doe."

"Doesn't he have a family?"

The sisters shook their heads.

"No one ever comes. No one ever has", said Winnie.

"We will come", Rose said. "We will be his family."

She stood on tiptoes, bent into the crib, and kissed the shocking skull which until that moment she had blocked out.

"Nishime", Rose said. "Do you know you are mine?"

"He can't speak, Rose, dear."

"But he does", she answered. "He spoke to me."

"No, he never speaks. He never has."

Rose now realized that between her and the boy there was a great, indestructible secret. Their eyes met and confirmed it. Again he smiled at her. The radiation of his soul was such that she felt no desire to drink from it greedily or possess it. For whatever was in him was also in her. She was so full, so suddenly spilling over with whatever had been given and received, that she could not stop herself from returning to all the other cribs and meeting the people in them for a second time. Gazing through their exterior forms into their souls, she found that some were capable of looking back at her, of joining with her in the great singing. Those who were incapable of this quickened with excitement or grew very still, and all of them seemed to enter a state of supernatural peace.

When it came time for the visitors to depart, the boy's eyes followed Rose all the way to the exit. His face was the last thing she saw before the doors closed and the lock clicked.

Earl was waiting for them down in the entrance foyer. He was pacing back and forth, checking his wristwatch. The return journey to St. Peter's-by-the-Sea seemed to take only a few minutes. Rose sat in the back seat enfolded by the peace she had found. The sisters were quiet for a change, though they did ask Earl if he had accomplished all he had wanted to do in Sydney. He had.

When they arrived home, no one felt the need to talk. After sharing a quiet supper together, Rose, Minnie, and Winnie went their separate ways, each setting themselves to some task apart from the others. Minnie sewed in the kitchen. In the parlor, Winnie cut up old garments into quilt pieces. Rose went to the den and got out her pastel colors and a square of drawing paper. She worked on a picture until ten o'clock. When she heard the sisters climbing the staircase and calling good-night, she got into her nightgown and climbed into bed. Within minutes everyone was asleep.

The next day was Sunday. When Rose told the sisters that she would like to find a Catholic church and attend Mass, Minnie said there was a parish in the town eight miles farther along the coast. She phoned a neighbor and begged a ride for Rose.

"She's a Catholic, too," said Winnie with a bright smile, "really a very nice person."

So Rose went with the neighbor, attended Mass, and returned to St. Peter's just before noon. She had not had much solitude for several days, and so after lunch she told the sisters that she would like to take a walk alone on the beach. They thought that was a fine idea and sent her off bundled in one of their homemade scarves. Rose took a footpath across the salt-sprayed headlands, passing through stands of gnarled stunted spruce, ground juniper, and low shrubs of black crowberry. Arriving at the pebbled shore, she strolled along the water's edge for a time, staring at stones, breathing so deeply the pure cold air that her lungs ached.

The day was overcast, the humidity penetrating her bones. She felt her physical weakness anew and wondered if she could continue as an artist. It seemed to her that if she were to truly become a mother for the boy in the cage, she must live near him, and this meant she would have to find a way to make a living. But how?

As she ambled along, a mood of despondency gripped her, a feeling that everything she tried in life never amounted to much. She had poured out her life for her work, and it had come to nothing. She was defeated at every turn. Her beloveds were all gone, her life as an artist was gone, and maybe even her desire to adopt a little son would prove to be no more than an empty dream. The low mood steadily darkened into feelings of discouragement.

She stopped for a while on one of the sandy stretches to watch a band of red-beaked puffins clowning in the sea, diving and swimming expertly. Were they playing or fishing? She was not sure. Shore birds hunted up and down the strand on their stilt legs, whistling their prolonged *go-wit, go-wit, go-wit.* They were dressed in black-flecked cinnamon, cousins to the sandpipers that she had known along the rim of Threefinger Lake.

When the sun broke through the cloud layer over the Atlantic and lit up the cove for a few minutes, a sparkle of color attracted the corner of Rose's eye. She glanced at the spot where it appeared, and saw a braided line of reds, blues, and greens rolling at the high-water mark of a curl of surf. She walked to it and bent down to see what it was. At first she thought that the colors were pebbles, but on closer inspection she realized that the impression of a braid was created by numerous fragments of crockery, the smallest the size of her baby fingernail, the largest no larger than her thumb. There were hundreds of them, worn by the sea to a consistent smoothness, oval in shape, with ivory-colored rims. Their glazed surfaces were crackled, and beneath the network of hairlike fractures was a variety of designs: tiny flowers, geometrical patterns, random dashes, birds, and two miniature hands holding a heart.

Among them was a pale green stone the size of a large coin. It had been worn by the waves into the shape of an artist's palette, complete with a hole for a thumb and a half circle of dots, like dabs of colors. It was inexplicable. Rose had never seen anything like it. She put it into her pocket. As she bent again and again to pick up the little pieces of crockery, every find uncovered ten more, each unique, each an inspiration of the sea. She could not stop filling her pockets until they bulged. As her collection grew, so did a feeling of amazement and pleasure, as if she were salvaging the raw material of loveliness itself. She wondered if the sea had been assembling a vast mosaic throughout the ages. In its plenitude, it possessed more material than it needed and, from whimsy or generosity, allowed some of it to reach those solitary watchmen who strolled the shore.

Rose remembered the times when she and Tchibi had gathered the castoffs of the river, the sculpted woodwrack and the polished stones. So long ago it seemed—a memory, faded but not forgotten. She almost turned to speak to him, to show him the palette and the other marvels in her pocket gallery, then sighed ruefully at her foolishness, for he too was gone.

Was he gone?

"Io, Nishime", she whispered to the waves. "See what the world sends to us. See how there is no limit to its wonder. Ay, ay, my little brother, how I wish you were here beside me!"

But this sadness held no bitterness. The pain of absence was swept away by the promise given in these burnished, waterworn words: Nothing was lost, they said. Nothing. The forms changed but were not destroyed. They became other things and, in their new condition, were better able to take their true place.

She made her way slowly up through the rocks and dunes to the sisters' house and went inside. When they heard the front door close, they bustled out of the kitchen. They wanted to hear about everything she had seen on her walk. When she told them about the little runners crying *go-wit, go-wit, go-wit*, they threw up their hands in excitement.

"Oh, glory", Minnie exclaimed.

"You were *so* lucky, Rose", said Winnie. "Those were God-wits. A God-wit is a rare find. I've seen them only a few times in my life. They migrate, you know, and pass through here only for a day or so a year. Minnie, we must write this down in our bird book!"

"I'll do it this very minute!"

Over tea and shortbread, Rose emptied her pockets onto the kitchen table.

"What is this?" Winnie asked. The sisters bent over the collection just like the patients who had bent over the tin of saltwater taffy.

"It's little pieces of china", Rose explained. "I found them in the waves on the shore. I wonder how they came to be there."

Minnie sat back and removed her spectacles. "I think I know", she said in a musing tone.

"Tell us, Minnie, tell us", Winnie urged.

"Well, it would have been in 1898, I believe. Don't you remember, Win? Papa told us about it. A three-masted schooner out of Bristol, England, bound for Boston with a load of fine china. It went down in a terrible storm, just outside the bay."

"That's right! The *Princess Patricia*! She foundered on the rocks. You could see the masts for years, Papa said. He saw it when he was a boy."

"Yes, and remember when we were girls how he sometimes rowed us out in the dory on a calm day and we looked down on the ribs of the old ship. You could still see them under the water."

"I remember", Winnie shuddered. "It gave me a fright, it did. All those tommycods swimming in and out of the holes."

Minnie put her spectacles back on and peered at the china pieces. ·

"Imagine", she said. "After all these years, here's the jetsam at last. Oh, my, what a shipwreck it must have been."

"Yes", said Rose in a subdued voice. "The great shipwreck that went down before the beginning of the world."

They looked at her curiously.

"Minnie? Winnie?" Rose said. "I think I know what I was sent here to tell you."

28

Rose and the sisters talked long into the night. Rose told them about God, whom she called the Beating Heart. They said that was a lovely way to think of him. They told her that when they were little girls, they had been baptized.

"We were Presbyterians", said Minnie.

"No, dear, we were Methodists", Winnie corrected.

"Papa was Presbyterian, and Mama was Methodist."

"We used to love going to church at Christmas and Easter."

"But when Mama passed away, it took Papa quite a while to get over it."

"For the longest time he wasn't up to going to church."

"For years. Then we just forgot to go, I guess."

Minnie leaned forward earnestly. "But we do believe in Jesus."

"Oh, yes. Very much."

"We say the Lord's Prayer every morning." She looked shyly at her sister. "When we don't have company, of course."

"And the Psalm at night."

"The Twenty-third."

They smiled in unison at Rose and sat back, as if to say, you see, it's all settled.

"Do you go to your church at Easter and Christmas?" Rose asked.

"Some years we go. It depends on the rides and the weather. We do love Christmas. We had such lovely Christmases when we were girls. But it's an awful lot of effort for us now."

"We make dolls and things for Edgar's family."

"Easter morning, we bundle ourselves up warm and go down

to the beach just before dawn. Minnie insists on a little bonfire. Every year we have it."

"Every year we watch the sun come up."

"If there's a sun that year."

"There's not a sun every year. Sometimes it's stormy."

"But we always have the fire."

"That's right, every year we have the fire."

"Then we come home and make a special breakfast."

"Yes, there's such a feeling in the house that day."

"Light everywhere."

"And singing. As if the walls were singing."

"So you see, Rose, we like to remember", Winnie said shyly.

"The old rugged cross", Minnie said with a wistful smile, shaking her head at bygone days.

"And a closer walk with thee", Winnie contributed.

"Yes, and the lilies."

The sisters then launched into a discussion concerning the preservation of lily bulbs. It went on for a time, branched into the topic of what they wanted to plant in the garden come spring, then swerved back to feelings. They loved religious feelings, though they did caution Rose that people were sometimes, perhaps, a little *too* religious. Whenever that happened, they said, the feelings got all mixed up with unhappiness and unfriendliness and unneighborliness.

"And I don't think that's very good", said Minnie.

"He wouldn't want it", said Winnie.

Rose pondered their simple version of faith. Her dark eyes grew sad with an understanding of her own unrealized longings. Never had she known what these sisters had been given from birth: a father and mother, a secure position on the planet from which they could listen to the sea and watch the sun rise over the arc of the horizon. Year after year, the infinitely beautiful universe operated according to its dependable laws right before their eyes. They were content to be part of it. They asked for no more.

Rose saw how different her lot had been from theirs. Bush and city had been given to her, and in both places she had known little more than the broken dwelling, the broken family, and the broken heart. Why had God given her this kind of life and another to the sisters?

The face of Oldmary came to her as if in reply. Then Tchibi, and Fr. Andrei, Mère Jean, Hugo and Esther, and even, in her way, Euphrasia. God had not abandoned her, and in all places he had warmed her with the radiant heat of his presence in the sacraments. There had been times when he had spoken to her with words, words heard in the heart of the soul. There had been consolations. There had been charitable strangers aplenty, greater in number than those who had hurt her.

During that brief moment when Rose struggled to repudiate an upwelling of envy, of resentment, and of sadness, she admonished herself that her greatest fault might be, in fact, something that she had not considered wrong until now—the habit of forgetting. In the cold dark barrenlands through which the Presence had led her, this had been her abiding weakness: to forget in the desert what she had seen so clearly in times of plenty. Whenever she had indulged in regrets and dwelled on her losses, hiding in the dark burrow of self-pity, she had felt the shutters begin to close over her soul. One by one the windows were blocked. Then she was left alone with her fear.

Fear, her great adversary, had always prowled through the shadow forest surrounding her, ever seeking to spread its gloom over her, and worse, to fill her with its deception. Her mind knew it was deception, yes, but her heart sometimes forgot. And here again was her weakness: the forgetting. With faith and grace she had resisted it by doing those things that pushed back the darkness: praying, drawing, painting, and serving others. There had been times when the ecstasy of union with him had returned, so deep and so high that she had felt herself drawn up into the river of souls and beyond. But there also had been moments of defeat, of near despair.

Rose reminded herself that God often took his children on the darkness-way, the losing-way, so that they might arrive at the Promised Land with nothing but him as their strength, their treasure. Shaking away the envy, she smiled at the sisters and said, "How blessed you are to be given a life of peace."

"Oh, yes, we are very blessed", they nodded emphatically.

"We've often talked it over, Min and me", said Winnie. "And we don't understand why."

"We're the luckiest people in the world," said Minnie. "But why us?"

And why not me? The thought leaped unbidden into Rose's mind, bringing with it a trail of grief. Again she shook off the temptation.

She became aware that the sisters had fallen silent and were staring at her. Obviously they had asked her a question that she had not heard.

"Please, Rose, tell us more", Winnie said.

"About the Beating Heart", Minnie added. "That's Jesus, isn't it?"

"We know he's the one you meant, Rose. But we're not very smart people. You'll have to explain it."

Their earnest, open faces gazed at her in expectation.

"I—" Rose began, then faltered.

"Is it like Jimmy Doe?" said Minnie at last.

"And Melba?" said Winnie.

"Mr. Humbolt, too, and all the others?"

"Beating hearts—every one of them with beating hearts?"

"All inside the one big heart? Is that what you mean, Rose?"

"Yes," Rose whispered, "yes, it's like that. We're all inside. Held in his hands. But we don't know it."

"Yes," said Minnie, "I sometimes think it's just like that. I'm

Melba. He's bending over me, trying to reach me, but I can't hear him, I can't see him. Then he touches my head and my heart."

She made seven dots on her forehead and three on her heart.

Winnie took her sister's hand. "Oh, Min, dear, I've often thought the same. *We're* Melba."

"Win, you too? You should have said something."

"I was sure you'd think I was being silly."

Once again, they careened away on a side trail of conversation. When they had come full circle, they fell silent and looked at Rose. Winnie leaned forward, the toes of her slippers brushing the carpet like a tiny ballerina.

"Rose, we really shouldn't impose. But we'd like to ask you something."

"And you must feel free to say no", Minnie added.

"We were wondering if you've ever thought of living by the sea."

On the bus ride back to Montreal, Rose had a lot to think about. Minnie and Winnie had asked her to come and live with them. They were doing very well now, they said, selling their dolls left and right, the money was flowing in, they would hire Edgar to build an addition onto the house.

"For a slightly larger person", Minnie said.

"Though not overlarge."

"Then you can be an artist without fretting and fussing about where your next penny's coming from."

"We'd love it, Rose. Really we would. You're like our sister."

"Our daughter", Winnie corrected.

"No, more like our little sister", Minnie argued.

"*Younger* sister," Winnie said, "not little."

"She's rather a tall person, it's true, but not terribly tall."

The humor of jumbled perspective struck all three women at

once, and they burst out laughing. Rose took their hands and said, "Winnie, Minnie, I thank you for your invitation. Rarely in my life have I been offered something so generous and beautiful. I will go home to Montreal and pray to our Lord about it. If it is his will, I will return."

"Oh, goodness," said Winnie anxiously, "what if it's *not* his will?"

"Then we can visit each other", said Rose smiling. "We will always be friends."

"That's right", Minnie said. "And family. And our children are your children too. Jimmy Doe is yours now, isn't he?"

"Yes", Rose answered, lowering her eyes.

Thus as Nova Scotia melted into the hills and valleys of New Brunswick, the face of Jimmy appeared in the eyes of her heart. The thrumming pulse in her hand told her that he was with her and they would never be separated. She would return. She was certain of it. God could not say no to this. He would not have given her a child if he meant to take him away again.

She would pray for the Lord's will. Yet it seemed to her that his will was clear. She knew that some were called to the solitary path. Oh, yes, some. But souls needed other souls to lift hope on high, to console, and to remind each other of what was so easily forgotten. Moreover, she was growing older, her health was worse with each passing year. Although the sisters did not really need someone to look after them, they were older than she was, and in time their health would fail, and they might be placed in an institution. How could they bear such a thing? There was another way. They could all look after each other.

Now as the bus dipped down into a river valley and wound northward, Rose recalled their last meeting. At the bus station, Minnie had twinkled her eyes and squeezed her hands, saying, "Just imagine, Rose! One day, many, many little people may come to live together by the ocean. Think of it—a place where we all could live! We'll be happy together."

"We'll make beautiful dolls and pictures", said Winnie. "We'll teach others to make them."

"And at Easter," said Rose, "every Easter, on the day of forth-bursting, on the day of light and singing, we'll have a fire on the beach."

"Yes, yes", the sisters whispered. "Hundreds of us. Maybe thousands."

Rose took a tube of paper from her backpack and handed it to them. The sisters unrolled it together. Their mouths opened and tears sprang to their eyes.

"Oh!" breathed Minnie.

"Oh!" sighed Winnie. "Is it us, Rose?"

Rose nodded. Rendered in many colors, the pastel drawing portrayed two sisters, Minnie and Winnie, as little children. They lay side by side in a cradle, arm in arm. On their breasts they held small white birds, and in the center of each bird was a flame. The cradle was a bower of wild flowers and lilies. At the bottom of the image a bonfire blazed on a beach. God-wits ran whistling along the shore. A tiny sailing ship dipped its bow into a swell of azure waves, its pennants snapping, its canvas singing. Above, on the crest of rolling green hills, three little houses stood side by side: one yellow with white trim, another white with yellow trim, and a third, brown with white and yellow trim. Above the houses the sky deepened from cerulean blue to cobalt-black in which countless stars wheeled, a river of stars spiraling upward to the height of the image where two wings hovered over everything. From between the wings brown muscled arms reached down, the large hands enfolding, the fingers touching the foreheads of the twins in the bower.

"It's for you to keep", Rose said.

"Oh!" Winnie sighed.

"Oh!" Minnie echoed.

They threw their arms about her. She bent and held their small bodies.

Now the bus descended from the wooded heights, entered the flatlands beside the great river, and turned west. As the hours passed, Rose drifted into slumber and the image of her child came again and again to her, his brown eyes blazing with the powers of the soul. As he gazed back at her she knew that somewhere in the inner maze of the institution he was lying awake, thinking of her. He was seeing her face in the eyes of his heart.

Waking, she noticed that night was falling and the glow of Montreal now covered the horizon ahead.

"No longer will you be called Jimmy Doe", she whispered. "No longer will you be called forsaken. Io! Now you will be my son and I your mother."

Yes, though the cold and dark of the barrenlands seemed overwhelming, and though there were ten thousand times ten thousand Jimmy Does in this world, there were also many Roses. In all places the small beating hearts would make islands of light in the darkness, would grow and spread and join with others who kept vigil at the edge of the world.

"What is your true name? I will pray to the Beating Heart for the giving of your name. For you are known in his mind and are not forgotten. He alone knows who you are, he alone knows your task in the world. He alone sees the full measure of your burning heart, little son, little true son."

She wondered if this was his name: True Son. But there was an incompleteness to the thought. These words were *about* him, but they were not *him*, not the core of him. So she fell back into slumber and rested in the hands that came down from above, and when she awoke again, she heard the words-without-words. They rose to the surface of the sea, she saw their form and the meaning of them, and it was given to her that she must shape the meaning into a spoken word.

"Your name", she whispered to the child in the steel cage, "is Beloved of God. Your name is John."

Rose fell ill again after returning to her rooms on Rue Fauxjour. Fearing a recurrence of the flu and the specter of pneumonia, she remained in bed for two days. She tried to go out on the third in order to apply for work, but shortness of breath, dizziness, and a persistent fatigue drove her back to her room before she had walked a block. She slept a great deal, when she was not nursing a grating cough that seemed to have started all on its own deep in her lungs. Still, there was no bubbling, no sign of real infection. She attributed the sickness to the long journey and the onset of winter.

When she was able to get up again, she unpacked her bag and found inside it a little doll. The doll was about eight inches high, a short, broadfaced Indian woman with shiny black button eyes. The skin was made from brown cloth. The hair was gray wool. The dress was a dark green jumper on which one of the sisters had embroidered a wild rose. A little hump along the spine made Rose smile, then laugh.

Accompanying the doll was a tiny leatherette knapsack. Inside the sack was a hundred-dollar bill and a note.

Rose, dear,

This is from us to you.

It's an early Christmas present.

We hope it will help with your expenses and speed you back to us soon.

Winnie and Minnie and all the family

Rose determined that as soon as she was able she would go to the shrine on Mount Royal and ask St. Joseph to pray for her, especially that he might intercede on her behalf for the will of God to be accomplished in her life. She felt more certain than ever that her future now lay with the sisters on the coast of

Nova Scotia. She was so sure of this that she wondered if it was necessary to make special prayers for the intention. She reminded herself, however, that her feelings were not always reliable, and that if she had truly given her life entirely to God, she must not make hasty decisions. She wrote to Minnie and Winnie explaining that she was still waiting for an answer from heaven. She asked them to pray for her, that she would hear God's will correctly, and obey it without question.

On December eighth, she felt a little recovered and went to the Oratory of St. Joseph on the holy mountain. Because she did not feel well enough to walk all the way, she took the city bus instead.

Io, the air was rich with grace that day, and it seemed to her that the statues of the Mother were as radiant and gentle as those of her adopted father. The Beating Heart sent wave after wave to her during Communion and she was so completely saturated in it that for an hour after the final blessing she could not move.

Still, she wondered why the Beating Heart did not speak to her about her request. Surely, the third and final journey still lay before her. Was it not a return journey to St. Peter's-by-the-Sea?

As she made ready to leave the basilica, she fell to coughing, and brought up a bit of blood from her lungs, spattering a linen pocket handkerchief. She did not worry overmuch about it, though it did seem odd. There was no infection in it—only the blood—so bright red that she could not recall ever having produced such a thing before.

She coughed throughout the night, sleeping fitfully. The ache in her back was worse than usual, so much so that she began to groan from it. She got up to make herself a cup of tea, and the room began spinning. So she staggered back to bed. The sharp stabs in her spine kept her awake until dawn, when she decided that it would not hurt to see a doctor. He might prescribe a mild painkiller, and then she could sleep, speeding her recovery.

Around the corner from Rue Fauxjour was a street clinic run by doctors who devoted one day a week to serving the poor. In the reception room of the clinic, which was filled with several dozen other residents of St. Henri, she waited for three hours until a doctor could see her. He asked about her symptoms, and she told him about her cough. He listened to her lungs through his stethoscope and felt the sides of her neck.

"How long have you had this cough?"

"About a week."

"It's a dry hacking cough, isn't it?"

"Yes."

"Any other symptoms?"

"Yes, I've been rather dizzy."

"And are your thoughts sometimes out of the ordinary?"

"What is ordinary?" she asked, remembering something Hugo once said when he was in the mental asylum.

"A good question. Actually, a good point", he said, looking at her with new interest.

"What I mean is, do you find your mind acting in any way that's unusual for you? Do you sometimes wonder where you are or how you got there?"

"All the time", she smiled.

Thankfully, he seemed to understand that she was making a little joke. He returned her smile.

"I mean, more than usual?"

"No."

He frowned when she spat up a bit of blood into her handkerchief.

"It's a bad cold", Rose explained.

"Have you ever had pneumonia or tuberculosis?" he asked glancing at her with concern.

"Tuberculosis? No, I don't think so", she replied. "But I have had pneumonia more than once. And I usually get bronchitis at this time of year. That's probably all it is."

"It may be no more than you say, Miss Wâbos. Your lungs don't seem to be infected, but I'd feel easier if you'd go for some tests. Would you be willing to do that?"

"Yes, if you think it's necessary."

He wrote out an appointment card and handed it to her. "There's a free outpatient clinic at Mercy Hospital. If you show up there tomorrow morning at nine, and give them this, they'll do the tests. Come and see me on Friday, and we can discuss the results then."

When she saw the doctor again, he asked her to sit down on the visitor's chair in his office. He closed the door.

"Miss Wâbos", he began. He paused, cleared his throat, laced his fingers on the desk in front of him and began again. "I have some difficult news for you. You have a tumor in your right lung. The cancer has mestastasized, moved from the lung by the bloodstream into your brain."

"What does this mean?"

Looking down at his hands, he said, "It means no curative therapy can be applied because the cancer has spread from its primary site. Only palliative care is possible now."

"What is palliative care?"

He inhaled deeply and began to blink rapidly. He was a young man, and Rose now understood that he was not used to giving bad news to patients.

In a low voice he said, "I'm afraid it means you have between two and six months to live."

Rose took this information calmly, in fact, without any emotion. She was merely puzzled. She could not think of anything to say.

"I'm sorry", the doctor went on. "We'll do everything in our power to relieve any suffering you may experience."

"Two to six months?"

"Yes."

"That's all?"

He nodded.

"What comes next? Will I just get sicker and sicker?"

"I'm not sure exactly how it will progress. There are variations depending on the constitution of the individual. But you can expect the shortness of breath to increase. You'll feel confused at times and wonder where you are—even who you are. These episodes will pass, but they can be upsetting. I'll prescribe a tranquilizer if you wish. That's something to make you calm."

"I don't think I'll need it, doctor. What else will happen? I want to know it all. You need not hide it for the sake of my feelings."

"There may be swellings in your neck, the lymph nodes. Later, if the cancer spreads to the bones, you could develop tumors on one or more vertebrae—your spine—also the pelvis and femur could be affected. If multiple bone deposits develop, there'll be pain, perhaps a lot of pain. We'll help you with that. But it won't happen until closer to . . ."

"To the end?"

Again he nodded.

"Do you have family in the city?" he asked gently

"No", she said.

Rose returned to her rooms on Rue Fauxjour and lay down on the bed. She stared at the ceiling and watched the dappled colors of Christmas lights that came in through the window from the laundromat across the street. Car horns sounded, clacking hockey sticks and the shouts of small boys rang on the sidewalk outside. The radiator clanked rhythmically. The machinery of the world went on.

She felt nothing. The information was not real, though in a corner of her mind she acknowledged that it must be true.

Death. Hugo had called it "the old lover-monster". She subtracted the word *lover* and was left with the core of the matter: it was a monster. It ate. It devoured without prejudice. One and all fell into the open jaws of the great *neshiwed* itself, the *kinoje* that haunted the world, haunted every life, and materialized in front of one no matter where he turned to escape it, no matter how much he denied its existence.

It was bigger than she was. It was now so big there was nothing she could do to defeat it. She might delay it for a time, but in the end it would accomplish what it always set out to do.

Even so, something within her was greater than death. She knew this with her mind, and knew it also, to a degree, in her heart. Death's power lay partly in its terror. Men scattered before it or fought it or picked up the tools of malice as if to convince themselves that wielding death gave them power over it. She had no strength to do any of these. So she opened the tightly curled fists of her hands, realizing that the fingernails had been biting into the palms. She inhaled, feeling the alien mass in her lung for the first time, horrified by it, hating it. This was followed by anger. Then she sagged and closed her eyes, muted all sounds, and went down inside herself to the heart of the soul.

There, she spoke to the silence—a silence that had never been more silent than it was now—saying, "I accept. Do what you want with me."

For a time she floated in the pool of abandonment, letting go of her fear, letting go of her self, or letting go of the fierce grip on life that she thought was her self.

"Io, at last I am becoming a poor person. This I offer. Yes, this too I offer."

The next morning she awoke to the renewed ache in her spine, a soreness on the right side of her neck, and a return of the fear. She practiced letting go, floating. But the physical pain soon distracted her, and she could not stop examining her skin with her fingertips again and again. Lurking below the surface were the *neshiweds*, unseen, growing. There were no lumps yet. When she coughed, it produced only a few speckles of blood.

"How long?"

Two months at least? Six at best?

Beyond that, it was a sentence that would not be commuted. She might, of course, plead for mercy. Miracles did happen. The holy mountain was a place of miraculous cure, and she would surely go there to ask for one. But the real question was, did he want her to go on in life. Was it his will that she return to her new family, to be a mother for John, and to paint more images that would stir souls to look up beyond the barrenland?

"My work is not yet finished", she said to the silence. It never would be finished, she replied for him. Yes, she tried to fill his mouth with the answer she needed, wanted, hoped for. Never would death's arrival be opportune, never, not while the well of the heart overflowed. By supplying his response, she did not feel in any way reassured. Instead she felt the silence spread. Was he asking her to be silent, to permit without a struggle all that was to happen? She wanted to greet his silence with her own—the silence of perfect trust. But the thoughts would not cease. What if she were granted another ten years or twenty or thirty? In the end would she be brought to the same question: Why? Why now? Why now, when there is so much left to do? If you take me now, is it the same as if you take me thirty years from now?

Thus, the wrestling match began again, circling around and around the central blow that had been struck. After acceptance came doubt and fear. Then came the grief of losing all that she would have given were it not being taken from her. Who could explain this contradiction? Then acceptance again. Then grief. The cycle would not stop and it soon exhausted her more than the sickness itself.

Two months, the doctor had promised.

"I am certain of two months at least. I can do much during

this time. I can get ready. I will explain to my beloveds why I cannot continue in their lives. Minnie and Winnie will understand. But, Oh, my John! How will you understand? I will write to my sisters and beg them to be your mothers in my place. I will tell them your true name, that you *do* speak, yes, that there are thoughts within your mind, but most of all that you speak with the powers of your soul."

Rose got out of bed. Beyond the windowpane, snow was falling on St. Henri, whitening the streets. Footprints stippled the sidewalks, tire tracks unrolled ribbons. The children were at school dreaming of Christmas. The adults were working or searching for work. A garbage truck rumbled past, shaking the building's thin walls. Iron squealed on iron, then banged. Shouting men dumped metal cans into the jackfish jaws and threw them back empty onto the sidewalk.

When the noise had subsided she said her morning prayers. Then, in an effort to bolster her courage, she set on the window sill the little doll the sisters had made for her. She emptied her pockets of the countless china pieces scavenged from the beach of St. Peter's-by-the-Sea and put them onto the sill beside the doll, where the light could spark their colors. After that, she got dressed and went outside to search for help. A lady at the local welfare office listened to her story, read the medical report, stared at her, and gave her a voucher for food. Then she stamped a form that certified Rose to receive a relief check every two weeks from now on.

From now until the end, Rose silently added.

The shame she felt was no more than a passing thing. She had done everything in her power to look after herself, and now she was running out of everything, running out of life itself. Too swiftly, it seemed. Or too slowly?

On Sunday morning she took the bus to Mount Royal and spent the day at the shrine. She asked God to heal her and asked

St. Joseph to add his prayers for this intention. She begged this gift for the sake of her new family. But her emotions were mixed. For the first time, she entertained an attraction to death. Death would be like dropping down into a deep snow bank and falling asleep forever. Released from her lifelong pain, flying up at last into the *tchibekana* and beyond it to the many-gated city, she would meet the faces of love who would rush out to greet her. And foremost among them the hidden face of the Beating Heart. Did he want her to come to him now? If so, she would go without resistance. But if he was going to heal her, would it be for a year, a few years, decades? And if he did, would he give her strength as well, with which she could serve his children?

But he was only silent. The air of the shrine did not cease to be a radiant stillness, but it was no longer liquid gold. It was the visible shape of silence. There were no consolations after Communion.

Ay, ay, I do not understand!

Day after day, she returned to the shrine to pray. In the growing state of abandonment, she continued to ask for a miracle, yet three times during that week she coughed up bright red blood. The sore in her neck swelled into a hillock. A knife was permanently planted in her spine between the shoulder blades.

Once she took the bus across the river to the shrine of Blessed Kateri but found it locked, the building closed for a month of renovations. Leaning her head against the door, she prayed that her beloved sister would intercede on her behalf.

On the ninth day of her pilgrimage to the mountain she experienced a consolation after receiving the Eucharist, and during that brief ecstasy, she heard a final word:

Three journeys I give you, for the purification of your soul and for the good of many souls. Two journeys you have taken, the third and last is before you.

"Where, my Lord? Tell me, and I will go."

To the city of pride.

And without the benefit of further explanation, she knew that he was calling her to the capital, to that place of desolation through which she had passed many years ago.

Rose rested in bed for a day, gathering her strength. On the following morning, the twenty-fourth of December, she wrote a letter to the McCaul sisters. She stamped it and put it into her pocket. She coughed a large gout of blood, saturating the handkerchief. Dizzy, she fell onto the bed and dozed fitfully. Waking sometime later, she lay still for a while, uncertain about where she was. Only the laundromat lights illumined the room, spattering dots of color across the ceiling.

"My name—" she said. Several minutes ensued before she was able to finish the thought.

"—is Bineshi. I am a silver bird. Or a rose, I think. At least I once was a rose. Or a rabbit—"

"—Rose—yes, that's it."

"O—Oh—ghini—Wah—bose."

Struggling to her feet, Rose made ready to go. Into her parka pockets, she stuffed the remaining money and the doll the sisters had made for her. Recalling for a moment the salt-sharp wind beside the sea and the cries of the God-wits, she scooped up a handful of polished china pieces from the great shipwreck that had gone down before the beginning of the world.

Desiring a last look at her artwork, she opened the closet door, only to find the floor littered with shreds of paper. Mice had nibbled the bottom half of the roll of pastel drawings. There were holes in some of the paintings as well. Lacking the will to examine the extent of the damage, she closed the closet door.

Out in the street, the late-afternoon air cleared her mind a little, and she remembered that she had a work to do. After dropping the letter to the McCauls into a mailbox, she walked down Rue Fauxjour and left its graying half-light behind for the bright street lamps of Notre Dame. Her thoughts righted themselves, and she turned east. Half an hour later, she arrived at the central bus station, exhausted. She purchased a ticket for Ottawa and by five o'clock was riding on the Greyhound into the west.

The hub of power in the capital was a T junction. Wellington Street ran east to west, Elgin Street ran south to north and butted into Wellington at the Parliament buildings. On the alternate corners of the intersection were the huge Victorian railway station, the Chateau Laurier Hotel, the War Memorial, the end of the Rideau canal, frozen now, and, as if rebuking the grandeur of all that nineteenth-century architecture, the ultra-modern National Center for the Performing Arts. This was a cluster of cement cubes, its featurelessness relieved only by a few surrounding trees. Christmas lights danced in the bare branches, paler stars pricked the dome of the sky. People walked briskly along the sidewalks, ran for buses or taxis, passed with uneasy glances the Santas jingling bells in front of plastic pots full of coins. Others scurried in and out of the stores that remained open for last-minute shoppers.

Rose stopped in front of the glass display cases on the outer wall of the Arts Center. A poster in one of them announced a play that would be performed that night. Foot-high bold letters proclaimed: HURONIA.

Below it was a picture of a beautiful young native woman, half-naked, garbed in tatters of white deer hide. Weeping, she clung to a tree, while above her towered a sinister figure dressed in the long black cassock of the Jesuits.

At the base of the image was the following:

A play by Wolfgang von Falkenstein, produced and directed by Mark Chandler-Ross, performed by Cirque des Etoiles Theatre Company in conjunction with the National Ballet of Canada and the Ministry of Culture, Government of Canada.

This was followed by quotes from newspaper reviews:

The smash hit that took New York, London, and Montreal by storm comes home at last. A dazzling production!

Intense, shattering, deeply moving, this is an epic account of an oppressed people who refuse to be subjugated by alien values. Among the top ten plays of the decade.

Huronia is drama at its most pure and most powerful. When the Blackrobes come among the free peoples of North America, bondage, exploitation, and disease follow. Only one person dares to stand against them, the young Huron woman, Wildrose. Desired by the hypocritical missionaries and by the traders who collaborate with them, this courageous visionary rejects white, European domination, and rallies her people to their own life-giving culture.

Two thumbs up! Don't miss it!

Rose read the poster a second time, swaying on her feet, trembling. A bus slid to a stop at the curb behind her, its brakes hissing. Wheeling about, Rose saw the jackfish bolt away down the street carrying many souls in its belly. She cried out to warn them, but they could not hear.

As she trudged along Wellington toward the Market district, the music of Stravinsky faded in her ears. When she came to Sussex Street, she turned onto it, for in the distance a bell was ringing slowly in the steeple of a church. She followed the sound and entered a crowd of people leaving the church. They were shaking hands, hugging, kissing, wishing each other "Merry Christmas". The crowd dissolved in every direction, and Rose slowly climbed the steps to the front door. A sign informed her that it was the cathedral. She wanted to go inside. The warmth beckoned. Most of all, she desired the deep rest of his presence. To be reassured. To be consoled at the stable near his altar. And the manger. She would kneel before the Child and ask his pardon for the play.

Opening the front door, she was met by two custodians who were locking up. They stared at her.

"Please, may I go inside and pray?" she asked timidly. It came out as a croak.

"We're closed for the night."

"Just for a few minutes? I want to see him."

"Who?" one asked.

"There's a shelter down on the market you could go to", said the other. "Two blocks up, three blocks east. They'll give you something to eat."

"Nah, it's closed for the night", said the other man. "Besides, I heard it's full."

Turning away, Rose went down the steps.

The cathedral was situated on a corner. She turned onto a side street, and as she passed along one wall of the building she came upon an outdoor manger scene. The stable walls and roof were made of spruce logs. It was filled with hay. The statues were life-sized—Mary, Joseph, the Christ Child, shepherds, animals. She dropped to her knees before the crib. The colored lights suddenly went out. So did all the lights in the church windows. The traffic light at the corner illuminated the stable with a faint green glow.

Rose leaned over and kissed the forehead of the baby.

It felt as cold as ice on her lips.

"Io, my Lord", she sighed.

She reached inside and stroked the face, the little arms lifted to embrace the world. The tiny hands. She took the fingers of one hand in her own. At first they burned her with cold, then they gradually warmed as she warmed them, and they warmed her, and she warmed them—it was difficult to know which was which.

Struggling for breath, she began to shiver uncontrollably.

"I have no place to go", she said. "Baby Jesus, I have no place to go. I am in the no-place, I have become a no-thing. Only you remain."

Galaxies whirled across the orbs of his eyes, but he did not move.

"You are God", she breathed, dropping silent tears onto his forehead. "You are God."

Again and again she repeated it, inhaling the word, exhaling the word, whispering the forgotten word, the humiliated word, the abandoned word.

"You are God."

Her tears ran down from the crown of his head. When the traffic light turned red, the tears turned to blood.

Realizing that she was still shaking with cold, Rose crawled on hands and knees and burrowed into a mound of hay behind the statue of Mary. Wads of canvas swirled about a shepherd's feet. She dragged it over herself. Then more hay over that. She felt warmer, yet it was some time before the attacks of shivering ceased.

Seized with sudden longing, she reached into the crib and picked up the statue of the infant Jesus, took it in her arms, and wiggled back down inside the cocoon.

Slowly, slowly she rocked him, crooning the songs that Old-mary had sung to her, and the Huron Carol written by one of the martyred Blackrobes. When she could sing no more, from her lips there came the loon songs that Tchibi had sung and the wordless atonal chants of the cold dark barren lands crying out for a savior.

29

Bells were ringing as she awoke. The tower of the Parliament buildings bonged heavily, the cathedral cling-clanged its lighter bells, and the more distant churches added theirs to the general rejoicing. It was Christmas morning.

"But where's the baby?" said a woman's voice.

"Maybe somebody forgot to put it in the manger last night."

"I doubt it, Jake. Probably a thief made off with it."

"Ah, Mum, who'd do a thing like that?" said a girl's voice.

"They'd have to be crazy, Dad", said the voice of an adolescent boy.

Rose stirred and poked her head out of the hay. She saw before her, standing in front of the manger, a middle-aged man and woman and seven young people ranging in ages from eight to twenty. When they saw her face appear between Joseph and Mary, their mouths fell open.

Rose placed the statue of the Child Jesus into the manger, kissed its forehead, and got to her feet, shaking straw from her rumpled clothing.

"What on earth—" the man exclaimed.

The woman stared at Rose intensely. "I think I know you—" she murmured, straining to recall a lost memory.

"Huh? What? How could you know her?" said the man shaking his head.

Rose did not recognize them. Embarrassed, ashamed of her blood-spattered parka and hacking cough, she stumbled away down the street.

Rose walked on, head down, seeing nothing but her feet darting before her: in-out, in-out, in-out. Slush caked her boots. Her feet ached with the chill. The tips of her toes were numb. Three blocks down, she came to another church, where people were still arriving for Mass. She entered the welcome warmth of this small parish and slid into the back pew just as the opening hymn began. The singing was weak, for it was a poor parish, the congregation few in number, most of them elderly.

Trembling throughout the liturgy, she tried hard to concentrate, to form words of prayer, or at least to fix her attention on the altar. In this she succeeded only at the Consecration and the elevation.

Kije-kije-kije-Manito! her heart cried. *I have nothing to give you on this your day. Nothing do I give you but my self. Yes, I give all of it. Io, it should have been more, but it is less, it is the falling, the falling and dying. But this also I give to you.*

She joined the line for Communion, but when she reached the priest who was distributing the Host, he stared at her, held back the ciborium, and shook his head. In a split second she understood how he must see her—dirty, bedraggled, bloody, coughing—a street person, a madwoman. Horror passed across his face, followed by a silent inner struggle as he wondered if she was capable of receiving the sacrament worthily.

Rose knelt on the wet floor, closed her eyes, raised her face to him, and opened her mouth.

"Jesus", she exhaled. "You are God."

When the Host was placed on her tongue, the sweet-fire entered her.

A hand rested on the crown of her head. She looked up to see the priest gazing at her with pity. Because there were others waiting to receive Communion, he withdrew his hand. Rose got to her feet and returned to her pew at the back, behind a pillar where she could be invisible.

During the thanksgiving time, she was unable to say a thing

to the Presence within her. Nor did he speak to her, neither thought-words nor words-without-words.

After the final blessing and hymn, she went out into the streets.

It was snowing now. Large wet flakes dropped down from above, blanketing everything. She walked back in the direction from which she had come earlier in the morning, past the manger—the manger was now all inside her—past the cathedral, past the blood-red traffic light. On the other side of the street an immense glass structure towered above a plaza. Shining through the curtains of snow, it looked like a giant crystal.

Something drew her toward it, perhaps the promise of a public building in which she might warm herself for a time, perhaps an ancient memory of quartz. As she approached it, two stainless steel doors opened automatically. She passed between them and entered a lobby that smelled of heated air, fresh carpets, paper, canvas, and paint.

In the center of the lobby a sign proclaimed:

The National Gallery of Canada
wishes you a festive holiday!

This was repeated in French and surrounded by translations into several languages. She now recognized the presences in the air, the chorus of holy *anjeni*, and the discordant noises of the fallen ones. Painted words cried out from distant rooms, the galleries that lay beyond the main lobby. Rose turned hesitantly to the left and walked up a marble ramp leading deeper into the building. Because the guards were distracted, they did not see her pass with her bloody coat.

Reaching the end of the ramp, she turned right and entered through bronze doors into a wide open space filled with golden light. The floors were polished wood and the walls a non-reflective white.

The temperature in the room was hot. Rose began to sweat.

She removed her parka, folded it, and carried it in her arms. At the far end of the room a single guard paced back and forth, checking his wrist watch. He glanced at Rose then looked away. Other visitors strolled about, stopping for a few moments before each image.

In the first of several annex galleries, a room that was small but volatile with presence, Rose found glass-covered cases of chalices and ciboriums. She felt from them the radiant afterglow of the presence they had once contained. In this room there was also an ornate wooden altar, hand-carved two centuries ago in a Québec workshop. Its tabernacle door was open, the inner chamber empty.

On the surrounding walls were paintings of the saints. She wanted to pray before them, but reminded herself that she was in a museum. She was dizzy, and sharp stabs pulsated in her spine and chest. The lumps in her neck pushed against the distended skin. Though she was unable to make formal prayers, she spent long minutes before each image, eyes closed, seeing them internally, sadness flooding her as she realized that for many they were not windows on the infinite, but on the past. Taking her leave of them, she passed into another wing containing more annexes.

She entered a room of landscapes, rich in color and mood, painted early in the century. Many of the places were familiar to her, for they were variations on the land she had known from birth, the barrens, filled with both beauty and terror, the *ultima thule*, where one would go if one wished to be absorbed by absolutes, to be taken and seen no more.

"You would get lost", said little Ogini to Euphrasia of the Flowers.

"Yes, of course. It would be silly, wouldn't it, doing something like that? On a whim. On a sentiment."

"But if you did, God would be with you", said the girl with obsidian black eyes.

"God?"

Leaving this gallery, she entered the next and the next, continuing her journey through the century's decades. The sixth decade contained hundreds of images without recognizable forms. There she found the language that Hugo had sought to master during his lost years. Slabs of color among splatters of randomness, heaps of plastic, wriggling electronics, and photographs of nothingness. Absurdity and darkness and death and despair.

Rose groaned and hurried on.

A sign on the wall beside an entrance said *Contemporary Realism.* Rose went into a small annex and gazed about at the dozen paintings within. Facing her, a woman sold caged birds.

Esther's acid voice burned through the veneer of the canvas: "Denial is for those who do not value life as they should. Only as they are led to the place of execution do they awake."

"Esther, darling," said Hugo, "enough of this morbidity!"

"Large betrayals, Huggo! Large betrayals have their roots in small betrayals."

"And the lost? What of the lost? Can the delusions be reversed?"

"If recognized for what they are." Esther's voice climbed to a note of dangerous threat. "Then comes the choice."

"What choice?" Hugo demanded.

"To sink in bitterness, or to carry deprivation with love. As the price of love."

"Price? What do you mean price?"

"To give life, it costs. Always it costs. Sometimes it costs everything."

"To love", Rose interjected, "is to desire with your whole heart to give everything. To carry others on your back and in your heart. To exchange your strength for another's weakness, and this becomes the offering-way."

"Tell me, Rose," Hugo growled in his most ferocious tone,

"where is the one who designed this patched-up old motor of a universe. Eh? Tell me! As you journey into the cold dark barren infinity, *nothing* is seen in the eye of God, because there *is* no eye of God, except within the self."

"No, Hugo, no! You are deceived. It is the liar's art, it is the falsifier and the false fire, for you have not yet heard the singing!"

"Too much black, my rose-colored-glasses girl. Too much black paint splashed across the canvas."

Esther cut in angrily: "Huggo, be quiet! You are lecturing!"

"Nonsense! I was about to tell Rose the great secret of Art."

"She knows it already."

"No, she doesn't!"

But Hugo and Esther—sparring to the last—dissolved into thin air.

As Rose stumbled about the room, a guard eyed her, but turned away, yawning. It was Christmas Day, it was close to lunch time, he wanted to go home.

Then, miracle of miracles, she saw Tchibi. He was standing quietly at the end of the room, gazing at her.

"Nissime, little sister, do not be afraid. I am with you."

"Nishime, little brother, I will not be afraid, if you are here."

"I am here."

How changed he was! He was clean and strong and tall, the burn holes washed from his body. He was sane. He was in love with her.

"Oginiwâbigon Wâbos," he said with great tenderness, "let us never be separated again. Soon, you will come. You will fly up into the *tchibekana* and beyond it to the City of Light in the kingdom of love. And there we shall be as one in the great dancing and singing."

She reached for him, but heavy footsteps echoed on the hardwood floor.

"Please do not touch the paintings", said a voice.

Rose turned and saw a guard frowning at her a few steps away.

"He is my little brother", she explained.

"You can't touch", he said more firmly. "It's against the rules."

She looked at Tchibi, begging him to show the guard that he was real. For humans are permitted to touch each other. Tchibi gazed at her with love, but he did not speak. He did not move. He stood against a swirling background of sweet-fire. His bare feet were balanced upon a solid globe of white quartz.

"It's against the rules", the guard said again.

Startled, Rose stepped back from her painting. Satisfied, the guard went away.

Rose covered her face with both hands and crushed the wails that leaped to her throat.

"Anonymous", said a voice.

Looking up, Rose saw two elegantly dressed women standing before a painting to the right of Tchibi's portrait. One of them wore an identification badge on a chain around her neck. She was explaining the painting to the other woman, who wore a fur coat and exuded a powerful perfume.

"The aboriginal symbolism is obvious. The demon-spirit versus the archetypal lover. The black stone. Primeval forces struggling to reconcile the absolute tensions between darkness and light."

"Of course, that's quite evident", the other replied in cultured tones. "The primitive style as well."

"Yes, whoever the artist was, he or she was an autodidact."

"How did you obtain it?"

"It came last year as part of a bequest by a well-known private collector."

"Oh, really, who was that?"

"Estelle Morgan."

"You don't mean *the* Estelle Morgan?"

832

"That's right. During her lifetime she was one of the most generous benefactors of the Gallery. She was on the Board of Advisors for years and donated a Renoir, a Monet and an early Esther Dyson, among other works. These more obscure pieces came from the estate after her death."

"Strange that she didn't leave a record of who painted them."

"Well, her collection was rather large—esoteric *and* eclectic. Not everything was properly documented. Perhaps she wanted it that way."

"I suppose we'll never know. By the way, who is Esther Dyson?"

"Come, I'll show you the Dyson. It's a lovely little piece."

The two women walked away.

Rose glanced at the information plate beneath the image they had been referring to.

> *Woman Sleeping*, artist unknown
> Oil on canvas, circa 1960

"Euphrasia, let it go!" Rose whispered. "Let it go, for the black stone is the greatest weight of all, and it is pulling you down to destruction."

Footsteps echoed on the hardwood floors.

Rose reached for the black pearl. But even as she did so, she realized that such things could never be torn from another. They could only be given away by the one who possessed them, who was possessed by them, who sought to be free of them. Rose now offered her own death for Euphrasia, offered it in whatever form it would take. Though she was alive and Euphrasia had already died, God was beyond time. Could he not send the graces back to her, so that she might let go of this thing?

Of her own volition, Euphrasia now pulled the pearl from her chest. Blood spurted from her heart—it was a cleansing blood. She handed it to Rose. Rose took it and hurled it far and

833

high over the sea. The pearl hit the surface of the blacker waves and sank without a sound.

"You've touched your last painting, lady", said the guard in his severest tone of voice. He grabbed her wrist in one hand. With his free hand he extracted a mobile radio from a clip on his belt and talked into it.

"Trouble in contemporary realism", he said.

"We'll be there in a minute", came the electronic reply.

"Put on your coat, lady. It's time for you to go."

She coughed blood onto the guard's uniform. Disgusted, he let go of her wrist and stepped quickly back.

But two other guards arrived to take his place. They held her arms and walked her from the room, through annexes and side galleries, through decades and centuries, past astonished lovers of art, anjeni, saints, and demons, down the sloping marble ramp, and into the lobby. There she was brought before the director of security. When it was determined that the little woman was no more than a crazy street-person, they walked her out the front door and warned her never to come back; if she did, she would see the inside of a police car.

For several minutes, Rose stood without moving. She watched the traffic light turn colors several times. Dizzy, confused, she turned to the left, away from the city core. Instinctively she knew that she was now facing the north. When she had caught her breath and her heart ceased thundering in her chest, she steadied her thoughts as much as she was able. She glanced at the cathedral and bowed to the presence within it. Then she glanced at the Parliament buildings. "Now do I shake the dust of this city from my feet", she cried. "I go from this place of pride, never to return."

Rose began to walk. Walking, walking, walking with no goal, into the place of no-place. "Ay, ay, I go down, I go down. I am sinking", she muttered.

She came to a bridge that stretched across a frozen river. On the far side was a smaller city. Beyond it was a line of grey-purple hills dusted with snow. The afternoon was speeding to its close, the darkness near at hand.

"Where shall I go? If there is no place for me to go, what choosing is left to me?"

She turned onto the bridge's walkway and headed toward the opposite shore.

"My life is finished. My work is scattered and nameless."

"And all my thoughts," she said to the wind, "all my thoughts were written on you. You carry them off, the words and the names, the pictures and the songs. All my labors, Kije-kije-kije-Manito, all my labors."

She went on, sometimes speaking, sometimes thinking, sometimes sinking into a stream of words-without-words, and with grater frequency conscious of nothing but the pain in her flesh, like burn holes.

"Where has my Tchibi gone?" she said to herself. "I remember him, but not everything do I remember."

Reaching the French side of the river, she came to a long street, crossed against the traffic light, and entered a maze of narrower streets. She walked at strange angles across avenues and side lanes because the path seemed to make sense to her. Down alleyways, past cats rummaging in trash piles, through heaps of crumpled Christmas paper spilling from overturned garbage cans, past steaming sewer vents. Back onto another street, through more red lights, green lights, amber lights, squealing tires, angry drivers banging on their horns. The wind cruel on her face, for wind too, which was once a friend, had turned against her.

"I do not blame it, no, I cannot blame it, for life is a barren-ground, and the things which are done upon it are without meaning."

"No, this is untrue. It all has meaning, and whether or not

life has meaning, I can still choose a small thing. I will go north. Yes, I will go into the barren land. I will dwell in the Tent of Nowhere. Soon I will lie down in the Land of Little Trees, if I reach it. If not, I will lie down when the flesh has burned the last of its fuel. I will lie down beneath a spruce tree and look up through the branches, along the cord of its twisted spine into the necklace of the loon."

"But who will sing for my spirit? Tell me, *who*?"

"Is my Tchibi waiting for me there, or was it all a dream? Is he no more than a picture on a wall, a tale that none can understand?"

"Do not forget him, do not forget him, the one who was— is—my brother. I knew him! I knew him! I know him! I know him!"

"And do not forget John the Beloved, my son. O my son, my true son! Now I will never come to you, I will never hold you and speak with you, our two hearts shall not be as one, mother and child."

This caused a torrent of fresh sobs, for of all her grief, this was the most bitter.

She stopped and rubbed her face. She realized that her thoughts would not stay on their proper path. They veered thisway and thatway, white with black spots or black with white spots. Believing one moment, fearing and doubting the next, followed by the suction of despair.

"Ay, ay, is there a black pearl in my heart?" she wailed to the wind, but the wind ripped the words from her mouth.

By early evening of Christmas day, Rose was approaching the outskirts of the city. Though her feet were numb and her teeth chattered uncontrollably, the air was warmer. The snow on the sidewalk was melting into slush. Overcome with fatigue she stopped and leaned against the window of a grocery store.

Then black paint was thrown across the glass, and she felt herself falling down, down, down into the deep waters.

Ay, ay, now it is over. This too I give you.

As she closed her eyes upon the world, all seeing, feeling, and thinking faded into nothingness.

A hand shook her shoulder.

"Come on, lady, wake up."

She opened her eyes. An Indian face hovered over her with a worried expression. A brown-skinned man, neither old nor young.

"Tchibi?"

"Are you all right? Did you have a fall?"

He leaned toward her and sniffed, checking for the scent of alcohol.

"Are you hurt?"

She shook her head.

"Come on, let me help you up. There, easy now, easy now."

He put one arm around her waist and with his other hand held her arm firmly, drawing her to her feet.

"Nothing broken. But you don't look very well", he said. "Where do you live?"

"No-place."

"No place? Are you sure? I can drive you wherever you want to go."

"I must walk. I must go north, where one is taken into absolutes and is seen no more."

He stared at her, his eyes perplexed. She coughed blood on him, but he did not recoil. He looked more worried than ever.

"Hey, lady, you aren't well at all. D'you have any ID on you, anything with your name and address?"

She shook her head. "My deer-hide sack, with the rose on it. Oldmary made it. But it's gone. I don't know where."

"Someone steal it?"

"I think I lost it. I forget."

"Do you need a place to stay? There's a shelter not far from here. I can take you there."

Again she shook her head. "I am going to the place where I was born, in the Land of Little Trees. There I will lie down beneath the blanket of winter, and the moon's face will shine on me."

"Sounds chilly. Look, why don't you come with me. My wife and I can give you something to eat, and then when you're feeling better, you can think better. How about it?"

"Tchibi, is it you?"

"My name's Jack", he said.

"Will you take me to the north?"

He frowned. "Well, our apartment's just over there a few blocks away. It's on the north side of town."

"Near the Land of Little Trees?"

"Not quite."

Without waiting for her answer, he steered her toward a pickup truck that sat idling by the curb in front of the grocery store. He opened the passenger door and helped her climb inside. Then he got into the driver's seat.

As they drove down the street, he glanced sideways at her.

"What's your name?" he asked.

"I—I'm not sure. I think it's Rose. Yes, Rose is my name. Wâbos. Ogini Wâbos."

"Are you Mohawk?"

"I am Anishinâbe."

"Oh, from the north woods, by the Great Lakes, right? Me, I'm half Salish, part Dogrib, and part Slavey. Quite a combination. My wife's Mohawk from Kahnawake, the reserve near Montreal. You ever been there?"

Rose nodded.

He turned onto a side street and parked in front of a three-story apartment building. He helped Rose get out, then walked arm in arm with her to the entrance.

"We live on the top floor. Think you can make it up the stairs?"

She was too exhausted to reply.

Inside, the stairwell smelled strongly of meals being cooked. Christmas music came faintly from the apartments they passed. At the top of the stairs, the man rapped on a door and waited.

The door was opened by a young native woman carrying a child in her arms. The woman's face registered astonishment. The child, a four-year-old girl, smiled at Rose as if she had been waiting for her.

30

When Rose had been with them almost a week, sleeping through much of it, she sat up in bed for the first time. They told her it was New Year's Eve. She did not know what year it was. She remembered some things and not others.

The man's name was Jack Tobac. Observing him off and on for several days, listening too, she had learned that he was from the Rocky Mountains, far in the west. He was a wood-carver. He worked at a warehouse loading transport trucks at night, and he made carvings at home during the day. The room in which Rose lay was his workshop, though he had moved his tools and blocks of wood to the kitchen while she was with them.

The woman was Mari–Kahenta, his wife.

Their daughter, Kateri, they had named after the saint.

During one of Rose's waking periods, the woman came to her room with a towel and a basin of hot water and bathed her body. At first it shamed Rose, but the woman's kindness soon set her heart at ease.

"Do you not remember us?" Mari–Kahenta said.

Rose did not remember having met them. She could not answer.

"On the day we brought our newborn child to Blessed Kateri's shrine at Kahnawake, I saw you there in the church of the Jesuit Fathers. You cried out."

"Yes, now I remember it", Rose said.

"The doctor told us you would forget many things. He said that much of it will come back to you. Also, he said you must eat."

When Mari-Kahenta had dried Rose and clothed her in a soft white gown, she made her lie down under clean sheets and blankets that smelled of fresh wool. She brought soup made of onions and the meat of *wêwe* the wild goose, hot and salty. Also, bread. Rose felt her strength revive a little.

"I do not remember a doctor", she said.

"Jack asked a doctor to come see you, to tell us what is wrong. He came while you were sleeping, on the first day. He felt the lumps on your neck. He took blood away. This morning he called and told us."

"What did he tell you?"

"He gave us medicine prescriptions for you. Jack bought them. It will help with the cough and the pain."

"Did he tell you I am dying?"

"Yes", she nodded.

"I should go", Rose said. "I am a burden to you."

"You are not a burden. You are a gift to us. Did you not come to us on the day of his birth?"

Rose thought about what she said, then asked her, "Do you believe in him?"

"Iesos? Yes, we believe in Iesos Kristos. And his mother the holy Mari, and Yosheh the guardian, and all the saints."

She glanced at a wood crucifix hanging on the wall beside the bed.

"Jack made that", she said. "He is like Yosheh—Saint Joseph." She smiled. "That is why we took our Kateri to the shrine of Great Kateri. To consecrate her."

"The baby made small sounds. I longed to hold her."

"Why did you not come to us and ask?"

"Because I thought you would be frightened of me."

"Frightened of you? Why did you think such a thing?"

"Because I am a nothing-person—and ugly. My back—"

The eyes of Mari-Kahenta saddened. "Do you know, Rose, that I have often thought about you since that day we saw you at the tomb of our sister. Many times have I said to her, 'Look after that one, Kateri, look after that woman, for she is a servant of God'."

Unable to speak, Rose turned her face to the wall, and Mari-Kahenta quietly went out.

Later, the little girl entered the room and sat down on the end of the bed.

"Why is your back like that?" she asked.

"That's the way it grew."

She reached over and stroked Rose's spine.

"Can I kiss you?" she asked.

"No", Rose said.

"Why can't I?"

"Because I'm sick."

"I want to kiss you", she insisted.

Rose shook her head

The girl kissed her anyway, a wet smack on the cheek.

"Tell me a story!" she pleaded, bouncing up and down.

"What kind of story?"

"About when you were a little girl."

Rose gazed at the child, pondering. *What is a life?* she thought. *You cut the canvas, tack it to the cross-frame, pour out your blood on it. Io! How can I tell a child such things, for between the speaking and the hearing there is always a great distance.*

"Please!"

Rose shook her head.

"Please, Rose, please!"

Rose kept the tale as simple as possible. It took about five minutes to tell. Birds and stars and fish, the many waters. While she was talking, Jack came into the room and sat down on a chair in the corner. It was made of balsam saplings tied together by thongs. It smelled like incense. He spread a leather apron on his lap and opened a box of wood-carving tools. As he listened to Rose telling her story to his daughter, he sliced shavings from a block of wood. It was about two feet high, eight or ten inches wide.

"Then the silver bird goes up to the loon's necklace, doesn't she?" Kateri asked.

"She goes later", Rose said to her. "She's not ready."

"Why isn't she ready?"

"Because something weighs heavy on her wings."

"What is it?"

"She's afraid. She's afraid she's too small for the big journey."

Kateri giggled, "But she's *always* been small!"

"Yes, always."

Jack looked at Rose curiously. He turned the block of wood in his hands and held it up to the light, squinting at some flaw he wanted to correct. He resumed whittling.

"Does she see the partridge again?" Kateri asked.

"Oh, yes, she does."

"Does she see Mother Mari and Saint Yosheh and Baby Iesos?"

"Yes, they're all waiting for her to fly to them."

"Will she make pictures in heaven?"

"I hope so."

Kateri jumped to the floor. She went over to the window and crawled onto the chair in front of it. The glass was partly covered with frost, a garden of crystals glowing with silver light. She peered through a patch of clear glass.

"Oh, look", she said.

"Rose needs to rest, Kateri", her father told her. "She can't get out of bed right now."

"But it's the lady."

"The lady?" Jack murmured, paying her no mind, frowning over a difficult cut.

"Who is the lady?" Rose asked the child.

"She's the lady standing on the moon."

Her father cast a glance at the window. Rose struggled to sit upright, her heart thumping.

"She's gone", the girl said. "She smiled at me."

"What did she look like?" Rose asked.

"Like Mama, with stars all around her."

Singing to herself, she rubbed her fingers in the frost, melting it, scratching and rearranging, blowing on it with the breath of her mouth. With great concentration, she made shapes: rabbits, bears, fish. In the softer new frost that spread like a sheen of white canvas, she made a different shape. Pressing her warm thumb into it, then scratching delicately around it, she formed a bird. Its beak pointed upward.

"Time to say good-night, Kateri", said the girl's mother, entering the room.

Kateri got down off the chair, ran to the bed, and kissed Rose. Rose kissed her.

She put a stone into the child's hand. It was the palette stone she had found on the beach at St. Peter's.

"What is it?" Kateri asked.

"It is a thing carved by the sea."

"Is a story inside it?"

"Yes. I will not tell it to you, because the stone must tell it. Keep it, and when you are older you will understand the story inside it."

"Can I give it away?'

"Yes, at any time."

"To Papa?"

"Yes, if you want to."

She ran to her father and showed it to him. He smiled at her.

"Bedtime, Kateri", he said. Mari-Kahenta took the girl by the hand and led her out.

Jack set the carving on the floor, gathered the shavings in the leather apron, and folded it. He was not looking at Rose. He was thinking.

"The little stone", he said at last. "Did it really come from the sea?"

"Yes."

"Can you tell me its story?"

"If you want me to."

"I want you to."

Rose closed her eyes. She heard the surf and the piping of the shore-birds. Then she began:

"Once there was a woman who thought her life was over. She was ill and very tired. She had failed at everything. As she walked beside the waves, she said to God, 'All my sacrifices have come to nothing. I am defeated at every turn. What am I going to do?'

"As she said this she looked down at the waves licking the beach and saw many broken pieces of china that had come from a shipwreck. Among them was this stone. It was not from the shipwreck. It was something the sea had carved. She picked it up and wondered at it, for it was a perfect palette shape, with a thumb hole and dots to represent dabs of paint. The stone was like a miracle to her, for she was a painter.

"Then she understood. If God could patiently create this stone over thousands of years, seeing ahead to the woman who would one day walk on the beach with discouragement in her soul, he could do anything. If he could send her a message like this, he could bring a harvest from barren soil. He could bring dead things to life, and even a life that seemed a failure might become fruitful."

"So, he was speaking to her."

"Yes."

"Thank you for giving it to our daughter. She will understand it one day."

"Will she remember me?"

"She will remember you."

"I am glad. I will remember her too, if I do not forget. I

forget so many things now. I forgot the word the Lord spoke to me in the palette stone, and my heart grew heavy again. Then I got lost."

"But now you are found. See, he does not forget you."

Rose could not reply to this. Her throat closed, her lungs struggled to breathe.

Jack picked up the wood carving and brought it to her.

"This is for you", he said, placing it on the bedside table. He smiled and went out, closing the door behind him.

The carving was a manshape. It was like a totem, but more human. The trunk of the body and the head were simple forms, but the expression on the face was deep. The eyes gazed down with attention at something he held in his outstretched hands. It was a small wooden bird. It perched in his fingers with perfect freedom. It was thinking of flight. It was not ready to fly, but soon it would be.

In the palms of the hands were holes—pierced through from one side to the other. Light came through them. On the forehead were smaller holes. In the side, near to the heart, was the largest hole, and from it ran two rivulets scored in the wood, the overflow of the wound.

Rose closed her eyes.

So many words the Beating Heart sends me, she thought. *See, Ogini, you are not forgotten by him. A word of himself he sends. And a word of his mother he sends. The moon is sailing over the land, and upon it she stands. You cannot see her, though a child can see her very well.*

As Rose closed her eyes and drifted down into the deep waters, she felt the arms of the woman enfold her.

"My daughter, little piece of my heart, why did you doubt?" said the woman. "Why did you lose hope?"

Rose cried to her, "My Ningâ, my holy Ningâ whose face I have not seen. Why did you go away and leave me?"

846

"I have never left you. Never for a moment did I leave you. Though you felt alone, you were not alone."

"I was lost."

"You were not lost", the woman said. "Within you is a light, Oginiwâbigon. Within this family who have sheltered you are lights. The greater light is coming, and the darkness cannot overcome it."

"Ningâ, Ningâ", Rose whispered.

Then the woman pulled a blanket of peace over Rose's body. She stroked her head and held her closer.

Small, Io! We are so small! Rose sighed. *But this is how it must be.*

Author's Afterword

The tale of Rose Wâbos is fiction, but a fiction based on the lives of a number of people who have lived in my country. As one of the characters in the novel says, "There are many roses blooming in the garden of the Lord." Most of them are hidden, some have suffered more than my central character, some less, yet all of them know what it is to live in poverty.

This book was written under the intercession of Rose Prince, a woman of the Carrier people of northern British Columbia who died in 1949. Although this is not her tale, she was, like my Rose, a suffering servant of God. When her body was unearthed years after her death, it was found to be perfectly incorrupt, a fact attested to by the native witnesses and the priests and nuns who were present.

The intercession of Blessed Kateri Tekakwitha was also a constant source of grace for me during the writing of the story. To the extent that it expresses the mystery of poverty of spirit, Kateri and Rose are to be thanked. The flaws are all mine.

O Kateri, our mother-sister-daughter, blessed are you,
for you loved our Savior Iesos
with your whole heart, at great cost,
as now you continue to love and serve him
in the great harvest.

O Kateri, Kateri, *onkweonweke katsitsiio teotsitsianekaron!*

Novels in the *Children of the Last Days* series:

*Asterisk indicates a title forthcoming.

CHILDREN OF THE LAST DAYS is a series of six novels that examine the major moral and spiritual struggles of our times. Each can be read independently of the others. The first three of the following titles, however, are best read in chronological order, for they form a trilogy within the larger work.

STRANGERS AND SOJOURNERS, set in a remote valley of the interior of British Columbia, is about the lives of two exiles, an Englishwoman, Anne, and her husband, Stephen, an Irishman. Beginning on the first day of the 20th century, and concluding in the mid-1970s, the Delaneys' story is the foundational novel for the following two titles.

PLAGUE JOURNAL is set in the near future. The novel is composed of both written and mental notes made by Nathaniel Delaney, Anne and Stephen's grandson, who is the editor of a small-town newspaper. The story takes place over a five-day period as he flees arrest by a federal government agency, during the preliminary stage of the rise of a totalitarian state in North America.

ECLIPSE OF THE SUN describes the plight of Nathaniel's children, who are scattered and have become fugitives as the government seeks to eradicate all evidence of its ultimate goals. The events of this novel take place during the year following those of *Plague Journal*.

FATHER ELIJAH is the story of a Carmelite priest, Father Elijah (born David Schäffer), and his confrontation with the spirit of Antichrist. The events of this novel take place at approximately the same time as those of *Eclipse of the Sun*.

SOPHIA HOUSE is set in Warsaw during the Nazi occupation. Pawel Tarnowski, a bookseller, gives refuge to a Jewish youth (David Schäffer) who has escaped from the Ghetto, hiding him in the attic of the book shop. Throughout the winter of 1942–1943, the two discuss good and evil, sin and redemption, literature and philosophy. A novel that explores the meaning of love, religious identity, and sacrifice.

A CRY OF STONE is the life of a native artist, Rose Wâbos. Suffering from deprivation of several kinds, including a physical handicap, Rose is raised in the northern Ontario wilderness by her grandmother, an Indian woman named Oldmary. The story covers a period from 1940 to 1973, chronicling Rose's growth to womanhood, her discovery of art, her moving out into the world of cities and culture, her search for beauty and faith.